ONE CLEAR CALL

The Works of UPTON SINCLAIR

FICTION

THE JUNGLE
THE METROPOLIS
LOVE'S PILGRIMAGE
SYLVIA'S MARRIAGE
THE SPY
THEY CALL ME CARPENTER
THE MILLENNIUM
OIL
BOSTON
MOUNTAIN CITY
THE WET PARADE
ROMAN HOLIDAY
DAMAGED GOODS
THE JOURNAL OF ARTHUR STIRLING
MANASSAS
CO-OP : A Novel of Living Together
NO PASARAN !
OUR LADY : A Story
THE FLIVVER KING
LITTLE STEEL

The World's End Series

WORLD'S END (1913–1919)
BETWEEN TWO WORLDS (1919–1929)
DRAGON'S TEETH (1929–1934)
WIDE IS THE GATE (1934–1937)
PRESIDENTIAL AGENT (1937–1938)
DRAGON HARVEST (1938–1940)
A WORLD TO WIN (1940–1942)
PRESIDENTIAL MISSION (1942–1943)
ONE CLEAR CALL (1943–1944)

GENERAL

THE PROFITS OF RELIGION
THE BRASS CHECK
THE BOOK OF LIFE.   Mind and Body
THE GOSLINGS
MENTAL RADIO : Does it Work and How ?
MONEY WRITES
CANDID REMINISCENCES
THE WAY OUT
THE FASTING CURE
THE BOOK OF LOVE.   Love and Society
MAMMONART
DEPRESSION ISLAND
THE GNOMOBILE
WHAT GOD MEANS TO ME
MARIE ANTOINETTE.   A Play
LETTERS TO A MILLIONAIRE
TELLING THE WORLD
A GIANT'S STRENGTH.   A Play

ONE
CLEAR CALL

BY

UPTON SINCLAIR

Sunset and evening star
And one clear call for me
TENNYSON

T. WERNER LAURIE LTD.
187 PICCADILLY, LONDON, W.1

FIRST PUBLISHED August 1949

PRINTED IN GREAT BRITAIN
BY R. & R. CLARK, LTD., EDINBURGH

ACKNOWLEDGMENTS

A HISTORICAL novelist is dependent upon many sources for his local colour, scenery, costumes, and what not. The present writer is indebted for a few such details to several excellent books which he is happy to recommend : for Palestine, Fulton Oursler's *A Skeptic in the Holy Land* (Farrar and Rinehart) ; for the Third Army in its Nancy headquarters, Robert S. Allen's *Lucky Forward* (Vanguard Press) ; for the liberation of Paris, A. J. Liebling's *The Republic of Silence* (Harcourt, Brace) ; and Milton Shulman's *Defeat in the West* (E. P. Dutton).

I present this ninth of the Lanny Budd volumes, together with all the others, to my beloved wife, Mary Craig Sinclair, without whose patience and wisdom none of the series would have pleased its public so well. I learned about women from her !

CONTENTS

BOOK ONE
POWERS THAT WILL WORK FOR THEE

PAGE

1. WHO WILL GO FOR US?   9
2. DO WELL THE DUTY   38
3. WHO WORSHIP THE BEAST   65

BOOK TWO
THE NIOBE OF NATIONS, THERE SHE STANDS

4. WHEN YOU ARE IN ROME   90
5. THE LIGHT THAT LIES   113
6. TRUTH CRUSHED TO EARTH   136

BOOK THREE
THE ENEMY FAINTS NOT, NOR FAILETH

7. SLAUGHTERS OF THE RACE   168
8. PATHWAYS EAST AND WEST   199
9. HERE A DIVIDED DUTY   226

BOOK FOUR
TILL DANGER'S TROUBLED NIGHT DEPART

10. WHEN FORTUNE FLATTERS   248
11. SPOILS OF THE ENEMY   277
12. DESTRUCTION FACE TO FACE   304

BOOK FIVE
MOVING ACCIDENTS BY FLOOD AND FIELD

PAGE

13. HARD LIBERTY 333

14. IN WORST EXTREMES 347

15. CAMPO CORAGGIO 367

BOOK SIX
MUCH HAVE I SEEN AND KNOWN

16. CALIFORNIA, HERE I COME ! 396

17. ALWAYS TO BE BLEST 426

18. PROMISED LAND 452

BOOK SEVEN
HUMANITY WITH ALL ITS FEARS

19. LULL BEFORE STORM 476

20. RED LAUGH OF WAR 502

21. INTO THE CANNON'S MOUTH 527

BOOK EIGHT
ACTION IN THE TENTED FIELD

22. THOU HAST GREAT ALLIES 552

23. OUTRAGEOUS FORTUNE 579

24. TONGUE IN THE THUNDER'S MOUTH 605

25. LE JOUR DE GLOIRE 629

BOOK NINE
FEATS OF BROIL AND BATTLE

26. A HOUSE DIVIDED 654

27. A FRIEND IN DEED 680

28. THE PATHS OF GLORY 693

BOOK ONE

POWERS THAT WILL WORK FOR THEE

I

Who Will Go for Us ?

I

THE small catboat slapped the waves of the gulf, and the salt-laden spray flew over the man and the woman; they were clad only in bathing suits and smiles, and it was the same as an early morning swim. They leaned out to windward, to keep the boat level, and gazed over the blue water, glinting with sunshine. Here and there a small flying fish rose from the water in front of them, sailed along like a toy airplane, and then plunged into the sea. " Look ! " Lanny would exclaim, and Laurel would be amused by his eagerness. Along the shore, lined with palm trees and small houses of white, blue, and coral pink, flew a procession of pelicans, grey birds which moved their wings with slow dignity and permitted nothing to disturb their course. Being early, it was pleasantly cool; later on the visitors from the north would seek shelter from a subtropic sun.

There is time to think while you sail, especially when someone else does the sailing and the course does not have to be changed often. Laurel Creston thought, What a lovely vacation ! And then, I ought to be so happy ! But there could not be a single note of joy in her symphony without its accompaniment of pain. She thought, He may have to go any day, and I may never see him again ! Such was the fate of women in wartime ; and in her heart she raged at the vile Nazi-Fascist creed that had caused millions of men to be torn from the women who loved them on all the five continents of the earth. Mothers, wives, and sweethearts everywhere had faced this war with anguish and then steeled their hearts to endure it.

9

She did not voice these thoughts to Lanny. To all appearances he was serene ; he had lived through wars most of his life, world wars and civil wars all over Europe, and had adjusted his mind to them. He would go back to his job and be so wrapped up in it that he would have no time to grieve. But she would stay at home and think about him with heartache. She would cry, I must not love him too much ! Some of my love must be given to mankind ! But she found to her surprise that she was loving him more, and it was harder to give him to mankind.

Now and then she had expressed this thought to him and had found that, manlike, he took it merely as a compliment. She reflected that he had had two wives before her, and she could never be to him what her only man was to her. She wanted to ask him, Do you love me wholly ? And will you always love me ? But she had learned that men do not like these questions ; that they want to take love as a matter of course, and not to pull up the plant by the roots to make sure that it is growing. The woman wants to be wooed over and over and studies arts to bring about that pleasant experience.

On the shore was a baby boy, and Laurel knew he was a bond between them ; Lanny had a daughter some thirteen years old, but this was his first son. A man wants a man child to bear his name and carry on his work ; to be and think like himself, and Laurel was enough in love to want it to be that way. She looked at the father—easy to see, in bathing trunks and a pair of slippers. He showed few signs of his forty-three years, for he had taken care of himself. His face and neck and hands had been browned by the sun of Africa ; he played tennis whenever he got a chance, and pounded the piano with vigour. Now he was happy as a boy, leaning backward over the side of a leaping sailboat. Laurel knew that he really was a boy in his thoughts, back in the Golfe Juan, where he had swum and fished and sailed from his earliest days. He had had a happy childhood, and Laurel was determined that if he did not have a happy manhood it would not be her fault.

Ashore there was a breeze off the gulf, and if you stayed in the shade it was endurable. Lanny still wore his trunks, and his wife wore a crepe slip. The baby wore nothing, unless you counted a mosquito netting which covered the basket in which he lay. He was restless, because there were a number of little red swellings on his skin, and they itched. The parents had developed the same trouble, and had thought it must be hives, due perhaps to the heat ; but the people of this small fishing village told them that the trouble was caused by a tiny bug called a chigger, which burrowed under the skin. Lanny had driven to Tampa to consult a doctor and had got a lotion which was supposed to help.

Now he was discussing the information he had gained ; the chigger was a small red flea, and what it did was to bore a little hole and inject a drop of a digestive juice which was intended to prepare your flesh for its sucking apparatus. Usually its purpose was foiled because you knocked it off by your scratching—but that didn't help you much, because the bit of your flesh went on being digested. The creatures climbed up the stalks of grass or weeds, waiting for you to brush against them, so it was better to wear leggings, and never to lie on the ground. Laurel listened to all this, and was amused to observe her husband's interest in entomological details. She asked him why, and he said he was fascinated by the problem of what nature could have meant by creating so many strange forms of life, each struggling desperately to survive at the expense of others.

When the couple had exhausted this subject, they turned to the sponge industry of the Florida west coast. They had engaged a small powerboat, which was to present itself at the two planks which served for a dock and take them out to the sponge beds. It was their plan to start at dawn and return before the worst of the heat, for early June was midsummer here. They were in love with the marvellous clear water, green in the shallows and blue in the deeps, in which you could watch innumerable strange forms, both animal and vegetable. Here was more material for speculation about Mother Nature and her reasons or lack of them. The world of men was at war, and that fact pained and grieved you ; but here was a world that had been at war for millions of years, and no creature in it could have any sense of friendship for any other.

II

Their talk was interrupted by the arrival of a small boy. He was barefoot, and what he did about the chiggers was not clear ; his clothing consisted of a pair of khaki shorts, all patches. He had wavy black hair, dark eyes, and skin the colour of the pecan tree which grew beside his father's house. For his two rows of pearly white teeth many a rich man or woman would have paid a fortune. He showed them when he smiled, and still more when Lanny gave him a small coin for his errand.

Now he said, " Telephone call for you, Mr. Budd." Laurel caught her breath. She thought, Oh, God ! But, being a well-disciplined lady, she made no sound.

Lanny replied, " Thank you, Toni," and to his wife, " Excuse me, dear." He got up and walked fast, the youngster trotting by his side. Along the unpaved road which served this little cove were scattered a few houses, and one of them was the café where Toni's parents lived and laboured. Both of them were large, and in the sunlight they shone with exudations of good living. America had treated them well, and their only trouble was that the land of their birth had got into a miserable war with the land of their adoption.

The café served a concoction called a gumbo, with crabs and shrimps and oysters and fish, peppers and onions and tomatoes and celery ; a big bowl of it was a meal, and the three visitors from the North—husband and wife and the nurse who was the wife's friend—had come every evening, to save the need of cooking in their rented cottage. Big Toni— Dantone was his name—was enraptured to meet a gentleman who had been raised on the French Riviera and had played with fisherboys who spoke the Ligurian dialect of Italian ; he would stand and twist his handle-bar moustache and gossip with Lanny all through the meal. Toni came from the Bay of Salerno, in the south, and took the same delight in Lanny's phrases that an inhabitant, say, of Savannah, would have taken in the twang of Cape Cod. He seized the chance to learn—in Italian, and safe from American ears—what this war was about. Was it true that the American Army was going into Sicily, and even to the mainland, and would Napoli and the other beautiful cities be entirely destroyed ? They were being bombed now—you could hear it over the little radio which was kept going in the café, and the large and slouchy Signora Toni would stand listening, the tears gathering in her eyes. *Ah, i poveri !*

This agreeable gentleman from up north came striding quickly, and gave his name over the telephone, and all the Dantones, big and little, heard words which made them sad. Yes, he could come at once ; he could leave in half an hour. He wouldn't save much time by flying because he might be delayed in getting a plane. He had his family with him and would drive day and night ; his wife would take a turn at the wheel. If all went well, he should reach Washington the next day, certainly by evening ; he would send a wire in the morning to report what progress he was making. Yes, he had coupons for gasoline, and his tyres were good. So long !

III

Lanny shook hands all round with his " dago " friends—he didn't call them that, but others in the South did, and meant no harm by it ; it was a name, like " Joe " for a soldier, and you grinned when you said it. Lanny promised to come back some day. Then he strode back to the cottage. Laurel wasn't too shocked by the news ; she had guessed long ago that her husband was doing some kind of secret work in a grim and terrible war, and that his duties took precedence over love and marriage. They threw their things into suitcases, and the other odds and ends into carton boxes, and stowed them in the trunk of the car. The baby, asleep, was laid on a pillow in his travelling basket ; Agnes Drury, trained nurse and mother's helper, would ride in the rear seat with him and keep watch. The cottage was locked up and the key left with the agent.

Northward along the coast, through the bay city of Tampa and beyond. By nightfall they were speeding across the peninsula of Florida, through seemingly endless forests of pine. The road was smoothly paved, and a mile a minute was standard—but you had to watch the shaft of light ahead, for a cow might wander out into the highway, and deer were plentiful, and would stand in the road, dazzled by the glare. Before midnight the car was speeding up the east coast, along which resorts were strung like beads on a thread. They had been through the usual cycle of boom and bust and then boom again, and now many of the great hotels were turned into military hospitals.

The travellers did not stop for meals but ate what they had in the car and bought more the next day. Lanny drove while the others slept, and when daylight came they were in the interior of Georgia, land of red clay and unpainted shacks. Two hounds, chasing a rabbit, dashed madly out of a pine wood, one of them directly under the wheels of the car. They did not stop ; it was another casualty of war.

Laurel drove for a while, and her husband slid down in his seat and took a long nap. By mid-morning they were in North Carolina, and he sent a telegram saying that he would reach Washington by dinner-time, and that two rooms should be reserved for him. That was necessary, for the city had become the capital of the world, and important business men were sleeping in chairs in hotel lobbies, in washrooms, taxicabs, and sometimes on park benches.

It was Highway Number One, all the way from Key West to the northern tip of Maine. They were coming into a district where war industries had been set up, and heavy trucks escorted them, behind and before. Lanny kept a space in front of him, so that if he were hit in the rear there would be room to slide. The highways of America had been transformed and would never again be the same ; nothing in America would be the same, after this dreadful ordeal by battle. As they drove they listened to the radio, familiar voices of men whom they had never seen, telling them the events of the hour and explaining their import. The Japanese were being cleaned out of the Aleutians, and the Americans were holding on desperately at Guadalcanal in the Solomons ; the Allies were bombing the island of Pantelleria in the Mediterranean, also various cities in the Ruhr ; the Russians and Germans were sparring like two boxers, all along a two-thousand-mile line, and it was a problem which of them would begin the expected major onslaught. The air-waves echoed with Russian clamour for a second front and their refusal to accept the Mediterranean attack as an equivalent.

IV

The car came into Washington on schedule. Lanny had had another nap in the afternoon, and felt fine, he said. He telephoned Baker, the President's man, and learned the name of his hotel. There was time for a bath and a shave, then to dress and have dinner—room service was prohibited in wartime, so Agnes had to stay with the baby and then dine by herself. Lanny said no word to his wife about where he was going or what he expected ; he was under pledge and kept it strictly. But he couldn't keep his wife from observing that these rush calls to Washington invariably preceded flights to Britain or North Africa and absences of several months.

Lanny sat and read the papers, with his watch on the table beside him. At ten minutes to nine he got up, put on his linen coat and his Panama hat, gave his beloved wife a more than dutiful kiss, and said, " Don't wait up for me. I may be late." He strolled out into the blacked-out city and, walking slowly and carefully, arrived at a certain corner promptly on the second of nine. A familiar car drew up at the kerb, a voice said, " Hello," and he stepped in.

He wasn't supposed to talk to Baker either ; but in the course of several years they had acquired a certain number of topics in common. Lanny said, " How is the Boss ? " The answer was, " The doctors say he's O.K., but you don't have to be a doctor to see that he's tired." Lanny said, " God help him ! " And that wasn't just a conventional phrase. The burdens which this great man carried in his soul, the problems he carried in his mind, were a cause of brooding sorrow to his secret agent.

1600 Pennsylvania Avenue was the address. It was a sort of little park, an oasis in downtown and crowded Washington. A high fence surrounded it, and Lanny was glad to see Navy men in little white caps patrolling. The Navy was in charge at the entrance drive, and the car stopped and Baker said, " A visitor on the President's orders." That was enough, and they went up the drive to what was called the " social door," used only on formal occasions. Two secret service men stood in the shadow of the high columns, and now they came out and flashed torches; when they saw it was Baker, they stepped back. The pair went in, climbed a side stairway, and went down a corridor to the door of the President's bedroom, where Prettyman, the Negro, sat on duty.

All this was routine to Lanny Budd; he had been here a dozen times in the same way. But his heart would never fail to beat faster, for he considered Franklin Roosevelt the greatest man in the world, and everything of a public nature that Lanny hoped for depended upon his decisions and commands. Lanny hadn't enlisted in any of the war organizations, he wore no uniform and bore no title, but he had given his word, and keeping it was his supreme duty. The forty-three-year-old presidential agent had an earthly father, whom he loved, but there were limitations to his admiration for that father. In the past six years F.D.R. had come to be a sort of super-father. Lanny had never tried to formulate it, but if he had been asked to do so he would have called him a Father of the Future, a Father of Victory over Fascism.

V

Baker tapped on the door, and a cheery voice called, " Come in." The crippled man lay on the ancient mahogany bed in which a long line of presidents had slept. Lanny had never seen him in any other position in this room : propped up by pillows, wearing a striped pongee pyjama coat, his spectacles on, some papers in his lap and a stack of them on the table beside him. Always there was a hard day's work behind him, a schedule of callers demanding decisions that would affect the fate of the world. In this room he could be quiet and comfortable ; here he received a few of his trusted friends, and many times stole hours from his sleep for the pleasure of companionship which meant so much to him.

It was a hot night, and an electric fan was playing on the bed, making it necessary to keep a book on top of the papers. The great man called a cheery greeting ; when Lanny had come from China he had been " Marco Polo," and now, browned by the sun of Florida, he was " Ponce de Leon." He grinned and exchanged a warm handclasp, then sat in the chair beside the bed and studied the aspect of his Boss. A big man physically; a big head, and powerful arms and shoulders which he had developed of necessity, by untiring discipline. His hair had become entirely grey, and there was only a little of it left above the temples. The face was deeply lined, and Lanny's heart ached to see it; but he must not give any sign, he must meet the cheery smile and the jest. Business as usual!

"Well, Governor, what's up this time?" The P.A. knew that the hurried summons meant something special, and he thought it an act of kindness to take as little from the great man's sleep as possible.

Roosevelt came directly to the point. "I had a man whom I especially trusted, and I sent him on an important mission to Italy. Yesterday morning I got word that his heart had given out, and they are shipping him home in a box."

"Hard luck!" replied the other gravely. He hoped his own heart could be trusted.

"How well do you know Italy, Lanny?"

"I wouldn't claim to be a specialist, but I've lived most of my life within an hour's drive of the border, and I've visited a few times and motored over the whole country. On the Riviera people come and go, you know, and prior to the war the fashionable world didn't pay much attention to national boundaries. I must have met hundreds of Italians off and on."

"You speak the language?"

"Enough to get along. I wouldn't be able to pose as a native."

"That isn't what I have in mind. I want somebody to meet a few of the top people."

"They all speak French and many speak English."

"Can you think of any who might be sympathetic to our side?"

"I might, but I'd have to give thought to it. The aristocracy submitted to Mussolini only because they had to, and they surely don't like what they're getting now."

"And what they see coming! I can tell you that we are going into Sicily. I don't know the exact day, but it should be next month. Our military men expect it will take us three months to clean out the island. I'm hoping it may be quicker."

" You sound as if you were asking my opinion, Governor."
Lanny smiled as he said it. " I have no idea how many
divisions the Germans have there, but it's a safe bet the
Italians won't put up a desperate struggle."

" That's what we are hoping ; and of course our agents
are working there to persuade them that we'll be good
customers."

" The bombs are helping too, I'm sure."

" What we want is to convince the Italians on the mainland
that they've been backing the wrong horse. We've got the
big airfields in Tunisia in working order, and we're turning
on the heat. We have grave questions to consider—for
example, shall we bomb Rome ? We'll take pains to avoid
hitting the Vatican and the churches ; but the immense
marshalling yards of the railroads are there, serving the whole
peninsula to the south. Putting the railroads out of order is
our most important single job."

" That ought to be easy," Lanny ventured, " because they
have so many tunnels."

" Tunnels have proved to be difficult targets for airmen ;
but saboteurs can get them, and we have people working on
that. What I want is to have someone make contacts with
the governing class and explain what unconditional surrender
will mean to them. We don't want to humiliate them, we
don't come as conquerors, but as liberators of the Italian
people."

" In other words, Governor, we want somebody to do
another Darlan." It was a touchy subject, and the younger
man forced himself to a grin.

" I know you didn't enjoy what you had to do in North
Africa, Lanny, but you ought to see that it worked. We got
the government, we got the army, and we have the French
fighting with us instead of against us."

" You win, Governor. But it won't be so easy in Italy,
for there the government people have the Germans on their
necks. They'll be scared as the devil, and they're not the most
dependable people in the world."

" I know the difficulties, and I'm not giving an order. I
hesitated before putting it up to you. It's a dangerous
mission."

It'll be a useful one, so I'll take a shot at it. But I have to tell you about a misadventure I had with the Fascists at the start of their career. I was in Rome with a lady friend, Marie de Bruyne, nearly twenty years ago. A newspaper-man brought me the news about the murder of Matteotti, and I tried to telephone it to the outside world. The result was I got called up before Italo Balbo, head of the Fascist militia, and they put me out of the country, not too politely. Whenever I have gone in since then I have expected that somebody would look me up in the files; but it never happened, so I decided those old files must have got buried. If anybody dug them out, I could explain it as a youthful aberration. I could point out that Benito called himself a Socialist when he was twenty-two years old."

" I hate like the devil to send you back into enemy territory, Lanny."

" Don't worry for a moment, Governor; I have what amounts to a command from Hitler to return. I'm supposed to be interviewing American crypto-Nazis right now, working on a plan to have you assassinated."

" Have you been making much headway ? " This over-burdened man always managed to spare some time for a smile.

" I was planning a motor trip to interview some of them, just so that I could make up a plausible story for the Führer. But I suppose this new assignment takes precedence."

" Italy happens to be our line of march," said F. D. R.

His P.A. recited, " We'll hang Il Duce on a sour-apple tree, as we go marching on ! "

VI

The arrangement was that Lanny was to report to " Wild Bill " Donovan in the morning, and the Italian section of the Office of Strategic Services would give him a thorough briefing. How he was to get into Il Duce's realm, where he was to go, and whom he was to meet, all that would be talked out, and then Lanny would report to the Boss for final instructions. His reports would have to come through O.S.S. channels, for, alas, the United States had no ambassador and no consuls anywhere in Italy. F. D. R. said that he would arrange for the reports to come first to him, and the son of Budd-Erling

Airplanes would still be classified as a " P.A."—presidential agent.

Lanny went back to the hotel and told his wife that he would be going abroad very shortly—something that she knew already in her heart. He would not say where he was going, and she would not ask. War changed marriage, as it changed everything else in the world. People discovered that they had a country, and that its survival was more important than their own. The husband said, " It won't be dangerous, what I'm doing " ; and maybe that was true and maybe it was what is politely called a fib.

At nine in the morning he presented himself at a rather dingy building in the slum section of Washington. Except for the fact that there was an armed soldier posted at every door you would never have guessed that it was the head-quarters of one of the most important war agencies. In the O.S.S. were combined all the Intelligence departments of the Armed Forces. The genial, rosy Irish-American who headed it had just been promoted to the rank of general. Someone had told him that Lanny Budd was coming, and he had two of his top " Italian " men present—one of them a young New Orleans lawyer of Italian descent, and the other a middle-aged importer of ceramics who had been going to Italy and back most of his life. The General sent them away to an office to stay shut up until they had solved the problems of getting Lanny into enemy land, whom he was to meet there, and what he was to bring out.

They spent the entire day discussing a score of different plans, none of which satisfied the fastidious art expert. Lanny asked for time to think matters over, and then he telephoned Baker to request another appointment with the Boss. Close to midnight, when that tired man had been reading and signing documents for a couple of hours—some of them directing the spending of hundreds of millions of dollars—Lanny Budd was escorted to the second-story bedroom. One glimpse of the care-lined face, and he came at once to the point.

" Governor, those fellows know their kind of job and they're doing it well ; but they don't know my kind, and they are stumped when I confront them with my facts. They want to send me into Italy with false papers and have me pose as John

Jones or Tom Smith. But where can such an unknown get among one of the oldest and most aloof aristocracies in Europe? They overlook the fact that I have met members of that aristocracy through the years, and some of them are bound to find my face familiar. I have met literally hundreds of German officers and Nazi party leaders—remember, I have been a guest in Hitler's home for a couple of weeks at a time. To the first one that recognizes me, I'm a spy, and I'm caught, and I have no possible defence."

"You are right, Lanny," said the President. "I ought to have realized it."

"You have a million things to realize, Governor, and let me realize this one. I have promised the Führer to come back and report to him, and that's my entrée. It would be foolish not to make use of it. I'll tell him that I have come on the trail of treason in Italy—I have got the secret out of the Italians in America, and I want to run the thing down in Rome."

"Can you get him to believe that?"

"I can make it impossible for him not to believe it, because the O.S.S. can give me facts about loyal Italians here. That won't do them any harm because Hitler can't get at them, and his Intelligence doubtless knows about them anyhow. Meantime I have an excuse to meet the Roman governing class and play my double game with them."

"You'll have to give Hitler some results to justify such an effort, won't you?"

"I won't tell him anything that will do him any good, or our friends in Italy any harm. If I tell him that some of his Italian supporters are double-crossing him, how is he going to be sure? In his heart he doesn't trust any Italian that breathes, and I might find a way to ball up his affairs for quite a time."

"All right, Lanny. Have it your way. What do you want from us?"

"Just to be set ashore from a patrol torpedo-boat on some beach near Ostia. They'd better carry one of those little kayaks, because I'd like to be dry-shod—there's a lot in first appearances. I present myself to a German patrol and ask to be taken to Marshal Kesselring—he was a guest at Berchtesgaden the last time I was there. He may remember me, for there were a lot of both Nazis and Junkers who didn't approve of the Führer's having an American in his home at that critical time. When I meet him I'll ask him to call Berlin 116191, and he won't fail to be impressed by my having the Führer's private telephone number. I'll give Hitler my spiel, with the General listening, and the Führer will order me turned loose to do his work."

" That may be all right with the Germans, but what about the Italian police ? "

" Kesselring will give me a pass that will be good throughout the country. The Nazis are running it more completely every day."

" But that will mean you are stamped as a German agent, and you will meet only the wrong sort of people."

" That will serve the purpose pretty nearly as well. It's like the negative of a photograph—it shows the same details, only everything is in reverse. The pro-German Italians will know who the pro-Americans are and will talk about them. General Donovan will give me the address of our ' post office ' in Rome, so that I can send messages to you, and if there should be an important reason for my meeting any of our friends in Italy I can make myself known to the ' post office ' and ask them to check on me with Donovan."

" All that's going to be pretty risky business, Lanny."

" I'll promise to use every precaution. I'll be guided by circumstances and not take any steps that won't pay off. When I've done all I can, I'll see what I run into at the Führer's headquarters."

" You'll run into a madman, Lanny. I can say that, because I know what we and the Russians are going to serve up to him in the next couple of months."

" Adi is never entirely mad ; he's like Hamlet, mad only north-north-west. He'll rave at me because of what my countrymen are doing to turn the world over to the Bolsheviks, and then he'll stop and ask penetrating questions about what sort of fellow this Jewish-Red Rosenfeld is, and finally he'll send me out by way of Sweden to find out how much money Colonel Generoso Pope is raising among the New York Italians to buy General Badoglio in Rome."

"I see you've got the picture, Lanny. Go ahead and do it your way. Tell Donovan to give you the dope on the American-Italians—the many good ones and the few bad ones. And use as much as you need of that money I gave you."

"I don't need any of it, Governor. I sold the two paintings I brought out of Germany for three times what they cost me ; and so long as you will let me go on breaking the law, I can get along nicely—I could even afford to pay you a commission." You could say anything to this democratic aristocrat, provided you employed the right sort of chuckle. He would throw back his head and laugh in a hearty explosion, revealing his somewhat uneven teeth, and also his happy disposition. If only he didn't have to work so hard, thought the son of Budd-Erling !

VII

One of the President's last remarks was, "Jim Stotzlmann was here this evening." Lanny said, "Oh, good ! I was going to look him up in New York." Jim was at the Mayflower, and when Lanny got back to his own hotel he telephoned. This playboy was a night owl and hadn't come in yet, but Lanny tried an hour later, and there he was. Characteristically he offered to come over right away, but Lanny said, "We sleep in my family. Come and have breakfast with me."

This scion of a famous wealthy clan was just the man for Lanny's problem, for he knew everybody who was anybody. As an officer in the Reserve Army, he was now a major, busy with the protection of docks and shipping in New York harbour. As an old friend of the Roosevelt family—F. D. R. had been present at his christening—he had long been a presidential agent ; he hadn't mentioned the fact to Lanny, and Lanny hadn't asked, but each could be certain that the other had guessed. Jim was a big fellow, full of conversation and chuckles, and what secrets he kept were hidden behind a veil of extraordinary frankness. You would have thought him the last person in the world to be a spy.

He looked handsome in his major's uniform, with service decorations from World War I. He gave his friend a warm handclasp, saying, "The Boss told me you've been having adventures." After they had given their orders and the waiter had departed Lanny said, " I'm having an adventure now, and it mustn't be mentioned. I want to find out something about the Italians in New York—those who are with us and those who are against us."

Jim's face lighted up. " Good ! I'll introduce you to a dozen."

" No," Lanny said, " I don't want to meet them through you. It has to be by accident." One secret agent didn't have to say more to another.

The heir of the Stotzlmanns thought for a moment, then said, " I'll tell you. Come to Mrs. McLean's shindig tonight. Everybody comes, and there'll surely be one or two sons of sunny Italy among them."

" Can you get me an invitation ? "

" You won't need it. She lets her close friends bring their friends. When you have a couple of hundred guests you can't even remember."

Lanny hesitated, then added, " We've just motored up from Florida. My wife is with me."

" Bring her along of course."

Lanny still hesitated. " My wife is a bit on the formal side. I don't think she has ever been to an affair where she wasn't invited."

" All right, I'll get Evalyn to send her a note." He pronounced the name " Eevalyn," and Lanny made note of it. " It won't come till afternoon, because she sleeps in the morning."

So, later on, Lanny went upstairs and told his wife what was coming. Her first remark was, " I have no clothes ! "

Lanny said, " Go and get yourself an outfit this morning. This is a show you mustn't miss."

" I'm nobody to those people, Lanny."

" Yes, but they're somebodies to you. Some day you'll be writing a novel about Washington, and Evalyn Walsh McLean is made to order for you. Get yourself the right things so that you can look like one of them and feel at home."

" That might cost a thousand dollars, Lanny."

The figure did not startle the son of Beauty Budd. " It'll come back to you in royalties," he declared. " Cast your bread upon the waters ! "

VIII

Lanny established his credit and got the hotel to cash his cheque, and Laurel went shopping while he reported at the old brick building near the gasworks, and told the genial head officer what he had decided to do. It was arranged that he was to be flown to the city of Tunis, through which he had passed four months ago, when it had been in German hands. From there the victorious American Navy would be requested to drop him off at one of the beaches which have served as summer resorts for Roman citizens for a couple of thousand years. The P.A. received and memorized the location of the American " post office " in the Holy City—the ultra-secret address at which American agents left communications to be forwarded to the O.S.S. He also received a stack of documents, some of which he was free to take with him and study on the journey ; others were marked " top secret " and had to be read in the office, and without making notes.

He found that they had done a thorough job on the aloof Roman aristocracy, also the military, the big industrialists, the political personalities. They had done it for every city, town, and village which could by any chance be involved in the war, pro or anti. Hundreds of thousands of Americans had hunted through their scrapbooks and their attics for photographs and letters, guidebooks, railroad timetables, hotel circulars—everything that might by chance yield a scrap of information useful to a secret agent or to the Armed Forces. Thousands of people had searched in the libraries, in museums, in the records of business concerns, in consular reports. Millions of details had been gathered and classified, and a P.A. might have sat in that little cubicle for a month or two and compiled material about the places he was going to visit and the people he would meet. But by that time it would be too late. His Boss had allowed him only two or three days in Washington and New York, in order to collect a few yarns to tell to the Führer of the Germans, who was mad north-north-west.

IX

When the P.A. came back, toward seven o'clock, he found his wife transformed. She was wearing a lovely pale-blue evening gown, of that kind of simplicity which costs the skies. She had followed his instructions and gone to a " good " place ; she was proud of herself because she had found a dress that became her and had cost only three hundred dollars. Fortunately you didn't wear a hat to an evening party, and all she had had to buy were shoes and gloves to match, and, of course, stockings, and a little handbag that had cost fifty dollars, and a handkerchief for thirty-five. She would not attempt to compete with Mrs. McLean's Hope diamond, said to be worth several millions ; Laurel would appear without jewels.

It had taken a couple of hours to get the dress properly fitted ; so this sensible woman had lain down and read and rested, and now was ready to make a night of it. When Lanny said that he had been getting up data all day, she accepted the statement and asked no questions. He hadn't had to do any shopping because he had his white dinner jacket and black trousers in a suitcase in the car, and the hotel valet had pressed them. Jim Stotzlmann was coming for his friends ; he had a Cadillac and a chauffeur, and that was the way to approach the homes of the wealthy.

When the pair came down to the lobby, Jim took one glance at the lady, whom he had never met before ; he saw that she was " right," and Lanny saw that he saw it. That is the way matters go in the smart world ; you are " right," and your woman is " right," and if you're not you only go once.

On the drive genial Jim told about the place to which they were going and the hostess who was to entertain them. Evalyn Walsh was the daughter of a wretchedly poor miner who had wandered through the Rocky Mountains knocking off chunks in a search for gold. That was no secret, because Evalyn herself had told the details in a book called *Father Struck It Rich*. It was a sort of Aladdin's-lamp story of a sudden rise in the world, far too violent for comfort or even sense. Evalyn, sole heiress to a score of millions, had married the heir of the McLean fortune, derived from a newspaper in Cincinnati. Ned McLean, a loutish fellow with an almost insane temper, had come to Washington and built a monstrous palace in the Victorian style, calling it Friendship House. When Evalyn couldn't stand him any more she had gone to Riga—an odd choice—and got a divorce. Ned had contested it, and there had been a lively scandal. Evalyn, victorious, had sold the mansion and bought herself an estate in Georgetown, where she had built a still more monstrous place, calling it by the old name. It stood on a hilltop, and behind it was a swimming pool as big as the house ; inside it was such an assortment of junk as had never been in the world before—for example, an " animal room," full of miniature creatures made of glass, porcelain, and even plaster.

Long lines of cars were lined up in the drive. Evalyn couldn't endure ever to be alone, and had four huge dining-rooms in which to entertain her guests. " It's all terribly vulgar, of course," said the scion of the Stotzlmanns, whose fortune had come from his great-grandfather and therefore was established and respectable. " Everybody comes because Evalyn really is warm-hearted and likes people. It's a place to meet the people you want to talk to, and have everything in the world you want to eat and drink."

" How can she manage that in wartime ? " asked Laurel, and the answer was, " Some of the more expensive things aren't rationed ; and I suppose she gets poultry and meat and butter and such things from her other estates. No doubt she has a staff who manage it for her, and it wouldn't be good form to ask questions."

" I won't," said Laurel with a smile. She couldn't explain that her curiosity was that of a novelist ; she kept that fact as closely guarded as a war secret. Her story about life in Germany under the Nazis bore the pen-name of Mary Morrow, and was now being praised in papers all over the country ; but nobody knew who this writer was, and nobody had any suspicions about a quiet little woman with a slow smile and soft brown eyes ; nobody guessed what was going on in the busy brain behind those eyes. That suited Laurel, for she wanted to watch people and not to have them watch her. If she were introduced as the author of a popular novel, the people at Friendship House would crowd around her eagerly ; but they would be afraid of her too and would try to pose before her. Let her be plain Mrs. Budd, daughter-in-law of Budd-Erling, and let them be occupied in showing themselves off ; she would go home and make notes about them, and when she put them into a story they wouldn't recognize themselves, since what they read would not coincide with what they believed.

X

Driving into the Friendship House estate was like approaching the opera on opening night ; entering the mansion was like catching the 5.38 at Grand Central Terminal. A line of elegant ladies and gentlemen waited to greet the hostess, and Jim and his pair of pals waited their turn, chatting meantime with others whom Jim knew—there were few he didn't. The hostess proved to be a tall bony lady dressed in pink marabou, satin, and ostrich feathers. She had heavy eyebrows and drooping eyes and mouth, as if she weren't awake yet ; she would tell you that this was her waking time and that she never ate anything until dinner. She would tell you anything about herself, and made it a point not to let riches and fame tone down her mining-camp language and manners. When the party was breaking up, in the small hours of the morning, Lanny heard the hostess screaming to the butler, " Call a car and take these two bums to the station." The " two bums " were leading newspaper columnists, and the hostess wasn't meaning that they were drunk ; she was just kidding them because they had come in a taxicab. The hostess was slightly drunk herself, and so were the majority of her guests, for they had been plied with food and liquor over a period of five or six hours.

You couldn't avoid noticing the great lady's jewelry, nor were you supposed to. Two pear-shaped diamonds hung from her ears, and a great ruby surrounded by diamonds hung by a gold chain across her forehead. Chains of diamonds dangled all over her, and miscellaneous jewels gleamed from her fingers. The *pièce de résistance* was the famed Hope diamond said to be the largest in the world. It hung from a chain over her bosom and was set off by diamond sunbursts, one pinned to her dress on each side. If you expressed interest in the Hope —and of course that was why it was there—you would be invited to lift it by the chain and feel its weight ; but you had to promise not to touch it, because there was an old tradition that ill luck befell anyone who so presumed.

Washington society agreed in polite whispers that this tradition had surely been vindicated in the case of the present owner of this treasure. Evalyn's marriage had gone on the rocks and her husband had died in an insane asylum ; her daughter, a frail and melancholy girl, had recently become the wife of " Buncombe Bob " Reynolds, one-time circus barker who had become senator from North Carolina and was one of the most ardent propagandists of that brand of hundred per cent Americanism which could hardly be distinguished from Nazi-Fascism. Lanny and his wife had no means of knowing that the young wife of an old man was going to poison herself within a year or two, but when they were introduced to her they realized that she was a far from happy person. Lanny had met so many sons and daughters of the rich who were maladjusted that it had become a sort of formula to him.

The heir of the Stotzlmanns wasn't happy either ; he had had four marriages and four failures, and on the drive back home he poured out his heart to the wife of Lanny Budd. It had occurred to him that she might know some girl who was what he called " nice " ; that is to say, a girl who was old-fashioned and believed in love ; who wouldn't have her head turned by an awesome family name and attempt to buy out the contents of Tiffany's in the first month of marriage. Laurel said that was a difficult problem and she'd have to think it over. Before she had finished this thinking, she read in the papers that Jim was married again, and the next time she met him she learned that he was on the way to his fifth divorce.

XI

But meantime, here he was, a deputy host and loyal friend. Lanny had expressed a desire to meet some Italians, for a reason too important to be explained. All right ; Jim wandered about in the crowded drawing-rooms, something that was difficult because so many people knew him and grabbed hold of him, and he couldn't hurt their feelings, being kind of heart. Especially the ladies ; there were scores of them who had spent the day as Laurel had spent it, making themselves beautiful and getting ready for whatever adventure might come into sight. What better than this unattached heir of Chicago's famous family ?

Jim persisted and presently came upon what he wanted— no less a personage than Signor Generoso Pope, which the Italians rhyme with " ropy," but which the Americans say as one syllable. He was indeed a sort of lay pope to well-to-do and conservative Italians of the United States ; publisher of the newspaper they all read, and counsellor and guide in matters of business, politics, and finances. Signor Pope had told his readers that Mussolini was the heaven-sent regenerator of *la patria*, destined to restore the glories of the ancient Roman Empire, and they had believed him, all save a few malcontents. Now, alas, the Signor and his subscribers were in an embarrassing position, and he had to use more weasel words than had ever crawled backward out of any hole in the earth.

There were many people of that sort here tonight, for Friendship House was the council hall of all the New-Deal haters in the national capital. Here Lanny shook hands with the all-powerful Mr. Harrison Dengue, who not long ago had been working on a plan to have President Roosevelt kidnapped from his Hyde Park home and kept under the orders of persons who wanted to stop lend-lease to Russia. Here he shook hands with a Congressman who had allowed the Nazi agents in this country to use his congressional frank to mail out literature written by a Nazi agent. Here he met multi-millionaire Jimmie Cromwell, and publisher Cissie Patterson, and Igor Cassini, her satirical " society " columnist.

But Lanny was looking especially for Italians ; and by extraordinary good fortune, when he and his wife entered one of the four big dining-rooms, he discovered himself seated next to the person of all persons whom he would have chosen. What had happened was that Jim had got the ear of the hostess and mentioned that his friend, the son of Budd-Erling, was interested in meeting this product of the melting-pot ; and Evalyn had beckoned to her steward, or whoever it was that stood near awaiting her orders. The place-cards were shifted, and thus Signor Generoso Pope found himself in conversation with an agreeable gentleman who had been raised almost at the front door of Signor Pope's native land, who had travelled all through it by motor-car, knew its cities, its art treasures and cathedrals, and had met pretty nearly every distinguished person the Signor could name.

Lanny Budd put himself out to make himself agreeable, and he had what it took. He was an art expert who had had the choosing of several collections of paintings for wealthy Americans ; more than that, he was the son of one of America's great industrialists, whose airplanes were flying all over the world and helping to win a war which the son insisted ought never to have been started. It was one of the tragedies of history, and whichever side won, both sides would lose. That was exactly what Signor Pope thought, and he wished he could say it in such eloquent language. He was a naïve-appearing gentleman, with a round face, dark hair, and prominent eyes.

A warm friendship was struck up ; and when the Signor learned that Mr. Budd was proceeding to New York next day, he asked the pleasure of taking him in his car. Lanny said he was delighted, and didn't mention anything about having a wife and baby and a car of his own. Laurel would drive that car to New York, and Lanny would ride with the publisher ; he would deplore the war, and also the New Deal and its extravagances, and lead this exuberant son of the South to pour out his troubled soul. When the ride was over, Lanny would know pretty nearly everything he wanted to know about the near-Fascists and the crypto-Fascists of the Italian colony of New York ; and about the nine Italian generals who had been captured in North Africa and were now interned in Tennessee, from where they were diligently working for a separate peace. All this for the price of one evening ensemble, which his wife would carefully preserve for other occasions when it might be necessary to help her husband meet the " right " sort of people.

XII

Laurel did not fail to notice her husband's sudden interest in the Italian publisher, and the fact that he had upon his reading-table an assortment of literature—pamphlets, clippings, typewritten and mimeographed sheets—all dealing with that country. With an Anglo-American army poised just across the strait of Sicily, and with radio and newspapers speculating as to when it meant to cross, Laurel had no trouble in guessing her husband's destination. When tears welled into her eyes, she would turn her head and go into the next room and pull herself together. As old as human history is the fact that men go away into danger while women stay at home and weep. But in this case the woman had to want him to go ; she had to value the overthrow of Nazi-Fascism more than she valued his life and her own happiness.

Only once did he mention the data he was storing in his mind. That was when he came upon a pamphlet bearing the imprint of the Italy-America Society of New York ; reading it, he began to chuckle, and then to laugh. " Listen," he said, " here is your guide and guardian, Otto Hermann Kahn." He liked to tease her about a strange circumstance which had developed in her life : an intimacy with a departed spirit, one-time possessor of a vast fortune upon which he could no longer draw. A thing almost beyond imagining, for in real life Laurel Creston had met this urbane and elegant gentleman only in the most casual way, and it was with consternation she had learned that he had taken up uninvited residence in her subconscious mind.

The son of Budd-Erling had long been interested in what is known as " psychical research," but only four years had passed since Laurel had learned that she was a possessor of the gift called mediumship. From that time on the former senior partner of Kuhn, Loeb and Company, Wall Street bankers, had been her " steady company." Whenever she went into a trance, he would speak without waiting to be invited. Laurel herself had never heard this " spirit " voice and knew about him only what Lanny or others told her he had said while she lay in a deep kind of sleep. Of late she had feared to enter this state with any person other than her husband present, for Lanny had so many secrets to hide, and Otto seemed to know them. They could not take the risk that he might mention forbidden matters at the séance.

What Lanny now had in his hands was an address which had been delivered by the great or ex-great banker, revealing him in the role of social philosopher and prophet. Nearly twenty years ago, on November 15, 1923, he had betaken his cultured and affable self to Wesleyan University, in Connecticut, and there before the faculty and students had spoken *ex cathedra* concerning the events of the time. Benito Mussolini had taken power a year and a half earlier, and America wanted to know what sort of man he was. Otto Kahn told them :

" The credit for having brought about this great change in Italy, and without bloodshed, belongs to a great man, beloved and revered in his own country, a self-made man, setting out with nothing but the genius of his brain. To him not merely his own country but the world at large owes a debt of gratitude. . . . Mussolini is far from fomenting class hatred or using class animosities or divergencies for political purposes. . . . He is neither a demagogue nor a reactionary. He is neither a chauvinist nor a bull in the china shop of Europe. He is no enemy of liberty. He is no dictator in the generally understood sense of the word."

There was a whole discourse along those lines, and a memorandum attached to the pamphlet stated that the Italy-America Society had printed it in both English and Italian and given it wide circulation in both countries. When Lanny got through with it he remarked, " I ought to remind Otto of that, and hear what he thinks of it now ! "

" He might resent it," his wife objected. " He might drop us from his calling list."

" Well, he hasn't had anything useful to tell us for some time, and it might be well if you had a change of ' controls.' Let's try a séance and maybe he'll bring it up himself."

XIII

It was in the autumn of 1929, during the dreadful Wall Street panic, that Lanny had learned about this strange mode of procedure from an old Polish woman whom his stepfather had discovered in a New York tenement. Lanny had taught it to his wife, and now she lay on her bed in a half-darkened room, while he sat close by with a writing pad on his knee and a pencil in his hand. Laurel began to breathe heavily ; she moaned for a while and then lay still. Lanny waited. At length he asked in a quiet tone, " Is anyone present ? "

There came at once the voice which claimed to be Otto Kahn. The way to get results from that voice was to take it for what it called itself, and be as urbane as the most urbane of Maecenases had been on earth. " Well, Otto, happy to meet you again. Where have you been keeping yourself ? "

" I would tell you if I knew, Lanny."

One couldn't be sure whether that was banter, or whether it was a fact concerning the strange limbo in which these subconscious entities had their existence. The banker-being wouldn't state explicitly, but at times it appeared that he wanted Lanny to believe that he existed only when Laurel invited him to exist. At other times he would know things that Laurel didn't know, or at any rate that she didn't know she knew. Since the learned psychologists agree that the subconscious mind never forgets anything, how can you know what you know ? To be accurate, you can only say, " I don't know it so far as I remember at this moment."

Lanny and the banker-being chatted for a while as two gentlemen might who encountered each other in a broker's office or the smoking-room of a club. After a bit Lanny said, " By the way, Otto, I just happened to come upon a copy of an address which you delivered at Wesleyan University almost twenty years ago."

" Indeed," said the other. " I hope it didn't bore you as much as it did me."

" It didn't bore me at all. I thought it an interesting example of precognition. Do you remember that you said, ' Mussolini is far too wise and right-minded a man to lead his people into hazardous foreign adventures ' ? "

" Did I really say that, Lanny ? "

" It stands in print ; and you went on to say, ' Mussolini is particularly desirous for close and active co-operation with the United States. I feel certain that American capital invested in Italy will find safety, encouragement, opportunity, and reward.'"

"Dear me!" said the ex-banker. "I am embarrassed."

"Did you put any of your own funds into Il Duce's bonds, Otto?"

"As you know, my friend, we international bankers took foreign bonds in large blocks and sold them to the public. If we had any left over, we considered that we had exhibited bad judgment."

"I believe the record shows that before he marched on Rome—in a sleeping-car—Mussolini got the assurance of the American Ambassador, Richard Washburn Child, that he would get a loan of two hundred million dollars from J. P. Morgan and Company."

"We bore no affection for that firm, but it may be that we handled a portion of those securities. That was, no doubt, the reason I made the speech. You know how it is, Lanny—no man who plays the races can say that he never backed the wrong horse."

Exactly the way it would have been in the smoking-room of the club! Lanny could imagine the smile on the banker's face and the twinkle in his eyes. Otto knew perfectly well that he was being kidded, and he was giving change in the same currency. Lanny added to his amusement by remarking, "You ought to be ashamed of yourself! My father bought some of those bonds."

"Well, Lanny," was the reply, "they will always be good for wallpaper. I used to have a friend who had covered one wall of his rumpus room with souvenirs of his wrong guesses. It turned out that he had to spoil the job by peeling one of the documents off the wall. It was mining stock, and it paid the cost of the whole house. Tell your father to hold on to his bonds, because Fascism may come back—someday we may find that we need it in our own business."

XIV

Enough of banter! The P.A. had a serious purpose in mind. "Listen, Otto," he said in a different voice. "I'm not blaming you. I know that many of our greatest thinkers were sure

Il Duce had solved the problem of labour unions once and for all ; I know that Nicholas Miraculous, almighty president of Columbia University, told the world it was so, and turned the university into one of Mussolini's transmission belts. But now our country is at war with the rascal, and you have a chance to do a patriotic service."

" What can that be, Lanny ? "

" I'd like to talk with somebody who knows the insides of Italian affairs as they stand at the moment."

" *Santissima Vergine!* Do you suppose I keep Italian statesmen on ice ? "

" I don't know how you do it, Otto, and you don't seem to want to tell me. See if you can't find me some Italian who has recently come over. The American armies are going into Italy, and they will need help there."

A pause, and Lanny waited patiently for this strange psychic machinery to grind. Suddenly Otto spoke again, and with no mockery in his tone. " There is a man here who was young when he died ; he is dark, smooth-shaven, an intellectual ; handsome fellow. He says you tried to help him."

" What did I do ? "

" He was murdered, and you tried to tell the world about it. He is very grateful."

" That must be Matteotti. Can he speak directly to me ? "

" He says he will try, but his English is not good."

Lanny replied in Italian, " My Italian is not good either, but I understand it. You must know that a martyr does not die in vain. The name of Giacomo Matteotti is known not merely in Italy, but also to liberal-minded people throughout the world. They have learned that the cowardly Mussolini ordered your murder because he dared not face the exposure of his regime that you were making in the Chamber of Deputies. The world understands that you spoke for democratic Socialism, the hope of all enlightened elements in Western Europe now."

A grave man's voice replied through the lips of the entranced woman. " The proof of Mussolini's guilt exists. It is in a memorial of Filippo Filippelli, who was editor of the Fascist newspaper, *Corriere Italiano,* and the man who provided the assassin Dumini with the car in which I was carried away. That memorial has been suppressed for nineteen years. You should try to get a copy of it. My son Matteo will help you."

"I cannot take the chance of meeting members of the underground at present. What I need is the names of those in power who are ready to break with the tyrant."

"Galeazzo Ciano is a scoundrel, but he sees that his father-in-law's days are numbered, and he will seek to save his own skin. One of the men who carried Mussolini's orders to Dumini is Giovanni Contarelli, and he is one you should meet. He was then Parliamentary Secretary of the Fascist party and served his master well, but now he knows that his idol is about to tumble."

Lanny repeated these Italian names as he wrote them down: Filippo Filippelli, Galeazzo Ciano, Dumini, Contarelli. Then he asked, "Are there others?"

The voice replied, "Cesare Rossi, head of the Press Bureau, and Aldo Finzi, Under-Secretary of the Ministry of the Interior, also prepared memorials concerning Mussolini's guilt. It is necessary to be careful in dealing with these men. They are like weathercocks which turn quickly, according to the shifting of the wind."

"I shall know about that wind," replied the P.A. There came a sigh from his wife, and he knew what that meant. She began to groan as if she were having a nightmare; then she opened her eyes and blinked once or twice. The trance was over. She asked, "What happened?"

"Otto came," was the reply, "but he just kidded me. Said that my father should use his Italian Fascist bonds to paper the walls of his rumpus room."

"What an epitome of the spirit of our time!" exclaimed the literary lady. "I believe I shall put that into a book."

She went to bed, but lay awake, and while he slept she went into the next room and sat at her desk. In the morning she put a paper into his hand, saying, "I wrote a poem. Read it when you have the leisure."

He took the leisure at once and read:

> The world lies like a stone upon my heart
>   With all its urgencies and vast despair;
> The world from which so soon I may depart,
>   Not knowing when I go, or where.

2

Do Well the Duty

I

LAUREL drove her husband out to Port Washington on Long Island. He was being flown in a big Douglas, known as a C. 54. It had a crew of six and was supposed to carry a score of passengers, but there were only half a dozen and the rest of the load was mail sacks, covered with canvas and laced in position with ropes, like a spider web. The P.A. had a seat upholstered in snakeskin, the latest thing in elegance. Laurel saved her tears until after the plane was up in the air ; then she dried them and drove the car back to New York.

As for the P.A., he read the Italian material he had brought along. The sea beneath him appeared as smooth as a sheet of glass, and the white clouds were close and cool-appearing. Once there was excitement—they were passing a convoy, and the passengers gazed out upon tiny-seeming vessels, scattered in regular rows like a newly planted vineyard. The plane dropped a smoke flare as a recognition signal, and took the precaution to give the convoy a wide berth, for freshly trained crews manning anti-aircraft guns were apt to shoot first and inquire afterward.

The first call was Bermuda, which had been a tourist paradise and now was a busy naval and air base, taken over from the British. A couple of hours stop and they were off to the Azores, where the British had charge of the job of hunting submarines and escorting convoys. The farms were tiny, and from above had as many colours as a crazy quilt, the border stitches being fences of piled-up stones. Coming down, Lanny could see brown, barefooted peasants cultivating their toy plots with bullocks. The houses were of volcanic rock, plastered with adobe, resembling those he had seen in the valley of the Rio Grande. Centuries ago Texas and the Azores had been part of the great Spanish Empire.

The same plane but with a new crew carried him on the next leg of the journey, to Marrakech in French Morocco. This oasis in a desert land had been made into an airport for American bombers, which now flew the Atlantic without a stop. Lanny had been here just after the Casablanca Conference, and had spent a night in a sumptuous villa along with Roosevelt and Churchill. Now he was to have a night in the town, and he was pleased, because his mother and stepfather were at the Hôtel Mamounia.

II

Beauty Budd had never thought that she could face the ordeal of having her sixtieth birthday. But somehow, when it came, it was like any other day ; she had avoided mentioning it, and nobody but her husband knew about it, and it didn't bother him because he was a religious mystic who had learned that time was only a form of thought, and his thought was that it didn't matter. His hair had become snow-white and made a nice combination with his rosy complexion and bland and benign countenance.

Beauty had never been much for the outdoor life, not even on the French Riviera where she had spent most of her days. She considered the sun an enemy of a peach complexion, and when she went out to cut roses for her dinner table it had always been with a big straw hat and a white veil. For years she had had her reward and been able to justify her name with only the normal amount of cosmetics. But now the wrinkles had gathered, and she had given up counting them ; skin enamel and other devices did no good, and, besides, it was becoming impossible to get the stuff at any price. There was nothing for poor Beauty to do but turn to God, according to her husband's advice.

Now came her only son, with whom she was well pleased. Only terror kept her from gossiping about his wonderfulness, his ability to meet the great ones of the earth in whatever land he visited, even in wartime. He had warned her with the utmost seriousness that talk might cost him his life ; so

all she could say was, " My son is one of the most celebrated
art experts. The museums accept his authority, and some of
our greatest millionaires employ him to purchase paintings
for them." She was free to pile that on as thick as she pleased ;
she might name the Taft collection, and the Winstead collection, and the Vernon collection of Moorish mosaics and doorways and fountains for ablutions. Everybody knew him in
Marrakech and points north-east, and hopes would rise among
the owners of cultural treasures.

This time Lanny could only stay overnight. He was bound
for Algiers, and beyond that he would not say. He had
dumped his printed matter about Italy into the sea, and
Beauty could not get any clues from his baggage—even if she
had had a chance to peek into it. They sat up most of the
night while she plied him with questions about families and
friends. How was his wife, and how were they getting along ?
Lanny said they were doing fine, and that Beauty's judgment
had been vindicated. She swallowed that, as she had swallowed
all compliments all her life—most of them had been true, and
why should she bother to sort them out ? The fact was, she
had accepted Laurel Creston only in the last extreme, after
trying one heiress after another as bait for the most eligible
of men. She had given up gracefully at the end, and now,
since they had a baby, the matter was settled.

How was the baby ? Had his blond hair changed colour ?
No, it hadn't. Were his eyes still blue ? No, they were brown
now, like those of Lanny and his mother. Had he spoken any
word yet ? Had he made any effort to get up on his feet ?
And so on and on, as you might expect from a grandmother
who was being kept by a cruel war four thousand miles away
from the most precious of her possessions.

And then Robbie Budd, and his family in Newcastle, Connecticut. Several years had passed since Beauty had seen
Lanny's father ; but Lanny had talked with him over the
phone just before flying and reported that all was well. Budd-
Erling was turning out the fastest pursuit plane in the world,
and doing it wholesale now ; the planes had helped to win
the battle in Tunisia and were doing a job over Sicily that
you could hear about every hour or two over the French
radio. Beauty did not fail to listen, because it was a question

of when she would be free to return to her home in Juan-les-Pins.

Did Lanny think that little bit of heaven was going to be blasted into ruins ? Lanny didn't think so, at least not soon. That was as far as he would go, and he warned her not to repeat even that much to anybody. In the present situation of the Armed Forces his words meant that the next destination must be Sicily. Beauty complained that other people talked so much more freely than her son. He answered, " Those who talk freely don't know what they are talking about."

In the morning there was Marcel, child of Lanny's half-sister Marceline. He had an Italian father, and looked it, with lovely dark eyes and hair. In Florida, not long ago, listening to an overseas broadcast, Lanny had heard this father, a major in the Italian Army in Tunisia, referred to as a war prisoner. He told Beauty about it, and they agreed in hoping that the bad egg whom Marceline had divorced would be put away for a long period. The child, nearly five, had taken this splendid hotel for his playground, making friends equally with guests and staff. His mother was in Germany, and he had pretty well forgotten her ; he knew Uncle Lanny better, and was grieved because this delightful person couldn't stay and teach him dancing steps.

Beauty Budd knew better than to ask where her son was going, or on what errand. She was one more woman who had to be left behind—not to weep, because that was bad for the complexion, but to fear and if possible learn to pray. She was the daughter of a Baptist preacher, but hadn't liked his way of praying and had got away from it at the earliest possible moment. Now she had to learn all over again from her husband, who had an entirely different lingo and technique. Parsifal Dingle didn't believe there was any hell, or that you had to be totally immersed in water to have your sins washed away. He believed that all the religions had one God, even when they didn't know it ; also that that God was in you, even when you didn't know it. Parsifal occupied himself with loving everybody, even when they didn't desire it and gave few signs of deserving it. This was an interesting experiment and gave evidence of success, particularly unexpected in a city made up of Moorish fanatics, French soldiers and traders, wealthy idlers, poverty-stricken refugees, and international spies.

III

A new plane took the P.A. to Algiers, and no questions asked. This white city on the hilly slopes of a beautiful bay had become one of Lanny Budd's numerous homes ; he had spent months here off and on, helping to prepare the way for the landing of the American troops. He had made many friends, real or pretended ; and some of them were now in jail, and some were in the French Army, and others were scattered to new posts of duty. Lanny reported to Robert Murphy, diplomatic representative of the American government to the government of French North Africa—which meant the whole of France, since Hitler had put the Vichy crowd out of business. F. D. R. had said, " You won't need any word from me. The less there is in writing the better." Lanny repeated these words to Murphy, and Murphy raised no objection, for the two had worked together and shared their secrets.

" Italy ? " said the genial careerman. " That's a pretty tough assignment ! "

" I know," replied Lanny, " but I have some connections there from the old days." He didn't hint what they were, and he certainly wasn't going to tell Bob Murphy or anybody else that he had been into Germany and spent a night in Hitler's headquarters. The last the diplomat had seen of the P.A., he had sent his car to convey Lanny to the Maison Blanche air-field in Algiers. Lanny had departed in an English " recce " plane for Cairo, and neither the plane nor the pilot had been seen again. How Lanny had escaped and got back to Washington was a mystery, and Murphy would have listened to the story gladly ; but Lanny didn't see fit to tell it, and the tactful diplomat forbore to ask.

He answered questions about various persons. Lanny's old-time friend, Raoul Palma, was no doubt working for the O.S.S. Murphy had no idea where, and Lanny wouldn't try to find out, because Raoul had no connections in Italy. The same thing was true of Jerry Pendleton, once Lanny's tutor. Captain Denis de Bruyne was in the new French Army, somewhere in Tunisia, and had taken part in the fighting. Lanny didn't try to meet any of his other friends in Algiers, for he wished to avoid talk about his destination. As for Murphy, he was up to his ears in the squabbles of the various groups of French politicians. A preposterous situation, with General Giraud running the French Army and General de Gaulle running the government. Robert Murphy could hardly have helped feeling uncomfortable if a perambulating art expert had been going about asking questions as to the situation, which dated back through several centuries of French history. The son of an Irish-American railroad section-hand surely had but slight responsibility for it. Lanny asked no questions.

IV

From the familiar Maison Blanche airport a bombing plane made room for a mysterious American traveller and the small suitcase in which he carried his toothbrush and comb, handkerchiefs, socks, and a change of underwear. The only papers he carried were the passport in his pocket and a couple of Nazi pamphlets in his suitcase. Lanny wasn't going to pose as a German in Italy, but he was going to look and talk like one, and let the man in the street, *l' uomo qualunque*, take him for that. He didn't know just how the Germans mutilated Italian, but he knew the consonants over which they stumbled in English, and it seemed safe to assume that they would have the same trouble in another language ; Lanny would say *ja* and *nein* on occasions, sprinkle in a *Donnerwetter* and an *um Gottes Willen*, and assume that the average cab driver, café waiter, and policeman in Rome would dislike him heartily but be afraid to express his feelings.

The trip to the port of Bizerte took less than an hour. First the Italians and then the Germans had seized it, and both had built fine airfields and had had no time to wreck them. Now a steady stream of planes was pouring in, the bombers flying all the way from America with only one stop at Marrakech, and the smaller planes being landed from carriers and ships at Casablanca. The field was as busy as the deck of a carrier in action. Each plane circled until it was ordered in, and the moment it came to a stop it was rushed off the field and another came gliding down. There was an incessant hum of high-up fighters guarding the base from German raiders ; but these came rarely now, having learned the rate of exchange. " Three for one," said the field officer of whom Lanny asked this question.

The arriving passenger was met by an alert young Naval Intelligence man. An order had come through, and he put Lanny into a jeep and proceeded to brief him even while they were driving. What precisely did Mr. Budd want ? When Mr. Budd said he wanted to be deposited dry-shod on the black volcanic sands of the beach resort of Ostia, the officer said that would be too risky a journey in a P.T. (patrol torpedo-boat). The P.T.'s were making such runs, of course, but they got shot up by planes, and the Navy didn't want to take risks with a V.I.P. (very important person). The job would better be done by a sub. Lanny asked if there was one handy, and he was told they didn't often come into port ; they were refuelled at sea, and when one did come in it took time to refit and supply it.

" My orders are to get to Rome at the earliest possible moment," said the mysterious civilian. " They allowed me only three days to be briefed in Washington and New York. Couldn't you put me aboard a sub by seaplane ? "

" The trouble is, the subs never radio their whereabouts except in an emergency. You understand, that would be too helpful to the enemy. I'll have to consult my superiors and see what can be done for you."

V

The officer drove his guest into the country and parked him in the shade of an acacia tree. He wouldn't let him be seen in Intelligence headquarters, which were in a com- mandeered hotel in the city. " There are spies everywhere," he said, and Lanny was duly grateful.

This Lieutenant Ferguson was not a regular Navy man, he explained ; the reason he knew so much about Italy was that he was a painter and had spent a couple of years in Rome and Florence. That had been up to the time of Mussolini's declaration of war on America, and Ferguson had been interned

with the newspaper-men, first in the Regina Coeli prison—
what a name for a hellhole, the Queen of Heaven !—and then
in the ancient city of Siena. Apparently his father had been
a man of means, for he had met many of the " right " people
in Rome—" right " in the political as well as the social sense.

Ferguson didn't ask questions about whom Lanny knew,
or how he expected to get by with both the Italian and the
German authorities. He understood that this was somebody
special, and he just told what he knew about conditions in a
land unwillingly at war. He had heard the Germans speaking
what they called Italian and could give an imitation of them,
very comical—and there was no harm in laughing heartily
under an acacia tree. The young officer had brought a basket
of lunch and they made a day of it ; Lanny asked questions
and the other poured out answers. He liked the Italians but
loathed the Germans, and the Italians shared both these attitudes. Lanny had heard the phrase " friendly enemies," and
now he learned a new phrase—" unfriendly allies." Italy had
been at war for three years and hadn't been able to beat even
the Greeks ; the Italians were humiliated, hungry—and
helpless.

The Navy had a policy, derived from the State Department
or from the Combined Allied General Staffs, Ferguson didn't
know which. We were not asking the Italian people to revolt,
because we knew they couldn't—the Fascists had all the
weapons. We didn't want to throw the country into tumult,
for that would make it harder to manage and in the long run
wouldn't help anybody but the Bolsheviks. The programme
was to knock out the Mussolini gang and make a deal with the
higher Army officers and the big business crowd, who would
be ready to come over to our side as soon as we were ashore
in force. That was the way to take advantage of the anti-
German sentiment in Italy ; the way to get the fleet and the
air bases and save the lives of American soldiers.

" In other words, just what we did in North Africa," said
the P.A., and the ex-painter said, " It worked there, and all
the Italians know it, and the higher-ups aren't thinking about
anything except to be the lucky de Gaulle or Giraud."

" I notice you don't say ' the lucky Darlan,' " replied
Lanny with a chuckle. He didn't say how he had been worried

by the prospect of having one of the worst of the Vichyites put in charge of the first of our military conquests, and how lucky we had been in having that incubus knocked off our necks by several bullets from an assassin's pistol. Lanny wasn't here to carry out his own policies ; he was taking the orders of his Boss, and he tried not to worry, because they were also the orders of Winston Churchill.

VI

The P.A. was driven back to the city of Bizerte and left to find himself accommodation in one of the hotels which had not been taken over by the military. Lieutenant Ferguson gave him a pass which would serve if he were stopped by the Military Police. At nine next morning he was to walk past the Hôtel-de-Ville, the city hall of Bizerte, and Ferguson would be there if he had any news. If not, Lanny was to come again at noon and again at three. All that was an old story to a secret agent who had been posing as an art expert all over Europe for six years.

He said, " I would like you to do me one favour. I have an old friend who is an officer in General Giraud's army ; his father is an extremely wealthy man, and they may know people in Italy who will be of use to me. Captain Denis de Bruyne is his name, and if he happens to be anywhere near by he will come to see me at once."

Lieutenant Ferguson said it should be possible to find him ; it was arranged that after getting settled in a hotel Lanny would go outside and call Ferguson on the phone—not mentioning his own name, but merely the name of the hotel where he could be found. If Ferguson was able to find Captain de Bruyne, he would give the code message that " Annette " was in town and where she was staying. Annette was the name of Denis's wife, and he and Lanny had used it as code in Algiers. There was, alas, no chance that the real Annette could be anywhere within reach, for she was in Seine-et-Oise, in the hands of the Germans, and Denis had not seen her since he had made his escape after being wounded in battle three years ago.

Lanny found a room, not without some difficulty ; then,

after eating a rather skimpy dinner in a café, he went back to the room, took off his clothes—for it was not merely hot but muggy—and stretched out on the bed, not to sleep, but to recite to himself the lessons he had learned during the day. Not for anything would he have made notes of them ; he must go over them and impress them upon his mind—names, places, dates, and the details which would have been gossip under other circumstances, but which in the near future might be the means of saving or losing his life. Dino Grandi had been popular with the Cliveden set when he had been ambassador in London ; Federzoni, chairman of the Italian Academy, was rumoured to be getting ready to desert Il Duce's sinking ship ; the same for the Count of Turin, cousin to the King ; Marshal Cavallero had been involved in a shipbuilding scandal during the war and had been ousted by Mussolini ; ex-Premier Orlando—good God, they were even thinking of resurrecting that aged stout souvenir of the Paris Peace Conference of 1919 ! The grandson of Budd Gunmakers, as Lanny had been then, had met an American lady who had sat next to the then Premier of Italy at a dinner party, and had been struck dumb by his statement that his wife never got out of childbed without having become pregnant again. Now these hastily begotten sons were at an age to be knocked out of the skies by American airmen, or bombed in Taranto and Spezia because they did not dare to bring their ships out to sea. What a world !

VII

In the midst of this came a tap on the door and a voice telling Lanny there was a gentleman to see him. He replied that he would come, put on his clothes hurriedly, and went down into the lobby. There was Denis, his face worn, and looking not too spruce in his uniform. They did not embrace as they would normally have done ; Lanny made a motion with his finger, and they walked out and down the street together until they came to the park near the waterfront. There they found themselves a seat, and the light of a half moon made it possible for them to be sure that no spy was in reach of their low voices.

Until recently the P.A. had been able to go into Vichy

France and to meet Denis's younger brother, Charlot, who
was one of the hated pro-German crowd. But now those days
were over, and Lanny had no news of the erring young officer.
The Vichyites had set up a mock government somewhere near
the German border ; their Army men might now be on the
Russian front, or they might have been sent into Sicily.
Poor Denis was obsessed by the dreadful idea that he might
meet his brother on the field of battle. Such things had
happened in all civil wars, in France as in America, and the
elder imagined himself turning a dead body over and seeing
the face which had been dear to him from infancy up to the
time of *la patrie's* tragic collapse.

Presently he said, " I heard that you were lost, Lanny.
I was dreadfully upset."

" I was down in the desert," the other explained ; " but
I got out all right. I had the fortune to meet a camel caravan."
He didn't say that he had been brought into the German lines,
or where he had been since parting from his friend. Instead
he remarked casually, " I gather that we are going into
Sicily." This, of course, would be no secret to a French officer.

" You should pay a visit to our troops, Lanny. You would
be delighted by what you would see. The honour of France
has been saved."

" You have seen real fighting. I learned from the radio."

" All the way from Kasserine to Cap Bon. We have stood
up to the enemy, with weapons as good as his own, or better,
and we have driven him back, foot by foot. We had to storm
one hill after another, for a hundred miles—positions the
enemy had been preparing for half a year."

Lanny encouraged his old friend to tell this story. For
three years Denis had lived in humiliation, not merely because
la patrie was under the conqueror's jackboot, but because to
a clear-sighted Frenchman it was apparent that his own bad
judgment, and that of his family and his class, had been
responsible for the débâcle. But now Denis had helped to
wipe out the stain, with his own blood and that of his men.
He had got a bullet through the shoulder and had stayed in
action for a whole day with merely two chunks of cotton
poked into the wound at each opening. He looked like a
much older man.

"Tell me," said the P.A. as casually as he could, "how do your men feel about the prospect of fighting their way through Italy."

"They are dancing with impatience, Lanny. They will consider that they are on their way home. Do you suppose there is any chance of our landing on the Riviera?"

"Nobody tells me things like that, *cher ami*. But there seems a good chance of your marching to Rome this year. Do you know anybody there?"

"I have a cousin in Rome, the Marchesa di Caporini. She visited Paris not long before the war."

"I heard your mother speak of her, but that was before the Marchesa's marriage. What sort of person is she?"

"A very elegant lady, but not very happy, I believe. The Roman aristocracy must be in a bad way by now; as you Americans say, they have got a bull by the tail."

"Your cousin's family is committed to the regime?"

"She was when we saw her. She did not make a success with us because she thought Italy ought to have Nice and Savoy. We couldn't see that such an issue was worth fighting about, but we considered it decidedly bad taste. It is painful to realize what fools we were in those days, Lanny. We really believed the dictators were generous men, planning to bring in a new regime of order and prosperity."

Lanny replied, "You must keep that in mind when you think about Charlot. Both you and your father taught him to believe in the New Order, as you called it. You must not blame him if he cannot change his mind as fast as you."

"Believe me, Lanny, I think of that all the time. If only I could get hold of him, to reason with him, to make him see what satanic actions his Nazi friends have performed!"

The other smiled. "I am afraid he would reply by citing the satanic actions of the Russians. He would not fail to add what the British Fleet did at Oran, or Mers-el-Kébir, as you call it. I do not know what he would cite against us Americans, because he was too polite to mention that subject to me. He would surely not be pleased by our invasion of the soil of Algiers, which is called a part of Metropolitan France and therefore is sacred."

VIII

In the morning the P.A. strolled past the Hôtel-de-Ville at
the hour specified, and then back again, but there was no sign
of the Intelligence lieutenant. Lanny walked and inspected
the great naval base of Bizerte, which was now British and
American, and which would live in Army history because it
rhymed with " dirty Gertie." (It didn't, but the G.I.'s weren't
going to bother their heads or tongues with the correct pro-
nunciation of any foreign name.) These khaki-clad heroes
were performing prodigies of labour, restoring docks and cranes,
and at the same time unloading mountains of stuff from ships.
Six times in the course of a morning stroll Lanny was stopped
by M.P.'s and required to show his papers. These were in
order, so he got a respectful " O.K., sir."

The immense basin and its complexity of docks were full
of craft of all sizes and shapes—a wonderful target for bombers,
but not one showed up that morning. A new expedition was
in preparation, and nobody here could have any doubt where
it was going. He had seen a great flotilla arrive to take Algiers,
and he knew what prolonged planning and preparation had
been required. Now here was another " amphibious operation "—" Husky " it was called. This time the distance was
short, one or two hundred miles across the strait to the large
triangular island of Sicily. There would be enemy planes in
the air, and enemy submarines in the water, and enemy guns
large and small in the hills which covered the beaches. How
many there would be and what forces to man them were
perhaps known to those who planned the landing, but surely
not to the plain " Joes " who were in near-by camps, resting
before going on board the vessels.

Only a year and a half had passed since the attack on
Pearl Harbour had dragged America into this war. Miracles
of production had brought an armada here, equipped with
something like a quarter of a million different articles, from
tiny ball-bearings of the hardest steel, so small that the eye
could hardly see them, to huge tanks, self-propelled tank-
killing guns, and L.S.T.'s especially built to slide up on beaches
and let down ramps on which the monsters could roll ashore.

Most of the soldiers had but the vaguest idea of why they were in a war, but they had been told there was a job to do and they were doing it. They had seen pictures of a fellow with an ugly mug, standing on a balcony and throwing out his chest like a pouter pigeon. They called him " the Deuce," and didn't mean any pun, but thought that was the way his title was pronounced. A generation ago their fathers had come over and helped to put the Kaiser " in the can " ; and now there were two more, a Deuce and a Führer. A Seabee from Texas with whom Lanny got into conversation thought that the leader of the Germans was called Führer because he was in a fury all the time.

At noon there was still no lieutenant, so Lanny got his onion soup and bread and fruit in an obscure French café, meantime studying diligently a small Italian dictionary he had picked up in a bookstore. This was a proper thing for either an American or a German to carry, and he would not merely refresh his memory on phrases he would need, but would practise his saying them like a German. The land of Dante and Leonardo was swarming with Teutons, both military and civilian, and no matter how much the Italians disliked them they took their money and let them alone—and that was al a secret agent needed.

At three o'clock there was the lieutenant, saying, " The Navy reports that it would hardly be possible to set you down on the beach at Ostia. It is well fortified and patrolled. There are barbed wire, mines, searchlights, and no doubt radar ; any craft approaching would pretty surely be detected and fired on. The nearest unguarded shore is more than ten miles to the south."

The P.A. replied, " O.K., let them land me there, and I'll find transportation."

Said the lieutenant, " Here is a map for you to study. You will be flown in a seaplane, and I will be in front of your hotel at twenty hundred." Lanny replied, " I'll be ready " ; and that was all. He went back to his room and learned about the roads and villages south of Ostia, then strolled and looked at more of the spectacle of Operation Husky. He had supper in another café—never the same, lest anyone should get his features fixed in mind. He returned to his room and studied until five minutes before eight, or twenty hundred as the Armed Forces called it, when he took his bag and went down to the lobby of the hotel, paid his bill, and went for a stroll.

It was just about dusk, and he didn't have to return to the front of the hotel, because the officer in the jeep saw him and swung round to the kerb and took him in. Hundreds of thousands of young Americans had read mystery stories, spy stories, "thrillers" of one sort or another, and now they were getting a kick out of being called to enact in real life what they had read. There wasn't any play-acting about it, because this polyglot port had been in the hands of the enemy only a few weeks ago, and any hotel waiter, cab driver, or Arab wrapped in a dirty white bedsheet might be a spy, reporting to a technician with a sending set hidden in a barn, or a fisherman's hut, or even a load of garden produce being brought into town.

IX

It was all right to talk in a moving car, for no one could get near enough to hear above the sounds of the engine. Ferguson put into Lanny's hands a large wad of Italian money which he had got in exchange for American money Lanny had entrusted to him. Then he remarked, "The Navy is paying you a compliment in lending you a seaplane." Perhaps that was a hint from a young officer whose curiosity had got the better of his discretion. But Lanny did not take the bait ; he said politely, "I appreciate the honour." In order not to seem uncordial he added, "Some day when this is all over, fate may bring us together again, and then I'll tell you a story that will interest you."

"I hope it may happen," replied the younger man, who had been deeply impressed by his good-looking and friendly passenger.

Against a badly wrecked concrete pier lay the small, fast seaplane. Lanny was introduced to the pilot, a lieutenant, and the co-pilot, an ensign. Each of these had a seat, and Lanny was invited to sit on an inverted bucket with a folded blanket on it to make it less hard. He shook hands with Ferguson and thanked him for his kindness. Two sailors pushed the plane away from the dock ; its engines, already warmed up, were put into gear, and it glided out into the wide main basin of the harbour. Darkness enveloped the plane, but several small guide lights were turned on ; the engines began to roar and the propellers to whirl, and the seaplane forced its way through the water. A ticklish moment, for you couldn't see ahead, and what if some small boat, sneaking out without permission, happened to lie in the path ?

But it didn't happen ; the rocking and splashing ceased, and the ship was airborne. After that Lanny was in the hands of the two aviators, who had maps and ingenious instruments by which they could find a certain stretch of shore in darkness. Lanny might sit and recite his Italian lessons in his mind, or he might spread the blanket on the floor and have a nap. He did a little of both, and was fast asleep when he felt a jar, and started up to discover that the plane had settled down upon the water. He asked, " Did you find the right place ? " The reply was, " We said our prayers."

One thing was sure : the weather had been kind. There was very little sea, and the P.A. didn't have to contemplate the prospect of having to swim for it, and perhaps lose his small suitcase. The seaplane was hardly rocking at all, and the pilot had shut the engine off and was letting her drift. Lashed fast to the struts was one of those collapsible boats called a kayak, because of its shape. General Clark and his fellow officers had used several to land on the shore not far from Algiers for a conference with French officers who were secretly favouring the American invasion. That time the sea had been high, and it had been all but impossible for the Americans to get away again.

Now the two aviators untied the package with swift fingers and spread the hinged wooden frame with the attached water-proof canvas. The three men laid the tiny craft upon the water, and first the ensign and then the passenger got in, holding tight to the seaplane so as not to upset the kayak. There was just room for two, facing each other and with their legs drawn up close. Lanny rode backward, his suitcase in his lap. The ensign paddled vigorously, and soon they came to the shore.

A ticklish moment when they touched the shore, for it was rocky, and to get out of this craft was as hard as to get into it. Lanny had explained his desire to keep his feet dry, not because of discomfort, for that wouldn't have amounted to anything in warm weather, but because he did not wish to betray the manner of his coming. The ensign stepped into the water and managed to keep the kayak from capsizing ; he dragged it up so that his passenger might step out safely. Lanny whispered " Thank you," shook hands, and waited while the craft was launched again. He was prepared to strip and help if necessary, but the young fellow managed it alone and disappeared into the darkness.

X

There was the son of Budd-Erling with his little suitcase and a pocketful of Italian paper money of all sizes—mostly large, because the lira was even lower than the franc and going down fast. It was dark, but from the stars he could guess that it was after midnight ; he couldn't see the ground, but had to stumble along, ascending from the sea over rocks and weed patches. He had not brought a flashlight and would not have dared to use one. The success of his plans depended upon his getting to the German military authorities before he was picked up by the Italians. The Germans were the masters ; but if the Italians got him first they might jail him as an ordinary spy, look up his past record, and never let the Germans know anything about him.

Buildings loomed before him, outlined against the stars ; he kept one hand before him as he walked, because barbed wire was to be expected. He kept waving his hand up and down in front of him, so that if he touched electrified wire it would be a quick stroke and might not be fatal. Every few steps he halted and listened for the footsteps of a sentry. It seemed most unlikely that any shore this close to Rome would be unfortified and unguarded ; he knew what had been done to the beaches of Britain. But apparently hard-pressed Italy didn't have any electrical power to spare, and not much wire ; and they had an awful lot of rocky coast. Surely there should have been sentries along the shore ; but although he held his breath and listened he heard nothing. Perhaps the sentry was taking a nap ; anyhow, the invader, stepping softly and crouching low, came to a road, climbed onto it, and stood listening in the shadows of some sort of building.

The entire shore was completely blacked out, and Lanny had no way to see his watch. By starlight a moving figure can be seen plainly enough for a shot, and Lanny's heart was pounding; but he could gain nothing by staying in hiding. Apparently this was a summer cottage; it was unoccupied, the windows closed. What Lanny wanted was a taxicab or motor-car to take him to Rome; but how could he find a garage in the darkness? If he saw a person walking he would be afraid to speak to him, for fear it might be a policeman or a soldier; he had no papers that he could show, and his hope was to escape attention until he got away from the shore.

What would he do if he were challenged in Italian? He had not failed to work out a course of action. He would demand to be taken to the highest police authority; there he would say that he was an American agent of Herr Hitler, desiring to be permitted to speak with the German authorities at once. He would not tell how he had got into Italy—he would say that Herr Hitler had arranged it and had forbidden him to reveal the secret. He would demand the right to telephone, at his own expense, to the Führer's private number in Berlin. If the Führer was not there, he would call Air Marshal Göring, whose art adviser and agent he had been before the war.

A most unlikely story, but the very boldness of it might cause its success. Great names would overwhelm any local official; and when it came to higher authorities, the son of Budd-Erling had a long record as a Fascist sympathizer to expatiate upon. He had been married to Irma Barnes, now Countess of Wickthorpe, whose home had been known before the war as a Fascist hideout. In Paris he had been intimate in the home of Denis de Bruyne, wealthy industrialist who had helped to finance the Cagoulards; at the time this conspiracy had been exposed, Lanny had sought refuge in the palace of Graf Herzenberg, of the Nazi Embassy staff. The glib art expert could tell stories like that by the mile, and all the Italians would have to do was to ask their German friends about him. But suppose the Italians who got hold of him didn't have any German friends and didn't want any? Then indeed a double-crossing agent might wish that he had stayed on his own side of the war fence.

XI

The wanderer was in a settlement of some sort apparently. One shack fronting the highway had chinks of light behind black curtains ; Lanny guessed it might be an all-night eating place and tapped on the door. A voice called, " *Entrate.*" He stepped in and closed the door quickly, as regulations in war-stricken lands required. There was a lunch counter with an elderly Italian behind it, and Lanny greeted him with his best German imitation, saying " *Roma,*" and then " *Macchina, automobile.*" The proprietor, who was alone, pointed in a direction where he said there was a garage. Lanny took out a twenty-lira note and pointed to that, saying, " Come, show me." The man, who wasn't apt to make that much in the rest of the night, put out his light, locked his door, and escorted the stranger down the street.

There was a garage, and apparently the proprietor slept in the rear. The café man knocked, and presently a sleepy voice called from inside, and the café man explained that a *signor tedesco* demanded to speak with him. So presently another old man opened the door—they were all old, because some four hundred thousand young men had been shipped to Naziland, and two or three million taken into the Army. When the man heard that a traveller wished to rent a car to take him to the capital, he threw up his hands in dismay ; " *Assolutamente impossibile !* " he said ; there was no *petrolio,* and besides, it was forbidden by the police ; it was necessary to have a permit, and that took many days, and so on.

Lanny invited himself into a bedroom which apparently had a large family, who had awakened and were listening. He spoke large words : government, military affairs, state business, *molto importante.* Every time the man said " *impossibile,*" Lanny replied, " *Quanto costa ?* "—how much ? These, he knew, were black-market days, when anything could be done if you paid for it ; but you mustn't pay too much, because that awakens suspicion and exposes you to blackmail and even to crime. First, he said "*Mille lire,*"—a thousand lire—and then,

"*Mille cinque*," which is fifteen hundred ; he thought that should be sufficient for a forty-mile drive.

When the proprietor said he didn't have the gas, Lanny guessed that he was bidding for the passenger to buy it. When the man said two thousand lire, Lanny said, "*È troppo*," —too much—and after arguing back and forth for a while he started to leave. The man, weakening, objected that it was forbidden to enter the city between the hours of ten at night and sunrise. To that Lanny replied that he didn't want to enter the city, his destination was in the suburbs. He had studied a map and could specify the locality ; the man said if that was the case he would take a chance, but it was *molto, molto illegale* and might get him a heavy fine. He wanted Lanny to agree to pay the police ; but Lanny took his turn saying "impossible," and stood by his fifteen hundred lire. At last the man said, "*Bene, signor*," and proceeded to get into his pants and shirt.

He unlocked his garage, and there was a battered yellow Renault which some tourist must have left behind ten years ago. It sputtered and spat, but it started, and the old man put it out on the street, locked the garage again, and invited the passenger and his suitcase inside. He drove through the deserted streets without lights, slowly but accurately, as if he had the eyes of an owl. Once out of the town, he turned on only the parking lights, and these were carefully hooded. He did not make any pretence of getting gasoline—that had been just a bargaining point. They drove at ten miles an hour, and that was all right, because Lanny could do nothing more until daylight. The road was a modern speedway, one of the gifts Il Duce had made to the Italian people out of their own money—this in the early days when he had been trying to please them. He had drained the swamps, killed the mosquitoes, built model houses, and caused the trains to run on time ; so the tourists had spread his fame and his wonderful new ideas among the money-spending classes of all lands.

Arriving at the suburb, Lanny picked out a dwelling at random and told the driver to stop there. He spoke his German-Italian thanks, paid his debt, and went up the steps of the building and pretended to ring the bell ; he stood and waited, and the driver waited to see if anyone came to the door. Lanny's patience was the greater, and finally the man drove away. Lanny was sure he would not report the strange episode to the police no matter how suspicious he might be ; by his own admission he had broken several regulations and in all probability the Fascist police would bleed him white.

XII

The P.A. strolled and found a park with a bench, and there he sat. Dawn was coming, and soon people would be about, and then it would be all right for one more to join them. There was nothing suspicious about this traveller's appearance ; he looked like a gentleman, but not too elegant ; his English-made tropical worsted suit was considerably rumpled and he would be needing a shave. He might have been an agent taking orders for sewing machines, had any such thing been available in war-tormented Roma Immortalis. More probably, he was a bill collector, or possibly a doctor. In a city of a million and a half inhabitants the police cannot question everybody on the street every day.

Nor can they block all the roads and lanes and alleys that lead into such a city. It was the P.A.'s idea to stroll on obscure streets among plain people on the way to their jobs. He would keep watch ahead, and if he saw any signs of a roadblock or even a policeman, he would turn off to another street. So, with as many windings as the Tiber River, he would make his way among the Seven Hills and arrive at his destination, the Hôtel de Russie—surely an odd name for the headquarters of the German High Command. He had to find it without delay, for he couldn't stop at any hotel without being reported to the police, and he couldn't buy food or even eat in a café without having a ration book. He might have asked the people at the O.S.S. " post office " to hide him—but he didn't want to be hidden, he wanted to get a legal pass and travel about.

It all worked out according to his careful plan. He came to the wide Piazza del Popolo, where he saw the grey gun-metal cars of the German staff parked. The familiar S.S. men stood on guard at the door of the hotel, and Lanny knew how to deal with them. His hand shot up in the Nazi salute and he snapped out, " *Heil Hitler!* " The response was obligatory, and the effect semi-hypnotic ; the dummies found it difficult to distrust anyone who had put them through the ritual. Lanny said, " I have business with Marshal Kesselring " ; and the commander of the guard replied, " *Ja, mein Herr,*" and signed one of the others to accompany the visitor inside.

At the desk where once had been an obsequious hotel clerk now sat a red-faced and severe-looking Feldwebel. Lanny approached and said, " Will you kindly oblige me with a small envelope." He took a visiting card from the case in his pocket. " Mr. Lanning Prescott Budd," it read, and with his fountain pen he wrote underneath, " *Geheimer Agent des Führers, einen Bericht zu erstatten.*" He put the card in the envelope, methodically sealed it, and wrote on the outside, " *Dem Herrn Marschall Albert von Kesselring, oder dem Herrn General Enno von Rintelen. Persönlich.*" He handed that to the Feldwebel and watched the man's eyes pop. He tapped a bell, and a soldier came. " *Neunzehn,*" he said, and the man took the card and went to the elevator. Lanny picked up his little suitcase, went to one of the big leather chairs, seated himself, and crossed his legs nonchalantly. The S.S. man watched him discreetly from near by.

XIII

There emerged from the elevator a tall, monocled Prussian of high rank. He came toward the visitor, and the visitor rose and gave the Nazi salute. Many of these old-time masters of Germany hated having to return this salute, but they wouldn't let a stranger know that. This one introduced himself as " Oberst von Horn," and Lanny said, " Herr Budd," and bowed. The Oberst said inquiringly, " You wish to speak to the Marshal or the Chief of Staff ? " The visitor, knowing the exact measure of courtesy and coldness to use with these proud gentry, replied, " I sent them a written message, marked personal."

It was a challenge, and the officer would not fail to know it. Said he, " Will you be so kind as to give me an idea as to the nature of your business with these officers ? "

" *Leider,* Herr Oberst," replied Lanny. " I am under strict orders that what I have to say is to be said to them alone."

" Under whose orders, may I inquire ? "

" I have told them that in my written message, Herr
Oberst." Lanny might have added, " Did you open it ? " but
that would have been rude, and when you are dealing with a
haughty person you are as rude as he, but no ruder.

" You must understand that they are very busy, Herr
Budd."

" *Selbstverständlich*, but I will take no more of their time
than they care to give me."

" And suppose they are not here ? "

" I don't mind waiting until they come." There was a duel
of the eyes ; Lanny stared straight into a cold blue Prussian
pair, and wondered what they were making of a brown
American pair.

Apparently not much, for the Oberst said, " May I inquire
of what nationality you are, Herr Budd ? "

" I trust that you will not take it as a discourtesy, Herr
Oberst. I am under strict orders to give no information except
to Marshal von Kesselring or General von Rintelen. You must
surely realize that a man would not enter the Mediterranean
headquarters of the Reichswehr unless he had something that
would justify his intrusion."

The haughty one realized that he had met his match. " You
confront me with an embarrassing responsibility," he said, and
his eyes moved to the suitcase on the floor beside Lanny's chair.

" I understand what you mean, Herr Oberst. The bag
contains the few necessities of a traveller, and I shall be pleased
to have you examine it. Since I have to ask the privilege of
speaking in private to either the Marshal or the General, I
expect that you will have me searched."

" *Ausgezeichnet*, Herr Budd," said the other, obviously
relieved. " *Bitte, kommen Sie mit mir*." He signed to the
S.S. man, then led the way to the elevator.

XIV

In a room which had once been a hotel bedroom, and now
appeared to be a conference room, the S.S. man opened Lanny's
small suitcase, while the Oberst sat stiffly in a chair and stared
through his monocle at each article as the other held it up.

The man ran his hands over the lining of the suitcase, felt the
seams, and did a thorough job. He handed the Italian dictionary and the two Nazi pamphlets to the officer, who leafed
through them without comment. A well-educated man, he
doubtless thought the pamphlets were rubbish and realized
that they might be a blind ; but he said nothing. Lanny took
off his coat, shirt, and trousers, and sat in his shorts while the
S.S. man made an examination of the clothing and contents
of the pockets. He took off his shoes and handed them over ;
he stood up and let the man pass his hard hot hands all over
him. In these days science had constructed so many subtle
poisons and cunning weapons that it was hard to distinguish
between an innocent civilian and a deadly assassin. A fountain
pen might shoot a poisoned bullet, so the S.S. man first made
sure that it would write, and then he took it apart and made
sure that it wouldn't do anything else.

He took a large wad of Italian bank-notes out of the
stranger's wallet and another wad out of his back trousers
pocket and handed them to the officer, who glanced at them,
still without comment. Lanny's passport revealed that he
was an American, or at any rate that he was posing as one.
When the Oberst had looked through this elaborate document
he knew also that the stranger had come by way of North
Africa ; but still he kept silent. Lanny took the liberty of
saying, " I suggest that you caution this man not to mention
my name or to talk about anything he has learned."

The officer addressed the S.S. man sternly, " *Hören Sie !
Über diesen Vorfall darf weder jetzt noch in Hinkunft das
Geringste verlauten.*" The man saluted and replied, " *Zu
Befehl, Herr Oberst.*" Lanny put his clothes on and got back
his property. When the officer condescended to apologize for
the inconvenience, Lanny answered, " Some day we may meet
in peacetime and exchange a smile over this odd manner of
introduction."

The P.A. was escorted to a suite on what Americans call
the second floor of the hotel and which Europeans call the first.
He entered a reception room where a secretary and a filing
clerk were busy. At a word from the Oberst the secretary
tapped on an inner door and then opened it. The Oberst went
in first and stopped, clicked his heels, bowed, and announced,

" Herr Budd, who wishes to speak with you." Lanny entered
and saw a man in a grey-green uniform seated at a large flat-
topped desk. " Marschall von Kesselring," announced the
Oberst with stateliness ; and Lanny bowed politely and said,
" Herr Marschall."

" Smiling Albert " was the Marshal's nickname ; he was
a Bavarian, noted for the bonhomie common to his land. But
he wasn't smiling now, being in the midst of desperate days.
He nodded his head to the extent of perhaps two inches and
demanded, " You have a message for me ? "

The reply was, " My orders are to speak with you in private."

The commander of all the land, sea, and air forces of the
Axis in the Mediterranean area glanced at his staff officer, who
spoke quickly, " Herr Budd suggested that we should search
him, and this has been done. He carries an American passport
and has come by way of North Africa. He is not armed."

" You may wait outside," said the Marshal, and the Oberst
clicked, bowed again, and withdrew. The S.S. man had been
left out in the hall, and the secretary had not entered the room.

" Herr Marschall," began Lanny, when the door was closed,
" I had the honour of being a guest at Berchtesgaden just
before this war broke out. Many generals came and went, and
I believe you were among them."

" Oh, so you are *that* Herr Budd ! " The great man's
manner changed quickly.

" I was commissioned by the Führer to carry out certain
investigations and to come back and report to him. His
instructions were that wherever I succeeded in entering Axis
territory, I was to seek out the highest German authority and
request him to notify the Führer at Berlin 116191."

" I see that you have been entrusted with the Führer's
telephone number."

" He did me that honour. So far I have used it only
three times."

" May I ask when and where you last saw the Führer ? "

" The time was last February, and the place was his field
headquarters. I was flown blindfolded. My guess was western
Ukraine."

" This is very interesting. Are you at liberty to tell me
how you got into this city ? "

" *Leider, Herr Marschall*, my orders are to talk with no one until I have reported to the Führer. It is possible that he may send me back here, and if he does, no doubt he will instruct me to talk with you. Meantime, I have one thing to ask, that you will be so kind as to notify the Führer that his American agent is here."

XV

The heavily burdened officer sat gazing fixedly at this unexpected caller : obviously a cultivated man and accustomed to good society—no raw upstart like the Nazis, whom an officer of the old army had a hard time tolerating. Well-dressed in spite of the wrinkles and well-groomed in spite of needing a shave ; the visitor spoke an elegant German which must have come in part from books. He seemed at ease in spite of having put his head into a tiger's mouth. His story must be true, the Marshal reflected, or this would have been the last room in the city of Rome to which he would have sought entrance.

Casual as he seemed, Lanny too was studying his auditor : a man of sixty or so, smooth-shaven, with round, puffy cheeks, giving the odd effect of a chipmunk. He had bags under his eyes and other signs of the strain under which he was working. His manners were polished ; but besides being " Smiling Albert " he had been called " the Crazy Butcher," because of the way he had sacrified his men in the desperate fighting in Tunisia. Before that he had been Luftwaffe Chief of Staff and had directed the bombing of Poland, Holland, Belgium, France, and London. Chat with him pleasantly, but don't forget that your head is in the tiger's mouth !

The tiger pressed a button and spoke to his secretary in the next room. " Get me the Führer at his headquarters." The woman's voice said, " *Zu Befehl, Herr Marschall*," and then he turned to his guest. " Would you be at liberty to tell me, Herr Budd, how you came to know the Führer so well ? "

" Surely, Herr Marschall. I am an American because my father was, but I was born in Switzerland and have lived most of my life in France and Germany. I visited the Fatherland as a boy, because of my friendship for Kurt Meissner, the *Komponist*."

"Oh! Then you doubtless know his brother, General Emil Meissner."

"I know him well. Can you tell me how he is?"

"He is all right, so far as I have heard. Perhaps the Führer will tell you where he is serving."

The other continued, "At Schloss Stubendorf, Kurt's home, I met a lad who became one of the Führer's earliest followers, and so I learned about this wonderful man. In my youth I thought I was something of a Socialist—you know how generous-minded young people tend that way. It happened to both the Führer and the Duce, I have been told." Lanny wasn't just gossiping when he said that; he was preparing for the time when some German or some Italian authority would uncover his bad record in Rome. He went on to tell how Heinrich Jung had given him literature, and so he had learned the difference between sound National Socialism and the evil Marxian variety. Heinrich had been to visit Adolf Hitler in prison, and later had taken Lanny to meet the great man in Munich. From that time the American had been one of his ardent supporters and had brought information and aid for his cause. All that was a story which the P.A. had told to so many Germans that it was like a gramophone record.

A buzzer sounded by the desk, and the Marshal took up the "far-speaker," as the Germans call it. "*Guten Morgen, mein Führer,*" he said, and a familiar voice replied, "*Was haben Sie?*" Hitler had the habit of talking very loud into a telephone, and Lanny, sitting by the desk, could hear the voice clearly. Adi had never entirely lost his Innviertel accent, and he snorted his gutturals as if to make the German language as Germanic as possible.

Kesselring spoke slowly and precisely. "There is a gentleman in my office who has just arrived in Rome. He appears to be important, and it may be the part of discretion not to mention his name. He tells me he is a friend of Kurt Meissner and Heinrich Jung and has known you from the early days. He visited your field headquarters last February and you commissioned him to make certain inquiries and to bring you information."

Lanny held his breath as the voice from a thousand miles

away made the receiver rattle. *" Ja, ja, ich kenn' ihn gut. Das mag wichtig sein. Schicken Sie ihn zu mir so schnell wie möglich. Mit Flugpost."*

" Zu befehl, mein Führer."

" Ist das alles ? "

" Das ist alles."

" Gut. Sie werden den Feind ins Mittelmeer werfen. Sieg heil."

" Smiling Albert " hung up the receiver. For the first time since the visitor had entered his office he was justifying his name. " He says to send you by airmail ! " Not realizing that Lanny had been able to hear the distant voice, he repeated the rest of the master's words. " He says I am to throw the enemy into the Mediterranean ; but evidently that doesn't mean you. He says you are important, and I am to send you to him as quickly as possible. A dispatch plane usually leaves at noon ; I'll see if it cannot be speeded up. Is there anything you would like in the meantime ? "

" Thank you, Herr Marschall. I should like very much to wash and shave, and I could eat a bite if you have it to spare."

3

Who Worship the Beast

I

HISTORY was repeating itself when Lanny Budd rose into the air above the city of Rome and flew northward to meet Adolf Hitler. The previous time it had been winter, and the mountains had been covered with snow. Now it was summer, and every tiny plot of earth had its colour ; the hill slopes were terraced high up and tended by patient, loving hands. When the young men were torn away from their homes, the old men and women and the children carried on, keeping the vines alive and planting wheat or barley or vegetables in every

nook and cranny of soil, some no bigger than a fine lady's
handkerchief. Italy was a poor land, and ever since the dawn
of history its life had been a war between the peasants on the
one hand and the military lords, the landlords, and the tax
collectors on the other.

The fast plane carried one pilot, one passenger, and a
couple of sacks of mail, carefully sealed and chained. It rose
higher and higher, until there was a crackling in the passenger's
ears. Snow-clad peaks lay ahead, and the plane sped between
them, up the Brennero, a pass which Lanny had known from
boyhood. He put on the overcoat which had been lent him
and looked down on the long blue lakes. In days of peace
luxury hotels had been built on these pine-clad shores, and
now they had been taken for military headquarters, for barracks and hospitals. A few, Lanny knew, housed officer
prisoners, treated according to the polite Geneva conventions,
each side afraid that if it broke the rules the other side would
break them even more.

The plane sloped downward over Austria, and Lanny took
off the overcoat. He asked no questions, but guessed that the
first stop would be Nürnberg, as before. The old city was
being bombed more frequently, and he could see more signs
of damage than in February. A landing was made, fresh fuel
was taken on, and one mail sack was exchanged for another.
They rose again, and the course was still northward ; this time
the passenger's guess was Berlin, and it proved correct. No
objection was made to his looking down upon the results of
the terrible air raid he had witnessed on the first of March ;
there would have been no sense in objecting, since the enemy
sent reconnaissance planes frequently and took photographs
of everything.

Lanny had heard that Adolf Hitler had made himself a
wonderful air-raid shelter in the garden of the New Chancellery,
and he looked forward to visiting it. But no, the plane stopped
no more than five minutes on the great Tempelhoferfeld.
Enemy " mosquito " planes might shoot over at any time, so
the field men rushed the refuelling job. Before they left for
the third lap, Lanny was politely told that he would have to
be blindfolded, and he politely said, " *Natürlich.*" He noted
how the plane was headed, and the pressure on his entrails

told him which way it was turning ; they were headed east. The Führer would not be far behind the Russian front, the only one that counted in the early summer of 1943. The Germans and the Russians were still sparring, feeling each other out along their two-thousand-mile front ; but the main attack had not come, and no one, perhaps not even the commanders, knew which one was going to begin it.

II

The plane landed, and Lanny was assisted out and put into a car. The car drove fast, and presently was in a forest—you can tell a forest because the echoes are intermittent and quick. In the earlier days, headquarters had been in a *Schloss,* for Göring had solemnly promised that no bombs would fall on German soil, and all good Germans had believed him. Now there was no part of German soil that was safe from bombs, and the brains of the government and the Reichswehr were hidden in inconspicuous places. Before this visit was over Lanny learned by accident that he was in the neighbourhood of the ancient city of Königsberg.—King's Mountain—where a century and a half earlier a small-sized professor named Immanuel Kant had sat in his room, his eyes fixed upon a church steeple outside his window, thinking up the *Ding-an-sich* and the Categorical Imperative and the Four Antinomies and the other foundation stones of modern idealistic philosophy.

The car came to a halt, and the foreigner was led up some steps and into a building where he heard footfalls and voices ; the echoes told him that they were walking on wood, not on the stone or concrete floor of a castle. The blindfold was taken off, and he found himself in a room with a couple of S.S. men wearing the green uniform of the Führer's own bodyguard, the Leibstandarte. They told the visitor that everyone who saw the Führer now had to be searched, and he told them that he had been searched once but was happy to be searched again.

This time they made an even more thorough job of it ; one of them carefully washed his hands in Lanny's presence and then ran his finger around Lanny's gums and looked into his throat ; then he put on a rubber glove, put vaseline on it, and ran it as far as possible up the visitor's rectum. Lanny had never asked questions about the attempts on the Führer's life, but he had heard rumours that several had been made. Uneasy lies the head that wears a crown—and this even though the crown may be an invisible one. The P.A. was escorted to a room where there were two secretaries whom he knew of old and greeted politely. One of them tapped upon an inner door, opened it, and ushered Lanny into the presence of the Great Man of the Germans.

The P.A. knew exactly what to expect. He knew that last January Adi had lost more than half a million of his best troops by slaughter or surrender at Stalingrad, and that in May he had lost three or four hundred thousand more in Tunisia. Adi must know that the attack on Sicily could be only a matter of weeks, and that when Sicily had fallen, Italy would be only a few miles away, and Southern Italy had airfields from which his native land of Austria and his adopted land of Bavaria might be bombed day and night. F. D. R. had told his agent that America had turned out more than seven thousand airplanes in the month of May, and would raise that to eight or nine thousand during the summer ; Adi might not have those figures, but would know exactly how much damage was being done to his airplane plants, his synthetic-oil plants, his coal mines and steel mills and other means of war production. He would learn about them from reports which were specially prepared for him in large type, so that he could read them without revealing the fact that he was near-sighted.

He was a man being driven beyond endurance and sustained by a fantastic variety of drugs administered by a quack doctor of venereal diseases. He was subject to wild fits of rage and might drive himself into one in which he was impelled to punish the one American whom he happened to have at hand. Knowing this, Lanny had prepared a series of communications so intriguing that the Führer's attention would be held by them. Had he not himself laid down the dictum in *Mein Kampf* that the bigger the lie the easier to get it believed ? People would say that nobody would have the nerve to say such things if they were not true. Had he not appointed the Prince of Lies as his propaganda minister, the crooked little

Herr Doktor Goebbels, who had persuaded the German people to swallow more absurdities than had ever been thought up by a statesman in modern times ? Lanny hadn't come here to tell Hitler any truth that was avoidable ; he had come to try out a set of inventions which he hoped might be better than Hitler's and Goebbels' combined.

III

Die Nummer Eins, the Germans' number one hero and Lanny's number one foe, was a man of medium height, wearing " the simple soldier's tunic " which he had put on at the beginning of the war and had promised the German people never to remove until victory was won. That, of course, was a symbolical statement ; it didn't mean that he would never take a bath, but merely that after the bath he would put on the same kind of costume.

He had grown stouter, and it showed unpleasantly in his cheeks and nose. His flesh was flabby and his complexion pale. He wore a harassed look, and the cordiality which had been in his manner in days of peace was lacking. He could not forget that it was Lanny's countrymen whose crude material power was threatening the foundations of his noble thousand-year Reich. The last time he had launched into a tirade on the subject, and Lanny now wanted to keep that from being repeated. He clasped the Führer's moist white hand and exclaimed, " This time I have brought you really good news ! "

The Führer needed news of that sort ; so he said, " *Wirklich, Herr Budd?* By all means, let me have it. *Setzen Sie sich.*"

It had been the P.A.'s intention, before taking this trip, to motor or fly across the United States and pay a call upon half a dozen of the most powerful opponents of Franklin D. Roosevelt. He would visit San Simeon again and see how near a powerful publisher could be brought to a programme of action in defence of the " free enterprise " system. He would make the acquaintance of Colonel McCormick, who controlled the thinking of several million Americans in the Middle West, and who, during the last presidential election, had counted the days left to "save America" from the calamity of a third term. He would call on Mr. Du Pont and Mr. Pew and Mr. Gannett, wealthy gentlemen who put up the campaign funds for the reactionary wing of the Republican party. He would lead them to vent their fury, and then would take it to the Führer and multiply it by ten.

Circumstances having blocked that programme, Lanny had to fall back upon the evening and part of a morning he had spent at Friendship House, meeting a dozen of the most bitter anti-New Dealers and Nazi appeasers in the United States. He had had a talk with Mr. Harrison Dengue, the super-industrialist with a scheme to kidnap the President. Mr. Dengue had introduced him to a general who could control home defences and the Army in the New York military district in which the President's Hyde Park home was situated. Also, Lanny had renewed his acquaintance with Senator Reynolds, who was Mrs. McLean's son-in-law and published a paper and headed a movement. Lanny had listened to the talk of Cissie Patterson, Colonel McCormick's cousin and publisher of a reactionary newspaper in the national capital. And, of course, there had been the hostess, with the biggest diamond in the world on her bosom and a mule-skinner's angry language pouring from her lips.

A large group of the friends of Friendship House held the conviction that the present war was playing into the hands of the Bolsheviks, and if fought to a finish would leave them in control of all Europe. These friends believed that F. D. R. knew this and didn't care, because he was no better than a Bolshevik himself, only he was too shrewd to put the label on. What he had done was to promote income taxes that were confiscatory, and a whole set of other measures calculated to lift the poor up and pull the rich down. The Friendship rich loathed him and had no hesitation in calling him names and suggesting that "somebody" ought to kill him. That was as far as they would go in public; what they would whisper in private Lanny took the liberty of imagining, and when he poured it out to Adolf Hitler he gave that chief of counter-revolution the happiest hour he had spent in many a month.

It was all a pipe dream, of course; but Adi was living on drugs these days, and he swallowed dose after dose and called for more. Evidently he was watching American affairs closely ; he had an extraordinary memory for both friends and foes, and had heard of every person his visitor named. He wanted the details regarding each one's wealth and position and activities, and even his or her personal appearance. Lanny was careful not to name anyone he couldn't describe ; having reinforced his own knowledge with that of Jim Stotzlmann, a walking encyclopaedia of social gossip, he was able to pour out a flood of " really good news." Never in the fifteen years that he had been dealing with this genius-madman had he enjoyed such a sense of making a hit.

IV

What was to be done ? The Führer had his programme, and the only problem was to get the masters of America to understand it. There must be immediate peace between Germany and Italy on the one hand and America and Britain and France on the other. All three of the so-called democratic nations would be left with everything they had, and the smaller nations, Belgium and Holland and Denmark and Norway, would be set free. America would be at liberty to conquer the Japanese and to take the whole Pacific, and South America too if she wanted it. All that Hitler wanted was a chance to go at Russia. He wouldn't ask help from anybody ; he would put the Reds out of business and keep them out for a thousand years, and what more could any American capitalist or man of great affairs desire ?

It was all so obvious to the Führer, he could not understand how anyone could fail to see it, and he wanted Lanny to tell him how and why they did fail. The experienced P.A. knew better than to try ; he said they were coming to understand the situation now. The class lines were forming rapidly in America, you could almost see it happening.

" But there is no time to spare," insisted Hitler ; " the issue will be decided this summer ! " He didn't say that his armies might not be able to hold the Russians, but Lanny knew well what was behind the desperate urgency in his voice. Lanny had been in Berlin in February, when the Reichswehr and the Nazi party had been combing countryside and city slums for new manpower ; they had taken the sixteen- and seventeen-year-olds, the fifty-five-year-olds, the once- and the twice-wounded, the tubercular and the syphilitic. All these were now in the lines, and how long would they be able to hold ?

"It is the most perilous crisis in the history of the world, Herr Budd. And you and the British are making it, compelling me to send seventeen divisions to stiffen the backbone of the Italians." Lanny did not fail to take note of the figure ; it was the same that his Boss had given him a few days previously. The Führer's lack of discretion was the despair of his generals ; but perhaps he was indiscreet only as Lanny was, by forethought, telling those things which he could be sure the other person already knew.

Lanny followed this technique and told his chief enemy what he had observed of Allied preparations in Algiers and Bizerte. There could be no question that a landing in Sicily was being prepared, and it was hardly to be imagined that the joint armies would resist the temptation to cross the narrow strait to the Italian mainland, where they would find so many airfields, easy to repair. Lanny had obtained Roosevelt's permission to say this, not merely to Hitler, but to the Italians he might meet. The island of Pantelleria had just been bombed into surrender, and all the airfields of Sicily and the tip of the boot were being bombed day and night ; this pattern of gaining air control before attempting a landing had become standard, and no military man would fail to recognize it. Of course it was possible to bomb two areas and thus create uncertainty as to which was to be invaded ; but in this case the Allies were not bothering with any such device. Their every move spoke Sicily.

V

The Führer wanted to know by what route his messenger had come, and Lanny narrated how he had hired a fisherman to sail him in a boat from a small place on the Tunisian coast, La Calle. You could do anything with the Americans if you were willing to spend money, and the same was true of the Italians. This led, by Lanny's intention, to the subject of Hitler's exhausted and reluctant ally. Lanny didn't say that

the Italians had been dragged into the war against their will ;
he said they were now frightened and sick, when they realized
that they were scheduled to be blasted, first with bombs and
then with artillery. The Italians in New York were as busy
as bees, trying to figure out a way to prevent this, and they
had evolved the idea that Italy might make a separate peace
on condition that the Allies would not use the peninsula as a
base from which to attack Germany or German-held territory.

"You must tell me what would be your attitude to such a
proposal, *mein Führer*," said the respectful agent ; and Hitler
replied that he might be willing to consider it, but he doubted
if the Allies would consent, or would keep their word if they
gave it. "You know well that it is Churchill's programme
to attack through the soft 'underbelly' of Europe."

Lanny answered, "Yes, but supposing my friends should
succeed in putting Roosevelt out of the way—it is not likely
that Churchill could hold out very long."

"In that case, of course, it would be a different matter ;
we should negotiate a peace as quickly as possible—with
every country except Russia. Meantime I should say that
the idea of peace between Italy and the Allies, on the basis
of the inviolability of Italian territory, might make an excellent
talking point, especially among Italians."

"You would be willing for me to tell them it is your idea ?"

"Surely. It will tend to convince them that we are reasonable, while it is the Judeo-democracies which plan to destroy
the treasures of Italian art and culture in the vain effort to
break through our southern defence wall."

VI

This was an important point the P.A. had gained. It
would enable him to pose as Hitler's representative in Rome,
and to have something definite to propose and to ask questions
about. One more thing he wanted, and that was for Hitler
to want him to go. Then he would be safe against all enemies
—save only Hitler's enemies. He began, "I must not fail to
warn you, *mein Führer*, that there are many Italians, and
some of them high-placed, who have treason in their hearts ;
fair-weather friends who got fame and wealth by espousing

your cause, but who now are getting ready to desert what they believe to be a sinking ship."

" I am not unaware of that situation, Herr Budd, and am taking steps to protect our sacred cause. Any information you can give me will be carefully noted."

" Unfortunately, *mein Führer,* all that I know is second-hand. I had only a few hours in Italy. I went straight to Marshal Kesselring, because I wished to take no risk of falling into the hands of the Italian police with an American passport in my pocket."

" You were wise in that. What do you intend to do now ? "

" I promised Signor Pope, one of my influential Italian friends in New York, that I would meet some of his friends in Rome and find out how the land lies there. I have been told that the Duce's own son-in-law has begun to weaken, and that is the reason Il Duce removed him as foreign secretary and sent him to the Vatican, where intrigues are indigenous and do no harm."

" I have a whole dossier on Ciano on my desk now, Herr Budd, and you may assure your friends that their suspicions are fully justified."

" I have heard also that Dino Grandi has begun to listen to the song of the sirens."

" That too is no idle rumour."

" And General Badoglio, the old dotard, of course hates Il Duce, because Il Duce made him carry the blame for the collapse of his armies in the Greek war."

" *Stimmt auch !* "

" There are other names I might mention ; but, as you know, I have never been accustomed to deal in second-hand information. Since there is nothing more I can do in the States at the moment, it has occurred to me that I might spend some time in Rome and see what information I can pick up for you. It happens, by a fortunate circumstance, that I can get access to the right circles because of the fact that one of my oldest friends in France has a niece who is married to a member of the Roman nobility. My French friend is Denis de Bruyne, the wealthy industrialist who helped to finance the Cagoule. He was arrested by the French police at the time their plans were exposed, some six years ago. He is a man to be trusted."

" I know of him by reputation, Herr Budd. I do not forget the friends of our cause. If he could have had his way, it would not have been necessary for me to invade and conquer France."

" His niece is the Marchesa di Caporini, and if the son of Budd-Erling Aircraft were to show up in Rome, with plenty of money in his pockets and confidential messages from important Italians in New York, he would have no trouble in reaching the right persons and gaining their confidence."

" May I have the pleasure of furnishing the money, Herr Budd ? "

" No, *mein Führer*, I want to be listed as one of those persons who really believes in your cause and thinks no more about personal gain than yourself. I am still able to carry on my profession of art expert. Would you believe it, with the help of Reichsmarschall Göring's staff I was able to purchase a couple of paintings from a Jew in Berlin and to store them in Sweden ; when I got to New York I was able by paying a sum to the right party to get permission to bring them into the country, and I made enough to pay for the trip."

" *Herrlich, Herr Budd !* " For the first time that day the Führer permitted himself a chuckle. " Do you expect to do that sort of thing in Rome ? "

" That is part of my camouflage, *Exzellenz*. Every Italian will understand the desire to make money, and all take it for granted that American millionaires do not care what they pay for anything."

" Then there is nothing I can do for you ? "

" Yes ; you will have to give me a letter to your Marshal, telling him that I am all right ; and it might be a good idea to drop a hint to Il Duce, so that his police will let me alone."

" Kesselring will attend to the Italians for you. Mussolini is a difficult man to deal with, and he is in a contrary mood at present. I am going to have a talk with him soon and put him in his place."

The P.A.'s face wore an understanding smile. " A lower place than he feels entitled to, I am sure. Il Duce would not remember me, but when I was young I had two encounters

with him. One was at the San Remo Conference, just after
World War I. I saw him in a violent dispute with some of his
comrades who resented his too sudden change of front. A
year or two later at Cannes I was present when a friend of mine
interviewed him for an English newspaper. You know, *mein
Führer*, in those days we young fellows imagined we were
Socialists."

"I am still a Socialist, Herr Budd."

"Of course ; but I refer to the international variety. It
was you who taught me the difference between sound National
Socialism and the bogus Marxian kind, and for that I owe you
an eternal debt of gratitude. For a while, if you remember,
I held myself aloof ; I didn't want to admit that you were
right, but events forced me to do so. I think it was the riots
I saw in Paris that made up my mind. Heinrich Jung and
Kurt Meissner helped to make your ideas clear to me."

"Kurt came to see me not long ago," put in the Führer.
"I was saddened to see him crippled by wounds, but his spirit
is undaunted, and it strengthened mine."

This gave the visitor a chance to pour out a mouthful of
words about the strength of the Führer's spirit, and how it
stood like the Brandenburg Gate, a monument to war which
so far the war had not touched. Such remarks went down
as well with Adi as with all dictators and despots through the
ages ; his ability to absorb compliments increased with the
years, and it had become less and less possible for him to
tolerate the presence of persons who disagreed with him.
The fact that this gracious and elegant *Kunstsachverständiger*
came from abroad lent weight to his praise ; his voice represented what the judgment of the Anglo-Saxon world would
be when it had come to its senses and realized that Adolf
Hitler had been from the outset the staunch defender of
Western culture against the advancing hordes of the East.
Lanny was in all probability the only American whom the
Führer had met in a long time, and it was balm to a tormented
soul to be told that the powerful nation was preparing to switch
from the side of incarnate evil to that of incarnate righteousness.

VII

The sweet interlude was broken by a buzzer on the desk. The Führer took up a telephone receiver, listened, then said, " Put him on." He listened again for a few seconds. Lanny could not hear the voice at the other end and dared not appear to be trying. But he could not help seeing Hitler and the transformation which the few seconds produced in the listener's face and manner ; he frowned, gritted his teeth, clenched his free hand, and when he spoke again it was the bellow of a bull. " *Der gottverdammte Schurke ! Was für ein Betrug !* Take the *Schweinehund* out and shoot him ! No, you don't need any written order. Shoot him first and get the order afterward." There followed a string of epithets which Adi had learned in the Innviertel, some of them filthy words of which Lanny had to guess the meaning.

The Führer of the Germans slammed down the receiver and sat glaring at his imaginary foes in empty space. Lanny shrank inwardly, not wishing to divert that Stygian wrath upon himself. But there was no escaping ; an auditor was required, and there was only one at hand.

" There is your Prussian *Adel*, your *Junkertum !* " he burst out. " These proud gentry think they are the masters, they are the rulers of Germany for the past hundred years and they dare to set themselves against my will, they disobey my explicit orders, they plot together like so many Bolsheviks. *Aber, Gott sei mein Zeuge*, I will teach them their mistake ! *Ich bin es, ich*, whom the German people have chosen as their guide, and those who oppose me I shall crush to the last scoundrel, the last traitor ! "

That was the start. Every time Lanny had been in the Führer's home he had witnessed one or more of these outbursts, and wondered *in Gottes Namen* when they would stop, and how could a human organism endure the expenditure of such quantities of energy. Here was a man who might speak to fifty million people any time he chose—indeed he might speak to the whole world with the certainty of being heard or read by all the thinking portion ; yet again and again he was willing to expend the same amount of effort in addressing

one or two persons—could it even be *no* person ?   Lanny
wondered if he had these frenzies when he was all alone in
that eagle's eyrie which he had had built for him on the top
of the Kehlstein ?   Did he there make orations to God, or to
posterity, or to that German *Geist* who was his dream companion ?

Now he was talking to his American agent, and he wasn't
content to denounce the Prussian nobility, the arrogant caste
whom he was breaking to his will ;   he must go on and tell
why they were wrong and why he, the divinely appointed
Führer of the Aryan world, was eternally and everlastingly
right.   Lanny never did find out who it was that was being
shot at this moment ;   but apparently the victim had spoken
or written something about having the Führer shot.   It didn't
occur to Adi that he himself had just been planning to have
Roosevelt shot, and if he had been reminded of this he would
have seen no resemblance between the two cases.   The Jewish-
descended Rosenfeld was the representative of democratic
licence and Bolshevik depravity, whereas Adolf Hitler was
the white knight of Aryan purity and virtue.   His cause
was holy, and those who opposed it were devils or disciples of
devils.

All this the one-time wastrel from the home for the shelter-
less in Vienna explained to the son of Budd-Erling Aircraft
in detail.   A note of frenzy came into his voice, almost of
despair ;   he was surrounded by these diabolical foes, and they
were crowding in upon him, he was being forced to face the
fact that they might bring him to complete collapse and ruin.
It was too awful, too wicked, too far beyond belief.   This
marvellous Third Reich that he had built, this thing of power
and goodness beyond compare, this structure that was guaran-
teed to last a thousand years and that had triumphed over
one foe after another — Austria, Czechoslovakia, Poland,
Holland, Belgium, Norway, France, and then Rumania,
Hungary, Bulgaria, Greece, Yugoslavia, and at least half of
Russia—wonderful, wonderful beyond all the tales of history !
And all this was to fail, all this was to collapse into ruin,
because of two despised rotten democratic lands and one
obscene ghoulish Asiatic land ruled by its *Lumpenproletariat* !
No, it was beyond belief, it was the victory of Satan over God.

Adi, who had so far relied upon himself alone, became religious in his language when he contemplated this cosmic calamity.

Apparently he had the idea that this grown-up playboy from overseas was the god out of a machine who could save the situation ; he implored the divine messenger to go at once and have Roosevelt carried down to Hell—to do it himself if necessary ! And Lanny, scared white in the presence of this foaming tirade, could only keep murmuring, " *Ja, ja, mein Führer ! Wie recht haben Sie ! Die reine Wahrheit aus Ihren Worten ! Wie klar ist Ihre Voraussicht !* " and so on, anything that would indicate his lack of opposition to this genius-madman, this wretched gutter rat whose inferiority complex had evolved into a Messiah compulsion beyond anything that any psychiatrist could have conceived. One man's mental disorder had knocked down a dozen nations of Europe and had forced the rest of the world to assemble twenty or thirty million men in arms, and to convert their economies from the production of useful goods to the means of wholesale killing. The son of Budd-Erling thought, Dear God, all I want is to get out of this place alive !

VIII

The tirade ended as Lanny had seen others end ; for the Führer was only half mad, and the other half watched what he was doing and did not permit him to wreck himself. One moment he was pacing the room and slapping his thighs violently ; the next moment he stopped, wiped the perspiration from his forehead and the spittle gathered in the corners of his mouth, and said quietly, " You know all that, Herr Budd." He did not apologize, for that was contrary to the principle upon which he ran Germany : " *Hitler hat immer recht.* " He was always right and his critics always wrong.

He continued, " You know, Herr Budd, I am by nature a sociable man, and in the old days it would have been my pleasure to spend an evening with you and have you play the piano for me, and have Kannenberg sing some of our old Bavarian songs. But now I have no time for any sort of recreation ; I carry the fate of Germany in these two hands " —he showed the hands, clenched into fists. " Now with the barbarous foe pressing close to our gates, I have to make a hundred decisions in a day."

" I quite understand, *mein Führer*," said the respectful visitor. " I am honoured that you have given me this much time."

" Is there anything you wish to do in Germany ? "

Lanny replied, " As you may know, I have a half-sister living near Berlin ; she is Marceline, the dancer, daughter of Marcel Detaze, the French painter whose works you possess. If I am going back by way of Berlin, I should like to take a few hours to visit her and tell her about her little son, who is with my mother. After that you may send me straight on to Rome, and I'll report to you as quickly as I can get anything of importance."

" *Richtig*," said Hitler. " You will report directly to me through Marschall Kesselring."

" I trust, *mein Führer*, that you will let the Marshal know that you have reason to feel sure of my good faith. It must have been surprising to him to have an enemy alien walk into his headquarters."

" I will make the situation clear ; and you, Herr Budd, may be sure of my gratitude, and my willingness to do anything in my power to repay you."

" What I want from you, *Exzellenz*, is to prove to your opponents, and especially to the people of my own misguided land, that the system you have established is here to stay. You must have some idea what a moral strain it is to me to return to America and listen to the talk I hear there. What a relief when the day comes that I can be free to speak the truth in that land in which Jewish lies are enthroned."

" *Das kann ich mir vorstellen, Herr Budd. Leben Sie wohl.*"

IX

Lanny was flown the same evening to Berlin and was met at the airport by an Oberleutnant of the Waffen S.S. who had been appointed as his escort in order to avoid possible inconveniences. *Absolut korrekt*, this young officer betrayed no trace of the curiosity he must have felt. He drove the American visitor to a small hotel in the suburbs, where dangers from bombing would be slight. Lanny's first act on arrival was to telephone his old friend Heinrich Jung, who was all but speechless with delight at the sound of Lanny's voice. He showed up for breakfast in the morning, and it turned out, most agreeably, that Oberleutnant Harz was one of his pupils from a long time back.

It was a huge educational machine which the Führer and his aides had built for the purpose of training millions of young Germans to take delight in marching, singing, wearing uniforms, carrying banners, and wielding " daggers of honour " : the Hitler Youth, if they happened to be of the male sex, and otherwise the Hitler Maidens. They couldn't all be made to look exactly alike, but they could be made to think exactly alike, and it interested the visitor from overseas to observe how Heinrich, whom he had known for thirty years come next Christmas, had managed to train a whole generation who looked like Heinrich and thought exactly as Heinrich thought. The S.S. Oberleutnant regarded the Jugend official as a semi-divine being because he had known the Führer in the early sanctified days and had actually visited him in prison ; he was thrilled to be pledged to secrecy on the subject of a secret agent of the Führer—it was the greatest honour of his life, he said, and his blushes backed up his words.

Heinrich was a desk official and belonged to a favoured caste so far as rations were concerned, so he still had an expanding waistline. He hadn't much news, except that his office had been bombed out, fortunately at night while he was at home. His numerous family were well and his wife sent her regards. He told about Kurt Meissner, who had a crippled arm and could no longer play the piano, but who composed National Socialist music of extraordinary fervour. Kurt's spirit was undaunted, and so was Heinrich's, and when Lanny asked the Oberleutnant, he reported that it was the same with himself. Things were going badly at the moment, and the military and party people could not help knowing it, but they had been taught a formula which they recited publicly on all occasions and doubtless said in place of prayers : Frederick the Great had been beaten on more than one occasion, but had refused to know that he was beaten, and in the end he had triumphed gloriously.

"We must prove that we can endure longer than the enemy," said Heinrich; and Lanny, who was part of the enemy, replied, "The American people have been used to an easy life and do not yet realize what they are in for." The Jugend official went on to talk piously about Blood and Soil —*Blut und Boden*, which in pre-war days the busy wits of Berlin had abbreviated to "*Blubo*." But nobody talked that way now; all Germans who were not in concentration camps were solidly united in defence of their sacred heritage.

X

Marceline Detaze, like the Germans who had money and were free, had removed herself to the country, as far as possible from bombing objectives. Being the daughter of a Frenchman and deriving her citizenship from him, she was not classified as an enemy; being the cherished *Freundin* of a Prussian nobleman and Wehrmacht officer, she had obtained permission to come and go as she pleased. An hour's drive from the city she had found what had been a school for young ladies and now was a hospital for wounded officers. The extensive grounds had been turned into potato fields; but one corner had been spared because of big shade trees, and there was a gardener's cottage which Marceline had leased for a year. She lived with an old woman for a maid, and read fiction from the school library—every afternoon she read aloud to the patients, because it was a bore to be alone. She said this apologetically, not wanting her brother to think that she had turned into a humanitarian or anything of that pretentious sort.

Marceline had been born in the middle of World War I, and everything she had heard in later years had caused her to hate it. Now she hated World War II, for one sufficient reason, that it had ruined the career of a girl who had worked hard to have her own way, and now in the midst of her triumph had been knocked out. It was all right to talk to soldiers about Frederick the Great, but that had no meaning to a night-club dancer; the clear-sighted Marceline knew that there would be no more dancing in Germany for a long time, and that by going into Germany she had made herself hated in most of the countries that had money.

Here she was, compelled to do her practising in a room about fifteen feet square, and to music that came over the radio ; at first she had had the use of a small stage at night, but now it was filled with beds ; everything in Germany was being filled with beds for wounded men, and Marceline had to hear their stories and write letters for them. " And of course when they get anywhere near well, they want to sleep with me," she said, having the European frankness on this subject. Lanny knew as well as she the code of the Hitlerites, that it was every woman's duty to give sexual comfort to a soldier, and to bear a future soldier or mother of soldiers for the Fatherland whenever and however that might be possible. " I tell them that I have a lover," she went on, " but that doesn't mean much to them. I am afraid the doctors of this institution consider me an alien and disturbing influence."

It was easy enough for Lanny to believe that she was disturbing. She was twenty-five and at the height of her carefully cultivated charms. She had been fashion's darling from the age when she had learned to stand in front of a mirror, to turn this way and that and survey herself. At the age of five she had sat at her mother's dressing-table, examining her hair, her skin, her eyes, and applying a variety of substances out of ornate expensive bottles. Later, when all these operations were completed, she went among the right sort of people, those who were wealthy and socially prominent, and when they turned to look at her the purpose of her life was achieved.

There was no use trying to change her—Lanny had learned that. Perhaps, he reflected, that was what it took to make a successful artiste ; that was what she expressed in the dance —pride and worldly glory ; that was all she had to express, and all that her audience would have understood. Sex, yes, but not its physical side ; that would have been crude and vulgar. Sex idealized, transmuted into pride and worldly glory ; the sex of the ruling-class woman, whose price was not a meal but a kingdom—that was what her charms represented.

She wanted to hear all about her little boy ; but Lanny had observed that when she was with the child she quickly became bored. She had been shocked to hear that he had been taken out of the Axis world, but Lanny had persuaded her

that it was unavoidable. She wanted to know all about
Beauty, and when Lanny mentioned the wrinkles she was
politely sympathetic. However, this feeling did not go very
deep ; it was inconceivable to Marceline that such a calamity
could ever befall her own fair skin, which a poet in Paris had
once raved about. When Lanny told her about her stepfather
and his faith-healing of Moors, that was like a fairy story out
of another world.

Then there was the news of her love affair, which she was
prepared to tell in detail, even though it was humiliating to
her *amour-propre*. After her marriage to a Fascist aristocrat
who had exploited her, she had sworn off love ; but here she
was, involved with a Prussian nobleman and Wehrmacht
officer, the most arrogant being on earth. She would fly into
rages with him, but presently she would be in his arms,
shuddering with delight and at the same time calling herself
a slave and a fool. When he was wounded, she had nursed
him, and she knew that she would do it again ; what she half
hoped was that he would be killed in battle and set her free.
Then she exclaimed, What a dreadful thing to say ! Women
were born to misery, and men were born to war, and what
was the choice between them ?

XI

They were sitting under one of the shade trees, and trees
do not have ears. The young Oberleutnant was entertaining
himself with the village barmaid and there was no one else in
sight. " Tell me," said the P.A., always on the watch to do
business, " what does Oskar think about the war ? "

" Until recently the idea never occurred to him that his
wonderful Army could meet defeat. But Stalingrad broke his
nerve, I think ; he was there, and barely got away, and lost
three of his toes from frostbite. He was here a month ago,
and defeat made him easier to get along with. He is sure
that the Americans are going into Italy, and that the Italians
will turn traitors. Do you think that will happen ? "

" Anything is possible," replied Lanny.

But that sort of thing doesn't go down with someone who
has lived in the house with you and watched you, especially

someone who is of the female sex, observant of details. "Tell me, Lanny," demanded the half-sister, "how is it possible for you to come into Germany and travel about, with things as they are?"

"Well, you know," he began his rigmarole, "I made a lot of friends in Germany before the war, and so did my father. Some of them are high-up Nazis, and they are making money as fast as they can."

"You mean that you can buy paintings and take them out of the country now?"

"Göring is making a huge collection, and those that he discards he sells for cash and buys others that he prefers." That, too, was not a direct answer, but he hoped it would do.

The woman lowered her voice, and her brown eyes looked straight into his. "Listen," she said, "you ought to know that you don't have to give me any double-talk. I know you haven't any love in your heart for this set of low-caste fellows who have thrown the world into war."

"Marceline, you musn't talk like that," he whispered, and looked all around him and even up into the tree.

"*Mais c'est à toi que je parle*," she said, and after that she spoke French and so did he. "I like gentlemen," she went on, "and I hate noisy rowdies, and I never had any reason to think that your taste differed from mine. I can tell you something that ought to be of interest to you, and you don't have to say that you got it from me."

"No, of course not; and for your part, don't say that you told it to me."

"I don't ever talk about you. Rightly or wrongly, I've been convinced for some time that you are not just buying and selling *objets d'art*. If you get into any trouble I don't want it to be my fault."

"Right, old darling. Tell me what's on your mind."

"You know what the Americans mean when they talk about 'Mr. Big'?" She first said it in English, then repeated it in French, "Monsieur Gros," and when he answered that he was familiar with this linguistic device, she went on, "There are some highly placed persons who have become convinced that he is responsible for the present bad situation and are planning to get rid of him by the quickest way."

The P.A. answered quietly, " That is important news indeed. Can you tell me, are these highly placed persons in the political world or the military ? "

" The military. As you know, perhaps, Monsieur Gros insists upon determining strategy and giving orders, even as to details. Men who have been studying problems of strategy all their lives naturally think they know more about them and resent having an amateur step in and take control away from them. It has always been the first maxim of German policy never to become involved in a two-front war ; and he got them into it. And when things go wrong he blames them, calls them foul names, shakes his fist in their faces, and has even had several of them done away with."

" I don't want to ask anything that you don't want to tell me ; but naturally I am supposing that you got this information from your *ami*."

" That is correct," replied the sister without hesitation.

XII

The P.A. sat for a while in thought. He had had long training in not showing any state of excitement. " As you say, Marceline," he began, " this is important news, and interesting. The highly placed men you speak of would naturally wish to know what will be the attitude of their enemies in the event that they manage to carry out their programme."

" They have discussed that question at great length, I know."

" Well, then, it might be a service to your *ami* if someone were to carry a message for him and bring back the desired information."

" Could you do that, Lanny ? "

" You know well that Robbie Budd has access to the highest circles. He could see our own Monsieur Gros and get a quick and dependable answer."

It was Marceline's turn to be silent. " It might be some time before I can see my *ami* again," she said at last.

" Wouldn't he come to you if you wrote him that you were in trouble and needed him."

" Just the contrary. He has troubles of his own, and his country has more."

" Surely there ought to be some way to give him a hint. When you see him, don't mention me. Tell him that you have contact with a person who could be of use to him."

" He would guess, Lanny ; he remembers you and asks about you, but I have never told him that I have seen you in Germany. All this is frightfully dangerous, and I shall lie awake half the night, shivering at the thought of what may happen to us both. Are you sure it is worth the trouble ? "

" It's a matter of some millions of human lives, Marceline."

" Those people have never given me cause to love them, and I can't get up enthusiasm for their lives. I prefer to say that this war is damned inconvenient to me and I'd like to see the end of it before I'm too old to have any fun."

" Put it that way, but be careful where you say it." He looked about him again. " Is there anything more you want to tell me about your friend's programme ? "

" I don't know very much ; I only found it out by accident."

" Does he know that you know it ? "

" He does. He is not worried about me because both my nationalities make me an enemy of his enemy. It amuses me to observe that his attitude to me is less insulting since he knows that I have this whip over him."

" Don't ever use it," Lanny said. " Do you know how many persons share the secret ? "

" It is quite widespread. It is not merely a plan to get rid of one man ; it is to possess the government. You understand, these men are not idealists. They want power, and if they get it, the Army will rule."

" It is an old story," said the P.A. " There was once a Bismarck. One thing more : you say that you were able to write to Beauty ? "

" You remember the Dohertys, whom we entertained at Bienvenu ? They are living in the Engadine, and I wrote to Mrs. Doherty and asked if she would be so kind as to pass on a message to my mother. Apparently the censor does not object to that ; I received a reply a month or so later."

" You might send a message to me by the same route.

Let us have a code. The message should have to do with paintings, and it had better be something real, which you can explain to anyone who might question you. Do you know of any paintings, or have an interest in any ? "

"There are some in the main hall of this one-time school."

"Do you know what they are ? "

"They are paintings of peasant scenes, three of them. I never paid much attention to them."

"I will look at them and express interest in them, in the presence of the Oberleutnant, and perhaps of others. That will make it a true story. You can write me by the Switzerland route that your effort to get a price on them is going well, or that you are delayed, or that you fear you cannot get it. Let us agree that a hundred marks represent a day ; so if you write that you think the price will be about three thousand marks, I will understand that the great event is expected in a month. I will keep Beauty informed as to my whereabouts and she will forward the message."

Marceline smiled. "I might make a guess that you have been doing this sort of thing for quite a while, Lanny."

"Don't think about it," he said. "You might talk in your sleep."

XIII

The young officer returned from his amours and was introduced to Herr Budd's sister. He had seen her dancing in a Berlin night club, and made it plain that he would have preferred her to any village barmaid. That was an old story to Marceline, but it never bored her ; on the contrary, it was like a drink of champagne—and this was an old story to her brother. The same thing had happened six years ago in Paris, when Lanny had been cultivating Graf von Herzenberg, the German diplomat, and had invited him and his son Oskar to a smart night spot where Marceline was beginning her career. The young officer had "fallen for her," as the saying goes, and the father had, to all appearances, considered it the proper sort of liaison for a young aristocrat—though of course he would never think of marriage with a Franco-American danseuse, even though she happened to be the daughter of a famous painter.

Marceline explained to Oberleutnant Harz that her brother wished to inspect the paintings in the hospital entrance hall, and the three went in together. Lanny was introduced to the *Intendant*, and he accompanied them. The *Kunstsachverständiger* took one glance at the paintings and exclaimed, " These should be Defreggers ! " He looked at the signatures, and sure enough, they were. This gave Lanny a chance to produce one of his suave and elegant discourses, especially impressive to this audience, because it included the statement that Defregger was the Führer's favourite painter, and a story of how Lanny had found several examples in Vienna, and these now hung in a place of honour in the Berghof, the Führer's Berchtesgaden retreat. If Lanny had really been buying paintings, all this would have been the last thing in the world he would have said ; but he wasn't buying paintings, he was establishing a code for Marceline.

He asked who owned the paintings, duly noted down the address, and asked his sister to communicate with the person ; this story would go the rounds of the place, and many who had barely glanced at the paintings previously would now know that they were great art and would be proud of being able to tell others about them. And if ever it chanced that Herr Himmler of the Gestapo developed an interest in the letters which the daughter of Marcel Detaze was receiving from Switzerland, all he would have to do would be to send to this hospital and the matter would be explained to his full satisfaction.

When they parted Lanny had a minute or two alone with his sister. " Better make it a thousand marks a day instead of a hundred," he said. " Those paintings should be valuable ! "

BOOK TWO

THE NIOBE OF NATIONS,
THERE SHE STANDS

4

When You Are in Rome

I

SET down on the Guidonia airfield in the Eternal City, Lanny Budd was met by another S.S. officer, who introduced himself as Hauptmann Schnabel. They both heiled Hitler, and the Hauptmann said that he had received instructions to take care of the Führer's friend. He drove him to a part of the city which resembled the Quartier Latin in Paris, being given up to art studios and garrets and the small shops which serve that poor but proud sort of folk. The guest was escorted into a large building by its rear entrance ; he later discovered that it was the Braunes Haus, the Nazi party headquarters on the Via Margutta. Lanny had been in Brown Houses in Munich and Nürnberg and other cities and was used to seeing swastikas on furniture and balustrades and mantelpieces, and to watching overfed busybodies hurrying this way and that, carrying brief-case and barking salutes. In whatever town the Nazi armies entered, there was a Braunes Haus next day, and the population learned to cross to the other side of the street to avoid passing it.

Lanny was escorted upstairs and made comfortable in a council chamber. The armchairs were upholstered in red leather with brass swastikas on the backs—a standard pattern, copied from the original in Munich. Lanny was introduced to an attentive little gentleman in civilian clothing, Herr Güntelen, whom he immediately spotted for a Gestapo man. They were exceedingly polite and told him they had received orders to afford him all possible assistance ; Lanny assured them that he needed a lot of it and would be most grateful. They produced cigarettes and brandy, and Lanny told them that the Führer had converted him to the Führer's ideas as to these indulgences, but that he had not the slightest objection to others following their own ideas. The Hauptmann, red-faced and hearty like a village butcher, partook stealthily of the brandy ; the other man sipped occasionally and smoked incessantly.

Lanny said, " *Meine Herren*, it must be a little puzzling to you to have an American among your associates ; and I for my part will feel happier if I am sure that you know me and trust me. So, if it wouldn't bore you I should like to take some time to tell you about myself and how I came to be a friend of your cause."

They assured him promptly that they wouldn't be in the least bored, so Lanny began his spiel—a German word which the Americans have taken over and given a meaning which the Germans do not understand. He said at the outset, " The only way I can tell this story is by mentioning the many Germans whom I have known and who have influenced me. It happens that these are prominent persons, not merely of your party but of the *Kaiserzeit*. To tell about them may sound like boasting, and I beg you to believe that I have no such motive. I will tell you the facts because they are facts and explain my ability to serve your cause."

They promised to attribute no *Prahlerei*, no vainglory, to him.

II

" I am," said Lanny Budd, " the son of a beautiful American girl who came to Paris with her brother and became an artist's model. My father was then the European representative of Budd Gunmakers Corporation, which Americans thought was a great affair, but of course it wasn't great according to German standards. I was raised on the French Riviera, where I met all sorts of people, artists and musicians and the fashionable set, including, of course, Germans. When I was thirteen I studied Dalcroze dancing at Hellerau, near Dresden, and there I met Kurt Meissner, a year older than I and already an accomplished musician. We became friends, and I spent several Christmases at his home in Schloss Stubendorf. It was there that I met Heinrich Jung, whose father was *Oberförster* of the estate, and it was through him that I first heard about Adolf Hitler and his ideas. At that time I thought myself a Socialist, though I didn't know very well what the word meant ; I was full of generous impulses and was sure that all the evils of the world could be remedied overnight. At the age of nineteen I became secretary-translator to one of President Wilson's advisers at the Paris Peace Conference, and there I got my first disillusion. I became outraged by the unfairness of the Versailles *Diktat* and resigned my position as a protest against it. That is a matter of record—it was in the newspapers and you can look it up."

"We have already done that, Herr Budd," replied the Gestapo man.

"No doubt you have quite a dossier on me," replied the P.A. with his genial smile. "If there is anything in it that disturbs you, I trust that you will mention it to me and give me a chance to explain. I have learned much and changed my mind in many ways in a quarter of a century, but I have never had to apologize for my objections to the Versailles peace terms. I said then that they would cause another world war and they have done so. It has been a tragedy for me, because I have friends on both sides and I have had to make up my mind, something that is difficult, since I am rather lazy and easygoing and would rather get along with everybody than fight anybody. It needed your Führer with his dynamic personality to make me face the issue. He took me up into his retreat on top of the Kehlstein and spent a couple of hours telling me what was coming and what he wanted me to do for him. Have either of you gentlemen ever seen that extraordinary place ? "

"No, Herr Budd," said the S.S. man reverently. "You have had an honour vouchsafed to very few Germans." Lanny decided that this was a party hack and a good deal of a fool ; but the other man was something different and had to be handled with care.

"I have been able to run various errands for the Führer. I visited Vienna and Paris and London and New York in order to get information for him ; I even travelled out to California to talk with Mr. Hearst and find out how far he was prepared to go in the effort to put a stop to the so-called lend-lease to England. Also I have bought paintings for the Führer—I am by profession an art expert, and Marshal Göring has seen fit to trust my judgment. I trust that you have not failed to ask him about me."

"We have done so, Herr Budd," said the Gestapo man.

"I have been a guest at Karinhall many times and have met many of his friends. I spent a couple of weeks in the Führer's home just before the present war broke out and met a number of his higher officers. Some of them, I fear, were not able to understand why the Führer should have an American in his house at such a critical hour. I was not able to give them the long explanation I am giving to you."

"We appreciate it," said Herr Güntelen. "The more we know about you, the better we shall be able to help you."

"Do go on," said the other.

So Lanny talked. He was naturally glib, but he tried not to appear so. He told straightforwardly about his many German friends—a carefully screened list, of course. He told how Kurt Meissner had been his friend and mentor, and had lived in Lanny's home on the Riviera for seven or eight years after the first World War and there had developed his musical genius. All Germany knew how the Führer honoured Kurt Meissner, but few knew how much the *Komponist* owed to an American lady of wealth and wisdom. Lanny had only to look back upon those days, when he had really adored a great German musician, and he could speak in a way that would convince even a Gestapo man that he was in the presence of something genuine and significant. It was a shame to speak such words fraudulently; but Lanny had learned from the Germans one of their sayings, that when you are among the wolves you must howl with them.

III

This session lasted part of an afternoon and the greater part of a night. Food was brought in and they stayed on the job. After Lanny had told about General Emil Meissner, and Heinrich Jung, and Graf Stubendorf, and Graf Herzenberg, and General-Major Furtwängler, and other proper Germans who were his friends, he invited the two hosts to ask him questions, and Herr Güntelen brought up the delicate matter of Lanny's father, who was making so many fighter planes in an effort to drive the Germans out of the air.

Lanny said, " Yes, it is indeed delicate, the most painful in the world to me. Marshal Göring knows my father well," he added, " and knows his real attitude ; others know it, for my father is a Republican and a bitter opponent of the Roosevelt administration. But he is its prisoner ; his plant has been in effect commandeered. The Army tells him what to do and Army officers are there to see that he does it. But that is not all of the story ; the reason the Führer sent me to America four months ago was to get the most highly secret information in the world, the moves that are under way to bring about an overturn in the American government. I am sorry that I cannot talk about that, being under the Führer's explicit orders. You may, if you wish, call him up and ask about it."

" *Nein, nein, Herr Budd*," put in the startled S.S. man. " *Befehl ist Befehl*, and certainly we do not want to ask you about any matters that you do not feel at liberty to talk about."

So, they knew their places, and the friend of the Führer was their master. He didn't want them to hate him, so he hastened to add, " We all have one loyalty and serve the same cause. Is there anything else I can tell you that might be of help to you ? "

He waited, not without inward trepidation. As the Greek hero Achilles had a vulnerable heel, as the Aryan hero Siegfried had a similar spot in his back, so Lanny was wondering if either of these men would ask, " What about your wife ? " Both he and Laurel had done their best to keep the dark secret of Mary Morrow, anti-Nazi novelist far too well informed. Not even her publishers knew that she was Mrs. Lanning Prescott Budd ; she had even taken the precaution to open a bank account in her pen-name, so that she could cash royalty cheques without detection. But the Gestapo had spread its nets so widely !

They didn't speak the word " wife." But that didn't mean that they didn't know he had one. They might be waiting to see if Lanny would mention the subject. They might have come upon other reasons for doubt and refrained from mentioning them, just waiting and watching. In this dreadful game of espionage and counter-espionage there could never be any security, any relaxation ; the moment a man began to think of such a thing, to long for such a thing, might be the moment of his end. And Lanny Budd did so hate this war and long to shake this burden of lies from his back !

IV

The Gestapo man said, " I think we understand you clearly, Herr Budd. Will you tell us what you plan to do and how we may be able to help you ? "

Then began the second stage of the interview. Something that amused Lanny deep in his soul—only a few days ago he had been briefed by the Office of Strategic Services in Washington, and now he was being briefed by the Geheime Staats-Polizei in Rome ! And on the same personalities, the same set of facts ! Surely a P.A. ought to know Rome and the Romans when he got through !

He told the story that he had told the Führer and set forth in detail what the Führer had asked him to do. To find out who were the traitors among the Italians, those who were preparing to cast Mussolini out and turn the country over to the invading Americans. The S.S. man shook his head sadly and remarked, " It might be better, Herr Budd, to list those who are still dependable. The number would be so much smaller and easier for you to remember ! "

" Do you agree with that, Herr Güntelen ? " Lanny asked, and the reply was, " We are giving the traitors enough rope to hang themselves."

" I hope that I can help you, at least with information. If you will give me a list of the individuals you suspect, I will do my best to meet them."

" But how can you expect to circulate in Rome when so many people know that you are an American ? "

" The fact that I have lived most of my life in France will make it plausible to say that I have acquired French citizenship. Would it not be possible for you to provide me with a French passport, real or fictitious, and to fix it up with the

Italian authorities not to raise any question about the document ? If you told them it was genuine, I doubt if they could find out otherwise in the present disorganized state of France."

" I suppose that could be arranged." The gimlet eyes of the Gestapo man were boring into Lanny, and he felt uneasy, lest perchance he was being too plausible, too clever. " You understand," he continued, " I am here as an art expert. I represent American millionaires who are assembling great collections in order to cheat the conqueror death and immortalize their names as the donors. I cannot ship paintings out of Italy at present, but I can perhaps buy them and arrange for their safe storage ; at any rate, I can talk about doing this and inspect examples and discuss prices. All that is an old story to me."

" You have credentials in your profession ? "

" I could call up Reichsmarschall Göring, or Baron von Behr, head of the Einsatzstab, which as you doubtless know is your government's organization in charge of valuable art works. But I do not think that will be necessary, for the reason that I have in mind a French lady in Rome who is a cousin to some of my close friends. You probably know her, the Marchesa di Caporini."

" We know of her."

" Tell me, if you can, her political position at present."

" She has been outspoken in favour of the Fascists, and so far as we have heard she is not one who has gone over to the enemy."

" Let me explain, she is a cousin of the de Bruyne family, whose head is one of the leading industrialists in Paris. His wife was my *amie* for many years, a gracious and lovely person. On her deathbed she charged me to watch over her sons, and I did the best I could. The younger son, Charlot, became an officer of the Légion Tricolore, for the purpose of protecting the Vichy government against the intrigues of its enemies. The father and both the sons were active in support of the Cagoulards, and when their efforts were exposed I tried to hide them from the French police ; as a result, I got into trouble myself, and Graf Herzenberg, then with the German Embassy staff, hid me in his country place until the storm had blown over. I tell you these things so that you will understand that, while I have never met the Marchesa di Caporini, she will undoubtedly know about me and introduce me to the people I wish to meet."

" That sounds reasonable, Herr Budd. The trouble is that through her you will be apt to meet only our own side. Social life here in Rome is sharply divided."

" If I listen to the talk of our friends, I shall soon learn who our enemies are."

" Yes, but it will be second-hand evidence. You will not gain the confidence of the important traitors."

" It has been my practice to pose as an ivory-tower art lover and to leave the painful subject of politics to the politicians. My story is that it would ill become a Frenchman, in the present condition of my country, to come into Italy and give advice to the Italians."

The P.A. paused. There was something he wanted very much to have said, but he wanted it to come from Herr Güntelen. This shrewd and observant man—he had been, as Lanny learned, an agent of the I.G. Farben cartel in the pre-Hitler days—sat thinking hard, and Lanny was trying to guess his thoughts. When the German spoke, it was suavely and persuasively. " You know, Herr Budd, there is a certain type of mind that has become very common here, the person who shades his political opinions according to those he is with. Could you not be that sort ? "

Deep inside Lanny Budd was laughter. The most dreaded spy organization in the whole world was inviting him to do exactly what he most wanted to do—to take sides against it ! He had a right to look surprised, and did so. " You mean that I should pose as an Allied sympathizer, Herr Güntelen ? "

" I wouldn't say anything quite so definite. There are shades of opinion, and you might say just enough to encourage the other fellow to open up."

" That would be a pretty dangerous game to play, I fear."

" We are living in dangerous times, Herr Budd, and we all have to take our share of risk."

" Perhaps you do not get just what I mean. If I should go out into Roman society and pose as being any shade of Allied sympathizer, how long would it be before reports began to get out about me—and not merely in Rome but to my

D

friends in Germany and France ? It might not be long before you yourselves would begin to wonder whether I was not playing my part too well."

"You would be reporting to us occasionally, I hope."

"Unfortunately that is what I cannot do. My orders are to report directly to the Führer, through Marshal Kesselring. I would be glad if you would check that statement with the Führer, so that you will not think that I am unappreciative of your kindness."

"*Auf keinen Fall*, Herr Budd. We have confidence in your statement, and we are not so fortunate as to have access to the Führer personally."

"If I get anything of value I will ask him to let me tell you. As to your suggestion that I might shade my opinions, I will bear it in mind. If I meet some especially important figure, such as Dino Grandi, and find that I could gain a point by whispering words of friendship, I might try it. But I must have the pledge of both you gentlemen that if rumours come to you that I am keeping the wrong sort of company, you will understand that it is at your suggestion, and not of my own impulse." He managed to put a smile upon his face while he said this, but it was a somewhat wry smile ; he knew that he was walking on eggs, and would be all the time he was in Rome. He was preparing to venture that most tricky of courses, known to the O.S.S. as " turning "—that is, pretending to go over to the enemy and work for him. He was not fooled for a moment by Herr Güntelen's politeness. He knew that what was going on in this gentleman's mind was the gentleman's secret. *Achtung.*

v

Duly equipped with a valid French passport, a card of identity, a permission to " circulate," a food-coupon book, and other necessities of life in wartime Italy, the son of Budd-Erling sallied forth to find himself living quarters. The Germans might have done this for him, but it wouldn't have looked right. They had warned him that he would have trouble, for the situation in Rome was the worst in all the country. Everybody who had the means was getting out of the lower half of the boot, and it was literally true that all roads led to Rome. This was the one safe place, for who would dare to desecrate the Holy City, the Eternal City, headquarters of Holy Mother Church ?

The Regina-Carlton Hotel was crowded, Lanny was told ; but his father had taught him in boyhood how to deal with such a situation. A few gracious words to the hotel clerk and a few more to the porter, explaining how urgent his business was, and then a couple of hundred-lire notes to each of these functionaries, and Lanny had a comfortable room with bath. Only cold water ran, but that was enough in midsummer. There was no soap or toilet paper, but there was a black market in the Piazza Vittorio Emanuele, and the porter would get you what you wanted at no more than half a dozen prices. That was the way, if you had the money ; if you didn't have it, you slept under a bridge and starved, or begged, or stole, or tried to sell " feelthy postcards " on street corners.

Lanny sat down and wrote a proper letter on the stationery of a proper hotel. " My dear Marchesa : I am an old friend of the de Bruyne family and am hoping that my name will be known to you. I had the pleasure of meeting Charlot several times in Vichy during the past year and so can tell you news of the family. I am in Rome for the purpose of purchasing old masters for an American collection and would appreciate the privilege of calling upon you at your convenience." He dropped that into the mail, and next morning waited in his room, reading the *Osservatore*, the Vatican newspaper, which gave more news of the outside world than Mussolini would permit in any of his Fascist papers. Naples had been bombed, and the systematic bombing of Sicilian airports and shipping was continuous.

The telephone rang, and there was the voice of an agreeable lady, inviting him to call that afternoon and expressing the usual regret that the coffee would of necessity be imitation. He made the gallant reply that it was herself and not her coffee that would interest him. The hotel valet pressed his clothes, and he made himself presentable and was driven in an aged *vettura* to a weather-beaten Renaissance mansion not far from the Colonna Palace. An aged manservant in faded livery opened the door and escorted him into the drawing-room.

All rooms in Rome are kept dark in summer, but there was light enough for him to see that there were paintings on the walls, and he satisfied his professional curiosity while waiting for his hostess.

VI

Marie de Bruyne had been some years older than Lanny, and he had assumed that her cousin would be the same. He was surprised to see a buxom lady, appearing no more than middle-aged, but of course that might be due to hair dye and dim light and other devices which the son of Beauty Budd had had ample opportunity to learn about. He had imagined a quiet, reserved lady, like Marie, but this cousin was hearty in manner and talkative; that too might have been put on for the occasion, a matter of morale in a time that tried the souls of women. Anyhow, Lanny was going to have no trouble making friends; the lady knew the story of his left-handed membership in the family and was eager to hear the rest. She wanted to know all about Charlot, what he was doing and thinking, and what news there was of Denis, *père et fils*. "Lanny —may I call you Lanny?" she said. "We miserable Romans have nothing left but gossip, and not enough of that to go round."

He brought out his store of the commodity. He told how Charlot had been organizing the Légion Tricolore, the Fascist military group to put down the underground resistance in Vichy France. He did not say that he had met Denis junior in North Africa, but repeated what Charlot had told him about the ideological chasm between the brothers. "That is just the way it is with us Romans!" exclaimed the Marchesa. "All split up into warring groups, and no one has the patience even to hear the other person's point of view." That did not sound like the statement of a Fascist fanatic, and Lanny began to wonder whether this lady too was in the process of "turning." He was there to find out, not to commit himself, so he said, "I decided years ago that the problems were too complicated for my powers, and I confine myself to making sure whether Giottos and Correggios are genuine or not."

She wanted to know how it was possible for him to travel and buy paintings in wartime Europe, and he told her that he was so fortunate as to have influential friends. The elder Denis had introduced him to Pierre Laval, and he numbered other members of the Vichy government among his friends. There were American millionaires willing to spend large sums to save Europe's art treasures from the wreckage of war. " I have been commissioned to purchase anything that Hermann Göring may overlook." That, of course, was in the nature of a feeler, and the response was immediate, " Oh, the Germans have been dreadful ! They have stripped the country bare."

The woman asked what kind of paintings he was interested in, and he told her—anything that was genuine and good. He wondered if she was going to refer to her own ; but she was a tactful lady and said she had a friend who possessed a genuine Giorgione. " That ought to be worth a great deal of money," he commented ; then he told her the favourite story of his friend and colleague, Zoltan Kertezsi, who, during an exhibition of paintings he had conducted, had been approached by an elegantly dressed lady who said that she had been told not to miss the " George Oney," but she couldn't find " Oney " in the catalogue.

All this made good conversation, and Lanny was adept at it ; he offered to leave more than once, but he was urged to stay. She wanted to hear the details about his love for Marie de Bruyne ; how he had met her, and how he had adored her for a matter of seven years. Marie had taught him, so he stated, the greater part of such wisdom as he possessed. It had been a love story in the French manner, she and her family being Catholic and having a horror of divorce. Marie had been unhappily married, and the free-spoken Marchesa knew all about it—she mentioned that the elder Denis was one of those unfortunate men who had to have virgins, and of course the mother of his sons could not qualify. Julie—that was the Marchesa's name and she told Lanny to call her that—Julie knew about the recent tragedy which had befallen the old man in Paris, and she discussed that with the same frankness. At the age of eighty plus, he had fallen under the spell of a designing young woman who was stripping him of his property. Lanny said that appeared to be one of nature's ways of punishing old men for their sins ; in his youth he had met the sculptor Rodin whom the same calamity had befallen.

When he left Julie told him to make this place his home. He need not worry about eating her food because her husband owned much farmland not far away and they were able to get things into the city. " I am a lonely old woman," she said, " and you bring me a breath of fresh air from France. In return I will tell you all about our corrupt fashionable world, and I'll help you to see the paintings you want and not to be robbed too badly."

That was certainly a fair offer, and Lanny went away reflecting that Julie, Marchesa di Caporini, could hardly be a very staunch Fascist. He could guess that like the rest of her class she had been terrified by threats of revolution within Italy and without, and had accepted Mussolini as her saviour ; but the Germans had come and she had not liked them, and now she was getting her mind ready for the coming of a new invader with a different ideology. Anyhow, she liked this Franco-American visitor and promised to make arrangements for him to inspect the " George Oney " next morning.

VII

On his way back to the hotel, Lanny stopped at a kiosk and acquired a load of newspapers and magazines ; the city was blacked out at night, and there was a curfew, so he would undress, stretch out on the bed, and learn what the dictatorship was telling its public. Lanny, who had espoused unpopular causes since boyhood, had become expert at reading between the lines of kept newspapers, deciphering truth from the falsehoods of its enemies.

Julie kept her promise and phoned about the appointment. She could not use her car because the tyres were worn out and it was impossible to get gasoline ; but Lanny would come in a cab and take her to the place. Then, would he come back to lunch at her home and meet her husband and children ? He said he would and thanked her. He could go to sleep peacefully on this hot night in the middle of summer, knowing that he had got access to the very centre of the social fortress of Rome.

Next morning he visited another palace, where he was introduced to an elderly commendatore named Cesare d' Angelo, with white hair and handle-bar moustache and most elegant manners. Lanny was escorted into a basement and from there down another steep flight of stone steps into what had once been a dungeon ; it had been provided with fireproof doors and turned into a temporary art gallery. Among the paintings was a fine " Descent from the Cross," and Lanny was permitted to inspect it at his leisure ; he was told that its price was a hundred and fifty thousand dollars, to be deposited in a bank in New York. He promised to report the offer to his clients ; he did not think it was a Giorgione, but a Titian, done by that painter when he was under the influence of Giorgione, with whom he worked.

Lanny and the Marchesa sat in the Commendatore's fine library, two-storied, with a balcony having elegant carved railings running all the way round. Iced drinks were served, and they talked politics ; Lanny hadn't planned it that way, but the old gentleman was determined, because he was sick with the fear that Rome was going to be bombed and his treasures destroyed. Here was a visitor who came from America and whose father manufactured military planes ; surely the father must have talked about how they were going to be used, and the son must have heard the talk. The old man, abandoning all dignity, all pretence of aristocratic aloofness, stretched out a pair of trembling hands and besought the visitor, " Tell me what you would do, Monsieur Budd, if you were in my place." They were speaking French, because that was the Marchesa's native tongue and she and Lanny used it.

The guest replied, " I honestly do not know, sir. If the Allies fight their way up the peninsula, it is hard to see how any place in the country can be safe, because every hill will be a military objective and every stone hut a machine-gun nest. For that reason I should think this city might be your best bet."

" Do you think that the Allies will grant our plea and accept Rome as an ' open city ' ? "

" They will lay down stringent conditions, and I doubt if the Germans would consent to them. You may be sure the

Allies will do what they can to avoid damaging the churches
and historic buildings ; the main target will be the railroad
yards."

" Your bombers can be counted on for such accuracy,
Monsieur Budd ? "

Lanny smiled. " When our Air Force started out they
used to boast of their ability to drop a bomb into a barrel ;
but now, under actual conditions of wind and weather, they
have had to reduce their claims. I should think, however,
that they could be counted on to distinguish between a place
of worship and a tangle of railroad tracks."

There was Lanny, talking learnedly about the very subject
he wanted to—and he hadn't been the one to bring it up. He
told the anxious old landlord—that was what he was, an owner
of latifundia—that the best way to save his property was to
get Italy out of the war. The landlord in return pointed out
the terrible complications—the Germans were here, and
wouldn't get out, they wouldn't give Italy up to the Allies,
because Italy was peppered with fine airfields from which
Germany and her satellites could be laid waste. When Lanny
brought up Hitler's idea of having both sides retire and leave
Italy alone, the Commendatore smiled sadly and remarked
that it was unlikely indeed that the Allied military men would
consent to such a deal ; they hadn't brought all those fleets
of ships and landing craft into the Mediterranean in order to
hold parades, nor yet to prove that Winston Churchill had been
right in trying to take the Dardanelles in the last World War.

Lanny, listening with half his mind, was thinking with the
other half, This is the place where I ought to be able to meet
Marshal Badoglio.

VIII

The art expert went back to the Caporini palace and lunched
with the family in a stately dining-room of panelled and
hand-carved walnut. On one wall hung a fifteenth-century
tapestry showing Romulus and Remus with their wolf, and
against another wall was an immense sideboard loaded with
silver and crystal from the days of Benvenuto Cellini. The
meal was served by the aged manservant, not without difficulty
because his hands were showing signs of palsy.

The family was hardly to be called exhilarating ; its head, older than his wife, was partly bald, thin, and sallow of complexion ; he did not talk much, and when he did, he told stories having to do with horses, dogs, and other country-gentleman appurtenances. There were two children ; the elder a girl who sat silent and started when you spoke to her ; from her remarks Lanny decided that she was not " all there." The boy, on the contrary, was eager, and anxious to impress the visitor ; a product of the Balilla, the Fascist organization for the training of youth, he seemed to Lanny to embody all the disagreeable qualities of that system ; he was cocky, self-assertive, and ignorant. The fact that his mother was a Frenchwoman, and that the guest was supposed to be French, did not keep him from asserting that France was an enemy and was wrongly withholding from Italy Nice, Savoy, and Corsica.

Against these handicaps the mother struggled to make her guest enjoy himself. He saw that she adored the children and yet was ashamed of them. He saw that she did not love her husband and that they had no intellectual congruity. As a man of the world, accustomed to all sorts of human situations, he parried gently the boy's impertinence and questioned the country squire concerning the state of the wheat crop and the prices the government allowed for it. Such facts had their bearing upon the war situation, and all was grist that came to a secret agent's mill.

To a fond mother such behaviour meant that the guest was kind, and this kindness warmed her heart and caused her to take still greater interest in his purposes. She thought of several friends who had paintings and strove to interest her husband in making suggestions, although it could hardly be expected that Lanny would lend much weight to his judgment in matters of art. The expert wondered if she had told her husband about Marie de Bruyne, and what reason she had given for taking so much trouble for a wandering *conoscitore d' arte*. They were speaking Italian, since the Marchesa admitted that her husband's French was not good, and the boy, Lanny guessed, would scorn the language of a defeated and humiliated people.

After the meal the elders repaired to the drawing-room

and there Lanny referred to Commendatore d'Angelo's fear
of bombing raids as a means of drawing out his host.   No
excuse was necessary, because the subject was the one which
every person in Rome from the Pope to the lowliest beggar
was most disposed to discuss.   The position of Italy was
frightful, and everybody from the Pope to the beggar knew
it.   Lanny had never seen a cyclone, but he had read about
them and could imagine standing on the prairie watching one
bearing down upon him, with no cellar in which to seek refuge.
A cyclone is only wind, and, as a rule, it destroys only wooden
buildings, but the cyclone of war was fire and blast, and the
more solid a structure, the more apt it was to be used as a
fortress and knocked to pieces by the invaders.   Wood was
scarce on the peninsula, but rocks were plentiful, and the
buildings had been patiently put together to last for centuries
—if only the mailed fist of war could be kept away from them.
The Italian boot was long and narrow, and destruction would
sweep over it like a scythe.

Such was the picture in every Italian mind, as the visitor
was to discover.   They were a clear-sighted people, realistic
and sceptical, even cynical.   Mussolini had laboured mightily
to puff them up with pride, love of glory, the dream of a new
Impero Romano ; he had succeeded with part of them,
especially the young, but now that dream was dead and
stinking in their nostrils ; their Duce was a bald-headed old
lecher, suffering from stomach ulcers and syphilis ; he had
dragged them into this war, and Lanny would have a hard
time finding anybody who would admit that he had ever
wanted it.   The P.A. was astonished to find how sick ordinary
people were of Fascism as well as of the war, and how outspoken they were, high or low, rich or poor.

Here was this nobleman and landowner who had thought
only of protecting his property.   Fire-breathing Red agitators
had come into the rural districts, poisoning the minds of the
farm labourers and organizing them into unions, which in the
landowner's eyes were mere bandit groups.   Mussolini had
promised to end all that, and he had done so, and they had
had a decade of reconstruction.   But then Il Duce had led
them into foreign adventures and had brought in the Germans,
who were like a swarm of locusts, covering the whole land.

Now the Allies were coming, and they were still another sort of locust, a sort that dropped fire and destruction out of the air upon cities and towns, ships and harbours, railroads and bridges—everything that Mussolini had constructed and of which he had boasted too loudly.

Here, also, was the nobleman's wife, a Frenchwoman who, in the days of Fascism's pride, had visited her native land and offended her relatives by suggesting that the way of peace for France was to give up her border lands at her neighbour's demands. Now there was nothing left of that pride at all; the Marchesa said that the war was a tragic blunder, and that the Italians should give up whatever they had to in order to get the German masters out of it. Lanny had come expecting to hear these things in whispers, as he had heard them in Germany, where people went suddenly and opened their doors to make sure their servants were not spying, and put the tea-cosy over the telephone because they had been told that the police had a secret device enabling them to hear even when the receiver was on the hook. But in Rome he found that the people's discontent had reached the boiling-point, and the only ones who pledged you to secrecy were those whose livings depended in some way upon the regime.

IX

He went out and walked in this Eternal City, much changed in the two decades since his ill-fated visit. Il Duce had put up some showy government buildings and monuments and had built a great boulevard, leading to a new Forum, named for his work. He had played a cruel joke upon his own *gloria*; on this Via del Impero—the Road of the Empire—he had erected a marble wall and on it had put large bronze maps, showing what the old empire had been at its height, and what the new empire had been at its start, and how step by step it had grown. He hadn't yet got up the courage to take down the North Africa maps, and there they stayed, mocking him. Lanny took one glance and walked quickly; it was no place for a foreigner to linger.

To the visitor this Eternal City was Eternal Capitalism, the exploiting of the poor by the owners of the land and the means of production. This city, called "holy," contained some of the vilest slums he had seen in all Europe. That had also been the case in all the great capitals he had visited, not merely in the Mediterranean lands but in London and New York. Everywhere he had seen the shrines of Mammon, decked with the images of the humble and lowly Jesus, and had recalled the burning lines of the English poet Buchanan:

> Great Christus-Jingo, at whose feet
> Christian and Jew and Atheist meet.

The young men and the middle-aged of Rome were gone, all save the Fascist *Militi*. The women and the children were gaunt and half-starved, sad-eyed and silent. They came early and formed long queues, waiting for bread, for oil and greens; often they waited half the day, only to be sent away because the supplies were exhausted. They hid in their stifling tenements from the glare of the day, and when the sun went down they came out on the hot pavements for a breath of air. In peacetime they would have spent half the night outside, but now there was a curfew at dusk and the law was "martial."

Lanny had no way to find out what these people were thinking, for he was an elegantly dressed stranger and they would bear him no love. The hotel porter had warned him against venturing into the slums; crime was rampant—it thrives in war, like poverty and its evil sisters. The filth was appalling; the children had apparently no place to relieve themselves but in the streets, and they did this by daylight; the adults for the most part waited until night. Furtive beggars pursued the stroller, whining out of the corners of their mouths; children pestered him with offers of every sort of vice. The men were gone and the women were hungry; he could have bought young girls or boys for a bar of chocolate or a couple of cigarettes. Everywhere amid this misery and corruption walked the black-robed priests—"black beetles," the hate-filled workers called them. Lanny pitied them, for he knew that many were men of conscience and had no idea of what had caused this avalanche of suffering, and would not have been allowed to do anything about it even if they had found out.

X

Lanny telephoned Commendatore d' Angelo and asked the privilege of calling upon him again. The request was granted, and they sat alone in the old gentleman's study. The visitor's pretext was that he was concerned about a safe place to hide the alleged Giorgione if he bought it, and that led quickly to the subject of peace and how to get it. Lanny had only to listen and put in a few words now and then. The landowner took it for granted that the son of a great American capitalist would have the point of view of his own class; the question was how to save that class amid all the storms which were buffeting it. Fascism in Italy represented its effort to save itself from the Reds; but now Fascism was a prisoner and a pawn of Nazism, and that had shown itself as bad as communism. What did America have to contribute to that situation?

Lanny knew that he was talking to an influential person, one who was honest within the limitations of his point of view. It was necessary for a P.A. to trust someone if he was ever to get anywhere; he decided that this was the man. " I am going to ask you to let me speak to you in confidence," he said. " It happens that my father is a man of considerable power, and when he learned that I was planning this trip he asked me to make inquiry as to the attitude of the Italian people toward the problem of ending this war."

To a man of experience in affairs that was equivalent to saying, " I am an American agent." The Commendatore replied promptly, " I am glad you came to me, and you may surely count upon my good faith. We Italians have been dragged into this war, and we learned with consternation that we were supposed to fight Americans, whom we think of as wealthy relatives overseas."

Lanny could say that the American people surely did not think of the Italians as enemies, but as victims. He told about his friendship with Italians in New York, in Florida, and in Newcastle, and did not mind exaggerating this intimacy. His host showed his confidence by saying that the Italians and Americans had a common enemy and should be fighting him together. " That enemy is a dangerous beast, an old one, but he still has his teeth and claws." Lanny knew whom he meant and did not ask him to name names.

The Italian continued, " I do not think that anything can be done until the Allied Force has actually landed on our soil and made it plain that a serious invasion is meant. So long as there is any possibility that Italy will be by-passed, our people will continue to hesitate and dally."

Said the art expert, " I am not in the confidence of our military, but the situation appears obvious. The Italian air-fields are being used by the Germans against us, and we can have no security in the Mediterranean until we have taken them over."

" *Hélas, hélas !* " replied the old gentleman—they were speaking French, as before.

The question was, what was going to happen to Italy when the Nazis were prised off her back. Lanny said it would of necessity depend upon how this operation was performed. If the Italians did it themselves, they would naturally have more voice in deciding their future. He pointed to what had happened to the French in North Africa ; he revealed that he had been there and had been able to watch events. Admiral Darlan, General Juin, M. Lemaigre-Dubreuil of Huiles Lesieur, and other leading Frenchmen had had to make the same decision which now confronted the Italians. They had come over to the Americans, and as a result they enjoyed security.

The old gentleman declared that he and his friends had not failed to make note of this precedent. He revealed himself to be a monarchist ; he did not think the Italian people would accept the old King, who had too closely allied himself to the Fascist regime, but the King's eldest son, the Prince of Piedmont, was an excellent young man, handsome, not too intelligent, and in every way adapted to become a constitu-tional monarch on the English pattern. Lanny pointed out that British armies would undoubtedly be in the forefront of any invasion, and it was to be assumed that Winston Churchill would favour a government of the British sort ; certainly he could be counted upon to oppose the setting up of any Red or even Pink regime. Wherever the Allied armies came there would be law and order and respect for all property rights. To hear this suave gentleman talking you would have thought he was a member of the Comité des Forges—he knew many of them, and had managed to satisfy them just as he was satisfying Commendatore d' Angelo.

XI

This proved to be a long conference. The cultivated Roman revealed that he and his friends had been consulting together for months as to what they could do in the crisis they foresaw. He did not name these friends, but as the conversation developed Lanny took the liberty of mentioning various persons, and it turned out that the Commendatore knew them all. When Lanny asked, " Do you suppose that General Badoglio would be willing to discuss these matters with me ? " the reply was, " I think it would be an excellent thing for him to do."

When Lanny went out from this mansion he possessed a complete picture of the mind of the *haute bourgeoisie* of the Italian capital, their hopes, their fears, and their plans. He was surprised by the freedom with which this wealthy gentleman had spoken, just as he had been surprised by the attitude of the Caporinis. He took it as a sign that the situation was far more ripe than either he or Roosevelt had imagined. A good field for a P.A. to work in, and a chance to please the tired man in the White House !

The information was important enough to justify a report. Lanny did not want this to be in his handwriting, so he went for a stroll in an obscure part of the city and picked out the office of a real estate agent ; he went in at noon and asked permission to use the typist's machine while she was at lunch, paying for the privilege of course. He looked very much the gentleman, spoke with his German accent, and his request was granted. He sat and picked away, one sheet of plain paper which he had in his pocket, and no carbon.

He had devised a code and left a copy which F. D. R. had tucked away in a drawer of the reading table by his bed. Lanny had taken the first names of the presidents of the United States and assigned them a new meaning ; George was Roosevelt himself, John was Hitler, Thomas was Göring,

James was Mussolini, Andrew was Badoglio, and so on through a list of the various persons Lanny was likely to meet on his trip. For the further confusing of an enemy who might get hold of one of the reports, German cities and Italian cities were to exchange names. Thus Lanny wrote that Traveller —his own code name—had been in Rome and was now in Berlin ; he had seen John and John was greatly excited over the programme to put George out of the way. As it happened, there was a definite programme to put John out of the way ; it was a military plan and the persons were of top importance. He went on to tell about the attitude of the well-to-do Berliners, and said that he was expecting to meet Andrew very soon and would report again.

Lanny had two envelopes, one larger than the other, and each purchased in a different store. Making sure that no one was looking over his shoulder, he addressed the smaller " To the President, Personal and Confidential, from Traveller." He carefully sealed the letter in this, and then sealed it in the larger envelope, which was addressed to Pietro Padrone, and no street address. Lanny went out and walked again, this time to the American " post office," the secret address which the O.S.S. had given him.

This was the most dangerous part of a P.A.'s duties. He could not entrust this letter to the mail ; he had to put it into the hands of the right person. And for all he could know, this person might now be in the hands of the Gestapo or under their observation. Lanny knew that the American Intelligence Services would never arrest a spy until they had watched him and all his activities and had made note of all his associates. He had to assume that the Germans would be no less thorough ; and it might be that they had staked themselves out on all sides of this " post office " and had set up cameras in rooms across the street to take photographs of everyone who entered.

It was a chance that had to be taken. Lanny had walked past the place once and noticed that it was a small stationery store, a business that must have been difficult to keep supplied in this time of universal scarcity. Now he strolled, and turned in, calm in appearance but with heart thumping. There was a young woman at the counter, and no one else in the place that he could see. He asked, in Italian of course, " Have you any sepia carbon paper ? " The word sepia was code, and the girl was supposed to say, " I beg pardon, sir ? " She said it, and Lanny repeated, " I would like some very good quality sepia carbon paper."

The girl appeared nervous, but she couldn't have been more so than this middle-aged American gentleman wearing a tiny brown moustache and a brown suit of linen, neatly pressed. She said, " I will find out, sir." Lanny waited, and in a moment there appeared a short stoutish Italian, rosy-faced and wearing spectacles. He said, " I am expecting a shipment from Livorno." That was the code answer, and Lanny replied, " I would like to book an order for some." He took the envelope from his pocket and handed it to the man, then turned on his heel and went out, looking anxiously around to see if there were any suspicious-appearing characters lurking in doorways or peering from windows. He saw none and guessed that he had got away with it this time.

5

The Light That Lies

I

LANNY BUDD was doing what is called " moving " in fashionable Roman society. This wasn't as much restricted by the curfew as he had expected, for these rich and clever people had always been above the law and still found ways to be. They had permits of one sort or another, and when Lanny had been properly vouched for, he too could have one. What astonished him was the cynicism of this society, and the freedom with which its members expressed themselves. Fascism, in order to survive, had to succeed ; and here it was, failing before the eyes of the dullest. In " smart " society nobody is willing to be counted among the dull.

The P.A. had imagined his role as secret and subtle; he would meet only the key persons and keep himself as obscure as possible. But he found that he had chosen the wrong sponsor for that sort of career. Julie Caporini, all kindness and helpfulness, could not be made to understand his idea. "How can you expect to buy paintings," she exclaimed, "if you do not meet the right people and find out what they have and whether or not they need money?" And when Lanny couldn't find a satisfactory answer to that, she added, "Oh, you *must* meet Isabelle Colonna! She is our social queen, our *arbiter elegantiarum*; if she approves of you, everybody will take you up. Let me take you there for coffee—she may have the real thing!" Lanny had to say yes.

The Colonna family was one of the oldest in Rome, and the Princess Isabelle lived in a palace that was a show place in a city with a hundred palaces. It was humiliating to have to arrive at such a place in a cab, but Julie said that many of the very best people were reduced to that state. On the way she talked about their hostess, who had conquered Roman society by her wit and charm, despite the fact that she came from the Levant. She had chosen Galeazzo Ciano as her political guide and was standing by him even now when he had fallen from grace. "That is very unusual in our world," explained Julie, "so you see that she is a person of courage and honour."

To this Lanny replied, "If the rumours I hear are true, Galeazzo has not responded in kind."

"Oh, well," said the Marchesa, "that would be too much to expect from a man in his position." She said this without the trace of a smile, and Lanny assented in the same way.

The magnificence of the marble palace led him to expect a stately person, well on in years and conscious of her social responsibilities. He was surprised to meet one who was young, or at any rate who appeared so, and sprightly and frivolous, in the mood of a decadent time. Like all the others, she was bored by this time of strain and privation; so many men were away, and travel was so difficult. It was the first summer she had ever spent in Rome, she assured her guests. She wanted above all things to be entertained, and here was a visitor who had been in a dozen countries and had met many persons whom she knew. In short, he was an acceptable man, and she proposed to give a card party at the golf club, where "everybody" would meet him. She served real coffee and explained that it had been brought to her from Turkey by an attaché of the embassy in his diplomatic pouch.

II

The name of the institution was the Acquasanta Golf Club. In this most pious of cities Lanny had got used to the idea of a Queen of Heaven Prison, and now he was taken to a Holy Water Golf Club. (Some wit had said, "In Rome the Faith is made; elsewhere it is received.") The club was a beautiful spot, with lawns kept green in spite of summer drought and smooth in spite of the scarcity of labour; there was a view of rolling hills, and between them the arches of a red stone aqueduct built by the ancient and stern Romans. Here, at the summons of their queen, came the new Romans, the *crema di la crema*, the *gratin*, the upper crust; three times as many women as men, for in these desperate times even the most highly placed officials had to do some work.

Mostly young women, as beautiful as any that Lanny had ever seen, and in costumes showing no diminution of elegance. They were the young matrons, chosen because of their various charms, not physical perfection alone, but gaiety, *esprit*, ability to entertain the men who had position, wealth, and power. The men were in their offices, dealing with multiple troubles; the ladies were bored and looking for entertainment. They had heard of a new curiosity, an American in Rome. Nobody was fooled very long by his claim to be a Frenchman; they knew he was an enemy alien—and how had he got here, and who was protecting him, and what was he trying to do? Did it mean a hope of peace?

Nobody was more skilled at social banter than the son of Budd-Erling; he had learned it as the grandson of Budd Gunmakers, at the age of four, or perhaps five, by listening to ladies and gentlemen. These were the same kind of ladies —in one or two cases they were granddaughters of the same ladies. But the process of social decay had gone on for forty years, and the witty remarks these new ladies made would have made their grandmothers blush to the roots of their hair. Jokes about other people's sexual affairs, and sometimes about their own ; jokes about men with men and women with women ; there was nothing they did not know and touch upon with airy cynicism. Lanny, who had frequented smart society on the French Riviera, and in Paris, London, and New York, was familiar with this butterfly attitude and did not have to be naïve or puritanical ; it was his role to be reserved and mysterious, and be sure that interest in him would increase.

There is an old song about " the light that lies in women's eyes," and some modern wit has added the tag, " and lies, and lies, and lies." Lanny knew that light, and he saw it now in more than one pair, ranging in shade from dark to azure ; he knew that he could choose among this assortment of delicate creatures, one or even several, and divert himself agreeably during his sojourn in this Holy City. He guessed that he was expected to do so and would be considered an ungrateful guest if he refrained. He did not intend to do it, because he had a code about which these people knew nothing. He would deal with them on the basis of polite jesting ; he would be interested in them all, and each would wonder if he was serious with some other. The guessing would mount to a mild rage ; they would try to find out about him from the higher-ups, and whether they succeeded or not wouldn't matter, provided that he played his hand shrewdly.

So, when he was told that the lady who had just been his bridge partner was a " Galeazzo widow," he did not look either shocked or puzzled, but let his features expand into a delighted grin. All Europe, and indeed all the polite world, had known of Count Ciano's habit of keeping a harem of young and lovely women always at his service. It had been his practice to loll on the beach at Ostia with half a dozen of them about him, and others trying to get near. He would make appointments with the diplomats of other countries to meet him there, and sometimes it had happened that these gentlemen were elderly, and had paunches, or spindly legs, or other characteristics which they did not care to expose in bathing trunks. It had become something of a scandal that Italy's Foreign Minister had thus abused the diplomatic proprieties, and had been known to offer his cast-off lady loves not merely to members of his own staff, but to visiting statesmen who had wives and families at home, and who, if they had *affaires* on the side, preferred to keep the matter out of their business discussions—and out of the newspapers.

III

The deposed cabinet member, now Ambassador to the Vatican, came to the Holy Water Golf Club late in the afternoon and met the new American friend of his very dear friend, the Princess Colonna. He was swarthy and black-haired ; his ancestors, like Isabelle's, had come from the Levant. He was short and thick-set, handsome in an animal way, with broad shoulders of which he was proud and a paunch of which he was ashamed ; he tried to conceal it as his father-in-law did, by drawing it in and elevating his chest. He had risen in the world by aping his father-in-law in all ways, sticking out his chin, barking at his inferiors, and being very delightful to those whom for any reason he wished to please. Like Mussolini, he had also cultivated athletics ; but the present hot weather was too much for him, and he preferred to sit on a club piazza and kid those who came in exhausted and sweaty from their round of the links.

As always, he diverted himself with the ladies. They still gathered about him, and Lanny could guess what was in their minds : the wheel of fortune turned fast these days, and who could tell when it might bring their dear Galeazzo on top again ? So long as Isabelle still stuck to him, he was surely not to be considered a dead duck. So they beamed upon him and exchanged witticisms with him and with one another, and once more Lanny was astounded to discover that they were as free and easy on the subject of politics as they were with one another's sexual amusements. They teased the ex-minister about his demotion and asked him if he had chosen the post because of the well-known Vatican extra-territoriality. Neither Italians nor Germans nor Americans could get him so long as he stayed there ; but unfortunately there was no golf course, and what would he do for society ? They would come to visit him, but what would Il Papa say about that ?

" Il Papa " didn't mean Galeazzo's papa, nor the papas of any of the ladies, but that august personage, the Holy Father, Pope of Rome.

Evidently the ex-minister had been told about the Franco-American art expert. How much he knew was a question, and Lanny, prepared in advance for the meeting, was resolved upon extreme caution. But Ciano knocked all that out with a few sentences. What was the use of diplomatic protocol in a time when the guns and bombs had taken charge ? Sitting in the presence of half a dozen of his ladies, he defended himself by asking this visitor what he, the visitor, would have done in such a set of circumstances as Ciano faced, and he described them in detail. When Lanny said he could not imagine, that was Ciano's vindication. " I couldn't imagine and nobody else could imagine ; but there I was."

" Trying to foresee history is like trying to foresee the stock market," ventured the polite guest.

" Hell ! " was the reply. " I could foresee the stock market all right, because I could make it go where I wanted it to." As the ladies laughed he went on, " I did so, and I made a fortune at it. But who could foresee what was going to happen in Greece ? "

" They told us that you had bought all the Greek leaders," put in the lovely Rosaura Forli.

" So I did," declared her hero, " but the scoundrels wouldn't stay bought. I protested against the invasion ; I protested against every step up to the last madness. Could anybody that lives have imagined such a joke as Italy declaring war upon America ? David going out against Goliath, and without a single stone in his sling. But we are prisoners of the Germans, and we do what we are told."

Lanny hadn't expected anything like that, and all he could lamely say was, " It is indeed a tragic situation."

Ciano, turning his dark eyes upon the visitor, said, " They tell me you know the Führer, Signor Budd."

Lanny admitted it. " I have done business with him as an art expert."

" Then perhaps you know what is in his mind at present and will tell me."

" He is a man of frank speech. He would be pleased if the

Allies would make peace with Italy on the basis of an agreement by both sides to keep Italian territory inviolate."

" *Davvero!* Wouldn't that be lovely, if the Allies would agree! Have you heard any of them suggesting that bright idea ? "

" Alas, no, Count Ciano. I fear they have designs upon your airports."

" Quite so ; and we are caught between two artillery barrages. Have you any suggestion of hope for us, Signor Budd ? "

" I fear that lies outside an art expert's province. But I sometimes meet persons of influence, and if you have any idea that you would like to have communicated, I will be a faithful messenger." Lanny said this, inwardly wincing—as many other diplomatic persons had done—at being called upon to discuss affairs of state in the presence of half a dozen pretty young chatterboxes.

" Be so good as to report this for me," responded Il Duce's errant son-in-law. " I have washed my hands of the mess and leave it to be cleaned up by those who made it. And you know whom I mean."

IV

At the home of Commendatore d' Angelo Lanny had his promised meeting with Il Maresciallo Badoglio. This old gentleman—he was seventy-two—had served as Mussolini's scapegoat in the Greek campaign ; he had been ordered to take his ill-prepared armies up into those wild mountains, and he had done so and got soundly thrashed by tough fighting men armed with British weapons ; then, of course, he had been blamed and kicked out. Somebody besides Il Duce had to be wrong. Pietro Badoglio had retired to his country estate ; he was an immensely wealthy man and represented the top of Italian society, the white hope of the monarchists, the aristocracy, the landowners, and the great manufacturers. He had been given the Supreme Order of the Annunziata, which made him a " cousin " to the King and entitled so to address him.

This eminent personage came to the d' Angelo palace

wearing his elaborate uniform with a broad Sam Browne belt and many pockets. He wasn't willing to have the American come to him, the Signor had explained, since every other person in Rome was a spy. The Marshal was rather small, dapper and elegant, with colourless skin and a little white moustache. His voice was low and his manner reserved; caution was his watchword, and for the most part he sat quietly and let his host tell the American stranger how the Marshal had opposed the alliance with Germany and the attack on Greece, to say nothing of the insane declaration of war against America. "Now," said d' Angelo, "the Germans hold our country in a tight fist, and our problem is how to pry that fist open."

Lanny had expected this sort of reception. "*Monsieur le Maréchal*," he said, "permit me to speak frankly, and in strict confidence. I bring you no credentials; it will be obvious to you that an American could not come into your country carrying credentials—except of the wrong sort. I have to convince you of my good faith by my personality and my moral tone, so to speak. At the time this war broke out, I enjoyed the confidence of Marshal Pétain, and at the home of Madame de Portes he commissioned me to carry a message to the King of the Belgians, in a last effort to stave off the calamity. I did not succeed in the mission, because the German armies marched into Belgium that same night. I only tell you the story to make it clear that I wanted peace for France and Belgium as I now want it for Italy."

"*Je vous accepte dans ce rôle, Monsieur*," said the Marshal. He spoke French fluently, and that was better for the guest.

Lanny continued, "At the time preceding the Allied Army's invasion of North Africa I happened to be there, making a collection of Moorish art for a wealthy American. I had enjoyed the friendship of Admiral Darlan for some time, and I came to know General Juin, and M. Lemaigre-Dubreuil, and other important Frenchmen in both Algiers and Casablanca. They entrusted me with their plans and hopes, and I was able to get word to prominent persons in Washington and to work out arrangements which were very advantageous to the French. You must understand that my father is a leading American industrialist and is in position to get word to persons in authority and to get their answers. If I can persuade you of my good faith, I may be able to do for the Italians what I did for the French."

Il Maresciallo's watchword remained caution. "Our situation is an extremely complicated one, Monsieur Budd," was his reply.

"I know that well, *mon cher Maréchal.* As you no doubt know, the Allied armies are about to invade Sicily. I have not been told the exact date, but it cannot be far off now. I know of my own knowledge that the French military men were sure that Casablanca could not be taken from the sea and that an army which attempted that feat would be met with disaster. As you know, we solved that problem. Sicily offers no greater difficulties."

"I grant that you can do it, Monsieur Budd ; but it will be a slow and costly adventure."

"Our military men allow themselves three months for the job ; but I happen to know that President Roosevelt believes it can be done in half that time. We have five thousand planes on hand for the invasion, and half as many vessels."

"I warn you, the Italians will fight for their native soil much harder than they fought for Africa, which many of them never wanted."

"We allow for that, *mon Maréchal.* But our warships and bombers will reduce the shore fortifications, and we shall put tanks ashore as quickly as we did in North Africa. We know that the Germans have brought the Hermann Göring Division to Sicily, and that they have one or two other divisions there ; but their troops are tired, while ours are fresh—and we do not have to fight a war with Russia at the same time."

"The German military men have had very bad advice, Monsieur Budd," said the Marshal, and his visitor replied promptly, "You of all men should know what that means to commanding officers." That was pressing the argument closely, and for the first time a trace of a smile crossed the old gentleman's mask-like face.

V

Lanny went on telling secrets, for he had decided that this was the man who had the right to hear them, and he had been authorized to use his judgment. Said he, " The Strait of Messina will offer no obstacle to an invading army, and we shall take the great air-base of Foggia and be in a position to bomb not merely the whole of Italy, but also Austria and Southern Germany, which the Führer will not like."

The former commander of all the Italian armies showed signs of warming up. " Since you seem to be so well informed," he said, " will you tell me whether they intend to bomb Rome ? "

" I am told that the decision is in the hands of our military, and that as soon as they have secured a foothold in Sicily they intend to bomb the railroads of Rome—what the British call the marshalling yards. These are considered a key point in the communication system by which the German armies are supplied."

" Many poor people have their homes right beside those yards, Monsieur Budd."

" It is because of those poor people that I have sought this interview. We have several million Italians in America and we find them good citizens, and surely do not wish to bring death and ruin to their relatives and friends. We want the quickest possible peace with Italy."

" And yet you hold out nothing but unconditional surrender ! "

" That phrase, *mon Maréchal,* is for our enemies, not for our friends. We are perfectly willing to tell non-Fascist Italians what we mean to do when we enter their country. You have seen us come into North Africa. We did not kill the men or rape the women, and we paid fair prices for everything we had to take. Once the people understood this, they have welcomed us ; you hear no complaints from the Italians of Tripolitania and Cyrenaica."

" Those are colonies, Monsieur Budd ; but Italy is an independent nation and a great one."

" You will hear the same thing from the people of Sicily

as soon as we have taken it ; the girls will be throwing flowers to our troops and the boys will be exchanging chocolate bars for eggs. We are bringing freedom to all decent Italians, and we ask nothing of them except that they will set up a decent government which the rest of the world can respect and live with."

"As you doubtless know," said the precise old gentleman, "I am a believer in our monarchy and a servant of our King."

"I am aware of that, and if we were not willing to accept your help and the King's help, I should be talking not with you but with the resistance groups in the mountains. I have the definite instruction that after this war there will be a provisional government comprised of all the groups which are willing to aid us, and that when the war is won the people of each nation will choose the form of government they desire. Government by popular consent is the principle upon which our American nation was founded, and we have abiding faith that if the people are trusted they will choose peace and order and not conquest."

These were not precisely the best words to warm the heart of an aged monarchist, but they were the words Lanny had been told to say and he said them. The airplane bombs and the artillery shells were behind them, and nobody knew it better than this ex-commander. He swallowed whatever pride he had left and inquired, "What, precisely, does your government desire me to do ? "

"First, to consult with your friends and others who can be trusted, and then send a representative to Lisbon to meet with a representative of our government to decide when and how Italy is to withdraw from the war. The time for action, we believe, will be after it is clear that Sicily is lost and that Naples will be next. Also, we think the bombing of the railroads in Rome may help to make people realize the need of peace."

"Be careful, Monsieur Budd ; it may work just the other way. It may infuriate the people and harden their will."

"Our strategists do not think so, *mon Maréchal*. Men fight because they hope to gain something ; but the Italians have nothing to gain even by winning this war. Only today I heard the jesting remark that in Rome all the pessimists are studying German while the optimists are studying American. You see how it is, the Italians turn even the language over to us ; they do not like the English so well, I am told."

" We have heard rumours, Monsieur Budd, that Winston Churchill looks upon Sicily as a place which might have strategical importance."

" *Cher Maréchal*, Churchill has to have American help in taking Sicily. I am quite sure that if you will send a representative to Lisbon, you will have your mind put at rest on the point that Italy will not be dismembered."

VI

" I think you have convinced him, so far as concerns yourself," the Commendatore whispered ; and Lanny went away to await results. They were not long in coming, for that same evening the landowner called on the telephone to ask if his " French " friend—so he was careful to refer to Lanny—could come to his home again in the morning. This time it was a very old gentleman named Luigi Federzoni, who had been fixed in the P.A.'s mind as a former leader of the Nationalist party, a reactionary political group which represented the great latifundia and had favoured all the expansionist and imperialist aims of the Italian monarchy. Two years after the Fascists had seized power, this group had come over to them. Federzoni was now chairman of the Italian Academy and a powerful figure. Lanny knew that if he was ready to desert the ship of Fascism it must be close indeed to sinking.

The visitor told his story all over again, a bit more cautiously in this case ; but evidently it was good enough, for Federzoni expressed himself as satisfied, and next day the secret agent was invited again. This time it was Count Volpi, who had until recently been Mussolini's Finance Minister and had negotiated the loan which the Morgan bank in New York had made in the 'twenties, by which the Fascists had been enabled to retain their control of Italy. Count Volpi was a man who knew the financial world of both London and New York, and it would have been impossible for Lanny to fool him, assuming that Lanny had had such a desire. But Lanny really was the son of Budd-Erling and could tell about the great institution and how it had been founded and run. He knew that he was passing an examination, and he told about his father's friendship with Zaharoff, and with Schneider of Schneider-Creusot —Lanny had been a guest in his Paris home and had there met the heads of the Comité des Forges, and could name them and tell what they had said. He knew London too, and had been married to Irma Barnes, who was now Lady Wickthorpe —and suddenly the Count Volpi di Nisurata remembered, oh, yes, the Wickthorpe people had been very friendly to Italy and he had heard about Signor Budd—" so you are *that* Signor Budd !" Then Lanny told about his friendship for Generoso Pope and the other New York Italians, and after that he was established.

It was a dangerous game he was playing, but he had come prepared for it and found it easier than his fears had suggested. The wretched Duce had kicked out the men of real influence and power from his cabinet and got himself a bunch of party hacks. The men of influence were uniting against him ; and of course the day-and-night bombing of Italian airports and seaports and shipping was having its effect. The people of Rome were living with something more terrible than a sword of Damocles hanging over their heads. Suppose one of those bombardiers were to slip and miss the railroad yards and hit a palace or a de luxe hotel instead ! Refugees by the thousands had been pouring into the Holy City, and now they were getting out again and fleeing to the country. You no longer saw the Fascist insignia worn by anybody on the streets, and people like cab drivers and waiters would say to a foreign visitor, " Il Duce ? I spit on him ! "

VII

After two or three of these conferences Lanny would stroll and find an available typewriter ; he would never go to the same place twice. He would type a report—no carbons—seal it in the usual way, and deliver it to the " post office." Each time was a fresh danger ; but nothing ever happened. Clearly the O.V.R.A., the Italian secret police, had not yet discovered the American spy centre. Perhaps they didn't want to discover it ; Italy was so riddled with dissent that you couldn't be sure of anybody, either way ! One thing was certain—and Lanny would put it into his report—the Germans had broken one of the codes used by the O.S.S. head in Switzerland. This agent had sent in a report about the doings of Count Ciano. It had been decoded, and Hitler had had a copy of it laid on Il Duce's desk. It was a fair guess that that was the reason why Italy's free-spoken Foreign Minister had retired to the Vatican.

However, the Germans were still pretty sure of themselves, and he had to use the utmost care in dealing with them. He decided that it was time to make a report to the Führer ; he didn't sit down and dash that off, but lay on his bed and thought hard about every sentence. All had to be exactly right, definite-seeming and yet not too definite, true and yet not dangerously so, weighty enough to justify Lanny's sojourn in Rome and yet not enough to do real harm to the Allied cause. F. D. R. had said that his P.A. would be justified in revealing some secrets to the enemy, provided it was a means of getting more important secrets from the enemy ; the question was one of balance.

Lanny wrote this letter by hand, and since it was to pass only through German hands, he wrote in German :

Mein Führer :
    This is the first of the reports I promised you. I wish that I could send good news, but I know nothing but the truth would be of any help to you. I find the situation in Rome very bad. The main factor is the fear of bombs. As you know, these people do not have the stamina of the Germans ; they think of saving their own skins. They are cynical and have discovered all the weaknesses of their Duce, so that he is no longer able to inspire them. Peace at any price is the sentiment I hear everywhere, from the ignorant poor to the frivolous rich. I dare not try to counteract it, because in that case no one would talk to me.
    You cannot imagine a more disgusting spectacle than I witnessed at a golf club in the suburbs of this city at war. Rich men, it appears, still have nothing more important to do than to knock little balls about a field ; and meantime the elegantly dressed ladies sit and gossip about their amours. The centre of attention is Ciano. I am told that you called him to his face an ass and the son of an ass, and

I thought of that as I listened. He did not hesitate openly to sneer at his father-in-law and to wash his hands of Italy's troubles.

This appears to be the general mood and prevails even among members of the Duce's new cabinet ; I am told that Pavolini, Bottai, Galbiati and Renato Ricci are far from dependable. [This was not true, and was meant to sow confusion.] I am planning to cultivate these men and see if I can win their confidence. I had a private meeting with Marshal Badoglio, and that shrewd old fellow tried his best to get information from me without giving any in return. He professes to have withdrawn entirely from political activity, and that may be true, but I will not guarantee him. I plan to meet him again and hope to gain his confidence.

There is general agreement here that the Allies are about to invade Sicily. It is expected in Vatican circles that the Americans will attempt to bomb the railroad yards of Rome. The Pope, of course, protests against this.

The one bit of good news I can tell you has to do with your own troops, whose conduct is magnificent. I see them everywhere, and they are correct, dignified, and more polite than this light-minded population deserves. This is particularly true of the S.S. men. With such loyalty your cause cannot but prevail in the end. I fear that this report will not be of much use to you. I hope to do better with more time. It is difficult for a stranger to gain the confidence of persons in important positions, especially when they are by nature as suspicious as the Italians. They do not trust one another and tell a different story to each person they meet.

With assurances of my devotion,

LANNY BUDD

This letter, of course, was meant not merely for Hitler's eyes but for those of Herr Güntelen and others. Lanny addressed the envelope to " Reichskanzler Adolf Hitler, by courtesy of Marschall Kesselring," and did not mark it " personal," lest that should seem discourteous to the Wehrmacht commander. He could be sure that in any case the letter would be steamed open, read, and perhaps photographed. The Führer wouldn't want his Army and his Gestapo to take any chances ; and even if he did, they wouldn't. Lanny took the letter to the Hôtel de Russie and laid it on the desk before

the red-faced Feldwebel, saying, "*Ein Bericht*." Then he
walked out, not wishing to meet any of the Reichswehr
officers. He had nothing to get from them and no desire to be
questioned by them. His report would be judged a poor one,
but harmless; and as an amateur, he was not obliged to be
efficient.

VIII

The Marchesa di Caporini had come to think highly of her
Franco-American friend. He had been to many parts of the
world, met the right people, and told interesting stories. There
could be no questioning the fact that he was having a social
success in Rome; he was meeting the right people here, looking at paintings, and expressing opinions that carried weight.
This reflected glamour upon the lady who had introduced him,
and she wanted more of it. She suggested that he might leave
his hotel and become her guest; there were many vacant
rooms in her palace, and while it would have been a problem
to heat them in winter, this would not apply in the month
of July. She was one of those fortunate ones who had food
and could offer hospitality, and it would save a *conoscitore
d' arte* a good deal of money. The great lady did not suggest
that he should pay board, but possibly she expected that he
would insist upon doing so.

This courtesy caused Lanny embarrassment. He could
not tell her that his presence in her home might be a cause of
danger to her; and still less could he tell her that he feared
she might be coming to take too great an interest in him.
This was a free-spoken world, and Julie had talked about the
peccadilloes of the ladies he was meeting and had warned him
in a playful way against some of the more designing and the
more brash. She had even gone so far as to tell him of her
own unhappiness; her husband was under the necessity, or
at any rate thought he was under the necessity, of having boys.
They could be purchased very cheaply, it appeared, and Lanny
knew it from approaches on the streets. That left Julie with
an empty heart; and what more likely than that she should
be thinking of him as eligible to fill it?

There was a peculiar set of circumstances which drew this
pair together. Just as Galeazzo Ciano had "widows," and as

his wife, Edda Mussolini, had a pack of " widowers," so Lanny might be thought of as the " widower " of Julie's cousin, Marie de Bruyne. He had loved her devotedly for seven years, and this constituted romance according to all the French novels that Julie had ever read. She was several years younger than Marie had been ; and what more likely than that she should dream of taking Marie's place and of enjoying seven more years of honourable fidelity ? Not even her worst enemy would have censured her.

She had asked him if he was married, and he had had to lie to her. He dared not take even the faintest chance of causing inquiries to be made that might lead to Mary Morrow ; and besides, he had learned that it didn't do any good to say that he had a wife. Visiting the Fürstin Donnerstein in Berlin only six months ago, he had thought to solve the problem by inventing a wife for the occasion, young, beautiful, and rich ; but that hadn't kept an unhappy widow from crawling into his bed on a cold winter night. Hilde, an old friend, had taken his refusal in good part, but he surely mustn't take such a chance with a comparative stranger.

The strains of war had driven the women crazy, he told himself. Here in Rome there were probably two or three grown women for every grown man ; and that competition put a strain upon female virtue which it had not been equipped to withstand. The P.A. was afraid to go to the golf club any more, because the young women there made such efforts to carry him off ; and he suspected that their efforts would have been still more violent had not most of them taken it for granted that he already belonged to the Marchesa.

Lanny took a long walk amid the weather-beaten temples of ancient Rome and the new and gleaming monuments which Il Duce had erected to his own glory. He gave his best thought to the problem and realized that it might seem a strange thing —it would have seemed a hilarious thing to all the smart people of the world—that a man should be willing to risk his life for his country but should be unwilling to risk his virtue. Surely when men were dying or about to die by the thousands it was not too much to ask that a secret agent should permit himself to be seduced by an aristocratic lady. Surely it was attributing too much importance to the sexual act, and

E

especially in these days when methods of contraception were so well understood!

There could be no question that the noble lady had helped Lanny in his work and would be able to help him more. And hadn't he said that this work would come first? Hadn't he promised that to F.D.R.? But the image of Laurel stood in his way; he had made a promise to her too. Should he go back and tell her that he had broken it, and why, and ask her to forgive him? Or should he just say nothing about it, on the principle that what she didn't know wouldn't hurt her? Great numbers of men in the Army were doing that, and what difference would one more make?

But he couldn't do it. The image of Laurel just wouldn't let him. He went back to his friend and employed a device which he had used after World War I, another time when the ladies of the fashionable world had been importunate. He confided to Julie Caporini the fact that he was a victim of a strange malady, the nature of which none of the doctors had been able to discover, which made it impossible for him to be satisfactory as a lover. It was because of this that he had parted from his wife, Irma Barnes, half a dozen years ago. He didn't say that as concerning Julie directly; he asked her to communicate it tactfully to a couple of ladies who had invited him to their apartments. Julie was sympathetic—she was really a kind person—but she could not fail to realize that he had provided her with an extraordinary titbit of gossip. She no longer pressed him to become a guest in her home, and once more it became safe for him to use his guest-card at the Holy Water Golf Club. He had always been an amiable person and did not mind it in the least when the Galeazzo widows made playful allusions to his affliction and dubbed him " *Il Monaco*," the Monk.

IX

D-day of Operation Husky was July 9. At carefully calculated hours there set out from the ports of North Africa the greatest armada in the history of the world; and other fleets from Gibraltar, Britain, and the United States joined it precisely on time. The island of Sicily has a triangular shape, a hundred miles or more on each side, and the Americans approached the southern side and the British the eastern. There happened to be a high wind that night, and the commanders suffered agonies of worry; but it was too late to change the plan, and fortunately the storm abated toward morning. The newly devised landing craft of all sizes approached the beaches in the darkness, and desperately seasick young fighting men staggered ashore with their heavy packs, too weak to be frightened they afterwards reported.

Lanny Budd got the news in the hotel when he came down to breakfast. There was a radio set in the lobby and a crowd of people about it. The official government station was reporting that the Americans were attempting a landing in Sicily in bad weather and that many of their craft were being wrecked; many thousands of parachutists had been dropped on land, and these had been scattered by the wind and were being captured in large numbers. People listened to this without comment, apparently afraid to trust one another. Lanny went into breakfast without being worried, for he knew the Nazi-Fascist radio and could have dictated what it would say. He knew the Mediterranean from boyhood and reflected that its waves were deep and steep, not too bad for landing craft; also, he had met some of the G.I. paratroopers, and he was quite sure they were not of the surrendering kind.

He betook himself to Julie's home, where there was a radio set that he could run for himself. First, he heard the official radio admit that the Americans had got ashore at Gela; they were being attacked and driven back by an armoured division, but still he didn't let himself be troubled. He had seen the big hulks called L.S.T.'s—landing-ship tanks—and knew that they followed right behind the L.C.I.'s—landing-craft infantry. The first men who got ashore were sharpshooters, and they spread into the town, or the hills, or whatever was in front of them, and took shelter. Some were double teams and carried a wondrous object that looked like a piece of stove pipe and was called a bazooka; it was a sort of rocket gun, and it liked nothing better than to see a tank approaching. All these matters had been provided for, and Lanny had the firm conviction that Americans had never lost a war and seldom a battle, except when they were fighting one another.

Patience was necessary, for the Axis radios made the situation worse and worse, and the American radio in Tunisia didn't tell very much, not wishing to give information to the enemy. In Axis lands you had to learn to read the news backward, so to speak; you were told that the Allies had been repulsed, and you made note of the place where the repulse occurred and observed that it was farther in Axis territory than the last place of repulse. First, Lanny heard that the Americans had been repulsed at Gela and Licata and Scoglitti, and that the British had been repulsed at Avola and Pachino; then he read that both had been repulsed at Ragusa, which was inland and between these points, so he knew that the two armies were coming together and pinching off a chunk of Sicily, doubtless with airfields in it. Airfields were all-important, because North Africa was so far away that fighter planes coming to protect the landing forces had only a few minutes to stay overhead. But let the paratroopers take a landing field, and planes would swoop down, and the big D.C. 4's would bring fuel, and Operation Husky would begin to justify its name.

X

The invasion was what Lanny had been promising his new friends, and now he could say " I told you so," but he didn't. A tactful person, he remembered that it was Italians who were being made prisoners of war; he must never show satisfaction, but use the opportunity to point out that the Italian officers would soon be residing in American summer-resort hotels, while the *soldato semplice* would be working on an American farm for a wage, and some of the food would be coming back to feed the starving Italians.

General Eisenhower helped the secret agent by delivering over the radio a proclamation in which he told the people of Italy and Sicily the same things that Lanny had been telling Signor d' Angelo and Marshal Badoglio and other leading citizens. The document was signed by Roosevelt and Churchill, and Eisenhower read it in English and then had it repeated in Italian. The General's voice was friendly and persuasive, and he told the people that Fascism was their real enemy, and that as soon as they had thrown it off they could be friends and allies of the Americans and English. The Axis radio did not repeat this message and their newspapers did not print it, but they undertook to answer its arguments, and as it happens you cannot effectively answer arguments without revealing what they are. So was vindicated once more the ancient Hebrew saying that truth is mighty and it prevails.

To help in the process American bombers came at night and showered the towns of Sicily and Italy with leaflets containing the proclamation ; they did not omit Rome, and this not merely gave the Romans something to think and argue about, but it reminded them that planes that carried packages of printed matter might bring packages of T.N.T. on the next trip. Lanny Budd was too polite to mention this himself, but he heard it several times from the lips of others. He walked the streets of this half-old and half-new city and listened, making a remark now and then to draw people out. He was fascinated to observe that when he spoke with a German accent, the reaction he got was one of sly pleasure in what was happening in Sicily. Nobody shook his fist in the stranger's face, but many planted little darts of malice in his skin. Not all the radios in Axis Europe could persuade the Roman *uomo qualunque* that he had any other enemy than Germans.

Among Lanny's rich friends the reaction appeared to be : " Why don't they come quickly and get it over with ? " He could understand that feeling, because he had watched the invasion of North Africa through all its stages ; it had taken a full six months, and he had suffered agonies of impatience. The military men had explained to him what a giant task it was to put several hundred thousand men and all their equipment ashore on enemy soil and keep them supplied with all the goods they would consume. Each of those clumsy landing craft would have to make a hundred, perhaps two hundred, crossings in the course of Operation Husky. The island of Sicily is a mass of hills and mountains, plus one great volcano, and the Germans would defend them all. They would not make the mistake they had made in Tunisia and let themselves be penned up, but would retreat from one position to the next and fight a " delaying action."

" We must cultivate patience," said the elderly landowner

who had become Lanny's trusted confidant, attending conferences with the other conspirators and bringing Lanny word
of what happened. " Our leaders are old men ; they hesitate
and postpone, saying that tomorrow may be better than today."

Lanny argued, " They must see that we are now firmly
established in Sicily, and that it's only a question of weeks
before we shall be ready to cross to the mainland. What
are they waiting for ? "

" They are waiting for someone to make up their minds
for them. I hate to say it, and you must not quote me, but
I don't believe they will move until Rome has been bombed."

" That makes it rather hard on us," pleaded the P.A.
" We have to do it, and then be blamed for doing it."

" There is nothing rational about war so far as I have been
able to observe," said Commendatore d' Angelo. " I suggest
that the end might come more quickly if one of your bombardiers were to miss the railroad yards and hit one of the
palaces." The old gentleman smiled as he said it, because
that was what urbanity required. The word, derived from
the ancient Romans, means that you have lived in a city and
acquired those gracious and easy manners which city folk
have leisure to invent and to practise.

XI

The P.A. needed no further hint. He prepared another
report, telling of the reaction of various groups of Romans
to the invasion. He added, " I have good authority for the
belief that our friends will take no action until their hand
has been forced by the bombing of Rome." He sealed the
letter in the usual way and took it to the " post office."

When he entered, the stoutish rosy-faced Italian, who presumably was Pietro Padrone, said to him, " Would you mind
stepping inside, sir ? " Lanny was startled, but there was
nothing for him to do but comply.

Behind the stationery shop was a passage lined with shelves
on each side and with a door at the end. It seemed a good
place for conspiracy, and the man murmured, " I have a
message for Traveller." Lanny replied, " Thank you," and
the man went into the back room and returned in a few

seconds and laid in the caller's hands a tiny strip of paper with typewritten words. Lanny read, " Traveller one to five received."

All Lanny's reports were numbered, and this of course was gratifying to him. He thanked the man and then added, " I don't want to ask anything I shouldn't, but I have a letter here which is important, and I would like to know how soon it is likely to be delivered."

The answer was, " It is impossible to say exactly, but it should take about a week. Perhaps I should add that we have a wireless sender now, and if the message is urgent I can send it by way of Sicily."

" Does it go in code ? "

" Oh, surely."

" Then I think perhaps you had better send it to Robert Murphy in Algiers, with instructions to forward it from Traveller to the President. He will understand." Lanny opened the two envelopes and handed the message to the Italian, who slipped it into his pocket.

" It does not go from here, but from another place," he explained. " It will be sent within the hour."

" And what will be done with the paper ? "

" It will be burned and the ashes well broken up. We do not keep files."

" You are unique among all the government services," replied the P.A. smiling.

The other had been speaking Italian, but now he grinned and said, " Is dem Bums goin' to win de woil' series ? " That also was code and meant, " I am from Brooklyn."

6

Truth Crushed to Earth

I

THE Marchesa had a friend who possessed some modern paintings and wanted to have them viewed by the art expert from the French Riviera. This lady had a villa in Frascati, a summer resort in the Alban Mountains to the south-east of Rome. Lanny had to maintain his camouflage, so he couldn't say no. An appointment was made and he set out one morning by what the Americans call a trolley and the Italians a *tram elettrico*. Motor-cars were scarce, and besides, he welcomed chances to watch the people and listen to their talk. In Italy you do not sit in solemn state, as in an English railway compartment ; you chat with your neighbours, and before you leave the car you know all about their lives, and especially their troubles.

This car was packed not merely with humans but with bundles. Many people were moving away, and others had baskets which they expected to fill with country produce if they could find it ; they had small objects which they hoped to trade, and the woman who sat next to Lanny, wife of a government clerk, showed him a small trinket and asked his advice as to how many eggs it should be worth. He was using his German accent, but she showed no hostility and asked if he really thought the Americans would drop bombs on Rome. Poor soul, her cheeks were sunken and her hands trembled ; she had three children, and it was hard to keep them alive on the ration permitted—especially when you could not get it, she added.

The woman left and her place was taken by a man who came from the back of the car and whom Lanny had not seen previously. He wore the rough clothes of a working man and carried a parcel wrapped in newspapers ; a glance out of the corner of Lanny's eyes told him that the man had a black beard and moustache turning grey. Wearing beards had come back into fashion because steel was being made into a thousand kinds of war *matériel* and there was none left for razor blades. Lanny said, " *Buon' giorno* " with his careful German accent.

The man answered curtly, making it plain that he did not like the new masters of his country. The pretended German tried several topics—the weather, the scarcity of food, the events in Sicily—and each time the replies were in monosyllables. But that was enough to start an idea in Lanny's mind : he knew that voice ! He stole a look and then turned his head and took a better one. He looked away quickly and murmured out of one side of his mouth, " Hello, Pete ! "

The man sat rigid, but Lanny thought he could feel him start. " My name is not Pete," he replied, likewise in a low voice.

" O.K., Pete," whispered Lanny ; then, in a normal voice, in his German-Italian, " Do you think the enemy is going to bomb the city ? "

The reply was, " Don't know," and again silence. Lanny whispered, " Better to talk," and then, in Italian, " It will be pleasant to get a little higher up, away from the sultriness of Rome." He went on to remark that the ancient Romans had discovered that fact and had built themselves a fine road to the near-by mountains. Did the stranger know that what was taken to be a chain of mountains was really the rim of an immense volcano, and that Lake Nemi had been one of its several craters ? Had he seen the ancient Roman trireme which Emperor Tiberius had built on this small lake and which the great new leader of the Italian people had rescued from the depths and restored ? To each of these questions the bearded labourer replied with the monosyllable no—which happens to be both English and Italian.

II

The car stopped and several people got off. Just as it was about to start again the man sprang up and stepped quickly to the door. Lanny, prepared for this manœuvre, did not hesitate, but followed behind him and swung off the moving car. There they were, at a small station, a mere box, the car rolling away, and the people who had got off going their separate ways, paying no heed to them. The pair were about fifteen feet apart, and Lanny reduced the distance to one foot and whispered, " You don't have to worry, Pete."

The man insisted again, " I don't know you."

The other people were out of hearing, so it was safe to speak in English. " I am Lanny Budd," said the P.A.

" You are mistaken about me. My name is Arrigo."

" A beard may be a disguise for some, but not for me. Let's take a stroll, away from everybody, and have a talk. That can't possibly do you any harm."

They started away on a country road. " I can guess what you are doing," Lanny said, " and you probably have orders not to reveal yourself to anybody. So I won't ask unnecessary questions. But I may be able to help you, or you to help me."

For the first time the man replied in English. " You speak with a German accent."

" That is *my* beard, Pete."

" I have heard reports that you have become a Fascist sympathizer."

" That is my moustache. The last time we met you entrusted me with an important secret about Hitler's demands on Czechoslovakia, and I smuggled it out to the British press for you. How could you imagine that I would change ? "

" Many have changed."

" Nobody but idiots and knaves have gone over to Mr. Big. I assure you I am neither."

They came to a great oak tree which offered welcome shade and they sat beneath it. Pete Corsatti looked about carefully, then said, " I am in your hands, Lanny."

" So am I in yours. We are in the enemy's country. Are you in any special danger ? "

" Nothing more than usual."

" Just one more question. Does the name Padrone mean anything to you ? "

" Yes, it does."

" O.K., then. I asked because I thought maybe you might need a means of communication. Were you one of those

American newspaper-men whom Mr. Big locked up when he went to war ? "

" No. I hadn't been in Italy for several years."

" I see. Then there is less chance of your being recognized. I wondered how you could risk it."

" I had just got on that trolley when I sat down next to you. I belong back in the mountains."

Lanny quoted Milton, " ' The mountain nymph, sweet liberty ! ' "

III

Nineteen years had passed since these two men had first met, and six since their last meeting. It surprised Lanny to realize that Pete was fifty and had greying hair. Brooklyn-born, of Italian parents, he had been the representative of an American newspaper in Rome when the grandson of Budd Gunmakers had come on an unsanctioned honeymoon with Marie de Bruyne. This had been rudely interrupted by the kidnapping of Matteotti and the trouble that Lanny had got into.

Lanny had promised not to ask questions about what his friend was doing, so he brought up another subject. " I want to tell you a strange story, Pete. I have no idea whether you know anything about what is called psychical research, and maybe you'll think I'm nuts, but anyhow, this is what happened to me. I have a friend who is a medium ; she goes into trances and doesn't know what is happening, but she speaks, and the voices say they are spirits, and maybe they are and maybe they're not—I've never been able to make up my mind. A month or so ago I was leaving on a danger-ous mission, and we tried a séance to see if the spirits would have anything to say about it. Does this sound crazy to you ? "

" A little bit, but it's interesting. Go ahead."

" Well. I sit listening, and I am told that Giacomo Matteotti is communicating. You remember him ? "

" I have had no chance to forget him. His name has become a symbol for the whole Italian underground."

" Well, I'm told that he is present and is telling me the secrets of his death. He says that the proof of Mussolini's guilt exists. There is a memorial written by Filippo Filippelli, editor of the *Corriere Italiano*, who lent Dumini the car that the gangsters used."

"That is true, Lanny. We know about this memorial. There is said to be only one copy."

"I was told more. The man who carried Mussolini's orders to Dumini is Contarelli, parliamentary secretary of the Fascist party."

"That might easily be the truth. I don't know."

"Memorials were also prepared by Cesare Rossi, head of the Press Bureau, and by Aldo Finzi, secretary of the Ministry of the Interior."

"He was under-secretary, I believe."

"I was making notes of the words spoken and I had to write fast, so I may have got it wrong. I was warned that these men were weathercocks, who turn quickly, and that I must be careful in dealing with them."

"That is surely correct, and the story is very astonishing. Are you sure the medium did not know these facts?"

"I did not mention the subject to her either before or after the séance, because I was not at liberty to tell her that I was coming to Italy, or why. From previous experience I know that in her trances she reveals all sorts of things about which she cannot possibly have conscious knowledge. Of course it may be that she gets it out of my mind, or the mind of someone else who is present. I speculate about the possibility that there may be a level in our subconscious where all our minds are one. I know about Dumini, of course; Matteotti's wife had named him to me when she telephoned me that her husband had been abducted. But I can't recall that I ever heard the other names. Did you ever tell me about those men?"

"I learned about them later. I'm sure I didn't know about them before you were escorted to the border. Of course we may have talked about the case years later, when we met at the Stresa Conference."

"That's the devil of trying to probe these psychic mysteries. You're up against the fact that the subconscious mind never forgets anything—all the psychologists appear to agree on that. But the conscious mind forgets and can never be sure what it has forgotten. Even on that basis I'm confronted with the fact that a medium can go into a trance and dip these things out of my mind and present them to me in the form of a little drama, a dialogue so real that it would take a novelist to create it."

"All this is new to me," commented the journalist. "I took it for granted that mediums were fakes and I never paid any attention to them."

IV

Lanny had said that he might be able to help Pete, or vice versa, and so it turned out. Pete knew a lot about the Matteotti case, and since it was in the past, it was a subject about which he could talk freely. He had taken Lanny into the press gallery of the Parlamento, where they had witnessed the scene in which the young leader of the Italian Socialists had defied the fury of the Fascists, reading off a list of the crimes by which they had seized power and were gradually stifling the liberties of the nation. It had been the most stirring scene that young Lanny Budd had ever witnessed, and it had made an indelible impression upon him. Afterward he had paid a visit to Matteotti in his office—he was editor of the party newspaper—a frail, sensitive man with a mournful face, as if he had foreseen what was coming to him. Gentle, idealistic, and kind he had been, and five ruffians had seized him on the street in daylight and dragged him into a Fiat car, carried him out to a lonely place, stabbed him thirty-six times, and left his half-burned body in a ditch.

"An interesting thing to observe," commented the newspaper-man; "it seems to take martyrdom to make history. Matteotti's name has become a battle-cry to Mr. Big's opponents; he is the symbol of what they are fighting for. If Socialism ever comes to Italy, he will have more to do with it than any other one man."

"He has had a great deal to do with my life," the P.A. replied. "There are times when I am afraid, and then I think of him and become ashamed of myself. He voiced the conscience of a whole people."

"Is that really the way you feel, Lanny?" asked Pete. And then, without waiting for the answer, he said, "You know how careful I have to be, not merely for myself but for a lot of other people."

"Sure thing, old man. Don't trust me with anything you don't have to. I have no idle curiosity."

"This you ought to know. Matteotti left a son, and a widow who trained the son to worship his father's memory. The dirty dog, Mr. Big, overlooked them. The son was a little toddler when the father died ; now he's a man, and has only one thought in life—I won't say to avenge the father's murder, but to end Fascism in Italy and to complete his father's work. He is one of the leaders of the underground, and I am here to help him."

"How long have you been at it, Pete ? "

"About eight months."

"And you haven't been recognized yet ? "

"I don't come into the towns very often. This was a special job and I took a chance."

"Am I delaying you ? "

"I was through and on my way back. But my friends will begin to worry if I stay very long."

Lanny said, "It may interest you to know that I was in North Africa and saw the show there. I was able to help a little. Is there anything I can tell you ? "

"There are questions that everybody asks me. Is Rome going to be bombed ? "

"The railroads, yes, I'm pretty sure. Not the rest of the city."

"And will the Allies come on to the mainland ? "

"Of course they will. How could they leave that huge Foggia air-base in the hands of the enemy ? I am guessing they'll come as far as Rome, for the moral effect. Whether they'll go beyond that, I've no idea." There was a pause, then the P.A. said, "Tell me something in return. Will the Partisans be strong enough for an uprising ? "

"We warn them against it. The Germans have all the weapons. Our job is sabotage, especially on communications. We destroy bridges and block tunnels and we hold up trucks. Often we get stuff that we can use, the rest we set fire to. All that will increase as the armies come nearer ; they will drop stuff to us."

"I know about that," said the P.A. "I was briefed by O.S.S., though I'm not directly under them."

V

These two old friends had many things to talk about. Pete had played an important part in Lanny's life, having had to do with his marriage to Irma Barnes ; Pete had talked to her and told her that Lanny was too proud to ask a very rich woman to marry him ; so Irma had come after Lanny. It had turned out not to be a happy marriage, but that wasn't Pete's fault. Now he said, "I heard reports that you had gone back to your class, and I thought it must be Irma's influence. I was sad about it, but I didn't blame you too much."

"I caused those reports to be spread, Pete. I found that my best service was to get information from the top fellows among the enemy. Only a very few of my closest friends share that secret ; you must be careful and not breathe it to anybody. If you hear my name mentioned, just sigh and go on being sad."

"There's one person here who ought to know about you. I've been wondering if you wouldn't like to meet Matteo Matteotti."

"What good would it do ? "

"He could tell you a lot about the underground, its state of mind and its problems—more than I am free to tell. And you might be able to cheer him up ; you know it's no easy job living the life of a criminal when you have no inclination that way but are a noble soul and something of a saint. I take it that you are in a position to state that the Americans are coming in force and will bring whatever it takes."

"They have five thousand planes for the Sicily campaign, and they are turning out eight thousand a month now."

"If I were to say that to Matteo, he couldn't be sure that I knew it. But if *you* told him, he'd be a happy *banditto*."

"Could I trust his discretion, Pete ? "

"You could trust him to the death, or to the O.V.R.A. torture chambers."

"Could I meet him alone ? I mean, just with you ? "

"Of course. But you'd have to take a trip on a donkey.

There are reasons why he couldn't come out into the open at present."

" Well, six months ago I rode on a camel, and I don't suppose a donkey could be worse."

" Tell me how I can reach you in the next two or three days."

" I am going back to Rome tonight. I'm at the Regina-Carlton. Drop me a line and tell me where to meet you."

" I'll tell you the place now. You know Tusculum ? "

" I have never been there, but I know it's near Frascati."

" There's an ancient Roman theatre there, a famous ruin ; the theatre, not the amphitheatre, which has not been excavated. Anybody can direct you to it. When you get a letter giving the day, you walk there just at sundown, and I'll pick you up."

" You had better have a code name when you write me. I prefer a woman's name because the spies think that is innocent."

" Lady-killer ! " exclaimed Pete with a grin. " How will it do if I be Irma ? "

" O.K.," said Lanny, returning the grin, " provided my new wife doesn't hear about it."

VI

Lanny resumed his journey to Frascati, very happy. The luxury of being able to speak the truth for one hour had set him up for another month's campaign of falsehood. He inspected the paintings, made proper comments, and asked the customary tactful question—whether the lady could be persuaded to part with any of them and what price she would expect. Then he rode back to Rome.

Reading the Axis newspapers and listening to the Axis radio, he learned that the American armies had been victoriously repulsed from just north of the town of Enna, and from the map he learned that this was an important communications centre in the middle of Sicily. He also learned that the Germans had victoriously driven a salient into the Russian lines at Kursk and had victoriously repulsed the effort of the Russians to drive a salient at Orel. This meant that the huge battle of the Ukraine was at last under way; Hitler was pouring in his last reserves, except those that he was pouring into Italy, to set up a series of defence lines across the innumerable mountains of this volcanic land.

Two days later there came a letter addressed to Lanny's hotel, informing him that he could meet "Irma" on the following evening. Once more he took the electric car to Frascati, and he strolled on the grounds of a show place once owned by Lucien Bonaparte and said to be the site of Cicero's villa. From the back of this he proceeded by a shady road to the ruins of ancient Tusculum, birthplace of Cato the Censor. He went down into an underground chamber so old that it preceded the invention of the arch. He climbed upon a height from which he had a magnificent view of the mountains with the sun setting behind them; after which he walked, like any casual tourist, to the open-air theatre where the comedies of Plautus and Terence had been presented more than two thousand years ago.

There came the black-bearded working man, riding one donkey and leading another by a cord. Lanny mounted—no saddle, only a blanket tied on with ropes. The sight was familiar and attracted no attention whatever. The pace was slow and dignified, and they went into the sunset and presently were ascending a pass between two mountains. Darkness enveloped them, but apparently the donkeys knew the way; Lanny couldn't have interfered if he had wanted to, because he had no bridle rein and didn't know how to speak to donkeys in any language. All he had to do was to sit and with his knees firmly clamp the creature's heaving sides. He was afraid to talk to Pete for fear of being overheard. He breathed the cool mountain air, laden with the scent of pine trees, and thought what he would say to Matteo Matteotti and what questions F. D. R. would wish him to ask of a leader of the Italian Partisans.

VII

Lanny's thighs were beginning to ache. It seemed a long ride, but perhaps it was no more than two hours. Heavy forests surrounded them, and at last there appeared through the trees a dim reddish light. It was a charcoal burner's fire, with a hut near by; they did not stop, but went on, and presently there was another gleam of fire, and this time they turned off the trail to it. In a small cleared space a little pile of sticks was burning, and near it a blanket was spread on the ground and a man sat on it.

When he heard the hoof beats he rose and stepped back into the shadows until Pete spoke; then he appeared again, and Lanny saw a tallish, slender young man with dark hair, expressive eyes, and a sensitive, intellectual face, surprisingly like the one that Lanny remembered from two decades back. A strange and fascinating mystery, those patterns which nature keeps in her storehouse and reproduces with such fidelity. A materialistic age thinks that it has answered the question when it gives a name to the agents—chromosome or gene. But a little more thought might suggest that a pattern is nothing without a mind to read and understand it; and where was the mind that read and understood the patterns of heredity and provided sons who were like the fathers and the mothers, yet different from both and from one another?

The ex-journalist introduced the two, and they squatted, Hindu fashion, on the blanket. They spoke Italian, Lanny having refreshed himself in the language by this time. The young Partisan—he was twenty-two—said, "Call me Matteo, if you please, Signor Budd. I remember that my mother told me about you, and any friend of my father is an old friend of mine."

Lanny told the story of that visit to Rome, and how Pete Corsatti had taken him into the press gallery by the simple expedient of slipping five lire to the custodian—in those days five lire had been a dollar, and now, alas, they weren't much more than a cent. Lanny had sat and listened to the Socialist leader's speech and to the wild-beast cries of his enemies; he had been so impressed by the lion heart of this so gentle-appearing man that he had gone to call on him in his editorial office and express his sympathy. Lanny told every word he could remember of that interview, and the younger man listened as if it were to a Gospel. He had been brought up to reverence his father as a hero, a statesman, a martyr to the cause of human justice and freedom. Here was a new religion in the making, one that was to be kept for ever free from the superstitions and delusions that cumbered the old religion of Italy. This would be a religion based upon modern science, and its priests would be experts who understood how to make freedom and peace for human beings instead of exploitation and war.

Matteo told what the enemies of Fascism were doing to help the Allies. "For the first time in twenty years we have hope," he said. "More and more men are taking to the mountains, and the Germans are greatly annoyed by our raids. But we must have more arms, and also food. We cannot live off the peasants, because the tax collectors and the landlords leave them barely enough to keep alive."

Lanny was not authorized to speak for the Air Force, but he pointed out that its bases were still far off. "They are getting nearer now," he said, "and it won't be long before their planes are over these mountains."

"We are in the hands of your President," declared Matteo. "Do you know him?"

"I have met him," replied Lanny modestly. "You must not expect too much of any one man. The Italian people must arouse themselves, take their own freedom, and keep it."

"Believe me, Signor Budd, they are eager for the chance. They have learned their lesson, and I do not think they will soon fall under the spell of another dictator. Tell me, if you know, what will be the policy of the Allied armies when they enter our country."

Lanny told what Roosevelt had instructed him to say, that each and every people would be permitted to choose its own form of government in a free democratic election. "But you must not be surprised," he added, "if during the war period you see us making terms with anyone who will help us. First and foremost, we have to save the lives of our soldiers, and if Badoglio, or Grandi, or Ciano will give us aid, we shall not refuse it."

"But what promises will be made to such men, Signor Budd?"

"The same promises as to you, Matteo—that the people of Italy will decide. It will be up to you to do what your father was doing, to awaken the masses and educate them, and see that they choose wisely."

"What troubles us is that once a government is in power, armed with modern weapons, the people are helpless against it. The monarchy, the landlords, the great capitalists, and the Church hierarchy—they are all one, and they are as much our enemies as the Germans."

"I have lived in Europe, Matteo, and understand all that ; but the American people do not understand it, and you will have to give them time."

"I know that America is a capitalist nation ; but if they insist on restoring the old system of exploitation over here, they will have won the war and lost the peace again. There will be the same greedy masters buying up governments and getting ready for the next war."

"Nothing can be more certain than that ; but it is for you and your friends to bring the change in Italy. You will come down from the mountains and speak with your father's voice."

VIII

They talked all through the night, for this ardent young Socialist wanted to know everything about the progress of the war. He and his followers rarely heard the truth, and Lanny had to tell about the twelve million Americans under arms, and the eight thousand new planes every month, and the twenty-five hundred ships serving the armies in Sicily ; about the conquest of the submarine, about the glider planes and the paratroopers, the tank-killers and the bazookas, the rockets and other weapons that were on the way. Why was the Socialist party so weak in America, and was the Republican party really supporting the war, and what was the basis of Roosevelt's strength ? Lanny told about what F. D. R. had called his *troika*, the three-horse team he was driving,—the Southern reactionaries, the Catholic machines of the big cities, and the leftist forces of labour—a strange combination which had to be driven with a carrot in front and a club behind. All that was like a wild dream to the son of a humble Italian lawyer ; it frightened him, because he knew that the fate of his own country, and perhaps of the world, depended upon the skill and good luck of that teamster.

Pete said, " It's time we were leaving. It will be better

that we get into town before daylight." So the P.A. and the Partisan shook hands and promised to meet again when the happy days came. Lanny mounted his patient donkey, and with Pete leading they went into the outer darkness. Pete judged it safe to talk, since there was no one apt to be about at that hour. He said, " What do you think of him ? " And Lanny replied, " He has what it will take."

" You would have thought so," remarked the other, " if you had seen the demonstrations that occurred last month on the anniversary of his father's death. People risked their lives in all the cities."

After some thought the P.A. added, " He is the man our government ought to use in reorganizing Italy. But I fear they won't."

" No such luck," was the other's comment. " They will pick out some old fuss-budget who hasn't had a new idea in fifty years. But of course anybody will be better than the Duck." Such was the disrespectful name which American newspaper-men in Rome had employed among themselves.

They came out of the forest at dawn, and from the top of a ridge Lanny could see the ruins of Tusculum. " No need for you to come any farther," he said. " The less we are seen together the better." He got down from the donkey and gave his friend a long handshake. " Take care of yourself, Pete. I heard over the radio that they shot an American spy the other day."

" We think we know who it was," replied the other. " Poor fellow ! We know that arrests for what are called ' security reasons ' are going on all the time."

" I ought to have some way to get in touch with you, Pete. There's always a chance that something might turn up."

" My name here is Rinaldo. You can drop me a note in care of Padrone. But it may be some time before I get it. We don't stay in one place, you know."

IX

Lanny rode into Rome by the first morning car. Even that early he noticed that the cars coming the other way were packed with people, some even hanging on to the steps. When

he entered the city he found out the reason—American airplanes had showered leaflets warning the population to get
out, the city was about to be bombed. Some were taking that
advice, but of course it was a small proportion of a million
and a half population. Those who could go were the fortunate
few who had money and could leave their jobs ; women took
their children and worried about what was going to happen
to their men. Anxiety was written on the faces of all, and
Lanny renewed his hatred of war and his wish to see the war-
making power taken out of the hands of reckless and greedy
men.

For his own part, Lanny trusted to the aim of the American
flyers, of whose training he had seen a good deal. He went
to his hotel and made up for his lost sleep. Then he had a
bath, put on his clothes, freshly pressed, and went down and
read in the morning papers how the Americans had been
victoriously repulsed while trying to reach the north coast
of Sicily. The news of the bombing announcement had to be
printed of course ; it was accompanied by such words as
" dastardly " and " criminal," and by a protest from Il Papa.
But no one who read the news expected the protest to have
any effect upon the Allied Combined General Staffs.

Lanny wrote a brief report and took it to the " post office."
On his return to the hotel he found a telephone message from
the Marchesa. He had expressed a casual desire to meet
Count Grandi, and now, calling back, he was asked if he could
come late this afternoon. He said, " Always gladly," and
thanked his friend. The day was stifling hot, and he went up
to his room and took off his precious clothes—they were all
he had, and more would have cost him a fortune. He lay
down on the bed and thought hard about what he was going
to say to the second most dangerous man in all Italy.

Dino Grandi had been Mussolini's Chief of Staff on that
famous " March on Rome." There was a photograph of it,
expected to occupy in Italian history the place that " Washington Crossing the Delaware " occupies in American. It showed
Grandi at the head of the parade, wearing his blackshirt
uniform, while Mussolini walked by his side wearing civvies.
(The others had walked from Milan, but Il Duce had come in
a sleeping-car.) Grandi had been a handsome, erect young

man, educated, and what is called a gentleman—but that had not kept him from being one of the most cruel of the Fascists. One of his jobs had been the exterminating of the Italian co-operatives, by the method of administering castor oil to their leaders; from Lanny's point of view that made him one of the major criminals of the time. Grandi had gone to London as Mussolini's Ambassador, had joined all the " best " clubs, and had used his charming manners upon the Cliveden and Wickthorpe sets.

Lanny delayed meeting him in Rome until he had made sure what role to play with him. Grandi had broken with his master and was no longer Minister of Justice; people who were in the know talked freely about his desire to replace the head of the government. His rival for that honour was Badoglio, and one of Lanny's tasks was to make up his mind which of this pair would make the safer ally for Lanny's country. If it were Grandi, Italy would keep its Fascist form; if it were the old Marshal, the monarchy would get back its power. The idea that the Italian people might want to try something new would hardly appeal to Admiral Leahy and Admiral King and the other elders who were the President's advisers.

x

The P.A. did not have to feel too greatly honoured because important persons came to meet him instead of summoning him to their offices or homes. They did this because Rome was a boiling cauldron of intrigue, and few persons were sure whom they could trust. Everyone guessed that a Franco-American art expert must have some political purpose, but no one had been able to decide what he represented, and important persons with dark secrets locked in their bosoms deemed it the part of discretion to meet him at the house of someone else, where it could be called an accident if things went wrong.

Count Dino Grandi came to have coffee at the home of the Marchesa di Caporini. He had graciously sent her some real coffee in advance—he could do that because he had become one of the richest men in Italy. He had set to work at the moment the Fascists took power; he had got the oil monopoly as his perquisite, and the enormous graft of this had been one of the things which Matteotti had been exposing when the five gangsters had closed his lips. A palace, servants in livery, a Mercedes limousine, a private black market—these had been the stakes for which the " March on Rome " had been undertaken. Just so Caesar had behaved in Egypt, Alexander in Persia, Genghis Khan in large parts of Asia and Europe.

Dino Grandi was a tall, bulky, football-player type; stouter since Lanny had last seen him, but his face was still young though he was nearing fifty. He wore a small moustache and beard, the beard cut square across the bottom, as you see it in Assyrian sculpture; it was so black that it seemed to have a tinge of blue. His voice was soft and his manner most agreeable, especially to the ladies. They chatted about the wonderful iced coffee while they drank it, and then Lanny told the news about the Countess of Wickthorpe and other friends.

It developed that the Count had had Lanny's youthful indiscretion looked up, and he made a joke about it, but it was one of those jokes which have a serious purpose behind them. Lanny related how he had become a Socialist in boyhood, and how Hitler had converted him to National Socialism. That went in Italy too, because they called their regime a form of Socialism; they had a " corporative state," and the labour unions were supposed to be a part of the government. It looked fine on paper, and the fact that it had no relation to reality was never mentioned in polite conversation. Lanny told how he had been lectured and scared by Generalissimo Italo Balbo, and the Count commented upon the sad fate of that able soldier, who, while flying to Tobruk in the previous summer, had been shot down by mistake of his own anti-aircraft gunners.

XI

The hostess discreetly withdrew and left the pair of conspirators to make what they could of each other. Grandi spoke English—he knew the language perfectly and liked to display the fact. He chose the role of friendship, saying, " Let us speak frankly, Mr. Budd. Tell me your purpose here in Rome."

Lanny did not say " I am here to buy paintings." He

knew that wouldn't go down. He replied, " It has happened in the course of my work as an art expert that I have made friends in different countries and have lived so long in half a dozen of them that I count them all as home. This war drives me to distraction ; I can see no end to it but the laying open of Europe to barbarism from the east. I do not see myself in the role of statesman, but I am a friend to some of them, and I have tried to serve by taking messages from one to another—always quietly and in the strictest confidence."

" You are protected by the Germans here, I am told. You enjoy the friendship of Hitler ? "

" I have visited him now and then over a period of fifteen years. Both he and Göring have invited me to enter their service, but I have declined. I would like you to understand that I have never taken one cent from either of them. What Hitler means to me is that he stands as a bulwark against invasion from the east, and if he goes down I cannot see who else will save us. Whom can you suggest ? "

That put it up to Grandi. Let *him* be frank for a while ! Having met Lanny at Wickthorpe Castle, and knowing all about Budd-Erling Aircraft, he knew that whichever side the visitor was on, Dino might be on that side before the war was over. They talked about the methods by which Italy might be removed from the war, and by which Italy's present masters might save their necks. Grandi revealed that Il Duce had gone to the border for a conference with Hitler, a meeting in which history might be made. He was due back soon, and then the pot might boil over, for Hitler's demands would be likely to drive the Italians to desperation.

The conversation lasted a goodly time, for the shrewd Fascist wanted to extract every item of information he could. Lanny, for his part, talked freely, because the more he revealed, the more quickly the Italians would realize that they were on the losing side. He dropped a hint : he feared that the Duce's health was breaking under the strain and that he was no longer equal to the demands of this crisis. To this the Count replied that he, Dino, was still a member of the Fascist Grand Council and had made up his mind to demand a meeting of that body and bring up the subject of a change. No modern state could endure to be governed by such a group of incom-

petents as Mussolini had taken into his cabinet. That was
indeed talking turkey, and Lanny thanked his powerful friend
and promised to watch these historic events with prayerful
attention. " I wish I could help you," he said ; and the other
replied, " You may be able to ; we shall see." That was more
than a hint and gave a P.A. plenty to think about.

XII

Late on Sunday evening Lanny was called to the home of
Commendatore d' Angelo. There were no secrets in Rome, it
appeared ; the old gentleman knew that Lanny had had a
meeting with Grandi and wanted to find out what had happened. Lanny told him, with seeming frankness, but kept
back what he thought might involve himself too greatly. In
return he learned that the Army was going to stand by the
King, and the King was going to put Badoglio at the head of
the government ; at least that was the programme. Mussolini
was expected back from Feltre, scene of the conference with
Hitler, in the morning ; already the Badoglio partisans knew,
or claimed to know, that Hitler was demanding more Italian
troops for the Russian front, and was proposing to give up
the whole of the Italian boot to the Allies and base his defence
line on the River Po. It was to be hoped that Mussolini had
refused the demands ; certainly, to accept them would mean
his own downfall.

Next morning Lanny arose late and had his breakfast in
a sidewalk café under an awning ; very agreeable, except that
people whose daily bread ration was one-third of a pound
stopped and followed with their eyes every forkful of food
he put into his mouth. But he had lived through two wars
and several depressions and had put the necessary hard shell
about his feelings ; you can help one or two people in trouble,
but when there are one or two hundred millions all over the
earth you have to practise to do your best in the world as it is.
Lanny read the morning news, in the leisurely fashion of the
Mediterranean lands, and noted that the Americans had
reached the north coast of Sicily, thus cutting the island in
two ; they were being " victoriously repulsed " from Palermo
with its fine harbour.

The P.A. was preparing in his mind a report to Hitler, and meant to take a stroll and think it out ; but the sun was hot, and he decided that his room would be a better place. He paid his bill and was about to rise to his feet when he heard the scream of sirens. Some patrons ran to the inside of the restaurant, leaving their food ; others went out to the sidewalks and stood staring up into the sky. Presently Lanny heard a distant murmur which he knew well : planes were coming. The sound grew louder, and he knew that it was made by many planes, and could be only the Americans. There were few, if any, air-raid shelters in this Holy City, and one place was about as safe as another.

Lanny knew that the freight yards lay some two miles to the south of where he stood, and he had that much confidence in his country's Air Force. Undoubtedly the pilots had been carefully briefed, had studied maps of the city, and knew every detail of the targets. Reconnaissance was in charge of one of the President's sons, Colonel Elliott Roosevelt, and the maps his men brought in were said to be marvels ; they were studied under a stereoscope, which caused every detail to stand out as if you were just above it. The millions of Catholic voters in the Democratic party were guarantee enough that the Air Force wasn't going to hit the Vatican or any of the famous shrines.

The planes were Liberators and Flying Fortresses, great four-engine bombers painted a uniform olive-drab. They flew in small V formations, each V behind the next, making a long train, as far back as you could see. They were four miles up in the air, yet the sound was like the roar of freight trains close by. To this was added the racket of anti-aircraft guns and the bursting of their shells ; this was dangerous for the people in the streets but apparently did no harm to the bombers ; they came on majestically, varying not an inch. There were half a dozen Italian fighter planes darting here and there overhead, but they manifested no stomach for the fight, and from first to last did nothing but fly. It was the first time in history that a large flight of bombers had come unescorted in broad daylight, and some Americans had had misgivings, but they proved to be unjustified.

Fragments from the bursting shells injured some of the

people below, yet many stayed out of curiosity. The planes passed directly over the heart of the city ; perhaps that was a bit of propaganda, or perhaps a way to make sure of not hitting the city. It made a wonderful show, and in the two and a half millenniums of its history the city of Romulus and Remus had surely seen nothing like it. The great gliding birds passed, and a second or two later you saw the bomb-bay doors of the first flight open and the grey bombs shoot out ; each carried five hundred pounds of a new and deadly explosive, but they looked very small and pretty ; they came, twelve from each plane, in a graceful parabola, gradually straightening out. You felt the earth shake beneath your feet a couple of seconds before you heard the explosions, heavy, crumping sounds. They became unceasing, and the ground under your feet trembled even as did your knees and your spine. Huge clouds of smoke and dust arose from the bombed district.

There were some two hundred planes in the first flight, and everyone knew what they had hit, the San Lorenzo railroad yards. The crowds started in that direction, but again the sirens sounded, and there came another flight, this time farther to the east ; the target was the Littorio marshalling yards, and again there was a tumult, and a cloud of destruction, and curiosity seekers starting in that direction. A third warning and another flight, this time of Marauders and Mitchells, smaller planes, flying lower ; they were after the Ciampino airfield, which lay to the south of the city ; they would smash many planes on the ground, and those planes would never again fly to attack American ships on the way to Sicily and American-captured airfields on the island. Altogether the " show " lasted over two hours, and of nearly six hundred bombers which passed over the city only five failed to return to their bases.

XIII

It was Lanny's business to observe the reaction of the Roman populace to this peace hint, and he spent the rest of the day wandering about, using his eyes and ears. He found that with few exceptions the people had got its meaning ; he heard cries of terror and of grief, but few of anger, and no desire for anything but an end to this senseless war. Just as

Marshal Badoglio had predicted, the raid had destroyed the tenement homes all about the railroad yards, and the people in the neighbourhood were in a pitiable state ; many were digging frantically in the ruins, trying to rescue the survivors —a sight that Lanny had witnessed in many cities of this old Continent, beginning with Barcelona seven years before.

While Lanny was there he came upon a strange sight, the Holy Father's visit to these panic-stricken people. The P.A. stood and watched him, a small, scholarly figure in a white dress, scattering his prayers and blessings in every direction ; the people bowed their heads and were comforted, for they were certain that he had some magic power ; he could forgive their sins and save them from Satan if not from Air Chief Marshal Tedder. Lanny bowed his head with the rest and kept silent. Never was there a better time for applying the ancient adage, that when you are in Rome you must do as the Romans do. Some four thousand of them had been killed, and it was Lanny's countrymen who had done it.

Two churches which were near the railroad yards had been damaged ; and back in his hotel Lanny listened to the Nazi radio denouncing what it called "a barbarous assault on a sacred shrine." He could smile over this, knowing that the Nazis had bombed more than four thousand British churches. But he wouldn't let anybody see that smile, and he would be careful to agree with everything that everyone said. In the evening he paid another visit to Signor d'Angelo, and there he agreed that the American flyers had done an excellent job. They hadn't hit a single palace, but they had suggested to the Roman aristocracy that they might hit some palaces next time, just as they had done in Berlin.

Mussolini had come back from his border conference ; and what a beehive of gossip the city had turned into ! For a long time "the Duck" had been kept on a diet of rice and milk ; but in the presence of Hitler and his staff, whether from bravado or greediness, he had eaten everything that was put before him, and as a result, on the way home, he had rolled on the floor of his private car in agonies of acute indigestion. "Sometimes it kills people," said the elderly landowner, "but, *hélas !* he seems to be getting over it."

More important was the news concerning the demands

which Hitler had served upon his partner. He wanted to withdraw the Hermann Göring division from Sicily and let the Italians defend it as best they could. The same for the whole Italian boot—he proposed to abandon Rome and destroy the huge shipment of ammunition which had just been delivered there. And Mussolini wouldn't say what answer he had made to these proposals; he wouldn't even confirm the reports of Hitler's demands, which had been derived from members of his staff. Apparently the Duce had given in to the Führer and wanted to conceal the fact even from his dummy cabinet.

So, in the morning, Lanny had to prepare another report for his Boss in Washington, and then, at another place, one to his Boss in Berlin. He was playing a dangerous double game and meant to keep it up as long as he could; each message that got through was that much gain for his side. He wondered whether his call for the bombing of Rome had had any effect. Of course the airmen must have been training for weeks; but the last word had to come from higher up, and it might well be that Lanny's advice had tipped the scales. Anyhow, he wrote now that the moral effect of the raids had been excellent and that the railroad yards would be out of service for several weeks. He told about the plight of Il Duce —using his code name, of course. He expressed his belief that the victor in the struggle would be Andrew, that being Badoglio.

Then he wrote to the Führer, saying that the effect of the bombing had been to infuriate the Romans and make them more determined to resist. He pictured the Duce's collapse, both physical and moral. The political pot was boiling fast, and no one could be sure what would come out of it. He expressed his fear that Badoglio might be the next premier, a weak and indecisive leader. He told of his talks with Grandi, a man who knew what he wanted and might try to seize it. From this the Führer would know that this devoted friend was meeting important people; but no mention of the son of Matteotti up in the mountains!

XIV

The Italian boil was coming to a head, and it took no skilled physician to see that it was going to burst very soon. If the two German divisions were withdrawn from Sicily, the defence would collapse overnight; and if the Allies got into Rome, they would surely use the airfields, and the Germans would begin bombing them, and without much regard for sacred shrines. Lanny went daily to call on his carefully chosen friends and collect the gossip. He hadn't told anyone definitely, but they apparently assumed that he had some way of getting the news out; perhaps they thought he had a radio-sending set in his room at the Regina-Carlton Hotel on the Via Veneto!

As a matter of fact, he kept his room without a scrap of evidence in it and left it unlocked for the convenience of the O.V.R.A. whenever they chose to call. He carefully fixed his small suitcase so that he could tell if it had been opened, and he came to the conclusion that somebody was looking his things over on a twice-a-week schedule. They had a chance to inspect a list of the paintings he had looked at, the names and addresses of the owners, and the prices quoted, if any. It was highly educational, because there was a description of each painting by an expert whose opinions cost a lot of money. Lanny was careful to add to the data now and then so that his inspectors would know that he was not wasting his time in this storehouse of old masters. Two of the art lovers on Lanny's list told him they had received visits from the police, and the art lovers had praised the French visitor's international reputation. This, Lanny didn't have to be told, would increase the price he was expected to pay for the paintings belonging to those good friends.

Dino Grandi carried out his threat to demand a session of the almost forgotten Fascist Grand Council to hear and consider the demands of Hitler upon the country. Grandi had a copy of the demands, and instead of trying to hide it he went boldly to the Duce and told him what he was going to do. That was indeed bearding the lion in his den; and afterward the bold Count visited the homes of other members of the council to discuss the problems with them. Police kept watch while these sessions were being held, but they did not interfere. Mussolini had his uniformed bodyguard, known as the Moschettiere del Duce, and he also had three hundred and fifty plainclothes men who kept watch over the Palazzo Venezia where he lived, and over the palaces occupied by his family and the various ladies whom he visited. These guards would obey any orders he gave, and Roman society buzzed with speculation as to when he would use them, and how.

News spread with the speed of lightning—literally that, meaning the telephone. Julie had gradually come to realize that Lanny was collecting more gossip than art, and she set herself to helping him. She would phone, saying, " I have just learned of a very fine Vannucci which you might get." He would go to her home, and the " Vannucci " would prove to be an inside story of the meeting between Il Duce and the Führer, straight from the lips of Ciano's latest *innamorata*. It bore all the signs of authenticity, because it described Adi as shouting down the Duck and giving him no chance to speak for several hours. The Italian was always at a disadvantage in dealing with his German ally because he thought he could speak German, was proud of the fact, and insisted upon showing it off ; his blunders irritated Hitler, who knew no foreign language and had too much sense to try to pretend otherwise.

The situation between them was an impossible one ; both were on their way down and neither could help the other. Mussolini had presented a request for forty-nine tank divisions and three thousand planes to hold Italy against the Allies ; he might as well have asked for the moon. Hitler blew up, and from that time on did nothing but rage and storm at a braggart and pretender who had been nothing but a handicap from the beginning. Mussolini had done nothing against France until Hitler had brought that country to its knees ; he had rushed into his crazy attack on Greece and thus dragged Hitler into the Balkans and fatally delayed his invasion of Russia. Of course the Führer would say nothing about the fact that Il Duce had taught him his whole bag of propaganda tricks ; not merely how to seize power, but how to hold it, and the banners and slogans and salutes and songs whereby the children of a nation might be made into a horde of deadly little robots.

XV

Five days of plotting and scheming, of confidences and betrayals, proposals and counter-proposals, followed upon Il Duce's return from that ill-fated conference that was nothing but a row. Lanny had another talk with Grandi, who was determined that the Fascist Grand Council should meet. It had been a part of Mussolini's window dressing, like the labour " corporatives " ; it had never had any authority, but in this crisis the deposed Minister of Justice, one of its members, was determined to use it. He succeeded in beating up such a demand that the Duce was forced to call it, and on the afternoon of Saturday, the twenty-fourth of July, the twenty-six members assembled in the famed Balcony Room of the Palazzo Venezia, from which for twenty years Il Duce had been proclaiming glory to his followers massed in the Piazza below.

Lanny got the story the next day from the Commendatore, who had heard it from one of the councillors. It had been a frightening ten hours for those Fascist old-timers, many of whom had become grey-haired, or bald like their Duce, in the course of twenty-one years. They had entered the Palazzo through lines of Il Duce's musketeers, who wore fezes with death-head insignia, and who now carried tommy guns by way of warning to presumptuous political dummies. In the Balcony Room their master, in full uniform with all his decorations, sat at a magnificent desk, while the dummies sat on the outer side of two long tables which made a " U " with the desk.

Mussolini opened the proceedings by reporting on the meeting with Hitler, and said that he had rejected Hitler's proposals. Then he launched into a tirade, blaming Italy's failures upon everybody but himself. He said that the war was not popular, but no war ever was. He predicted that the Allies would not invade the Italian mainland. Italy must fight on.

When he finished, Grandi arose and delivered an attack upon the head of the state, accusing him of having usurped

powers and brought the country to ruin. Then came Ciano,
supporting the charges against his father-in-law—and what
deadly hatred there was between these two men ! The debate
became furious, and they called each other vile names out of
the gutters of Rome. White-bearded Marshal de Bono leaped
up and brandished an automatic in defence of the honour of
the Army, but he was persuaded to put it back into its holster.
Grandi presented a motion that the King be asked to take
command, which meant, of course, the deposing of Il Duce.
The wrangling lasted through the night ; these elderly men
turned grey with fatigue—and that included the Leader with
his stomach ulcers. They almost came to fisticuffs several
times, and one cabinet member, Pareschi, who had a weak
heart, fell into a faint.

" *Votare !* Let us vote ! " Dino Grandi kept insisting, and
that was something that had not been heard in twenty years.
Mussolini, white with rage, stormed and threatened ; but the
former Minister of Justice went on insisting, " *Votare !*
Votare ! " At last the vote was taken, each member rising
in his seat and announcing his decision. Many had not spoken
previously, and it was their votes which decided. The council
stood nineteen to seven in favour of Grandi's motion, nearly
three to one. Grandi had the motion in writing and called
upon the members to sign it ; they did so. Mussolini bowed
his head and said, " *Va bene* "—very well.

Why did he not use the power he had and order the
Moschettiere del Duce to arrest those rebel dummies ? This
was a question which Lanny heard discussed by all his friends
in Rome. None questioned that these well-trained gangsters
would have obeyed their master ; they would have taken
Grandi and the other recalcitrants out and shot them in the
courtyard of the Palace. The Mussolini of ten years ago would
have given the order ; but the Mussolini of today was a sick
and broken man and lacked the nerve. He could not even
address his people over the radio because his voice quavered
and gave him away.

He was caught between two fires, the Germans in the north
and the Americans, British, and French in the south ; his star
was setting, and, more important yet, his stomach ulcers were
getting worse. He had taken a fearful licking from his German

master, and he had come back after a night of physical agony to find that his capital had taken a licking from enemy bombers. His people had turned against him and thought of nothing but of getting out of the war. Crowds were demonstrating all over the city, demanding peace, and if he had ordered a wholesale murder, the population would have risen and torn him to pieces.

Apparently he had the idea that the King would stand by him. When the King summoned him, he took his time about going and went with an escort of a hundred and fifty of his bodyguards in a long train of cars. But he made the mistake of posting them outside the grounds of the royal villa. Inside the grounds the Army officers had hidden some fifty of the *carabinieri*, also an ambulance. When Mussolini entered to the King he was told abruptly that he was dismissed, and when he went outside he was forced into the ambulance and driven away, to the Braschi Fortress, outside Rome. The cabinet resigned, and Marshal Badoglio was appointed the new Premier.

It was eleven o'clock on Sunday night when that news was made public, and then Lanny Budd witnessed one of the strangest sights of his life. It was a moonless night, very dark and very hot; the people poured out into the streets to celebrate, many of them in their pyjamas. The wild demonstration went on until morning, dancing, singing, shouting, blowing horns—it was like New Year's Eve in Times Square, New York. People built bonfires, and what a strange sight in a blacked-out city which had been bombed less than a week ago! Soldiers in trucks raced through the streets, waving the tricolour flag —green, white, and red—of the monarchy and singing the songs of twenty years ago. Crowds gathered before the Palazzo Venezia, where once they had cheered a uniformed pouter pigeon spouting defiance to the whole world; now they kicked on the gates, spat on the walls, and cursed it. Others gathered before the Regina Coeli prison, by the Tiber bank, demanding the release of the prisoners whom the tyrant had put there. Everywhere men wearing Black Shirt uniforms were attacked on the streets.

So it has been through the ages when the mighty have fallen; and Lanny, who considered Benito Mussolini the vilest of men, wasted no sympathy upon him. He had watched the career of false glory since its beginning, and to see its end had been one of a P.A.'s goals in life. Now he watched the crowds and read the leaflets which the Socialists and the Communists were distributing, promising the people a new and better world; then he went into the drawing-rooms of the privileged few and listened to their schemes to take control of this revolution and turn it to their own ends. That too was an old story.

XVI

President Roosevelt issued a statement, broadcast by the Algiers radio, saying that the Italian people would be allowed to choose the form of government they preferred, and that the Allies were ready to deal with any group which would co-operate against the Germans. His P.A. took that as an instruction and went to his friend Signor d' Angelo, seeking a private and confidential meeting with the new Premier. That wasn't so easy, since the Marshal was busy choosing his cabinet and forming his policies. At any rate, that was what he said; but Lanny knew that he had been thinking about his cabinet for weeks, and as for his policies, the Allies were going to settle them.

Pietro Badoglio was riding on top of the wave of fortune, or so he believed, and it was a great concession for him to drop in at the home of an old friend and meet a secret emissary of an enemy's government. He could not stay long, he apologized, for many important matters were pressing for his attention. He did not stand up and spout, as Mussolini would have done under the circumstances; he was a gentleman of the old school and his voice was low. But Lanny quickly saw the difference between a politician seeking office and willing to make promises to everybody, and a politician who has got office and has to think of the consequences of every action, even of every word. " I am not yet prepared to be quoted on that, Monsieur Budd "—so spoke the hero of Abyssinia half a dozen times during the interview.

The substance of his communication was that the Germans were here in Rome, and he was in no position to break with them. If he made any sort of deal that was unacceptable to them, they might do what they had done with the Vichy government—set it aside. It was necessary to wait until events had revealed themselves more clearly.

"Suppose, *Monsieur le Premier,*" said the P.A., "that the Americans were to send an amphibious force to the beaches of Rome and at the same time land several thousand paratroopers in the night, as they have just done in Sicily. They could take and hold the city, and you and your government would be safe."

"That seems to me a typically American idea, Monsieur Budd—somewhat extravagant, if you will pardon me. Even if the coup succeeded, it would leave the major part of our country in German hands. They might choose to wreck it entirely, in punishment for what they would consider betrayal by us."

"But if the Allies have to fight their way up the peninsula they too will be forced to wreck the country."

"You say ' forced,' Monsieur Budd ; but we insist that they do not have to invade our country at all ; they can wait and effect a fair settlement with us."

So there it was. "Caution" was still the old gentleman's motto ; he was going to stall and let his soldiers be used by the Germans to kill American and British and French soldiers. "The war must go on," he had said publicly, and now he said it privately, and he had nothing else to tell an American emissary, except that he protested against the bombing of Rome and that he hoped the Allies could be persuaded not to trespass upon the sacred Italian mainland.

Oh, yes—and one thing more ! Conversing with his friend the Commendatore, he complained that one of his political opponents had rebuked the newspapers for listing him as " Duke of Addis Ababa," when that capital was now in the hands of the British. The elderly warrior showed more feeling over this question than he did over the bombing of Rome. He had conquered Abyssinia, his government had awarded him the title, and according to all precedents he would hold the title for ever, regardless of anything that happened later on. Said Badoglio, " Napier continued to be known as Baron of Magdala even after Magdala was retaken by the Abyssinians. Marshal Ney continued to be addressed as Prince of Moscow even after Napoleon's retreat." Lanny Budd realized that he was dealing with a vain old man who was more concerned about one of the ribbons he wore on his chest than about the thousands of his countrymen who were going to perish in futile battle.

XVII

Lanny went away from that conference with his mind made up that his usefulness in Rome was over, at least for the present. He had been here about six weeks, and the length of his stay had been left to his own judgment. He decided that it was time to report and get fresh instructions.

How best to get out ? He had no way to summon a seaplane and meet it off the beach of Ostia. He might have sent a message by the new wireless system and got instructions in reply, but that would have been dangerous ; and anyhow, what would Herr Güntelen and Marshal Kesselring think if he were to disappear suddenly from the scene ? He had made what amounted to an agreement with Hitler and he was under obligation to keep it, at whatever risk. Hitler would send him out, as he had done once before, by way of Lisbon ; and that would suit a world traveller, because it might give him a glimpse of Paris and Madrid, and he could proceed by way of England and see his daughter. All he needed to do was to think up a satisfactory set of fairy tales to tell the Führer.

By this time the Americans had taken the entire western half of Sicily and were beginning the final great battle. So when Lanny went to the Hôtel de Russie and asked to see Marshal Kesselring he was not surprised to be told that this officer was not " available " ; Lanny could guess that he was in Naples, or even nearer to the front. He explained to Oberst von Horn that it was his wish to send a message to the Führer, and he was told that the staff had instructions to send whatever message Herr Budd might request. Herr Budd wanted the Führer to know that Herr Budd had information for him ; the staff officer promised that this important statement would go at once.

Lanny returned to his room and wrote notes to several of his acquaintances, telling them that he was leaving town for a while and thanking them for their courtesies. He left them to guess where and how he was going. Within an hour he received a message from the Oberst, saying that if Herr Budd would be in front of the Hôtel de Russie at fourteen hundred hours, a car would be waiting.

Lanny went, and was driven to the Guidonia airport, which the Americans had not yet put out of use. There was the same dispatch plane, with the same pilot who had flown him the last time. Herr Budd and his little suitcase were strapped into the co-pilot's seat and the plane rose. Lanny had a bombardier's-eye view of the smashed railroad yards, and then the plane swung round to the north, over the winding brown river—" O, Tiber, Father Tiber, to whom the Romans pray ! " A few minutes later the passenger was looking down upon the bright blue of Lake Bracciano, and from there was unrolled a panorama of mountains, all brown or rock-grey on top, terraced and bright green on the sides. How many poets had sung about this land, and how many armies had marched over its roads ! Up to a generation ago only the birds had enjoyed the view which Lanny was enjoying ; but he soon forgot it, thinking up the fairy tales he was going to tell to Adi Schicklgruber !

BOOK THREE

THE ENEMY FAINTS NOT, NOR FAILETH

7

Slaughters of the Race

I

"THIS is too easy!" Lanny Budd kept saying to himself. "This can't go on. Watch out!" That he should have spent forty days and nights in Rome, playing both ends against the middle, and with a hundred pairs of sharp eyes watching him, a hundred sharp tongues criticizing him—that was tempting fate too much. And now he was going back into the tiger's den, and at a time in the tiger's life when it had so much to make it irritable. The British and Americans were driving the Germans out of the Mount Etna defence line in Sicily, and the Russian advance had taken two of the Germans' most strongly defended positions, Orel and Bielgorod. It was a time for Lanny to study every word that would pass his lips; he had not merely to guard against blunders, but to practise the offensive defence, by thinking up something novel, something that would sweep the Führer off his feet—if he could!

The first time he had come to Hitler's headquarters it had been the Ukraine, and the second time it had been Königsberg, far to the north. Where would it be now? He didn't wish to show any curiosity, but watched the sun and judged that they were heading due north. It is difficult to recognize mountains from above them, and there are many lakes in the Alps, most of them long and thin. National boundaries do not show, and he could not be sure when he was over Italy and when over Austria or Germany.

It wasn't until the plane had begun circling an airport that he realized he was coming to a place of many memories. Far to the west was the great spread of a city—that was

Munich. To the east was the town of Salzburg, with the river cutting it into halves ; below were villas perched on mountain slopes, and in the valley a village with a great hotel. Lanny knew the shape of the clump of buildings that comprise the Berghof, the Führer's country home ; and reaching up toward the plane was the famous rock, the Kehlstein, on top of which the inspired man had built for himself a secret retreat. He had taken Lanny Budd up in a great bronze elevator, a 700-foot shaft, and had revealed the basis of his religious belief, which resembled, so he said, that of the Arab camel driver Mohammed.

Yes, it was Berchtesgaden, and Lanny could guess that Adi had been found in need of rest after the excitement of overcoming his Italian ally. When the plane came down there was a car waiting, the driver in the green uniform of the Führer's bodyguard, the Leibstandarte. Lanny saluted. *" Heil Hitler ! "* the man responded, and they rolled out of the village and on up the road which climbed along the mountainside. The dark green of fir trees covered the slopes —*auf die Berge will ich steigen, wo die hohen Tannen ragen !* Clouds white as snow moved majestically overhead. The breeze was cool and laden with forest scents. Lanny drank them in and wished that he might stay here, away from all thoughts of war. But he knew enough about the plans of both sides to be sure that the war was coming here—indeed, it might end here.

The first time the art expert had driven up this road it had been at night, and he remembered the car lights sweeping over these tree-clad slopes. Irma Barnes had been in the seat beside him, and Trudi Schultz had been in the back seat— being smuggled out of Hitlerland by the least suspected of all routes. That had been the end of Lanny's first marriage and the beginning of his second, though he hadn't known it until later that night. The last time he had come here had been with Laurel, and that had been the beginning of his third marriage, though he hadn't known it either. It had been almost four years ago, in the last dreadful hours before the German invasion of Poland ; the two Americans had made their feeble effort to stave off the calamity, but in vain.

II

When they came to the gates which barred the road into the estate, the car halted and was searched. Then they drove in to the main building and waited a minute or so until the roly-poly Herr Kannenberg emerged. This former restaurateur of Munich was the Führer's steward and entertainer; also, apparently, his official greeter; Lanny always suspected that he was sent out in order to make certain that the person who came in the name of Herr Budd actually was that person. The greeting was effusively cordial, just as it would have been in the café if the son of Budd-Erling in evening clothes had been giving a dinner party that might cost a thousand marks at their old valuation.

Lanny was taken in by the side door and searched again, but it was less unpleasantly thorough. He emerged into the main hall, a great, almost square apartment with heavy beams overhead; there were panels of the same beautiful wood and a masterpiece of painting in the centre of each panel. At the far end of the room was a sight for Lanny Budd's sore eyes—if by any chance he had got them from the bright sun over the Alps. Pacing up and down in front of the immense window that looked out over the mountains was a tall erect man in a dark-grey suit, with a long solemn face and close-cut blond hair—Lanny's boyhood friend, the *Komponist*, Kurt Meissner.

Lanny hastened to him with a glad greeting; he would have had to simulate that emotion even if he had not felt it. A strange psychological conflict when a friend of one's youth goes wrong in his later years; one cannot forget the old sentimental feelings, and at the same time one cannot ignore the present divagation—at least not if it is along the lines of Nazi-Fascism. For this is a creed of anti-tolerance, and it does not let you rest, it does not permit of neutrality, it compels you to be actively for or against. Lanny hated Kurt Meissner's creed with all his heart and soul; it was a deadly thing, a creation of the devil or whatever served that role in the modern world. Yet Lanny loved Kurt Meissner; he loved the genius he had watched evolving, he loved the teacher who had quoted to him the phrases of idealistic philosophy. That these phrases could be used in the service of racial bigotry, of fanaticism and wholesale murder, was the most tragic discovery of Lanny's life. He should have learned it from Shakespeare, who had warned that the devil could cite Scripture.

The fact that the old feelings were still in his heart made it easier for Lanny to play his role. He had only to remember how things had been from the age of thirteen to nearly twice that. He could quote Goethe and Schiller, even Heine ; he could play music, even Mendelssohn and Chopin—for Kurt was " broadminded " and did not carry his distrust of Jews and Poles into the world of the arts. He must not quote the more crude and brutal Nazis, for Kurt was ashamed of these and would expect Lanny to continue as the young idealist—a year younger than his self-appointed mentor.

So now Lanny caught Kurt's right hand—the uninjured one—and wrung it, saying, " *Welch frohes Wiedersehen !* " Kurt explained that the Führer's secretary had telephoned to Schloss Stubendorf, instructing Kurt to come to Breslau by train, where he would be put on a dispatch plane and brought to the Führer, the place not specified. Here they were, and Lanny cried, " *Wunderbar !* " They settled in two chairs in front of that famous large window, and Kurt told the news since their last meeting, and Lanny told such news as it was safe for a Nazi zealot to hear. Kurt considered it amazing that Lanny was able to get into Germany, and Lanny didn't say how he had done it, but took refuge in the statement that the Führer had a way of getting what he wanted. The other asked no questions, for if the Führer wanted him to know, the Führer would tell him.

III

Presently the godlike one came in. He was in a pitiable state of nervousness ; the others saw it, and Lanny understood that Kurt felt the same grief that Lanny felt when he saw the weariness of his own leader. Both leaders were wearing themselves out in the service of the cause they believed in ; and which of them was right the future would decide. The Führer's flabby face twitched, and his left arm had become helpless ; Kurt's was partly helpless too, though for a different reason, an injury in an air raid.

Hitler greeted his new guest and said, " I am here at the Berghof by Dr. Morell's orders ; he insists that I need a rest." This was the nearest he could come to an apology ; he meant that it distressed him to be away from military headquarters in the midst of a double crisis. The American visitor replied that our bodies could be a great nuisance at times ; he himself had been all but knocked out by the sultry heat of Rome, which rarely let up. It was a delicate way of saying to the great man, " Do not blame me if the information I bring you is not all that you expect."

" Tell me what you have learned, Herr Budd," said the Führer ; he could not wait for even a minute or two of social preliminaries. Kurt offered to leave, but the master said, " *Nein, nein !* I keep no secrets from you "—which of course wasn't true, but was most gracious.

Lanny delivered his prepared story. He didn't have to vary greatly from the truth, it was just a matter of selection. He told of his interviews with Badoglio and with Ciano and Grandi ; he had reported in writing, but now he could tell in more detail, describing the personalities and giving his estimate of the characters. He was careful not to hint at those persons who didn't want publicity, such as d' Angelo and the Marchesa ; he implied that he had penetrated to the higher-ups on the basis of his father's reputation.

He said that the effect of the bombings had been to infuriate the populace of Rome and to prolong resistance ; he could safely say that because nobody could disprove it, and it was what Hitler would choose to believe. For ten years Adi Schicklgruber had been living in a court ; which meant that he had surrounded himself with persons who would tell him what he wanted to hear and nothing else. It was surely not up to Lanny to change that regimen.

" Grandi and Ciano are dead ducks now," said the visitor, and explained the American phrase, thus bringing the first smile to Adi's worried face. Badoglio was the man of the hour, and Lanny answered a string of questions about this " Duke of Addis Ababa." There could be no question that he meant to go on with the war ; he had declared even stricter martial law in the city, and he had given Lanny positive assurances in the presence of a third person, an old friend. Of course no one could tell how long he would remain of that mind, the Italians were a volatile people, knowing nothing of German *Zucht und Ordnung*. The riotous scenes which had occurred in the Balcony Room of the Palazzo Venezia were a mockery of statesmanship ; Lanny told the details, and apparently Hitler had not heard them, though, of course, he may have been pretending as a means of checking on his agent.

Lanny praised again the conduct of the German troops in Rome ; even the natives could not deny that they were magnificent. The natives, of course, were thinking only of themselves. The rich wanted to play and gossip at the golf club, as if there had never been a war in the world ; the black marketeers wanted to reap their fortunes, the politicians wanted to keep on the winning side, and the poor took what was given to them, which was not much. How tragically different from Germany, where everybody was cared for alike ; where all knew they could trust their government, and did so ! *Deutschland über Alles !*

It was a good report, and its effect was heightened by the presence of Kurt Meissner. Most of it was new to him, and he listened with deep interest, and was proud of the American friend whom he had introduced to the Führer fifteen or more years ago. Kurt voiced his opinion, and it carried weight because Adi always found it easier to trust those persons who had known him before he took power and therefore were less open to suspicion of self-seeking.

He asked, " What are you planning to do now, Herr Budd ? " And Lanny replied that he had in mind to return to America and inquire into the affair with which the Führer had charged him. He didn't hint that it was the affair of getting President Roosevelt kidnapped, for that might have shocked Kurt and he might have been unable to believe that Lanny was attempting such a job. Hitler didn't mention it either, and Lanny wondered if he too was afraid of offending the moral sensibilities of his great *Komponist*. A statesman has to learn to live on different levels—and he must not get them confused.

IV

Lanny could guess that the Führer's quack doctor had told him he was worrying himself ill over the turn in the tide of battle, and that the tormented man had planned to get himself an evening of happiness with two old friends who would remind him of the good days when everything had been coming his way. He took the pair up to his elegant study, saying, " We are going to have dinner by ourselves ; it will be more *gemütlich*." Lanny was glad, because he was an enemy alien, well known to the domestic and military staffs, and he did not relish the ordeal of facing them all.

The host pressed a button, and Herr Kannenberg came running. " *Schicken Sie Eva*," said Adi, " *und das Essen—schnell !* " The little roly-poly hastened out, and presently there came into the room a young woman about whom Lanny had heard on his last visit but whom he had never seen. She was in her twenties, a brunette, somewhat plump ; she was pretty, kind, and placid, and wholly untroubled by brains. " *Das ist meine liebe Freundin, Eva Braun*," said the Führer. That was introduction enough, and Hitler didn't bother to name the two men ; Eva gave them the briefest possible smile, then seated herself on the couch beside her master, and thereafter devoted her attention exclusively to him. Kurt did not address a single word to her during the evening, and Lanny made note of this example and followed it. Eva was a part of Adi's rest cure.

Kannenberg came running again, followed by an S.S. man wheeling a table with dishes, cutlery, glasses, and a covered soup tureen. A larger table was placed in front of the couch and a meal was quickly got under way ; the steward helped, something that would have been beneath his dignity had he not been doing it for the greatest man in the world. Perhaps he hoped that he would be told to set a fifth place for himself, but that did not happen. There was, first, the inevitable noodle soup ; and while they were eating it—Hitler not without sounds—the wheel-table was rolled off and came back with the second course. The Führer's vegetable plate with a poached egg on top and two slices of whole-meal toast were ceremoniously placed before him. The others had generous helpings of roast chicken, with rich gravy, and potatoes and turnips. The food was hot and well cooked, and made an acceptable wartime meal.

The Führer's partner, the Italian Number One, had been dumped off his seat of power, and this was an event of enormous significance to Hitler. " Tell us how it came about," he said ; and that set for the secret agent a task of no little delicacy. He had thought much about it and had decided that the way of safety lay in emphasizing all those factors which made Italy different from Germany, and Il Duce different from his opposite number. The instability, the inefficiency, the cowardice of generals who had come home from the field of defeat and of admirals who did not dare go out and give battle—these things excluded the possibility that Italy might be taken as a precedent and that there could be any warning for a Führer in the downfall of a Duce.

Lanny referred lightly to the sexual corruption, being in the presence of a lady whom he hardly knew. But Hitler said, " Tell us about that jackass Ciano and his widows." *Esel, und Sohn eines Esels !* Thus commanded, Lanny described the ladies at the golf club and in the salons ; he gave one or two samples of their spicy conversation, and Adi was diverted thereby. " Tell us all," he insisted. " We are no prudes here."

Lanny understood that the worse he made Rome appear, the more he would justify Hitler for being unable to prevent its bombing, so he proceeded to shoot the works. He told about Edda Ciano, Mussolini's daughter, the sharp-faced hysterical woman who, it was reputed, quarrelled with both her husband and her father and chose her lovers from all classes of the population. He told about Mussolini himself, so proud of his amours that he had his secret service keep an official record of them, and the score to date was seventy-three. The latest flame was named Clara Petacci, and she had been set up in a palace, and what a hellcat she was ! Her horde of relatives all had to be given official positions, and her father, a doctor, had waged a minor war to have the ambassadorship to Spain given to a friend whom Ciano, in Lanny's hearing, described as " an old jailbird, an ignorant man, a swindler, and obscene."

Chuckling over this story, Adi patted his Eva on her plump

knee and remarked, "*So etwas würde meiner Eva nie ein-fallen!*"

V

The meal was eaten and the table cleared. Herr Kannen-berg lingered, obviously hoping to be requested to bring his accordion and favour the company with his Bavarian *G'stanzln*. But no, this was going to be a highbrow evening, and the round little steward was not invited ; he took himself sadly away, and Hitler said to his American guest, " The first time you came to this house you played for us. Will you do it again ? " Lanny replied, " I played the first movement of the *Moonlight Sonata*. I know it is a favourite of yours." When Hitler said yes, he added, " My fingers have grown rusty of late, but I don't think I shall forget any Beethoven that I ever knew."

He seated himself, and there came forth those sorrowful notes, so laden with grief, yet so beautiful—oh, surely, there must be some balm for human suffering, some meaning to all the sacrifice and the failure ! You could think of men giving their lives by the thousands on the sodden, rain-soaked fields of Central Russia ; you could think of the hopes of mankind for beauty and peace that have never come to fruition ; you could think of noble spirits who had longed to assuage human pain and had seen only greed and cruelty prevailing in the world. You could think such thoughts in the moonlight, of course, or you could think them in a room with a genius-madman who had aspired to dominate a continent and had almost succeeded—but who, because he was ignorant and deluded, had brought only ruin and misery where he had hoped to bring prosperity and joy.

Such were Lanny's thoughts as he played the slow, mourn-ful composition, product of one of the great souls which Germany had given to mankind. Were there other Beethovens perishing in the lonely steppes of the Ukraine tonight ? Had they died in frozen Stalingrad, or in the blazing hot desert of North Africa ? Were they being gathered up now by the *Razzia*, the raids which desperate Wehrmacht men were making every night upon the civil population ? How much of German genius, of wisdom and scholarship and scientific skill, was being lost to mankind for ever because the one-time inmate of a home for the destitute in Vienna had gambled on his belief that Britain and France would not dare come to the rescue of Poland, and that the New World could not arm itself in time to save the Old ?

Woe, woe, and sorrow beyond all imagining, sunk for ever into the abyss of time, swallowed by eternal forgetfulness ! When the sad notes died away, they sat silent for a while ; then Kurt, the musical authority, remarked, " Very good, Lanny "—and it was kindness, not condescension. Kurt could have done much better, but his skill was one of the casualties of war. When Hitler remarked, " How I wish that you could play for us ! " Kurt replied, " I can play the treble part only." It occurred to the host that he had a four-hand arrangement of the *Führermarsch*, which Kurt had written in his honour, following the precedent of Wagner's *Kaisermarsch*. He said, " You might play it three-handed." And that, of course, was a command.

Lanny got the music out, and set it up, and they played a piece which Lanny thought was wholly uninspired, unworthy of Kurt's true self. Kurt played with his right hand, and Lanny with his two hands more softly, and it sounded not too bad. It told Adi Schicklgruber that he must not yield to grief, that he must have the stamina and *Beharrlichkeit* of Frederick the Great, and then his name would be written on the scroll of history alongside that great conqueror's. In short, it said, " Get to work again ! "

The Führer took up the house telephone and asked if there were any dispatches. They were sent up ; he sat reading and frowning, and then he read them aloud : the Russians were continuing their relentless pressure beyond Bielgorod and the situation was serious there. After that they talked about the war, and Lanny couldn't see that the Führer was getting any rest out of this meeting with old friends. To be sure, Eva leaned her head on his shoulder and he petted her as he talked, but it was an absent-minded sort of love-making, and Lanny wondered about it. Had this amiable, slow-minded girl been able to win Hitler away from those abnormalities which had caused so much distress to other women, and had driven his niece, Geli Raubal, to take her own life ?

VI

The master of the Third Reich talked about the new divisions he was pouring into Italy, and the shock the Anglo-Americans would get if they dared attempt a landing on the toe of the Italian boot. Lanny said that he had heard talk at his father's about the idea of landing farther up on the boot. He thought that might cause a bit of confusion in the Führer's mind; but if it did, it didn't show. "We shall be ready for them, wherever they come," declared Adi. "We are getting new weapons, and I hope you won't be around when they start to work, Herr Budd."

The real danger was the Russians, the host went on; there seemed to be no limit to those hordes, they bred like the vermin they were. The Führer's General Staff assured him that the enemy had used up his last trained divisions in taking the Orel salient, and there was no more to be feared from him this summer. Lanny had been told otherwise in the White House, but he surely wasn't going to mention it in the Berghof. He sat with his deeply hidden thoughts—an odd thing, for he was firmly convinced of the reality of telepathy, yet here he sat, staking his life upon the idea that neither of the other two would be able to get any of the treasonable thoughts that were swarming in his mind. Thoughts of Oskar von Herzenberg getting ready to take the Führer's life! Thoughts of going to Berlin to get the latest news of this conspiracy and carrying it to the Führer's enemy overseas!

Hitler was a wretched sleeper and never wanted to go to bed. Eva Braun began to doze on his shoulder, and he told her abruptly to go, and she went, without a word of good night to anybody or from anybody—she just went. Lanny knew that his host would want to sit and talk till almost dawn, and that seemed a cheap price to pay for information. What might he not tell when he got good and tired?

So Lanny stayed awake and told more about the degradation of Italy and the pitiful state of Mussolini's health. Hitler mentioned that the silly fellow's pride had been wounded by having to eat rice and milk in the presence of hearty Germans, so he had made it a condition of coming to the conference that he should have his food served apart ; but at the last moment he had decided that this was even more humiliating, and he had eaten with the rest and made himself ill. Lanny said, " I think it was you who made him ill by refusing him forty-nine tank divisions and three thousand planes." That, of course, pleased Adi enormously.

But Hitler couldn't keep away from the subject of the Russians. How he hated them and feared them—and how hard he tried to pretend that he despised them ! He called for more dispatches and showed by his comments that he knew the position of every division and indeed every regiment of his three million Germans at the front. Lanny didn't try to remember any of this because he knew that positions changed quickly in a war of movement, and he was sure the Russians needed no reconnaissance services from him. The fighting was on Russian soil, and every last man, woman, and child behind the German lines was a spy. Hitler knew that too, and said they were being shot freely, and their numbers reduced.

As the hours passed his mood grew melancholy. " I speak to old friends in confidence," he began. " I have been forced to confront the possibility that this heroic effort of the German people may end in failure. These barbarian hordes may sweep over the most highly civilized land in the world. Have you thought what you will do, Kurt ? "

" Grosser Gott ! " exclaimed the musician. " I have never dreamed of such a thing, mein Führer ! " He said it with fierce conviction, but all the same Lanny guessed that it wasn't true. Kurt was just trying to keep up his great master's spirits.

" Think of it now," the master commanded. " It is the duty of every man to make a will, even though he may believe himself in the best of health. Will you accept a commission from me, Kurt ? "

" Natürlich, verehrter Führer. When have I ever refused one ? "

" Very well. You will not stay in Upper Silesia, to be enslaved by the barbarians. You will take your family to Switzerland and establish a home there. I will see that money is put to your account in that country. Your commission is to compose the saga of our German effort, the greatest hope of mankind, and to preserve the traditions for its rebirth and reawakening. Germany will have that, rest assured ; the National Socialist spirit will never die, and in the end it will conquer. You agree to that ? "

" *Gewiss, mein Führer.*"

" And Herr Budd will no doubt do what he can to help you."

" Anything in my power, *mein Führer.*" This from the reverent *Ausländer.*

" Have you ever thought of composing an opera, Kurt ? "

" I have often thought of it, but I have been awed by the achievements of Richard Wagner."

" *Ich bin sicher*, you will rise to this high occasion. You will have a theme as great as any in our old Teutonic legends. Be sure that I will never give up, but will die sword in hand ; it will be a new Götterdämmerung, the greatest ever seen in the world."

There was a solemn silence. Kurt's long face wore an expression of consecration, as if he were a humble priest receiving the blessing of the Holy Father. " I accept your command, *mein Führer,*" he said. " I will do my best."

VII

Lanny waited a decent interval and then he interposed, " We must not let our imaginations run away with us, *Exzellenz.* The German Third Reich is a long way from defeat."

" *Das ist wahr, Herr Budd,*" responded the Führer in a changed tone. He went on to name the factors that might bring victory, and this involved a long exposition : the strategy of the war, the resources of the various countries, the morale of the populations as he conceived it. He had got most of his ideas about America from his youthful reading of Karl May, a German novelist who had written long romances about the immigrants and Indians of the Wild West. Adi had had more chance to know the German people, but to Lanny it seemed that he didn't know them much better ; they were not what they were, but what their Führer was determined to make them.

It was a long, long session. Hitler talked and talked, asked questions without awaiting answers, and almost put the P.A.

to sleep several times. He told the history of Europe as he saw it ; he discussed the diplomacy of the two World Wars and explained why it had been necessary for him to conquer Russia. When Molotov had come to Berlin in November of 1940, after the conquest of France, he had demanded as the price of a deal not merely Finland, the Baltic States, half of Poland, and all of Bessarabia, but also the Dardanelles. " Of course I couldn't give him that," said Hitler. " That would have meant turning the whole Mediterranean over to him. How can Britain and America fail to see that, and to realize that I am fighting their war ? "

Lanny's mind was working hard, preparing an answer to this, but it was quite unnecessary ; the Führer went on to tell how *he* meant to remake the map of Europe : there wouldn't be any Bolshevism and there wouldn't be any democracy or any Jews ; the Slavic race would be the serfs and do the dirty work.

Then came the subject of philosophy, and Hitler told what a bad thing it had been for Germany to fall under the spell of materialistic monism. That led to the subject of religion, and he told God what to do in the present crisis. Again he expressed his esteem for Mohammed—another self-made prophet—and Lanny took the chance to tell Kurt how he had once been taken up the shaft through the heart of the Kehlstein, and on the top had been honoured with an exposition of a great master's views on God and human destiny. A delicate compliment, letting the master know how carefully his words had been cherished.

Somehow the subject of art came up. Hitler's tastes ran to the simple and obvious, the early Aryan, so to speak. He had forbidden all the modernist stuff as decadent. Lanny agreed with this judgment, though not with the banning ; he thought the public had a right to be fooled if it wished. But he didn't say that. He, a well-known art expert, bowed to the decisions of a one-time painter of greeting cards at twenty-five pfennigs apiece. And when the talk turned to music, Kurt Meissner did the same. Wagner was first, and the rest nowhere. At three o'clock the Führer saw fit to release his auditors. He did not apologize for keeping them up, but said, " I have work to do in the morning and must try to get some sleep." Etiquette through the ages has established the fact that the safety of a whole people depends upon the ruler, and therefore his wishes and welfare must be the sole consideration. It was an ancient idea—see the *Alcestis* of Euripides !

VIII

Lanny and Kurt were being flown to Berlin, where Kurt had business with his publishers. Lanny, travelling on his French passport, genuine or forged, didn't have to worry, because he was to be met by an S.S. officer in Berlin and again in Paris. He had asked for one day in each city, explaining that he wished to talk with his old friend Denis de Bruyne, who was in close touch with the financial and political world of France and might reveal something of importance. " If he does, I will mail you a report," said the P.A.

The Führer replied, " Send it to Berlin. I am leaving here this morning and will be at my military headquarters in the Forest of Görlitz." That was an important secret from the point of view of the Allied Air Forces. Lanny wondered, was it a slip, or was Adi letting his American friend know what complete confidence he had in him ? Lanny wasn't going to pass on the secret, because he knew that the forest in question was a big one, and the headquarters would be well hidden. Also, if it were bombed, there might be a flash in Adi's memory.

There was no ceremony of parting, for the Führer was locked up in the map-room with several of his generals ; the dispatches continued to be bad. Nor could Lanny have much talk with Kurt, because the plane was noisy. He devoted himself to remembering the important things Hitler had said, and the important things that Lanny himself was planning to say to Reichsmarschall Göring, if by good fortune *Der Dicke* was in Berlin.

Arriving at the Tempelhoferfeld, they found that it had been thoroughly pasted with bombs during the night, so they had to fly to another field in a distant suburb. That disarranged matters, because Lanny's escort was not on hand ; but meantime he got the official Residenz of his fat friend on the phone. He asked for General-Major Furtwängler, but was told that he was " at the front." The secretary, who knew Herr Budd of old, said *Seine Exzellenz* was sleeping after a bad night, but would surely want to see Herr Budd, and would Herr Budd promise to call again the moment he arrived in Berlin ? Herr Budd promised.

An S.S. Leutnant arrived in a car with a uniformed chauffeur, and the *Komponist* and the *Kunstsachverständiger* were driven to the city, by a route which gave them opportunity to observe much bomb damage. Kurt was delivered to his music publishers, and Lanny to one of the smaller hotels, where he was not known. He telephoned from there, and heard the booming voice of the old-time Teutonic robber baron : " *Um Himmels Willen, wie kommen Sie hierher ?* " When Lanny said he had spent a night at the Berghof, *Der Dicke* wanted in the worst way to see him. " *Kommen Sie so schnell wie möglich !* "

Lanny replied, " I wouldn't let anybody see me till I have a chance to clean up." He agreed to come to lunch.

He got a room, and had a bath and a shave, and his one suit was sponged and pressed. He got a copy of the *Völkischer*, and had time to read that the German troops were victoriously retreating from both sides of what had been the Bielgorod salient ; also that the German and Italian troops were victoriously retreating into the north-eastern corner of Sicily, inflicting terrific losses upon the Americans and British. Then Lanny went for a stroll and observed the results of the bombing which he had witnessed during the previous winter and many other raids since then. At thirteen hundred hours he approached the Residenz, by the plebeian method of shanks's mare, which he hoped would be considered patriotic because of war shortages.

IX

There were no shortages inside the Air Commander's office, of that you could be sure ; no shortage of breath for a welcome and no shortage of comfort for the inner man. Lanny was received in the sumptuous private office, an enormous ebony table in the centre and gleaming gold curtains at all the windows ; everything as it was when he had first come here, nine years ago—except that there was no lion cub, all the animals in the zoo having been killed and eaten. *Hermann der Dicke* had taken a fancy to an American art expert and had amused himself by displaying his glories to this visitor. What was the use of having glories if no one saw them ? And who better to impress than the son of Göring's former business associate, used to all kinds of luxury and really knowing the difference between true elegance and the crude imitations which Hermann the aristocrat saw about him in parvenu Naziland ?

On a hot day at the beginning of August the way you displayed elegance was to hang the coat of your latest sky-blue uniform over the back of a chair, so that all the decorations and medals could be seen ; then you could be comfortable in a white polo shirt and enjoy a silver pitcher of beer resting in a bowl of ice. You could press a button and have a table wheeled in with pheasant in aspic and endive salad and iced peaches with cream, and you could gobble this with much smacking of the lips, and enjoy it more because three million of your fellow countrymen were floundering in the mud of Central Russia. There had happened to be a long spell of rain before the Orel salient, and *Der Dicke* explained that this favoured the defence, which was falling back upon its own supplies while the enemy had to drag his forward through the swamps.

Lanny had a story to tell : the Führer had ordered him to Rome and he had been able to meet the top people and have confidential talks. Hermann had been to Rome the previous winter, so he knew the scenery and the personalities. He had laid down the law to that decadent people, and they had hated him but had to obey ; where they had failed, they were now paying the penalty, and *Der Dicke* made no secret of the fact that he hoped the bombing had done them good. He fully shared Hitler's opinion of Ciano and took delight in the scandalous tales. " Galeazzo's widows—*famos !* " The old pirate leaned back in his chair and laughed until he half choked himself. He slapped his fat knees, covered by soft shiny black leather boots.

Things were going badly, he was too good a military man not to know it, and too free-spoken to try to fool his guest. The Number Two could take satisfaction in the fact that he had no share of the responsibility ; it had been a long time since his advice had been asked, and still longer since it had been taken. Lanny could bear witness to the fact that he, Göring, had tried hard to prevent the fantastic attack upon Russia ; and Lanny said yes, surely he could. He knew better than to blame it upon the Number One, and chose instead an unnumbered person whom he knew that Göring regarded with abhorrence. " Too bad the negotiations had to be left to Ribbentrop," he said, and this warmed the fat man's heart. He told of the desperate efforts he had made to persuade Hitler that the one-time champagne salesman was as incompetent to deal with Russian statesmen as he had proved himself to be with British. Said Göring, " The Führer pointed out that Ribbentrop knew Lord This and Minister That, and I answered, ' Yes, but unfortunately Lord This and Minister That know Ribbentrop.' "

They condoled together for a while, and then, to cheer his host up, Lanny brought up the subject of paintings. If Hermann Göring had been in Palestine in the year thirty-three or thereabouts he would have had a Jewish agitator crucified without bothering to have a trial, and with him would have hanged all his disciples, save only Judas. But a " Descent from the Cross," gorgeously painted several hundred years ago, possibly by Giorgione but more probably by Titian, that was something else again, and as *Der Dicke* listened his mouth watered. He collected paintings by the acre of gallery space, and that anybody else should have a good one was intolerable to him—and especially in Italy.

On the subject of Giorgione the American visitor was really a delight to hear, for ever since he had reached his majority he had been practising smooth and elegant statements about old masters. " In my opinion," he said, " there is only one certain work by that master, and that is the ' Madonna ' at Castelfranco, his birthplace. Others are ' attributed ' to him by one or more experts, but I personally have my doubts regarding even the famous ' Tempesta,' which is in the public museum of Venice and for which the late Lord Duveen offered a million dollars." Lanny went on to tell the story of how Prince Giovannelli of Venice was fleeced of this painting by the Italian government, and Hermann listened with interest, because he had done a lot of fleecing himself and might get some pointers.

Lanny went on, " I believe that this ' Descent from the Cross ' was painted by Titian when he was still under the influence of Giorgione—he worked with the master, you know. I am offered the painting for a hundred and fifty thousand dollars, and I think that is a reasonable price under the circumstances. I will make you a free gift of the information, because I am not here to collect a commission from you."

" *Unsinn !* " responded the host promptly. " If I buy it, you shall have your share. I have plenty of money in New York, you know, and some in other cities."

" It might be that I would get into trouble if I took it, Hermann. Anyhow, we can decide about that later."

X

Like his Führer, the Number Two got dispatches from the various fronts. He read them to his guest, even though they were bad. " I have no secrets from you, Lanny. You know that I want peace, and I know that you do. My Luftwaffe is being wiped out. Because they cannot supply me with planes they are taking my paratroopers and other highly trained men and putting them in as ground troops, and there is nothing I can do about it. I am supposed to be satisfied with the fact that they continue to wear my blue-grey uniform instead of the Army's field-grey ! "

Lanny could guess that this Air Commander was following Lanny's own technique of telling some secrets in order to get more ; and Lanny was willing for that to happen, for he knew that F. D. R.'s policy was to frighten the enemy and break his nerve by telling him the worst. When *Der Dicke* hinted to know how many pursuit planes the Budd-Erling outfit was turning out now, and whether it was true that they had a new model about to go into production, Lanny told exactly what he knew. He told about the armada of ships that was serving the Sicilian campaign, and about the estimated number of submarines that were being sunk—about one a day all summer. Hermann would know the real figures, but it would interest him to know what the Allies believed.

All these things Lanny said with a grave face, and they both agreed that the Fatherland was in a serious position, and that it would be the part of wisdom to get out at any cost. "*Dieses verdammte* unconditional surrender!" exclaimed *Der Dicke*, using the English phrase; and Lanny agreed that it was an uncivilized and indecent formula. But it wouldn't necessarily mean just that—all kinds of terms and modifications were even now being demanded by the Italians. Lanny had picked up that information in Rome, and he named the people, but of course he was careful to name the wrong ones. If it could lead to the Gestapo's distrusting their best friends in Italy, that would be all to the good.

"*Leider!*" exclaimed the *Nummer Zwei*. "I have lost my influence by urging reasonableness. The Führer would not hear of such suggestions, no matter who made them. We have to go through to the bitter end, and we are using up our human resources, which cannot be replaced. Stalingrad was our Gettysburg I fear." The bemedalled commander's mouth drooped, matching his jowls and the folds under his chin. His complexion had lost its colour, he belched frequently and gave other evidences of ill-health. Lanny could feel certain that he had gone back to his old habit of taking drugs; there had been a bottle of pills on the table with his food, and now he was restless, looking about as if he needed something. "I wish I could stay and talk about paintings the rest of the day," he said; "but I have to meet my generals and decide what to do about your increasing bombing. *Zum Teufel mit Ihnen!*" He said it with a melancholy grin.

The son of Budd-Erling replied seriously, "I am ashamed to be so helpless, *lieber Hermann.*"

XI

The S.S. Leutnant was waiting in the car outside the Residenz. He was enormously impressed by an *Ausländer* who could come from the home of *Die Nummer Eins* to the home of *Die Nummer Zwei*. His name was Apfeldorf, and he had grey hair; Lanny took him to be forty, and learned that he was twenty-two. He had fought all the way from the Polish border to the suburbs of Moscow and part of the way back. He walked with a decided limp, and revealed to his guest that he had a wooden leg and it did not fit very well; there were so many who needed this sort of help. When Lanny indicated his interest, the young Nazi devotee told his experiences in this first campaign, when the Army had been hurled into that vast semi-barbarous land—so he described it—and had failed in its main objective; the troops had been caught by the most severe winter in many years, and the government had had to beg for blankets, fur coats, gloves, and woollen scarves from the civil population. "Now I am nothing but a desk man," sighed Leutnant Apfeldorf.

Lanny had telephoned to make sure that Marceline was still at the one-time school. She had said, speaking German, since that was required by law, "*Oskar ist hier, Vorsicht!*" That word of warning meant that she had not told her lover that she had shared his deadly secret with her half-brother. When Lanny arrived at the cottage she was sitting on the porch, waiting for him; Oskar was asleep inside, so she had an excuse for taking Lanny off under the shade tree in the garden. He assured her that he would be careful; he had met Oskar a number of times in Paris, and knew his father still better, and his officer caste better yet.

The Oberst—he had been promoted recently—was slightly younger than Marceline. His father, the Graf, now had a minor job in the *Auswärtiges Amt* in Berlin, which presumably meant that Ribbentrop didn't trust him too much. Oskar's regiment had been sent into the Orel salient, which certainly indicated that nobody cared what happened to him. He had lost his left arm from a shell burst, and had got a splinter in his abdomen, so he had had a narrow squeak; there would be one more desk man in the Reichswehr, which already had more than it could use. He was able to move about, but feebly; Marceline was taking care of him, and she made a little *moue* and asked, "How could I say no?"

The young officer hadn't been able to do anything about the conspiracy; but he hoped soon to be active again, and then a Franco-American dancer would be in the very middle of it. "Should I go elsewhere?" she asked, and Lanny replied, "That is a matter you will have to make up your own mind about. This much is certain, you may be able to render an important service to your country."

" But you know how I hate politics ! " she exclaimed.

" This isn't politics, Marceline ; this is war. Some twelve millions of our best young men are risking their lives for you and me."

" Oh, you were always like that, Lanny ; imagining that it was your duty to do something for somebody else. I'm not like that, and I never expected to get myself into such a position."

" The world right now is full of people who find themselves in positions they never expected. Be sure of this, if you know about the scheme and don't reveal it, you will be held just as responsible if it should be discovered. Make up your mind one way or the other, because it's very serious, and if your heart isn't in it you'll have a hard time."

" Could you take me with you to America ? "

" No, old dear, I couldn't. Your position is a peculiar one : under American law you have the right to choose the citizenship of your mother, but you would have to be in American territory to have that right recognized. Under both French and German law you are French because your father was. I suppose that if you could get to Sweden, the American Ambassador would have power to recognize your status ; but I doubt if he would, because you came into Germany after the war broke out and you have performed here after Germany declared war on your country. You will remember that I warned you at Juan."

" Oh, you were always warning me," said the dancer with another *moue*. " But I would have had to be a different person to take all that advice."

XII

It had been Lanny who had introduced Oskar von Herzenberg to Marceline ; he had invited father and son to a night club in Paris where she was dancing. She had taken a fancy to the handsome stern-faced Junker with the duelling scars on his left cheek. She had danced for him, and then with him, and he had proved a good partner ; he could be charming when he chose to forget his exalted social position. In those days he had had rosy cheeks and the glow of health all over him ; the dancer, recently divorced, had been looking for something to fill her empty heart, and this had appeared to be it.

Oskar joined them ; and there were no roses in his cheeks. He was deathly pale, and when he got up out of his chair he stood for a minute to see if he was going to be dizzy. His face was set for the continual endurance of pain. Lanny thought, Oh, God, how much needless suffering in this world ! He had to remind himself that Oskar hadn't in the least objected to inflicting suffering upon Poles and Frenchmen and Dutchmen and Norwegians and so on through a long list. Now that this suffering had bounced back upon himself it was a different thing.

Behind those cold blue eyes there was passion of revolt against the Nazi upstarts who had taken Germany away from its long-time Prussian possessors. By a strange turn of the wheel of fate, Oskar was now on Lanny's side, and it was up to Lanny to work out a tactful way of making Oskar trust him, without giving any hint that Lanny already knew the dread secret. Lanny had to let Oskar know that Lanny wasn't what he pretended to be, and then Oskar would let Lanny know that Oskar wasn't what *he* pretended to be. It might take more than one visit, and it mightn't work out at all ; but if it did, it might be of importance.

Lanny began by telling about his visit to Göring, and about *Der Dicke's* low state of mind. *Der Dicke* was a top Nazi, but he came of a " good " Prussian family and had been an *Armee* lieutenant in World War One, so he was a person worth consideration. His remark that Stalingrad had been the Reichswehr's Gettysburg was an acute one, which any military man would be interested to discuss ; when Lanny pointed out that the politicians of the Confederacy had insisted upon fighting the war to the bitter end, but that Lee, if he had been consulted, might have been willing to recognize the inevitable much sooner, Oskar knew that Lanny had read history and had an understanding of the present plight of the Fatherland.

The visitor said, " I want you to understand, I am in this country as an art expert. I have known Hermann for a long time and have done a lot of business with him. He is a little bit cracked on the subject of collecting paintings which he doesn't have time to look at, but he owns them."

" How on earth can you get permission from your own country to do business in wartime ? " Many persons had asked that question, and Lanny had his answer pat. " My father is a man of influence, and he had important business dealings with Göring before the war. They became friends, and now are able to arrange matters. You know how it was with the Comité des Forges people during World War One."

" I suppose I am very naïve," said the Junker. " I would not have supposed it possible that business men would have such power."

Lanny smiled most amiably. " It is like the black market ; if you operate on a small scale the police pick you up, but if it's a matter of millions, the police demand what we in American call a ' cut.' "

" You Americans have changed the world greatly," replied the other. " If you have your way, I won't know how to get along in it."

" Let me teach you," said the P.A., still smiling.

XIII

Marceline was pleased with the way her brother was getting along with her lover. They helped Oskar into the house and he lay on the couch where Lanny was to sleep that night—he could stay because his plane for Paris did not leave Berlin till mid-morning. The maid-of-all-work prepared a simple evening meal, and while they ate it Lanny told about the Reichsmarschall's sumptuous ways. He told about life in Italy, with special emphasis upon paintings, of course. He made it amusing, but he also revealed that Italy was not to be counted upon as an ally much longer. He didn't have to put this forward ; the Oberst brought it out by questioning. Several times while Lanny was strolling in the flowery fields of the Muses, Oskar dragged him back into the smoke-blackened smithy of Vulcan. The Junker wanted to hear everything that Lanny knew about the world situation, and Lanny could imagine him retailing it to his associates in the plot to get rid of the Number One usurper.

In the course of the evening Lanny thought it safe to say, " I want you to understand, Oskar, I have been a friend of Germany since boyhood, and when this present regime came in I accepted it as so many of you Germans did, because I believed what they told me. But the Germany I love and want to help is the old Germany, governed by gentlemen such as I met at Schloss Stubendorf, where I visited Kurt Meissner. I say this in confidence, of course, for if I said it openly I could not continue to come back. But strictly between you and me, I think that Göring has begun to realize that he has got into the wrong *galère*, and it is only his personal loyalty to Hitler that keeps him where he is. You would be surprised to know how many of the Reichswehr officers have dropped hints to me of the same attitude."

That was like dangling a bit of red cloth in front of a frog in a pond ; he cannot help jumping. Said Oskar, " I would be very much pleased to have you tell me who they are."

" Believe me, I would if I could, in honour," replied the P.A. with warm friendship in his tone. " Men speak to me in confidence because they know me as an art expert, not involved in political affairs. I could not name them without their consent."

He decided that matters were going a bit too fast, and this had better do for the present. He was living in a world of plots and counter-plots, and could not exclude from his mind the possibility that some chief of the Gestapo, Herr Güntelen in Rome or Herr Himmler in Berlin, might have decided to check up on this plausible American friend of the Führer. What more obvious than to call upon his half-sister's lover and instruct him to pose as being in a plot against the Führer's life to see what would be the reaction of the son of Budd-Erling to this nefarious scheme ! And, on the other hand, Oskar von Herzenberg would be turning over in his head the possibility that a rich American playboy, a friend of the great, might have taken offence because a Prussian aristocrat considered his half-sister good enough for a mistress but not good enough for a wife, and might be thinking up a scheme to lead him on and get him put out of the way ! Such things had happened.

When Oskar slept again, Lanny walked in the garden with this woman whose childhood had been a delight to him. He said, " Tell me, just how long has Oskar had this attitude toward the *Regierung* ? "

She answered, " He has always hated them in his heart because they have taken his place in the country—I mean, the place of his class. The Junkers will never give up." She went on to talk about the extraordinary human phenomenon, the Prussian officer-aristocrat, product of discipline impossible for an American to imagine. Their minds had been so drilled that it was easier for them to think of suicide than of disobedience of an order. The aim of their training had been to make them all exactly alike, in ideas as in appearance, in private life as in professional conduct. Marceline told of looking through an album containing souvenirs of her lover's cadet days, and of coming upon a circular having to do with social behaviour. Visiting hours were limited to one specified hour, week-days only. " On entering the room, carry hat in left hand. On taking a seat, lay the hat down. Length of visit should be about ten minutes. Do not look at your watch. No reason should be given for termination of visit. On leaving, do not turn your back on the company when opening the door." And so on through a long list of minutiae. White wine was to be drunk from tall glasses and red wine from short. In presenting flowers, the stalks were to be held downward. The whole being of a man so trained was absorbed in the effort to be *korrekt*, and the idea of rebelling against authority almost unhinged his mind.

Marceline promised, " I will take more interest in what he is doing and he will tell me more. If he asks about you, I will assure him he can trust you."

" You mean to stay then ? "

" Stay ? Where can I go ? "

XIV

In the good old days Lanny would have taken from dawn to midnight motoring from Berlin to Paris, and his friends would have thought he had done a remarkable stunt. Now a passenger plane carried him in less than three hours and set him down at Le Bourget airport. There was another S.S. Leutnant to meet him. The Führer's staff had done every-

thing to make matters easy for him; they had changed his
Italian money into German, French, and Spanish, and he
didn't have to have his French passport examined, nor to
expose the meagre contents of his little bag to the customs
authorities.

He was motored to the office of Denis de Bruyne *père*. He
had phoned to make sure the old man would be in town; the
secretary had undertaken to arrange it, since Lanny wouldn't
have time to drive out to the château, some distance away in
Seine-et-Oise. He didn't want to meet people and have to
explain his presence in Paris; he just wanted to keep his
promise to the younger Denis and find out how the family
was. If there was anything of significance going on in the
political world the father would know about it and would tell.

This man of money came of a distinguished family which
had fallen upon bad times and had to part with its ancestral
home. Denis had made a new start and bought the home
back. When Lanny had first met him he had owned a good
part of the taxicabs of Paris; later he had branched out into
other activities, including banking, and now was counted
among the " two hundred families " so hated by the *sans-
culottes*. Lanny's own relationship to the family, as faithful
lover of the mother up to the time of her death, was one
difficult to explain outside France, a land which has no
Reno, and whose social élite have worked out a substitute
called *la vie à trois*, dignified and decent in their eyes. Lanny
had walked side by side with the *père de famille* in the funeral
procession of Marie de Bruyne; he had been constituted a
sort of lay godfather to the boys, and had been a friend and
political confidant of the old man ever since.

Three years had passed since their last meeting; years of
trial and strain, and Lanny had half expected to learn that
Denis had gone under. But here he was, his face wizened and
looking like a mask of what it had been, his little goatee white
and somewhat wispy. He got up on trembly legs to welcome
his visitor—he was somewhere in his eighties. He asked the
usual question with the usual bewilderment. " *Nom de Dieu,
comment ?* "—how, how, how did an American manage to
visit Paris ? Lanny gave the stock explanation, the relations
between Robbie Budd and Hermann Göring, and the amazing

potency of this combination. Denis at once proceeded to make a business man's application of the matter. He was a stockholder in Budd-Erling, and there must be great sums due him. Wasn't there some way for matters to be arranged so that the money could be got into France?

Business before pleasure! Lanny described the miracles that were being wrought in Newcastle, Connecticut, and in the Middle West and the Far West. Everything was being put back into the Budd-Erling business, and Denis no doubt was becoming the owner of more stock, which would compound his interest in the end. " Take care of yourself until the war is over," Lanny said with a smile; to which the old man answered wryly, " What the Germans leave the Reds will take."

Lanny changed the subject. " I have had several meetings with Denis *fils*." The Frenchman, who adored his sons, forgot everything else and plied the guest with questions. Lanny related how he had been commissioned to purchase examples of Moorish art and had made several trips to North Africa; he had met the elder son, first in Algiers, and the last time in Bizerte. He was recuperating, he was doing his duty as he conceived it, and he had besought Lanny to obtain news of all the members of his family.

The father said he had had no word from his elder son, except in the previous year the postcards which the Germans had printed for use between Vichy France and the portions which they held. These cards contained statements such as " I am well," and a tiny square in which you made a tick to indicate that it was true. If you wrote anything else the card was thrown out and you might get a visit from the police. That system had applied to French North Africa until the Allies had taken it; now there was no communication whatever.

Lanny answered the questions, and asked those which the younger Denis would have wanted to ask. Charlot was a *capitaine* in the Légion Tricolore, maintaining order on the French Riviera, and living—of all places in the world!—in Bienvenu, Lanny's old home. He had written his father, explaining that he had picked out this place for commandeering, so that he would be able to see that it was protected.

Lanny promised that before he left Paris he would write a letter to Charlot, saying that this was good news and thanking him.

And then the two wives : they were well, and the children were well, and life in the old place was going as usual, though, of course, there was apprehension as to what might be coming later.   There were few portions of the old Continent free from that apprehension.   Denis said he didn't get out to the château very often ; business kept him in Paris.   He offered to take Lanny, but the other said his schedule did not permit it ; the truth was, he didn't want to meet those women and have to answer questions about the husbands, now on opposite sides of a war.   The women had dutifully accepted the near-Fascist views of their families in the old days ; were they divided now, and if so, how did they manage to live in the same red-brick château, direct the same kitchen—commodious but without modern conveniences—and the same garden with fruit trees trained against its walls ?

The visitor told of meeting the two sons alternately and trying to explain each to the other, but in vain.   What did the father think, and what should Lanny tell the sons about his political views ?   The old man hedged—what else could he do ?   These were terrible times ; the Führer was carrying out his publicly declared policy of seeing that every people in Europe starved before the Germans did.   He wanted to make friends of the French, but he also wanted their wine and fruit and wheat and oil, to say nothing of munitions and machinery ; when these two motives clashed, it was generally the latter which prevailed, so said the head of this wealthy and prominent family.   " It would appear that I backed the wrong horse," he admitted.   " You Americans have behaved well in North Africa, and I have no doubt you will behave equally well with us, provided there is anything left of us when you get here."

" Is that the way your friends feel, Denis ? "

" It is the way all men of property feel.   We are helpless in the hands of one army, and shall be helpless in the hands of the other when it comes.   We can only sit and wait."

It was an aged man speaking, one who had learned caution in a hard school.   He was too shrewd to accept his friend's reasons for being in Paris ; he must have guessed that Lanny was on one side or the other, and if Lanny didn't choose to say which, that was his privilege. Denis was taking care of his own ; that had been his business, also his politics, and he wasn't going to change at this late day in the midst of this paralysing confusion. If his sons, and perhaps his daughters-in-law, had got on opposite sides—well, that was part of the confusion, and one reason more for keeping quiet.

There was another subject, the most delicate in the world. The elder son had besought Lanny to bring him word about the old gentleman's " unfortunate entanglement " ; Lanny said, with as much delicacy as he could command, " The boy is very unhappy because of rumours he has heard that you are involved in a situation which may cause you trouble and at the same time endanger the family inheritance."

The elder didn't bat an eyelash. He was a Frenchman, and he knew all the plain words in his own language. " Lanny," he said, " remind my boys that I have been a widower for sixteen years and might as well have been for many years before that. I had the sense to find out what I needed. Now I am at an age where sexual satisfaction is difficult to obtain, and when I find a woman who can give it to me and is willing to take the trouble, I know what she is worth to me and I pay her accordingly. I have seldom in my life paid too much for anything, and my sons should have confidence in my business judgment. Assure them that I am not yet in my dotage."

Lanny thought that the way to take that was with a chuckle. " *Bien, cher ami,*" he said ; but he wouldn't be any more sure of Denis's story than Denis was of Lanny's.

XV

The P.A. wrote the promised letter to Charlot, saying that he hoped he was comfortable in his new home and promising to come and visit him some day. Also he wrote the Führer what the English-speaking world knows as a " bread-and-butter letter," thanking him for his hospitality and telling him that, from what a visitor had been able to gather, Frenchmen of great affairs were reasonably satisfied with the treatment they were getting from Germany, and that production was under full headway, which is what all business men like. These duties done, he took his S.S. escort on a tour of the art shops to see what the French painters were doing under the Führer's protection. Then they dined, and went to a cinema, where they saw a German picture and a French, and compared the hearty sentimentality of the former with the *crime passionnel* of the latter. " Of course, the French are what they are, and the Germans cannot change them," said Lanny in his best German.

In the morning he was put on board the plane for Madrid, and from there he sent a cablegram to his father, saying that he would arrive in Lisbon the next day and desired two days in London and then home. This message was addressed to " Robert Budd, President, Budd-Erling Aircraft Corporation, Newcastle, Connecticut "—this for the benefit of censors, Spanish, British, and American. The arrangement was that Robbie would notify Baker, also Laurel. Baker would make arrangements, and Lanny would have a seat on the next plane to England, something for which long lines of ordinary folk were waiting in vain.

The P.A. succeeded in getting a plane to Lisbon that afternoon, and he gave up his plan to call on his old friend, General Aguilar, in Madrid. The Allies were no longer afraid that Franco's Army might fall upon their left flank in North Africa ; the pudgy little martinet had seen that the wind was blowing strongly from the west, and all that F. D. R. was concerned about now was to limit the amount of tungsten that Hitler could get from Spain. The way to do that was to pay higher prices, and the bidding was terrific.

Arriving in the city by the Tagus, muddy brown like the Tiber, Lanny put up at the Avenida Palace Hotel and sent a duplicate cablegram by way of precaution. He enjoyed a bath and a good dinner—Portugal offered every luxury to those who had the price, and piteous starvation to those who hadn't. He took a stroll on the broad Avenida da Liberdade and purchased London newspapers a week old and New York papers three weeks old, but full of news for a man just out of Axisland. He read himself sleepy with them.

He had to control his impatience, for cablegrams might

be long delayed in these times. He breakfasted, and read the morning papers—Portuguese was easy if you knew Spanish, French, and Italian. He strolled in hot and languid Lisbon and resisted the efforts of spies from half a dozen lands, including even Japan, to strike up an acquaintance and worm out his secrets. After four days wasted he was just starting an effort to call Baker on the transatlantic telephone when a message was brought to his room. He had a seat reserved the next morning on a seaplane, and he went down to the harbour to inspect it and make sure that everything was O.K. When the flying boat lifted itself from the waters of the Tagus estuary, he wished the afflicted old Continent no harm, but he was glad to get away from it and thought with delight of meeting a few persons to whom he could speak the truth.

8

Pathways East and West

I

LANNY was wondering what he was going to do, arriving in Britain from enemy lands. But the all-remembering Baker had attended to that also. Lanny was relieved when he saw his friend Fordyce of B4, the British Intelligence Service, waiting for him at the dock. The Armed Forces of the two nations had become one and were working together in all departments. Fordyce shook hands with the mysterious arrival, and without customs or other formalities whisked him out of sight.

They were taking a plane to London ; and on the way to the airfield the friendly Englishman remarked, " I have news that may surprise you. You are flying to Quebec."

" Am I ? " said Lanny, surprised indeed.

" There is something going on there, rather secret, so don't say where you are bound. It is known as Operation Quadrant."

" I hope we are not taking Canada," replied Lanny.

" Our forces to oppose you left a couple of days ago," said the Englishman, returning the smile. " It will be a great fight."

" What am I supposed to do when I arrive ? "

" Baker will be at the Château Frontenac, and you are to call him there. We were told that you wanted two days in London, so I arranged for you to be flown by way of Iceland, three days from today, early in the morning. Will that be convenient ? "

" Thank you, I will make it so. There is one matter in which you might oblige me. I have a little daughter in England, thirteen years old ; she lives with her mother in Wickthorpe Castle. I have been planning to take her for a visit to my father in Connecticut. Do you suppose it would be possible to get me two passages instead of one ? I will pay for hers, of course."

The B4 man said, " There is always more traffic from America than there is returning."

" Let it rest until I phone you tomorrow," replied the other. " I have to make sure that it will be agreeable to Lady Wickthorpe."

II

The ex-husband had never failed to call up Irma and make sure that his presence at the Castle would be welcome. He had never been able to let her know when he was coming, and little Frances could never have an idea when her delightful father would descend out of the sky—quite literally in a fiery chariot, even though it was " internal combustion." She was told that he purchased paintings, but she had rarely seen any of them.

Irma said, as she always did, " Oh, good ! Come right out. Frances will be so glad." Six or seven years had passed since she and Lanny had got their divorce, and they were holding to the determination to carry it off in the modern manner, without fuss or hard feelings. Frances must know that her mother and her father were friends, and likewise her father and her stepfather. Everything in her life must be gracious and serene ; only common, low-class people ever quarrelled, or drank too much, or used bad language, and wars were fought only against peoples which did not have Anglo-Saxon standards of good manners.

Lanny took the next train out of London, just in time to miss a " tip-and-run " raid by the Luftwaffe. Göring had accumulated sufficient forces for a few such attacks, and it was important to assure the German people that the British were being paid back for what they were doing to German cities. The train was crowded, and the passengers heard the sound of the bombs while passing out of the suburbs north-west of London. Lanny was interested to observe how much as a matter of course they took the event ; few stopped the reading of their little four-page evening papers. In the compartment with Lanny was a girl of five or six, an age which meant that war was her natural environment. She looked up at her mother and asked a question which would stay in Lanny's mind for the rest of his life : " Mummy, was the bombing as bad as this in peacetime ? "

Frances was at the station with her little basket pony cart. She ran to greet him, but not too exuberantly—she was becoming a dignified young lady now, carefully repressed by a mother and a grandmother from Long Island. Nearly half a year had passed since Lanny had seen the child, and she was approaching the age where changes come quickly. She had lived on this great estate where there was never a shortage of food, and where the war had been far-off thunder or the chatter of machine-guns high up in the air. She had been taught that it was all in the order of nature and that she mustn't let it trouble her too much ; she mustn't let anything trouble her, for she was one who, in the phrase of Kipling, had " inherited that good part." She had rosy cheeks, a trim figure, dark-brown eyes and hair—she was going to be the same brunette beauty that her mother had been when, at the age of nineteen, a great heiress, she had picked the grandson of Budd Gunmakers for her mate.

A trustworthy groom, a war cripple, sat in a little high seat in the back of the basket. Frances drove, and Lanny squeezed his long legs in beside her. She bubbled over with pleasure at seeing him and, as always, plied him with questions as to where he had been and what he had done. He couldn't mention either Italy or Germany, so he told about Florida; she knew that he was married again, and he talked about his baby boy, and about the pelicans and the bright-coloured fishes and the diving for sponges; also about his visit to North Africa, and to Frances's other grandmother, whose memory must not be allowed to grow dim in the child's mind. Also, there was her little cousin, Marcel Detaze, who lived in such romantic surroundings, a palatial hotel in an oasis of the African desert, with date palms and orange groves all around it, tremendous snow-capped mountains behind it, and British and French and American soldiers, white-clad Moors, and other strange people inside it.

Frances was old enough now to have dinner with the grown-ups; she would sit quietly and only speak when she was addressed. There were two members of the " county families " who had been invited at short notice, and the little girl observed that they had come to hear what her wonderful father had to say. She did not miss a word, because she had been taught that ladies of the English ruling class took an important part in public affairs; she might some day find herself the wife of a cabinet minister, or even of a prime minister.

She did not hear anything about Operation Quadrant, now getting under way in Quebec, but she heard about Operation Husky, now nearing completion at the north-eastern corner of Sicily. It would be only a few days before the last of the enemy had been driven across the narrow Strait of Messina—they could go in rowboats if necessary. Everybody wanted to know if the Allies would follow them to the mainland, and how far they would go. Englishmen who had to stay at home naturally wondered how an American art expert could carry on his business in war-torn lands, and they would have been stupid indeed if they had not guessed that he had some sort of mission. Being well-bred and well-instructed, they wouldn't hint at such an idea.

Lanny, for his part, was interested to observe how the Wickthorpe set, once so militant, had been tamed by events; they still disliked Jews, and were still certain that some day we should need the help of the capable and vigorous Germans in putting down the Reds; but they confined their peace talk to criticism of the unconditional surrender formula, and confessed sadly that nobody paid any attention to their wishes. Lanny was amused by the thought of what a sensation he could have caused by telling them that he had just come from Hitler. He had promised Hitler to tell them ; but he wasn't keeping promises to Hitler.

III

In the morning the visitor was taken for a tour of the estate, at least the parts that were nearest. Every square foot that could be spared was growing food of some sort, and everything was in the full green of midsummer ; Ceddy, the host, boasted that this one-time show-place was now almost paying its way. He meant before taxes, of course ; he couldn't possibly have kept it together if it hadn't been for Irma's fortune. The Castle itself, dating from Elizabethan days, had outlasted many wars, and inside it had all been made over, both elegant and comfortable. Irma, loving her role of great lady, saw to it that everything was kept in order, even with none but old people for servants.

The fourteenth Earl of Wickthorpe was about Lanny's age, but showed his years more ; his blond hair was beginning to be scarce on top and his closely trimmed golden moustache had traces of grey. He worried a great deal about the war, and still more about what was going to happen after it. A country gentleman, he hated and feared industrialism even while he enjoyed its products and the income his wife derived from the street railways of the Middle West. Lanny had the idea that Ceddy would have liked it better if the work of the world could be done by bands of well-trained chimpanzees instead of the slum denizens who, his Lordship was convinced, were planning to rise and take possession of England when this war was over.

Nothing to be done about it ; so cultivate your acres, and let your wife reinvest her income in America, and train your sons and heirs to make the best of whatever might come to them. Lanny renewed his acquaintance with a sturdy rosy-cheeked youngster aged five who bore the title of Viscount and the name of James Ponsonby Cavendish Cedric Barnes Masterson. He was called Jimmy, and his brother, two years younger, the Honourable Gerald Cedric Barnes Masterson, was called Jerry. Also, Lanny would not fail to pay a courtesy call on the redoubtable Mrs. Fanny Barnes, his ex-mother-in-law, who was just as glad to see him as if he had been a tarantula, but who was compelled by circumstances to pretend to admire him ; also on her brother, " Uncle Horace," who had two ideas about the visitor, that he might be lured into playing a game of contract, and that he might take some tips on the stock market and let the tipster in on a share of his winnings—but not of his losses.

But mother and daughter knew what Lanny had in mind, for he had talked it over with Irma the last time. Fanny had been doing her best to make Irma promise to say no, but Irma wasn't in position to say it, and Fanny had consulted a lawyer and made certain that no British court would refuse to recognize a father's right to partial custody of his child. Irma had had the child all the time since the divorce, and now surely the father could claim his turn. And besides, it mustn't be allowed to get into the courts ; they were friends, and Lanny's arguments must be met fairly.

IV

The pair had their conference in the library of the Castle, while the grandmother sat chafing in her little cottage, for Frances was her chief happiness in life, and she said it was like waiting to be told that she was to have her eyes cut out. Lanny was explaining to his ex-wife the danger which hung over the English people. " I cannot tell you how I know ; you must take my word that I do. Hitler is speaking the truth when he says he has a new weapon ; whether he is right in the idea that it will give him victory I can't say, but I know that he believes it and is turning a great part of German science and industry to perfecting and producing this weapon."

" How soon will these things be ready, Lanny ? "

" That I cannot tell. There is no secret more carefully guarded. It might be a month and it might be half a year. We can be sure only that these flying bombs will come in showers, perhaps by the hundreds, and they will continue to come until we land and capture that French coast. They may even be improved so that they can come from Belgium or Holland."

" They will be aimed at London ? "

" That is the biggest target ; but no one can be sure how accurate they will be. Who can guess how wind and weather may divert them ? I am told that before the German scientists get through, they will have a bomb that flies faster than sound ; then there will be no warning whatever, only a terrific explosion."

Irma sat staring at this man to whom she had once been so close, and who was now a man of mystery to her. What did he really believe ? What did he want now ? And could he be trusted to keep his word ? She had lain awake long hours, thinking about this, and had built several lines of defence. One of them was, " The children could be taken to Scotland, Lanny."

" Yes, but how many people will be fleeing to Scotland, and what will be the conditions there ? You have a right to subject your own children to such risks, but you must remember that Frances is only half yours, and I am asking the right to take better care of my half."

He went on to tell of his talk with Robbie and Robbie's wife ; how eager they were to have the child, and what a happy environment they would provide for her. She would go to school with her half-dozen American cousins and have a life free from fear. When Irma mentioned her special phobia, American kidnappers, Lanny grinned and said they were all in Sicily now, kidnapping Germans and Italians to their hearts' content. " Surely you don't expect Frances to be an entirely English child ; surely you know that she is really American, and that her American relatives have a right to know her."

There was no answering these arguments, and Irma fell back upon her own unhappiness and that of her mother. Lanny answered that this wasn't fair ; it was putting pressure on both him and the child. Of course, Frances wouldn't want to go if it would make her mother miserable ; she wouldn't enjoy the visit unless she could take it as a holiday. She would write a letter once a week and have plenty of news to tell. If she was given a fair chance to be contented, and then wasn't, Lanny would agree to bring her back on his next trip.

"You will swear to do that, Lanny?" Irma had tears in her eyes, something he had rarely seen, for she was a proud and self-contained woman.

"I will give you my word of honour," he answered gravely. "That is better than swearing. I want the child's happiness, and I would like her to think of this as a wonderful adventure, and without any idea of anxiety."

V

Lanny phoned his friend Fordyce that the deal was on, and he came up to London and got the child a passport at the American Embassy. Under American law Frances was an American because her father was, and the fact that she had been born in France and had lived most of her life in England made no difference. Since she was going by way of Canada, there had to be a Canadian visa. How long would it be before the world returned to the blessed state it had known prior to 1914, when it was possible to travel all over the world without filling out blanks and standing in line and paying sums large or small to have stamps put on documents?

The newspapers that morning broke out with the tidings that Winston Churchill, who had been travelling between Hyde Park and Washington, was on his way to Quebec. Roosevelt was coming, and there was to be a full-dress military conference. So the secret of Operation Quadrant was dead before it was born, so to speak; Lanny chuckled when he mentioned the matter to Fordyce. The "brass" had fondly imagined they could repeat what they had done in Casablanca, where the population had been kept guessing as to who was hidden behind the barbed wire surrounding the Hotel Anfa and its cottages. But it just couldn't be done in the capital of a Canadian province, so close to the border of America with its ten thousand newspapers and its "sleuths" hungry for tips and skilled at hinting secrets. No, there would be the usual fanfare, and the cameramen would have their half-hour's free-for-all, taking close-ups and angle shots, and telling presidents and premiers and admirals and generals where to sit or stand and how to look pleasant.

"But," said the B4 man, "just you try to get by that

double cordon of guards and find out what they are saying inside ! "

Lanny would have liked to say, " I'll make you a wager," but that wouldn't have been cricket. Instead, he explained, " This makes a difference in my plans, because it makes the word Quebec taboo. I can't tell Lady Wickthorpe I am going there, and I don't want to tell even my relatives. Is there any way I could fly on to Montreal and then come back alone to Quebec ? I would have my father send someone to meet the child in Montreal."

The B4 man said that could be easily arranged. It was possible that he got some pleasure out of playing the role of omnipotence. Anyhow, he was friendly in his quiet English way ; he didn't know where this American art expert had been and he scrupulously avoided any approach to the subject. It was enough that the son of Budd-Erling was helping to put down the Hun, and that the President of the United States wanted to see him quickly.

Lanny cabled his father to have Cousin Jennie or some other trustworthy lady motored to a hotel in Montreal, to bring Frances to Newcastle. He telephoned Irma about this, explaining that Cousin Jennie was an elderly spinster of the Budd tribe whom Irma had met on her honeymoon with Lanny but would hardly remember. She had come to Halifax in the spring of 1941 to read to Lanny while he lay in hospital with both legs broken. She was the most conscientious lady imaginable, and the child would have a motor trip through scenery not so different from that of Scotland. Irma could find no fault with any of these arrangements.

VI

One more duty and pleasure the P.A. had in London, a meeting with his friend Rick. For years now these meetings had taken place in an obscure hotel, for Rick was a Socialist writer, and Lanny was supposed to be a near-Fascist and had to be choosy about his company. Lanny would phone and say, " This is Bienvenu," and Rick would say, " Will sixteen hundred be O.K. ? " They would take off their coats and stretch out on the bed ; Rick would remove the steel brace

which supported the knee he had got smashed in the First
World War. Thus made comfortable, they would settle the
outcome of the present war and the destiny of the world for
years to come.

Just thirty years had passed since Lanny Budd had made
a friendship with Eric Vivian Pomeroy-Nielson and Kurt
Meissner at the Dalcroze School in Hellerau ; and what a lot
of world history they had seen since then ! The fates had
divided them, and Rick remarked, " I wonder what has
happened to Kurt." Lanny replied, " I heard a report that
he had been injured by a bomb and cannot play any more.
Poor fellow ! " Rick countered, " Poor fool ! " for he had
lived closer to Germany than Lanny and couldn't afford as
much tolerance.

These two agreed in all their political ideas and hopes.
Rick was working as hard as he knew how to build that movement of social protest which his neighbour the Earl of Wickthorpe so greatly dreaded. He had written several plays
designed to undermine the prestige of the British privileged
class, and he had written hundreds of articles and letters in
support of the labouring masses. He had met many disappointments, but insisted that now the mind of Britain was really
changing, and when this war was over it was going to be shown
at the polls. Lanny told what Ceddy had just said on this
subject, and remarked with a smile, " God must be puzzled
to have two English gentlemen offering him such different
prayers."

" Count me out of the list of gentlemen," responded the
other. " I am a Left-Wing journalist, very poorly paid."

" What are you going to do, renounce the title ? " inquired
Lanny. This question was in order, for Rick's father, the
baronet, was in failing health and not likely to last much longer.

" I'm not sure," said the son. " I'll ask the party. They
talk of having me stand for Parliament."

" Hurrah ! " exclaimed Lanny. " I'm wagering they'll tell
you to become Sir Eric. It will get you a lot of votes by
mistake, and it won't lose you many by intention."

Lanny joked, but at the same time he was stirred by the
idea that his friend from boyhood might obtain power to carry
out his ideas. What a different England it would be if men

of social vision had a chance not merely to speak but to legislate, and to abolish from that ancient land not merely the old aristocratic privileges, but the newer privileges of economic royalism. Roosevelt had coined that phrase, and how the economic royalists hated him for it—some enough to talk about killing him ! They would hate Sir Eric in the same way, and call him a traitor to his class ; but that wouldn't worry him, because he had had it all his thinking life. He would quote from a public platform the lines of the English poet Mackay, answering the man who boasted of having no enemies :

> You've hit no traitor on the hip,
> You've dashed no cup from perjured lip,
> You've never turned the wrong to right,
> You've been a coward in the fight.

VII

Lanny didn't go back to Wickthorpe to witness the shedding of tears ; the little girl was brought to town by her music teacher. Two light bags held all the possessions she would take ; the rest of her clothing would be given away because she was growing so fast. Her eyes still showed traces of red when she met her father, but even so she was agog with excitement ; she was going to have her first plane flight—oh, wonderful ! " Do you feel it when you first go up, Father ? " and " Can you see out of the windows ? " and " Will there be any Germans ? " and so on.

They were taking a night express to the town of Prestwick on the west coast of Scotland, which had become in a short time one of the great airports of the world. From there they stepped into a large comfortable plane. Its engines had been " revving " for some time, and when the passengers were safely strapped in, it moved onto a concrete strip, then put on speed and rose, so gently that Frances wouldn't have known it had she not been looking out. She could look all she pleased, and see planes in the air and little fishing boats on the water, but no Germans.

On board were military men and others, very important with large leather brief-cases ; good-looking young airmen in the blue uniforms of " Pan-Am," and a very agreeable young stewardess on whom Frances immediately developed a " crush." Poor little rich girl, she had spent most of her life inside a great estate, and while she was supposed to have " everything " there, she had had little freedom, and the experience of meeting new sorts of people and saying what she pleased to them was all but unbelievable. From now on she would be plain Frances Barnes Budd and not " your little ladyship " ; nobody would know that she was a great heiress, forbidden to walk on a street alone for fear of kidnappers.

They were flying into a region where the sun set only for a couple of hours, and not that long if you were high in the air. Their first stop was Iceland, which seemed misnamed, for in August the ice was away back in the glaciers, and they saw only barren rocks, and steam now and then from what the stewardess said were boiling springs. They came down near the harbour of a small clean city, and paused only for new fuel and to exchange a few sacks of mail. This time, because the weather was reported good, they were not going to Greenland, but straight on to Newfoundland. Lanny had a weak feeling in his stomach, for it was somewhere over this cold sea that he had crashed and got his two legs broken. Frances knew about it, but he told no details, for she was supposed to have left fear behind on the tight little island of Britain.

They slept peacefully during most of the eight-hour trip. Then they had breakfast, and watched the plane descend at an airport by a long lake called Gander, in Newfoundland. How amazingly it had grown since Lanny had last seen it ! It now had ten million square feet of concrete runways, and the only trouble was the wild moose that insisted upon walking on them.

The plane rose, and flew over the large wooded island, while Lanny told his daughter about the man who had refused to get into the plane with him two years and a half ago, because the man had had a premonitory dream about an accident ; he had disappeared into these woods, and Lanny wondered what had become of him. Lanny was not permitted to tell Frances about his unorthodox views on politics and economics, but he could tell her about psychic phenomena and the strange things that happened, of which he hoped some day to learn the meaning. Perhaps when she grew up she would help him.

VIII

They came to the great city of Montreal, on an island in the St. Lawrence ; and there at the Ritz-Carlton Hotel was the tall thin New England spinster, old-fashioned English in her manners and ideas ; her features had many wrinkles, but they were wrinkles of benevolence. She was pleased with this lovely child, and kissed her warmly, thinking that she must be homesick and shy in a strange land ; but Frances wasn't like that, she was observant of a new world and interested in everything it had to show her. Her father had to go about some of his picture-buying affairs, so she was going to ride to Newcastle with this nice old lady, and there meet her grandfather and her step-grandmother—or would it be grand-stepmother ? There would be a lot of cousins and uncles and aunts, great-uncles and great-aunts, and it sounded " topping."

Lanny saw them off in the car, and then called his wife in New York to tell her that he was safe and well and ask how she and the baby were. He said that he had business in Canada which might detain him a couple of days ; he would keep her informed. He said " I love you " several times, and only after performing this marital duty did he ask her to call Robbie and inform him that Frances and Cousin Jennie were on their way to Newcastle. " We'll go up and see them," he said, and then hastened to ask more questions about Baby Lanny, for never must the idea start up in Laurel's mind that he might be more interested in his first child than in his second.

Arrangements at the airport had been made, and Lanny just had time to acquire a bundle of newspapers. What marvellous things, those Montreal and New York papers, with such a generous spread and a seemingly unlimited number of pages, with all the news of all the world ! Lanny, in flight to Quebec, read that the Allies were closing in on Messina, and that the Americans had bombed Rome a second time, including the airport from which Lanny had taken off. They had bombed Milan and Turin, Genoa and Berlin, all in the same day. How Adi must have raved !

IX

Of more immediate concern was the account in the local papers of the opening of the Quebec Conference. Since the conferees could not keep it secret they had apparently decided to go the whole hog and make it a demonstration. Churchill had arrived by special train at the Wolfe's Cove Station—where the British general had landed his army for the famous battle nearly two hundred years ago. Roosevelt had arrived in another train, and they had formed a motor cavalcade up the winding road which leads to the Plains of Abraham, some three hundred feet above the river, along which the greater part of the city is situated. There had been a public parade, led by the red-coated band of the Royal Mounted Police, past the old battlements and moats to the Citadel, the summer home of the Governor-General.

The two chiefs were to be housed here, in comfort of an old-fashioned sort—with only one bathroom to each corridor. There on the " deck " they had sat, with chiefs-of-staff and marshals and admirals and generals standing in a row behind them, and let the photographers do their worst ; there was a full-page spread, including the Prime Minister of Canada and the Governor-General, and all the big " brass " whose faces had become familiar to the Allied world.

And after that, silence ! Roosevelt, Churchill, and King were, as Churchill's secretary said, " three oysters." The hundred and fifty newspaper-men who were housed at the Hotel Clarendon had nothing to do but bite their fingernails and make up " think pieces " with scattered bits of local colour. The military men were established in the immense Château Frontenac, for which the Canadian government was paying the Canadian Pacific Railroad the sum of ten thousand dollars per day. The place was so crowded that colonels were sleeping two to a bed. The space between the Château and the Citadel was protected by a double line of guards, and you had to show your pass to each line.

At the airport Lanny got the President's man on the phone and was told to call back in an hour. That gave him time to be driven into town in an old-fashioned horse-drawn *calèche*, all that he could find. He was in no hurry, and was interested to look about and enjoy the bracing cool air—what a contrast with the climate of Rome ! A great modern city had spread over this plateau, and below it was the usual " Old Town," with crooked narrow streets ; here everybody spoke a French patois, amusing to Lanny ; one of the shop clerks said to him admiringly, " Oh, you speak *French* French ! "

Lanny telephoned at the time set and was told that a room had been reserved for him at one of the smaller hotels ; his name was " Harrison," the same which he had taken when he had set out from Newfoundland and had been wrecked on the way. " Meet me in front of the hotel at nine this evening," Baker said.

Lanny found the hotel, had a bath, and got his clothes pressed. He had time to go out and buy a few necessities, and then come back and have dinner and read the evening paper, full of gossip about the personalities at the Conference and guesses about what they were planning. Then he went for a stroll ; the sun sets late in this northern climate, and he surveyed the monuments and show-places of an historic city. The public square is called the Place d'Armes, but what really dominates the scene is the great hotel, built in imitation of a French château, grim and grey, with numerous sharp-pointed turrets. It is taller than any château ever seen in *la patrie*— this because it had *ascenseurs*, possible only in a machine age.

X

Lanny's walk took him past the Clarendon, haunt of the newspaper-men. He didn't think anyone there would recognize him ; but forth from the entrance burst a large middle-aged gentleman in a major's uniform, and upon his round amiable face appeared a beaming smile. " Well, of all people ! What on earth are you doing here ? "

" Pretty much what you are doing, I venture," was the response, and Major James Stotzlmann linked his arm in Lanny's and walked off with him, out of sight and out of mind of the gossip hunters.

" I was with the Boss yesterday," he said, lowering his voice. " He is enjoying this show, but it won't give him much rest."

" I'm supposed to see him this evening," Lanny replied. " I'll try not to keep him too long."

" He will tell you what's going on, no doubt. We are hoping Winston Churchill will agree to the landing across the Channel."

" Good Lord ! Is he still holding out against that ? "

" Winnie is a bulldog and never gives up. He argues, what is the good of winning the war if it leaves Stalin in the Balkans ? The Boss, of course, wants to make friends with Stalin."

" That's the difference between the two of them," commented Lanny. " I watched them in a polite battle at the White House. The First Lady helped her side."

" Eleanor is true blue ; she ought to be here now. But the Boss has most of our 'top brass' behind him, and I think he'll win."

The pair strolled on, exchanging opinions for which a baffled press would have paid large sums of money, but they weren't for sale. Jim Stotzlmann was by way of being a millionaire, and the son of Budd-Erling had all the money he would ever want in this world. Jim said, " I am here on security work, and that pleases me, because the Boss needs it. This time I could bring him proof."

" You mean there are people here in Canada who might do him harm ? "

" Anybody can come into Canada, with or without papers. It only needs a small skiff to cross the St. Lawrence."

A sudden idea struck Lanny Budd. " Look, Jim," he said, " you know all about what's going on in the matter of F. D. R.'s safety."

" I know enough to stir up quite a fuss if I were free to tell it."

" I have a plan, something that might be very important if the Boss will agree. I might talk to you after I see him."

" I'm at the Clarendon. There are a couple of mavericks among the newspaper-men, fellows who will bear a bit of watching."

" Maybe I'll call you up. It depends upon what the Boss says. Make note that I'm going under the name of Harrison. Don't speak my real name."

" I'm going under the name of Mum," said the heir of the Chicago Stotzlmanns.

XI

Promptly on the stroke of nine Lanny walked past his hotel and stepped into a car which halted for him. Baker said, " Glad to see you," and then, " The Chief has made an agreement with his opposite number that they won't work late at night, but the agreement may not be kept. You may have to wait a while."

" That's all right," replied the other. " I have plenty to think about." That was especially true at the moment, because the meeting with the other P.A. had started a train of ideas in Lanny's mind. He would have been glad to have all night to follow it up.

They parked near the Citadel, and he was expecting red tape with the guards, well-trained soldiers who were fully armed and were pacing conspicuously in two rows, not far from each other. Signs gave warning to intruders ; but evidently Baker had arranged matters in advance, for at the first guard-house by the drive all he had to say was " Baker and Harrison," and at the second guard-house it was the same ; they walked on into the ancient grey-stone fortress, through chain gates that were famous examples of the ironwright's art.

At the desk Baker signed his name and also " Harrison " and they went into a gold-and-ivory reception room where Lanny was left in the company of several military gentry loaded with gold lace ; they manifested no desire to converse, and the P.A. took a seat and closed his eyes, leaving them to assume that he might be dozing. What he did was to think as hard as he knew how about what he was going to say to the busiest man in the world. He had the habit of going over things in his mind until he knew his speeches almost by heart ; but the trouble was, the genial Franklin might have plans of his own and lead the conversation into regions not mapped in Lanny's geography book.

At last Baker came and gave Lanny a nod ; he led the way to another gold-and-ivory room, a large one on the upper floor, looking out on the court. Every room had a name, and this one, the Governor-General's, was " Frontenac." Propped up in a big bed was the man whom Lanny served, and he greeted his servitor with, " Hello, how's my Boy Scout ? "

Lanny was pleased, as any man of forty-three going on forty-four would be to be taken for a boy. " Sitting on top of the world, Governor," he answered. " I believe this second bombing of Rome ought to do the business for us."

" Sit down and tell me," commanded the Governor, " what is the matter with this guy Badoglio ? "

Lanny took a chair by the bedside and did his best to explain a very old gentleman who had believed in his Pope and his King since early childhood and was extremely jealous of his own glory as defender of these potentates. " Italy " meant that to him, and " honour " meant the same. He wanted to use modern weapons to take the world back to the twelfth century, when the Faith had really ruled. " I've no doubt he believes literally in the Devil, and the reason he hesitates so long is that he cannot make up his mind whether the Devil is Hitler or you."

F. D. R. gave one of his chuckles. " Just now the Devil is saying ' unconditional surrender.' "

Lanny looked serious. " I know that's your formula, Governor. I have thought about it a lot ; it was a good formula for Mussolini, but not so good for Badoglio. The Latin peoples set much store by their *amour-propre*, and it's no good humiliating them unnecessarily."

" Well," said the other, still grinning, " we're perfectly willing to specify the conditions for unconditional surrender. We've just been given to understand that we may get such a request through the Vatican."

" It won't do much good for me to say anything about the Vatican, because you will attribute it to prejudice ; but I ought to say it."

" Shoot ! "

" The Vatican is the world's biggest gossip centre. It is full of agents from all over, and it's impossible to keep any secret there for twenty-four hours. The first essential with Badoglio is secrecy, for the reason that he's in the hands of the Germans and so is his royal family. If any of them are to be of use to us, we'd have to get them out alive. So I say a double-nix on the Vatican."

" Would you like to go and do the negotiating, Lanny ? "

" I can't see myself as a diplomat, but you know I'll go for you wherever you say and do my best. I came home because I thought I ought to get up-to-date orders. It took me nearly two weeks to get here, because I had to come by way of Germany. I met Hitler and Göring."

" You don't tell me ! Begin with them ! "

So Lanny told about his evening at Berchtesgaden and his luncheon at the Residenz. He described *Die Nummer Eins* and *Die Nummer Zwei*, their mental and physical condition, their growing fears and their declining hopes. F. D. R. always enjoyed a good story, and this apparently was one. When the narrator came to his half-sister and her lover, the other said, " We have got some hints of that plot from the O.S.S. We can't have anything to do with it, at least not directly."

" The Reichswehr officers won't need weapons from us. But they will want what Badoglio wants—information as to what our attitude is going to be if they pull it off."

" It will be the same as it was in North Africa and will be in Italy. We will sign an armistice with anybody who has power to stop the fighting, and we will specify the conditions of unconditional surrender. Then the people will decide what sort of government they want."

" You mean immediately after the war's end ? "

" Of course not. The country will be demoralized and industry will be in chaos. We shall have to feed the starving, and get things going again, and let public opinion have a chance to form. Then there will be democratic elections, and if the people want to be governed by their Army officers, it's all right with us—only we'll see that they are kept disarmed."

" God grant that we don't go to sleep again ! " exclaimed the pious P.A.

XII

They came back to the subject of Italy. Lanny was required to tell the story of what he had seen and to describe the various personalities he had met ; he told about his talks in drawing-rooms and at the golf club, and also with people on the streets. Hatred of the Germans was universal, and also hatred of Mussolini. Lanny described the scenes on that hot Sunday night when the news was given out that Il Duce was in prison. Lanny said, " That dirty dog," and Roosevelt agreed that that was the right phrase.

Then the P.A. told about his trip into the mountains and his talk with the son of Matteotti. The President said, " We shall get help to them, and soon. I don't mind telling you that the decision has been taken, we are going over to the mainland as soon as the landing craft can be assembled. It is my hope that we can be in Naples within a month."

" Oh, good ! " responded the P.A. " It will mean that thousands will take to the hills and become guerrillas."

" I hope they won't be too greatly disillusioned if we make a deal with Badoglio. I could not turn Italy over to the Partisans even if I wanted to. Congress would not let me and public opinion would not support me. What Matteotti and his friends will have to do is to come down from the hills and educate the people, showing them how to get the landlords and the economic royalists off their backs."

" That is what I told him, Governor, so there's no mis-understanding about that."

" Free speech and honest democratic elections—that is the programme for all Europe ; that is the thing we have to give them, more important even than food. And meantime, while our boys are fighting, we will take the help of anybody who comes forward. If the old Marshal and his King will turn against the Germans, surely we can't say no."

" The problem is, they will ask for the status of allies. That would give them equality with the French, and I suppose absolve them from having to pay reparations."

" I doubt if what they can pay will amount to a hill of beans. We'll be feeding them, not taxing them. And we ought to assure them that neither France nor Britain will take any of their territory. Can you wait here a day or two, Lanny, and let me have a chance to consult about the matter ? "

The reply was, " Of course, Governor ; I am here to get orders."

XIII

It was time for the caller to depart and let this tired man have some sleep. But he made the mistake of remarking, " I ran into Jim Stotzlmann today," and that started the Boss talking. He loved his friends, and the longer he had known them the more he thought of them—unless they had proved false. Jim's mother had been a friend of the Roosevelt family before Franklin was born, and Jim was the dearest fellow, warm-hearted, loyal, and not so erratic as he seemed. His ghastly experiences in the First World War had broken his nerve and made him restless—he couldn't be happy to stay in the same place very long at a time—but as errand boy and collector of inside stories he was tops. Lanny mentioned the party at Evalyn McLean's, and the President said, " That incredible woman ! I wonder if she has any idea what an influence she is."

The P.A. thought that he might as well get the subject off his mind, so he put in, " Meeting with Jim brought me an idea. If I'm going back to Italy, I have the problem of getting in. Being set down by a seaplane is dangerous, and if I show up there a second time without any explanation, the Germans are bound to become suspicious. I ought to protect my friendship with Hitler and Göring because it might prove important. Göring might develop into another Darlan, or Hitler himself might begin to weaken—assuming that he isn't bumped off."

" By all means, Lanny, keep up the connection."

" Well then, I ought to go into Italy by way of Germany, and with Hitler's approval. I can go to Madrid or Stockholm any time and get word to him. The only problem is, I have to bring him something, in the currency he values ; that is, information he can use. And it has to be something true, otherwise I have swindled him."

" What's on your mind, old man ? "

" Hitler is just as fascinated by the idea of having you bumped off as you are by the reverse. I have been feeding it to him, but without anything definite to show him ; I simply can't go again without some new development. And when I met Jim, it flashed over me. Jim insists that he has uncovered a conspiracy of some V.I.P.'s against you——"

" Some V.G.D.I.P.'s I'd say, Lanny, if you know the phrase. But Jim is more alarmed about the situation than I am. There is a lot of that wild talk going on in different parts of the country. The Westchester train that brings the Wall Street men into the city in the morning is known as ' the Assassination Special.' "

" Jim insists that these are men of action. He insists that military men are in it, and if they carried you off from Hyde Park and had you in their power they could issue manifestos in your name and have the country helpless."

" They don't know me, Lanny ; our big-money men are men so drunk with their own importance that they can't see anything else as it really is."

" Whether it's so or whether it isn't makes no difference so far as concerns my plan. Jim can make a report about it, and the more lurid he paints the situation, the better."

" He has already made two or three reports, and the colour has deepened each time."

" All right then ; that will save bother. Let us assume that you have the reports copied on official paper, with your letterhead and so on. You write a note to the Chief of Staff, or to Admiral Leahy, or somebody, calling attention to this dangerous situation ; the documents are marked ' top secret,' and I take them to Hitler and tell him I paid a clerk a thousand dollars or two to have them stolen. I believe he would swallow that, and it would let him know I'm a top-notch agent."

The President sat with his brows wrinkled in thought. " I can't see how that could do harm," he said at last. " But wouldn't the fact that the plot is known to me tend to reduce its value to him ? "

" You might have Jim prepare a new report, one that would be still hotter ; I might take the original to Hitler and say that it had never reached you. There is this further possibility : I might drop a hint to Hitler that his own agents in this country should take the matter up with the plotters. It is possible that he might give me the name of one of them. He gave me a contact in the days before Pearl Harbour ; later I gave the name to General Donovan and learned that the fellow was safely locked up."

" Let it ride, Lanny, until I have a chance to think it over. Meantime, don't mention it to anyone."

" I'll never do that, Governor. Nobody knows that I have been in Germany except the O.S.S. people, and Ambassador Johnson in Stockholm where I came out the time before last."

" One person more, Lanny. I want you to talk with Harry Hopkins. Tell him the whole story, both Italy and Germany. He will probably be the one to make the decisions."

XIV

Lanny went back to his hotel with his head buzzing and lay awake for an hour or two, thinking up wild things that Major James Stotzlmann could put into a report to the President of the United States on the subject of a plot to kidnap and replace him. The beauty of it was that it didn't have to be true ; anything would go, however preposterous. Jim could bring in all the prominent Roosevelt haters. Adi would get his greatest thrill since he had stood at the tomb of Napoleon in conquered Paris. Adi would come up certain that the glorious days of January 1933, when National Socialism had romped into power in Germany, were about to repeat themselves in the land of Judeo-pluto-democracy overseas !

In the morning Lanny called up his millionaire friend and they went for a walk in the country back of Quebec. Such marvellous country, where the vegetation had only three or four months every year in which to grow, and made up for it by growing sixteen hours a day. They saw red clover standing as high as their shoulders, and they were both tall men ; the scent of it was intoxicating. But presently they forgot it, for Lanny brought up the subject of the " junta," as Jim called it. Jim was tormented with worries about it, and not at all content with the measures F. D. R. had taken in removing some of the evil men to remote posts in the Far West. In these days of flying, conspirators could get together in a few hours—see how Franco had managed it when he had been exiled to the Canary Islands !

" Right now they are quiet," Jim said. " Darlan in North Africa wasn't so bad for them, and Peyrouton isn't, and maybe Badoglio and the King in Italy won't be. But wait till the war's over, and the countries of Europe vote Red or Pink, as they're sure to do, and the Boss stands by them, as I know he will. Then you'll see these big fellows foaming at the mouth, and that's the time they will act. We'll discover then that American Fascism is more deadly than either Italian or

German, because our masters have more money, and believe more in money power, and are more used to having their own way in all things."

The Major needed no encouragement to pour out the story in greater detail. He had been with the son of one of these economic royalists when the son had got drunk and had boasted that the country would soon be rid of that So-and-so in the White House. Jim, expressing incredulity, had stung the young fellow into boastfulness, and he had revealed the plot and all the persons concerned in it. Since that time Jim had been working at his own expense with dictaphones and telephone tapping, and had a record of conversations which would have sufficed to send several prominent persons to the gallows for treason—if F. D. R. had been willing to move against them. But the Boss was easy-going, and talked about " hot air," and the right of his enemies to shoot off their mouths, and the danger of splitting the country and giving encouragement to the enemy by taking such shooting too seriously. He would move quietly against the dissidents who were in government service, and they would take the hint that they were being watched and would pipe down.

Lanny listened and made note of details which he might use in his little private conspiracy. He told his anxious friend, " You are right that we are coming to rough times. What will save us, I hope, is our democratic tradition. You and I and others must do what we can to keep it alive."

But the scion of the Chicago Stotzlmanns was not to be comforted so easily. " What chance does the democratic tradition stand when its enemies control ninety per cent of the press and the radio and the money—plus all of the weapons ? I tell you, there are fellows who could take over the government of this country in twenty-four hours if ever they get mad enough to try it. And believe me, they're going to get madder every hour in the economic crisis that will come after this war."

XV

In the evening Baker took the P.A. to the Citadel again, and he spent an hour in the room called Madeleine de Verchères, in the company of " Harry the Hop." The President's friend lay on a Georgian period bed, clad in a dressing gown which did not suffice to conceal the emaciation of his frame. Seven months had passed since Lanny had met him in Marrakech, just after the Casablanca Conference, and he looked more than ever like a death's head ; nearly all his stomach had been cut out on account of cancer, and he could hardly assimilate any food. But what a spirit blazed in that sickness-racked body, and what a brain informed it ! Lanny's greatest pleasure in life was to talk to a man like this, who really knew the facts and got instantly the significance of what was said to him.

The P.A. told the story of Rome, omitting no important detail. Harry said, " Just as in the case of France, the first aim is to get the fleet out of reach of the Germans. We have a brother of the commanding admiral in our country, and this brother has written urging him to come over to us ; we are trying to get the letter to the admiral, and if other efforts fail it might be a job for you."

" I'd be glad to try, of course," answered Lanny, " but it would be a difficult assignment. I was searched twice, from the top of my head to the soles of my feet, and my belongings were searched twice every week, apparently on a schedule."

" Only the Germans would have worked that way," replied the other with a smile. " The next thing is to get Badoglio and the royal family into our camp. So long as the Germans have them, they have to speak German, but if we get them, they can speak American. A large percentage of the Italians still listen to them."

Lanny told about his trip into the mountains and his talk with the young Matteotti. " A lot of Italians would listen to him too."

" I know," said Harry, " but all those persons are with us anyway, and have to be. What we want at the moment are those who have power and who could use it for either side. Be sure, the Boss means to see the common people win out in the end ; but the first job is to save every American life we can. We'd never be able to sleep nights if we were failing to do that."

Lanny told about Berchtesgaden, and then about the fat boy in the Residenz, and then about the plot to take Hitler's

life.   That meant answering many questions about the
characters of a night-club dancer and her Junker lover. " You
and I never dreamed we'd get tied up in things like this,"
remarked the harness-maker's son from Iowa. " I made
myself into a social worker, doing what I could to save lives,
and now here I am, scheming to kill people, wholesale and
retail." He added, " You'd better leave that Hitler thing to
the Germans. It's loaded, and you're too valuable to be
wasted."

" Thanks," was the reply, " but you know how it is—if
someone told you that you were valuable and ought to get
more sleep, you wouldn't take the advice."

This was preliminary to an offer to depart, but Harry
wouldn't have it. He was a sociable fellow and fond of his
friends ; and besides, the Boss had given him a hint regarding
the Stotzlmann matter, and he had to hear all of that. He
had one of those steel-trap minds that don't take long to
make decisions. " That strikes me as a bully idea," he
declared. " It can't hurt our leading S.O.B.'s to tell tales
about them to Hitler, and anyhow, I wouldn't care if it did.
I don't see why we shouldn't provide you with a lot of real
inside stuff, provided it's carefully selected—say, production
reports, and we might hop them up a bit and help to scare
the wits out of the Führer."

The P.A. answered, " I have no means of knowing what
source of information he may have in this country, so that
he'd be able to check up. I find it's a good rule to tell the truth
where I can."

XVI

Lanny spent another day catching up with his reading and
writing letters to various friends, which he would mail when
he got away from the scene of the Conference. He kept in
touch with Baker and was told that the President would see
him that evening, but it would be late. Then he was told that
he would have to wait until the next evening. He could guess
the reason, that Winnie the Night Owl wasn't keeping his
promise to let his opposite number get some sleep. Rick had
told his friend in London that there was a saying : the only
persons who had influence with the British government were

those who stayed up all night so that the Prime Minister could call them on the telephone between midnight and four in the morning.

Lanny waited. When you had been in the Axis world for a couple of months there was a lot you wanted to know about the real world, and you would read all the back newspapers and magazines you could lay hands on. Also, there were the Stotzlmann notes to write out, for it was safe to make notes in Canada, and Lanny had the idea that he might write the report himself. What difference would it make so long as only Hitler and his gang were going to see it ?

Another summons came, and Lanny sat in the ivory-and-gold bedroom once more and was told right pop out of the box that he mightn't have to go into Italy again after all. Scarcely two hours ago there had come from the British Embassy in Madrid the news that the Italian General Castellano had arrived there in civilian clothing, and with a false passport under the name of Raimond Imas. Ostensibly he was there as a member of the Italian mission to Lisbon, for the purpose of welcoming the Italian Ambassador to Chile on his return from that post. He had announced himself to the British Ambassador, explaining the secrecy by saying that if the Germans got wind of his mission they would have him shot forthwith.

Lanny was tempted to say, " That sounds like me." But it was no time for joking ; instead he remarked, " I did not meet Castellano, but he was named to me as one of those who favoured capitulation. He is, I believe, a Sicilian, and is on the Italian Joint Staff—that is, the Army, Navy, and Air Force."

" He brought a letter of introduction from the British representative at the Vatican. He claims to have full power to negotiate an armistice."

" Well, that's what we've been waiting for. Hurrah ! "

" You think he is genuine then ? "

" There is every reason to think so. Badoglio is caught in a nut-cracker, and he has to give way."

" We have sent word that we will meet him in Lisbon. It is a matter for the military to handle, and we are sending a British officer and an American."

H

" Well, that's fine, Governor. You won't need me on that job."

" Not if it works out. You might go home for a few days and we'll see."

" My wife won't object," said Lanny with his cheerful smile. " How long do you expect this Quebec show to go on ? "

" About a week more, as well as I can guess. And now we have an agreement—" F. D. R. stopped suddenly, as if he had meant to give the date but had thought better of it.

" That's grand, Governor," said the P.A. quickly. " That will please everybody, including the Russians. The newspapers seem to be worried because Stalin isn't here."

" Stalin has a good excuse—we are settling the problem of the Japs too, and Russia wants to keep out of that. But we shall have to get together with Stalin soon. It won't do us much good to lick the Nazis unless we can make friends with the Russians. We surely don't want a Third World War ! "

9

Here a Divided Duty

I

LANNY took a plane which delivered him to New York in a couple of hours, and he telephoned Laurel from the airport there. He heard a little catch in her voice when he said he'd be at the apartment in an hour. He added, " It's nice to have somebody to come home to." These wartime home-comings were always an event, for no woman who parted from her man could ever be sure that she would see him again, and every time the doorbell rang it might be a telegram telling her that she was another war widow.

Agnes expressed a sudden impulse to go shopping, and the couple had the little place to themselves. Laurel had developed a passion of which she did not altogether approve intellectually; she was determined to be a feminist and not have her happiness dependent upon any man. But here was her man, and she was in his arms, and how could she persuade herself that she wasn't happier than she had been a couple of weeks ago, before she had got word that he was coming out of the Nazi hell once more?

For she knew perfectly well where he was and what he was doing. Had she not been to the Head Devil's home with him, and seen exactly how he had fooled the Head Devil and got what he wanted? How could she doubt that he was playing the same game for his country's sake? But he wanted her to pretend that she didn't know, so she pretended, and her novelist's imagination was busy with a hundred secrets he might be getting, a hundred risks he might be running. Her only escape from these terrors was to pour her feelings into stories; very real stories, because they had been lived before they were written, and they interested numbers of other women who were living the war day by day.

Lanny, the perfect lover as well as the perfect husband, thought first about Laurel; he read all the clippings about her book and talked about them. And then about the baby! All babies were fascinating and, indeed, incredible—large pink worms that were destined to evolve into human beings, with capacities and energies impossible to foresee. Most fascinating of all was one's own baby, flesh of one's flesh and soul of one's soul, with so many delightful resemblances and so many disturbing differences. This Baby Lanny was eight months old, and he was at the crawling stage, and the looking-about stage, and the putting-things-into-his-mouth stage. This last-named is a most disturbing development; impossible to see how the human race has survived it, yet, indubitably, it has done so.

The advantage of being married more than once is that you can make the mistakes and learn the lessons in the first experiment. The disadvantage is that the shadow of the first marriage hangs over the second. Lanny, thrice-married, had learned this from Trudi Schultz, his second. Trudi had agreed with Nietzsche in pitying the lovers who had nothing but their love; Trudi had been devoted to a cause, but she had never been able to forget Irma Barnes, so rich, so elegant,

so different from a poor Socialist artist. The old devil jealousy
had entered her marital heaven by the back door and was not
to be driven out just by saying he had no right to be there.

So now the thrice-married husband observed every detail
about his little son and remarked that his smile was exactly
like Laurel's. Laurel showed him a sample ; and when she
said that the baby's eyes were like Lanny's, he rejected the
compliment and compared them to hers. " Even my family
will tell you so ! " he declared, thus tactfully reminding her
of the existence of the many Budds. " Don't you think you
ought to call Robbie ? " asked the wife ; and he told her to
come and sit by the phone, so that she could hear the words
of this other family and never have a chance to feel that it
was really " other."

II

The president of Budd-Erling had had a cold, but now he
was over it. The doctors insisted that he needed a rest, so he
was staying at home for a few days, trying to understand the
ideas of his son and daughter-in-law by reading Dr. Rhine's
New Frontiers of the Mind. Lanny knew, of course, that
Robbie would be running his huge plant over the telephone,
answering a hundred questions a day. Robbie reported that
they were all delighted with Frances ; she was a lovely child,
and just starting school and much excited over it. " When
are you coming out ? " And Lanny said he would talk it
over with Laurel and decide. Robbie added that he would
send the car at once, and Lanny said, " Thanks, as ever. It
looks as if Italy is trying to get out of the war."

That is the way a perfect husband brings up the child of
his first wife to his third wife—sandwiched in between Dr.
Rhine's book and a car and the war news. And all quite
casual, with no excitement expressed or expected. Laurel
said, " I am so eager to meet her." That, of course, was the
thing for a perfect stepmother to say.

Laurel had begun weaning the baby as soon as she heard
that Lanny was coming. Agnes came back from her shopping
and was ready to assume her duties. When the car arrived
at the garage, Laurel said, " Why not go out and see the
family now ? " Lanny countered by saying, " I'd rather wait

a day or two if it's all the same to you. I want very much to read your manuscripts." So it is that love and marriage may go smoothly if both parties understand human nature and if they have their arguments in reverse, so to say—the husband insisting that the wife should have what she wants, and the wife insisting that it should be the other way. And don't forget the faithful friend, the mother's helper, who has to have her share of kindness and appreciation !

Partly it was that Lanny was tired of moving about and meeting so many people ; he could think of nothing pleasanter than to lie on a couch in light pyjamas and read the newspapers or listen to the radio telling about events in Sicily under Allied occupation. Then he would pick up one of Laurel's stories and follow that shrewd and watchful mind, making use of experiences and ideas that had come to her, many of them from Lanny or in his presence. When lunchtime came, what could be more fun than to search the pantry and find whole-wheat bread and peanut butter, and in the refrigerator orange juice and milk, red tomatoes and yellow peaches ? Lanny Budd, who had been everywhere and seen everything, decided that what he liked best was home.

III

In due course Laurel phoned Esther and made sure that a visit would be welcome. They drove along the shore road to Newcastle, leaving the baby, for the first time in the baby's short life. There was that large Budd family, scattered about on a hilltop estate looking out over the town of Newcastle, the river, and two immense industrial plants, Budd Gunmakers and Budd-Erling Aircraft. Robbie had had the life satisfaction of seeing his own plant, his own dreams, outstrip in size and prosperity the plant which his grandfather had founded and which his father had run and had refused to turn over to Robbie. The two sons of Robbie and Esther had been exempt from war service because they were essential to an essential industry ; this wasn't favouritism, for they were carrying tremendous loads and Robbie couldn't have got along without them. Robbie, Jr., was thirty-eight and Percy thirty-seven, and they had provided the family with half a dozen

grandchildren ; the Budd tradition was like the law of the
Medes and Persians, which altereth not.

The whole tribe, old and young, had come to meet Frances
and inspect and approve her. They came now to have another
look at Lanny's wife and to ask how the baby was coming on.
Nobody knew that she was Mary Morrow, and many would
have been shocked if they had been told. As to Lanny, they
knew there was something strange about him and his journeys,
and they hoped it was not anything that would disgrace them.
They pretended to accept the idea that he was permitted to
travel and purchase art works in wartime.

Lanny had achieved the feat of remaining friends with
Irma Barnes, who had deserted him for a title—or so Laurel
was firmly convinced. Manifestly, she thought it was up to
her to achieve the same feat with Irma's daughter. It wasn't
the child's fault that she had a stepfather and a stepmother,
and the future happiness of all of them depended in part upon
Laurel's kindness. So she kissed Frances at their first meeting,
asked how she liked the land of her forefathers, and listened
to her account of her first days in school. A happy child,
unspoiled in spite of luxury, well trained yet not repressed,
she would never tread on Laurel's toes, and Laurel would
carefully keep off hers. With a reasonable amount of caution
one could be a stepmother.

IV

Lanny said, " Let's take a trip." So quickly had he forgotten the joys of staying quietly at home ! Laurel, who knew
his restless spirit, was ready to go. He phoned to the comfortable " camp " of his old friends the Murchisons in the Adiron-
dacks and learned that Harry was abroad on some war mission,
but Adella was there with the children and a couple of friends.
Adella said, " Do come ! " So they put their belongings into
the car and drove up the Newcastle River and through a pass
in the hills to upper New York State.

The mountains were at their most pleasant, the mosquitoes
gone and the snows not yet come. Lanny and Laurel greeted
old friends, walked on paths through spruce and pine forests,
slept on balsam pillows, ate freshly caught trout, and watched

the moonlight making a path of silver across a cool mountain lake. It was all so lovely they wanted to stay ; they looked at a place near by, and talked of buying it, and thought what fun it would be to line the walls inside and double the windows and stay through the winter. They had plenty of money, they could have been comfortable for the rest of their lives—and what fate was it which drove them out into a deadly cruel world ?—

> Swept with confused alarms of struggle and flight,
> Where ignorant armies clash by night.

These lines had been true when Matthew Arnold wrote them, and they had been still more true when Lanny read them during the First World War. They were written on Dover Beach—and what would the poet have thought now if he had come back from the spirit world and inspected that beach, sowed with deadly mines, blocked with barricades of concrete and barbed wire, and with rubble blasted from the cliffs and houses above ? It was " Hell's Corner ! "

Lanny Budd climbed on a mountain trail, thinking about this all the way. He loved his life as much as any man, and he hated brutality and lies, apparently more than most men. He had been born too young to be drafted for the first holocaust and too old for the second, but he had surely given his share of warnings and incurred his share of voluntary risk. Why shouldn't he lay off and rest for a while ? The world's wrongs were ancient, and what any ordinary man could do to diminish them was assuredly small in comparison. Why not learn to shrug your shoulders in the French fashion and say with Matthew Arnold again :

> Let the long contention cease !
> Geese are swans, and swans are geese !

But Lanny thought of that tired man whom he had left in the Citadel of Quebec. The burden he was carrying was that of Atlas, and there was no way he could get from under it save by death. Lanny had commented on the stacks of tiresome documents, and the patience it took to meet the streams of bores. " Patience ? " F. D. R. had said. " You acquire patience when you spend two years learning to wiggle your big toe."

That would be something for a sound man to remember
all his days. A cripple had been elected President of the
United States—the first time that had happened in our history
—and he had been elected for three terms, that also being
without precedent. He carried two colossal wars in his head,
and had room enough left for all his friends, and also for his
enemies ; a cheerful smile for the former, and a whiplash for
the latter.

Lanny thought of the three dictators whom he had watched
arising during his mature years : Mussolini, Hitler, and Franco,
in order of appearance. Two of them were foxes whom he had
pledged himself to hunt down, and to hang their brushes from
his mantel. He had just seen the end of Mussolini—or so he
thought at the moment—and it was " view halloo " for the
other. Lanny knew that he could never be happy in the
Adirondack Mountains, or in New York or any other place,
if he were to drop out of that chase. Not with a wife and a
baby and all the gold that was buried under the ground at
Fort Knox, Kentucky !

v

Laurel phoned each day about the baby. Agnes had a
reliable baby-sitter to help her, and all was well. But she said,
" A Mr. Alston called up and wants to see Lanny. He is at
the Hotel Commodore." And that was the end of the holiday.
Lanny called the hotel, and Alston said, " I'll be here until
tomorrow, and it's rather important." Lanny said, " I'll
leave in a few minutes, and it ought not take more than five
or six hours."

Laurel's heart sank, and she had to draw a long deep
breath. However, she hated the dictators as much as Lanny
did, and she had as strong a sense of honour. They threw
their few belongings into their bags and stowed them in the
car and set out down the Keene valley, and out of the mountains by the valley of the Hudson, there a tiny stream. It
grew wider, and when the Mohawk joined it at Albany it was
a real river, with war traffic of barges and steamers. Adella
had put some food into a basket, so they did not make a single
stop, but sped down the west bank of the river, the less
populated, and crossed the great George Washington Bridge,

and so into crowded Manhattan. It was night by then and Lanny phoned Alston again, who said, " Get your sleep, and I'll set everything else aside for nine in the morning."

Lanny replied, " Take a drive in the park with me." He didn't have to say more ; the President's " fixer " would have confidential things to impart.

It was at the age of nineteen that Lanny Budd had become translator-secretary to this one-time professor of geography whom Woodrow Wilson had brought to the Paris Peace Conference as one of his advisers. This experience had determined the rest of Lanny's life, for it had accustomed him to meeting eminent persons and watching history being made, not to his satisfaction. " Open covenants openly arrived at " had been a magnificent promise, but it had been forgotten before the Conference had got well under way. No matter how willing democratic statesmen might have been to negotiate openly, there was no getting the representatives of the British and French and Japanese Empires to come into a goldfish bowl.

Alston, who had introduced Lanny to Franklin Roosevelt, was one person to whom the P.A. could talk frankly. They didn't meet often because both had travelling missions and seldom knew where they would be. Now Lanny's car drew up in front of the great hotel, and the ex-geographer stepped in without a word. Rolling up Park Avenue and into Central Park, they could say what they pleased without thought of dictaphones or keyhole listeners.

" Charlie " was about the age of Robbie Budd, with whom he had been at Yale. He was one of those wiry small men who eat lightly and live long. Lanny had seen him tired, but never discouraged, and always too busy to talk about himself. Perhaps he kept notes, but Lanny never saw any ; he listened attentively and remembered what he heard. He was a piece of walking loyalty, and F. D. R. had learned to appreciate it. When his advice was asked, he would give it ; when the Boss said, " Let this be done," Alston would make sure that it was done. It was wonderful what a clear, keen mind, rigid honesty, and a quiet voice could accomplish in the management of men.

VI

Now the manager said, " I have just come from Quebec. Tell me about Italy."

So Lanny went through that story again. When he came to his last talk with Badoglio, and his suggestion that the Americans might drop paratroopers into Rome and keep the Germans from seizing it, Alston declared, " That is exactly what we plan to do. Our information is that there are four Italian divisions in or about Rome, and only one German division near it."

" That one is a Panzer," the P.A. warned. " But I suppose we have learned to deal with German armour."

" The Italians of course want to get out of the war. We shall get the Fleet and a considerable part of the Air Force, and that will be bad news for the Japs, because it will release many of our warships for the Far East."

Lanny asked, " Did the Boss tell you about my little scheme of taking some documents to Hitler ? "

" He did, and he told me to have them prepared for you. The question is, what use are you going to make of your visit ? I have an important suggestion."

Lanny indicated his interest, and the " fixer " first cautioned him as to secrecy—something that wasn't necessary but was required by protocol. Then he said, " We are coming on well with atomic research and are satisfied that the Germans are out of the running in this field. As matters stand today we have only one serious worry, and that is in the field of jet propulsion. The British are ahead of us, but the Germans are far ahead of the British ; they have been working on it in the greatest secrecy for more than ten years."

" You may remember, Professor, I was asked to find out where they were working on this, and someone else got ahead of me with the information."

" We have bombed Peenemünde several times this year, and our airmen come back and report that they have knocked the place out. But we have learned that airmen are inclined to optimism in regard to their achievements. Our information is that the experiments are going on and that rocket bombs are now actually in production. I don't need to tell you how important that is to us ; it might result in victory being snatched out of our hands. We cannot take the chance of having a shower of these frightful weapons falling upon our ships while our men are coming aboard in the English Channel ports."

" I understand, Professor, and I'll make a try. But that won't be an easy assignment."

" My point is, stick to that, rather than in helping with a job on Hitler. Neither Hitler nor any other German will surrender if he has such a weapon in his hands, and if we can get it in our hands we can knock out the whole kit and caboodle. Put your mind on getting anything you can—blueprints, technical descriptions, the formula of the combustibles they are using."

" How did we come to be so far behind in this matter, Professor ? "

" It is the custom to blame everything on the military mind, which is bent upon being ' practical,' and understands by that doing everything the way it has always been done. You cannot imagine what battles it has taken to force the adoption of new ideas. Nothing but a direct command from the President was able to get work started on atomic research, and I doubt if the general in command really believes in it to this hour. He is required to spend hundreds of millions of dollars at the demand of a bunch of young college professors who sit around and jabber mathematical formulas that sound like pure gibberish to him. He must feel himself in the position of Alice with the Mad Hatter and the White Queen and the Knave of Hearts and the rest."

VII

So there was Lanny with a new job, and a new subject of study, what the graduate students in a university know as a " major." This time he didn't go down to Princeton and live *en prince* on a millionaire estate, and play Mozart's violin sonatas with Professor Einstein by way of recreation. This time he took a suite in an obscure hotel, and one of those young professors of physics came and stayed with him, bringing a heavy brief-case full of " blueprints and technical descriptions and formulas of combustibles." Last January at Casablanca F. D. R. had provided Lanny with some of this, but it had all been intentionally wrong, designed to fool somebody; this time it had to be right, and Lanny had to know why it was right—because otherwise somebody might fool *him*.

He had to understand at least the elements of what the Americans knew about rockets and jets, and what they wanted to know from the Germans. He had to read, and then ask questions about what he didn't understand, and then answer questions to be sure he had understood the answers. He was allowed to make notes, under the pledge that he would keep them pinned next to his heart and would destroy them before he landed anywhere on the continent of Europe. Neither he nor young Professor Elbridge went out of the suite while this " majoring " was under way; their meals were brought to the room and they watched the waiter to be sure he didn't pick up any papers. They had carefully searched the rooms for wiring, and now and then they opened the door to see if there was a listener in the hall. All this was melodramatic, and they made jokes while they did it—but they did it.

The P.A. learned the difference between a rocket missile and a jet missile: the former carried its supply of oxygen in a tank, while the latter got its oxygen from the air. This meant, in effect, that the jet was limited to an altitude of some eighteen miles, beyond which there is no oxygen; the rocket could go to any height, but it was limited by the weight of the oxygen it required to get it up into the stratosphere. " Don't bother to try to understand the mathematics," said the young professor, " but just learn the fact that rockets fuelled with liquid oxygen can never travel farther than five hundred miles, and perhaps not quite that."

" Do they need to go any farther ? " asked the pupil, and the answer took his breath away. " We have reports that the Germans are working on a *Raketenbomber* that will be capable of carrying a load of explosives half-way round the earth. They will not be satisfied with bombing London; they expect to wipe out New York and Chicago and Detroit."

That might take some time; but now in production and immediately to be feared were guided missiles capable of travelling a couple of hundred miles, and at speeds faster than any Budd-Erling pursuit plane. Launching platforms for these were being built all along the coast facing England, and while these sites were being bombed, no one believed they had all been discovered. More alarming yet were experiments being carried on at Peenemünde and other places, aimed at the production of larger jet missiles, which would be able to rise into the stratosphere and there attain speeds faster than sound. The victims of such a missile would have no warning and no chance of escape ; the tremendous explosion would come first, and the sound would come later—and in reverse, the louder sounds and then the less loud, as if the missile were going away instead of coming.

Still more terrifying was the certainty that this knowledge of jet propulsion was being applied to airplane engines. Our "brass" hadn't believed it could be done, and as a result we were behind the British, and the British were behind even the Italians. " Some of us are to be flown to Italy the day the armistice is signed," reported Elbridge, " to see what we can learn. The Italians, no doubt, have many of the German secrets, but surely not the most important."

Such frightful dangers here, and such a mass of technicalities to be met ! If airplanes were to be flown faster than sound —seven hundred and sixty miles an hour—they would compress the sound waves in front of them and thus generate turbulence which would shake them to pieces. They would have to have different shapes, with knife edges ; and quite possibly the shapes which flew at supersonic speeds might not fly at subsonic speeds. What kind of fuel would they use in such jet engines, and of what materials would the engines be made in order not to melt in the tremendously high temperatures that would be created ? Here, indeed, was mankind confronting a new future and terrified by what it saw !

Said this young physicist, " We have seen a report by Professor Wernher von Braun, the scientist in charge of jet propulsion research in Germany, in which he suggests the building of a new satellite to be launched from the earth and to circle about it, making a complete circuit in an hour and a half. Once it got above the atmosphere, about two hundred miles, it would encounter no resistance ; centrifugal force would balance gravity, and it would continue in its course

for ever. It could be supplied by jet vehicles shot up to it,
and the technicians who lived on it would be in position to issue
orders to all the nations of the earth and to be obeyed. That
is what war may come to, Mr. Budd!"

VIII

Lanny went down to Washington, and in that old brick
building near the gasworks he sat down with General Donovan
and that section of his organization which had to do with jets.
Orders had come from above—the P.A. was to have everything
they could give him, and so the top-secret drawers were
unlocked. Lanny learned a number of things that even Professor Elbridge hadn't known. He gave the O.S.S. people
the names of all the persons in Germany, important or obscure,
whom he was in position to meet, and they in turn gave him
the names of various persons from whom he might get something if he could meet them.

There was, for example, that Professor Schilling, whose
name—"the English coin"—had been haunting Lanny's mind
for the past two years and a half. It had been on the way to
visit this German physicist, a secret sympathizer with the
Allies, that Lanny had set out to fly from Newfoundland and
had landed in the North Atlantic with two broken legs. Later
on Bernhardt Monck had visited the man, so he had told
Lanny, and got what he had. Schilling was a nuclear physicist,
working at the splitting of the atom ; but he would know men
who were working in jets and might know one who was secretly
anti-Nazi. Lanny went through a whole dossier on "the
English coin," including photographs of him which he studied
carefully. Also he got the password, Raffaelli, which would
tell the scientist that Lanny was to be trusted.

Then there was Professor Salzmann, of the physics section
of the Kaiser Wilhelm Institut. Hitler himself had sent Lanny
to this gentleman, and Lanny had promised to come back and
bring him more information on his *Specialität*. That, as it
happened, was jet propulsion, and now it was Lanny's
Specialität also. Salzmann was the perfect type of cold-blooded
Prussian, with a shaven blond head and a double chin, and
a neck and head straight up and down behind. Lanny looked

him up in these files to see if by any chance six months of bombing had changed his mind ; but he found no indication of any such development.

Also, there was Professor Plötzen, one of the theoretical physics men of the same great institution : a very different personality from Salzmann, a man of wealth, a man of the world, interested in world culture ; it had been a pleasure to spend an evening with him. In his home the startled Lanny had found Bernhardt Monck, acting as butler and stealing the eminent scientist's papers. The Gestapo had come for Monck but he had got away. Now Lanny wondered, had Plötzen by any chance connected Monck with Lanny, and what would be his attitude to the American visitor next time ? Lanny had to recur to this again and again ; many Germans were bound to have suspicions, and how long would it be before they put this and that together ? " Better take along a cyanide capsule," advised one of the O.S.S. men ; but Lanny answered, " I can't ; they search me too thoroughly."

Most important of all was Bernhardt Monck himself. Lanny had lost contact with him since they had parted in Stockholm ; in this secret work you didn't ask about anybody unless you needed him for the job you were doing. Now Lanny would need him very much, for Monck, an old-time Social Democrat, had contacts with the anti-Nazi underground, now coming to life again. Inquiring, Lanny was told that Monck was living in Stockholm and in the pay of the O.S.S. The organization had a " post office " in the Swedish capital as it did in Rome, and they gave Lanny the address. All he had to do was to write a note to " Anton Vetterl " and deliver it to this place, and he would hear from his old friend if he was in town. Lanny said, " I'll wait for him."

IX

All this took time, and meantime the Quebec Conference had come to an end. A statement was issued telling the world that harmony had reigned and unanimous decisions had been reached ; the world would learn about these when they were put into effect. Both Roosevelt and Churchill came back to the White House, and Lanny called Baker and reported, " I am ready to leave. Does the Chief want to see me before I go?" He was told to call back in three hours, as usual, and when he did so he was told to be at their regular street corner at twenty-one hours. (Everybody was using military time now.)

It was dark at that hour in Washington, though it hadn't been in Quebec. Baker said, "I am to arrange for you to fly to England by way of Newfoundland. The British will have you flown to Stockholm." Lanny's reply was that he would like to have a day in New York, and Baker told him, "I'll arrange for you to fly tomorrow morning, if that's O.K." Lanny said, "I was to get some papers from Professor Alston." The answer was, "He spoke to me about them, and I am to get them tonight." The P.A. remarked, "Apparently none of you people ever forgets anything." Baker said with a smile, "We are not encouraged to."

In the White House the Boss lay in his big bed, with an especially big stack of papers alongside him—always the case when he had been away. The P.A. resolved to come right to the point; but, as it turned out, the busy executive was in one of his human moods. "Lanny," he said, "I hate like the dickens to send you into that den of snakes. But you keep asking for it."

Said the other, smiling, "I get a great kick out of being the Führer's only American friend."

"You think you can keep that up indefinitely while we go on knocking the stuffing out of him?"

"I haven't said that. Very likely the time will come when he'll go crazy and I'll be afraid of him. But not until we cross the Channel."

"Well, it's settled that we're going to cross. This is our number one objective from now on. Also, you'll be glad to know, Italy is about to sign on the dotted line. And on our terms."

"Unconditional Surrender Roosevelt," smiled Lanny. He knew that his history-minded friend would appreciate being compared to General Grant.

"Funny story," continued the other. "General Castellano was so afraid of the Germans that he got himself lost on the way back to Rome, and his own people didn't know what had become of him. They sent another man to Sicily to try to fix things up with us. But now Castellano is in Sicily too, and things are shaping up all right : the Fleet will come out and surrender, and all the planes that can get away will do the same ; the rest will be destroyed."

" And Badoglio and the royal family ? "

" Apparently they are going to make a sneak into our lines. They will be the government of Italy for the duration. By the way, would you like to talk to Churchill ? "

" I'd like to listen to him," replied Lanny dryly, " if he has time to talk."

" He always has time in the evenings. You keep him busy, and I'll get a chance to go over all these papers."

Lanny had been called on for that service once before, and he knew the situation. Winston was a trying guest ; he wanted to have his own way, politically and militarily, and he would never give up arguing—not even after the matter had been " settled."

" Have you got everything you need for your journey ? " inquired the hard-pressed man, and Lanny answered that Baker had promised him the papers and everything else was O.K. The President took up the phone and called for the Prime Minister ; he said, " Our friend Budd is here," and then, " O.K."

He hung up and said, " He knows where you have been and he wants to hear your story. You know which is his room. Good luck to you, Lanny, and take care of yourself." A warm handclasp, and the P.A. went out from the presence.

x

The Right Honourable Winston Spencer Churchill, His Majesty's Prime Minister, sat in a large overstuffed armchair which fitted his plump frame as snugly as if it had been made to order. He was clad only in his shorts and a pair of straw slippers ; he made no attempt to extract himself from the chair's embrace, but said, " Hello, Budd," and waved his hand toward the stand beside him. " Have some ? " On the stand were whisky and soda, also several of the long dark cigars which had become, as it were, the great man's trademark. Lanny squirted a little soda from the siphon, just to

have something to hold in his hand, and the host remarked,
" As a world traveller, you should be free of the abominable
American practice of having everything ice-cold."

" First I was in Rome and then in Iceland," smiled Lanny,
" so I had to take things as they came. Washington, I observe, is very much like Rome." It was a muggy evening.

" Tell me what you saw there," said the P.M.

Lanny began his story, the same that he had told to Hitler
and Göring, to Roosevelt and Hopkins and Alston. But he
didn't get so far this time, because his auditor had been to
Rome and knew the city and its leading people of the old
regime, and was impelled to impart his knowledge. The Right
Honourable Winston, grandson of the seventh Duke of
Marlborough, was not only a statesman, orator, and military
strategist, but also a man of letters, author of a dozen books
of what he called " hist'ry." He talked int'restingly about
Roman his'try, both ancient and modern, and when Lanny
described the scenes on the night of Il Duce's fall, Churchill
said, " They go crazy with delight when they get rid of a
tyrant, and then they get another."

There was a lot to be said about Benito. Churchill called
him " Johnny Jump-up," and Lanny told of interviewing him
at the Cannes Conference, just after the end of World War I.
He was then a journalist-agitator, travelling around with a
couple of thugs to protect him ; a little fellow, only just learning to puff up his chest and stick out his chin, he appeared
undernourished. " ' Yon Cassius has a lean and hungry
look,' " quoted the P.M.

After this modern Cassius had seized power and got his
promised loan from the House of Morgan, Churchill had
praised him as statesman and builder. Now this was embarrassing, for his political opponents liked to quote what he had
spoken and written. He defended himself to his visitor.
" You know how it was, Budd ; the Reds in Italy were
seizing the factories, and they had no idea how to run them.
Mussolini was the only man in sight with a programme and
the power to save the country from chaos. So long as he
stuck to that programme, I was for him of course. There was
no way for anyone to know that he was going off his chump
and set out on a course of imperialist adventure."

Lanny said, " Your course has been perfectly consistent, and only the ignorant would fail to understand it. I was at the Paris Conference, and I can testify that you were the first to understand the perils of Bolshevism and the need to unite Europe against it."

" I am still sticking to that course," said the P.M., as pleased as Punch. " I wish to God there was some way I could get your President to realize it. He is playing with sticks of dynamite, and he's as unheeding of their danger as any child."

" There are a great many children like that," said the super-Tory. " They see that Hitler has to be beaten, but they don't see what they may be setting up in his place."

" The idea of letting Stalin into the Balkans ! " exclaimed the other, and he spent an hour or more in expounding the strategy of this war to a man whose father was a producer of war goods and therefore might have influence with the American "brass." " A tragedy, Budd, a blunder which may negate all the gains of this war ! "

XI

Deep inside himself Lanny Budd was smiling. He asked just enough questions and interposed just enough arguments to keep the Prime Minister talking ; for Lanny was thinking about the tired man in a near-by room who wanted time to sign important state papers and then go to sleep. Winnie wanted an auditor ; all right, here was one who would stick it out until the cock crowed, or even until the sun rose.

Churchill wanted to hear about Hitler and about Göring, and Lanny described his last visit and others. If that led to detours, and to accounts of Winnie's interviews with Ribbentrop, " that disgusting bounder," Lanny was pleased to hear these. When the talk came to paintings, an art expert listened respectfully to the P.M.'s opinion of the Führer's opinions on this subject. Winston himself was a painter, and it was talking shop. When it was a question of getting the Führer shot or blown up with a bomb, the P.M. manifested deep interest, but declared, " We can't have anything to do with that of course. Assassinations are off the British political line."

" Quite so," replied the other. " I don't think there is any need for you even to express an opinion. These Wehrmacht officers are capable of taking care of their own business. All they will ask me is, what will be the attitude of the Allies toward them if they should do the job."

" That is an important question, Budd, and I have given due thought to it. I'd rather you didn't quote me personally on the subject——"

" Oh, of course not, Mr. Churchill ! "

" You can make the statement that so far as the British government is concerned, we shall be willing to sign an armistice with any group of men who are in a position to make it effective. We shan't trust any of the beggars, and we only hope that this time your own government will stand the watch with us. Is that clear ? "

" Quite so ; only I shall have to put it in a little more polite language to a son and heir of Graf Herzenberg."

It was after three o'clock in the morning before the mouth in that round cherub's face opened in a wide yawn. His Majesty's Prime Minister ground out the stub of his last big brown cigar and remarked, " Well, I guess we'll have to get some sleep."

" You were too interesting, Mr. Churchill, and I have over-stayed my welcome."

" Not at all, not at all. You have been good company, and your President will thank you for keeping me out of his room. We have trouble in getting our hours to agree. Is there anything I can do to further your undertaking ? "

" One thing occurs to me, sir. The President is to provide me with some papers which will help me to convince Hitler that I am really his friend. Those papers would look strange to any of your officials who examined them ; and, of course, you know that I do not wish to reveal my true role to anyone unless it is absolutely necessary."

" Quite so, Budd. What shall I do ? "

" Your B4 man, Fordyce, knows about me and has been most helpful. If he would meet me at the airport and see me off on the plane to Stockholm, it would be a favour."

" Right-o. I'll give the order before I go to sleep. My best regards to Adolf ! "

XII

Next morning the President's man came to the art expert's hotel, bringing a passport and the plane tickets, also a peculiar object, a light athletic shirt of the kind that slips over the head; it fitted Lanny, and the front of it had been made into a sort of breastplate, or sewed-in pocket, filled with papers, not folded, but laid flat and wrapped in oilskin to protect them from perspiration. The top of the pocket was open, so that Lanny could slip the papers out to study them in the privacy of his room. Then he would make them secure with a couple of safety-pins and would wear that shirt until he was in the presence of the Führer, or at any rate of the Führer's guards who would search him. This wouldn't be a comfortable garment for summer wear, but Lanny reflected that it was a lot more so than the packs which the G.I.'s had been carrying on the hot and dusty mountain roads of Sicily.

The P.A. was flown to New York in a little more than an hour, and there he had an afternoon and evening at home, one of those distressing periods when he was going away and might never return. Laurel couldn't think about anything else, but was too proud to weep, and had to give an excuse to get up and leave the room so that Lanny would not see her tears. They couldn't find anything to talk about that seemed adequate to the occasion. Lanny couldn't tell where he was going or what he was doing; he couldn't even mention the past, Italy or Germany or Quebec. Even if he had broken the rules and told her, what good would it have done?—for the reality was as bad as her imaginings, or worse. They talked about the baby, and about the family in Newcastle, and about relatives of Laurel whom Lanny had avoided meeting because they would have been bound to ask questions which Lanny couldn't have answered. They talked about Laurel's ideas for stories. Then they decided to go out to a show, so that they would get at least the physical distraction of new scenes, new faces, and new voices. But it was a poor show, and perhaps the best wouldn't have held their attention.

In the bedroom Lanny took off his strange undershirt, folded it, and put it under his pillow without a word. Laurel didn't need any words—she was a novelist and knew them all. Secret documents having to do with the war, and if he were caught with them he would be shot! She lay there by his side, brooding, not sleeping; in the middle of the night she broke down, weeping, "Oh, how I hate war!" Over and over again, "How I hate war!"

They talked about it for a long time; what could be done about this war, and about the next which would be so much worse? He hadn't said anything about the new weapons, but she had heard about atomic fission before the blackout had begun, and she had not forgotten it as one of the possibilities; also rockets, and planes in the stratosphere, and poison gas, and death rays, and war with germs—these horrors had been guessed about and talked about in the old days, and all thinking people knew they must be on the way.

Both of this pair were agreed that war could never be abolished while the present economic system endured. Capitalism was war carried on like a game, under a set of rules and conventions, but its end was the same, the taking away from the other person of the means of life. Capitalism was a game of "freeze-out" poker; when you had lost all your chips, you were out of the game for good. Commercial competition inevitably tended to monopoly, and monopoly froze out whole classes and whole nations from their chance of life.

But how were you to change this system and get a co-operative world? The Socialists appeared to be too polite and inclined toward compromise; when they took power they seemed to shrink from the immensity of their task and were tempted to show that they could run capitalism better than the capitalists—a fatal mistake, for the capitalists knew the game. But the only alternative to that was violent revolution, a Communist dictatorship; and from that all people with kindness in their hearts shrank in dread. Truly the alternatives were difficult; they were ashamed of their own comfort and ease and spent hours wrestling with their consciences, trying to decide where their social duty lay, and which were the more important values in life.

Since sleep was denied them, Lanny said, "Let's try a séance." He was going on a long journey, and it was always fascinating to see if those entities which called themselves "spirits" would lift the veil of the future even for a tiny gap. Laurel agreed, and composed herself; there was a technique of going into a trance, she had discovered—you made your mind a blank, excluding all thoughts but the thought of emptiness. She began to breathe heavily, and the husband waited for the strange voice that would come. He waited, and her breathing became quieter, but no voice came, and he realized that she had taken the other fork in the mental road; she was asleep. So he too went to sleep—and if there were any creatures of the subconscious world waiting to tell him secrets, they went away thwarted.

BOOK FOUR

TILL DANGER'S TROUBLED NIGHT DEPART

10

When Fortune Flatters

I

THE Swedish plane, travelling by a secret route from Scotland, circled the clean stone city of islands and bridges and settled on the fine Bromma airport. The passenger from America was driven to the Grand Hotel, where he had stopped earlier in this same year ; he knew well that it was a spy nest. His breastplate of documents for Hitler were safe over his heart, and when he went to his bath he took the precious shirt with him and locked the door. When the valet brought his freshly pressed suit, Lanny already had the undershirt on and covered by a clean overshirt. Nobody was going to get a glimpse of that breastplate until he was in the Führer's home or headquarters.

He had the address of the American " post office " in Stockholm ; it was in a business building and was known as the " 21 Club." He would take care never to be seen in its vicinity. It must pretty certainly have been there since the beginning of the war and to be under observation by the enemy. After the P.A. made himself presentable he went for a stroll. He stopped in a stationery store and bought an inconspicuous sheet of paper and an envelope. In Stockholm all clerks and others who deal with the public know some English or German, so he had no trouble in finding an obscure office where a visiting foreigner was permitted to use a type-writer for a few minutes.

He wrote, " Bienvenu will be at the Geneva place at twenty." He addressed the envelope to " Anton Vetterl " at the 21 Club, and dropped it into a post-box. If an enemy agent opened and read that, he would hardly know that

"Bienvenu" was the name of Beauty Budd's home on the Cap d'Antibes, which Bernhardt Monck had visited years ago. Nor would he have had an easy time finding a "Geneva place" in Stockholm; but Monck would understand, having been accustomed to meet his American friend at the public library in Geneva.

II

This was duty number one. Number two was to get in touch with Eric Erickson, Swedish-American oil man; a simple matter, because Erickson was in business in the near-by city of Norrköping, and all that was necessary was to call him on the phone and say, "This is Lanny Budd." The big fellow voiced his pleasure, and asked, "Will you come and stay with me?" When Lanny explained that he expected to have only a couple of days in Stockholm, Erickson asked, "Are you free this evening? I'll come up and take you to dinner. It's a date!" Having been born in Brooklyn, "Red" Erickson knew American modes of expression. It amused him to remark, "I am the Erl King that Goethe wrote a poem about."

There are people you meet whom you like from the first moment; and if they happen to have the same feeling toward you, that adds enrichment to your life. Lanny had not expected to meet such a person in Hermann Göring's crudely lavish Karinhall; he had been puzzled to find a generous-minded man doing business with the Nazis and on intimate terms with the fat man's circle of friends. Lanny himself was doing it, but that was only camouflage. Only after coming out of Germany had he learned, through a slip of the American Minister in Stockholm, that the oil man was "one of us." Later he had inquired from the O.S.S. and learned that "Red" had given help of importance by listing and describing all the synthetic oil plants of Germany.

Now Lanny would have liked nothing better than to say, "I, too, am one of us." But that was forbidden. Every agent in this war against Nazi-Fascism worked with the certainty hanging over his head that if he were caught his enemies would do everything in their power to compel him to betray his associates. They would subject him to the most dreadful tortures invented by modern science, tortures which were supposed to be beyond the power of any human organism to withstand. The agent carried a little capsule of cyanide, which he was instructed to chew up and swallow if he was caught. There was a still better precaution, depending upon the fact that what an agent didn't know he couldn't be made to tell. So they worked in small teams, and outside of their own team knew only the people in the home office.

Lanny did not forget that Stockholm rivalled Lisbon as the world's greatest spy centre. No stranger could come in by airplane and register at a de luxe hotel without being noted and inquired about by the agents of several countries. So now, while waiting for his friend to motor a hundred miles, Lanny donned his camouflage and went forth to exhibit it. He was a well-established art expert, and had already made himself known to the leading dealers ; now he went to see what they had on their walls, and asked whether they had located any " examples " in which his wealthy clients might be interested. He could talk learnedly about great American collections, what they had and what they lacked, and about prices now being commanded by the works of old masters and modern favourites. It was a high-class and elegant kind of " shop," and exactly what all dealers enjoy. Word would spread that there was an American millionaire in town, representative of American super-millionaires and son of one of them. The political spies would hear of it ; some of them, Americans, would hasten to send word back to Washington, and people in the old brick building by the gasworks would get a mild kick out of the reports.

III

Red was a typical oil man, as Lanny had learned to know them when his father had been dabbling in the " black gold " a quarter of a century before : big, husky, full of energy and self-confidence, genial and generous with those they liked. Erickson had begun at the bottom in orthodox American style, having been a " pipe-line walker " all the way between Negley, Ohio, and Bayway, New Jersey—a goodly stroll for the most able-bodied young Swedish-American. He had saved money and gone through college and then become assistant manager of an American oil company in Japan. Now he was buying German synthetic oil and bringing it to Sweden, and telling the world, whether Allied or Nazi, that Sweden had to have this product, otherwise its industry would come to a halt and its workers would starve.

In return for this oil Germany got Swedish lumber, paper, iron ore, steel. The business men concerned got their profits out of the trade and that kept *them* from starving. Stockholm had become a " boom town " and everyone was getting rich. Lanny guessed that Red had taken Göring in on his deal—that was the way to get action. He had become the fat man's friend, and was not merely a guest at Karinhall, but had been taken to inspect the Fatherland's marvellous plants which made oil out of coal and had been so carefully hidden that it was only recently that the Allied bombers had been able to find them. Strange things kept happening in this war !

Erickson showed up at about dinner-time and took Lanny to his club, where they had a private dining-room. Lanny said he had been " home " ; he wouldn't mention Italy or Quebec of course. He had been looking for paintings for Göring's collection, and had found one, asserted to be a Giorgione, but more probably an early Titian. " That ought to be worth quite a bit," remarked the oil man, and Lanny said, " They are asking a hundred and fifty thousand dollars." When Erickson asked if Göring would pay sums like that, Lanny told the story of the Vermeer, for which *Der Dicke* had traded other paintings, estimated to be worth a million, six hundred thousand Dutch guilders. The subject was " Christ and the Adulteress," and some authorities had doubted its genuineness, thus greatly annoying the Reichsmarschall.

Erickson had been in Germany again and was planning another visit soon. He reported on Göring's highly irritable state of mind ; the German leaders were worried about the progress of the war, and they had cause to be. News had just come over the radio—Erickson had got it while motoring—that the Allies had made a successful crossing of the Strait of Messina. They had been practically unopposed ; the Germans had got away with some of their big guns and had destroyed others. The oil man gave it as his guess that the Italians would soon be trying to back out of the mess, and Lanny quoted his father's opinion that negotiations for an armistice were probably now under way. Lanny always leaned on Robbie whenever he was dealing with business men; they would take it for granted that the president of Budd-Erling would have inside knowledge, and also the power to arrange for his son to travel abroad and buy paintings.

The son of Budd-Erling remarked, " My father is especially interested in jet propulsion at present. He thinks that is the only means by which it might be possible for the Germans to pull themselves out of the hole."

" I agree with you," replied the oil man, and went on to discuss the subject freely. Lanny wondered, did this mean that he had guessed Lanny's true role and wanted to help him ? Or did it mean just that he liked to make his conversation interesting ? He reported that the Germans were making real progress with jet-propelled weapons, and the Allies had not been successful in their efforts to stop the experiments at Peenemünde. He said that some projectiles, believed to have been shot from that Baltic island, had fallen in the forest-covered mountains of Sweden. It was a subject the Swedes didn't like to talk about because of their ticklish position, caught between the two fires. What did the president of Budd-Erling think about the possibility that the British and Americans might be planning an invasion by way of Norway ?

Lanny said he had never heard his father discuss that subject ; but he had heard an amusing story in England. A year or so ago, when the Allies were about ready for their landings in North Africa, the authorities in London had advised the press correspondents who were going with the expedition to obtain fur coats and gloves and sleeping-bags. The luckless fellows had taken this tip and lugged this stuff on board the ships. The military people had guessed that German spies would learn of this and would transmit the tip that the invasion was aimed at Norway. The oil man said, " Apparently the plan worked, for we heard here that the Germans were rushing troops to meet an expected attack. They were using our railways, you know."

This was a point of vital importance to the Scandinavian world. The Swedes had not felt strong enough to refuse the

Nazi demand for transportation to Norway. The Nazis had agreed that the troops would go unarmed, but of course they had made a farce of that agreement, as of every agreement they had made with anybody since their seizure of power over ten years ago. In the previous month the Swedes, seeing Stalingrad and the surrender in Tunisia, had decided that their dangerous neighbour would not be looking for any more enemies ; they had summoned courage to refuse military transport through their country, so now the troops went in as " tourists," in civilian clothing, and their uniforms and arms went by sea to Oslo. Thus an oil man from Brooklyn indulged himself in the luxury of saying what he thought !

IV

Lanny was waiting for a chance to bring up his own subject again. Presently his host inquired what Robbie Budd thought about the prospects of a Channel crossing. Lanny quoted his father : it depended upon whether the Allies could keep control of the sea and the air. So far they had held both ; but what if the Germans could turn loose showers of rocket bombs against ships being loaded with troops in British ports ? What if they could do the same thing against the beaches, and against a thousand or two of ships lined up in front of the beaches ? Who was going to win the race for that new weapon ?

The host said that he knew something about oil but not much about jets, and that little was at second hand. He knew the difference between jets and rockets, and that the Germans were working with frantic haste on both types ; the Führer was staking his hopes on this method of getting at his foes. Short-range rockets were easier to make and therefore were further advanced, and London was undoubtedly in for a pasting. " I am told that more than a thousand test flights have been made," said Erickson, " and that the weapon has a range of forty miles. The Germans call it *Vergeltungswaffe Eins* —reprisal weapon number 1—shortened to V-1. Several of the rockets have fallen in our mountain forests, and the fragments have been carefully gathered up. It's all very hush-hush of course, but I know one of our government experts who has studied them, and I might find out a few details if it would interest you especially."

" It would interest my father very much," said Lanny, and added, " Needless to say, I won't mention the source of the information, to him or anyone else."

This was pretty nearly telling a shrewd man of affairs that Lanny Budd was more than an art dilettante or even an art authority. But he had to reveal it to someone, and who better than this secret friend of his cause ? Following his plan of telling some things in order to get more, he mentioned Professor Wernher von Braun of the University of Berlin and his extraordinary idea of constructing a man-made satellite to fly for all eternity about the earth, balanced at a carefully calculated point between the earth's force of gravitation and the satellite's own centrifugal force. If humans expected to live on this unprecedented vehicle, they would have to have fuel in order to keep themselves balanced between the deadly cold of space and the equally deadly heat of the sun. Assuming that the space ship was so launched as to make the circle about the equator in an hour and a half, there would be something less than three-quarters of an hour of sunshine and then something more than three-quarters of an hour of eclipse. To figure this exactly would be a simple matter for the astronomers ; but far from easy would be the task of shooting up man-carrying rockets that would connect with the space ship and be clamped fast to it, so that they could deliver their loads and then be released to return to the earth.

Lanny said, " When Morse made the telegraph his first message was ' What hath God wrought ! ' I doubt very much if the men who complete the first space ship will have that much piety."

The other corrected him, " That much modesty."

v

Erickson said that he expected to be in Berlin very shortly. He would be at Karinhall part of the time, and they might meet there. He added, " I'll see if I can bring some jet-propulsion man for you." That was practically saying, " I know what you are up to ! " But so long as Lanny hadn't said anything definite, he hadn't broken the rule. Before they parted the host remarked, " I am staying in town tonight, and I'll talk to the V-1 expert at lunch-time. He wouldn't talk frankly to you, but he will to me. We Swedes help the Allies wherever we can without getting caught. We are a free people—and besides that, we all have relatives in America."

Lanny agreed to come to the club in mid-afternoon to see what his friend had found out. At the appointed hour he presented himself, and the oil man put into his hand a legal-sized envelope, well stuffed. " This will tell you what we have been able to learn about the projectiles which have fallen in Sweden. Don't say where or how you got it ; and I advise you to get it out of the country quickly." Lanny promised to heed this advice.

Back in his hotel room he went without his dinner in order to study that report. The *Vergeltungswaffe Eins* was a robot plane; that is, one that flew without a pilot. It was jet-powered, scooping in air at the front, compressing it and heating it and then shooting it out at the back. It was estimated to have a speed of about three hundred and fifty miles an hour and a range of about forty miles. The war load it would carry would be about a ton.

These lessons learned, and the diagrams and drawings impressed upon his mind, Lanny wrote out the additional details which he had got from Erickson. He sealed all these papers in one envelope and pinned the envelope in the inside breast pocket of his coat, where he would be aware of it every moment. He took a taxi to the Royal Library of Stockholm, and in the large reading-room he got a German magazine and placed himself where, by lifting his eyes, he could watch the main entrance. While waiting, he learned what the Nazis were willing to let their countrymen know about their own affairs and about the outside world, a *Weltanschauung* which grew more out of focus each passing week.

VI

Promptly on the stroke of eight o'clock, called twenty in many European countries, Lanny glanced up and saw Bernhardt Monck, alias Anton Vetterl, entering the room.

Their eyes met for the fraction of a second, and Monck went to the shelves and consulted a book. Then he went out again, walking slowly, and after a proper interval Lanny followed. They went across the park and through several streets, turning corners according to their custom to make sure they were not being followed. When at last Lanny came up to his friend, the latter said, " Do not let anyone see us together, Lanny. I am a marked man in this city."

They strolled on obscure streets, not too well lighted, and Lanny explained that he had the address of the American " post office " but was afraid to use it. The German said, " You are wise. The place is watched." Lanny asked, " Do you use it ? " And the reply was, " Yes." Lanny took out the envelope with the data and put it into Monck's hands. " This contains especially important data on the German V-1." The reply was, " I will put it through at once." And that was all. Lanny knew that a trusted courier would take it, along with other documents, by plane.

He continued, " I am working on jet propulsion and am going into Germany. Can you give me any contacts ? "

Monck walked for a bit in silence. " That is a very dangerous job, Lanny."

" I know ; but I think I can get an invitation again."

" To meet top persons, yes. But can you meet ordinary Germans ? "

" I can pass for a German under everyday conditions ; I mean, with waiters, taxi drivers, and so on. I can go to some place at night, provided that I know I'll meet the right person."

" That's the trouble ; people change, they lose their nerve, they swallow the propaganda. You know, it is hard for any German to think of letting the Russians into the country. Then, too, spying is universal ; people disappear, their homes are watched, and anyone who asks for them disappears also."

" We have to take a gamble ; it's very important. Tell me about Professor Schilling."

" Schilling is a nuclear-fission man ; he wouldn't know anything about jets."

" Yes, but he might be able to send me to someone else."

" Schilling is a timid little gentleman, very much wrapped up in his speciality, and horrified to discover that it has become a war issue. He had never dreamed of such a possibility; he keeps saying that he thought only of discovering truth and now he finds himself a servant of the prince of lies. He used to be a free man in his laboratory, but now rough people pull him and haul him and give him orders, they spy on him and clamour for results. 'I am a goose that they hope will lay a golden egg,' he said. 'Then they will kill me.' "

"There are a lot of scientists who feel just that way, Monck. They have become class-conscious all of a sudden, and when the war's over, I shouldn't wonder if they went into politics. Tell me, did you have much talk with Schilling? "

"Only once. I had a hard time persuading him that it was his duty to give me anything. Finally he wrote out a lot of stuff. I've never been told how good it was."

"Tell me about Plötzen. Do you think he connected my visit with your presence in his house? "

"I don't see how he could; but how can I be sure? "

"You have no idea who betrayed you? "

"I had four different contacts; and I go over them in my mind, one after another. The gangsters must have seized one of them and broken the poor devil's nerve. Some day I may know, but I have no way to inquire at present."

"Tell me about Plötzen. I found him a congenial person. Is there any possibility that he may be nursing hatred of the Nazis in his heart? "

"I don't doubt that he is doing just that. But I can't believe that he would act on it. Plötzen is a coward, and also a snob. He is a man of wealth and means to hang on to it. He is proud of his ability to be a leading theoretical physicist and at the same time preserve his social standing."

"How funny! " said Lanny. "We have always been told that the Germans honour and glorify science."

"Yes, but not that solid-gold Berlin plutocracy, the Herrenklub crowd. To them a scientist is a higher sort of menial, useful and necessary, but kept in his place."

"You were a menial in Plötzen's house. I wouldn't expect a Social Democratic butler to love his master very ardently."

The German chuckled. "That might have something to do with it. But I wouldn't advise you to put your life in Plötzen's keeping—at least not until he has become sure that

I

the Nazis are on the skids." They were speaking German,
but now and then Monck put in an American slang phrase.
He had been a sailor and then a labour leader before the
coming of the Nazis ; he had become a captain in the International Brigade in Spain, and then had risked his life going
more than once back into Germany. Americans had the idea
that German Socialists were timid slaves of legality ; they
had no way to hear from the thousands who were sticking it
out in Nazi concentration camps, or from the other thousands
who were living double lives, helpless to rebel openly, but
doing secret work in constant peril of detection.

Monck gave his friend the name and address of one of
these determined men. His name was Johann Seidl and he
was a watchmaker and Nazi block leader in Berlin. He was
one of a group of half a dozen Socialists who had seen the Nazi
power on the way to victory, and had sworn an oath of loyalty
and secrecy to one another, and then had pretended to be
converted to the ideas of National Socialism. Thousands had
done the same thing for various reasons ; some because it
was the easiest way, others because it was the hardest—so
Monck phrased it. Three of these conspirators were no longer
heard from, he reported ; but if Johann was still alive, he
could be trusted ; he had had wide contacts in the past, and
he might know someone who was working in the field of jet
propulsion. It was not such a slender hope as it might at first
seem, because you couldn't go into mass production of any
article without having thousands of workers, and these frequently knew more than they were supposed to. " The young
Germans are no good to anybody," said Lanny's friend ; " but
when you get an old fellow who has had Socialist training you
have someone to depend on."

" What shall I use for a password ? " asked the P.A.

" Tell him that you were married to Trudi Schultz," was the
reply. " He knew her, and he may have some of her drawings
hidden away."

VII

Early next morning Lanny took a sheet of the Grand
Hotel's grand stationery, and wrote in the German language
a letter to the German Minister in Stockholm :

Exzellenz !

The undersigned, a long-time personal friend of the Führer, by the Führer's explicit orders, transmits to you the following requests : (1) No one is to be told about this letter and it is to be destroyed promptly. (2) You will oblige by telephoning personally to the Führer at Berlin 116191 informing him of my presence at this hotel. If the Führer is not available, you will inform his personal secretary, Ista Schröder. Further instructions may come from the Führer. You have no responsibility in the matter except to convey this information with all possible secrecy.

Respectfully,
LANNING PRESCOTT BUDD

Lanny sealed this letter and addressed it to " *Seiner Exzellenz dem Herrn Botschafter, Persönlich, Privat.*" He carried it within a block or so of the Legation, and waited until he saw a boy on a bicycle, stopped him, and made a proper-sized offer : fifty öre in advance, and another fifty after the performance of the service. Since the boy knew only Swedish, and Lanny only English, German, French, Italian, and Spanish, this took some gesticulating and pointing, but finally it was made clear. Lanny watched from a cigar store across the street and saw the boy admitted to the Legation ; he purchased an evening paper, and when the boy came out, followed him, paid him, and went his way, fairly sure that his manœuvre had not been observed by any Allied agent. His pretended treason made both sides his enemies.

Returning to the hotel, he read comfortably for a couple of hours. The Swedish newspapers gave the Allied communiqués, and fortunately the names of places were the same ; also, the scientific and technical terms which have Latin or Greek roots could be read by a foreign visitor. Lanny learned that the signing of an armistice with Italy had been announced, and he could make out some of the terms. He looked in vain for anything about the landing of American paratroopers in Rome, and was left to speculate about the reason for this disappointment. His guess was that the old *Maresciallo* and his still older, pint-sized King had had a failure of nerve ; later on he learned that this guess was correct. They had been afraid of that terrible armoured division of the Germans and had preferred to sneak away to the Allied lines and leave it for the Allies to take Rome by the weary, grinding process of mountain by mountain for two or three hundred miles.

VIII

There came a tap on the door of the P.A.'s room, and there stood a mild-looking little man in civilian dress. "*Ihre Name, mein Herr?*" he said, and when Lanny gave his name the man placed in his hands an envelope sealed but without writing. Lanny found in it a ticket to an airplane that was scheduled to fly to Berlin that afternoon. He was not surprised, because he knew Adi Schicklgruber and knew that he had not got where he was by patience, but by its opposite. The man said, "I have a car to take you to the airport." Lanny replied, "*Danke schön*," and proceeded to put his belongings into his one suitcase—a larger one this trip, since he hadn't had to come in a seaplane and land on a beach at night.

The man spoke not one word on the journey. Doubtless he had his orders, and Lanny surely had his. He guessed the man to be of a humble sort, and offered him a tip, which he took with thanks ; then he sat watching, presumably having orders to see the mysterious passenger off. Lanny sat in the sunshine at a great airport and watched planes arriving and taking off, and his own big liner warming its engines. His ticket had some initials on it, and these probably accounted for the fact that no questions were asked of him. Promptly on schedule the plane rose into the air and flew southward, and two or three hours later was set down on the immense Tempelhoferfeld—bombed every now and then by the Allies and promptly put in order again, all but the burned hangars and offices.

Modern civilization has made everything easy for those who have the right pieces of paper. In peacetime these had been, for Americans, oblong and pliable, green in colour and having the faces of old-time statesmen on them. In wartime they had changed in shape and character and had dates and other things put on with rubber stamps, also signatures of various functionaries. The Führer's long-time friend was without anything of the sort, but he feared no trouble and had none. A snappy young S.S. officer met him and took him in charge, putting him into a car, and driving him at high speed to the New Chancellery building on the Wilhelm-strasse.

That immense long ugly pile of granite had been hit by bombs and partly destroyed ; this part included the upper section, where Lanny had been shown the marvellous models which the greatest architect in the world—name, Adolf Hitler—had designed for the glory of his thousand-year Reich. But Adi's own offices had not been hit, and Lanny entered the familiar doorway, guarded by Leibstandarte men who saluted him and his escort. They went down the red marble hall-way to the heavy doors with the initials " A H " in bronze letters.

Inside the office Lanny was surprised to see his friend Heinrich Jung seated, waiting. He leaped up, heiled, and explained quickly that the Führer had meant to be here but had been unfortunately detained—Heinrich didn't say where, and Lanny was left to guess that it was at his headquarters in the Forest of Görlitz. Heinrich had been told to come and act as Lanny's escort until the Führer himself was free. Lanny expressed his pleasure at meeting one of his oldest German friends, and Heinrich escorted him to a guest chamber which they were to share ; it had two single beds and every comfort, for Adi took good care of his guests, even allowing them luxuries, such as meat and wine, which he denied to himself. But no tobacco inside his home !

The visitor asked about Heinrich's family and listened to all the details. He told about Irma, whom Heinrich had met as Lanny's wife. He told about his last meeting with Kurt Meissner, whom Heinrich hadn't seen for some time. Then they talked about this war. The devout and devoted Jugend official knew only what the Goebbels propaganda machine furnished him to be passed on to the young people of Germany ; Heinrich believed every word of it, and couldn't have been happy otherwise, for he was an honest fellow, though not very bright.

It would be thirty years this Christmas since Heinrich first had met Lanny Budd, and in those thirty years he had become the perfect bureaucrat, with constantly increasing duties, and

a family and a paunch of which the same could be said. He
stood in awe of his American friend, not merely because Lanny
was rich and elegant, but also because he was rendering
important services to the Führer. Heinrich was made
supremely happy by Lanny's assurance that he, Heinrich,
was the person responsible for Lanny's having become a
convert to the Führer's cause.

IX .

Four days and nights the pair spent renewing this friendship. They went for walks, and Lanny observed the bomb
damage and the condition of the people ; he made comments,
and Heinrich answered with items of information. The hard-
working bureaucrat didn't know any military or industrial
secrets, but he knew the everyday life of Berliners. They were
a sophisticated and smart lot, as sure of their superiority to
other Germans as Germans were of their superiority to other
races. The average Berliner still had confidence, because the
Führer had promised him a " wonder weapon " that was
certain to bring victory. *Wunderwaffe* it was in their language,
and in conversation they shortened it to *Wuwa*, pronouncing
it German fashion, " voo-vah."

There were, Heinrich had to admit, a few weak ones who
despaired, and even dastards who shirked their duties ; the
papers of soldiers who died were stolen or sold, and used by
men who went about pretending to be on leave. Others caused
it to be given out that they had been killed in bombings and
then went into hiding and escaped the draft. How they
managed to exist without food cards was a mystery, but it
was known that they did. There was a black market, even in
the Fatherland.

The Führer was keeping one of his promises, that the
Germans would be the last people in Europe to starve. Lanny
saw no signs of under-nourishment, but many signs that people
had to stand long hours in queues to get the food allotted.
Their clothing was neither new nor stylish, but was neatly
patched and clean. The widows and the orphans were not
permitted to appear in mourning, but you could see the grief
in their faces, and you saw crippled men in large numbers.

There was a gigantic sausage machine in the east, grinding up German manhood and making thousands of new widows and orphans every day.

The newspapers published the official bulletins, full of ingenious double-talk to make defeats sound like anything else. There would be strategic retreats, elastic defence, the straightening of lines and advantages gained by such moves ; all that may have served with the ignorant, but every thinking person must have known that the Reichswehr was being steadily driven back across the vast plains of Central Russia and the Ukraine. It had been that way all through the month of August, and now in early September it was the same, day after day : Konotop and Slavyansk, Stalino, Bakhmach, Mariupol, Nezhin, Novorossisk, Lozovaya, Romny, Novogorod-Severski —all of them odd-sounding names to Western ears, but you could find them on the map and measure the distances and figure how long it would take to reach the borders of the Fatherland. You weren't told how many dead were left on each field, to be buried by the advancing enemy ; but you knew there were windrows of them, and they were the *Herrenvolk*, the hope of the future. The world's most precious blood was being poured out to fertilize the soil of barbarians, and it was difficult indeed to understand the ways of Providence.

What was causing the Führer's delay was a series of defeats in the Don Basin, the great coal region upon which the Soviets' industrial progress had been based. The untimely rains had ceased, the steppes had dried, and there was ideal weather for the manœuvring of vast armies. The Germans were falling back ten miles a day, and manifestly the commander-in-chief of the German forces couldn't leave his headquarters in such a crisis, and he wouldn't have time to study the documents of his American agent. Anxiety pervaded the New Chancellery, like the miasma which arose when cool nights followed warm days on the many lakes and streams of the Berlin district.

X

There was nothing for Lanny to do but to wait, and go on wearing his breastplate of papers, regardless of the fact that the undershirt was in need of a washing. He explained the situation to the worshipful Heinrich, who was awed to be in the same room with such a secret, and thereafter was unwilling to leave Lanny alone, lest by chance someone might try to kidnap him or hold him up, even in the Führer's official residence.

The news that there was an American in the building could not be kept from spreading, and several visitors asked to see him. The first was an officer of the Führer's staff, Major Feldmann, who had met Lanny at Berchtesgaden in the dear dead days before Munich. He had been a mere Leutnant then, one of three whom Lanny had driven to Nürnberg for the *Parteitag*, the " day " which had grown into a full week of speech-making, shouting, singing, and parading. Lanny was glad to see him, and they talked about those wonderful times. With such a man Lanny of course talked only the official party line ; when the Major ventured timid words of anxiety, Lanny had no means of knowing but that a trap was being set for him ; he hastened to turn himself into another Heinrich.

The second caller was more diverting. His name was Dr. Heubach, and Lanny had forgotten the name but remembered the man. He had been the physician at the Berghof when Lanny had taken Laurel Creston there in the critical days just before the outbreak of war. Then, as now, Lanny had had to spend a lot of time sitting around waiting, and the young doctor had taken a liking to him, and in strict confidence had invited him to his room, where they could sit with the door partly open and hear the dressing down the Führer was administering to the British Ambassador, Sir Nevile Henderson. A curious custom had come into existence in the Berghof : whenever there was reason to expect a Führer-fury, the guests in the main hall would quietly retire to their rooms on the second floor and listen to the shouts and yells echoing down the corridor from Adi's private study.

Four trying years had passed, and Dr. Heubach had grown flabby like his master. He was not the Führer's personal physician, he explained ; that was the great Dr. Morell—and Lanny wondered if there wasn't a touch of sarcasm in the word " great." Dr. Heubach was here to take care of the large number of persons employed in the New Chancellery. He enjoyed talking, and he wanted to know what it was like in the outside world. Lanny, in the presence of Heinrich Jung, mentor of Nazi youth and model of Nazi orthodoxy, thought of all the bad things to say about the Allied world. In Britain there was a shortage of everything, and in America there was political discord, so intense that the de luxe train which carried the Wall-Streeters from their offices to their suburban homes was commonly known as " the Assassination Special."

The three found a more cheerful subject in the scientific progress being made under the pressure of war emergencies. For a century Germany had led the world in this field, and Dr. Heubach was pleased to report that progress was continuing at a pace never before dreamed. For the first time in the modern world scientists were set free from the restraints imposed by Puritan and Jewish superstitions ; for the first time rationality had become the criterion of research. Said this blond and bland Nazi physician, " For ages men have known that cattle and dogs and poultry should be bred only from the best males ; but superstition has prevented this obvious course being taken with human breeding. Now for the first time we have a generation of young women trained to understand their highest service to the Fatherland ; and the absence of men at the front need make no difference in our birth-rate, because we can use the method of artificial insemination."

Lanny expressed interest in this point of view, and the doctor went on to point out that hitherto science had been compelled to get its knowledge of human physiology by experiments upon animals, all of which differed to greater or less extent from humans. But now, thanks to the Führer's fervent belief in racial superiority, the scientists of the National Socialist world had an unlimited supply of human subjects, male and female, old and young, for whatever experiments might be useful to the state. The visitor from abroad said that that was a new idea to him and it seemed the most important that had yet come out of the *Neue Ordnung* ; whereupon the doctor went into details about the wonders he had witnessed in the laboratories.

Lanny had a hard time to keep from being sick to his stomach, but he managed to wear a look of proper scientific curiosity while Dr. Heubach told how men, women, and children of the sub-human Jewish and Polish races were being used to determine how long they could exist without food, without water, without air, and at what stages they could be revived from collapse induced by such deprivations. How much heat could they stand and how much cold? What would be the effect upon their metabolism of the removal of the gall-bladder, of the large intestine, of the spleen. And so on.

All this would be worth a report, so the P.A. encouraged his friend to talk freely. The doctor himself had watched experiments at the Dachau concentration camp, which was under the charge of the Death's Head S.S. Lanny had vivid recollections of this camp, where he had once made an attempt to arrange for the escape of his friend Freddi Robin. It was an immense place, with ten or fifteen thousand political prisoners—though that term was never used in Germany, since prisoners were not told what they were there for, and it made no difference. A large hospital just outside the grounds had been set aside for a scientist who was seeking to develop an anti-malaria serum for the troops in North Africa. First he would inoculate the victims with his serums and then with the disease. In all he had given the disease to two thousand persons, and had succeeded in saving about one-third of them —which Dr. Heubach did not consider a notable success. Mostly they were Polish priests, because the head scientist called himself a " neo-pagan " and hated Catholicism.

Next had come the Luftwaffe experiments of Dr. Rascher, an S.S. major who was disturbed by the number of valuable pilots found frozen when they were rescued from the North Sea in winter. They rigged up a freezing tank, with an iron collar to put around the victim's neck, and chains with handcuffs to keep him from trying to get out. The water was lowered to the temperature of the North Sea, and so it was learned how long the victim could remain conscious. Then it had to be determined how best to revive him. Some were plunged into hot water, and came out " red as lobsters," so said Lanny's informant, who had been present. Sometimes the victim was just left in a room of normal temperature, to live or die as might happen. Other victims had quantities of sea water poured into them, in order to determine how much of the North Sea the Luftwaffe pilots could endure to swallow and how they could be helped to recovery.

No less important to these flying men was the question of air pressure. A number of the wretched inmates of Dachau were put in an iron box and the air pressure was raised or lowered and the effects observed through a quartz window. Sometimes they would take the victim out when his nose started bleeding ; at other times they would wait until he was unconscious and then they would experiment in reviving him. Other victims would have fresh made-to-order wounds for the doctors to study ; when they died, there was a large crematorium, and the bodies were slid in through the furnace door. Always their gold teeth and fillings were knocked out, and Dr. Heubach remarked in passing that the income from these had paid the cost of the experiments.

XI

The next visitor caused excitement in the tender bosom of Heinrich Jung. An awe-stricken orderly came, announcing that *Seine Exzellenz*, Reichsminister Himmler, desired to call upon Herr Budd. Herr Budd did not show that he was startled ; he replied that the visit would give him pleasure. The orderly departed, and Lanny's pal exclaimed, " *Um Himmels Willen*, be careful what you say to him ! "

" What could I say to him ? " inquired the American, affecting surprise he was far from feeling.

" He is such a very suspicious man, Lanny, and you are an enemy alien."

" He is trying to protect the Führer, Heinrich, and he has reason to be suspicious of many persons. If he wants to make sure about me, I am happy to assist him."

Seine Exzellenz—he had just been appointed Reichsminister of the Interior—entered the room. He was a man of about Lanny's age and of Hitler's height, which was slightly below average. He had pinched features, a receding chin, a mild expression, and wore old-fashioned metal-rimmed spectacles ; a perfect picture of a German schoolmaster of the lower grades, so much so that the rich black S.S. uniform seemed like something put on for an occasion, say, an evening of charades or amateur theatricals. Many persons had made the mistake of taking Heinrich Himmler for what he appeared. He was a man of the people and shared their ignorance and childish naïveté. His conduct was guided by an astrologer named Wulf, and his other intimates were his masseur and a jockey, who was also Hitler's intimate. His S.S. men adored him, calling him " Reichsheini," and there were half a million of them ready to commit any horror that his stars might call for.

" *Heil Hitler*," said Lanny. " I have often wondered how we happened to miss each other these many years."

" I have heard a great deal about you, Herr Budd, from the Führer and others." The speaker's voice was as mild as his face. If it had been anybody else, Lanny would have said, " I hope nothing bad." But one did not make jokes with the head of the S.S., an official entirely serious in his attitude to life.

Neither did one show any trace of nervousness ; to do that might be to awaken the impulse of the cat which pounces upon the mouse. Suspicion was the food upon which this one-time poultry-raiser lived, and by which he had risen to the status of Number Two in a mighty empire. Hermann Göring had been officially assigned that status some years ago, but had fallen from favour and now rarely saw his master. Himmler was the one who had the task of keeping that master alive, and of putting down every trace of rebellion, or even of dissatisfaction, wherever it might show its head in the Third Reich.

" You have known our Führer a long time, I believe, Herr Budd ? " queried the mild voice.

" I first heard him speak more than twenty years ago, in the Bürgerbräukeller on the Rosenheimstrasse in Munich. That won't seem early to you, who, I am told, hold card Number Seven in the *Partei*."

" That is true, Herr Budd."

" That means you joined a group of six obscure men who were setting out to make the world over. To the learned and powerful of Munich, that seemed an insane idea ; but the seven persisted. It must have been early in the year 1919. Would it interest you to know what I was doing at that time ? "

" *Selbstverständlich, Herr Budd*."

"Because I had lived nearly all my life in Europe I had become secretary-translator to a professor who was on President Wilson's staff of advisers. Thus I had an opportunity to watch the peace negotiations from the inside ; and when I saw that Clemenceau and Lloyd George were prevailing over Wilson and that the settlement was going to be a *Diktat*, I was one of half a dozen members of the staff who resigned in protest ; at least, half a dozen protested and agreed to resign, but several backed out at the last moment. My name was in some of the American newspapers at the time, and it would be no trouble to find it."

This was " fishing " in a way, for the chief of the S.S. might have said, " I have already done so." But he didn't, and Lanny realized that he was there to listen, not to talk. The P.A. resumed, " From that time on I have been a friend of the German people. When my friends in other nations ask me why, I tell them that the Germans are the least apt to fall victims to the spirit of anarchy which has arisen in our time and threatens to destroy our civilization. The Germans not merely know what discipline and order are, they put them into practice, and for that reason they are the people who have most to offer to our time. I presume that I do not have to defend that idea to you, *Exzellenz*."

" Hardly," replied the other dryly. Could it be that there was a trace of a smile upon the almost blank countenance ? Could it by any possibility be that the man who directed the nefarious activities of the Schutzstaffel was susceptible to social charm ? The son of Budd-Erling was doing his best to find out !

XII

De l'audace, encore de l'audace, et toujours de l'audace, had been the motto which had carried Danton to the top in a revolution ; and now Lanny was giving it a trial. Watching this most dangerous of men, he remarked, " I have heard a story about you, *Exzellenz*. Most stories about eminent personalities have been made up to fit their character, but this one may be true. I should be interested to know."

" What is the story ? "

" It has to do with Gregor Strasser, whose secretary you

became. A group of your inner circle was drinking beer in
Munich and the talk fell upon the subject of what qualities
were most important in the National Socialist character.
Strasser laid his hand upon your shoulder, calling you 'gentle
Heinrich,' and predicting that you would never get far in the
movement because you were too mild, you looked and thought
' like a little bookkeeper.' Did that happen ? "

"Yes, Herr Budd, it happened about as you tell it."

"No doubt that had an influence upon your career, since
Gregor Strasser was the Number Two man in the movement
at that time."

"What has influenced my career is the desire to promote
and protect the National Socialist party, as the organ for the
building of the world's future. I can truly say that I have
never had any thought about myself."

"I believe that, *Exzellenz*. I have sometimes been asked
to explain you to the outside world. People imagine you are
cruel, a sadist, and so on. I have ventured to make the guess
that you are as mild a man as you appeared to Gregor Strasser ;
that you have no pleasure in the infliction of pain, and think
about nothing but the movement."

"You are correct, Herr Budd. I have never had any
emotions in the matter. I couldn't carry on my work if I did.
I am a man with one conviction, and anyone who shares that
conviction is my friend, and anyone who opposes it is my
enemy, and I do to him what I would do to a scorpion or other
deadly insect."

"We live in dangerous times," commented the visitor.
"It might interest you to know that I once met Gregor
Strasser—or rather, I was in the same room with him. It
was the first time I went to call on the Führer in the apartment
he occupied in Berlin. Gregor came in ; the Führer had sent
for him, I gathered, and in my presence he proceeded to give
the presumptuous man such a dressing down as I had never
listened to in all my life. That was when I learned who was
the master of the N.S.D.A.P. and who was going to be the
master of Germany."

"Yes, Herr Budd, and it was unfortunate that Gregor did
not learn the lesson when you did. When one starts a political
movement, all sorts of men swarm into it, from all sorts of

motives. As soon as it shows signs of meeting with success, some of them dream of taking it over and running it their way instead of the Führer's way. We had our critical time, and Gregor was one of those ill-advised men who had to be stamped on."

Lanny remarked, " I happened to be in Munich at that time, and I observed the process." He didn't say that he had seen an ardent young S.A. man, friend of Heinrich Jung and himself, shot in the face by one of Himmler's S.S. men and left lying where he fell. Lanny didn't ask whether by any possibility there had been in the mind of the S.S. head any trace of personal satisfaction at ordering the murder of his former employer, the man who had predicted that his secretary's " mildness " would keep him from having a career in the National Socialist movement. Lanny didn't point out that those twelve hundred victims of the Blood Purge had merely been demanding that the Führer should carry out the economic programme upon which he had built the party and won the votes of the poor and humble Germans—whereas Hitler had preferred to sell out to the steel and coal men of the Ruhr, who had given him the money and the weapons to seize power and kill off his old associates who had taken seriously the Socialist part of National Socialism.

What Lanny said was, " It was a severe lesson, and it seems to have been learned."

XIII

The son of Budd-Erling was exhibiting his best bag of tricks, but he had no idea what effect they were having, or what was going on behind that narrow forehead. Placid, blank-faced Heinrich Himmler was inscrutability itself in a Schwarzes Korps uniform. Was that his pose ? Or was he really a machine that did its work without emotion ? Always in the back of Lanny's thoughts was the realization that this was the greatest killer in the history of the world ; the largest-scale wholesale dealer-out of death. Genghis Khan doubtless had been equally willing to kill, but he couldn't have had so great a population to work on. This S.S. Reichsführer had ordered the deaths of several millions of Jews and several millions of Poles—Lanny had no means of estimating how many, but he knew they were being disposed of in immense extermination factories, their bodies shoved into furnaces and their bones ground up to make fertilizer for the German fields. Also there were the hundreds of thousands of Germans and other pure-blooded Aryans who did not happen to agree with Nazi ideology ; they were shot, or locked up behind barbed wire to die by slow stages. No outsider knew their number, and it might be that no records were kept.

This was the man who sat in front of the machine and pulled the levers. He said, " Let this one die, and that." He said, " Let this group die, this class, this race." No court in the land could stop him, no court had anything to say about the matter—such was the Nazi ordainment. Nobody but Hitler could interfere, and Hitler didn't. This was Hitler's man, whom he had put here to do this double job, the extermination of every individual who disapproved of National Socialism, and the extermination of those nations and races whom Hitler considered sub-human. For these purposes they had built the Schutzstaffel and the Gestapo, the secret state police ; there were now something over a half million of these, perhaps the most highly organized and most perfectly indoctrinated body in the world. They could go to any place in the Axis domain, seize any person and do anything they pleased with him, without charge or even explanation. They had some five thousand agents in foreign lands, and no doubt many secret agents in Allied lands.

This last was the thing for the son of Budd-Erling to worry about. How closely had these agents been watching him ? If they had wanted to do a real job, they could surely have found out where he went to stay when he came to New York, and who was the woman he lived with. They could uncover the fact that she was the author of bitterly anti-Nazi novels and short stories ; and possibly even the fact that she had got her material in a Berlin *pension*, and was that psychic medium whom Herr Budd had brought into the Führer's home under the name of Elvirita Jones ! Whenever that thought popped into Herr Budd's mind his heart began to thump, and it would surely have gone badly with him if there had been a lie-detector apparatus attached to his wrist or wherever they apply it.

If the S.S. or the Gestapo hadn't done these things it could only have been because of Adi Schicklgruber's orders. Adi had a sort of religious superstition concerning everybody and everything that had had to do with the early days of his movement. The blood flag, as it was called, the flag which had been carried in the Beerhall Putsch in Munich twenty years ago and which had been dipped in the blood of some of the martyrs who had died in that march—that flag was holy, and all other Nazi flags were touched to that flag in solemn ceremonies, and that made them holy too. It was the same with the few persons who had stood by Adi during his very comfortable incarceration in the Landsberg Fortress after the Putsch; Heinrich Jung had come three times to visit his Führer in that fortress, and that made Heinrich Jung holy, and to doubt his love and honour would have been a sin. It had been Heinrich Jung who had introduced Kurt Meissner and Lanny Budd to the Führer in the old days, and that had been like the touching with the blood flag.

But would that attitude continue, now when Americans were killing German soldiers in Italy and American airmen were bombing German cities and killing men, women, and children ? It was hard to believe—and much easier to believe that the very busy Reichsführer of the S.S. Heinrich Himmler, had said to himself, " I'll have a look at this fellow." And what if he didn't happen to like the fellow ? What if he decided that the risk was too great ? Would he order the fellow's arrest then and there ? Was it inconceivable that this most loyal of fanatics might decide to take matters into his own hands and save the Führer even in spite of the Führer's own wishes ? This modern Torquemada—a man who killed wholesale for the salvation of souls, for the overcoming of the Devil and the protection of the Faith—would he suddenly decide to take this too plausible art expert off to a dungeon and wring his secrets out of him ?

Not a dark dungeon, in the ancient style, but one of those modern laboratory dungeons that had a brightly shining light, so arranged with mirrors that the victim could never get it out of his eyes ! A dungeon made of concrete, in such a shape that the victim could not quite stand up and could not quite sit and could not quite lie, but was tortured in every position he might choose ! And then the relentless questions, by a relay of inquisitioners, keeping the victim always awake and with the bright light in his eyes, for hours, for days, for nights. Whom do you know in Germany, and who has helped you here? Heinrich Jung? and Kurt Meissner? General Emil Meissner? General-Major Furtwängler? Eric Erickson? Graf Stubendorf? The Fürstin Donnerstein? Your half-sister, Marceline Detaze? Her lover, Oskar von Herzenberg? Do you know Bernhardt Monck, alias Vetterl? Do you know his wife and children in France? Do you know Captain Charles de Bruyne, now living in your house at Juan-les-Pins? Do you know his wife and children? And Raoul Palma, alias Bruges, in Toulon? Do you know his wife? So on and on—and with the certainty that every one of these persons had already been seized or would be seized and subjected to the same horrors.

XIV

The military men have a maxim, that the best form of defence is an attack; and this, no doubt, applies to warfare of the mind as to that of the body. Lanny said, "I am extremely glad of having a chance to meet you, *Exzellenz*, because my position in Germany is such an extremely difficult one, and I have often wondered what your attitude toward me must be. I am an enemy alien and I have come several times into your country and moved freely about at the Führer's command. It can hardly be that you relish that, and I welcome the opportunity to explain myself to you."

There was nothing the Reichsführer of the S.S. could say except, "I shall be happy to hear what you wish to tell me."

"I have been in an uncomfortable position with my own countrymen ever since this war broke out, and even before that. Americans were divided sharply on the question of National Socialism from the time of Munich on, and most of the wealthy people whom I knew took the British side. I had become known as an ardent defender of the Führer and had been bringing him information for several years; but I saw that I could no longer get information if I kept that attitude and continued to associate with Forrest Quadratt and Hauptmann Wiedemann and other friends of National Socialism in New York. I was forced to take refuge in my role of art expert and pretend to lose my interest in political questions. The Führer understands that attitude, and it has enabled me to circulate among his enemies and bring him facts which he has found of use. But I am not sure if you, the Führer's friend and protector, realize that situation."

"It is a common one, Herr Budd, and not at all hard for me to imagine."

"For example, when I was in Rome recently, Marshal Kesselring turned me over to Herr Güntelen, who, I assume, is one of your men. It was he who suggested that I would not be able to get much information unless I shaded my opinions to the Allied side. I hated to do that, because I don't like the Badoglios and the Cianos and the other turncoats; but I met them, and I managed to hear them talk freely, and I reported on them to the Führer. Herr Güntelen promised that no matter what I did he would have no doubt of my good faith. But I cannot tell what reports may have come to you, and to old friends of mine like Heinrich Jung here."

The Jugend official had been sitting all through this interview, not opening his mouth, and probably shivering in his boots. For who in Germany was not afraid of this modern Torquemada, this man who could send even high generals to their death, and had done so? Even now Heinrich Jung didn't dare to speak, but waited for his superior to give the decision.

"Believe me, Herr Budd, I have not been left uninformed of the situation." Could it be that there was a smile on the tight thin lips? "Believe me, all true friends of the Führer are friends of mine," added the Gestapo chief. This was a careful answer and somewhat cryptic.

Following the motto of Danton, Lanny said, "If there is anything about my activities that seems to you to require explanation, I should esteem it a favour if you would let me give it to you at this time."

"Thank you, Herr Budd. I have accepted the Führer's faith in you because the Führer is the best judge of human nature I know. But since you make the offer, I will ask you about your relations with a man who makes such excellent airplanes for combat with our Luftwaffe."

"A very natural question. My father is a lifelong Republican, and put up large sums of his own money in the effort to defeat Roosevelt on three different occasions. He was, as you probably know, a business associate of General Göring, and he then conceived a great admiration for German efficiency and order ; he was an ardent isolationist, as the friends of Germany were called.. But after Pearl Harbour the government moved in on him, and he is to all purposes their prisoner ; they tell him what to do and he does it. My father is not an idealist like the Führer and yourself, *Exzellenz* ; he is a business man and conceives it his duty to protect the interests of his stockholders."

" He is well paid for it, I imagine."

" Not so much as you might think. The gross income of the company is immense ; but there are corporation taxes and excess profits taxes ; then, when my father gets his share, he pays about eighty-two per cent of it in personal income taxes. It is that way in war, in all countries. My father hates this war and vents his feelings by giving me items of information which I pass on to the Führer."

" Your father knows that you come into Germany ? "

" I have never told him because I do not wish to put that responsibility upon him ; but he is a shrewd man and I am sure that he guesses."

" You have information for the Führer at present, Herr Budd ? "

" I am bringing him some papers which he commissioned me to try to get."

" Would you be willing for me to see them ? "

Lanny had been prepared for this, but pretended to hesitate. " I will put it up to you, *Exzellenz*. If the Führer had instructed you to get certain information for him and him alone, and if someone else asked to see it, what would you do ? "

Again there appeared the trace of a smile on the thin tight lips. " I should give them to the Führer."

" No doubt he will show them to you if he thinks they have value." Lanny, extremely anxious not to offend this dangerous man, went on to suggest, " If you would call him on the telephone and ask him to change his instructions——"

" Never mind, Herr Budd ; the wait will not be long. I

am pleased to learn that the Führer has a friend who is to be depended upon."

Was that sarcasm or was it piety? Had the P.A. made another friend or another enemy? He had no idea which. It is the nature of despotism all over the world that no man can trust any other, or be sure of the meaning of any spoken word. The land of Beethoven, of Goethe and Schiller, had become Turkey under the Sultan Abdul Hamid, Russia under Ivan the Terrible, Spain under Torquemada, chief of the Holy Inquisition.

II

Spoils of the Enemy

I

LIFE changed in the New Chancellery when the Führer stepped across its portal. The Führer flag was raised over the building—a dangerous thing to do, but it was an act of defiance to the foe, a cry of hate. The sentries at the door stood more erect, the officials walked more smartly, the humblest *Diener* wore a smile and felt a thrill in his heart, knowing that he was part of the wonder. Such was the power of this genius-madman over the German people—all but a sophisticated few. The great indoctrinated masses loved and honoured him as a projection, a perfect archetype, of themselves. Amid all the suffering and grief they believed what he told them, that they were the greatest people on earth, and had only to hold out and victory would come to their banner. *Sieg heil!*

Even Lanny Budd felt the stirring. For him it would mean getting out of jail—the company of Heinrich Jung, of whom he was so awfully, awfully tired. Poor Heinrich, he truly loved Lanny and thought him a superior person; by way of proving his devotion, he talked to him and asked questions about the outside world. This kept Lanny under strain all the time, for fear that he might say something good about that world, might give some hint that in some way it was better than the Nazi world.

The only escape was to read the newspapers and magazines, and they were poisonous things, full of lies and hatred. In this huge imitation barracks that the Führer had built were no books but Nazi books ; the Führer was interested only in literature that was an extension of his own mind. Lanny was reduced to raiding the Karl May collection and reading one of these romances of the American Far West. They were fantastically out of drawing, but they had the feeling for adventure in strange surroundings. " Old Shatterhand," the scout, had a rifle that could fire forty-eight times and wipe out a whole herd of buffalo. To read about him was part of a P.A.'s job, for Adi wouldn't be able to believe anything really bad about a man who admired his youthful literary idol.

Heinrich Jung brought the news : the Führer was here ; and then Professor Haushofer had come ; then Franz von Papen, and Dr. Krupp von Bohlen und Halbach—evidently there was going to be a council of the elders, a very miscellaneous lot. There came Professor Pröfenik, astrologer and mystic, a white-whiskered old rascal, as Lanny knew well, having co-operated with him when trying to find out what had become of Trudi Schultz in the hands of the Gestapo. Heinrich brought one name after another, and Lanny realized that his turn was still distant. He went on reading about German immigrants on the prairie, and Winnetou, chief of the Apaches, smoking a peace-pipe with them. The Nazi doctrine, taught in all the schools, was that Germans had been responsible for most of the progress in America from the earliest days. Unfortunately there were not enough of them to control the bad behaviour of the Anglo-Saxons and other savage tribes !

There came Artur Kannenberg, bubbling over with welcome ; he liked Herr Budd—it was his business to like everybody, and to feed them. He brought the tidings that they were to have a little party, late at night, after all *die Grossen* had departed. Herr Kannenberg was going to give them a roast goose, and besought their aid in persuading the Führer to partake of it. He never ate red meat, but now and then could be tempted to taste fowl. The Führer's abused stomach was giving him endless trouble, and his steward's remedy was meat, in all the different forms which he knew so well how to prepare. *Aber leider*, it went untasted most of the time, and Dr. Morell continued to shoot glucose and caffeine into the unhappy great man's veins. Herr Kannenberg's whispered opinion of Dr. Morell's medical treatments amounted to *Majestätsbeleidigung*.

It was a whole series of indiscretions, but he thought of Lanny as an old friend, and one who could surely be trusted. "*Der arme Mensch!*" exclaimed the steward. "No one can ever get him to go outdoors. He paces the room; he frets and worries, day and night. He is sick of the very sight of generals; he distrusts them all, and yet he has to trust some of them! Three times last winter he went to Berchtesgaden, but he could not stay, because of the snow."

"Snow?" exclaimed the visitor. "Surely they could keep the road clear!"

"He could not stand the sight of it, Herr Budd. It made him think of Stalingrad, and our poor fellows freezing and suffering. Those dreadful Russian winters! Never must anyone speak of snow in his presence!"

II

It was about ten in the evening when Lanny Budd was summoned to the presence. He was searched, but not so thoroughly as last time; perhaps it was that Heinrich Jung was present, as a sort of guarantee of respectability. When the young S.S. men came to Lanny's undershirt he told them, "This package contains papers which are for the Führer's eyes alone. You are at liberty to leaf through the papers, but always with the typewritten side turned down. If you fail to do this, it will be my unpleasant duty to report the fact to the Führer." That was the way to talk to Nazis, and under Herr Budd's watchful eyes they handled that package as if it had contained poisonous snakes.

The conference took place in the Führer's private apartment. The one-time inmate of a shelter for the homeless did himself well as regards furniture and decorations, but his taste was decidedly bourgeois; he liked big overstuffed chairs, heavy curtains, and a collection of knick-knacks, which to an

American suggested the days of his grandfather. The Führer looked wan and exhausted, but showed eagerness to welcome this visitor who brought promise of excitement.

Sunk up to his neck in upholstery, Lanny told a wonderful story, which he had been reciting for weeks, about the efforts he had made to get real information this time, and how he had come upon the trail of a secretary who had been in Robbie Budd's service for many years and shared Robbie's abhorrence for this fratricidal war ; this man was now in Washington and his son was employed in the White House office. A couple of thousand dollars had done the trick, and Lanny now had the latest authentic figures as to American military production ; also, he had reports fresh from the hands of the authorities, showing the widespread efforts of wealthy and powerful persons to get America out of the war.

Hitler's hands trembled with eagerness as he reached out for these papers. They were in English, and anyway he couldn't have read them, being unwilling to put on his spectacles in the presence of a foreigner. But he pretended to look them over, and then asked Lanny to summarize them. When the procedure was finished he exclaimed in amazement, " How is it possible, Herr Budd, that the government does not move against such conspirators ? "

Lanny had the answer to that one carefully thought out. In a decadent democracy the government was afraid of public opinion, and the scandal that would result from the exposure of a spirit of revolt so widespread among the most influential persons. The government did not dare to defend its own existence ; it temporized and argued with its foes, tried to frighten them, and was itself frightened by their bold resistance. No one who listened to Lanny's detailed story could escape the conclusion that the Judeo-pluto-democracy overseas was on the verge of a revolution replacing its Jewish-descended Rosenfeld with a regime that would turn American arms against Asiatic Bolshevism and in support of Aryan order and property rights.

Lanny talked at length about his researches among the great capitalists of his country. He didn't have to be restrained by fear of libel suits from telling Hitler that some of America's leading newspaper proprietors were loyal friends of Nazi-Fascism, operating under democratic disguise. Their tens of millions of readers were by now thoroughly indoctrinated, and the mothers of America wanted nothing but to get their sons out of this world holocaust.

Lanny revealed also the terror which prevailed among government circles in Britain, which had learned about the jet bombs now coming into mass production. Lanny told some of the things they knew, and the Führer rubbed his hands together, a characteristic gesture when he was pleased. "Tell them the worst!" he said. "Tell them that our *Vergeltungswaffe Zwei* will carry more than a ton and a half of explosive, and in full production will cost only a tenth as much as a bombing plane. Tell them it won't be long before we build them so that they will release their cargo and then turn and fly back to their base; they will fly so fast that the British will not hear them until after they are gone."

Lanny promised faithfully that he would tell all this.

III

For a full hour the P.A. answered questions of his Führer: what he had seen in America, the attitude of the different classes, the delays in production, the rationing and the black markets, the possibilities of a *coup d'état*. Lanny's answers were such as to bring comfort to a harassed soul, and put him in a mood to yield to the temptation of roast goose. He sent for Heinrich Jung, and also for his dear "Evi"—so he called her. This was an honour for both Heinrich and Lanny, for the very existence of this Bavarian damsel was known only to a few intimate friends. The women of Germany had never heard of her; to them the Führer had to be a celibate and saint, whom each in her secret heart imagined as her special, heaven-sent Lohengrin.

Herr Kannenberg came, bursting with cordiality, and singing the praises of the feast he had prepared. The odour of the hot goose assailed the nostrils of all four of the party. Impossible to resist it, and Adi consented to have one small slice of breast; a large slice was put on his plate, together with a pile of stuffing. They talked about the food, and other feasts they had enjoyed in the old days; Lanny, who had partaken of *Weihnachts* cheer at the home of the Meissners thirty years ago, told how he and Heinrich and Kurt had shot hares in the snow and Lanny had learned about real German *Hasenpfeffer* and the kind of bun called *Dresdner Christ-stollen*. Anything to keep the Führer's mind away from the terrible thought of German armies being crushed, and German blood poured out, on the dust-blown Russian steppes !

After the meal was eaten and Adi had sunk into a soft sofa with one arm about his *Schatz*, Herr Kannenberg asked if he might sing for them, and the offer was accepted. The little round fellow seated himself on a small stool, overflowing the sides of it, his ivory-inlaid accordion clutched over his belly. He began to play, keeping time with one foot and turning his enraptured eyes to the ceiling. He played the Bavarian *G'stanzln* which Adi had learned to love in childhood, and which called for no intellectual effort disturbing to digestion. "*Hab' oft die ganze Nacht bei ihrer Hütten gewacht,*" wailed the minstrel.

But just when everybody had got into the proper sad mood for a story of unrequited love, there burst upon their ears a rude, screaming sound, the air-raid siren. For a few moments the singer tried to keep on, in an effort to maintain morale, but his Führer rose, so he had to quit. There was danger in delay, for the British had fast bombers called Mosquitoes, and these delighted to make sneak raids, flying close to the ground to avoid the German radar. Thus the bombs often fell a few seconds after the warnings were heard, and this kept everybody anxious—which was what the malicious foe desired.

Walking as fast as dignity permitted, Hitler led the way to the *Führerbunker*, a private apartment underground. It was the first time the American visitor had seen it, and he was astonished by its elaborateness. The entrance was through an almost solid block of concrete, the size of a small cottage, standing in the Chancellery garden. You went down thirty-five or forty steps and found yourself in a central hall which contained a long table, upholstered chairs, paintings on the walls—everything as above ground, though on a smaller scale. On one side was a drawing-room, Hitler's bedroom, and his office ; also Eva's bedroom and a bathroom ; on the other side was Dr. Morell's office, an operating-room and a hospital room with several beds ; a telephone room for three operators and a telegraph room for four ; file rooms, a storeroom, a lavatory, and an elaborate engine room providing light and air conditioning.

They sat in the drawing-room, with the customary long, overstuffed sofa, the cuckoo clock, and the bric-à-brac—all according to the taste of a customs official named Schickl-gruber from the Innviertel in Austria. This *Führerbunker* must have cost a million marks at the least, but it would not be complete without gimcracks which had cost several marks each. It might be, of course, that these were Eva's contribution. She had been a photographer's assistant in Munich, and had studied to be a dancer, so she considered herself an artiste, and possibly had appealed to Hitler on that basis.

Anyhow, here they were, safe and sound in the most elaborate rabbit warren or gopher burrow ever constructed. Bombs began to fall on the city above, and the ground shook under their feet, but there was nothing to fear. Lanny tried to make conversation, but gave it up because he saw that it wasn't considered the proper thing. The Führer couldn't sit still ; he jumped up and paced the floor, snapping his fingers and muttering to himself. All the millions that had been spent to give him physical security couldn't give him mental or moral peace. This was an outrage, a crime, because it was destroying German property and German lives ; worse than that, it was an insult, because it was coming to the Reichs-hauptstadt, it was bearding the dragon in his own den ; it was doing what he and his *Nummer Zwei*, the Luftwaffe commander, had said could never be done by any foe. It was the behaviour of barbarians, an affront to civilization, and as it went on, bomb after bomb, the Führer worked himself into one of his tantrums, racing up and down in his drawing-room, in front of the guests lined up on the long sofa against one wall. Lanny could only sit and keep his eyes averted, finding comfort in the thought that these were British planes, which did night bombing, and not American planes, which came by day.

IV

The trembling of the earth ceased and the company climbed the stairs. But the evening was spoiled ; the Führer went to the telephone to learn what the damage had been, and the guests retired silently to their rooms. " It is like that all the time now," deplored the mournful Kannenberg. " For four years he has had to work all day and nearly all night. There will be dispatches from the front, and they will be bad. *Ach ! Du lieber Gott ! "*

Lanny Budd did not see his Führer again ; he was never to see him again in this life—though he had no means of knowing that in advance. The P.A. would carry with him the image of a half-insane man pacing up and down in a room, and some nineteen or twenty months later he would read that the same man had paced that same room and then had shot himself in the head, while the one-time photographer's assistant had swallowed cyanide in her little bedroom adjoining. And was Lanny to believe this—or was he to suppose that it was one more trick which Loki, god of lies, was playing upon mankind ?

In the morning the polite Major Feldmann came to Lanny's room and said that the Führer had instructed him to find out what Herr Budd wished to have done for him. Lanny said that on a previous visit to Berlin the Führer had been kind enough to provide him with a letter of permission to stay in the city for two or three weeks, and he had got along quite well with that letter. He had a half-sister living near Berlin and several old friends in the city whom he would like to see. A week would be sufficient, if that would be agreeable, and then Lanny would ask to be flown back to Stockholm. He had some Swedish money which he would like to have changed for German, and he would ask permission to take out what he had left when he was ready to depart. The polite staff officer came back to say that all this could be arranged, and a couple of hours later the much-travelled art expert walked out of the New Chancellery with a pocketful of marks, food cards, and a police permit entitling him to sojourn within the limits of the Province of Brandenburg for a period of ten days.

There were columns of smoke rising from various parts of the city, but Lanny had witnessed many bombings and the sight aroused no curiosity in his mind. He strolled around the corner to the official Residenz of Hermann Göring, his friend and his father's friend, whom it was his duty to see next after the Führer. The secretary, who knew him, told him that the Reichsmarschall was at the Air Force headquarters, a place to which Lanny had once been taken blindfolded, and which he guessed to be in Belgium. The secretary offered to get him on the telephone, and this took only a few seconds, for there was no place in' the world that had quicker communications.

Once more Lanny listened to that bellowing voice, which made the receiver rattle. But no surprise this time, for *Der Dicke* had learned that Lanny was the Führer's messenger boy. Having himself lost his position at the right hand of the throne, he clutched eagerly at one who still had the entrée. Now he said, " I'll be in town in a couple of days. You will spend the week-end with me at Karinhall." It was a command, and the other replied, " *Ausgezeichnet! Besten Dank!* "

The visitor went out to the Wilhelmstrasse, carrying his suitcase. He did not care to register at one of the fashionable hotels because his presence would be bound to attract attention. He took a street-car to the Dahlem district in the south-west, where the Kaiser Wilhelm Institut was situated. To his surprise, he found this was the worst-bombed part of the capital, almost completely wiped out. But the Institute had not been hit, and not far away Lanny found an obscure hostelry where no one would know him. He showed his police permit, secured his room, and left his bag unlocked. He would check out in the morning and thus avoid having to register with the police—for the regulation said " within twenty-four hours." He had to bear in mind that Himmler's men might be following his every move, or trying to, and he didn't want to give them more aid than necessary.

V

The Physics Building of the Institut is a large, homely structure, with a rounded entrance on the corner, a tall tower above, and a row of small dormer windows all along the top. There were semi-basement windows along the bottom, all with steel bars, and S.S. men with tommy-guns walked in front of the building watching every passer-by. One followed Lanny inside and waited while he gave his name at the window of the booking-room and asked to see Herr Professor Doktor Salzmann. Lanny's name and address—the obscure hotel—were entered in the book, and when the message came for the visitor to be admitted, the guard followed him to the proper room to make sure he did not wander to some other.

Lanny had been here the previous winter at Hitler's request, because he had told the Führer he had picked up in his father's home and elsewhere some information as to what the Americans were doing with jet propulsion and atomic research, two of the most important subjects in the world. His real hope had been that Salzmann might inadvertently reveal something to him. He hadn't got much, and didn't expect to get much this time, but he was there because he had promised, and more important yet, because it would serve as camouflage to cover the visit he planned to make to Professor Schilling. In case the Gestapo were to make note of that visit and ask questions, Lanny could say, " The Führer asked me to meet Salzmann and Plötzen, and one of them mentioned Schilling to me last winter, as a person I ought to talk to."

So now the P.A. sat in the office of this Prussian *Gelehrte* of the old school, with white military moustache and hair closely cut where he still had it ; he wore black broadcloth, beginning to turn green at the seams because you couldn't get that good stuff any more ; also gold-rimmed pince-nez, and a double chin and thick neck in spite of food rationing—no doubt the scientists were in a special category. Salzmann had been puzzled to receive a visit from an enemy alien, but by now had got used to the idea ; he was cordial and encouraged Lanny to talk about jet propulsion and what the Americans and British were doing with it. Lanny's orders were to say that they were making progress, but he had to be cautious in this because it would make him the bearer of bad tidings, and it had been the custom of kings to order the death of heralds who committed that indiscretion. Adi Schicklgruber had gone back to so many ancient customs !

What Lanny did was to plead the inadequacy of an amateur. He had listened to technical men talking and had done his best to remember what he heard for the benefit of his German friends. He knew that the Americans were badly scared on the subject and were working hard and spending a lot of money; perhaps they were cautious in talking in Lanny's presence because his National Socialist sympathies had been well known before the war. Lanny watched this stern old-fashioned martinet and wondered what was going on inside that round head with the pink scalp and short white hair. Quite possibly he regarded his visitor as a combination of rascal and crackpot; anyhow, he guarded his words and revealed none of the Fatherland's hard-won secrets.

From his office Lanny was escorted to another, occupied by Professor Plötzen, as different a type as you could imagine: urbane and somewhat cynical, a *Weltmann* and darling of fortune, keeping his position in the smart world even while he worked hard at an exacting speciality. He and Lanny had liked each other from the start and talked about various mutual friends. Lanny could not get away from the thought: Does this man suspect where my sympathies are? And where are his own?

They chatted about atomic research, which was Plötzen's *Fach*. He was saddened because he and his colleagues hadn't been given funds enough for a real job, and of course he was eager for the smallest hint as to what was going on in the outside world. Lanny's talk, which seemed casual, had been carefully discussed with Alston and men at O.S.S. headquarters. Lanny would come right up to an important revelation and then fail to make it because he didn't understand the subject and couldn't be sure what he had heard; very tantalizing, but not the fault of a mere *Kunstsachverständiger*. Plötzen wouldn't give him anything positive, but he did confirm that Germany's atomic research was in the doldrums and that its one effort at nuclear fission was pathetically inadequate.

VI

When the American went out from that world-famous building—oddly enough, constructed with Rockefeller money

—he felt that he was established as a teller of Allied secrets on the subject of physical science. If now he were discovered to have paid a visit to the possibly suspected and closely watched Ernst Schilling, he could refer to his activities for the rest of that day as being all of one piece and in accord with the Führer's instructions. Even if his talk were to be overheard he could say that he was posing as an Allied sympathizer in accordance with the programme laid out by Herr Güntelen of the Gestapo. " To all intents and purposes I am one of you, *meine Herren !* "

Lanny thought these matters out while enjoying the sunshine in a little park, with children playing all around him and nursemaids watching the children and not overlooking the elegant but inattentive Herr. He strolled to a café and got a dinner on his food card ; a miserable meal of potato soup, ersatz sausage, warmed-over potatoes, and a dessert made of synthetics and referred to by smart Berliners as " genuine I.G. Farben." From there he walked to the modest home of the scientist, the address of whom Monck had given him. Fortunately it was in a detached house, so that there was no need to deal with a bell-boy or telephone operator. Lanny rang, and when an elderly servant answered he inquired if the Herr Professor was at home and then asked to see him.

The scientist proved to be a small-sized elderly man with grey goatee and moustache, horn-rimmed spectacles, and a suit of clothes which looked as if he had slept in it. His manner was timid and his voice gentle. He looked at his visitor inquiringly, and the visitor rose respectfully and explained, " I am an art expert, especially concerned with fine paintings, and I called on you because I was told of your interest in the subject."

" In *paintings* ? " said the man in surprise ; and Lanny didn't give him time to go farther. " It happens, Professor, that I have come upon an especially fine Raffaelli."

It was no coincidence that this eminent physicist had a code name that had to do with old masters ; two years back, when Lanny had taken the assignment of getting into Germany and memorizing and bringing out his atomic secrets, he had suggested that name and it had been accepted by the O.S.S. and presumably passed on to the old gentleman by some secret route. Anyhow, he knew it, and paled so obviously that Lanny could see it by the dim light of the room. "*Ja . . . ja!*" he stammered. "*Ja . . . gewiss.*"

The visitor continued quickly, "It happens that the painting is not far from here, and I am sure you would not wish to miss a chance of seeing it. The evening is pleasant and you might enjoy a stroll."

"*Sicher, es wird mich freuen.*" The scientist hastened to put on his black soft hat and his light overcoat, which looked as if he had been carrying scientific reports in it for the last ten or twenty years. He was a typical German scholar, serious, kindly, and no doubt absent-minded—but he hadn't forgotten the name that identified this stranger as an enemy agent.

VII

For walking at night in blacked-out Berlin you carried, if you could afford the price, a tiny electric torch. You kept it in your hand and, batteries being unobtainable, you generated electricity by working it like a pair of scissors. It sent a pale beam of blue light down to the pavement in front of you. But tonight there was a half-moon, so the professor put the torch into one of his badly stretched pockets. The pair walked close together and spoke in low tones, and when any other passer-by approached they fell silent. When they came to the little park where Lanny had sat with the children and nurse-maids, he suggested going in ; but the old gentleman led him away, explaining that the habit of people to resort to the parks for political conversations had become known to the police. They walked on streets which were lined with ghostly ruins, the silver half-moon shining through broken beams and rafters without coverings.

Lanny said, "I want you to know that two years ago I was assigned to visit you and ask about atomic fission ; but on the way I met with an airplane accident which laid me up. I have since been told that someone else interviewed you. Now I have been sent to ask you about rockets and jet planes."

"But that is not my subject."

"I know that ; but it is one which concerns us greatly,

K

and it is our hope that you may know someone from whom you can get the information we need." Lanny did not say "Herr Professor," and not once did they speak any name.

"That would be an extremely dangerous thing to attempt," said this "English coin." "It might well involve the heaviest penalty imaginable."

"I know," replied the P.A. "That applies equally to what I myself am doing. I put it to you as a matter of conscience. There is a clear possibility that one of our allies might be knocked out, and the consequences of that would be serious, possibly even fatal. Think it over, and see if there is not someone from whom you might get information on some pretext or by some device."

They walked for a while in silence. Then the old gentleman began, "Suppose that I were to get what you ask for, how would you handle it?"

"Physically, you mean? There would be nothing to handle. I never carry papers. You would meet me again, and tell me the facts, and I would learn them."

"You are an expert on this subject?"

"Unfortunately not; but I have studied it for this interview. I will tell you what we need to know, and when we meet again, you will tell me what you have found out, and I will carry it in my head."

"The subject is extremely technical and complicated."

"I have been well coached and have had considerable practice. Before I set out to ask you about nuclear physics I spent two months in learning what I was to ask you."

"We should say that it was characteristic of your countrymen to imagine that a man could come to understand that subject in two months."

"I did not make such a claim, *lieber Herr*. I said that I learned certain things by heart. My teacher was one of the greatest of living physicists, a man whom you know well. I recited my lessons to him and he gave me a passing mark. Thereafter I made a practice of reciting the lessons over to myself every night before I went to sleep and again before I got out of bed in the morning. I have done that with several different subjects, and so far I have managed to give satisfaction."

"All that is interesting and shows what the mind can do under the pressure of necessity. Tell me what you wish to know, and I will see if my memory will be equal to yours."

So the P.A. went through the lesson he had learned, and then, because there was a lot of it, he went through it again. He did not ask this learned gentleman to recite, but waited for him to ask questions. Lanny explained that he had got some elementary information about the V-1, and wanted especially to know about the V-2, which was a true rocket, larger and faster and therefore more dangerous. When he had finished his recital, the professor complimented him upon the mental feat he had performed and said, "Come to my home three nights from now, and if I can get anything I will give it to you."

Lanny replied, "I will try to come that night, but I have an engagement that will take me out of town, and it may be one or two nights later before I can get to you." He couldn't help smiling in the darkness as he thought what a tumult would have been caused in that professorial bosom if he had added, "My invitation is to Karinhall."

VIII

In the morning the traveller went to an outside telephone and called his half-sister. He asked, "Could I see that painting if I came now?" The answer was, "Yes, surely," and that was all. He went back to the hotel, paid the bill, and departed. He had no S.S. car to take him this time, so he would travel by a local train and learn more about what war meant to the German *Volk*. He found the Charlottenburg Station badly damaged, and on the train he stood for an hour, packed like a sardine with people who had done their best to keep clean in spite of the scarcity of soap. Some of the women still wore the finery which their husbands and brothers had taken from the French three years ago. Many talked about their troubles, but others kept their lips tightly shut, and Lanny was one of these because he did not wish to be spotted for a foreigner. He was far too well dressed for safety.

Leaving the train, he found a horse-drawn vehicle to take

him to the *Garnison-lazarett*. He sank back and surveyed the well-tended fields and hedges of the Province of Brandenburg. Cherry trees had been planted along this road, and that was evidence of the trust reposed in the population. In front of the farm-houses the shade trees were taking on their autumn colours. The trees drew the precious green chlorophyll back into the stems for winter storage ; the leaves turned, first yellow, then red, then brown, until at last the trees rejected them as worthless. Lanny had been reminded of how Hitler had treated his old comrade Gregor Strasser, and how he had treated Lanny's friend Hugo Behr ; thousands of others had met the same treatment during the past decade, and the P.A. reflected upon the way in which patterns of nature repeat themselves.

Marceline was waiting for him, seated under a tree in the garden, reading a German translation of *Gone With the Wind* ; it antedated the war, and the *Regierung* found nothing in it to object to. The pair could talk quietly here, and she told him the situation regarding Oskar. She had thought it safe to say that while Lanny had never shown any interest in politics, she was sure that in his heart he was not a Nazi ; he had important connections in America and could carry messages for the conspirators and perhaps bring a reply.

Marceline went into the cottage and summoned her lover. His health was coming back, and he had more colour, but he still walked slowly and with care. His left sleeve hung empty, and Lanny was careful not to glance at it. They did not sit close together, because that might have looked suspicious ; but there is no law forbidding gentlefolk to have soft voices, and a group of three is able to keep the entire surroundings in view and make certain that no one is getting close enough to overhear.

They talked about the grave position of Germany in the war : the bulletins had told of more " straightening " of the German lines in the Ukraine, involving withdrawal from two more cities ; the Allies were spreading over the toe of the Italian boot and had made a landing at Salerno, just below Naples. They were reported as being repulsed with immense losses, but thinking Germans could be sure that it wouldn't be long before they were being repulsed from places farther in the interior. Also, they had bombed Regensburg, deep in south-eastern Germany, and Oskar could say that there was a vitally important ball-bearings plant there. It must be that enemy spies were all over the land, picking out the best targets for the airmen. Lanny said nothing.

IX

The invalid officer expounded his thesis that his country had been brought to this plight by a set of gutter rats— "ignorant, low-class fanatics," he called them—and surely the outside world could not blame the German people for this calamity. The art expert replied that many Americans did blame the German people, but well-informed persons understood the terrible power of propaganda in this modern world. When you got hold of the press and radio, you could tell the people anything and be believed ; also, modern weapons were so deadly that insurrection had become impossible.

The end of this world struggle was a terrible thing to contemplate, Oskar went on ; Germany was being scientifically crippled and smashed—industry, transportation, communications. If the process continued unchecked, there would be nothing left for the people but starvation, or else to be fed by the charity of their conquerors. Lanny said that was perfectly true, and it was surely the duty of the old leaders of the Fatherland, the people of decency and education, to realize this situation and take action.

Marceline had told her Junker lover about the American newspaper-men's practice of talking about " Mr. Big." Oskar now translated it to " Herr Gross," a common enough German name, frequently Jewish, and therefore safe to bandy about. He said that this Herr Gross was the heart of the problem. He had made himself not merely head of the government and Minister of War, but also Commander-in-Chief of the Army. He trusted none of his generals, except a few Nazi incompetents like Jodl, whom he kept by his side. He ran the war from Berlin or Berchtesgaden or wherever he happened to be. He decided not merely great strategy, but the most minute details, and sent elaborate orders which were impossible to carry out. The effort to convince him of this would bring

instant dismissal. That was why the war was being lost, and
why the most honourable group of men in the whole world
was being driven to revolt.

Once this false leader was out of the way the entire evil
movement would collapse. And what would be the attitude
of the American government then ? Obviously, it was a
serious matter for any group of men to attempt to overthrow
the government of their country in the midst of war. Would
the enemy take that as the occasion to march in and complete
their conquest ?

Lanny was in position to say that he had discussed this
question with persons of the highest authority and could state
that the formula of unconditional surrender was meant for a
criminal *Regierung* and not for a government of responsible
persons with whom agreements could be made. Germany
would be occupied in any case, but the purpose of the occupation would be to see a representative government firmly
established. After having had opportunity for free and open
discussion the people would be called upon to say what sort
of government they wanted. " If you want official assurance
on that point," added the P.A., " it can be arranged for you
to get it through one of our diplomatic offices—I suppose
Switzerland would be the most convenient."

This pleased Oskar von Herzenberg, and it moved him to
confidences. He told an extraordinary story, of which no
hint had come out to the Allied world. Only two months
previously a group of men had made a carefully planned effort
to remove Herr Gross from the scene, and the effort had failed
through the merest accident. Oskar did not say who the men
were, but it became clear that they were Reichswehr officers,
and that Oskar himself had had knowledge of the affair. They
had planted a deadly bomb in a package supposed to contain
brandy, and got it on board a plane in which the Führer was
to ride. Everything went according to plan, except that the
detonator failed to work and the bomb didn't go off. When
the plane arrived in Berlin, the package was carried to the
Auslandsamt, its supposed destination. One of the conspirators
realized what must have happened and rushed to the office in
time to get possession of the package and take it away. So
Hitler had no idea how close he had come to death.

Oskar said with a wry smile, " That happened in July, but the men involved still get weak in the knees whenever they speak about it." He didn't say, " We shall try again," but hinted, " There are others who would work to that end if they could be satisfied that you speak not only for your own government, but for others which we fear even more."

The P.A. replied, " Might it not be a good thing if you and Marceline were to take a trip to Switzerland ? Cold weather is coming, and it might be an aid to your recovery to spend some time in a mountain resort."

" I will think it over and consult with one or two friends about it. How could I communicate with you, say, in the next three or four days ? "

" I will telephone Marceline. I remember that the younger Hans Holbein worked in Basel for many years, so let us use him for code. She can tell me that she has learned of an example of his work, say, an unlisted woodcut, and it can be viewed on a certain date. Let that date be not earlier than two weeks, to give me time to communicate with Washington. You register at the Trois Rois Hotel, and a representative of the government will contact you there."

Lanny added to his half-sister, " If there should be anything you want to tell me, you can do it by choosing a title for the painting and describing it. Holbein painted and engraved all sorts of subjects—landscapes, figures, portraits—so you can use your imagination."

Marceline was amused ; it appealed to her as a game. She was dreadfully bored by life in the country with nobody but wounded men around her.

x

Lanny spent the night in the cottage, sleeping on the couch as before ; he slept soundly, for his various missions were succeeding and he was pleased with himself. In the morning he went back to Berlin and from there called Göring's Residenz. He never had to parley with underlings ; it was evident that a busy man had left a standing order that the American art expert was to be put through whenever he called. Lanny had too much sense to be flattered by this ; it was made evident that what *Der Dicke* wanted was to ask questions about the Führer, everything he had said about everything, and especially about the one-time *Nummer Zwei* who had slipped out of position and was no longer sure what number he held. He had committed the crime of not wanting to attack Poland, and the crime of not wanting to attack Russia, and worst of all, the crime of not being able to keep the Allied Air Forces away from German cities. He was in the doghouse—a phrase which he had thought funny when Lanny had used it about Rudolf Hess, but would surely not have cared to hear applied to Hermann Göring !

He shouted, " *Wie geht's, Lanny ?* " And then, without waiting for an answer, " We are ready to leave for Karinhall. How soon can you be here ? " Lanny came, and saw in front of the building that six-wheeled baby-blue limousine with the military chauffeur, and the guard car with four armed S.S. men ready to follow. Two other guests were escorted to the big car and tucked in, for the sun had disappeared and a cold wind was blowing from the North Sea. *Der Dicke* was one of those restless spirits who have to supervise everything and can never give you any peace. He looked terrible, with flabby skin, corpse-like colour—and before the drive was over Lanny observed him surreptitiously swallowing a pill. Göring forced himself to be cheerful, however ; he had given final orders that would win the war, so now they had nothing to do but enjoy themselves, ha, ha, ha ! This old-style robber baron was not content to laugh, he bellowed.

One of the guests was a sister-in-law whom he had acquired by his marriage to a Swedish noble lady named Karin, whom he had privately canonized since her death. The other was Baron von Behr, head of the Einsatzstab, the organization which had been created for the purpose of plundering Europe of its works of art. Lanny had met him on a previous visit to Karinhall and had bought from him a couple of Göring's rejects. Lanny had the presumption to think that the Number Two Nazi's taste in art was far from infallible ; it ran to heavy nude female flesh and the costumes and jewels of the world's predatory classes. Lanny thought there were a lot more important things.

The car sped over the *Autobahn* to the north, the long

mournful horn warning traffic out of the way. The guests had an interesting topic of conversation, for one of the Baron's spies had recently discovered the hiding-place of a priceless collection of paintings belonging to a Jewish banker; the rascal had hidden them in a cave in the Thuringian mountains and then had sneaked away to Switzerland. Each of the treasures had been wrapped in oilcloth and tightly sealed against dampness; the list of them was a catalogue of famous names for the past five hundred years; and now the best had been brought to Karinhall, and a *Kunstsachverständiger* from overseas would have the delight of inspecting them. But he couldn't buy any of them because *Der Dicke* couldn't give him a clear title—not until he was able to get his hands on that " *jüdischer Schweinehund in Genf* " !

Lanny's thought went back to the White House and its occupant, who also had a hobby of collecting works of art. Engravings in this case, very small, but well executed, and reproduced by the billions—postage stamps ! F. D. R. had a large collection, and it rested his mind to get out one of the many volumes and insert new specimens. A harmless enough hobby—he didn't have to rob anybody or torture anybody to force him to reveal the hiding-place of his treasures. That was a difference between the Old World and the New, as Lanny saw it; the Old had far more culture, more subtlety, more taste—but it had also more cruelty and hatred. Take your choice between aesthetics and ethics !

XI

In the course of ten years Lanny had watched Karinhall expand from a hunting lodge into an immense rambling mansion. Its growth had not been stopped by the war; it was going to be the world's greatest art storehouse, and its owner had promised to leave it to the German people, and to build a railroad to it so that all the world might come and pay tribute to the name of Hermann Wilhelm Göring, master collector of all time. Even the enemy had apparently acquiesced in this arrangement; they had never bombed the place though it was in plain sight. Lanny knew what was in their minds, that after the victory the treasures would be returned to their owners, and the name of Hermann Wilhelm Göring would be expunged from the honour roll of art lovers.

You went into the place by a large entrance close to the ground, and walked through a hall, the oddest that Lanny had ever seen—like a tunnel, growing narrower as you advanced. He had never ventured to ask about that eccentric architectural idea. There were alcoves on each side where you could sit at a table and sip wine and admire paintings ; to Lanny it seemed more suggestive of a restaurant than of a home. Then you came to the biggest hall without pillars that he had ever seen, and he had travelled much. All the old familiar paintings had been taken down from its walls and the collection of the *jüdischer Schweinehund* occupied their places. Really it was a surprising thing, for every old master you could think of had a representative here. *Nennt man die besten Namen, so wird auch der meine genannt !*

So Lanny Budd could spend a pleasant week-end. The art of painting is one of the greatest of human inventions, a cultural instrument, a gateway to all other arts and branches of knowledge. When you have a collection of great paintings before your eyes, you can think of history, you can watch the pageant of the ages passing before your eyes. You can think of the poems and stories you have read, the legends, the traditions. You can think of religion, broaden your understanding of it, and learn that fundamentally all worship is one. You can travel in imagination and see the world without any of the discomforts and dangers of travel. You can enjoy the distilled essence of the beauties of nature. You can behold the works of man, " and manners, climates, councils, governments." You can study architecture, costumes, interior decoration, and, above all, peoples of all races and climes. You can study psychology in the faces of the proud monarch and the humble toil-worn peasant ; the great painter has read their secrets and told you more about them than they themselves knew.

Lanny could have enjoyed a full week at this country place, save for the fact that he was Hermann's guest. Hermann's idea of enjoyment was to gather his art experts and show them his trophies ; to spread his ego all over each canvas, and tell his guests what to tell him about it. That went on until his legs were no longer able to bear his weight; then he took his American friend off to his private study and told him what to think about the war, which was in a very unsatisfactory state indeed. Lanny knew better than to agree with this; he said that the Americans were surprised and alarmed by the fury of German resistance in Italy. All this week the German official communiqués had been describing the fighting on the Salerno beachhead, and now the Allies were in " headlong flight."

Said *Der Dicke*, " Don't let the little doctor fool you, Lanny "—meaning his fellow Reichsminister, Goebbels. " We knew that your armies were coming to Salerno, so naturally we had the beaches mined and our guns precisely laid. But that can't last long; you will make new landings, and Montgomery will force his way up the west coast and join you."

Lanny went on opposing. " I know that the Germans are laughing at the *Wuwa*, but all the same, I am satisfied that the Führer really has new weapons, and I'm waiting to see them in action."

" It's a race between us and your bombers, Lanny." In German, as in English, the word " your " can be singular or plural; and Lanny interposed quickly, " Don't say ' mine,' Hermann. You know if they were mine they wouldn't be fighting you. My father reports that our top people are terribly worried about rockets. The Führer told me they were coming, and he told me to say so in America."

" We ought to know that we can't frighten America out of this war. We ought to get peace, and get it at once, on the best terms obtainable. All that we are accomplishing is to turn the Far East over to the Japs."

So they had plenty to talk about for the rest of that session. Very soon *Der Dicke* began hinting to find out what his allpowerful Führer had said about his humble self. The fact was that Göring hadn't been mentioned; but Lanny thought it safe to say that the Führer had praised his loyalty and his indispensable executive ability. That made a new fat man of him, and he was able to get along for the rest of the talk without taking one of his stimulating pills. He beamed like a child.

Lanny decided that he really was going back into childhood, under the pressure of disappointment and defeat ; he was retiring into his own private world, where his vanity was the only law. When evening came the master of the household made his appearance in a costume of flowing white silk, like a Doge of Venice, studded with jewels, with the emblematic stag of St. Hubertus on his head, and—most fantastic of incongruities—a swastika of pearls set between the stag's antlers. Thus clad, he led his guests in a train about the mansion, showing them a domed library like that in the Vatican, with a desk twenty-six feet long, made of mahogany with bronze swastikas inlaid, and having on it two huge baroque candelabra of solid gold—so he told them—an inkstand of onyx, and a long ruler of green ivory studded with jewels. Next morning he showed the outside of the place, wearing a sky-blue uniform and carrying his jewelled baton of gold and ivory ; in the evening he was an oriental rajah, all in gold !

XII

Eric Erickson arrived from Stockholm by plane. Göring had a business conference with him, and that set Lanny free to enjoy the paintings in his own way. He was joined by young Bruno Lohse, Baron von Behr's assistant on the Einsatzstab, a Nazi who really loved great art and had discovered that Lanny loved it too. Later in the day this pair went for a walk in the magnificently kept forest, which had once belonged to the Prussian government, but which Göring had calmly taken for his own. Never had there been such graft.

They watched the stately stags at the feeding racks. As soon as the snow fell a certain number of them would be shot —a larger number than usual because of the shortage of choice meat for the Nazi chieftains. Lanny praised the stags, he praised the forests and the system of maintenance, he praised the wonderful thousand-year Third Reich, and the miracles it was going to bring about in the world's economic affairs, in the sciences, and, above all, in the arts. Young Lohse thought this was a wonderful American and asked naïvely if there were many more like him at home. Lanny replied that there were a great many who felt about Germany as he did, but unfortunately they had no way to express themselves at present.

In the evening they had a magnificent banquet, with venison and *Rebhuhn*, not to mention turtle soup and a turbot, and all the products of the country. Something to remember after the skimpy and tasteless foods which Lanny had been getting in Berlin ! *Der Dicke* announced that he had kicked all his doctors out and was eating what he pleased ; he made noises to prove his pleasure, and later his satiety. There was a huge log fire in the great hall, and after they were settled before it, they heard the war news over the radio—several more towns in the Ukraine had been surrendered to their former owners. Fru Lili Martin, the sister-in-law, asked Lanny to play for them, and he played one of Beethoven's *Contretänze*, which he had learned as a boy : it was *echt Deutsch*, and also short—Lanny knew well that his host wouldn't have stayed quiet for anything long.

Göring herded them all up to watch him run the elaborate system of electric trains which he had installed upstairs, a thing which would have given delight to any company of small children. Then he took them to the Karin shrine, where candles burned day and night, and where they were expected to stand with bowed heads and in silence for at least a minute. There stood the hostess, Göring's present wife, the large and impassive stage queen, Emmy Sonnemann ; Lanny watched out of the corner of his eye for any sign of her emotions, but she gave none. Emmy had never known the Swedish countess who had died of tuberculosis in the days when her husband was an inmate of an institution for drug addicts. Apparently Karin had been a sort of Patient Griselda and had earned the refugee officer's undying devotion. The second wife had the same need of patience, Lanny felt sure.

Next day, which was Sunday, the P.A. was standing in front of a Rubens, a group of those immense fleshy ladies reclining nude upon a bed of grass and ferns. Red Erickson came up behind and remarked, " There are seldom any ants or mosquitoes in paintings." When Lanny had stopped chuckling over that novel bit of art criticism, the oil man said in a low tone, " I haven't been able to get anything yet, but I may be able to. I'll be at the Hotel Eden for a couple of days."

Lanny said, " Thanks," and that was all. They didn't take
a drive together this time ; they had both decided that it
would not be the part of wisdom to call their friendship to the
attention of the Nazis.

XIII

That Sunday evening was a memorable one in an art
expert's life : he had a chance to get rich !

The son of Budd-Erling had been offered a lot of rewards
in the course of his extensive travels. Prior to America's
entrance into the war both Hitler and Göring had offered to
pay him for his services, an amount never specified because
he had not let discussion get that far. Mr. Hearst had offered
him fifty thousand a year to enter his service as a collector
of confidential information. F. D. R., too, had offered payment
for what Lanny preferred to do freely. Even Pierre Laval,
the butcher's son, had tried to buy him ! And now the chief
of the Luftwaffe, Reichsminister and Governor-General of
Prussia, put on his sky-blue uniform with broad dark-blue
stripes on the trousers and not less than two-score medals and
decorations on his bosom ; with all that magnificence he
summoned a Franco-American art expert into his study and
made him an offer of a million dollars. One million dollars in
paintings, to be chosen from the ten thousand masterpieces
to which Göring possessed a clear title—and Lanny himself
would be permitted to put the price upon them. Göring's old
and valued friend would be put upon his professional honour
and would state the true value of the works he wanted, and
he could have them up to a total of one million dollars !

And what did he have to do for that ? Just to bring to the
Luftwaffe chief the specifications and blueprints of whatever
jet pursuit planes the Budd-Erling Aircraft Corporation might
have in process at the present time. When Lanny looked
staggered and said he had no idea how he could get such
documents, *Der Dicke* replied, " Don't tell me that, Lanny !
They are there, and you have access to the place and must
know people there who feel as you do. With your father taking
the position that he does, might it not be that he would
help you ? "

Lanny was stuck, for here he had been telling all the leading

Nazis that his father was to all intents and purposes a prisoner of the Jewish-pluto-democratic government, compelled to serve it against his will ; and if so, why shouldn't he choose to help the German people whom he so greatly admired ?

Lanny said, " Hermann, my father is a man who has never learned to keep his mouth shut. For a matter of twelve years now his hatred of the Roosevelt administration has been known to everybody in the plant. His every move is watched, not only by spies, but by government agents who are all over the place. Moreover, he is a business man by his life's training. If it came to a showdown, I doubt if he could bring himself to do anything against the interests of his stockholders. If anything is done, it will have to be by me."

" All right then, Lanny, you do it ! " The fat man's eagerness made him seem like a greedy child.

" I think I know a man who might be approached. You know, when your own men were working in the plant before the war they made a few friends. I might have to spend some money on them."

" All right ; I have money in New York and can put it at your disposal."

" No hurry about that. I'll see what I can do for you."

" There must be no delay, Lanny. My information is that the project is far advanced ; and you know it takes time to get a new type of plane into production."

" I'll do my best, *alter Freund*. I'm expecting to go straight home. I admit that I am tempted by the thought of your paintings." Hitherto Lanny had proudly refused all bribes ; but a million dollars, and in the form of old masters—that was beyond the powers of human nature ! To refuse it could not be made to seem plausible.

Hermann's last words startled Lanny. " Take my advice," he said, " and be careful in your dealings with the Führer. He is under a great strain and is not always able to control his emotions. Believe me, I know ! "

When Lanny sank to rest that night on a *Rosshaarmatratze* in one of the guest rooms of Karinhall, he was saying to himself, " My days in Naziland are about over ! "

12

Destruction Face to Face

I

THE Reichsmarschall flew away to his forest-hidden head-quarters in the west, and Lanny and Erickson and a couple of the other guests were taken back to Berlin in the swiftly rolling limousine. It was on the evening of this day that Lanny was supposed to visit Professor Schilling, and he spent most of the interim thinking over the situation and how best to handle it. He had been nervous ever since his interview with Heinrich Himmler; he couldn't believe that things had really gone as well as they had seemed to. Naturally, it would be Himmler's game to have Lanny think so; but, on the other hand, it was Lanny's game not to be fooled.

If the " English coin " was closely watched, as Lanny had been warned, what more likely than that the woman who opened the door was serving as a spy for her Fatherland? Or perhaps there had been another servant listening behind a partly closed door. Or even a member of the family—that was one of the evil devices of the Nazis, to set a child to watching parents, or a sister to watching a brother. If it had happened in this case, there might be S.S. men waiting in the shrubbery for Lanny's appearance; or it might be that the frightened old physicist had already been apprehended and put to the torture. It might be that Lanny himself would be having that experience before the night was over. They had a drug called scopolamine, popularly referred to as the " truth serum "; it put the conscious mind to sleep, and the sub-conscious mind answered questions. When Lanny thought of all the things he might say under the influence of such a drug his bones turned to putty.

Of course he might telephone the professor and make an appointment somewhere else. To make it for a street meeting would sound suspicious, and to make it for a restaurant wouldn't help much, for the Gestapo could come there. If they were watching this specialist in one of the crucial subjects, they would surely not fail to tap his telephone. No, the thing to do was to go openly and rely on that bland geniality which had carried him through so far. He had the Führer's permission, not only to be here in Berlin, but to tell what he knew about those crucial subjects to the scientists who could make use of them. Also, he had just made a deal with Hermann Göring to bring him secrets about the jet-plane programme of America; and who was there that could question these orders of the Number One and the Number Two? Lanny asked this rhetorical question and was not pleased with the answer which came promptly: Heinrich Himmler!

II

With a mind full of such disturbing thoughts Lanny went to a new hotel in the Dahlem district. He had just got settled in his room with the morning papers and a couple of weeklies when there came the accursed screaming of those sirens. With ruins all about him—one corner of the hotel had been recently caved in—Larry jumped up and ran downstairs. The shelter was at the next corner, so he went down the street, following a stream of people, mostly women with young children; the men were at work and the older children in school. The shelter was underground, and you trooped down a flight of concrete steps. It was already crowded, and there was nothing for Lanny to do but sit on the floor against a wall. In these neighbourhood *Bunker*, he learned, the people had their own places pre-empted, and many kept bedding here and other necessities.

There wasn't light enough to read, and Lanny, desiring to attract no attention, sat hunched with his head in his arms, pretending to be asleep. He listened to the conversation, of which there was a great deal all around him, and discovered quickly that Dr. Goebbels and Reichsminister Himmler had not been able to keep the women of even middle-class Berlin contented with this war; if a poll could have been taken of the one or two hundred persons in this place, the struggle would have come to an end that day. When the crack of the ack-ack began to sound and the walls and floor began to shake, the women lost control of themselves and the block wardens gave more than one of them warning.

Next to Lanny sat an old gentleman, with straggly whiskers and a threadbare overcoat, playing with a pack of cards. When he discovered Lanny watching him, he invited the stranger to a game of bezique. Lanny had learned this game in childhood, so they played, and while the American airmen were missing a railroad station and bringing down several blocks of apartment houses, Lanny managed to lose one-mark-twenty to this sad-faced emaciated old man, who doubtless needed it. When they parted the winner said hopefully, " *Auf Wiedersehen*," and Lanny replied, " *Grüss Gott*," which was meant to suggest that he was a Bavarian.

The P.A. went out and stood watching the people from this shelter filing into a barracks built for the bombed-out— long sheds with small rooms and common toilets, most miserable. Then he returned to his hotel and resumed his reading of the *Völkischer Beobachter*. He did *not* read that the British had been driven into the Bay of Salerno, so he could assume that reinforcements had been landed on that bloody beach. Two more Russian towns had been given up, so he knew that the meat-grinder was still working in the Ukraine. The Americans had taken a place on the coast of New Guinea. That seemed a strange place to be fighting, but Lanny assumed that the General Staff knew its business and that there must be an air-base near.

Leaving Karinhall, Lanny had thought that he would never want another meal; but nature doesn't work that way. By evening he was hungry; he tried another café, and discovered that *Kartoffelsuppe* was the same potato soup no matter what fancy name was printed on the menu. He sat for a while reading Dr. Goebbels' afternoon budget of news, then got up and strolled toward the home of Professor Ernst Schilling, world-famous authority on the nucleus of the atom. The P.A.'s knees showed signs of not wanting to take him, but he gave them orders and they obeyed:

> When Duty whispers low, *Thou must*,
> The youth replies, *I can*.

III

The house was an old-fashioned one, a compromise between a villa and a cottage. There was a small garden in front, and some shrubbery ; a breeze was blowing, and every time it moved the shrubbery, Lanny Budd's heart gave a jump. There was a porch with pillars—and who might be standing behind them ? Who might be sitting in that big armchair in the shadowy corner ? The wicked flee when no man pursueth !

Lanny rang the bell, and the same elderly servant opened the door. What would she make of this well-dressed gentleman who came and took the Herr Professor for a walk in the moonlight ? The Herr Professor was an elderly man, and perhaps did not enjoy long walks, and might be exhausted after them. Lanny's fears had this woman all fixed up as an agent of Himmler. And what would she make of the un-German name of Budd ? Had he made a mistake in giving his real name ? But no, he was supposed to be there at the Führer's orders, and to have given a false name would have been wholly out of key. Take it easy and bluff it out !

"*Jawohl, der Herr Professor ist zuhause.*" Lanny sat in the little old-fashioned parlour, prim and spotless ; he wondered if this old gentleman was a widower, and how many years he had lived in this home, presumably once in the suburbs and now in the city. Did the household all run to the nearest air-raid shelter, or had they stayed here and just shut their eyes ? Every day, when the scientist went to his laboratory, he couldn't be sure if he would find his home standing when he returned ; every night, when he went to sleep, he wouldn't know if he would wake again. Such was the gift which Adi Schicklgruber had brought to his most-loved people, his *Herrenvolk*. *Blut und Boden*—now the *Blut* was scattered all over the *Boden* and the *Boden* was shaken day and night by T.N.T.

The *Gelehrte* came, saying, "*Guten Abend.*" Without another word he put on his worn overcoat and his faded black hat, took his walking stick, and showed his caller out of the door. Were his old knees likewise trembling, and not merely from age ? Had it occurred to him that his servant might be an agent of the Gestapo ? Did he have children or grand-children, and have to wonder whether one of them might be a Hitler fanatic, spying on the rest of the family ? When he glanced about at the shrubbery, was he thinking what Lanny had thought ? And had it occurred to him that this stranger who had pronounced the key word " Raffaelli " might have got that word by torturing a captured American spy ?

IV

They walked side by side, and close together as before. The elderly scientist looked behind him, then turned a corner and looked again. In a low voice he asked, " Are you ready for your lesson ? " When Lanny said yes, he spoke as follows :

" The thing you ask about is a true rocket, liquid-fuelled, about fifteen metres long and two metres in diameter, with an almost needle-pointed nose. It has four fins, sweeping back and serving as control surfaces. It has a jet engine which pours a tremendous stream of gases from its tail. One of its most important features is an extremely powerful pump which sprays the fuel into the combustion chamber. The engine burns for a little more than one minute, and in that time it consumes close to five tons of alcohol and more than five tons of liquid oxygen. That gives it an altitude of about twenty miles, and after that it flies of its own momentum. Its speed will be about one mile per second and its range is estimated at two hundred miles. It carries a load of a ton and a half of explosives. All this presents an enormous complexity of problems, literally hundreds of them, and as many different kinds of scientists have been working on them for more than ten years. They believe they have all the problems solved, and the thing is in production ; quantities are expected to be flying by next spring. They cost about a hundred thousand marks apiece. That is the story. Do you think you can repeat this ? "

Lanny tried. He left out several important points and made a couple of mistakes which the old gentleman corrected. It took three tries to say it exactly right. Then, " Do you think you can retain it now ? "

Lanny replied, " I'll spend a lot of time making sure. Do you know where the work is being done ? "

" Most of it at Peenemünde. There is another place, but I was unable to learn its name. I have told you everything I know."

" Very well, Herr Professor. I thank you."

" It is to save the world from a fate too dreadful to contemplate. And now, under ordinary circumstances I should be happy to make your acquaintance. Perhaps you will come to see me some day when all this is over. But for the present, we should not linger."

" Surely not." They had walked around several blocks and were not far from the old gentleman's home. Lanny said, " Gute Nacht," and turned back, then stood in the shadow of a tree and saw the other turn into his place. The P.A. went his way, repeating over to himself that terrible lesson, which spelled certain death for many thousands of British people. The P.A. had learned quite a lot about " wonder weapons," both at home and abroad, and was sure that nobody had any means of pursuing or stopping a missile that travelled at six or eight times the speed of sound.

V

It was a dangerous thing for a well-dressed man to be wandering alone about the streets of Berlin at night, and Lanny got to his hotel as quickly as possible. Near by was a public telephone, and from it he called his half-sister and asked, " Have you found that Holbein painting for me ? " Her reply was, " I expect to have word about it in the course of the morning. Where can I call you ? " He gave her the telephone number of the hotel, saying, " I won't be there later than noon. I may be flying in the afternoon, unless you can be pretty sure of getting me a chance to see that Holbein." If Herr Himmler's agents were listening in on telephones they wouldn't make much out of that.

Lanny went up to his room and lay on his bed, reciting his rocket lesson over and over until he knew it as well as the multiplication table. Then he fell asleep—for he had trained himself to plan but never to worry, and he had done his planning about these matters in advance. When he awakened, he found that the new multiplication table had not escaped his mind. He recited it again, and then had a breakfast of bread and apple butter and ersatz coffee brought to his room. He read the morning papers : more " straightening " of the eastern line, and more hard fighting at Salerno, but no more " headlong flight."

He didn't wish to leave this room until Marceline called. If she said yes, he would go to see the " painting." He wanted to see Erickson once more, and that was all, except to call the Führer's secretary and have arrangements made for his plane trip to Stockholm. All very simple, and nothing to bother a traveller's head about. It was like being in the still centre of a tornado.

There came a knock on his door, and surely that was nothing to make his heart leap. He was expecting a knock, for this was a third-class hotel, and in order to answer a phone call he had to go downstairs. Yes, it was the young woman who took the place of a bell-boy, and who had smiled at this obviously well-to-do man and made it plain that he wouldn't have to be lonely at night unless he chose to be—and he had chosen to be. Now she said, " *Der Fernsprecher, mein Herr*," and Lanny gave her the small piece of paper money he had ready and hurried downstairs, that being quicker than the elevator.

There was no booth, but it didn't matter, for he didn't expect to have much to say ; just " *Sehr gut, ich komme*," or else " *Schade. Auf Wiedersehen*." He took up the receiver and heard Marceline's voice, asking if he had had a pleasant night and if he was still interested in the Holbein painting. He answered that he was still interested. He knew that she was giving him a chance to make sure who was speaking, and he said, " I would like to take it to Bienvenu "—so that she could be sure who was her auditor.

She began a speech, slowly and very distinctly, so that he might get every word. This was the speech : " I have seen the painting. It is a grim and rather frightening thing, but there can be no doubt of its power. It is called ' Death in the Twilight.' I urge you to see it at once ; somebody else may get it, so don't delay a moment. I am no longer at home and cannot take you to see it, but don't fail to take my advice. Promise me."

"Yes, of course. Where can I see it?"

"It is at Neuschloss."

"Neuschloss?" he echoed. He wasn't usually dumb, but this quiet yet terrible series of sentences had set his heart to pounding and thrown his mind into confusion.

"Surely you remember!" exclaimed the voice. "The place where your translator lives."

Lanny's translator! He had no such person and had never needed one, except years ago in Russia. But he caught on: Marceline wanted him to translate Neuschloss. Newcastle! And that meant: Get out of Germany! It meant get out at once. Death in the Twilight! "*Ja, ich verstehe,*" he said. "*Ich werde mir das Bild ansehen—noch heute. Wie geht es Dir?*"

"*Heil Hitler!*" came the response. "*Lebe wohl!*" And that was all; the phone was dead.

VI

Lanny was standing by a wall-telephone in an alcove of the hotel lobby, where several persons might have heard his conversation and might be watching him. After hanging up he stood thinking for a fraction of a second, then walked towards the lavatory, that being a place where he could get out of sight and have a few moments to think.

His thoughts were in a tumult. Marceline had given him a warning that his life was in danger; that could be the only meaning of her words. "Death in the Twilight" had nothing to do with any painting by the younger Holbein. "Grim and rather frightening!" Rather, indeed! Marceline meant the Gestapo; she could mean nothing else. She had fled from them, and it might be that she had risked her life in order to warn her half-brother. Did it mean that Oskar's plot had been discovered and that Oskar himself had been caught? Or did it mean that Oskar was a spy and had betrayed the half-brother of his *Freundin*? Or that Himmler had found out something else about Lanny Budd and had sent his men to arrest him? Somehow or other, Marceline had found out about it ; perhaps a servant had warned her, as four years ago one had warned Laurel Creston in this same *Haupstadt* of terror !

Anyhow, Lanny had been warned, and in words there was no mistaking. " At once . . . don't delay a moment." That was somewhat out of key with the viewing of a painting and was as far as anyone would dare to go over a telephone in Naziland. The Gestapo was looking for the Führer's American friend ; and here he was in a hotel—which was like sitting down inside a trap ! Surely the first thing the Gestapo would do was to put their telephone system to work on the hotels. He was registered here in his own name and it would take but a few minutes to locate him. They might be entering the lobby at this moment. The clerk would say, " *Der Herr ist in der Toilette.*"

Lanny Budd was no longer in the *Toilette*. He was strolling out, as nonchalantly as he could. He did not go back to his room, but strolled out by the front door and down the street. He had no hat on, but it was a pleasant cool day, and a number of men were going without hats these days ; they were hard to get, and people wore no more of anything than the weather and the law required. Down the street, and around a corner, then around another corner and another, and now he was part of the crowd in a big city ; now he was no longer " registered " and easy to find. Of course he might run into someone who knew him, and who knew that he was wanted by the *Polizei* ; but that wasn't likely. The *Polizei* would have his photograph, but it would take them a few hours to get it reproduced and distributed, and meantime the son of Budd-Erling was just a good-looking middle-aged gentleman out for a stroll. There were plenty of Germans who looked like him, also Danes and Frenchmen and Swiss and others.

Lanny thought with a touch of heartache of the things he had left in his hotel room and that he would have to kiss good-bye ; they would be taken by the Gestapo, and some official would sell them in the black market. Lanny's other suit, his overcoat and hat, his clean underwear and socks and handkerchiefs, his toothbrush, his hair-brush and comb, his safety razor that was absolutely irreplaceable, his letters from American millionaires that he had carried with him on his many voyages in order that the police agents spying on him might be able to get through their dumb skulls that he was a really top-notch *Kunstsachverständiger*, *connoisseur d'art, conoscitore d' arte, conocedor de arte*—according to which frontier he had crossed. The spies used different words, but they all had the same ideas and the same techniques.

Lanny couldn't go on walking the streets of Berlin all day. He must have some place where he could sit down and think things out and wait until night. He bethought himself of a device he had used when he had been in danger in Toulon : a cinema ! There you could sit in nearly complete darkness, and for as long as you pleased ; there nobody paid any attention to you—being carried away into a dream world, the farther from reality the better.

Fortunately Lanny had his purse and his notecase, also his papers ; he must keep these latter for the present, for at any moment on the street he might be asked to show them. They would identify him as Lanny Budd, but there would be a chance that, for this day at least, the questioner would not have his name in mind ; whereas to be caught without any papers would inevitably mean being taken to the nearest police station and thoroughly investigated.

Lanny stopped at a small grocery, somewhat elaborately known in Germany as a *Kolonialwarenladen*. He bought a package of pastries called *Leibnitzkeks* and stowed them away in his pockets. They would last him for the day. The cinemas opened early in all German cities and closed early because of the blackout. Lanny went to the nearest, regardless of the programme, and found himself a seat at the side, where other people wouldn't stumble over him. There he sat and thought how he was going to get to Neuschloss, Connecticut !

VII

The picture on the screen was a version of the Strauss operetta, *Die Fledermaus*. It was done in technicolor, very bright and gay, well calculated to take the minds of Berliners off their troubles. Lanny watched it for a minute or two, then closed his eyes and tried to forget it ; *his* troubles required close attention. But he couldn't close his ears, and presently there came the loud tramping of soldiers, and the blaring music of the *Badenweilermarsch*, Hitler's favourite. A newsreel was being run; and then Lanny's ears were assailed by a shrill, penetrating voice—there stood that most odious of human creatures, Dr. Josef Goebbels, making a speech and calling down curses upon the heads of *die Meckerer, die Nörgler* of the Führer's holy Reich. Lanny had once attended a reception in the little doctor's home, and later had met his wife in Switzerland, where that lady had sought refuge from his infinite vileness. Since that time Lanny had kept away from him; but it was not possible to keep away from his voice, which filled a quarter of a million cubic feet of air with infernal sound waves.

Presently Lanny noticed another sound that surprised him; a murmur, rising louder and louder to hoots and jeering! The German people didn't like their crooked little Doktor any more, and were tired of hearing him call upon them for more sacrifices; they were raising their voices against him whenever he appeared on the screen. Lanny had been told about this by Oskar; it had become so common that the Gestapo had taken to raiding theatres, ordering the lights turned on suddenly and arresting the disturbers. Lanny surely didn't want that to happen to him and scrounged down in his seat, trying to be the most inconspicuous person in this *Cinemapalast*.

All newsreels have one virtue, they are soon over. Then came a biography of Frederick the Great, one of the Führer's favourite themes, and made just the way he would like it. Another costume picture, with gentlemen in perukes and short pants, and ladies with hair piled high and dresses full of flounces and flummery. Plenty of colour, and much dignity, bowing and scraping and announcing of titles. The Frederick of this film was never one of the leaders of the Enlightenment, loving everything French, speaking the language on all occasions, and patronizing such cynical personages as François Marie Arouet, alias Voltaire. No, he was an *echt deutscher Friedrich*, making patriotic speeches, choosing his six-foot Pomeranian grenadiers and disciplining them with his cane, berating his generals for lack of spirit and daring, holding out with all Europe against him, and snatching victory out of the jaws of defeat. In short, he was Adi Schicklgruber, grown dapper and wearing pumps on his feet and a powdered periwig on top of his head, but thinking the same thoughts and making the same speeches, almost two centuries ahead of time.

Such were the sights and sounds that tormented the senses of Lanny Budd while he sat in this large auditorium, trying to figure out how to snatch his own personal victory out of the jaws of defeat. He would lose himself in his thoughts for a while, and then would become aware of the screen, and quarrel with it in his mind, and then go back into his private world. Thus in snatches he saw the programme through ; then, instead of getting up and going out, he saw it through a second time. Now and then he munched one of his *Keks* ; as a boy he had been greatly amused to discover that this meant " cakes." It had been pointed out to him that this was the only way to get the Germans to pronounce it correctly ; otherwise it would have been *kahkays*, and that would have been harder still to recognize.

VIII

Lanny could think of stories more thrilling than anything on this screen ; they came swarming into his mind, one on the heels of another. " Death in the Twilight ! " What had Marceline meant ? Something that had actually happened, or just a name for a painting, suggestive of danger. Lanny saw Oskar coming up to Berlin and being seized by the Gestapo in the twilight ; he saw Marceline getting word about it next morning and fleeing into the forest. He saw Oskar having a quarrel with her—they had quarrelled almost incessantly ; in a fury he left her and reported her to the Gestapo. But no, he couldn't do that, because she would tell about the bomb in Hitler's airplane !

More probably, Oskar had been trying to find out about rockets, and someone had betrayed him ; perhaps even now he had been given the " truth serum " and was blurting out the facts about the Führer's American friend. Perhaps now every person whom Lanny had ever known in Germany was being questioned ; and what a turmoil, also what a lot to be revealed, and how many, many reasons for trying to catch this clever scoundrel before he got out of the Führer's domain !

Lanny saw them going through his belongings in the hotel room ; he saw them interviewing Salzmann and Plötzen, Heinrich Jung, Bruno Lohse, Baron von Behr—and the horror and alarm of all these different persons.

Yes, hundreds of scenes and stories, all of them melodramatic, and all of them perfectly possible, all of them things that happened again and again ! Lanny had been accustomed to say that the Nazis had supplied the writers of spy stories with material enough to last them for the next thousand years. And with villains—every kind of that story commodity imaginable ! Double-dyed villains, subtle sophisticated villains, maniacal villains, even unconscious and self-righteous villains.

They were here in Naziland, literally by the millions ; and Lanny was in the midst of them. How was he going to outwit them ? He saw himself going to Hitler and trying to brazen it out. But Hitler would refuse to see him ; or else Hitler would fly into one of his wild tantrums and rave at him and never hear a word he said. Hitler was one of the maniacal villains—also one of the unconscious and self-righteous villains! Was it conceivable that Lanny could persuade him to go against the verdict of Heinrich Himmler, the man upon whom he depended for the protection of his life, the man whom he most trusted of all men in Germany ? Was it conceivable that he would consent even to see the culprit, and to burden his mind and rend his sensibilities in the midst of all the calamities and slaughters on the eastern front ?

Or should he try to go to Göring for protection ? What chance would he have with that great lump of bluff and fraud, tormented by craving for drugs, and by wounded vanity, the fading of his glory, the failure of his hopes ? What would friendship mean to such a man in such a crisis ? Göring's faith in the plausible son of Budd-Erling would be as easy to crack as an eggshell—and exactly as impossible to restore ! And even if Göring wanted to help Lanny Budd, what could he do against Himmler and Himmler's machine ? Himmler would get hold of Lanny and crush him like the aforesaid eggshell, and nobody but Himmler's men would ever know what had happened to him. There might be a record somewhere that the American Army would discover—but who would have time to read it ?

One thing was certain, Marceline would not have given such a warning unless she had been sure that Lanny was in dire peril. She had made it as plain as words over the telephone could be ; and there was no other possible meaning for the words. If Marceline herself and Marceline alone had been in danger, she would have had no reason to risk talking. But it was Lanny who was to see the painting "Death in the Twilight," and Lanny who was to go at once to Neuschloss ! That being true, it must follow that the whole machinery of the S.S. and the Gestapo was at work to find Lanny Budd and arrest him. That was what the machinery was built for. A lesser offender might have called for a lesser effort ; but for a man who had dared to worm his way into the Führer's heart, to come into the Führer's home and try to steal his secrets, such a man would constitute a supreme challenge, and all the dreadful power of the *Geheime Staats-Polizei* would be set to work.

IX

What was Lanny to do ? The first thing that became clear in his mind was that he must turn over his priceless secrets to Red Erickson. Erickson was going out, and he would know the O.S.S. people and how to communicate with them. Erickson could fly to Stockholm, whereas Lanny might have to walk —or to swim ! Whatever might happen to Lanny, the secrets of *Vergeltungswaffe Zwei* would be known to the Allied Combined General Staffs, and to allied combined scientists and engineers and manufacturers !

Lanny waited through two complete programmes, and then, because it wasn't quite dark, he saw the second half of *Die Fledermaus* for a third time. Then he got up and strolled out into the blackened city street. He had no walking-light, and the moon was under a cloud ; it was necessary to move slowly, and to use extreme caution at crossings ; but he didn't mind that. He assumed that by now the Gestapo would have sent out an exact description of him, including his clothing and his lack of a hat.

He came to a public telephone. It was a risk to enter such a place, but once more duty was whispering, " Thou must." He went in, dropped his coin, and called the Hotel

Eden. He hoped that it was a likely hour to call the oil man ;
he would be dressing for a dinner. A sudden relief to hear
his voice ; and Lanny said, " Do you remember the joke about
the naked ladies and the ants and mosquitoes ? "

" I do," was the response, and no name. Lanny was pretty
sure that Red had him marked as a secret agent by now and
would understand cryptic ways of communicating.

" Could you make it convenient to see me for a few minutes
right away ?   It is a matter of importance."

" I have a dinner engagement ; but I can be late if necessary."

" It is really worth while. I can put you onto a good oil
deal. Do you remember the last time we were in Berlin, where
you met me on the morning of your leaving ? "

" I remember it."

" Could you find that place again ? "

" I'm sure I could."

" I'll meet you there. Whichever one arrives first, wait for
the other." Lanny hung up and got away from that spot as
quickly as darkness permitted.

He had quite a walk before him, but he didn't mind, for
the evening was chilly and he had no overcoat. His destination
was the Donnerstein palace on the Bismarckstrasse ; he had
stayed there with his friend Hilde, and had been in the cellar
when the building had been hit by a bomb on the terrible raid
of March first. Now the place was a burned-out wreck. There
might be somebody holed up in the basement, but it surely
wouldn't be the Fürstin Donnerstein, who had a summer camp
on the Obersalzberg, in the Bavarian Alps, and had even then
been on the point of seeking refuge there.

X

Walking in a blackout is no fun, and especially not when
every footstep behind you may be that of a police agent
seeking your life. Lanny kept watch for any flash of light
ahead, for it was only police who were allowed to use ordinary
flashlights, and if he saw such a sight he would turn quickly
and get away from the spot. Fortunately he had visited
Berlin off and on since his youth and needed no map ; he had

groped his way to the palace night after night, and he knew the very feel of the marble coping which surrounded its area. The high bronze railings had been carted away, no doubt to make munitions, but Lanny knew the spot. He saw no signs of life, but of course there might be caretakers, or even families of squatters underground.

Crouching in the area-way and waiting, Lanny heard a vehicle approaching and saw dimly a taxi with a shaded blue light. A man got out and paid his fare, then stood until the cab was gone. "*Sind Sie hier ?*" asked the familiar voice with a touch of Brooklyn even in German. Lanny climbed out and took his friend by the arm and led him away.

No need for beating about the bush in a time like this. Lanny said, " No names, please. I'm in trouble and I have to go into hiding."

" The devil ! " exclaimed the oil man. " Can I help you ? "

" I wouldn't let you. That wouldn't be fair."

" You let me help Vetterl."

" That was because I was there to take the rap if necessary. This time I'm on my own. What I want you to do is to take out an important message."

" All right, of course."

" It has to do with the V-2 that I asked you about. I got some facts from a top person."

" You have it in writing ? "

" I learned it by heart, and you will have to do the same. We'll go over it again and again until you can recite it."

" I'll do my best. Shoot."

The P.A. began : " This thing is a true rocket, liquid-fuelled, about fifteen metres long and two metres in diameter, with an almost needle-pointed nose. It has four fins, sweeping back and serving as control surfaces. It has a jet engine which pours a tremendous stream of gases from its tail. One of its most important features is an extremely powerful pump which sprays the fuel into the combustion chamber. The engine burns for a little more than one minute, and in that time it consumes close to five tons of alcohol and more than five tons of liquid oxygen. That gives it an altitude of about twenty miles, and after that it flies of its own momentum. Its speed will be about one mile per second and its range is estimated at two hundred miles. It carries a load of a ton and a half of explosives. All this presents an enormous complexity of problems, literally hundreds of them, and as many different kinds of scientists have been working on them for more than ten years. They believe they have all the problems solved, and the thing is in production ; quantities are expected to be flying by next spring. They cost about a hundred thousand marks apiece."

Lanny said this straight through, and ended, " Now see how much you can tell me."

Erickson was a business man, accustomed to putting his mind on what concerned him. He recited the lesson, about as well as Lanny had done when Schilling had given it to him. Lanny corrected the errors and filled in the gaps, until, after half an hour or so, his friend had it perfect. " You'll realize how important this is," the P.A. cautioned. " I have made a rule to say it over night and morning to myself."

" Don't worry," said the other. " I have it and I'll be sure to keep it."

" And you know what to do with it ? "

" Don't doubt that for a moment."

" All right, then ; that's all."

" Old man, I hate like hell to leave you alone."

" What I'd hate like hell is to have this message delayed ; that's why I don't mean to involve you. Get out as quickly as you can, because the Gestapo may be getting ready to question you about me."

Erickson said, " I'll take the first plane. You know some place to hide ? "

" I think I do. I can put my mind on it, now that I've got the message off. Good luck to you." They exchanged a warm handclasp, and Lanny turned and went off into the darkness.

XI

His course was northward, toward Moabit. Here, likewise, he knew the way ; before the war he had been coming here off and on for more than a decade. There had been a workers' school here, and Trudi Schultz and her husband had taught art in it. When the Nazis had come into power they had killed the husband, but Trudi had gone on with her anti-Nazi propaganda and Lanny had secretly helped her. It was his hope now to find one or more of her comrades and persuade them to help him.

It was a dangerous place for a well-dressed stranger, and not only on account of the Gestapo. Robberies were common in these blacked-out streets, far more common than the newspapers let the public know. The robbers would sneak up behind you and hit you over the head with a blackjack or a piece of pipe. Also, there was bitterness against foreigners, and many had been beaten up without having given any provocation. Naziland was a far different place from Deutschland of the *Kaiserzeit*. Lanny walked softly, and with all his senses alert ; no doubt he gave as many scares as he got. When he saw flashlights ahead he knew it was a *Razzia*, a raid to sweep up men for the Army. He back-traced a block and went around several blocks.

He had a name and address firmly fixed in memory. It was a street of tenements, homes of the poor, but he knew that in daylight he would have seen flower-boxes in most of the windows. He had no trouble in finding the street, but the number was another matter ; matches were difficult to get, and he wouldn't have dared to strike one anyhow. He made a guess and tapped on the door of a little shop. Many shopkeepers lived behind their places of business, and this one wouldn't open, but called from inside, " Three houses to the right."

Again it was a problem. There was a row of bells, and no doubt with names, but Lanny couldn't see them. Fortunately a man came out, and Lanny put on his best imitation of a guttural voice : " *Bitte, wohnt hier ein Herr Seidl !* " The answer was : " *Im dritten Stock, links, rückwärts.* " Lanny groped his way up in darkness, for gaslight was strictly rationed, and was expensive besides. When he came to the right door he tapped softly, and when he heard a voice from inside, " *Wer ist da ?* " he answered, " *Ist Herr Seidl zuhause ? Johann Seidl ?* " The voice asked, " *Wer sind Sie ?* " and he said, " *Ein Freund.* " Everybody in Germany was afraid, and doors were not readily opened at night.

This one came open a small crack, and in the dim light

L

Lanny saw the outline of a head. He asked, " Johann Seidl ? " And then, " I have a watch to be repaired." The man answered, " I do not do that sort of work. I work in a factory." Lanny whispered, " *Partei Genosse.*"

The word *Genosse* is the word used by German Socialists, meaning " comrade." The Nazis, who posed as being Socialists, favoured the phrase " *Partei Genosse.*" But it was possible for a Social Democrat to use that phrase, and an old working man wouldn't be sure which the visitor meant. But he would surely know that it wasn't a matter to be discussed in a public hallway ; he opened the door and Lanny came in.

XII

As in most workers' homes, there was one room, serving as kitchen and dining-room ; a gas stove against the wall, and a table, covered with an oilcloth, in the centre. The light was a single gas jet by the wall. By that light Lanny saw an elderly German working man, frail, with bowed shoulders, wearing an undershirt and patched trousers, a straggly grey moustache and old-fashioned spectacles with metal rims. The man saw a gentleman wearing a well-tailored suit and a closely trimmed moustache. He could hardly have been used to that sort of caller.

He said, " *Bitte, kommen Sie,*" and led the way into a tiny bedroom, without a light. He signed Lanny to sit on the bed —there appeared to be no chair. He shut the door, which left them in darkness ; then he came and sat by the visitor, close enough to touch him. " *Bitte, sprechen Sie leise,*" he said. Speak softly !

Lanny whispered, " I am told that you are a block warden for the National Socialist party."

" *Nein,*" was the quick reply. " I used to be but I could not do the work. My health is failing."

" But you still belong to the party ? "

" *Ja, natürlich.*"

" You used to belong to a different party, *nicht wahr* ? "

" *Ja,* but that was a long time ago."

" I remind you of that time, *Genosse.* I used to be the husband of Trudi Schultz."

Lanny could feel the old man start ; it took him a moment or two to catch his breath. Then he whispered, " How could that be ? "

" It is a long story. The Nazis got her husband and killed him. Trudi went on with the party work, as you know. She worked in a tailor's shop, but did no tailoring. When she carried bundles out, it was literature. You know, perhaps, that she got money from outside."

" *Ja.*"

" She said it was from a relative, but I was the one who gave it to her. You heard later, perhaps, that she had fled to Paris ? I was the one who helped her to get out of Germany when she learned that the Gestapo was on her trail. I had a wife at that time, but she divorced me, and I married Trudi in England. She went back to her anti-Nazi work in Paris."

" I never knew what had happened to her."

" The Nazis kidnapped her in Paris. I tried my best to save her, but I learned that she had died in Dachau. She was a noble woman, and might have become a great artist ; she had the talent. I was able to get some of her drawings published in *Le Populaire*, which at that time belonged to the Socialist party of France. I am by profession an art expert, so I know about such matters."

" You are not a German, *mein Herr* ? "

" I am an American. I have sworn vengeance against the murderers of my wife."

" How can it be possible for you to be in Germany now ? "

" I have done the same thing that you have done—pretended to go over to the enemy. I have been getting information for my government ; but today I learned that I have fallen under suspicion, and that the Gestapo is looking for me. I have come to my old comrades for help."

" This is a strange tale, *mein Herr*. It is a hard thing to ask of an old working man who is himself under suspicion. I have a grandson who lives with me here, and he belongs to the enemy in his mind. I tried to teach him my principles, but I failed."

" That is a story which I have heard many times. I know what I am asking of you, and I don't blame you for hesitating. You will wish proof, and what can I give you ? I could describe

Trudi to you, but you would realize that if I were an agent of the enemy I could have studied her picture and her work. Do you remember Bernhardt Monck ? "

" I remember him well."

" It was Monck who gave me your address. I have not the right to tell you where he is or what he is doing, except that he is working for the cause. He said, ' Tell him that you were Trudi's husband and that will be enough. He knew her well and may have some of her drawings.' I don't ask if you have them, because that might be dangerous. Tell me if you remember Hansi Robin."

" The violinist ? Very well indeed. He played at many party meetings."

" Hansi is married to my half-sister Bess. I have known him and his brother Freddi since they were boys. Johannes Robin, the father, was my father's business associate ; they made a lot of money buying war goods and reselling them—that was after the First World War. Johannes became a *Schieber* and made a fortune speculating in German marks, but the Nazis took it all away from him. Freddi had persuaded his father to give him money for a labour school here in Berlin. Trudi taught art in that school, and that was where I met her and her husband, Ludwig. Trudi and Ludi—we used to think that was a funny pair of names ; it sounded like a vaudeville team. All three of these persons, Trudi, Ludi, and Freddi, were destined to be murdered by the Nazi gangsters."

" I met Freddi, but I never heard what had become of him."

" He was tortured in Dachau, and when they turned him loose he was a broken man. I took him to my mother's home on the French Riviera, and we tried to save him, but it could not be done. Those are my reasons for hating the Nazis, and for appealing to an old comrade for help."

" You shall have it," said the watchmaker. He got up, opened the door, and put on his well-worn coat and cap. " I cannot hide you here," he said. " But I will find you a place."

XIII

They groped their way down the stairs and out into the street, somewhat less dark because there was a moon behind the clouds. The German led the way, and Lanny followed, close enough not to lose touch. No one saw them ; night is a blessing to all conspirators, and a handicap to all in authority. They turned a corner and went a couple of blocks, then the old man turned into an alleyway, and stopped and waited for the other to join him. He was standing in front of a door, on which he knocked, three times, and after a pause, three more. Lanny heard the door opened, but could see nothing ; under the strict blackout regulations no door might be opened when there was a light behind it. Seidl spoke low : " *Ein Genosse der auswärts schläft* "—a comrade who is sleeping out.

Lanny was led through a dark room. An inner door was opened, and there was a dim light by which he could see what was apparently a large workroom. He smelled leather, and later, when he thought it over, he guessed that it would be some work for the government, since it was hardly possible that anyone could get leather for private contracts at this time. His escort was a tall lean woman with grey hair and a drawn face, which gave her a severe expression. " *Genossin Anna*," said Seidl. " *Genosse Dreissig*." Lanny didn't know whether " Comrade Thirty " meant that he was the thirtieth man to be " sleeping out " in this place, or whether Seidl had just chosen the first name that came into his head ; Lanny had not given any name.

" *Willkommen*," said the woman, and she led the way to another door, which led by wooden stairs to a cellar. They went down, the woman leading the way with a candle in her hand. Matches were hard to get, and she lighted the candle from the gas-jet. A glance told Lanny that the cellar was full of packing-boxes, mostly stacked against the walls. There were several in the open space at the foot of the stairs, and the woman set the candlestick on one of these, and went up the stairs without a word, closing the door behind her. Evidently this was a place where one asked no questions.

The old worker signed Lanny to a seat on one of the boxes, and he took another. " Your hiding-place here," he warned, " is not much better than a doghouse ; but you will be safe."

" That is all I want," replied the fugitive.

" The worst will be that you cannot have a light during

the day. Late at night you may have a candle for a while ; but candles are hard to get."

"There is something I failed to tell you," Lanny volunteered. "I have some money."

"We are not doing this for money, but for the cause. You have earned it."

"Listen, *Genosse*. In the old days I used to bring money to Trudi, and she put it to use. I am authorized to distribute money where it can serve the cause, and there is no reason why I should not leave some with you. I am sure you have no food to spare on your own food card. You can buy some for me on the black market, and if you have money left over, you can use it to feed *Genosse Ein-und-dreissig*." Comrade Thirty-one !

The watchmaker assented, and Lanny took out his notecase and gave him several hundred-mark notes. "Do not spend this at any place where you are known," he cautioned. "There is a possibility that it may have been marked by the person who gave it to me. On the black market, I imagine, people come and go and do not ask names or remember faces. I must have a complete outfit of clothing that will enable me to pass for a working man ; and I'm afraid you will have to burn everything that I have on at present. It will be a temptation to hide it or sell it ; but I warn you, I have been in Berlin for some time, and have met important persons ; they will be able to describe my costume in detail, and there is hardly a single article that cannot somehow or other be identified as of American or English manufacture."

"I will put it into a furnace with my own hands," said Seidl. "But first we shall have to get other clothing. Also, we shall have to get false papers. Have you any choice of a name ? "

"Any name that suits a German worker."

"Let us say Schultz—you will not forget that. Hans Schultz. You will have an address that has been bombed, and you will be travelling, looking for your wife and children. We will fix up all the details. Your German is much too good, and you might spend your spare time recalling the common people you have known and how they talk. Two or three days' growth of beard will help a lot. You might be an office clerk instead of a labourer, and that will account for your hands."

"The papers that I have are very dangerous," Lanny suggested. "It might be well to get rid of them at once."

"*Richtig*," said Seidl. He took the candle and looked about, found a piece of tin, and set it on the concrete floor. Lanny took out his papers, including the precious food card. One by one he lighted them at the candle and held them until there was only a stub left. When the last scrap had been burned he worked the sole of his shoe over them until they were reduced to powder, and then Seidl scattered the powder over the floor. "It will be swept up the next time they clean," he said.

And so Lanning Prescott Budd faded out of existence in Naziland, and Hans Schultz, *Kanzleibeamter* was born—complete and ready for action, like the genie out of a bottle or Aphrodite out of a sea-shell.

XIV

The entrance to the "doghouse" had been made by setting a long packing-box on top of two smaller boxes with a space between them. This left a hole about two feet square, which had a box carefully fitted into it, so that no one looking at the stack of boxes would suspect that it was not solid. All that Seidl had to do was to pull the loose box out, leaving just enough room for a man to slide in on his belly. The candle was passed in to him, and he could see that he had a cell about seven feet long, four feet wide, and as high as the ceiling of the cellar, about eight feet. There was a pallet on the floor and two dingy blankets, also a pillow made of a gunny sack stuffed with straw. A slop pail with a cover completed the furnishings. The host had assured him that he need not worry about ventilation, as there were plenty of cracks between the boxes. "Some of our best comrades have hidden out in this place," said the old man ; and Lanny hastened to assure him that it was a very good "doghouse" indeed.

The visitor ventured to mention that his stomach was empty, and Genossin Anna brought him a pitcher of water and a sandwich made with two slices of bread, some margarine,

and a slice of *Wurst*. A part of the bread was potato meal
and a part of the sausage was cornmeal; but it was all
food, and he was hungry. Seidl had told him that runaway
soldiers had brought lice into the place, but they had been
able to get some insect powder, and this had been effective.
Lanny took his word for it; being weary from the long strain,
he stretched out and was soon fast asleep.

When he awakened there were footsteps overhead, and he
knew that it was daylight. He had been warned never to
light his candle while these footsteps continued, and he must
lie perfectly still when the cellar door was opened. He must
never remove the box that closed the entrance to his cell;
that would be done only by Anna or by Seidl. No one else
would share the secret—that was the way to be sure it was
kept. He prepared his mind for a stay, for Seidl had urged
that it was the part of wisdom to wait until the Gestapo had
had a chance to wear out their first impulse of determination,
and to get a list of new victims to hunt.

He made himself a routine. He would keep his body in
condition, for he knew that he might have to walk long distances and perhaps climb mountains; Seidl had said that it
was hard to get a man smuggled on board a ship to Sweden,
but they had an underground railway to Switzerland. A man
can exercise all the important muscles of his body while lying
on a bed, lifting his torso or his extended legs; he can turn
over on his belly and keep his arm muscles in condition by
lifting himself with them. And when he has got himself tired
out, he can lie still and think about a journey he is going to
take, and the obstacles he may find in his path, and how he is
going to get past them. He can make up a hundred adventure
stories, knowing that any one of them may come true. When
he has had enough of labour and needs recreation, he can
recall all the fine poetry he learned when he was a lad; or
he can play over the piano music he knows, striking imaginary
keys and hearing imaginary sounds.

XV

Still more fascinating, he can take the opportunity to try
out some of the obscure powers of his own mind. What is the

mind ? An accident in an inconceivable immensity of matter ? Some incidental product that rises, say, like a mist from a warm stream, and that carries the bright colours of a rainbow for a few minutes, then fades into nothingness for ever ? Or is it, as many philosophers have believed, something permanent and fundamental to the universe, that may even be the cause of the universe, the real reality, the *Ding-an-sich* ? That idea of a universal consciousness, an ocean of mind, a level where all our minds are one and may communicate with one another and with God ? " Speak to Him, thou, for He hears, and spirit with spirit can meet ! "

Lanny had talked a great deal with his wife about telepathy. What could it be ? Surely not any physical agency, like radio ; for distance appeared to make no difference. Lanny had decided that he did not possess this gift ; but how could he be sure ? Maybe it was because he had never taken time to develop it. Well, now he had all the time there was ; he had little *but* time. Why not make a few experiments ?

He had exchanged promises with Laurel that whoever died first would try to communicate with the other. But why wait for death ? Why not see what the living could do ? Lanny knew the difference in time between Berlin and New York, and he knew Laurel's habits ; when she would be falling asleep and her mind would be quiet, that would be the time to try to send her a message. He wouldn't try to appear to her, for that would frighten her, just as he had been frightened as a lad when he had seen the figure of Rick standing by his bed-side ; Rick had been flying in World War I, and had crashed and been near to death, but not dead. The books on psychic research are full of such cases, and it doesn't seem to make any difference if the two people are separated by half the earth. In Gurney's *Apparitions of the Living* Lanny had read six or seven hundred cases ; and if it could happen spontaneously, why might it not be willed to happen ?

Anyhow, he would try. He was going out by Switzerland, therefore he would concentrate upon that country. He knew Geneva especially well, and he would try to have Laurel think of him as there. He fixed in his mind the great Palace of the League of Nations, a stone structure built on three sides of a square, with square pillars along the front, an unmistakable building with a great flight of steps leading up to it. It was a tomb of human hopes, a monument to human futility, charged with all the grief and anguish of a tragic time. Lanny would concentrate his mind upon it and try to convey it to his wife; when he got home he would wait and see if she mentioned it; if not, he would casually put a photograph of it before her and ask if she knew what it was and if it had any special significance to her.

XVI

The fugitive spent nine days and nights in this doghouse. On the second night his protector came, bringing a razor and advising him to remove his elegant little moustache; this must be done without delay, in order that the hair might grow out uniformly on his face and give him a proper unkempt appearance. On the third night he received an exchange of clothing; the fastidious son of Budd-Erling replaced his shorts with a ragged and stained nightshirt. His overshirt was too small for him and had a frayed collar; his suit was dingy and shapeless and had several patches. He was assured that this was a proper costume for a filing clerk after four years of war.

There was the problem of his watch, an object altogether beyond the imagining of a white-collar subordinate. Seidl wouldn't dare to offer it for sale, he said, but he had a safe hiding-place, and after the war was won, the American comrade could come and get it. " The war *will* be won? " he asked in a tone of concern, and Lanny had no hesitation in assuring him that such was the case. It gave the P.A. something of a thrill to be able to speak frankly, and to realize that, once he had got out of Axisland, he would be able to say what he thought and to set himself straight with the world. It could do no harm to tell this faithful old German about America's gigantic military preparations—something which Dr. Goebbels' propaganda machine had carefully kept from his knowledge.

And what was President Roosevelt going to do with the victory when it was won? On that too Lanny could speak openly; he could say that he knew the President, and had his personal assurance that after the war the people of Germany would have a chance to choose the kind of government they wanted. " And what if they want a Social-Democratic government ? " asked this veteran of the class struggle. Lanny could assure him that that wouldn't frighten the President in the least. He was no friend of the economic royalists at home, and certainly would not worry about the expropriation of the cartel masters, who had been the paymasters of Hitler and his gang and were more responsible for this war than any other group. Those were wonderful words to Genosse Seidl, and he promised that when Lanny was safely out of the way he would cause them to be widely circulated.

The next night he came again, bringing an overcoat and a pair of shoes in keeping with the rest of the costume. He also brought news—being a former Nazi block warden he got inside information—that a police alarm had been sent out for an American spy by the name of Lanning Prescott Budd, and that a house-to-house search was being made for him. Lanny said, " *Das bin ich*," and the other replied, " I'd better not come again for a while. I might be held up and asked where I was going." He assured Lanny that all the clothing had been burned, even the priceless shoes ; the notecase had been burned, and Lanny's money was now tucked out of sight under one of the boxes of the doghouse. He was studying to disimprove his German, and practised a while on this elderly watchmaker.

After that for nearly a week the much wanted man lay in darkness, doing his exercises both physical and psychological. He shivered whenever the cellar door was opened during the daytime ; but it was only working men, under the direction of Genossin Anna, who appeared to be boss of the establishment. He had a bowl of hot soup with meat in it every evening, and on the whole he found the experience amusing. He set a burned matchstick aside in a pile each day, that being the orthodox way for a dungeon inmate to keep track of time.

When the morning and evening were of the ninth day, Genosse Seidl came again. " I have all the papers, and you are going tonight." By the light of the candle he showed the documents ; an identification card, a permit to travel, an exit permit, and a food card, all in the name of Hans Schultz ; all forged, but good enough to stand an examination by flashlight on a roadside. They had all been carefully rubbed by sweaty working-class hands, so as not to appear too new, and Lanny stowed them in the pocket of a dingy white-collar-class jacket. He had grown a brown underbrush on the lower side of his face, and had accumulated dust and grime on the rest of his exposed skin. The old man said he looked all right and would get by if he didn't talk too much.

"You are going in a farm cart," he explained. "You will have to get out and walk around places where there is apt to be a road-block. The farm people who will drive you are comrades and have done it before. The father of the family has been paid. I have brought you a needle and thread, and we'll sew most of your money in the lining of your coat." And so on for various details, which Lanny repeated until the old man was satisfied. Then they put out the candle, and Lanny said good-bye to his doghouse and groped his way up the stairs. He exchanged a warm handclasp with his hostess and then followed his guide out into the dark street.

BOOK FIVE

MOVING ACCIDENTS BY FLOOD AND FIELD

13

Hard Liberty

I

FROM the point of view of the European peasant, war has not always been a calamity. To be sure, it takes the able-bodied men ; but for the old, and the women and children, there are compensations. So long as they are behind the front, they have the land, and the products of the land which cannot be dispensed with. There is always plenty of demand ; and if the government takes to printing too much paper, the peasant can refuse to take it and resort to the ancient system of barter, loading up his house with cuckoo clocks and rugs and ornaments and even fur coats. If the government resorts to price fixing, there is always somebody around the corner ready to exchange the coat off his back for a sack of potatoes ; and if the government goes so far as confiscation, the peasant can bury his food in the forest and stop working so hard.

The market gardeners of the suburbs of Berlin were having that sort of easy time. They drove in their wagons to the public markets and sold a part of their products as the law required ; but meantime a member of the family would disappear with a couple of dressed chickens under her shawl and meet a black marketeer in an alley behind a *Bierstube* ; that might go on all day long, and when the cart came home it would look like a junk dealer's.

By nightfall most of these carts would have departed ; but one might delay, because the driver had got drunk, or had gone to a cinema or some place of less innocent entertainment. Lanny couldn't see where he was being taken, but his guide told him it was to a market square ; and presently there was a tiny blue light, shaded as the law required, and he saw a cart, with a stoutish woman sitting in the driver's seat and a boy of twelve or so beside her. " *Frau Mühlen*," said Seidl, and then, " *Genosse Dreissig*." The woman replied, " *Bitte einsteigen*," and Lanny climbed quickly into the cart. At the front, under the driver's seat, he found a pile of sacks and a horse blanket ; he was told to lie on the sacks and cover himself with the blanket, and he did so. All arrangements had been made in advance and there was nothing to be said. The old watchmaker gave the traveller a " *Viel Glück*," and Lanny, who had been told not to talk, returned a " *Vielen Dank*."

Pretty soon he wasn't going to be able to talk, on account of the jolting. The market-place was paved with cobblestones and in the course of a century the paving had developed waves. The horse began to trot—horses always know when they are headed toward home and bed. Lanny found that he had to let his jaw hang loose to keep his teeth from rattling. Apparently the cart had no springs, and when it crossed a railroad or street-car track Lanny went a couple inches into the air and came down with his full weight. But it was all right, he was headed south, and when he got to Switzerland he would go to the best hotel and get the softest of mattresses—so he told himself.

He wondered about these people to whom his fate was entrusted. He had been told but one sentence, and it wasn't ethical to ask more. This was the underground, and every person who had anything to do with it was risking his or her life. Monck had told Lanny that the Nazis had succeeded pretty well in exterminating it ; but apparently it was reviving again, no doubt under the influence of Stalingrad, and Tunisia, and Sicily, and Salerno. The dumbest person in Naziland could not have failed to be impressed when Hitler declared three days of national mourning for the huge army lost in the snows of Russia in January of this year. Only the dumbest could have failed to note that the Allies had landed and advanced wherever they attempted it. How long would it be before they set out to cross the Channel ? Surely not later than next spring !

Lanny knew that an advance guard of Americans were already in Germany : many kinds of Americans who could pass for Germans—students, teachers, travelling salesmen, technicians, most of them of German descent. They were being smuggled in, well provided with German money and sometimes with radio-receiving and -sending sets. They were getting information of a hundred sorts, and finding ways to get it out. They were building up a resistance, and it might well be that they had established this underground railroad on which Lanny was travelling. He had no way to know, and the railroaders themselves might not know ; to them he was just " Comrade Thirty." All Seidl had said was, " You will be passed along."

II

The cart came to a halt, and Frau Mühlen said in a low voice, " There are lights ahead. Get out quick." Lanny needed no second warning ; he was up and out of the cart in two jumps. " Go one block off the road to the right. Then go six blocks forward, and one block to the left, back to the road. There is an inn called ' Die weisse Gans.' We will wait there. If you miss it you can ask the way of anyone but the police."

Lanny said, " *Danke*," and disappeared into the darkness. He understood that there must be a road-block—the police perhaps searching for him. He had grown used to groping his way in the dark, finding a pavement and staying on it. There was always some light from the sky, and you saw better out of the corners of your eyes, in quick glances. Covering your head up with gunny sacks for a half-hour was an excellent mode of preparation, giving your pupils a chance to expand to the utmost.

He made his way, not too slowly ; he mistook alleyways for streets, and came out to the road too soon ; he saw the flashlights and retraced his steps and went farther. " *Bitte, wo ist Die weisse Gans ?* " was a natural question to ask when he heard footsteps passing ; so he found the place, even though he couldn't see the sign for which it was named. The cart was waiting, and he followed it a short distance and then climbed in. It was, he reflected, a convenience that only *die Polizei*

were permitted to use electric torches in the open ; that gave
the smugglers ample warning, and they made use of it.

They turned in to the small farm, and an elderly man came
out to welcome them ; he carried no lantern, which might be
because they were in the Berlin *Gebiet*, or else he had no
kerosene. Evidently he expected the passenger, for he asked
no questions, save, " *Rauchen Sie ?* " Lanny gave his word
that he was a non-smoker and would strike no match. Then
the man said, " You may stay in the hay." That sounded
fine to a traveller whose bones ached.

There was a small stable, and a loft with a winter's supply
of fodder ; Lanny climbed up a ladder and settled himself
in a corner, spreading enough hay to hide everything but his
nose. " *Hier sind Sie sicher*," said the old man—here you
are safe. Lanny took his word for it and went fast asleep.
The rats came, but apparently decided that he was not edible.
The war was fine for them, for it took all the chemicals for
explosives, and there was no longer any poison to interfere
with the conviction of rats that they are the *Herrenrasse*, and
destined to fill the world solid with their species.

Lanny spent the next day quite contentedly in that hiding-
place, finding it much better than a doghouse. He listened
to the barnyard sounds, which began at the first streak of
dawn. The rooster crowed, the hens cackled, and the birds
sang, as cheerfully as if there were no war. Several of the
hens flapped their way up and inspected the intruder, then
flapped their way down again. The farmer's grandson brought
him a plate of food and a glass of milk—the latter something
usually reserved for young children and black marketeers in
the *Hauptstadt*. The boy would no doubt have liked to question this mysterious caller, but he had been forbidden the
pleasure. Lanny contented himself with " *Vielen Dank*," and
then " *Wasser*." He stayed quietly in his loft, along with the
pigeons, the swallows, and the bats.

III

With darkness came a heavy truck, with lights that were
dimmed but that seemed extraordinarily bright. They went
out quickly and Lanny was summoned. The truck carried a

load of boxes—Lanny never knew what was in them. They were covered with a tarpaulin laced down with strong rope. The driver, elderly but vigorous, loosened some of these ropes and lifted the tarpaulin. A ladder was brought and two empty boxes about the size of soap boxes were laid on top of the load, about three feet apart. Lanny perceived that he was expected to lie between them and be laced over. He was dubious about it, until he saw the driver putting a strip of lumber on each side of the load to hold the tarpaulin away and allow circulation of air. "There is also air between the boxes," said the man, and Lanny had to take his word for it; he couldn't refuse to go.

He climbed up and took his place, with a blanket under him and his overcoat for a pillow. The cover was put over him and laced down. He realized that he was safe from observation, for a person would have to climb to the top of the load in order to see the projection which his body made. But it was darned uncomfortable, there being barely room for him to turn over. He had the choice of lying on his back and having his backbone bumped, or lying on his side and having his ribs bumped, or lying on his belly and having his whole front bumped. All trucks have springs, but they are meant to save the cargo, not the passenger.

Soon they were speeding, as Lanny could tell by the engine; he could guess that they were on the four-lane *Autobahn* that runs between Berlin and Munich. One of Adi's boasts, and one of his worst blunders, for he was short on oil and rubber, whereas he had unlimited coal, and he had neglected the railroads which could use it. Lanny knew this highway well, having motored over it many times in the old happy days. Then his running time had been eight hours, but now his sense of time was hopelessly out of kilter. He had read that to God a thousand years are as a day; now it was turned around, and a day would be as a thousand years.

Once the truck came to a halt, and Lanny held his breath. It was a road-block; he couldn't see the lights, but he could hear every word that was spoken. "*Ihre Papiere!*" The driver would be handing out his papers and an S.S. officer would be inspecting them. Other men with flashlights would be looking into the driver's compartment and under it, peering

under the tarpaulin and perhaps under the body of the truck.
Would they have a ladder and climb on top? If so, it would
be all up with Lanny Budd, and with the driver too.

But perhaps the man knew that they didn't take that
much trouble. Lanny heard the blessed words, "*Alles in
Ordnung.*" The engine of the truck started up and it began
to move; then faster, and soon it was humming, and the P.A.
murmured a message of thankfulness to that Providence to
whom a thousand years are as a day.

The next time the truck halted there was silence for a
while. Lanny heard the driver get down, and then he realized
that the man was untying the cover. Perhaps they were at
their destination; or perhaps the driver was making sure that
his human freight was still alive. It was, but not much more.
When the man whispered for Lanny to slide down one of the
ropes, his joints were so stiff that he had to ask for help. His
knees threatened to buckle under him when he stood on the
ground, and the man helped him to what appeared to be a
small cottage. Dawn was near.

Inside, the man lighted a lamp. There was no one else in
sight, and Lanny guessed that it was the man's home. He
was led to a small closet underneath the stairs; the man
unlocked it, and Lanny saw a clothes closet which had been
partially cleared. There was a pillow for him to sit on, and
another presumably for him to rest his head on. The man said,
"You will be safe here. The woman will bring you food."
When asked if there would be air, he replied that there were
holes in the floor and ceiling. "But be very quiet," he added.

Lanny ventured to ask, "*Wo sind wir?*" and the reply
was, "Regensburg." The man closed the door and locked it—
which might have been alarming, except that Lanny could
guess there must be members of the family who were not
supposed to know of his presence. Children, perhaps, who
might tattle, or who might be victims of the Nazi propaganda
and betray their parents.

IV

Regensburg! Lanny knew the city, with its tall, many-
gabled houses dating from medieval days. Motoring through,
soon after the Nazis had taken power, he had been witness of

one of the early pogroms against the Jews ; it had seemed barbarous and dreadful, but of course it was nothing compared to what was now going on, the deliberate extermination of a race. The city was the site of the greatest ball-bearings plant in Germany and recently had been the scene of one of the heaviest of the American daylight raids. Dr. Goebbels had claimed that more than half the bombers had been shot down, and that was all Lanny knew about it. It might be a good thing if, in passing through, a P.A. were to pick up some information as to what damage had been done.

But not in a clothes closet. What had to be done now was to rest his sore bones, and not to fall asleep for fear that he might snore. Presently there were footsteps and voices, and he could follow the life of a German truck-driver's family ; the children were being fed and got ready for school ; when they were gone the woman unlocked the door and handed in a pitcher of water, some bread and cheese, and, most wonderful, an apple. When he said that he was afraid to sleep, the woman told him that the little ones would not return until afternoon, and she would tap on the door and waken him before that happened. She said nothing else, and he was struck by the silence in which this underground railroad was working. He could understand it, of course—the people were terrified at what they were doing, so much so that ordinary human curiosity was suppressed. They knew that he wouldn't want to tell who he was, and they were afraid to tell who they were. Better that he should move on quickly and be forgotten.

He slept ; and then the woman brought more food and told him that the children were due soon. He offered money for the food, and she didn't want to take it, but he persuaded her to do so for the children's sake. All this in whispers, and then she locked him in until night. He sat fairly comfortably and thought about his problems. He was about two hundred miles nearer to his goal, and the woman had said that somebody would come for him after dark.

V

The children were put to bed and the place was still. Then a car came to the door, and the woman unlocked the closet, put a sandwich wrapped in a newspaper into Lanny's hand, and led him outside. " This is Dr. Franz," she said. " He is going to Munich." Lanny got into the car, a small two-seater, and they drove away.

This was the first of the underground people who wanted to talk. The doctor didn't ask anything about his passenger, but told that he had come to a hospital in Regensburg to attend some of the people who had been injured in the bombing raids ; now he had been called back to the Bavarian capital because there had been a more terrible raid there. He told what dreadful things these raids were ; Lanny might have said, " I have seen a lot of them," but he didn't. The doctor —a young man by his voice—remarked what a hideous thing all war was, and how he longed for the end of this one. His passenger agreed with everything, but apparently had no opinions of his own ; so presently the doctor fell silent.

Thus far all the luck had been with Lanny Budd, but perhaps it was being charged against him in the book of fate. They had driven about an hour at a fair rate of speed, and Lanny guessed that they must be within ten or twenty miles of Munich. There was heavy traffic on this *Autobahn*, for it was the route to Italy by way of the Brenner Pass, and Hitler was pouring in troops and supplies in a never-ending stream. None of it could go by sea and not much by air ; the great bulk was divided between railways and motor highways. They were passing through a stretch of forest, as you could tell by the echoes of the car's motion from the trees. Suddenly the car began to bump, a sound and a feeling familiar to the motorist, and bringing dismay to his soul : a flat tyre !

Quickly the driver drew up alongside the highway, as far off the paving as he could get, for the heavily laden trucks came roaring, and sometimes the drivers were tired and careless. The doctor got out, and Lanny too prepared to help ; but the man said, " You must not be seen. Go into the woods and hide until I call." There could be no argument about the matter ; Lanny groped his way and found a seat behind a clump of underbrush and munched his sandwich. This seemed as good a time as any.

Then it was that fate presented its bill for the good fortune this P.A. had so far enjoyed. A few minutes passed, and the doctor had just got fairly started at his work when two men in soldiers' uniforms came striding down the side of the *Auto-bahn*, in the same direction as the car had been travelling. Lanny was close enough to hear every word of the conversation; they offered to help, and when the doctor answered, not too cordially, that he didn't need help, they laughed good-naturedly and told him that of course he did—he was a gentleman and this was a dirty job. Without another word, one of them proceeded to crawl under the rear end of the car and place the jack, and the other picked up the wrench and proceeded to remove the wheel with the damaged tyre. Evidently they knew the job, and put it through in a jiffy, that being the way of Army men. There was nothing for the doctor to do but to stand and watch—which is what any " Herr " would have done under the circumstances, and paid them with a coin.

But, as it turned out, that wasn't what these men wanted. When the work was completed and the tools stowed away, one of them said, " We are going your way; you might kindly give us a lift." When the doctor explained that he wasn't going very far, the answer was that they would ride as far as he was going. When he started another protest, they just got into the car, one sitting in the other's lap, so as to make it plain that they would not crowd or inconvenience him. Such a thing would never have happened in the old Germany, but this was Nazi Germany, and wartime besides. They were quite good-natured about it, taking it as a bit of fun. " Come on, we are good fellows, and we have done something for you. We are late and out of money."

What could the doctor say ? If he had said flatly, " I do not desire your company," they might have become ugly. They were fighting for the Fatherland and surely were entitled to consideration from any civilian. They had no weapons visible, but might have some hidden ; anyhow, they were two to his one. They might take his car, they might even kill him —such things had happened, and there was much talk about a crime wave. They might be simple fellows on furlough, and again they might be deserters, doing what Lanny was doing, heading for the Swiss border, and in a mood of desperation. Certain it was that the night was cloudy and dark, and there were no cars in sight at the moment.

All this Lanny could understand as well as the doctor, and his heart sank as he saw the doctor get into the car and drive away. The doctor couldn't very well call, saying, " I will come back." He could be sure that Lanny would hear the talk and understand the situation. He would drive the men for a while, until he came to a village ; then he would say, " This is my destination," and so would get rid of the undesired passengers and then come back for the desired one. Meantime, the latter would wait.

VI

Lanny waited. He crept closer to the highway and watched the cars passing in both directions, for the doctor, returning, would have to travel some distance back to the next underpass or overpass, so that he could get on Lanny's side of the *Autobahn*—built for cars that know where they are going, and not for those that change their minds and want to turn around ! The doctor might have a hard time finding the right spot in the forest ; Lanny, realizing that, took the newspaper in which his sandwich had been wrapped and stuck it on a forked stick and set it in the ground close to the edge of the paving. Fast cars wouldn't notice it, but the doctor would surely be going slow.

Lanny waited the rest of the night. He saw hundreds of cars go by, but didn't see a single one going slow. None stopped, and no driver got out to call " Yoo-hoo " for a lost passenger. Lanny comforted himself with the thought that perhaps the doctor had had to take the two intruders all the way to Munich. Even so, that couldn't have taken him more than an hour or two. Could it be that he had failed to make sufficiently careful note of the locality ? But surely he would note the distance on his speedometer as he went south, and then the distance when he came back ! Could it be that the soldiers had slugged and robbed him ? Or that he had some engagement in Munich that he could not break ? Would he have to wait and come back the following evening ? Or would he break faith with his passenger and just forget him ?

Lanny would never know the answer to that riddle. He waited until dawn, and then he found a clump of underbrush in which he could lie and wait all day. He had no food or water, and missed the latter especially. He waited until the middle of the next night ; then he decided that he had been deserted and got up and started to walk. It wasn't long before he came to a stream and quenched his thirst. He didn't mind walking ; what worried him was the fact that he had lost contact with the underground. He couldn't just go into Munich and ask for its headquarters ; he was on his own now, without a friend in all Germany that he knew, unless he went back to Berlin and started over again with Johann Seidl.

VII

He kept on south, and worried every time a car swept by him. Sooner or later one of them would stop, and it would be a police or Army car, and they would ask to see his papers, and what he was doing there, and why wasn't he in the Army ? At the first crossing he got off the *Autobahn* on a country road. But he found that that too had its disadvantages, for the dogs at farm-houses were antisocial, and some were not content with barking, but rushed at him. It was not easy to find anything in the dark, but Lanny managed to find a dead tree branch and to break off a stick. He had never been a tramp before, and he was surprised to realize how many drawbacks the life had.

Walking, he thought of all the persons he knew in Munich, and whether there might be one whom he could trust. Wealthy people nearly all, lovers of art ; he hadn't been to the city since the war broke out, and couldn't be sure who was alive or dead. He could think of several who would surely be sick of the conflict now that their capital city was being plastered with bombs, but he couldn't think of a single one who might be willing to risk his neck for the sake of an American *Kunstsachverständiger*, be he ever so competent. No, there was just no sense in going into Munich at all, it would be pretty nearly as bad as Berlin.

The fugitive belonged out in the country, in spite of the dogs. Not many Gestapo cars roamed country lanes ; and he had money in his pocket and could pay for food at farm-house doors. He had a good story, prepared in advance ; his home had been bombed out in Berlin and he had come back after a week's absence to find his wife and children gone. They were reported to be—wherever Lanny decided that he wished to head for. As he thought it over he began to lose interest in Switzerland ; he knew how closely the Germans guarded that border, and how many people had lost their lives, either by falling in the dark or being shot in the daylight while trying to get across by mountain paths. It needed an expert guide, and how would a tramp office clerk find one on the German side ?

Austria was nearer, and Lanny guessed there would be no border, it being part of Naziland ; but he dared not count on this, for old habits hold. After that it was only a short way across to Italy, and since Northern Italy was in German hands, its border would be less closely watched. Lanny knew that in Italy the underground would be stronger ; all he would have to do was to climb into some high mountain pass and say to a woodcutter or a young peasant, " I am a friend of the Partisans, and where are they ? " They would soon come to look him over and hear his story, and then they would pass him on to some O.S.S. man, and Robbie and Laurel would get a message that Lanny was alive and well.

On the road to the Brenner there was one person of whom Lanny bethought himself ; that was his old friend Hilde, Fürstin Donnerstein. Hilde was in somewhat the same classification as Oskar von Herzenberg; that is, a member of the Prussian aristocracy who looked down upon the Nazis as *canaille*, and who, after four years of war and one year of incessant defeats, must be wholly sick of them. Lanny had stayed in the Donnerstein palace in Berlin, and had brought Monck there and hidden him for a couple of days, but without telling Hilde the truth about either of them. Now he would have to tell at least part of the truth about himself ; he felt quite sure that as a lady she would not betray a gentleman, and she might be able and willing to give him advice. He had done that for her, telling her to come to her summer camp on the Obersalzberg and make it fit for winter occupation. Bombers were not apt to come there, and food would be easier to get. It hadn't occurred to Lanny that he might be coming along to get some of the food.

VIII

The traveller walked until sunrise and then went to a farm-house and told his story to a sympathetic woman. It was a good story, and he was invited in to a warm breakfast with the family ; he was provided with a lunch in a bundle, and when he tried to pay for it they told him there was no charge. Such kind, good people they were, and Lanny had known so many all over this land ; he went away reflecting upon the mystery of how they kept falling into the hands of one set of military masters after another. Armies marching and fighting all over Europe, all through the centuries—and Lanny could not recall ever having met a single peasant or working man who liked war or expected to gain from it. War was a sport of ruling classes !

He went his way and came to a strip of woodland and lost himself in the middle of it. He was tired and craved sleep ; a chilly wind was blowing, and the best shelter he could find was on the lee-side of a great rock. The ground was covered with dead leaves, and he gathered armfuls, and then slept as soundly as the babes in the wood. When he opened his eyes again the day was far gone, but still chilly, and he got up and stretched his legs and then ate his lunch. He thought about his problems, and then about Marceline, and what might be happening to her. He imagined her in the hands of the Gestapo, and that was so terrible he had to put it quickly out of his mind. Instead he made for her an outdoor adventure story like his own ; a Rosalind-in-*As-You-Like-It* story, for once in amateur theatricals at Bienvenu she had tied a bandage over her breasts and put on boy's clothing and played a young apache to the great amusement of an audience.

Lanny was resolved to do his travelling at night, for he had got at the farm-house a hint that troubled him greatly. They had asked how he had managed to escape service in the Army, and he had to think quickly and say that he had been rejected on account of serious heart trouble. Up to that moment his thoughts had been fixed upon the notion that if the police were to get him they would discover that he was an American spy ; now for the first time he realized that his papers might satisfy them, in which case they would induct him into military service without a day's delay. To be sure, they would take his fingerprints, and they already had the fingerprints of Lanning Prescott Budd in Munich, where they had arrested him and thrown him into Stadelheim Prison for the offence of having been in the company of Hugo Behr, *Sturmabteilungsmann* shot down in the Blood Purge. That had been nearly ten years ago, but fingerprints do not grow old, and neither do police records. However, the bombings might well have disorganized the system, and they were in such a hurry for able-bodied recruits that they wouldn't bother to look up records. The age limits had been expanded again, and now stood from sixteen to sixty.

Lanny's active imagination saw himself being picked up in a *Razzia* and submitted to a medical examination, and they surely wouldn't find anything wrong with his heart ! They would send him to the German equivalent of a " boot camp," and he would put on a uniform that had been taken from a dead man, and a Nazi Feldwebel would drill him and kick him about for a month or two. Then he would be loaded into a cattle car and shipped off in the dead of winter to the Russian front, or perhaps to the Gothic Line, as the Germans were now calling their front in Italy. Lanny saw himself doing sabotage to that line, and then escaping into the American lines with a lot of valuable information. It made a grand story, but somehow he found difficulty in making himself believe it.

No, it seemed wiser to do his travelling under the protection of night, keeping watch ahead for flashlights and avoiding the towns. With the help of the friendly farm people he had got himself a sound stick and no longer feared the dogs. He was coming into the mountains, and it would be cold, and impossible to sleep outdoors at night without a blanket ; but by day he would find a place in the sun, or if it rained he might find a cave, or a hollow tree, or perhaps he could tell his touching story and get permission to sleep in a barn.

To Hilde's place was a little more than fifty miles, and from there between fifty and a hundred to the Italian border, depending upon where he approached it. He had no map, but had motored over this region for the past twenty years. Travelling by country roads increased the distance, but it was better to take longer and be sure of getting there. By now he had a thick brown growth on the lower half of his face, and when he bent over a stream to get a drink he hardly recognized what he saw ; so much the better, for if he didn't, the Gestapo surely wouldn't. He still had his pleasant smile and persuasive tongue ; he didn't meet a single farmer's wife or daughter who wasn't touched by his sad story of a home bombed to rubble and a wife and children being sought by a loving husband and father. To people in these foothills of the Bavarian Alps bombings were " old, far-off unhappy things," and they would have been glad to have him stay and sit by their large wood stove and tell them tales all evening.

14

In Worst Extremes

I

HILDE'S chalet on the Obersalzberg was one of those elaborate affairs which wealthy people build themselves in order to enjoy wild scenery without sacrificing the comforts of city life. It stood on the slope of a pine- and fir-clad mountain, looking directly across toward the slope where Hitler had his Berghof ; on a clear day you could sit in the Fürstin's summer-house with a pair of opera glasses and see the Führer come out of his hiding place, clad in the costume of the country —short black leather breeches, an embroidered green jacket, and a hat with a Spielhahn feather in it. In the old happy days he had delighted to walk on the mountain paths of his estate ; now he came rarely, and if you had been observed spying upon him you would have got into very serious trouble.

Lanny had been there in the days when the Munich Conference was being planned. He had stayed at the Berghof, and walked to Hilde's chalet, and also to Göring's, for *Der Dicke* had an elaborate place, with a forest fenced in and inhabited by wild boars which he delighted to chase and stick with spears from a safe seat on a horse. But not too safe, for he had fallen off several times, and once had been laid up for a couple of weeks. The son of Budd-Erling had had to plead ignorance of this noble sport, and content himself with the safer one of shooting stags from a high platform at Rominten.

Lanny knew the household at Hilde's, and knew that he had to be careful in approaching it. There was an older sister, a widow like Hilde, and by no means cordially disposed. There had been in the Berlin palace two elderly family servants who were loyal to the great and noble Führer of their Fatherland and were probably too ignorant to be changed by the events of the war. A most unpromising layout, and Lanny didn't expect to be a guest there, or even to make himself known.

Because other people in the neighbourhood knew him, he waited until after dark to come near the estate. He saw that there were lights in two of the second-story windows, and he guessed that Hilde had taken his advice and made some of the smaller rooms tight and habitable for winter. She had lost most of her income, she had told him, and would be content to keep alive, and not too much interested in that. He knew that she had never been a dog lover, and he was relieved to discover that his prowling was not greeted by any barking. He spent the night in a shed on her estate, wrapped in some potato sacks.

At dawn he was out and in the forest. Hilde's summer-house stood on a conspicuous point of rock, and it had been her pleasure to sit there and read on sunny days. Fortunately this was one, and he posted himself where he could be hidden by bushes and keep watch ; there he sat and dozed, and toward the middle of the morning, here she came, wearing a black dress, something that had been forbidden in Berlin. He was near enough to see that her beauty was gone, and her wrinkles impossible to hide, especially in sunlight. She had been a social butterfly, full of gay and somewhat malicious gossip ; she had flitted about the Continent, spending her husband's money in half a dozen capitals and speaking a smart jargon made up of German, French, English, and now and then Italian and Spanish words. Now her husband and her two sons were dead, her bright and clever world was dead, and so was her heart, she had told her old friend Lanny Budd.

II

The visitor moved carefully from tree to tree, keeping out of sight from the house. When he was near he stood behind a tree and said, not too loudly, " Hello, Hilde." He could not see her startled look, but got the impression from her voice. " *Wer ist da ?* " she said. He answered quickly, " Lanny Budd." She exclaimed, " *Um Gottes Willen !* " and he stopped her with the words, " Come for a walk. I must talk to you alone."

She got up and followed him into the forest ; when they were a safe distance away from everything he stopped and confronted her. He was prepared to see dismay in her face, for she had never seen this darling of fortune in anything but the right costume, and surely never without having washed his face or shaved for two weeks. " Don't be frightened," he told her. " I am in trouble, but I promise not to involve you."

" For God's sake, what has happened, Lanny ? " she whispered, having made up her mind that it was really he and none other.

" I came into Germany to buy some paintings from Göring, and one of his so-called art experts got into a rage because I exposed his having purchased some fraudulent stuff. He started the story that I was a spy, and a friend tipped me off that the Gestapo was going to put me through one of their inquisitions. I decided to get out, and I'm on my way to Italy."

" But, Lanny, *wie schrecklich !* You look dreadful ! "

" Well, don't worry, a part of that is camouflage. I have been walking at night and sleeping in the woods by day, and I'm a little short on food. The main trouble is, I wanted somebody to talk to, and I couldn't bear to go by without saying hello." He said this with his amiable smile, and there could be no doubt that it was the same old Lanny.

" *Aber*—you know how it is ! " she exclaimed. " My family —*c'est embarrassant !* "

" Of course ! " he replied. " I have no idea of imposing on you. I just wanted to have a chat. Are we safe here ? "

" Let us go a little farther, if you are not tired."

" I had a grand sleep in a shed on your place last night."

" Lanny, how perfectly appalling ! "

" *C'est la guerre*," he said, falling into her international mode of speech. " Nobody has much fun nowadays, and I thought you might be bored and glad to hear the news."

" How perfectly darling of you ! Of course I'm starving for news ! *Erzähl' doch !* "

III

They went deeper into the dark forest. Partridges flew up with a roar in front of them, and great hares scampered away. Hilde led him off the beaten path until she was sure there could be no eavesdroppers ; then they took seats upon a fallen log, and Lanny opened his delightful budget of gossip. Since he had last seen this fashionable friend he had been to Sweden, London, Washington, New York, Newcastle, Florida, then Marrakech and Algiers, Rome and Berlin, and in nearly all these places he had met persons whom Hilde knew and wanted to hear about. What was Irma doing and was she really happy as a countess, and had the war taken all her money ? And the little girl who had flown to America, which of her parents did she favour and how did she behave ? And Robbie and all that family and then Beauty among the blackamoors and Kurt Meissner and his tragic injury and that dreadful crude fat man—even out here in the forest Hilde was afraid to speak his name, and she looked about her as she listened to the story of his new lot of paintings, and his drug addiction, and his unhappy wife who was compelled to worship at the shrine of her predecessor.

This went on for an hour or so ; then suddenly this fashionable lady stopped and stared at her friend, so disturbingly altered. " Here I am chattering on ! " she exclaimed. " And you in such trouble ! How can I help you, Lanny ? "

" It is a help to see you," he replied gallantly, " and to be reminded of old times. I mustn't stay any longer."

" Lanny, it is perfectly putrid that I don't ask you into the house and take care of you, but you know my family situation. There would be gossip and it would spread fast."

"Certainly; and I wouldn't dream of involving you in my troubles. It wouldn't do me any good and it might do you serious harm."

"At least I can bring you food. There is an old woman near here to whom I sometimes take some, so it won't look suspicious if I bring out a basket."

"No basket, old dear. Small packages that I can stuff into my pockets. Wrap them in paper, and be sure there is no writing or printed labels on the paper."

"What a way to be living—and you of all people! Where are you going?"

"I need a little advice about that. I want to get into Austria. Do you know any trick for getting there?"

"How should I, Lanny? The roads are especially well guarded in this neighbourhood because of being near the Berghof."

"I was a guest there a couple of months ago," he told her. "I wanted to come to see you, but I had no chance. I was flown there and flown away again."

"We heard that you were there. There is no end of gossip about the place. The servants talk about what goes on. They say the Number One has a new girl, but nobody knows her name."

"Not so new, only the news is new. Her name is Eva Braun and he calls her Evi. She comes from Munich, and was an assistant to Hoffmann, that funny little man who follows his master around all day and takes snapshots of everything he does. Posterity will know all about this pretty but rather commonplace *Freundin*."

"Oh, Lanny, *quel morceau*! What a titbit, as you say! Our Sir Launcelot! Our holy one! That ought to be worth a dozen food packages."

"Be careful how you pass it on! You might have the Gestapo calling to find out where you get your titbits."

"We have a maidservant who lives in Berchtesgaden and brings us the latest. She—" The Fürstin stopped without finishing the sentence. "Wait a moment, Lanny. I believe I have a way for you to go south. This girl has a fellow who lives in the mountains and may be the sort of man you need. We have been worried about him because he comes here sometimes at night, and we are sure that he's a draft dodger, and perhaps something worse ; a smuggler or even a saboteur."

" Now you are talking, Hilde ! For a little money such a man might be willing to smuggle me into Austria, and perhaps farther. Is there any way I could get his ear ? "

" The girl would know how to reach him, I have no doubt."

" And is there some job that you could think of for him to do ? "

" Yes, there is always wood to be cut."

" Well, now, old darling, do me a real favour. Get this dubious *Bursch* into your forest, and I will hang around until I see him. I'll find a way to approach him, and of course won't give him any hint that I'm a friend of yours. I'll be just another draft dodger, and he won't have any trouble in understanding me."

" But Lanny ! It may take a while, and how will you live ? "

" I won't live in luxury, but I'll get along. There's a shed on the edge of these woods, and it seems to be deserted. I slept in one corner a part of last night and only a hedgehog came to bother me."

" My husband used to store hay there in the days when he took care of the deer and had shooting parties. No one will come there. But you will freeze, Lanny ! "

" I didn't freeze last night. I admit that if I were to find an old horse blanket hanging on a nail I could use it ; not a good blanket, you understand, for that wouldn't look natural. Besides that, all I want is food, and I'll get along beautifully. I'll wait until I see the man, or until you tip me off that it's no go. Send the girl at once if you can, because there's always a chance that someone may see me."

" *Tout suite !* " said the Fürstin, speaking New York French instead of Parisian ; and then, " So long ! " She gave him a quick kiss on the forehead and then fled to her house.

IV

The fugitive spent the rest of that day in the forest, cultivating the friendship of the chattering squirrels and the timid hares. He found wire snares set in their runways, for in these disturbed times there was a great deal of poaching. In one of the snares was a hare, strangled to death, and Lanny did not scruple to take it out and set the snare again, so as to avoid making enemies. He carried his treasure to a small stream, skinned it, opened it up with a sharp stick, and cleaned it in the water. He had two or three precious matches and needed only one to start a small fire of dry leaves and twigs. There he sat and patiently toasted one chunk of hare after another. It made a huge meal, even for a half-starved man ; he wrapped the two hind legs in clean leaves and tucked them carefully into pockets, for he wouldn't trust the squirrels while he went to sleep. He found a tiny clearing in warm sunlight and there slept peacefully. How delightful the earth could be if it weren't for the people on it !

When darkness approached he made his way to the shed. Food packages had been set on an empty box in one corner, and he made a supper of a *Schweizerkäse* sandwich and two cold broiled *Hasenläufe—ja, recht gut !* He groped and found a blanket miraculously hanging from a nail, and wrapped in this he made up for more lost sleep. At dawn he was out and gone, leaving the blanket on the nail, but taking the food packages in his various pockets.

He found a thicket from which he could keep watch, and a couple of hours after sunrise he saw a youngish fellow, in a country costume well worn and patched, come from one of the outbuildings of the estate with an axe over his shoulder. Lanny followed, not too close, for it would be easy to find him. Pretty soon there came the ringing sound of an axe on a fallen tree, and Lanny came up to the chopper and greeted him in the best Bavarian dialect he could muster, " *Allo, wie geht's, wie steht's ?* "

The *Bursch* stopped his work and stared, none too cordially ; he saw a tramp, as unprepossessing as art had been able to produce at three weeks' notice. " *Was wollen's ?* " he demanded.

Lanny came near and spoke low, lest even the squirrels and the hares might overhear. " Would you like to earn a bit of money, say, forty marks ? "

" I could use it," was the sceptical reply.

Lanny wasted no time, but took from his pocket two small

M

coins and two pieces of paper. He handed the coins to the fellow and held the notes up before him. " Two marks now ; twenty when we come to the old Austrian border, and twenty when you have got me well into the country."

" *Aha !* " said the *Bursch*. " *Das kann i verstehn.*" He thought for a while, then asked, " Would Hallein suit you ? "

" Hallein is all right," said Lanny. " You would take me a bit beyond and get me started off ? "

" It's a deal. I'll take you through the salt mines."

" You mean the one at Berchtesgaden ? "

" No, the Wolf Dietrich, at Hallein. It has tunnels that go for miles and some of them are under German soil. There are ways to get in, if you know the trick."

" That sounds all right. But won't they be guarded at the Hallein end ? "

" There are hundreds of workers, and they come and go. You can pass for one. I have friends there."

" *Das klingt gut,*" said the *Landstreicher*—tramp. " How soon can we start ? "

" The best time to come out in Hallein is when the work stops, at eighteen hundred hours. Then it will be dark. If we leave here at noon, we should make it."

" I don't want to be seen on the highways. I have my reasons."

" Don't worry about that. I have mine too. You stick around till noon. I'll have to take this axe to the chalet, then I'll meet you here. I'll tell them I sprained my wrist and have to let it rest for a day or two. My name is Willi. Do you happen to have a smoke on you, Kamerad ? "

V

Lanny found a quiet nest in the forest, and listened to the cheerful sound of the axe, and thought about Hallein. A small, dingy town in Austria, just below Salzburg and close to the old border, it was a place marked on Lanny Budd's mental map, for it was here that his marriage to Irma Barnes had come to an end. They had helped Trudi Schultz to escape from Berlin, and Irma had been in a fury with her husband not merely for having exposed her to such peril, but because

he kept such evil company ; it was " Red " company to
Irma, and no use for him to plead that it was merely " Pink."
Socialists, Communists, and bomb-throwing Anarchists were
all the same to the daughter of J. Paramount Barnes, railroad
king from Chicago. That had been six years ago, years laden
with great events in the life of Lanny Budd and his world ;
but nothing would ever wipe out of his mind the night scene
when Irma had told him that she was going back to her mother
in New York. They had parted at the railroad station, and
Lanny had gone to Salzburg to try to enjoy the music festival,
but not with much success.

Now he would see this little salt-mining town again. He
had known about the mines, and that they had a vast network
of tunnels and passages underground, but it had never occurred
to him that they might be used by smugglers and other law
evaders. Now he was going to entrust his life to one of these
men ; he had thought it over carefully and decided that Willi
could not afford to turn him over to the police, because the
fellow himself was a draft dodger, and while he might collect
a reward, he would inevitably be forced into the Army, and
the money wouldn't be of much use to him. Lanny's money
would be better ! To be sure, he might have a notion to hit
Lanny over the head in the salt mine and get more money ;
but Lanny would try to keep behind him at all times.

The cheerful sounds of the axe ceased, and after waiting
a while Lanny took post behind a tree near the chopping place.
Willi called him, and they started along a forest trail. It was
hard walking, up and down the sides of mountains, but Lanny
was well fed now and used to walking ; the man knew the
way and led off boldly, Lanny staying a few feet behind.
They saw a few country people in the course of the afternoon,
but no one showed any interest in them. There was some of
the finest scenery in Europe ; range after range of mountains,
with breath-taking views. But Lanny needed all his breath
to keep up with this mountain-bred man.

When dusk came they were in a deserted mountain meadow,
and there in a low shed was what you might call the backdoor
of a salt mine. Originally it had been the channel of a brook
by which water had been led into the mine ; now the water
had been diverted, and the channel was used by a few workers

who lived on the Bavarian side. Under an old treaty, they had a hereditary right to employment. The descent into the mine was by a slope, called a *Schurf*; it was a wooden toboggan slide for going down and small steps for coming up; but Lanny and his friend had to use the steps, because they had no *Arschleder*, as the miners called the heavy leather apron which you put on to protect your behind from the heat of the quick slide.

Before they went in Willi said, " You owe me twenty marks." Lanny put the note into his hand and he looked at it and then stuffed it away.

The steps were dark, but apparently Willi had been there before; he went down without hesitation. Lanny, at his heels, couldn't refrain from keeping both hands out in front of him. At the bottom of the steps was a tunnel about the width of an ordinary door and about as high, with timbers holding it up. There was hard-packed slippery clay underfoot, and from overhead came the ceaseless drip-drip of water. It seemed to Lanny they had walked two or three miles in this tunnel before they saw any light. He knew that these mines had been worked for two or three thousand years, but he didn't know anything about the process and was surprised to see no white or crystalline salt, as he had imagined; there was only clay, called *Kalkgestein*, and the salt was in the clay. Immense basins were dug or dynamited into the mountains, and water was let in, forming lakes; the water soaked the salt out of the clay, and then the brine was led out to the valley and evaporated there. Such was the process, and there were mines having as many as five or six galleries, one under the other. There was a whole district, known as the Salzkammergut, meaning the salt-department-property; the mining and selling of salt had been for centuries a monopoly of the government.

They did not turn aside to watch the working, or to see the abandoned lakes, which were emptied of water, lighted with coloured lights, and used for banquets, festivals, and shows. They went through tunnel after tunnel, lighted by widely spaced electric lights. They passed working men, who paid no attention to them, until Willi met one whom he knew. He stopped, and introduced his friend Hans, and then whispered to the fellow. Lanny produced a ten-mark note, and the miner hurried away and came back with two lanterns and two sets of miners' costumes—white, and including a hat that was a small round dome, trimmed with a scalloped white band. Thus equipped, they could pass anywhere, and Willi would return the property to the miner's home. Now they entered the wider concrete-lined tunnel which had a little mining railway and led to the main entrance. It was a mile or two long, and on the way was an old signpost having on one side the Austrian Imperial Double Eagle and on the other side the Blue and White of Bavaria's former kingdom. That was the no-longer-existing border !

Presently it was time for the shift to leave, and they trooped toward the main entrance by what was called the Wolf Dietrich tunnel. Lanny expected a ticklish moment, but nothing whatever happened. The workers were weary, and one heard only a few muttered words from them. They were taken up in elevators, a score at a time, and nobody paid the least attention to a pair of strangers. Old men died and younger men were called to the wars ; new men were taken on, and it was no concern of anybody but the boss. Lanny and his guide passed out through a marble portal bearing an inscription which they did not stop to read.

There was a long walk in darkness on a steep mountain road to the town of Hallein. On the outskirts of the town Willi asked which way his companion wished to go, and Lanny said, " Toward Salzburg," which wasn't true. The guide pointed towards the east, and then said, " *Zwanzig Mark*." Lanny put the bill into his hand, and Willi struck a match and examined it ; then he said, " *Glück auf !* " And taking the lanterns and the overalls, Willi disappeared into the darkness.

VI

The P.A. was in Austria, and that was a comfort, for the Austrians were characterized by what the Germans contemptuously called *Schlamperei* ; that is to say, slackness, easy-goingness. For example, they would rather be in a tavern, sipping their beer and singing songs about their *Schätzl*, than standing out on the highway on a bad night, waving flashlights and stopping travellers to examine their papers, even if it was wartime and the Nazi overlords had strictly enjoined it ! Let the Nazis do it themselves !

Lanny was bone-tired, and this was the coldest night he had yet encountered. Rain was starting to fall, and he decided that he must find shelter. He walked until he came to a farm-house that was dark ; he groped his way into the place, hoping that Austrian farm dogs would be more genial and more easily seduced with a bit of *Wurst*. He found a shed, and in the corner some sacks. He sat and devoured one of Hilde's food packages, and then covered himself up and fell fast asleep.

Anxiety awakened him at dawn, and he stood up, stiff with cold. He got out quickly, for he didn't want to have to make explanations. It was still raining, and this was a miserable prospect. He couldn't even tell which way was south—the road signs had all been taken down. He knew that he was less than a hundred miles from the Italian border as the crow flies ; but unfortunately he wasn't a crow. When daylight came, he saw a farm woman in a barnyard, and he guessed that she wouldn't be a very ardent Nazi ; he asked her the way to Golling, the next town south. She pointed, and he walked.

He was in beautiful country, the " Austrian Switzerland." It was the valley of the Salzach River, with low mountains on each side covered with pine trees, and behind them walls of taller grey mountains topped with snow. It was a historic land with many ancient castles ; it was also a vacation land, full of mountain chalets and hotels for the rich, now for the most part turned into hospitals. Such a country is difficult for a fugitive, for there is frequently only one road through a mountain pass, and you cannot travel off it without a guide. How Lanny wished he might find a friendly truckman who would strap him on top of a load and cover him up, away from the rain.

A car raced by him, blowing a horn. It was a military car with Nazis in it, and they looked at him as they passed and worried him greatly. What if they notified the next military post that there was an able-bodied tramp on the road ? Lanny turned off and climbed the slope of a mountain. There was

terraced land there and a peasant hut, and he decided to trust
the peasants ; he had never yet met one that liked being at
war.   Wars were made by people who went to live in cities
and there acquired wealth and power and a taste for more.

In this place, Lanny discovered, there was not a single
member of the male sex ; just an old grandmother and a
younger woman, pregnant, and with two little daughters.
They were frightened at first by the arrival of this stranger,
but he soon convinced them that he was a harmless person.
He had heard Artur Kannenberg sing scores of *G'stanzln* in
the dialect of this country, so he could speak it blunderingly,
of course taking his blunders playfully.   He had changed his
story ; his bombed-out wife was now an Italian woman and
had gone to seek refuge among her people in the town of
Dobbiaco, or Toblach in German.   He had decided that since
he had lost contact with the underground he would not dare
attempt to get through the much-travelled and well-guarded
Brenner, but would try one of the passes farther to the east,
but less infested with Nazis.

It was a touching story the traveller told, and the fact that
he had managed to keep out of the Army did not fill them with
distrust, only with envy ; their men had been taken.   They
let him dry himself by their fire, fed him a meal of potatoes,
turnips, and goat's milk, all they had, and consented to sell
him two valuable properties, a pair of mittens and a muffler,
both home-made.   His shoes were pretty nearly gone, but they
had none and couldn't tell him where to get any.   More
important yet, they told him about a relative in the town of
Werfen, a fellow who worked in an inn there, *ein guter Bursch*
who would show the road and maybe help.   They told him
about a wonderful place near Werfen, known as the Eisriesen-
welt, the ice-giant-world.   It was an ice cavern, said to be the
largest in the world, and it had frozen waterfalls, ice mounds,
ice men, and other wonderful sights.   These peasant women
had never seen it and Lanny didn't think that he would see it
on this trip ; he had found enough cold without going out of
his way, and his choice at present would have been Hawaii,
which was hot and hospitable all the year round.

VII

Warmed and fortified, the P.A. left the farm at dusk and
walked all night to the town of Werfen. He had no trouble
finding the inn, and the man there proved to be a good fellow
indeed ; in exchange for news about his relatives he introduced
Lanny to a man named Blech, who had spent the night at the
inn and was driving on to Bischofshofen in a wagon. For the
price of ten marks he was willing to have a passenger lie amid
a load of newly-made harness covered with a tarpaulin. It
was a bumpy ride, but it took Lanny more than thirty miles
on his way, and he was content to miss the fine scenery.

Here was your Austrian *Schlamperei* ; this Blech didn't
care a hang whether a man got away from the German Army,
he just wanted ten marks. If by an unlikely chance the
passenger had been discovered, Blech could have said that he
had crawled in unobserved. It was after dark when they
arrived in the town, and the man was sorry for this poor devil
who must have been pounded pretty nearly to a jelly, and
took him into an eating place where there were *gute Leute* and
saw him eat a hot meal. The talk in the place was excited,
for Mussolini, prisoner of Badoglio, had been rescued by paratroopers sent by Hitler himself. Now Il Duce was in Milan,
setting up a new government, which he was calling a " Republic." If there was anybody in this Austrian inn who wished
success to this government, he failed to lift his voice that night.

Lanny paid the bill, and in return the man hunted up
a map for him and showed him the shortest route into Italy.
The road led to Schwarzach, and from there on to Bad Gastein.
A bad place, Blech said. He was aware of no pun, because
he was speaking German, and to him Bad meant bath, and
the place was " *ein schlechter Ort.*" Very beautiful, in a gorge
between two waterfalls, and magnificent hotels had been built
there ; but now they were hospitals for officers, and the place
was lousy with the military—the man's own phrase, *lausig
mit Soldaten.*

This Blech had grey hair and talked as if he had had some
education. On a sudden impulse Lanny remarked, " I am
wondering if you mayn't have once been a Socialist."

The other looked at him sharply. " That is a question one doesn't ask nowadays."

" Suppose," countered the traveller, " I were to tell you that I am one ? "

" The answer is, I wouldn't know whether to believe you or not."

" Think a minute, *mein Freund*. Would a police spy be apt to ride all day on top of a load of harness ? "

The other smiled. " What's on your mind ? "

" Just this : I've been taking a walking trip, and all the way the road is paralleled by a railroad. I couldn't help thinking what a lot of trouble I could save if I could get in touch with some railroad man who would let me pay him a fare and open up a freight-car door for me."

" You would be asking a man to risk his life, you know."

" Yes, but you trusted me, and no harm has come to you so far. I'm going on my way, and neither you nor the railroad *Genosse* would ever see me again. Think it over."

" Just where do you want to go ? "

Lanny pointed to the map. " This place, Sillian, in the Pustertal, would suit me fine, and I would pay twenty marks to you, and twenty to the railroad man."

VIII

So it came about that after darkness had fallen Lanny was led to the railroad station. A freight train rolled noisily up the grade and came to a halt. Blech whispered to the station-man, and he in turn to a train-man ; one of the doors was opened, and Lanny was pushed inside and the door locked. There was just room for him to stand, or to sit with his legs drawn up ; the freight was heavy boxes, doubtless war goods, and he hoped they wouldn't shift as the train made its bumpy stops. Probably not, because it surely wouldn't go fast climbing toward the Hohe Tauern. He could imagine that he felt the engine toiling, and he could certainly hear the car creaking and groaning. He did not know this region or how high the pass might be. His clothing was of the poorest sort, and he had begun to suffer from the cold even before the sun went down.

It wasn't long before all Lanny's thoughts were occupied with that cold. He hadn't room enough for vigorous exercise ; all he could do was to practise alternately tensing and relaxing the muscles of various parts of his body. Thus he kept his blood in circulation ; and with his mind he speculated : How long would the trip take, and would the train-man forget him ? A human life didn't count for much in these days of world-wide slaughter, and the basis of Lanny's hope was an extra ten marks he had agreed to pay this man. That, presumably, would be more than the man would get if he carried his illegitimate cargo to the border and delivered it to the guard.

All the ill-clad Lanny was asking of fate was to get through this alive. He might have lost some fingers if it had not been for the mittens, and a pair of ears if it had not been for the muffler which he tied over them. Fortunately he had had enough food, and of that food he had made blood, and kept it in circulation for the twenty-four hours the slow wartime trip required. He was just about exhausted when the train came to a stop and the door was unlocked.

That might have been the border guard, but he was too cold to care. He heard a voice, " *Zehn Mark* " ; he had the note in his overcoat pocket, and fumbled for it and passed it out. Then the man helped him down and into the station, where there was a warm stove. The traveller crouched by it and would have stayed there even if the place had been full of S.S. men in uniform.

But no, it was only the station-master, and he proved a kindly old fellow ; they were all old these days—it was horrible to realize that wherever you went you found the countryside drained dry of men up to the age of sixty. Lanny fished out a five-mark note, and this entitled him to doze by the fire for an unspecified period. He ate the sandwich that had been in his overcoat pocket, and when the sun shone pink upon the highest mountains in Austria, he walked through the little town of Sillian and up the highway which runs through the high Toblacherfeld toward the Italian border, six or eight miles farther on.

He had plied the station-master with questions concerning the road, and what he had to expect from both Italian and Austrian guards. They were few, but alert ; you would have to have an exit permit to get by one set and an entrance permit to get by the other, and if you were seen on any of the mountain trails you would be shot, just as if you were a *Gemsbock*—that is, a chamois, or Alpine goat. Lanny hadn't said what he planned to do ; he just walked, and rejoiced in the warmth and in the magnificent sight, the sun shining upon a great glacier. He renewed his courage and hope, for just beyond this pass lay the goal of his long pilgrimage.

IX

The refugee walked until he could guess that he was within a couple of miles of the border. Then he picked out one of those peasant huts which cling to the snow-covered mountain-side. There a family earns a bare existence by building rock walls and carrying in loads of earth in baskets to make one more tiny garden ; that can go on for generation after generation, provided that the superfluous young males are shipped to America or the Argentine, or else are killed off in wars.

Lanny approached a hut. He had no stick, because you could not find such a thing in the inhabited parts of this land —they were all gathered up for firewood as soon as the winds blew them from the trees. However, there was small chance of there being a dog, for what would he eat ? There was an old grey-bearded man spading in the snow, and an old woman and a young one bent over some task that Lanny couldn't make out. Then he saw an unusual sight, a tall youth with health in his cheeks, and how could it have come about that the Army hadn't got him ?

The visitor made himself known, and discovered that this was an Italian-speaking family. Fine ! He could practise the skill he had acquired in Rome, and if he used a few German words it wouldn't matter, for they did the same. He told his sad story in this new language, and it proved equally effective. He explained that he could pay for a meal, and they invited him into the hut, where another lean and stringy woman was working over a fire. Here again were boiled potatoes and goat's milk, and this time marrow instead of turnips ; also dried garlic, and as a special favour to a guest, a few dried olives, which must have come from the southern side of the border. Lanny observed that bread was hardly ever seen, and he could guess that the grains were compact and handy for the armies, and therefore had all been commandeered.

After the traveller had made friends, he told what he wanted, a guide who knew the paths well enough to take him through the forest at night—this very night if possible. Then a little drama unfolded itself ; Lanny observed the people looking at one another, and then their looks seemed to concentrate upon the tall lad. The lad's face wore an excited expression, and a light came into his eyes. Suddenly one of the women, evidently the lad's mother, burst into tears and hid her face in her hands.

The patriarch of the family explained the situation : the boy was fifteen, and next week would come his sixteenth birthday, and they were debating what to do. He was due to report at Lienz for military service, and if he failed to do so the family would be heavily fined and that would ruin them and drive them from their home. Giulio himself had no interest in the war ; he had picked up some rebel notions, the old grandfather murmured apologetically. He wanted to go into Italy and join a group of young fellows who lived in the mountains, to evade the draft.

Lanny might have created a sensation by announcing, " That is what I too want to do." But he saw that he had the situation in his hands without taking any such risk. He asked, " Does Giulio know the forest paths ? " And the reply was, " Not well enough to travel them in the dark ; but he has an uncle who lives near the border and has earned his living as a guide. He has lost one arm in the war, so now the Army lets him alone."

So the problem solved itself. Giulio was crazy to go, and the women dried their tears. After all, wouldn't they have wept just as hard or harder if he had been drafted into the Army and carried off to the Russian front after three months' training ? The traveller would sleep for a few hours—in spite of the fleas—and at sundown they would go to the uncle's place. Lanny would pay the uncle twenty marks as soon as he was safely delivered to the town of Dobbiaco, or Toblach. Also he would pay twenty to Giulio, which would keep him going until he found the Partisans. It was a princely offer and seemed like a direct intervention of the Blessed One, the Queen of Heaven ; the son of Budd-Erling was surprised to find himself an agent of that royal personage, for the highest he had been able to reach in the social scale hitherto had been playing tennis with the King of Sweden and the exiled King of Spain.

X

There appeared to be no flaw in the programme, unless Lanny were to make a mis-step on a mountain trail in the darkness. Some bread resembling hard-tack was produced from a hiding place, and some cheese for sandwiches—the peasants are old hands at hiding food from tax collectors and military foragers. At the hour appointed the women finished their weeping, and Giulio wiped away the tears of which he was ashamed ; he swore to come back when the war was over —but of course he might not live that long. He led his *padrone* by a back snow trail to his uncle's place, and told that weather-beaten and crippled man about the bargain. The man was an Austrian, Gruber by name, and he said three words in German and three in Italian, and then three in between, but they all meant " O.K."

He took down three pairs of skis from the wall, and from under his bed two packages which appeared to be heavy. They had straps to go over the shoulders, and he put one on Giulio's and one on his own. That meant that he was a smuggler, but it didn't worry Lanny, who was something much worse. Gruber had a tiny pencil flashlight and an extra battery or two, something that only a black marketeer could have obtained in these days. They would use it only rarely.

The expedition set out, with Gruber leading, Lanny following as close behind him as possible, and Giulio bringing up the rear. They might be passing near sentries, so they would proceed in complete silence, pushing themselves up slopes and then gliding down others. The trail was through thick forests most of the time ; streams cut through it, and when there were gullies ahead, Gruber would give a whispered warning. If the stranger became dizzy or exhausted, he would ask for help. He must do his best to follow exactly in the guide's tracks, avoiding declivities.

So began six trying hours. The cold was endurable only because it was still. Lanny had done some ski-ing during his long life in Europe, but never in darkness and never in such fear. At one point, from a high clear slope, they could see the lights of motor cars on the road ; they stopped, and there were pinpoints of light, and Gruber whispered that that was the border station. Lanny could guess that he was at the place where he would have been shot at if it had been by daylight.

It was a hard trip, but men were doing it all the time, so Lanny was told. Men were subjecting themselves to every sort of test of muscles and nerves ; as Roosevelt had said, it was a war for survival. How far away Lanny's genial Boss seemed that night ! How far away was everything in this world but cold, and a wild forest covered with fresh snow and having hard-packed snow and sometimes ice underneath. A man would make this trip, there and back, for twenty marks, greatly depreciated. Lanny reflected : Perhaps he has something valuable in the two bundles ! Optical goods, for example, stolen from the Army, or explosives for the Partisans—who could guess ?

They came into a little valley, on a path beside a fast-racing stream. They stopped to get their breath, and Gruber whispered, " You are in Italy." They went on, and there were signs of dawn ; they were going down, and it was easier. When there was light enough to see, there was a broad valley, with many houses, and the guide said, " There, Signor, is your Dobbiaco ! " In Lanny's heart there echoed a song from older and happier days, a song of a German longing for Italy : " *Kennst du das Land wo die Citronen blühn ?* "

15

Campo Coraggio

I

THE three travellers spent the night on the floor of a cabin belonging to a friend of Gruber—probably a confederate, for he promptly hid the bundles and in the morning provided a new one to be taken back to Austria. During the night Lanny made the discovery that Italian fleas were of no more gentle disposition than those north of the Alps ; but the weather was far more polite, and for the first time in many nights he did not suffer from cold. In the morning it was marvellous to feel the warm sun and see fruit trees still green and water unfrozen.

He was interested to find out what these peasants thought and felt about the war. He discovered that the fall of Mussolini had caused them no pangs, and that men and women alike loathed the Nazis. Speaking to the Austrian, the old grandfather of this family remarked, " They took your country, and now they have taken ours." He added that they took everything in the country ; but the Allies had come, and they would take it from the Nazis and give it back to the honest Italians. While Lanny had been on his pilgrimage the Allies had moved into Naples ; soon they would be in Rome, and then in Milan—and Dobbiaco !

Lanny, of course, couldn't give any hint that he was an American ; but he asked about that land and heard wonderful stories. America was the land of riches, oh, unlimited riches ! These peasant people had but a vague idea of how the riches were gained, but they were there, and it was well known that any man who would go there when he was young, and work hard and save his money, could come back to Italy when he was forty and buy a small property and keep a cow and plenty of chickens for the rest of his days. Such was their dream of happiness for this world ; and for the next, you prayed to the

Blessed Virgin, went to mass two or three times a year, and left everything else to the Higher Powers.

Lanny had paid his guide, and in the morning this tireless one shouldered a new load and set out; he had a long way to go before he neared the border, and that part could be traversed in daylight. Lanny was supposed to go down to the town; but first he pleaded he was tired, and then he took Giulio aside and said that he was thinking of taking a trip with him to meet some of the Partisans; he knew people among them. Giulio was delighted to have company. He had been inquiring about the Partisans and had been told cautiously that they were somewhere in the mountains to the west; everybody had heard they were there, but it wasn't good to know too much. After a while, for a fee, the Italian grandfather said that he would guide them to the trail, and if they went far enough they would probably come upon one of the scouts; if they could convince him that they were good people he might take them to one of the camps. Naturally, the Partisans were afraid of spies and of raids by the enemy.

Lanny had had enough of mountain climbing to last him for a lifetime, so he thought; but he knew that he still wasn't safe from the Nazis, who held this country in a tight grip. He had taken his German papers and put them into the stove; Hans Schultz was no more, and Lanny's German career was ended. But what was he? If an American, he was a spy, and the Gestapo would surely get him and shoot their " truth serum " into him.

II

So, in the middle of the afternoon, a new expedition set out, skirting Dobbiaco through the surrounding foothills, and climbing into a new valley. When darkness fell they were in the heavy timber, and there, not far from the trail, they observed a small camp-fire burning. Oddly enough, there was nobody near it; but the guide called and gave his name, and there emerged from the shadows the first young man whom Lanny had seen in either the Austrian or the Italian Alps. He was, Lanny guessed, about twenty, with a scanty black beard, a pair of piercing dark eyes, and a stern manner; he wore a hunting jacket with a sweater under it, and a pair of trousers tucked into boots. He carried a shot-gun.

He asked what they wanted, and Giulio said that he had come from the Austrian side to avoid the draft and desired to join the Partisans. " This is my friend who wants to meet you," he added, pointing to Lanny, and Lanny spoke, " I have a confidential story which I wish to tell to your leader." The reply was, " Our leader does not meet strangers." Lanny smiled his well-rehearsed amiable smile and responded, " Tell your leader that I have the most important story he has ever heard. Tell him that he can hold me in his camp until he has verified my story, and if it is not true he can shoot me."

The young fellow called, and another chap came out, this one with a couple of old-fashioned pistols in his belt. " Watch these people until I come back," commanded the first, and then started off up the trail. The three travellers seated themselves by the fire and devoured the food they had brought. The old man wrapped himself in a blanket which he had carried on his back and fell sound asleep, snoring lustily. Lanny sat talking with Giulio in whispers, and the sentry stayed in the shadows, presumably with at least one of his pistols ready for action.

Perhaps an hour passed before there were footsteps on the trail and the light of an electric torch. Three men came into view, all armed ; one, older than the others, had a lean, stern face, a black moustache, and wavy hair, rather long ; his costume was riding breeches and boots and a camouflaged military jacket, obviously captured or stolen from the Germans. He came to the fire and looked the party over ; then, to Lanny, " *Bene, Signor* ; what is your story ? "

Lanny said, " First, this boy ; he is a peasant lad whose uncle guided me across the border from Austria. He has come to draft age and does not want to fight for the Nazis. He asks to join your group."

" We know his sort," was the response. " He will be welcome. But what about you, Signor ? " Lanny received this polite title, though he was a *vagabondo* who had not had a bath for a month and had a half-inch beard over most of his face.

" I would like you to have me searched and make sure that

I have no arms. Then I would like to talk to you privately. It will be for you to decide how much of my story shall be told to others."

The man turned to one of his associates. " Search him, Carlo."

It was a cursory job compared with what had been done to Lanny in Hitler's home ; but it was enough for ordinary purposes. The leader said, " *Vieni*," and led the stranger away from the fire. With his torch he picked out a fallen tree and they sat upon it—in darkness, for batteries had to be stolen from the enemy and were precious. In this high place it was cold, but Lanny didn't mean to take long.

Said he, " I am an agent of the American O.S.S. and have been working in Germany. I have information of the utmost military importance. I learned that the Gestapo had got on to me, so I got false papers and old clothes from the German underground and have hitch-hiked my way from Berlin. What I ask you to do is to find some way to get word to the O.S.S. I have a code name, Traveller, and if you can get that message to any American agent, he will send it to Washington and a way will be found to get me into Allied territory."

The man, a quiet and thoughtful person, took his time to consider the statement. Then he said, " This is, of course, an important story, and, assuming that it is true, we shall do what we can to help you."

Lanny went on, " I urge you to make my story known only to those who have to know it. I have been moving among the highest circles in Berlin, and getting information of top importance. The Nazis must know that and will be moving heaven and earth to stop me. If the word spreads that an American refugee is in these mountains they will do their best to catch him, and you might be tempted to suspect that I have somehow betrayed you. I beg you not to put either of us in that danger."

" I see your point, Signor, and I will do my best to keep the matter quiet."

" I ought to tell you this further fact : I was working in Rome last summer, and the Gestapo there knows me. So that is one more reason for caution. One of our agents took me to meet Matteo Matteotti and I had a conference with him.

The agent goes under the name of Rinaldo, and it may be that you know him."

" I do not know that name, Signor."

" It may be that he has never got this far north. I do not ask you to tell me anything about your methods of communication ; but I assume that somewhere you have access to a radio-sending and -receiving set, and so can communicate with American agents."

" These agents all know your name ? "

" None of them know it, Signor. My name is known only in Washington. What you are to tell the agent is to get word to Washington that Traveller is here. Washington will then send instructions."

" It shall be done, Signor. And meantime you will stay in our camp ? "

" Nothing will please me more. I am not a young man any more and I am tired out. For this last trip I had to tie the soles of my shoes on with wire. I hope that you will be able to get me a pair of shoes or boots."

" Such things are hard to obtain nowadays, Signor."

" It happens, fortunately, that I have money." Lanny took out a hundred-mark note—he was always careful to have the right amount ready in his pocket, so that he wouldn't have to show how much more he had. " You will have to feed me while I am here. I have funds, and when I leave I will turn some of them over to you, for I have been authorized to help the underground wherever I come in contact with it. Unfortunately this is German money, but perhaps you can get rid of it."

" *Certamente, Signor.* It happens to be the one German thing that Italians like." Then he added, " My name is Arnaldo."

" *Bene.* I suggest that you call me Pierre. I have lived most of my life in France, and I passed for a Frenchman in Rome. I suggest that you tell your men that I am from France, and also that they are not to ask me questions. Of course, if you yourself wish to ask me any, that is another matter."

" *Merci bien, Camarade Pierre,*" replied the leader, with a smile which Lanny didn't see but which he could hear in the voice. " *Il y a des Français avec nous.*"

III

The old peasant was left sleeping by the fire, and Lanny and Giulio were escorted up a trail for two or three miles. They turned off into a forest where there was no trail whatever ; they found their way by the light of the torch. Lanny could guess that they approached their hide-out by a different route each time to avoid leaving a sign for the enemy. The shelter proved to be a dug-out in the side of a slope, covered with logs and turf and carefully camouflaged with planted bushes. The entrance was through bushes at the side, and after you had entered a sentry on the outside covered your footsteps with a sprinkling of leaves.

Lanny was astonished when he went inside. It was a big place, and there were a score of men and boys in it. The youngest was sixteen, and the oldest could not have been more than twenty-five. Some were peasants, others students and factory workers. They were an enthusiastic and romantic lot, and nearly all good-looking. Lanny found subsequently that they represented every shade of political thought, being united only in their hatred of Fascism and especially of its German imitation. Oddly enough, they resented having even their country's bad ideas stolen by the barbarians of the north !

Arnaldo said, " This is Compagno Giulio, from the Austrian border, who wishes to join us ; and this is Compagno Pierre from France. He tells us a story which has to be investigated, and meantime he stays with us as a friend, but does not leave the camp until we have made sure of him." That was all the introduction.

The visitors were soon made to feel at home. First they were asked if they were hungry, and when they said that they had eaten, they were asked for news. This was the most precious of commodities here, for the group had no radio and were far from any town. Lanny had picked up information from the station-master at Sillian and could tell them that the Allies were at the Volturno River, some twenty-five miles north of Naples, and also had taken Foggia, the great airport. That news was shouted aloud ; it was taken to mean that

soon now the planes would be dropping supplies in this far
northern region. And the Army would arrive, oh, very soon,
for this wonderful people adored speed ; they would be in
Rome within a month, and in Milan within two months—was
it not so, Compagno ?

They demanded the opinions of this evidently well-educated
vagabondo, and he felt bound to warn them that they must
not expect too much, because Italy was just one mountain
after another to be climbed, and one river after another to
be crossed. When an olive-skinned young hero suggested that
the Allies could land on the coast, farther and farther up,
as they had done in Sicily and at Salerno, Lanny replied, " It
may be ; but you must remember that Italy will not be the
main objective in this war ; the Allies may be saving their
resources for a landing across the English Channel."

An argument started, and to this new arrival it was like
being taken back to his youth, when he had listened to arguments about World War I and how it was going to be fought
and what was going to come out of it. It was like being at
the labour school in Cannes, which Lanny had helped to
support, and where he had met youngsters who could hardly
be distinguished from these, except that they had spoken
French with a Provençal accent, while here they spoke Italian
with a Tridentine accent. And in Berlin there had been a
labour school where Lanny and the Robin boys had met youth
groups who had yet another language, but who had the same
hopes and, alas, the same disagreements as to how they were
to be realized.

Lanny had no trouble in making a place for himself in
this camp. He told about these labour schools, and also about
what he knew of the Partisans of France, who called themselves Maquis, a word meaning underbrush, where they hid.
He told how " Bruges," one-time director of a school, had
gone to Toulon to help organize the workers there, and what
they had done to make sure that the French Fleet did not
fall into German hands. He told of visiting a group of these
Partisans in the hills back of the great naval base, and again
in a cellar of the town. He told about two brothers, whom
he had known since their boyhood, who had split over the
problem of their country's destiny and were now in armies

on opposite sides. All this was in accord with the experiences of these Italian patriots, and they no longer had any doubt of the good faith of their mysterious guest.

He had twice the years of most of them, and they adopted him in the role of professor of world affairs ; they thronged about him, plying him with questions, and in the evenings, when most of them were in the dug-out, he would find that he was addressing the entire group. It did no harm for them to know that he had travelled all over Europe, and that he had visited America, and had been around the globe. He could solve problems for the lads, many of whom had but limited education.

IV

How eager they were for knowledge and how quickly they grasped whatever came their way ! They knew that there was something desperately wrong with their world, and with all the power of their hearts they meant to change it. To the last man they had this determination : there was going to be a new Italy and they, collectively, were going to be masters of it. Never again were they going to be made fools of by any dictator. Lanny gave them American phrases, a " stuffed shirt " and a " sawdust Caesar "—*uno Cesare di segatura*—and they received these with delight. *Mai piu!*

An old-time Socialist was heartened to discover that this new world was going to be his. Much as these lads differed about tactics, to a man their thinking was collectivist. There were going to be no more *cartelli* in Italy, and no more merchants of death, buying up politicians and preparing wars to enrich themselves. Even the Catholics, the most devout among them who wore scapulars and said their prayers, were strongly tinged with Pink. They would cite the encyclicals of Pope Leo XIII dealing with the rights of labour and the evils of inequality of wealth—those same authoritative documents which F. D. R. kept on his desk to read to archbishops who came to protest against this or that New Deal extremism.

There was agreement as to the goal, but the question of how to get to it was an open one. Lanny heard all the old arguments and discovered the same antagonisms that had so troubled him in both the schools. No matter in what language

—French, English, German, or Italian—the Socialists argued with the Communists, and never could they agree. Lanny had done his best to reconcile them; but how could you reconcile people who believed in the democratic process and the deciding of all questions by popular vote, with people who believed that the democratic process was a snare of the capitalist class and that the only way you could end capitalism was by the revolutionary action of an intelligent minority? Listening to the disputes, Lanny had decided that the Communists hated the Socialists even more than they hated the capitalists. The average Communist rarely saw a capitalist and knew him and his world only from pictures in the papers; but the Communist had the Socialists before him all the time, arguing with him, and blocking his success with the workers.

Among the Partisans, here as everywhere else, the discussions led to quarrelling and to splits. Lanny was told that many groups had been wrecked by this controversy, and as a result there were some Communist groups and some Socialist groups which refused to co-operate. But Arnaldo, a lawyer and man of firm will, had laid down the law that political controversy was barred in this camp, and anyone who came in had to accept that restriction. One thing they could agree upon, to drive the Nazis out of Italy, and to hang or shoot the spies and traitors who had helped them. After that the Italian people would decide what they wanted for their future. To this Lanny could say amen, and he would answer questions of fact and turn aside questions of theory with a smile.

V

It must not be assumed that this group had nothing to do but talk: far from it. They had to keep the camp in order, to carry water and cut wood and bring it to the fireplace which they had built of local stone, with cement carried up from the valley on the backs of men. They had to maintain strict sentry duty day and night on the trails which led to their camp. And since there was very little food in the mountains, they had to tote it up. In addition to such tasks of maintenance, parties large or small would go down to the villages to perform those secret tasks which justified their existence.

When the leaders became sure of Lanny's sincerity, they explained their problem. They couldn't do much open sabotage as yet, for they were too weak ; the Germans could send a military force into these mountains and drive them up beyond the snow line, where they would freeze or starve to death. But soon now the Allied planes would be coming over, dropping weapons and supplies. Arnaldo pointed to the gun-rack by the door ; there were a dozen different kinds, and for some of them they had only a handful of cartridges. But when the Allies would supply them with tommy guns—they used this American name—then they would be able to raid the enemy and to fight him if he ventured into the highlands.

Meantime, day by day, they were training themselves according to American Army instruction. They were learning to creep and crawl, and to move silently in the night ; to use the knife and the cord or wire to strangle an enemy ; to set dynamite and make road-blocks to wreck trains and trucks. Meantime they were going into the towns to distribute leaflets and paint slogans on walls, to maintain the morale of the population ; they were stealing supplies from the Nazis, boring holes in their tyres, and otherwise causing unpleasant things to befall them. The leader said, " If you will send us enough hand grenades, we can make it impossible for their trucks to travel on these highways ; and if we have enough ammunition, we can make a stand and keep their raiding parties from coming into the hills."

Lanny promised, " I will report the situation ; and I'm sure it won't be long now. You must remember that America is fighting two wars, on opposite sides of the world, and has had less than two years in which to convert its machinery of production to war purposes. There are thousands of groups clamouring for supplies, and questions of priority are the gravest the General Staff has to decide."

" Don't forget this," continued Arnaldo ; " most of the supplies the Germans fight with in Italy have to come on these highways and railroads."

The P.A. responded, " Take my word for it, Compagno, our staffs have good maps."

This unbidden guest was careful not to ask questions that bore upon the group's means of communication. He could come near to guessing what the process would be. They would send a courier to some near-by town to communicate with an American " post office." Sooner or later word would reach some agent who operated a radio-sending and -receiving set, used rarely, and only at night, and for a few minutes at a time ; then it would be packed up and moved quickly, perhaps in a pedlar's cart, perhaps in a secret compartment of a truck, perhaps in a doctor's automobile or a fisherman's boat.

The weak message from this set would be picked up by some more powerful set, perhaps a naval vessel cruising in Italian waters, or apparatus which would undoubtedly be in operation in Naples or Foggia. From there it would be relayed to Algiers, and thence to Casablanca and Washington, by radio or cable. The message would be in code and would not have to be long : " Traveller, Arctic, Hades," or something like that. In the secret book of O.S.S. Traveller would be Lanning Prescott Budd, P.A. 103 ; Arctic would be the " post office " in the Dolomite Alps ; Hades would be the radio-sending set that had started the message. In the old brick building by the gasworks in Washington men would jump into action, for that was what they were there for, to get their agents into enemy lands and to get them out when they were ready to come. The proper officers of Army, Navy, and Air Force would be consulted, and a way would be devised and a message sent : " Hades, Arctic, Traveller "—plus whatever instructions were to be given.

VI

Lanny spent five days in the idyllic surroundings of Campo Coraggio, Camp Courage, as this outpost was called. He was magically provided with a pair of new boots that fitted him, and that was all he really needed for the time being. He took part in the singing which was one of this company's ways of passing the long evening hours. He watched the magnificent scenery of the Alpine mountains in late autumn, and had the pleasure of seeing the first blanket of pure white snow laid down upon the land.

Then, on the sixth day, at early dawn, there came shouts from a sentry and a wild uproar : the sentry had heard a signal, six shots in three pairs at two-second intervals, which

meant that the enemy was coming up the trail. " Pack up ! "
shouted Arnaldo, and there followed a scene of confusion, or
so it seemed, but as a matter of fact it had all been rehearsed,
like a fire drill, and every man knew what he was doing.
Portable possessions were wrapped, tied tightly in blanket
rolls and thrown over shoulders, guns were taken down, and
within twenty minutes after the alarm was given the entire
band was ready.   A sentry came running in to report that
the Germans were coming in force with a pack train ; so the
band set out, on a trail that led upward along the mountainside and into heavier timber.   The snow was bad for them
because it made the trail easier to follow ; but they were
young and could climb as fast as the Germans ; they knew
all the paths, and if necessary could go down into the open
and scatter into the villages, to reassemble later.   They would
have been willing to stand and die, but the Americans had
told them to run away and live to fight another day.

All this was explained to Lanny by the leader, who brought
up the rear.   The P.A. had the uncomfortable thought that
the raid might be due to his presence ; but it was impossible
for the Partisans to suspect him of complicity since he had
not once been out of their sight.   He asked if it would make
a difference in his chances of getting a message, and Arnaldo
said that when a message came he, Arnaldo, would have a
way to receive it, and all Lanny had to do was to keep in
touch with the band.

They moved at top speed, and the trip was a test of wind
and muscle, not so easy for a man in his forties who had been
too busy to play tennis for a long time.   He had no choice
but to keep up, for even if he were able to evade the Germans,
he would not be able to survive in these mountains alone.
When darkness came they took shelter in a cave, where they
found other Partisans already in hiding.   Sentries were posted
a mile or two back on the trail, and no one could know whether
the band would be routed out and forced to flee in darkness ;
the enemy would have plenty of flashlights and, of course,
guns and ammunition.

At the first signs of morning Lanny parted from his friends.
Arnaldo had decided to send him down to be hidden in a
peasant hut, under the escort of two lads who knew the way.

The leader said, " Stay there ; or if you have to hide, the boys will keep in touch with the place." Lanny set out with his guides, and when he left the trail it was in a stream which came tumbling out of the high snow-covered mountain. He walked a quarter of a mile over slippery boulders, the three of them helping to hold each other up. That was to make certain that the enemy did not get their trail and follow them down.

VII

So once more the elegant son of Budd-Erling was quartered in a dug-out shed on the side of a mountain, in the company of the family goat and the family pig. He slept on a pile of straw, and his food was brought to him on a wooden platter. He was forbidden to go out except at night, and the two young fellows took turns doing sentry duty farther down the trail ; they had been told that he was precious, and that there was a possibility of the enemy raid having him as its objective. The Gestapo had its counter-espionage service, and no system of communication could ever be proof against the possibility of a leak.

The days were long, and the fleas were active. Lanny had only two means of recreation : the first, an Italian peasant boy of six or so, dark-eyed and melancholy in appearance, a fit subject for a painter of the poor. He was fascinated by this bearded stranger, who told him all the tales and legends he could remember, out of Grimm and Aesop, Uncle Remus and the Arabian Nights ; he told about Europe and America, and surely those were crowded hours in the life of a peasant child on the side of a lonely mountain. A high mountain it was, having a sharp-pointed peak ; the Dolomites are all like that. They are made of a kind of limestone, having streaks of colour as if a celestial painter had worked upon them after the Creator had pushed them up.

The other means of passing time was a small paper-backed volume which one of the propagandists of Campo Coraggio had slipped into Lanny's hand—an Italian translation of Lenin's *State and Revolution*. Here was the authentic gospel, and the P.A. took the opportunity to make certain that he knew what his Communist friends were driving at. It was a programme for social transformation, as carefully worked out as a series of theorems by Euclid ; there was no escaping its rigid logicality, provided that you admitted the basic premisses. But Lanny Budd had the advantage of four decades over Nicolai Lenin ; the latter had been predicting what would happen, whereas the former knew what *had* happened.

So he could say that a Russian refugee in Zürich had erred in laying too great stress upon economic processes, failing to allow for human ingenuity and personality, and the creative forces which these might release in the world. He had under-estimated the resilience of the capitalist system, and the psychological devices it would produce in its own defence. Above all, he had forgotten about genius ; he had failed to foresee the arrival of three masters of the arts of mass hypno-tism whom the big business men of Italy, Germany, and Spain would employ to flatter the collective egotisms of their peoples. A melancholy reflection, indeed ! This chilled and flea-bitten refugee from Nazi-Fascism now took his turn at trying to pierce the veil of the future. He saw General de Gaulle, fully equipped to play the role of dictator in France ; as for the great democracy overseas, could anyone doubt that the lords of press and screen and radio would manage to find themselves a new Huey Long, to save the system of their personal and private free enterprise ?

VIII

Four days passed, and four nights, and at dusk there arrived a sturdy peasant lad bearing a scrap of paper with a single word : " Mazzinni." That was the code name which Arnaldo had given to Lanny at parting, and he had added, with a smile, that he would put in the extra letter " n " to make doubly sure the message was from him and none other. Lanny emerged from his goat shed, bade good-bye to little Paolo and his mother and sisters and grandfather, and pre-sented the worn copy of Lenin to one of his guardians. Then, following the peasant lad, he made his way carefully down a trail in darkness, and in the middle of the night came to a small town of which he never knew the name.

He was escorted through dark streets to what appeared to be a fair-sized residence and was taken in by the rear door.

He found himself in the study of a scholarly person, perhaps a doctor, for there was an anatomy chart on the wall, two cases full of books, a pile of magazines and papers on the centre table, and a globe of the world under a floor lamp. More important, there was an elderly gentleman with a grey moustache and goatee, wearing spectacles, a black linen duster, and an amiable smile. " Signor Traveller ? " he asked, and that, of course, was code. " I am Dr. Moscichi," and that, of course, might be his real name or not.

From first to last neither of them asked an unnecessary question. The doctor said, " I have been asked to escort you to the coast not far from Venice. This is by no means an easy feat to perform, and we shall have to take precautions. We shall take a train tomorrow night ; I shall be feeble and in need of help, and you will be my servant. I have papers for you in the name of Guillermo Forli, and since we appear to be of about the same height, you will be able to wear a suit of my clothes. You are in my hands and I am in yours, and we shall have to consult carefully as to what stories we are to tell and what steps we are to take in various emergencies."

" I am deeply grateful," replied the P.A., " and will do my best to follow your suggestions."

" I know nothing about you, Signor, except that you are an important person, and that I am urged to do everything in my power to get you out of the country. I might add that ample funds have been provided."

" *Grazie, Dottore.* As it happens, I also have funds, more than I need to get back. It would be a good idea to leave some of them with you for the help of the next man who may come along."

" That I am willing for you to do. And now, first, you will wish to clean up."

" I have not had a chance to bathe in six weeks, and I am sorry to confess that I have fellow travellers."

" It could not be otherwise," said the old gentleman with a smile. " We will put your clothing into the fire, and I will help you to get your head clean. Also, I will provide you with a razor ; your whiskers are camouflage, I presume, but they will need trimming up, so as to look artificial instead of primitive."

IX

Lanny had his doubts about travelling as a passenger on a train, but the doctor said he had thought it over carefully, and it seemed to him a time for boldness. Gasoline was almost impossible to get, and private automobile travel was so rare that it would attract attention and they would be questioned at many road-blocks. But it was still possible to ride on trains, and he would have an excuse, that he was ill and needed to consult a specialist. He would need someone to escort him, and this would raise no questions whatever.

So Lanny scrubbed and polished himself and was properly " made up " and then briefed. The doctor didn't say how he had got the papers ; Lanny knew that the means of forging papers was the first need of every underground movement, and to prevent it was the number-one effort of every secret police. It required a print-shop, rubber stamps, an expert penman, and, of course, time. Lanny could guess that the orders from O.S.S. had come quickly and that the delay had been caused by the need for such preparations.

At about twenty hundred hours the doctor and his black-clad servant carrying a suitcase were transported in an old-fashioned cab to the railroad station. The train was late. The doctor sat conversing with a friend, telling about his sudden attack of illness. His servant was not called upon to speak and sat like a stone image in the darkness. When the train arrived—a small and poor one on a secondary line—the servant carefully assisted the sick man to his compartment. The conductor received a tip and was told they were not to be disturbed.

It was just as easy as that. The pair had done their planning in advance, and now lay down and slept, at least the P.A. did, for he had got used to a career of crime and put its worries out of his mind. The train was coming down out of the mountains, and in the morning would be in the warm flatlands, and Lanny thought that would be delightful for a change. Their tickets read to Venice, but when they came to the small town of Mestre, a railroad junction six miles above Venice, the sick old gentleman said to the conductor, " I have changed my mind," and they got off.

He recovered his health enough to negotiate for a carriage to drive them to a fishing village by the Adriatic shore, not far from the mouth of the Piave River. He had friends who had a villa there, he explained to the liveryman. His servant solicitously helped him into the vehicle, and they had an all-day ride, eating a little food out of the suitcase, without stopping at an inn. When they neared the village, the old gentleman had another attack of illness and asked to be taken to an inn there. The servant assisted him upstairs, and put him to bed ; and that was the end of the doctor's duties, as he had explained them in advance.

X

At eight o'clock that evening the dutiful servant left his master's room and went out for a stroll. There was nothing about that to attract attention. He had studied carefully a little sketch showing him where to go : down to the water-front, and eastward, past a couple of landmarks possible to recognize in the darkness, and then to the seventh cabin on the shore. He was to knock there and say the password " Traveller," strange to Italian ears, and he would be taken care of.

Lanny followed the instructions. He could not keep his heart from thumping fast when he tapped on the door, for this was almost the end of his journey, and it would be a cruel jest indeed if there had been a leak and if this door were to be opened by agents of the O.V.R.A. But no, it was a grey-bearded fisherman in a much-patched shirt who appeared in the flickering light of a candle.

When Lanny said " Traveller " he replied quickly, " *Si, Signor,*" and put on his jacket and called another old fellow. Their boat had been hauled up on the beach, on a couple of rollers ; they worked it down in a jiffy, and bade the traveller get in before it touched the water, so that he would not wet his boots. A lovely warm night, with a new moon in the sky ; they put up the sail, and the smelly little craft slid silently out into the Adriatic.

Lanny sat and thought : What a wonderful thing was the Office of Strategic Services, which General Donovan had built in a couple of years ! How well it was named, for this was surely a strategic service, a whole series of them, ever since " Mazzinni " had managed to get out a radio message from the Dolomite Alps. Money is no object, was one of their mottoes, and they operated literally on that basis. Wherever an American life could be saved, American money would be poured out like water. That was especially true when the Commander-in-Chief of all the Armed Forces had stamped his seal upon the life in question ; this was a presidential agent, and all the secret machinery had gone into action. An underground messenger had come up into the mountains, an underground doctor had left his duties, and now a red-sailed fisher-boat was gliding south into the darkness. Fishermen know the stars and how to use them in their business.

So, when the sun came up out of Yugoslavia, there appeared near the southern horizon a small speck which caused the men to point and shout with satisfaction. It grew larger, and soon they heard it, a seaplane ! How the connection had been made Lanny would never know. Perhaps there was a radio-sending set in Venice, or in that inn where the doctor had put up, or even in the fisherman's hut that night. There was sure to be one of the most powerful receiving sets in the world at the naval base of Bari which the Allies had taken a short time previously ; perhaps there was one even nearer, where the Allies had established their line on the east coast, about even with the Volturno line on the west. That would be only some three hundred miles south of the head of the Adriatic, no flight at all for a seaplane.

Anyhow, here it was. It slid down out of the sky and onto the water just ahead of the shirt-waving fishermen, and they put the boat about and put their passenger on the plane, again without wetting his boots. They pushed the boat away, and the engine started, and splash, splash, and then no more bumping—the plane was in the air and the P.A. was on his way home.

XI

The seaplane was noisy, so Lanny couldn't share his happiness with the pilot. He just snuggled in his corner and gloated over the luck he had enjoyed. He was out of Naziland and was never going back—unless it was in the wake of a conquering army. He would see Laurel again, and Baby Lanny, and Robbie, and F. D. R., and Alston, and other people who interested him. He would be able to tell these people what he had been doing, and would no longer have to have a dozen compartments in his mind, and remember what he was free to say to each one, and what lies he had told to Hitler and Göring and Himmler and Hess and the rest of those hateful fanatics.

He thought: What will F. D. R. give me to do now? And right away the old caution began to assert itself in his mind. Even though he couldn't go into Axis territory, there might be secret work that he could do. There were plenty of pro-Axis persons in the Allied lands, not excluding America, and it might be his job to keep contact with them. It wasn't likely that they would learn that he was no longer in favour with the Führer; the Gestapo all over the world would be informed, but they wouldn't publicize the fact that one of the Führer's intimate friends had turned out to be an agent of the enemy. So Lanny might continue to be the friend of the great newspaper publishers and others who in their hearts considered Nazi-Fascism the one last hope of the world. He might continue to take his wife to Evalyn McLean's soirées and to hob-nob with conservative senators of both parties.

He decided that he wouldn't say anything to anybody until he had had a talk with the Boss. When the plane came down in the harbour of Bari, now filled with American and British vessels of all types, the young Naval Air officer who greeted him was quite evidently full of curiosity. " So you got out alive, Mr. Budd! " The bearded gentleman in a shapeless black alpaca suit too tight for him replied, " Thanks to your wonderful efficiency." Nothing could have been more polite, or less satisfactory.

" You are to be flown to Washington," was the officer's statement. " How soon can you be ready? " The traveller answered, " As soon as I can get hold of something to read. Let me have some old newspapers and magazines if you can." He might have added, " I haven't seen an American newspaper or magazine for nearly two months," but that was the way

N

he had learned not to talk. As early as boyhood, in World
War I, he had learned the French motto, that enemy ears were
listening. *Les oreilles ennemies vous écoutent!*

A few details to be attended to; a shave by a barber, a
toothbrush and a comb from the commissary, and a contact
to be made with the O.S.S. man in Bari, who was glad to get
hold of some German money and to pay for it with good
American dollars. Then Lanny boarded a transport plane for
Algiers, and he was set down at the familiar Maison Blanche
airport. Here in the black market he managed to find himself
a proper suit of English tweeds at a very high price. He
had a chat with Robert Murphy and arranged for him to put
through a message to Newcastle, saying that Lanny was on
his way home; Robbie would telephone at once to Laurel,
and that would be a load off the minds of both. Lanny told
the Ambassador what he had observed about conditions in
Germany and Italy, that being of importance to the State
Department's leading man here. But the P.A. said nothing
about what he had accomplished in Germany or how he had
got out; that was for the President.

XII

Lanny requested a day in Marrakech, so he could see his
mother. On the plane flight he wrestled with the problem,
and at the last moment made up his mind that he wouldn't
tell her anything about Marceline. If there had been anything
that Beauty could do about it, the situation would have
been different; but there wasn't a thing on earth for her to
do, except to spend days and nights of anguish, and then
quite possibly find out that it had all been a mistake. When
Marceline had telephoned Lanny she had still been at liberty;
and Lanny knew that she had made many friends in Germany.
It was quite possible that she had sought refuge with one of
these and had been hidden; that had happened in the case of
Allied flyers, who had had no friends in Germany at all but
had found somebody willing to shelter them for months, and
had got out of Germany in the end. But Beauty inevitably
would imagine the worst and drive herself crazy brooding
over it.

So, when he appeared at the super-elegant Hôtel Mamounia, there was a happy reunion. He reported that he had been in the American zone in Italy—which was true ; and that all was going well there—which was also true. Pretty soon the Army would be across the Volturno River, and the march on Rome would get under way. There was surely going to be a landing in France before long, and meantime the Russians were driving incessantly ; so this dreadful war should be over in a year or two more. When Beauty said, " The Russians are going to take the whole of Central Europe and the Balkans, and who is going to stop them ? " her son replied, " Yes, old darling ; but the time to start worrying over that will be when Herr Schicklgruber has been put in the can."

What Beauty couldn't stop worrying about was the high cost of living in French Morocco, and the impossibility of getting liquid rouge at any price. The hotel had raised its charges, and Beauty had been unable to find a villa that could be rented for a price within reason. The Army took what it wanted and left nothing—and still the officers expected you to entertain them in proper style. The art expert was able to comfort his fashionable mother with the news that the general price rise was affecting old masters ; the sums which Zoltan Kertezsi was getting for Detazes in New York would enable his widow to go on living in the style to which she had accustomed herself.

There was that lovely little boy, the painter's grandson. He was now five, a delightful age, when they are full of intelligence but have not yet found out anything bad. Beauty adored him and spoiled him sadly, but he appeared to have a naturally sweet disposition. He had taken all this immense establishment for his playground and made no social distinctions ; he knew everybody both white and brown, and had picked up Moorish words as well as French and English. In this he was abetted by his step-grandfather, who had adopted all men as brothers, and had learned the language of the brown-skinned ones and went to their hovels to pray with them. He went also to the military hospitals and spent whole days with the soldiers. He got along with the doctors because he was willing to let them have the credit for what God had done. The doctors had a phrase that had come down from ancient times, *vis medicatrix naturae*, meaning the healing power of nature ; they admitted that they didn't understand that power, and Parsifal would explain it to them quite simply —it was God.

Lanny himself had never learned to pray, at least not well ; like many modern men he found the idea embarrassing. His stepfather said it was because he had had too easy a time in life ; and Lanny could smile to himself, for he had thought he was having some trouble not long ago. But, after all, he had got out ! How would it have been if he hadn't been able to ? He imagined himself in one of the dungeons of the Gestapo ; then, indeed, he might have prayed, and without embarrassment !

The great planes now made the flight from Marrakech without stop. From Washington they brought specialists and technicians—anyone who was needed in a hurry ; and on the way back their load was mostly wounded men. These men lay on pads, and it was not very comfortable, but then the flight took little more than half a day, and they were going back to God's country. They needed attention, and the P.A. helped where he could. All the time he thought what use Parsifal would have made of such an opportunity. The best that a mere worldling could do for these victims was to assure them that the war was being won, and that there were many forms of usefulness for crippled men.

Arriving at the Washington airport, Lanny's first act was to telephone Baker. He was told to call back in three hours. Having learned by painful experience that long-distance calls were slow in wartime, Lanny went to the hotel to which Baker had directed him and put in the call to New York from his room. He was in his bath when the call came through, and he stood on a bath towel while he talked to his wife. They were supposed to take only three minutes, and Laurel spent most of that time trying to keep from sobbing. But she managed to gather that he was in Washington, and perfectly sound and well, and that he hoped to be home in a day or two. The baby was thriving, she told him, and she had started a new novel. Lanny said, " Fine ! Fine ! " And added, " We've got the Nazis licked." He asked her to phone Robbie, and she told him that she had been to Newcastle recently, and all were well there, including Frances. The operator broke in, and he said, " So long ! "

XIII

There was a playboy in Lanny's Big Boss, just as there was in Lanny himself, and that was one of the reasons they got along so well together. Overburdened and exhausted as Franklin Roosevelt might be, he always had room in his mind for a good story ; and he knew that Lanny surely had one. He made room for him late that evening and Baker brought him in the customary way. In that bedroom in which nothing was ever altered, and of which the P.A. knew every smallest item, the big man gave the visitor an extra warm handclasp and exclaimed, " By golly, I have been worried about you ! "

Lanny grinned and said, " I was worried about myself, Governor. But here I am."

" You look thin," declared the other, and Lanny admitted that he had been picking up what grub he could, and not the kind he was used to. " Tell me all about it," commanded F. D. R., and pushed his state papers aside and settled back in his pillows for a holiday.

Lanny told about Hitler and his Evi, about Göring and his new costumes, about Himmler and his blank face and almost colourless eyes. F. D. R. said, " You make shivers run up and down my spine." Lanny answered, " I took it to mean that it was time to get out." He told about the different professors, and about Erickson. That message about the V-2's had come out, he was told, and it was tiptop stuff.

Then came the story of Marceline and her lover. When Lanny told about the telephone call, the Boss took his own phone off the receiver and called the O.S.S. They were on duty at night, of course, and he called the German section and asked if there had been any word out of that country having to do with either Marceline Detaze or Oskar von Herzenberg. The reply was, " Nothing."

Lanny offered to cut his story short more than once, but Roosevelt wanted everything. When he came to the happy ending, the traveller of course gave full credit to the O.S.S.

for its promptness and efficiency; and that pleased the Boss. "Wild Bill" was one of his favourites, and the organization had been his own creation, pushed through in spite of the opposition of half a dozen groups which resented being "merged." Said F. D. R., "There is nothing a bureaucrat hates worse, because in the process he may lose a title and some authority. But it is obvious that Intelligence has to be one thing, otherwise it is confusion."

So everything was hunky-dory, and Lanny had spent some money which he was ordered to take out of the funds the President had entrusted to him. He had got some important information, nearly all that he had gone for ; he was entitled to some kudos, but what he wanted was to be told that he had helped a bit with this war. It was coming along just fine, according to its genial Commander ; the Russians were making a terrible fuss about the lack of a second front, but we were getting ready fast now, and would soon show them, and the Germans too. Lanny said, "It will be a terrible blow to Hitler if we can get across the Channel and stay." The other replied, "Don't quote me, but that is exactly what we are going to do."

The next question was, what the P.A. himself was going to do. Lanny remarked, "I'm afraid I'm no good for Germany or Italy any more." The Boss replied, "Let's settle that. You are positively forbidden to go again." Lanny said, "That will please my wife, if I am free to tell her." The answer was, "Tell her it's final."

The first order was for Lanny to report to the O.S.S. in the morning and tell them everything he could about the German underground and the Italian Partisans. After that he was to take a rest ; a real vacation, a month or two. The President said, "I've nothing special for you right now."

"You once wanted me to go and see Stalin," ventured the P.A.

"I'm expecting to see him myself, Lanny, before this month is over. That is strictly *entre nous*, of course."

"Sure thing, Governor. I suppose I'll go to Florida again, or perhaps to California. There are some people there who will bear watching, as you know, and I might combine business with pleasure."

"That's the ticket! Take your wife along. From what my wife reports about her, she can be of use to you."

"Thanks, Governor. Tell me this: would it be proper for us to have enough gasoline to make a motor trip of it?"

"You have earned a tank-car," was the response. "Tell Baker to fix you up. Go and see what Willie Hearst is up to now. That will make it official business!"

Lanny looked at this careworn man, so eagerly providing a vacation for a friend, and so obviously needing one for himself. How gladly would Lanny have exchanged with him; but the Constitution of the United States did not permit it to be done. The fates were spinning the thread of Franklin Roosevelt's life, and when they were ready to cut it, no human hand could stay them.

XIV

In the morning Lanny paid his visit to the old brick building by the gasworks; he spent the day with the men who had handled the job of getting him out of Italy. He thanked them; and they, being human, would no doubt have been interested to tell him the story of how they had managed it, but that was against the rules. Oh, So Secret! Now and then it was, Oh, So Social!—for this office was staffed largely with men of means, who had been footloose and fancy-free and had been attracted by the idea of enacting in real life the thrillers which they had read in the small hours of the morning and which they had seen on the stage and in the movies—and had called "old-hat" and "ten-twenty-thirty."

They put him through a grilling as thorough as Heinrich Himmler could have provided—except that they didn't use scopolamine. The German section in the morning and the Italian in the afternoon—they had relays of stenographers and wanted to know everything he had seen, every word that had been said to him, and the names and addresses of every person he had met. For who could tell when some other "Traveller" might be coming through by that route? They might be sending somebody on it any day. The German section was enraptured by the information concerning the Wolf Dietrich Stollen, the salt mine under the Duernberg Mountain,

and began that very day a search in the Congressional Library
for data on the salt-mining industry of Austria. They
promised Lanny they would report any news about Marceline
Detaze and Oskar von Herzenberg ; also that they would
trace the matter of the young doctor who had deserted his
charge and would see that he was never again invited to act
as a conductor on the underground railroad.

Lanny was flown to New York that evening, and his wife
was there with the car which the ever thoughtful Robbie had
sent down. Laurel's emotion was touching to see. She had
been such a proud person, so reserved and independent, but
now she couldn't keep her voice from choking up. When a
woman has given her heart to a man, and especially when she
has borne him a child, he has become a part of her being,
and her welfare is irrevocably bound up with his. Now for
a couple of months Laurel had lived with the thought that
she might never see her man again ; that he might at this
moment be dead, or suffering things worse than death. To
have him come suddenly down out of the sky, veritably a god
out of a machine to her, was happiness almost beyond enduring,
and impossible to hide from passengers at an airport.

Driving back to the city, he told her of the programme
which the Big Boss had laid out for them. For the first time
he was free to name F. D. R., for he had said that Laurel
was to help. Lanny pledged her to secrecy, of course ; they
wouldn't even tell Robbie, but would just be two runaways,
travelling on bootleg gasoline. The only trouble was, how
would they get into the hotels ? All over the country everything was jam-packed ; people were leaving the country
districts and crowding into the towns, where wages were high
and war work was a patriotic service ; the women were
travelling to join their husbands near Army camps or wherever
the men might be ordered. " Is this trip necessary ? " read
the signs at railroad stations.

Lanny stood by the little bed where his baby slept, pink-
cheeked, warm, and blissful, utterly unaware of the cruelty
and wickedness of the world which surrounded him. Father
and mother stood with their arms about each other. What
would they not have given to be able to protect the child
from contact with that evil, from even having to know

that it existed. But, alas, there seemed no prospect that a
co-operative commonwealth, free, democratic, and humane,
would come into existence in the course of the next couple of
decades. War-torn and haunted by the spectre of bloody
revolutions, the world presented itself as a cause for grief and
despair, and Laurel had heard women say that they would
not bring a child into such a barrel of snakes. But here was
Baby Lanny, and they must do their best for both him and
the world he had to live in.

XV

They drove up to Newcastle. Never would Lanny hear
the name again without translating it—Neuschloss—and
thinking of poor Marceline and what might be happening to
her. But never would he breathe a word about it to anyone.
He would see Frances Barnes Budd, and be sure that she was
well and happy, and write a detailed letter to her mother,
as he had promised. He would meet all the Budd tribe,
taking what was good in them, as he had learned long ago,
and sharing with his wife a chuckle over what was eccentric
and egocentric. Old, three-hundred-year-old New England
they were, and the mighty megalopolis to the west of them
was a foreign land, mostly under the dominion of Satan. The
lesser megalopolis which was growing up around them was
likewise getting out of their control—an evil contrivance known
as the Committee for Industrial Organizations had moved in
and was taking it over, and the " right " people of the town
laid it all to " The Man," shortened from " That Man in the
White House." The world was going to the demnition bow-
wows, and the elder Budds lived in their old mansions and
grumbled at it. The ladies dusted every gimcrack every day
with their own hands, because you could no longer get a
servant at any price—Robbie had lured them all into his
monstrous airplane plant and was ruining them with two
dollars an hour.

Robbie was looking tired, but he had accustomed himself
to living in the midst of a whirlwind and would have missed
it if it had blown past. Robbie's life consisted of pay-rolls
and costs of raw materials and reports of output achieved and

expected ; also, of course, new blue-prints, new mockups, new ideas and theories. Lanny found that Robbie had got every item of the information which Lanny had sent out through Red Erickson ; but Robbie didn't know that it had come from Lanny, and Lanny had to resist the temptation to tell him. The P.A. gave information, but he had to say that he had picked it up in North Africa and Allied-held Southern Italy. If he had told Robbie about having been into Italy and Germany, Robbie might have trusted his other two sons with the secret, and one of these might have trusted his wife, and so the whisper would have spread in Newcastle and beyond.

Robbie had trained those two sons and they were carrying a good share of the burden. Since the day that Lanny had made his appearance in the world the father had never given up the hope that this first-born might help also. Now, the moment he heard that Lanny and Laurel were going to take a vacation trip, his busy organizing mind went to work to make use of them. An " executive " mind, it was, and though it wouldn't have said so in crude words, what it wanted was to execute art, music, literature, and even politics, and turn all the energies of mankind to the manufacture of material things—at present to be used for the taking of other men's lives. A painful necessity, the president of Budd-Erling would admit, but he would add, " There have always been wars and always will be, men being what they are." Lanny must have heard him say it several hundred times in forty years.

What he said now was, " Why don't you two go and look over our new plant in New Mexico ? " He said " our," because both Lanny and Laurel were stockholders, and he wanted to keep that fact in their minds. " It's beautiful country, and a delightful climate in winter."

" What would you want us to do ? " asked Laurel, who would never let anybody get anything by indirection.

" Just look the place over and meet the people in charge and give me your impression of them and whether they're up to the job. That's a stockholder's duty, isn't it—a public duty and a service in wartime ? " The sly old rascal !

" But we don't know anything about jet propulsion, Robbie."

"Lanny has picked up a lot about planes, and you are a judge of character. A report from you both would be a service to me, I assure you."

"Yes, but he's supposed to be taking a rest now."

"He'll get a rest motoring out ; and he doesn't have to do any more than he feels like. It will help you as a writer, because you'll meet new kinds of people—executives on a big job, scientists, working men from all over the country, Indians, ranchers, cowboys."

"You make it sound very tempting," admitted a lady who was tired of writing about Nazi criminals.

"It would give me an excuse to supply you with gasoline ; and I can solve the hotel problem for you, too—I'll give you a trailer, I'm having them built by the hundreds for my workers, both here and out there. They are made of aluminium, and very light ; they have a butane-gas heater and cook-stove, and connections for electric light and water ; two beds with the best mattresses, closets, shelves, everything complete. You hitch it on behind your car and it follows wherever you go, and only adds about ten per cent to your fuel bill. You can travel at night and never have to worry about getting accommodations. You can go to New Mexico and see the plant and then go on to California, and when you get tired of the trailer you can sell it for more than it cost you, because it won't cost you anything."

Laurel looked at her husband, and he saw the light of new enterprise in her eyes. "Let's have a look at one of the things," he said.

BOOK SIX

MUCH HAVE I SEEN AND KNOWN

16

California, Here I Come!

I

SO now Laurel and Lanny were going to have a honeymoon, nearly two years after they had been married in Hongkong. Maybe their trip through China had been a honeymoon, but it had been hard to enjoy while escaping from the Japs. A bride is supposed to have a veil and a train, orange blossoms in her hair, a trousseau and a going-away dress; but all Laurel had had was a pair of Chinese trousers and a loose jacket, and such belongings as could be stuffed into a duffel bag; that, plus deadly fear.

Now they drove back to New York and got their belongings. Laurel wouldn't let her husband bring the trailer into city traffic on his first trip, for she imagined all sorts of complications. They loaded up the trunk of the car with suitcases and bundles, and piled the back seat with clothing for both winter and summer; they were starting out in the midst of a chilly snap, and later on they would be crossing hot deserts. They made arrangements with Agnes to take care of the baby, whom she adored as her own; she had a friend who would serve as baby-sitter now and then. Lanny said, " It is not the American custom to take babies on honeymoons."

They returned to Newcastle, and one of Robbie's welders put the ball on the back of their car, the smooth steel ball over which the trailer hitch is fastened, leaving the trailer free to turn on it. Their clothes were packed in drawers or hung in the small closets; the suitcases were tucked away under the two beds—one bed at each end of the vehicle, crossways. It wasn't quite as if they were going through

darkest Africa, Lanny mentioned ; there would be towns on
the way, and they could buy what they needed. So off they
went, right after lunch on a Monday that happened to see the
first snowfall of the season. Esther stood and waved good-bye
to them, along with her butler and her parlour-maid and the
governess of some of her grandchildren.

It was a new way of life, of American invention. It had
become popular before the war and now was spreading fast ;
every working man who wanted to move to higher wages
wanted a rolling house to move in and to live in when he got
there. Some who couldn't find one took the chassis of an old
car and built a wooden box on top. ·Arriving at a new place
and unable to find even a chicken house to live in, some
would build themselves a shack in trailer shape, hoping to
put two axles and four wheels under it later on. Trailer parks
and " motels " sprang up all over the country, some of them
a new sort of slum, and others with modern conveniences and
even luxuries—swimming pools, dance floors, playgrounds for
the " kiddies."

II

Neither one of this bridal couple had ever tried this new
way of life. They discovered to their relief that the trailer
followed right along behind and didn't jerk or otherwise mis-
behave ; soon you came to take it for granted. The only
difference was that rounding corners in a city you had to clear
the kerb more widely, and when you wanted to stop you had
to put on the brake a few feet sooner. The trailer didn't slide
off the road in the snow any more than the car did. Observing
this, Laurel consented for the expedition to cross the George
Washington Bridge ; but they must approach it from the
north, avoiding the city traffic, and they must find a secondary
road westward, and not venture on a main highway between
speeding trucks loaded with heavy goods.

So began a six-thousand-mile journey that might have been
faster if they had wanted it so ; but Laurel was seeing her
native land for the first time and didn't care to rush past it
at a mile a minute. They crossed New Jersey and a corner
of Pennsylvania, finding their way by less-frequented routes.
They avoided the mountains, keeping in the Atlantic plain

until they got to the southernmost tier of states, and thus had little snow and cold.   They started early and did their travelling by daylight ; when darkness approached they didn't worry about finding a resting-place, for any good farm-house would do.   They would pay for the privilege of running their electric light cord to a connection, usually in the barn.   A bucket of water was the only other thing they needed.

Trailer life had its drawbacks, they learned.   The little room was crowded, and when you started off in the morning you had to stow everything away, otherwise you would discover that it had slid off the shelf or the table, and maybe had skidded under the bed where it was difficult to reach.   Trailer builders had learned this sliding business, so all the drawers had little notches which kept them from opening until you lifted them a quarter of an inch or so.

The apparatus for cooking and washing dishes looked most attractive, but this couple decided that they would have one hot meal in a restaurant in the middle of the day, and for breakfast and supper would make out with bread and milk and fruit, so they could use paper cups and plates and spoons and throw them away.   On trailer trips you rarely saw the same people for long, so you didn't have to dress—that is, you put on clothes for comfort and not to demonstrate your social position.   The name Budd was a fairly common one, and nobody guessed that these were *the* Budds ; so Laurel could wear a sweater and skirt and Lanny didn't have to have his trousers pressed.

This was really seeing America.   They could get out and look at the landscape, climb a hill, gather hickory nuts and wild persimmons in a wood, or buy cider from a farmer.   They could stand and talk when they met an amusing character, and then move on to the next adventure.   Goods were scarce in the city department stores, but in general stores at country cross-roads you would still find things that had been made before the war, and these were the best.   If you liked plain food well cooked, you could find it, and after a few mistakes they learned how to judge eating places.   When they had got settled in the evenings they would stretch out and indulge in the greatest of all luxuries, reading a good book.   They had accumulated many and never had time for them before.   They would take turns reading aloud, or read separately, and during the long drives tell each other what they had found.

Also, there was the radio, a powerful instrument of culture sadly misused. But you could learn to dodge the commercials and get the same war news anywhere in America, and the same commentators to tell you what it meant. The Russians were pressing steadily on, taking German fortified positions or by-passing them, chewing up German manpower and resources. There was the continuing clamour for a second front by the Russians and their friends, and the same secret fear in many hearts that the Soviets might make another deal with the Nazis and get out of the war. Lanny said, " Our salvation lies in the fact that Hitler has shown himself a man whom nobody can trust." He didn't have to say more, for Laurel had been in Hitler's home and knew him as a woman knows a man who has offered her the supreme insult.

That had been only four years ago, but it seemed ages away from these peaceful American scenes. Crimes were committed in this country too. Lanny had a Budd automatic in the car and took it into the trailer at night, just on chance ; but no such chance befell. It was a grand country if you had a little money, and pretty nearly everybody had it now. That was the irony of the free-enterprise system, so ardently praised by the enterprisers ; the system could keep the people in comfort so long as the energies of the community were being devoted to killing other people ; but the moment they settled down to enjoy the peace their valour had won, they found themselves heading into another depression, with bread-lines and apple-selling on the streets and leaf-raking on the country roads.

III

Down through the middle of Virginia, and then, avoiding the crowded Highway Number One, along the coast of the Carolinas and into the land of palmettos and magnolias and live oaks draped with Spanish moss. It was warm ; they dug out their summer things, and strolled in the moonlight and listened to the mocking-birds—a honeymoon according to the tradition of all romantic novels about the Old South. How long would they be able to enjoy it when they read in the newspapers and heard over the radio about American boys fighting in the rain-filled trenches in front of Monte Cassino, and in the terrible jungles of the Solomon Islands, where it had always been believed that no white man could survive ?

From Savannah they cut across to the western part of Florida and along the Gulf Coast. Laurel had got used to the trailer now and was no longer afraid that some truck was going to crash into the back of it. When they got a flat tyre, it was a sociable truck-man who stopped to help them out of their trouble, and tried to refuse the dollar bill which Lanny handed him. Now they rolled comfortably on Highway 90, dining on freshly caught shrimp and crabs, and forgetting that there was supposed to be a food shortage. Baker had supplied them with gas coupons, and Robbie had added more. To Los Angeles and back the trip would take less than four hundred gallons, which was only a small part of the " tank-car " full that Lanny was said to have earned.

This was the land of the " Tin-Can Club," as the trailerites playfully called themselves. They had worked all their lives on farms in Illinois or Minnesota, and in their old age had retired on a small competence and wanted to spend their days where it was easier to keep warm. They got their tin-can, old or new, and drove as far south as they could without wetting their feet. They lined up in rows in a camp—first a trailer, then a car, then another trailer, and so on. They put up an awning on two poles in front of the trailer to make a porch, and set flower-boxes along the edges to make a garden. The women sat in canvas deck-chairs and told one another about their families up north, while the men pitched horseshoes in the vacant space alongside. Every Saturday night they had a country fiddler and danced the Virginia reel to the tune of " The Arkansas Traveller," and on Sunday mornings they read a Hearst newspaper, printed a day earlier, and then attended a Four Square Gospel Church.

To Laurel Creston, brought up in the secretiveness, called reserve, of the wealthy, this was a delightfully different way of life. So easy for a novelist, where characters revealed themselves in a half-hour's conversation, and a whole family saga could be gathered in an evening ! But there would be another

camp just like it at the next stop, and so they moved on—
along the Mississippi Sound, and across Louisiana and into
Texas, which is an empire in itself and was preparing to win
a war all by itself. As the motorist clocks it on his speedometer, Texas is eight hundred miles across, and there is every
kind of scenery and climate and people. Most of it is outdoors,
and the people are glad to show it and tell strangers about
it. They are especially proud of their distances, and like to
recite a jingle on the subject: "The sun has riz, the sun has
set, and here we is in Texas yet."

IV

So they came into southern New Mexico, a land of tumbled
mountains and clear blue skies, of hot days and cold nights.
Rain fell in winter, but mostly in the high mountains, and
filled the dry arroyos with raging torrents. The mountains
were bare, and the rocks of every colour—grey, yellow, red,
brown, or black. The deserts were endless-seeming; with
irrigation they could be turned into prosperous farms. Jack
rabbits fled from you and coyotes kept up their shrill barking
at night. If you turned over a stone you might see a centipede
waving his tiers of legs like fringes, or a yellow scorpion
threatening you with his claws and long inverted tail carrying
a deadly sting. When these inexperienced tourists sat down
on a rug for a picnic they discovered that little round-bellied
ticks had crawled up their ankles and settled themselves for
their picnic.

There was a new town called Budd. The road to it turned
north off the highway—a paved road, and there was a spur
railroad near it, both climbing between almost white rocky
mountains to a high plateau. Trucks roared past them, just
as if it had been U.S. 1 between New York and Washington.
The war had come to this land of sage-brush and Indian reservations, and wherever the war came there was hurry, hurry,
hurry. The leisurely tourists climbed until there was a
crackling in their ears; then suddenly a landscape broadened
out, and there was the top of the world spread before them,
miles and miles, and painted hills all around, a blazing sun
and a sky without a cloud.

There was a road-block, and soldiers on guard, with side arms. Lanny gave his name, but it didn't impress anybody. " This is the Army, Mr. Jones ! " Contrary to what the song says, they had telephones, and a sergeant called the office. Then the barrier swung back, and a soldier on a noisy motor-cycle led the way to the administration building. Lanny had heard all about this dream town of his father's, but even so astonishment seized him. Two years ago there had been only sand and sage-brush, jack rabbits and coyotes, and now there was a settlement scattered over the landscape for miles.

This had been the way of it : Robbie Budd had got what his associates called a " bug," a stubborn determination to find out about jets, and what were then called rocket planes. The British were doing it, and why should America wait upon them ? Everything the British had was available, and Robbie had sent for it. Because he wanted to experiment with hundreds of the most dangerous chemicals known, he had sent his men to find a tract of land where there was nothing to set on fire and nobody to kill but the scientists and technicians whose job it was to take risks.

They had told him about this plateau that had water and power available from a government dam, and Robbie had bought it without ever seeing it—he hadn't seen it yet. He had paved a road and built a laboratory and about a hundred little cupola structures of concrete, in which to keep the fuels, far enough apart so that one could blow up without hurting the others. There were concrete sheds where such things as eighty per cent hydrogen peroxide as oxidant and methyl alcohol and hydrazine hydrate as fuel could be slapped together and burned, with measurements made of the " thrust " they developed.

And then, all of a sudden, somebody in the Planning Board in Washington had woken up to the fact that the Germans had jet engines actually in production ; presently they would have jet planes flying in combat—planes that couldn't be flown economically at less than four hundred miles per hour, and might go to six hundred. What then would become of our air supremacy, so painfully won only this year ? What would happen to the flights of daylight bombers we were sending over Berlin and Bremen and Hamburg, figuring that we could stand a five per cent loss but not a ten per cent loss on each expedition ?

The Army had stepped in and insisted on buying for Robbie about ten times as much desert as he had expected to need, and on running a railroad up to Budd. They sent in a swarm of workers to live in tents and lay out a city and build it in a few weeks. There was nothing new about any of this, it was being done all over the land, and the more remote and unlikely the place, the more important it might turn out to be. Had not Presidential Agent 103 sent in word about the V-3 which the Germans were planning and perhaps building, and which would carry many tons of explosives a distance of five thousand miles and drop them where it was told to ?

Disperse industry, was the Army's word, and here Robbie Budd had gone and done it. The town of Budd was ordered not merely to test jet engines, but to make them, and more important yet, to think them up in somebody's head. To that end hundreds of scientists were assembled from all over the country, and some from England, plus refugees from Germany and France and all the Axis lands. Trainloads of cement were brought in, and as for sand, you didn't have to look far for that in New Mexico. Laboratories and machine shops of concrete arose, almost literally overnight, and homes for the scientists and the workers. So here was a jet-engine centre, and soon it would be a jet-plane centre.

V

Robbie had written that his son and daughter-in-law were coming as his representatives, and to show them the works. That meant they were not merely V.I.P.'s, but V.G.D.I.P.'s. The manager of the plant took personal charge of them, and wanted to move somebody out of one of the best houses for their comfort. But Laurel laid down the law ; this was a camping trip, and they had everything arranged in their little aluminium trailer, named Bienvenu. There was no opposing a lady's will, and no accounting for the whims of the rich. A place was found for them among the workers, and they carried their trays in the cafeteria like everybody else.

It was good food, served hot and in a clean place—for

everybody had to be well and happy. They had crèches and kindergartens so that the wives and mothers might work in the plant ; they had movies every night, and community singing, and athletics, and dances, and home-made churches —everything that anybody could think of to keep workers contented in a desert wilderness. To keep them from packing up their belongings and driving down the trail ! And better yet, to cause them to write to their relatives and friends, saying that Budd, New Mexico, was the best war town yet !

The visitors were put into a jeep and driven around to inspect the wonders of the place. Everybody vied for Lanny's favour, for it was important that his report should be right. They had expected to meet a playboy, and were surprised to find that he knew something about jet propulsion and could ask intelligent questions. He didn't tell them that he had been coached on the subject off and on for a year, and had been boning up as hard as any would-be college students preparing for entrance exams. The scientists, old and young, took an interest in him and showed him what they had got from England, and what they had designed themselves ; what they had on the drawing boards, and then what they had in action. After talking and thinking about jets for so long Lanny found it thrilling to observe one develop its " thrust " in actuality. There was a tremendous " whoosh," but no sign of flame—the combustion was so perfect that the flame was all inside. The blast of hot air was terrific, and if you had stood within twenty feet of it you would have been burned to a crisp.

The P.A. sat in at conferences in which the top men discussed in highly technical terms what they were doing and hoped to do. They reported that the Germans had been two years ahead of us in getting the first jet plane into the air, and were now two years ahead of us in production. The Heinkel concern was putting out an engine with a straight-through combustion system with downstream fuel injection. The Junkers had in production what they called the Jumo 004B, with an eight-stage axial compressor. The German Army now had in service a jet interceptor plane called the Viper, which was launched by rockets and was capable of rising to thirty thousand feet in less than one minute.

Lanny asked, " How do you know these things ? " And the answer was, " The O.S.S. sends us information." Lanny felt chagrined because he had not been able to get any of this ; but he reflected that General Donovan's organization no doubt had scores of men working on the subject in the enemy lands. He had contributed his mite, and once or twice the scientists gave him items which he recognized ; but he said nothing about it, and nobody in this place ever knew that he had been inside the Kaiser Wilhelm Institut Physics Building in the winter and again in the summer of this year.

The American Armed Forces were preparing to spend twenty-five billions of dollars during 1944 on airplane production and development. It was a scientist's dream of heaven, for he could have anything in the way of resources and facilities that he called for—provided only that he could show the possibility of getting something new. Lanny met elderly bespectacled gentlemen who had spent all their lives in laboratories and had thought they were lucky if they could get a few hundred dollars for an experiment, but who now asked for tens of thousands and got them. He met young chaps just out of college whose eyes shone with excitement as they explained some oddly shaped piece of steel.

In the not very elegant language of the time, the town was lousy with new ideas. There was the " Jato " rocket unit, that could be mounted on the outside of a plane's fuselage, and be easily detached. It would " boost " planes to get them off the ground, and thus enable them to carry twice the loads they had formerly taken ; or it would enable them to rise from half the flight space, which would mean smaller carriers, or that large carriers could utilize more of their flight deck for storing planes, and thus keep more planes in the air. There were blue-prints for " composite-engine " bombers, and " jet-cum-propeller " fighter planes for carriers. Lanny listened patiently while a youngster who looked like a school kid explained a " reaction engine," as they preferred to call the jet, that was so beautifully simple you could cry over it, he said. It had only one moving gear, the compressor and the turbine being on the same shaft ; it had no vibration and very little noise to warn the enemy, it used little oil and needed no warming up, but could fly in thirty seconds ; and, best of all, in peacetime it could use the cheapest fuel, even kerosene. The only trouble was it went so fast that you were liable to be blacked out on the slightest turn ; also, they had had to put wire gauze over the air intake, because birds got sucked in out of the sky !

VI

The inspecting team spent a week at the plant, and so far as either of them could see, everything was all right. Lanny air-mailed a report, saying that all the people were wrapped up in their work, and their ideas appeared to be excellent. Laurel, who had spent her time among the wives, both in the trailer camp and in the villas, reported that there was the normal amount of backbiting, but none of the women knew what their husbands were doing—which was as it should be. Lanny knew that this would please his father, who was surely no feminist. Robbie's pride in life was his ability to find the right men and then give them a chance to show what they could do. Women made good stenographers and filing clerks, but nothing else.

The tin-can Bienvenu rolled again, and came into Arizona, which was like the rest of the South-west, except that more irrigation works had been built and more crops were being grown. The valley in which lay Phoenix, the state capital, had grown so fast that the highway was like a city boulevard. The trailer camps and motor courts were crowded, so they had to spend the night by the roadside ; because they had neither radio nor lights, they went to a movie, and discovered that many other persons were in the same fix and had found the same solution.

More mountain passes to wind through, and they came to a long bridge over the Colorado River, and on the other side was that dreamland of movie addicts all over the world— California. Seeing was believing, and the addicts all knew that in this Golden State everybody's kitchen was the size of a large drawing-room and had all the latest fixtures made of chromium ; also, that boys who were poor but honest and handsome invariably married the daughters of millionaires. Animated by this certainty, thousands of new people were pouring into California every day, and a lot of them had come by Highway 80 on the same day as Lanny and Laurel. All had to sit and wait, and then turn out the contents of their cars and trailers, for the state authorities took strict measures to prevent the importation of infected fruits and plants. It didn't constitute a cordial reception, but you could feel sorry for the poor inspectors, who worked long hours and still couldn't keep up with the procession of cars.

More mountains and deserts; it was Mary Austin's "land of little rain." A huge dam had been built on the Colorado, and an aqueduct brought the water some two hundred and fifty miles to the Los Angeles district—just in time to get the swarming new populations clean. Lanny told his wife about the political war going on over the name of the dam; the Democrats called it Boulder and the Republicans called it Hoover, and it was like casting a ballot every time you spoke the name. Lanny said that if the Japs were able to do a bombing job in this neighbourhood, all they would need was to destroy a couple of aqueducts, and Southern California would have to be evacuated; quite probably a million or two persons would perish while trying to get out.

They came to the Coachella Valley, the date country, and Lanny, who had been through here before, told the story of how a few shoots of date trees had been smuggled out of Arabia long ago—with difficulty, because the natives guarded their secrets closely. Now there were miles and miles of stately trees, each one resembling an enormous royal crown, and planted in rows as exact as a draught-board. Dates require an immense amount of water, but it has to be underground and not in the air; they were told that the general irrigation of Southern California might change the climate and make date-growing impossible.

They spent a night at Palm Springs, which had once consisted of a hotel and a few villas nestled in a niche of mountains and was now a spreading town, with factories and trailer camps like everywhere else. Next morning they drove up a long pass and into the orange country—a highway through fifty miles of orange groves, now loaded with blossoms and at the same time with ripening fruit. It was rapidly becoming a road-town with "hotdog stands" and "eateries" and "realtoriums"—you could learn a whole new language on the way. The traffic was heavy, and you had to watch out or you would end up in the hands of a " mortician."

With every mile as they approached Los Angeles, this traffic grew worse, and it was well that Laurel had got used to the trailer by now. From Pasadena it was one continuous city, whatever the name. Industrial plants had sprung up everywhere, and many thousands of them were discharging smoke or chemical fumes into the atmosphere. The result was an extraordinary phenomenon, a dense grey haze that sometimes made it impossible to see more than a few hundred yards. The plain was bordered on the east by a long chain of high mountains, the Sierra Madre, and apparently this " smog " couldn't get over them, but piled up against them, and from the ocean to the foothills people coughed and sneezed and wiped their eyes. Lanny said, " It's the price for licking Hitler."

VII

They had taken it easy on the way, and came into Hollywood toward sundown, the worst traffic hour. They found it as had been foretold ; everything was packed to the doors. Lanny tried one hotel and was told that people were sleeping on the billiard tables and in the chairs of the lobby. He went to the telephone and tried half a dozen other hotels and got the same response. They drove to a few of the trailer camps and found that these had illuminated signs : " No Vacancy." The visitors didn't have to worry, for they could go a bit out into the country and camp by the roadside ; but first they would have a meal, and do that in style.

They parked on a side street and made themselves as presentable as could be done by the light of a candle. Then they strolled on Hollywood Boulevard, and into Sardi's, one of the smart restaurants. They had to wait their turn, but they didn't mind, for this was one of the sights of the land ; people came from all over, even in wartime, just for the privilege of glimpsing in real life some of those faces and figures they had seen magnified and glorified upon the screen. The food would be good when they got it, and meantime it amused them to watch the flashily dressed crowd. They had no forewarning that it would be the beginning of an adventure.

In due course they were seated at a table, and it happened to be near the door. They had finished studying the menu and deciding what they wanted when they saw a woman come in and join the waiting throng. She was clad in a full-length mink coat, which tells the world that its wearer is at the top of the heap, at least financially ; she was a large woman and it took a lot of minks, even without the hat to match. She had some jewels too, and anyone could be sure that she was able to pay for her dinner. She was alone, which was unusual. Lanny glanced at the full and rather florid face and it seemed familiar, but he couldn't place it. The head-waiter came in the nick of time to spare him embarrassment ; the man bowed and said, " Just a few minutes, Miss Rector." Then Lanny caught the woman's eye and he saw that she recognized him. Good manners required him to make the first advance, so he rose and said, " How do you do, Miss Rector. I am Lanny Budd."

" How pleasant to see you here ! " she exclaimed, her face lighting up. They shook hands—it was the custom for ladies to shake hands with gentlemen here in the West. " We are a long way from Paris," she added. " And it must have been ten years ago."

" This is my wife," said Lanny. " Laurel, this is Miss Roberta Rector, for whom I had the pleasure of selecting some paintings in Paris."

" A pleasure to meet you," said Laurel cordially. " Won't you join us for dinner ? " She couldn't say less, since otherwise she would have left the lady standing.

Roberta Rector sounded like a movie name, and Laurel guessed that she must be an actress—one of those who have passed the *ingénue* age and have to take roles as mothers and aunts. But no, there were other kinds of people in Hollywood. Lanny said, " Miss Rector is a cattle princess," a remark which would have been crude in the extreme, except that Lanny knew his princess. He said it with his smile, and she took it with a still broader one.

" No," she explained. " No more cattle for me. I sold out and put my money into tax-free government bonds ; so I have nothing more to worry about in this world."

" You are wise," commented the man. " What have you done with the Monets and Cézannes ? "

" Oh, I got tired of them and gave them to the County Museum. I was living in the Beverly-Wilshire Hotel and had to have a separate room for them, and I was afraid the place might burn up or somebody might steal them. And then, you know how it is, so many people heard about them and wanted to see them ; I was always being bothered with letters and telephone calls. So I said, ' I'll put them where everybody can see them without having to see me.' "

" Mostly people wait until they are dead before they are that generous," remarked the art expert, who had known the rich from babyhood.

" Oh, well, I get tired of things, and I want something new to look at. I keep hearing about Detazes, and perhaps I might like to own some. Is there anywhere I could look at them ? "

" I showed you quite a number in Paris, Miss Rector."

" Oh, did you ? I had forgotten. I see so many paintings. People try to sell them to me."

" Fortunately the Detazes are in this country now—what we have left. They are in charge of my old friend and associate, Zoltan Kertezsi, in New York. You met him, a Hungarian."

" Yes, I remember ; he had a lovely soft brown moustache."

" It is grey now. He'll be happy to show you the paintings whenever you are in New York."

" I expect to go this winter. My life seems so restricted since Paris or London are out. I do hate this war. Don't you, Mrs. Budd ? "

" I hate all wars," said Laurel. She had realized by now that here was a " character," and as a novelist she took out her mental notebook and sharpened her pencil.

" I had covered my signs with slogans against war," continued the retired cattle princess, and a stubborn look came into her grey eyes. " Everybody objected to them, but I kept them, even after Pearl Harbour. Then people splashed tar on them, so I had to change them."

Lanny explained to his wife. " Miss Rector owns a hill in the heart of Hollywood, and on all four of her street corners she has bill-boards with her political opinions on them. You remember, you noticed one about India."

" I hope you agree with me," said the propagandist lady.

" I ask the world, what right have the British to talk about freedom when they refuse freedom to the people of India ? Don't you think I am right, Mrs. Budd ? "

" It's a complicated question," responded Laurel. " I am troubled by the possibility that if the British set the Indians free, they may soon be flying at one another's throats."

" Well, let them ; that's their business if they want to."

" Don't you believe in a police force, Miss Rector ? "

" Yes, but I wouldn't want a British policeman in my home and neither would you, I am sure. I see that you haven't thought these matters out, Mrs. Budd. You must let me introduce you to some of my Hindu friends and let them explain their cause."

VIII

This meal was served and eaten—with great gusto by Roberta Rector. Lobster à la Newburg, and a pitcher of buttermilk, and then a *coupe glacée*—neither Lanny nor his wife had ever seen such a meal, and they observed with quiet amusement that the lady let the gentleman take the bill without protest. Perhaps she was one of those many rich people who are extravagant in large matters and penurious in small. Certainly she was one of those many stout people who reiterate that they are " small eaters " ; they want you to believe that they are able to manufacture *embonpoint* out of water and air. " I only eat one meal a day," said Roberta, and failed to mention that she kept chocolates in her room and took a nibble every now and then, and visited her refrigerator for both buttermilk and beer.

This meeting solved a problem for the two travellers. When they mentioned that they were living in a trailer and had been unable to find a place to keep it, their guest said, " For heaven's sake, come and park it on my grounds. There is all the room you want, and I'll be delighted." They accepted, and the woman took them out to her big limousine with a waiting chauffeur, and drove them to the place where they had parked. They followed her car, and on the way Laurel exclaimed, " What a curious human ! What do you know about her ? "

Lanny said, " I know that her father was one of the big

cattlemen in Texas. You see the signs 'Rector Ranch Products,' and he was it. Also, I know that she bought half a
dozen paintings that cost ten or fifteen thousand dollars each.
I was told that she has never been married, but has a grown
son."

"What did she do that for?"

"I don't know; probably she's a feminist and thinks the
child should belong exclusively to the mother. She consorts
with anarchists and other radicals, and no doubt is considered
a dangerous character out here."

"I'm curious to know what's in her mind," declared the
novelist; to which the husband replied, "That ought to be
easy. She's certainly a free enough talker."

After they had climbed "Rector Hill" in the heart of
Hollywood, they parked their trailer alongside Roberta's house
and connected up the electric light with her back porch and
their water line with her garden hose. They went inside and
were shown through the house and were besought to occupy
one of the guest rooms. But Laurel said no, they had promised
themselves that this was to be a camping trip and they didn't
want to spoil their record. They were told about the house,
which had been designed by the man whom advanced and
art-loving Americans considered the greatest architect of the
time; the roof was so built that water didn't always run off
it, and the chimneys smoked, and the kitchen was incon-
veniently placed—but it was one of the most original and
beautiful of designs, and everybody wanted to come and see it.

Roberta said this without the faintest trace of a smile.
Whatever great architect had designed her mentality had left
out the sense of humour. If you made any sort of joke in
her presence, she would stop and look disconcerted, as if you
had stuck a stick between her legs while she was walking.
Then she would resume the conversation as if nothing had
happened. Her manner of talking seemed to say that she
had always had money and therefore other people had to learn
to listen.

First she told about her house, and then she told about her
hill. She had deeded it to the city for a park, and the mansion
on top for an art museum; but the city had not kept its part
of the bargain, and now she was bringing lawsuits, and was

tied up in quarrels with the politicians ; she talked at length about these most evil men. Then, too, she had the problem of her dogs ; she had eighteen water spaniels—they kept multiplying, after the way of nature, and what could she do about it ? The dogs raced all over the house, and when they were turned outside they bit somebody, and that, too, was a cause of lawsuits, and Roberta had had to appear in court, and worse yet, in the newspapers.

One more proof of the ancient thesis that the possession of wealth multiplies cares. Everybody knew about those tax-free bonds, and all wanted some of them, or at any rate some of the interest. In the beginning Roberta had been generous, but gradually she had come to realize that nobody was interested in her for herself, only in her money, and that hurt her feelings ; so she had made up her mind to refuse all requests. It had become a sort of phobia with her, and she said no even before she was asked. Certainly neither Lanny nor Laurel had any idea of asking her for money, but she appeared to be including them when she sounded her defiance. " It's no use to ask me, for I won't give ! I am sick and tired of giving ! My father killed himself earning that money ; he broke his heart valves. He left it to me, and I am guarding his fortune and his good name ! "

IX

The Budds retired to their tiny nest and sat for a while discussing this strange human soul which had fallen, as you might say, like a ripe peach into a novelist's lap. They spoke in whispers, for they were sure that curiosity had not been left out of the make-up of this intensely personal person, and it might be that she was standing in her garden trying to hear what these suddenly acquired friends might be saying about her. In the morning they were invited in to breakfast —anything they fancied, for there was a Chinese cook whom Roberta described as " the dearest old thing you could imagine," and a Filipino boy who was too delicate for the Army and who watched everything that went on with a pair of quick dark eyes.

Lanny went off in the car to look up a couple of his clients

and tell them about art works he had discovered in London
and Stockholm and Rome, for the Allies were soon going to
take that last-named city and perhaps the Nazis wouldn't have
time to sack it. That left a woman writer to pursue the
subject of psychology in what might be called field work.
When Lanny came back toward evening he found that Laurel
had decided to move into the house. The two women had
become fast friends and were deep in a conference, which
consisted in the cattle king's daughter telling everything that
had ever happened to her, and what she thought about it, and
what she knew, or thought she knew, about life. There were
men, and a few women, who called themselves psycho-analysts
and would charge you as much as fifty dollars an hour to let
you do that ; but here was a highly intelligent woman who
would let Roberta do it free of charge—or so Roberta hoped
and believed. Laurel Creston Budd hadn't said much about
herself, and surely not a word about being Mary Morrow.

The session went on for two days and might have gone on
for ever if Lanny had consented. This woman of "independent
wealth " was independent of everything on the whole earth ;
she had no obligations, no ties, and apparently no friends ; she
was frantic with loneliness, yet afraid to meet anybody,
because that person, male or female, old or young, rich or
poor, would sooner or later try to get her money. The poor
would want it for themselves, and the rich would want it for
causes, charities, ideas, whatever it might be they were
interested in and desirous of promoting. Roberta Rector lived
alone with her Chinese cook and her Filipino house-boy and
her eighteen water spaniels, and apparently she saw nobody
but her lawyers and the people who served her in restaurants,
stores, and banks.

X

Driving with her husband, Laurel retold a pitiful story.
Roberta Rector had not had a baby in order to defy society ;
just the other way round, she had defied society because she
had a baby. A rich man's daughter whose mother had died
young, she had been brought up in a splendid but lonely
home. She had been a beauty, and Laurel said, " She really
was, for she showed me the photographs ; and you mayn't

believe it, but I do, she hadn't been told a thing about sex and hadn't the remotest idea what it was. At the age of eighteen she came here from Texas, and she met a Russian stage director, a brilliant and fascinating man, who seduced her. She was mad about him, and thought he loved her, and found out little by little that all he wanted was to get her money to finance the world's most startling stage productions. When she learned that she was going to have a baby she was terrified ; but then she happened to meet Emma Goldman, who talked Anarchism and Libertarianism, and advised her to make having a baby into a crusade, and say that she had done it as an act of defiance. She said that, and so the radicals all thronged about her and got her money ; but she doesn't really understand any social theories—she just accepts what the last person has told her, until she decides that that person, too, has had too much of her money."

" What became of the man ? " Lanny asked.

" He has his career, and once in a while he shows up here. Roberta is still in love with him, but she also despises him. She used to give him money, but now she has shut down on him as she has on everybody else. She has never loved any other man, and never could ; she fears them, because they all want her money. She gets something over thirty thousand dollars a month and hasn't any idea in the world what to do with it, but she can't bear to give it away ; she wants to be loved for herself alone, and she can't find anybody who will do that."

" What about the son ? "

" The son is like everybody else : he wants money, more and more of it. He was sent to a so-called ' progressive ' school, and was allowed to do whatever he pleased because the head of the school wanted money from the mother. The son ran off with one of the girls in the school and married her and got a baby ; then he couldn't get along with the girl, so he divorced her and married another girl, and both girls and the boy are living in the same house—one of Roberta's. When I asked her about that she said, ' What can I do ? The first girl has no other place to live.' She summed up her maternal feelings in one sentence : ' I wish the whole lot of them would go to China and stay there.' "

So there was the story of a retired cattle princess who had an income of nearly half a million dollars a year, tax-free, and was the most frustrated and unhappy human being the novelist Mary Morrow had ever described. She was in a position to gratify her every whim, and got up every morning with no idea what she was going to do with herself that day. She would employ a famous architect to build her a lovely home, and when she had got tired of it she either sold it or just left it ; she had done that half a dozen times, and gone to live in a hotel. She had had a fine sail-boat built on one of the mountain lakes in Southern California, and when it sank at the dock, in a storm, she hadn't troubled to have it raised. She had taken up "causes," and then decided that they were mistaken. She had put up a fortune to help free Tom Mooney, labour leader jailed on a frame-up, and when he had got out he divorced his loyal wife and married a younger woman—and had come to Roberta Rector for more money !

Said Laurel, " Some day she will die, and then I will write the story. She is a living sermon on the evils of wealth inheritance."

Said Laurel's husband, " It wouldn't do any good, because nobody would believe it. They would say you had made it up to fit your propaganda."

XI

Lanny took his wife to meet his old friends, the De Lyle Armbrusters, wealthy people who had a sumptuous villa on a hill slope above Hollywood. They were the opposite of Roberta Rector—instead of shutting themselves off from all the world, they gathered all the world about them and aspired to be everybody's best friends. They were rather commonplace middle-aged people who sought distinction by surrounding themselves with celebrities. Lanny had known them of old on the French Riviera, and two and a half years ago, when he had come to Hollywood for the first time, he had made something of a hit with them because he had met Hitler and Göring and was able to tell about the private lives of these undoubted celebrities.

When they heard where Lanny and his wife were staying they were somewhat shocked. " Why do you tie yourself to that dreadful woman ? " And when Lanny pretended not to know what they meant, De Lyle went on, " A woman who consorts with Reds and Pinks, and Hindu and Irish revolutionists, and all sorts of riff-raff. Why don't you come and stay with us ? "

" We are travelling in a trailer," explained the son of Budd-Erling apologetically.

" But that's quite all right, Lanny ; people do what they please nowadays."

" But it's such a wee little trailer, made of aluminium."

" That's all right too ; we can put it behind the garage." De Lyle, like Roberta, talked without the faintest trace of a smile. He had a round, bland face, and was stout and growing stouter ; he was just as money-conscious as the cattle lady, but had much more than she, and he was willing to spend it for value received—that is to say, for social prestige and publicity in the society columns.

Lanny had expected this invitation and forewarned his wife. One of his jobs was to watch these people, so he would play his role of near-Fascist, and the thing for Laurel to do was to be a little mouse wife, with no ideas on the war or politics, just listening respectfully to the famous ones. Everybody in this town was playing a role, on and off the screen, and what Laurel as a novelist wanted was to store up material without giving any hint that she possessed a critical mind. They went back to the retired cattle princess and told her they had to be on their way ; her chauffeur hitched up the trailer, and the P.A. drove it up into Benedict Canyon and deposited it safely out of sight and out of mind on the Armbruster estate. Then he drove his wife to the shops in Beverly Hills, for she couldn't appear at " Genie's " parties in the clothes that had been all right in the company of eighteen water spaniels.

XII

The screen people you met at the Armbrusters were all very rich ; the poorest of them earned more than the President of the United States, and they all knew what the others were earning and talked about it frankly—and often. People were graded in importance according to their salaries, and if you dropped from the five-thousand-a-week class to the two-thousand-a-week class you were relegated to a different social group. There were many who would deny that this was true, but meantime it would be happening automatically, for if you had only two thousand a week you couldn't live like those in the higher class ; your liquor wouldn't be so choice or your swimming pool so roomy. There were some who talked about their money and retiring to do something worth while, but few indeed were able to achieve this, for the pressure to spend money like your friends and associates was irresistible. Here and there were little groups that got off by themselves and talked about " art," but, as a rule, that would be considered pretentious, and even a bit unkind, a criticism of your profession and your friends.

This Hollywood world had grown up in the course of some forty or fifty years, and money was what had made it and now maintained it. Money had brought talent of every sort from all over the world ; money-love and money-glamour had put its stamp on them and on every product they turned out. In the last great panic " the industry " had been on the rocks and Wall Street had stepped in and bought control ; now it exercised its silent but firm say-so, as everywhere else in American big business. Pictures were produced to make money and no nonsense about it, and if you didn't like that you could move out to the Mohave Desert and raise chickens, or up into the bare hills and walk behind a flock of sheep.

The couple from the east found the movie stars for the most part kindly and likable people. There were some among them who had a social conscience in spite of their high salaries. They defended the New Deal, and this was considered a sign of a disordered mind, for why shouldn't they be grateful to a country which paid them so extravagantly. The mass of the " colony " were normal Americans who wanted two things : to get more money, and to be allowed to keep it and not have to pay it to the government in the form of income taxes. There were some who were rabid on this subject. They damned the bureaucracy which spent their money for them ; and, above all, they damned " That Man," who was the " master mind," to use one of Hollywood's own phrases.

It was these people whom one met at the Armbrusters'

cocktail parties and evening affairs. They had no idea that the Budds were or could be any different from themselves. Lanny discovered that now, with the country at war and the Soviet Union an indispensable ally, they no longer expressed the hope that somebody " would shoot ' That Man.' " What they wanted was to get rid of him at the next election, less than a year away. They agreed that a fourth term would be absolutely fatal to American liberties ; they rejoiced in every mistake that Roosevelt made, even when it was one which might be costly to the nation.

What these near-Fascists wanted most of all was to revise and remodel the war, and find some way to get the Germans on our side and the Russians off. They had given up Adi Schicklgruber as being a hopeless bungler ; they wanted to get rid of him at the same time as they got rid of the Squire of Krum Elbow, and they questioned Lanny, knowing that he had been in Germany and actually knew the Nazi leaders. He was able to please them by revealing that many of the Wehrmacht officers wanted to oust Hitler and take over the government. These were the natural-born leaders of Germany, and Hollywood actors who had enacted their roles on the screen thought that was an ideal solution. They urged the son of Budd-Erling to stay and join the society they had organized to combat the many Red agents who were trying to seduce Hollywood and turn it to the ends of Moscow.

XIII

After a few days Lanny sent a telegram to the lord of San Simeon, reminding him that he had asked Lanny to bring him information whenever he could, and added, " I am here at your disposal. My wife is with me." It took no more than a couple of hours for a reply to arrive, saying that the lord would be pleased to receive them at any time. They could be flown from the Burbank airport in his plane if they so desired. Lanny replied that they would motor up the next day.

To bring a tiny trailer to a place where sumptuous accommodations were prepared for a couple of hundred guests would have been rather absurd ; so " Bienvenu " was locked up and left behind the Armbrusters' garage, and Laurel took her best clothes in suitcases. The coast highway had been opened up all the way to the north, and through the San Simeon property in spite of the lord's most strenuous opposition. The highway was costly, winding along the sides of cliffs; the scenery was of the finest, but you had to watch out with your driving or you'd find yourself in the Pacific Ocean.

Lanny warned his wife, " I have been asked to find out what this old man is doing and planning. Of course you call yourself a democrat, but you don't work at it. You mustn't say anything impolite about Hitler, or even about Mussolini; even though he's been kicked out he's still a great man, and he made the trains run on time."

" I've been reading the *Examiner*," said Laurel, " so I know his ideas."

" No, that's a mistake," replied the husband. " What the old man says in the *Examiner* is what he wants the public to believe about him. He calls it Americanism, and it sounds fine, but what he actually believes is something out of the Middle Ages. It will be wiser for you to keep quiet and watch me draw him out."

He told about the life of " Willie "—so his parents had called him, but now even his most intimate friends called him " Mr. Hearst." He was the son of a gold-mining king who had bought himself a seat in the United States Senate and had sent his only son to Harvard. Willie had been expelled, and from that experience he had conceived a bitter hatred of the so-called respectable world, and a determination to " show them." His father had bought a derelict San Francisco newspaper, and Willie's way of " showing " had been to fill it with crime, sex, and sensation. " Yellow journalism," it was called, and by appealing to everything base in the nature of the masses Willie had collected their pennies by the billions.

He had come to New York and bought a small paper called the *Journal*, and had set out to conquer that most haughty and sophisticated part of the world. He had built up an empire, with newspapers in a score of cities, including the most proper Boston which had kicked him out. Then he had taken up the idea of " showing them " in politics; he had dreamed of being Mayor of New York City, Governor of New York

State, President of the United States. To accomplish that he had become a " radical," espousing the cause of the masses and calling himself their friend and champion. But he found that while the masses would read his papers, they wouldn't trust him and didn't vote for him.

So William Randolph Hearst had become an embittered man, turning against all the causes he had espoused in his younger days. He had built himself the palace of an emperor, and retired to sit on his heap of gold and use it to dominate the lives of other men. In his heart he despised these men because they took his money and wrote not what they believed, but what he commanded. " All his life he has done that," Lanny said. " He would come into the office of the *New York American* shortly before midnight and throw out everything the paper had prepared in reference to some politician ; because that politician's wife had just insulted one of Hearst's friends, Hearst would order a cartoon portraying that politician in prison stripes. In politics, as in every other phase of life, he has been a strange driving force."

Laurel said, " What an introduction to a host ! "

XIV

There were gates, and a porter's lodge, and apparently a list of names which the porter consulted ; then they drove on a winding road to the hill on which this economic emperor had erected a monument to his own glory. There was a vast main building and half a dozen villas, each with a fancy Spanish name. A major-domo received them, much as if it had been a smart restaurant ; a servant brought in their bags and another took their car. The place looked and felt just like a de luxe hotel ; you had a suite with a sunken bath-tub, and you found a list of rules on the inside of the door, telling you among other things that if you wanted meals you must come on time. Exactly like the Berghof, except that in this place you were allowed to smoke, and there was a bar where you could drink all you wanted, but you were not allowed to take anything to your rooms.

San Simeon resembled Karinhall in that it was an art museum as well as a residence. There were cellars, occupying the entire space under the main building, packed with art works, most of which had never been uncrated. Hanging on the walls of the rooms were paintings enough to keep an art expert happy for weeks. The " Yellow Kid," as Hearst's enemies had called him during his early days, shared the blind passion of *Unser Hermann* for collecting for its own sake. Everything that anybody else wanted very much must belong to them, even though they had no use for it and hadn't time even to look at it. In Hearst's case it included everything from Egyptian scarabs to a twelfth-century monastery, which had been taken down stone by stone, boxed, labelled, and shipped to New York, but never put together again ! San Simeon differed from Karinhall in that it was also a zoo, with a great number of wild animals from all parts of the world, in cages or fenced enclosures. It was also a gym, with provision for a variety of games : handball, tennis, and squash courts, indoor and out, and swimming pools of fresh and salt water both warm and cold.

The Budds had arrived in the middle of the afternoon, and after they had freshened up they went down to the main rooms. Several guests were there, chatting, and Lanny introduced his wife to Miss Marion Davies, retired motion picture star, who was made-up as if expecting to be called before the camera. Laurel had been duly posted—this was their host's special friend and much depended upon her favour. In her company they strolled and looked at old masters, and Lanny poured out a fund of information surprising to people who had never realized that the history of art is a subject of study, just like the history of politics, or warfare, or other human activity.

In one corner of the great hall sat a large, tall, extremely wrinkled old man with grey hair and a long face which had been a boon to cartoonists for more than fifty years. He was diligently writing with a pencil on a pad, and it was one of the unwritten laws of this place that nobody ever disturbed him at such times. He was laying down the policies of the Hearst newspapers for the next day, and thus determining the thoughts of some ten or twenty million Americans for that period and longer. He didn't bother to retire to his study, but just sat in any chair that happened to be handy and set down whatever occurred to him. It might be a headline, or a directive for the handling of some news item ; it might be an editorial idea for one of his many writers to elaborate, or it might be a proclamation to be signed WILLIAM RANDOLPH HEARST.

When the writing on the pad was completed, a secretary would type it, if there was time, and then it would be " shot " from the telegraph office in this building. It would go to the nineteen Hearst newspapers in leading American cities, and in due course the air mail would bring copies of each of these papers, and " W. R." would check carefully to be sure his instructions had been followed. If it hadn't been done he would " shoot " a wire to the offending person, telling him in the plainest language what mistakes he had made ; if that happened more than once or twice there would come a wire saying, " Your services are no longer required."

Such was the life of an eighty-year-old journalist-emperor. This was what interested him, and if he ever talked or thought about anything else, it was just play, or politeness to some guest. His right to manage these papers in this precise way was what he meant by all the noble phrases he used : the free enterprise system, freedom of initiative, the American way, the Constitution, the Flag, and the Christian Religion. Above all, this was democracy, spelt with a small " d " ; for now the Democratic party was a prisoner of the New Deal, and the Hearst newspapers, calling themselves " Independent," gave their support to Hoover, Coolidge, and Harding.

XV

At the beginning of December President Roosevelt at last accomplished his desire to exercise his charms upon Marshal Stalin. Churchill had already been to Moscow, but Churchill's charms were of a different sort. Stalin had a good memory and knew that Britain's Tory leader had once called for war on Bolshevism. But the Squire of Krum Elbow was the author of the New Deal, the friend of the common man, and the enemy of the economic royalists ; more than that, he was the inventor of lend-lease and was shipping hundreds of millions of dollars' worth of supplies to the Soviet Union every month. Money talks, and F. D. R. was talking world order, peace, and prosperity in a voice loud enough for even the people of the Soviet Union to hear.

Stalin had been too busy to come to Allied lands, and they had compromised upon Teheran, the capital of what had once been Persia and now was Iran. There, in the Russian Embassy, the three top leaders had a four-day conference, and now as it came to an end a formal statement was issued. That was what Mr. Hearst had been so busy with ; and when he had finished he strolled over and welcomed his new guests, and after chatting for a few minutes took Lanny off to his study and spent the rest of the afternoon with him. On Lanny's earlier visit to San Simeon he had received the handsome offer of fifty thousand dollars a year to become one of this imperial person's political scouts, and to report to him privately what he could learn about the insides of world affairs. Now the lord of San Simeon had a chance to get some of it free of charge, and he wasn't failing to take the chance.

He talked about the news which had come over his private wire, and to which some of his guests were now listening over the radio. The statement issued from Teheran brought no satisfaction whatever to the owning and directing head of a great newspaper chain. It consisted of the vaguest and most empty generalizations. Complete unanimity had been reached on military plans, unity was to be maintained in the making of peace, and all freedom-loving nations would be invited to lend their aid in meeting the world's future problems. " Bunk ! " exclaimed William Randolph Hearst. " Pap for infants and imbeciles ! How much of Poland are they going to leave to Russia, and how much of Germany are they going to give to Poland to make up for it ? And what are they going to do with Austria, and all the Balkans ? Are they going to let Russia bolshevize them, and if not, how are they going to prevent it ? "

Lanny didn't have the answers to any of those questions and could only say that the situation looked dark indeed to him. There could be no question that the Russians were on their way to Berlin and would get there in a year or two, especially if the Allies attempted a Channel crossing next spring. Lanny could say that the Allied armies invading Italy were not being reinforced, and were even losing some of their

bombing units and landing craft ; and this was a sure indica
tion of a projected landing in France. The military men in
Berlin, the really competent ones, were becoming hopeless as
to their chances.

Naturally a large-scale vendor of news pricked up his ears.
How did Mr. Budd know these things ? When Lanny said
that he had recently been in both Berlin and Rome, he was
free to talk as long as he pleased and be sure of close attention.
How in the world did he manage such a trip ? Lanny replied
that it was his father's influence ; beyond that, unfortunately,
he was not free to say. But he talked about Ciano and
Badoglio and Count Volpi, and then about Hitler and Göring
and their entourages, both in Berlin and in Berchtesgaden and
Karinhall ; he made it plain that this was no fairy tale he was
making up. He told how Hitler had promised a competence
to Kurt Meissner to compose an opera about the collapse of
National Socialism, which showed what was going on in a
Führer's secret soul.

Adi, unrelenting opponent of the Reds, had sent Lanny
Budd a special message to his American friend and colleague.
What Herr Hitler wanted was to get rid of Herr Rosenfeld as
quickly as possible and by any means possible. The Hearst
newspapers were doing everything in their power to accomplish this by the constitutional process ; but that wouldn't
be soon enough—the election was eleven months off, and there
would be two months more before a new President could be
inaugurated. By that time the Russian barbarians might have
nearly all of Eastern Germany—and would they ever get out
until they had established a Bolshevik regime over all the
territory they held ? Hitler wanted the job on Roosevelt done
by some quicker process and had commissioned the son of
Budd-Erling to consult with all his friends in America and try
to arrange the matter.

Lanny said he was doing his best ; there had been a lot
of talk about the idea, and now, apparently, some action was
going to be taken. He dangled this bait before the publisher's
nose, but the cautious old fellow behaved like a fat trout that
doesn't rise to a fly. All he said was that the situation was
desperate, and he personally could see no basis for hope. He
went on to ply the high-class messenger with questions about

conditions in the Axis lands, and at the conclusion of the talk
he tried once more to get the messenger into his service. If
fifty thousand dollars a year wasn't enough, let Mr. Budd
name a price.

Once more Lanny thanked him and said, " What I am
doing, Mr. Hearst, is for the cause of free government and the
American way of life. Any help that I can give you is free
of charge." Speaking the words, he wondered : Would Mr.
Hearst decide that he had met a social equal at last ? Or
would he conclude that the visitor was an F.B.I. agent trying
to get something on him ? Lanny talked the problem over
with his wife, and that observant lady said, " This is a child
who has been hopelessly spoiled and will never grow up in
this life."

17

Always To Be Blest

I

TELEPHONE service was slow and tedious in wartime, but
Laurel had made it her practice to call Agnes once a week to
make sure the baby was all right. Back in Hollywood, Lanny
got his father on the phone and told him they were ready to
start for home. How was everybody and how was business ?
This last was meant for a joke, since never in anybody's memory
had there been such business as Budd-Erling was doing.

Robbie had an item of news. " Hansi and Bess are back."
Lanny exclaimed, " Oh, good ! How are they ? " Robbie
reported that they were claimed to be well but looked undernourished ; they were staying with Johannes Robin, Hansi's
father, until they could get the tenants out of their home.

Lanny's half-sister, Bessie Budd, and her husband had been
in Russia for more than two years, and Lanny hadn't seen
them since he and Laurel had passed through Moscow twenty
months ago. Then the war situation had been black, and these

musicians, friends of the Soviet people, had been heavy of heart. Now the tide had turned, and they ought to be happy ; but what had this long sojourn in a foreign land done to their minds and bodies, their musical technique and their careers ?

" Bienvenu " was hitched up and the Budds set out on the return trek. It was the second week in December, and they would stay in the south to avoid snow in the mountains. But they chose a different highway for the sake of variety. The novelty had worn off, and they travelled longer hours, to get it over with. Long ago an English poet had remarked that " man never is, but always to be, blest " ; and this pair who had everything to make them content spent their time counting the miles and the hours. They talked about the things they were going to do when they got back to the crowded city— their baby, their musician relatives, and what they were likely to hear about the new world overseas, the Soviet world, in which they were trying so hard to believe.

II

They were almost home, Trenton, New Jersey, when a snowstorm hit them ; impossible to see anything out of their windshield, and there was nothing to do but put up their trailer and car in a garage and themselves in a third-rate hotel, the only room they could get, small, dingy, and without a bath.

In that unpromising place they had an experience. They were tired of looking out of the window and seeing the soft silent flakes drifting down ; they had heard all the war news several times over on the radio ; they had read until their eyes hurt ; and then had taken a walk and got lost for a while. Back in the room again Lanny suggested, " Let's try a séance."

They had about given up their psychic researches, for the husband had got tired of the fashionable banter of Otto H. Kahn ; that important gentleman either couldn't or wouldn't oblige them any more, and he had a tendency to repeat himself. Lanny had the persistent idea that some tidings might come from or concerning Marceline or her Junker lover ; he asked about them, and about other friends who were or might

be in the " spirit world." But each time, when Laurel came
out of her trance, he had to report to her that he had got
nothing of significance.

Infinite patience is the number-one lesson that has to be
learned by every investigator in this strange underworld of
the mind. Laurel said, " All right," and stretched herself on
a bed which was covered with an old-fashioned crazy quilt.
Lanny put out the light, and sat and listened to her heavy
breathing, and then to the stillness which meant that she was
in her trance. The husband waited for more conversation of
the Algonquin Hotel type, but nothing came, and he thought
that Laurel had missed the bus again and fallen into ordinary
slumber. However, he said, " Is anyone there ? "

Then came a voice, a woman's, low and gentle. As a rule,
the imitation of voices is the weakest point in the case of these
mysterious entities ; but this time there seemed to be something vaguely familiar in the tone. " Is that you, Lanny ? "
And Lanny, being of long acquaintance in this other world,
did not ask rudely, " Who are you ? " but considerately,
" How are you, my dear ? " Love appears to be the prevailing
temper in that environment, and since there is supposed to be
no marrying or giving in marriage, there can be no harm in
endearments.

The voice said, " I have just arrived, and am a little confused." To this the obvious reply was, " No harm can come
to you here, and I hope you will stay and talk to me."

Lanny was thinking of Marceline, thinking of her intently,
with the idea that this might have some effect upon the
séance. But no, it wasn't Marceline ; there was a decided
foreign accent, and he thought of Hilde, Fürstin Donnerstein,
who might have got into trouble on Lanny's account. As the
conversation went on he decided that the tone was that of an
older woman, and he thought of Hilde's mother, who had
been killed in the heavy bombardment of Berlin last March.
She had hated Americans and had hardly been able to endure
having one in her home. Strange indeed if she were to make
her first appearance in a cheap hotel in the capital city of the
State of New Jersey !

Lanny followed the line of conversation which he had
learned from long contact with mediums and their " controls."

" You are not in any trouble, I hope," and " You will soon find friends where you are," and " Do come and talk to me whenever you feel able," and " What can I do to help you ? " This last brought a response that gave Lanny a jolt. Said the voice, " Deliver a message for me. Tell Baby Marcel that he is the one I miss the most."

Baby Marcel ! Lanny's mind leaped to the Hôtel Mamounia, where he had spent a night only four months ago. The voice was that of Madame Zyszynski, the stout and amiable old Polish woman who had been the cause of Lanny's taking an interest in psychical matters. He had been too rushed to have a séance with her on that last trip, and his conscience troubled him for fear that he had hurt her feelings. She had adored him as a son, and had been so pathetically happy whenever he told her that her work was good and that he had learned much from his sessions with her ; apparently it was necessary to her success that she should believe this. And now she had passed over into this new world, peopled with the beings who had used her voice, but of whom she had had no conscious knowledge. Would she know them now ?

III

Lanny recognized this as an event of importance to him, and he handled it with tact acquired during a lifetime of diplomacy. " Madame," he said, " this is the first word I have heard about the change in your situation. I am glad, because it saves me having to grieve about you. Can you be my friend in the new world, as you were in the old ? "

" I will try, Lanny." The voice was clearer, perhaps under the encouragement of love. He talked to her as he had done in real life, gently, affectionately, as to a second mother ; with a little humour, just a trace of scepticism, to stimulate her and keep her on her mettle. " Perhaps you will be my control now," he said ; and when she promised to try, he added, " I wonder if you will be able to find Tecumseh." Lanny would be sorry to lose that old Indian chieftain who had been Madame's " control " for most of her life and had carried on queer arguments and quarrels with the son of Budd-Erling over a period of fourteen years. Many people had told Madame about him, and she promised now to try to make contact with him.

One question more : " Have you seen or heard anything of Marceline ? " The voice expressed surprise at this idea ; had Marceline passed over ? Lanny explained that he did not know, but that she had been in trouble when he last spoke to her. He didn't say where or how—that would be for the " spirits " to report. Madame Zyszynski had lived in the household with Marceline off and on for years and knew well her virtues and her faults. How she would find her was a question that Lanny did not ask. Madame had passed away of a slowly creeping anaemia, she declared, and she still felt a confusion of mind. He replied that he would not press her any more. The voice died away, and Laurel began that quiet moaning which indicated her coming out of a trance.

He had a story to tell her now ! She too had visited Bienvenu and knew the simple-minded, rather dull old woman, an ex-servant who had married a butler, and who was wholly incapable of making up or even understanding the strange communications which passed her lips. If Lanny had been conducting a psychic investigation, he wouldn't have told Laurel what had happened ; but he wasn't trying to convince an uninterested world, he was dealing with the wife he loved. So he told, but of course without mentioning Marceline.

IV

The storm let up next day and they drove to New York. Robbie sent a man with a car to get the trailer, and the very next day it would become the home of a family which had come from Quebec or Oklahoma to put rivets in the newest Budd-Erling model. Meantime the travelling couple had hugged and kissed Baby Lanny, and grown-up Lanny had danced with him to music which magically filled the air or the ether or whatever it was, all over the North American continent. The same Toscanini and the same Bing Crosby, the same Major Eliot and the same H. V. Kaltenborn, and the same Franklin D. Roosevelt, followed always by the same " Star-Spangled Banner "—of which everybody knew the first three lines and the last two, but few knew the rest.

Laurel presented her faithful friend Agnes with a beautiful Navaho blanket which they had picked up on the outskirts of the town of Budd ; they had used it on the last stage of the journey, but that hadn't hurt it. They had bought Indian products for all the Budd tribe and for Laurel's relatives, none of whom needed anything ; also for the Robin family. The first telephoning they did was to the Hansibesses, who came in to town the next day, and what a time they had exchanging reminiscences !

Hansi Robin was now thirty-nine and Bess was thirty-five. They were a pair of finished musicians, and had played together in concerts in most of the capitals of Europe and in cities and towns all over America. They were devotedly in love after some eighteen years of married life, but they had been through a period of desperate strain because of their disagreement over the political problems of the time. The only daughter of Robbie and Esther Budd had become, to the utter dismay of her parents, a stern and Calvinistic member of the Communist party, while her husband was a gentle soul who demanded a kind and decent world right away and could not face the grim realities of the class struggle. They had been wearing each other out with arguments when the attack of Hitler upon the Soviet Union had solved the problem for the time being.

Of course the Russians had to defend themselves, and every right-minded person had to help them. A violin virtuoso and his accompanist wife had betaken themselves to this land of music lovers to play for them and express the sympathy that was in their hearts. For more than two years they had been doing this, all the way from besieged Leningrad to Vladivostok and back ; from the mining and factory towns of the Urals to the camps of the Red Army behind the front, where you could hear the guns day and night. And what had the experience done to them ? The P.A. and his wife were most eager to find out.

The first thing was obvious, the pair were thinner and paler. The lad whom Lanny had called a shepherd boy out of ancient Judea was a man, still slender and sensitive, with pain, his own and mankind's, written all over his features. The news of what the Nazis were doing to wipe out the Jewish race had been reported everywhere but it was something so monstrous that most people in America were unable to believe it. Hansi knew that it was true, and there was death in his soul ; in Russia he had put such sorrow into his music that tears ran down people's cheeks as they listened. He didn't know if that would happen in America, and talked sometimes of playing only for Jewish audiences. Only a people which had been persecuted for a score of centuries could understand what he was saying. " Even Bess cannot understand," he said.

V

This was meant half playfully, but Lanny guessed that it was half true. The attack upon the " Soviet Fatherland " had brought this pair together intellectually ; and now, what had been the effect of actual daily contact with that country over a long period ? Neither Hansi nor Bess mentioned the subject, and Lanny waited until he got Hansi alone ; the man would tell the man and the woman would tell the woman.

The violinist revealed that the breach had opened again and was as wide as ever ; they never spoke of politics to each other. " I love the Russian people," he declared ; " they are a great people, warm-hearted and generous, and their response to music is instinctive and overwhelming. But I can't bring myself to tolerate their government."

" Would you like *any* government, Hansi ? " asked the brother-in-law.

" You have to be there to understand the difference, Lanny. It is not like anything in our world. You meet some official, you visit his home, you like him, and play music for him ; and then some day you go to his office and find his desk vacant ; you ask where he is and nobody knows ; you discover that you are troubling them by your questions. You go to his home and learn that he has disappeared off the face of the earth ; his own family doesn't know what has happened. You can see that they have been weeping, but also you see that they wish you wouldn't press them ; they are afraid to talk to you. You discover that they are afraid to be known to associate with a foreigner ; they are embarrassed to say so, but they don't invite you to their homes any more. All their lives are dominated by fear."

" I have been told that, Hansi ; I thought it was explained by the national peril."

" America is at war too, but I meet all sorts of foreigners here in New York, and I hardly know the difference. In Russia I was welcomed by tumultuous audiences—you can hardly imagine such scenes ; but I had very few friends, and I had the feeling that most of those were selected persons. They were Bess's sort of friends, not mine ; they were the party-sort of people, who could not be corrupted by any unorthodox thing I might say. Some of them pretended not to be party members, but I had the feeling that they were playing a role, and of course I didn't enjoy that. Even your Uncle Jesse did not talk frankly to us ; and then he went away to Irkutsk, and since then has not written us a line. He too feels himself distrusted, I am sure."

Such was Hansi's story ; and Lanny argued with him, not for the sake of the Communist government, but for Hansi's marriage. " This war is a grim and terrible thing. It is my hope that when it's won the pressure may be relaxed. I have recently been re-reading Lenin's argument that under Socialism the state would wither away in the end."

" It may be, Lanny, and I hope so. But the way I see it, when men get power, they hold on to it ; they come to like it, and think they are the only people who are really capable of using it ; if anyone suggests otherwise he becomes an enemy, and he disappears off the face of the earth. I do not care about waging a war to remove one kind of totalitarian government and set up another. I think it is just as wicked to liquidate the bourgeoisie as to liquidate Jews and Poles."

VI

Lanny got Bess's side of the argument from his wife. Bess had spent the time trying to persuade Laurel to become a Communist. There was no other road to freedom for the workers, and it was childish to imagine that the capitalists would ever consent peacefully to giving up their grip upon the workers' lives and fortunes. Of course the Soviet govern-

ment used force ; all governments used force, whatever amount
was necessary to preserve their own power. The amount and
kind of force depended upon the resistance the government
had to meet. The American capitalist class didn't need much
because they owned practically the entire press, screen, and
radio, from which the masses derived their ideas. But how long
would the American political system endure if ever the workers
made up their mind to break the chains of the profit system ?

That was a subject for argument, and the two ladies had
it. Bessie Budd Robin had never heard, or had forgotten, that
Karl Marx had admitted it might be possible for Socialism to
be obtained by parliamentary means in the Anglo-Saxon lands ;
when she was confronted with this citation from the gospel,
she took the argument back to Russia, where the people had
never been accustomed to the use of the ballot and would
have to learn by slow stages. Or to Spain—the classic example
of what would happen when big business and the landed
interests was threatened by a political protest. The Spanish
people had trusted to the ballot and had won their freedom
and set up a people's republic—and what happened ? With
the tacit consent of the world democracies the capitalist groups
of Italy and Germany, acting through their Fascist agents,
had sent in gangster armies and destroyed the people's government of Spain, and had committed cruelties exceeding anything
ever charged against the Soviet Union.

" I had to admit that she has a case," said Laurel, and her
husband asked, " Are you going to let her make a true-believer
out of you ? "

" What I am going to do," said the wife, " is to wait and
see what happens. Bess is sure of her formula ; she insists
that after this war we shall see a dozen small nations having
to make a choice between a murderous White government and
a Red government. I asked her if that too would be ' murderous,' and she answered that it would do whatever was
necessary to protect the workers trying to break their chains.
You see how it is, each side applies all the bad words to the
other ; neither side will hear anything of the other side's case,
and if you try to present it you get called the bad names—a
Red or fellow traveller on the one hand, a reactionary or
Social-Fascist on the other."

Lanny replied, "I am putting my hopes in Roosevelt. He's been trying his charm on Stalin, and I'm eager to hear what happened."

Said the wife, "The man in the middle gets the bullets from both directions ; but I suppose we have to take our stand there all the same."

VII

Lanny Budd had business of his own to attend to. The art centre of the world had removed itself from Paris to New York, and the town was full of painters who wanted to earn a living, and of patrons who were making money by the hogsheadful. They wanted to decorate their homes, and at the same time make a shrewd investment, and they were willing to pay for the advice of an elegant and plausible gentleman who could talk about paintings in the same fluent way that they could talk about the food-packing business or the razor-blade business or whatever it might be. There were others who lived in Kokomo, Indiana, or Horsehead Gulch, Montana, who hadn't time to visit the metropolis but would look at photographs of paintings and pick out something that appealed to them. The fame of an art expert spread in mysterious ways ; letters would come, and Lanny would be surprised to discover that these people didn't mind paying thousands of dollars for a painting that had a proper certification.

With his wife and his old-time colleague Zoltan Kertezsi, he visited the exhibitions and inspected what the dealers on East Fifty-seventh Street had to offer. They knew him, and greeted him with carefully modulated cordiality ; it was a pleasant way to earn one's keep. Lanny would jot down the data he wanted, then stroll in the crisp wintry air to his home, and there dictate a few letters to a stenographer. Everything would be fine—until he turned on the radio and was reminded of American boys dying hour by hour in trenches on the rainswept hills of Southern Italy, of helpless Poles and Jews being packed into cattle cars and carried to some destruction camp, to be locked in a poison-gas chamber and then burned in a furnace.

Every night the couple tried a séance, hoping to get Madame again ; but, alas, it was only Otto Kahn, urbane and friendly but vague. When they asked about an old Polish woman named Zyszynski, he asked what was that, a sneeze ?—which was good fun but didn't advance the cause of psychical research, Lanny had sent a cablegram to his mother and received no reply, which did not surprise him, for he knew that there were censors who took their time and were suspicious of anything the least bit out of the ordinary. He was sure that Beauty would send an air-mail letter if anything had happened to Lanny's old friend.

Sure enough, a letter came, and he read it to his wife : the old woman had passed peacefully away just two days before the séance in New Jersey had occurred. Lanny said, " There you are ! Another case that we can have printed in one of the journals and bound up and put away to gather dust on the library shelves." He was pessimistic about the matter because he had read hundreds of such cases and knew from the books that there were thousands and tens of thousands recorded. But who would pay attention to them ? The learned ones, the literati, had their formulas, their systems of thought, and were by no means to be persuaded to revise these. Huxley said that Herbert Spencer's idea of a tragedy was a generalization killed by a fact ; but these modern wiseacres spared themselves such pain by the simple device of disregarding the fact. When Doctor Rhine of Duke University set patiently to work and by millions of experiments proved that some human minds could call a high percentage of cards that were going to be turned up in a well-shuffled pack, and could cause a high percentage of dice to fall the way they willed it, even when the dice were thrown by a machine—what did these rigid-minded ones do to get out of that trouble ? They proceeded to cast doubt upon the laws of probability, which prior to that time had been supposed to be as fixed as all the rest of mathematical science !

VIII

Just a week before Christmas Lanny learned from the newspapers that the President had come back from Teheran, after having travelled nearly eighteen thousand miles. He had come on the battleship *Iowa*, and Lanny knew that he enjoyed sea travel and would feel refreshed. He would have a string of people a mile long waiting for engagements ; but, even so, it was a P.A.'s duty to report, and Lanny did this. Baker called back, saying that the Boss would like Mr. Budd to have a merry Christmas and then report again.

An art expert permitted himself the luxury of spending several days in the Metropolitan Museum of Art inspecting the new treasures it had acquired. He took his wife to see *Life with Father*, a play that was to break all theatrical records. He drove her out to meet Mr. Winstead, his favourite client, who was in a state of excitement because Lanny had got him an option on a Correggio in Rome. When would the Allied Army get there, and what chance was there that the Germans would sack the city, as they had done with Naples ?

Carrying Indian products from New Mexico, they motored up to Newcastle and spent another of those plethoric Christmases ; too much of everything, and yet a great deal of kindness also, for most of the Budds were willing to put off their disputes for a period of ten days in honour of a Jewish baby born nearly two millenniums ago. Lanny counted back : it was twenty-six years since he had spent his first Christmas in this home ; it was thirty years since he had spent his first Christmas in Kurt Meissner's home in Stubendorf—and what a whirlwind of events had swept over mankind in those years ! For Lanny personally there had been successes, but for the human race mostly tragedies and failures. Lanny wondered, if he had known what was coming, would he have had the courage to go on with it ? Would the human race have had that much courage ? Lanny thought, if the scientists or the philosophers ever solve the problem of foreseeing the future, let them make sure that it is to be better than the past !

Early on Christmas morning Lanny sat by the very good short-wave radio set in his father's home and listened to a carol service from a village near the front. It was the British Army, and in the middle of it General Montgomery spoke a little piece to his troops. The English employed by the High Command is a something all by itself, and " Monty " was a character all by *him*self—extremely pious, and certain of the Lord's own personal guidance. The year's victories were the

Lord's doing, and peace on earth and good-will toward men were what the troops were all fighting for. The singing was hearty, and a sergeant said a short extempore prayer, exactly as it would have been on a normal Christmas Eve in an English chapel. To the listener in Connecticut it meant that nothing really made any difference to or in the English people, and that they would never be beaten except possibly by themselves.

Back in New York there came a telephone call from the President's man. Could Mr. Budd make it convenient to visit "Shangri-La" on the evening of the following day? Mr. Budd could, and made an appointment for eight in the evening at the little mountain town of Thurmont, Maryland. Lanny was now permitted to tell his wife a bit more about his doings, and she elected to go along for the ride. She could lie contentedly on a bed in a hotel room and work on her manuscript while her husband kept his appointment, and she would promise not to weep if he told her that he was going away on another mysterious errand.

They started early, so as to reduce the chance of being delayed by a storm. There being no trailer behind them they went by the Holland Tunnel and the Skyway to Newark, and on past Philadelphia on U.S. 1. They cut across a corner of Pennsylvania into Maryland, on a road that had been covered with snowdrifts but had been cleared. The President's summer hideaway, which he had come to like so well that he used it in winter too, was in a low range of mountains called the Catoctins, and the little hotel in the near-by village was enjoying a tremendous war boom, because of the military and other V.I.P.'s who came for conferences. Baker had seen to it that the P.A. had a room, and there the couple rested, then enjoyed a walk, and after that a dinner. Winter in the country is delightful to city folk who have money and can enjoy modern conveniences wherever they go.

IX

The P.A. went out in the darkness and strolled, and a car came along and picked him up. They sped out of town and into the hills, on a winding road that had taken a lot of labour to build. But labour had been the cheapest thing in America at that time, for this had been one of the C.C.C. camps, where idle young men were put to work during the great depression. Now labour was scarce in America, and so was everything else. As the car lights picked out the tree-clad slopes, Lanny asked, " How is the Boss ? " The reply was, " They are working him hard." And the visitor could be sure that was an understatement.

The camp had a military guard under the direction of the Secret Service ; but there were few formalities where Baker was concerned. There was a list, and Lanny's name was on it, and the car drove in. The main building of the camp was low, one-storied, and rustic in style. Lanny sat in the reception hall, with the burlesque map of Shangri-La on the wall. He had to wait only a minute or two, and then was taken to the President's room, which was small and plain, with half a dozen pieces of cheap white-painted furniture.

The crippled man was in bed, as always when Lanny saw him. He had on his blue crew-necked sweater that the moths had got into—but he still clung to it. The moths of sorrow had not been able to damage his smile that Lanny loved ; no matter how many cares he had or how tired he was, he would summon up a smile for a friend, and some joshing remark or amusing story out of the political and social world of Washington. Now his face was lined and his bed was piled with documents that required attention ; but he remembered Lanny's last visit and remarked, " I see you have got back your weight. Be careful you don't overdo it."

Lanny said, " You should have seen me, Governor, the day I came out of Italy. I had about an inch of brown beard. I'd have brought it home to show it, only I was afraid my wife would faint."

This time it was F. D. R. who had had the adventures, and it pleased him to tell them. He had been taken to Oran on the battleship, and a U-boat had been sunk trying to get him in the Strait of Gibraltar. He had been flown to Cairo, and before landing had been taken on a little side trip to see the Sphinx and the Pyramids. In Cairo he and Churchill had had their first consultation with Chiang Kai-shek—Stalin wouldn't meet him because there was no war between Russia and Japan. Madame Chiang had come to act as her husband's translator, and she had clapped her hands to summon the servants—in this case American G.I.'s, who didn't like it the least bit. Lanny remarked, " She has lived in America long enough to know that that is not our custom." To which the President answered, " Don't quote me, but I suspect that she may be getting a little bit too big for her Chinese breeches."

Next had come the trip to Teheran ; it was just a short flight over the Russian border, but was as far as the Red Marshal would come. F. D. R. told about the flight—over the Suez Canal, and circling both Jerusalem and Bagdad on the way. They had landed at a Russian airport on the outskirts of Teheran, and the President had gone to stay at the American Legation, in a walled area outside the city ; but the Russians were disturbed about this, because a number of German para-troopers had been dropped in the neighbourhood, and six of them were still at large. One sharpshooter would be enough for their purposes, so the President consented to move to the Russian Embassy, which was inside the city, and where the Big Three could meet without having to travel.

Lanny's Boss was as happy as a schoolboy telling the good story of how this transfer had been carried out. It was evident by now that the enemy knew everything that was going on ; so a cavalcade of armed jeeps was got up, and the route was lined solid with British soldiers, and a Secret Service man rigged up as the President rode solemnly through the main streets, acknowledging the applause of the populace. In the meantime the President was put into another car and, with only one jeep preceding, rode at high speed through the back streets of this aged and crowded city, and so to the Russian compound—without any German sharpshooter getting a crack at him.

At last the American Commander-in-Chief had had his heart's desire and met the Russian Commander-in-Chief face to face. " How did you find him ? " Lanny asked, and the answer was, " As you described him. He is a small man, but wears a big uniform. I had come determined to make friends, but it was pretty hard at first, for he seemed suspicious, and in a dour mood. I was not sure whether he liked Winston, so I had the happy thought to kid a British Tory, telling him that *he* was in a bad mood, and was an agent of imperialism. The more cross Winston got, the better Stalin liked it, and finally he burst out laughing. After that we got along famously."

"How did you make out with the banquets?" inquired the P.A.

"I observed that Stalin went easy on the endless toasts that seem to be essential; so I did the same. Winston, of course, could have drunk all the vodka in the house and never shown the effects of it. The party lasted for four days, and Uncle Joe got most of what he wanted; enough to make sure of keeping him in the war. He absolutely demanded a Channel crossing next spring. The Russians are to make the heaviest possible attack at the same time, and that is all we need. We agreed to be friends, and to meet again and work out details. If I can have my way it won't be in the capital of Iran, for that is surely one hell hole."

"From what I've been told," commented the P.A., "you were in more danger of typhoid and cholera than of German paratroopers."

"Imagine it, if you can. There are some modern business buildings in the city, but the only ones that have clean water are the legations, which have it piped down from the mountains. The rest of the town scoops up drinking-water out of the running gutters, which are also the sewers—there are no others. And yet the Shah and his court derive an enormous income from the American and British oil companies! Something will have to be done before long!"

X

So far the Boss had done most of the talking; he wanted it that way—it was his form of relaxation. Good form suggested that Lanny should wait, and he did so. At last the other stopped and said, "Tell me what you have been doing."

"You told me to take a vacation, Governor, and I obeyed. We took a motor trip to the town of Budd, New Mexico." Lanny told about the horrors he had seen preparing there, and then about the different kinds of horrors he had come upon in Hollywood and San Simeon. "I met a number of pro-Fascist and Nazi sharpshooters," he said, " but I think they have given up their idea of getting you with steel bullets ; they are preparing a battle of gold and silver bullets for next year. Take it from me, they are filling up their arsenal. The motion picture industry will raise more money to beat you than they did to beat the End Poverty in California movement ten years ago."

The other smiled. " By next year we should be in Germany, and we should manage to pick up quite a lot of campaign ammunition there."

Lanny's conscience troubled him when he kept this over-worked man chatting. So he chose the moment to inquire, " What did you have in mind for me, Governor ? "

" It may sound like another holiday to a man who has been in the Axis countries. Have you ever visited the Holy Land ? "

" Never."

" I suppose you have a general idea of what is shaping up there. For the past twenty years the agents, first of Mussolini and then of Hitler, have been stirring up the Arabs against both Jews and British ; there were five Arab revolts before this war began, and now the Arab lands have been getting together against the Jews in Palestine. The Arabs are fanatics and so are the Zionists, so it's a religious quarrel as well as economic. You know how nasty that can be."

" The nastiest in this world, Governor."

" It's Britain's problem ; but we are discovering day by day that all Britain's problems are ours. A few days ago we learned that two of the most violent Arab agitators have escaped from British custody in Jerusalem, and that will mean more trouble. The Axis is spending money to bring about another revolt, and we surely don't want any during this war. I have promised that the next time I go abroad, which will be in a month or two, I will have a meeting with King Ibn Saud and other Arab rulers. I shall have to know what I'm talking about."

" You have to know about too many things," put in the P.A. with friendly sorrow.

" Harry Hopkins is worried about the situation and thinks that something will have to be done in the way of mediation.

He suggested you as the man to go there and stay for a while and give us an impartial report."

" Well, Governor, I can surely promise impartiality. I'll be starting from scratch."

" What we want is to lick the Axis, and after that to settle disputes on a reasonable basis and get the nations together to protect the peace."

" Would I go as an official agent ? "

" I think you should slip in unobtrusively and talk with all sides as a friend. If you went as my representative, everybody would stand on ceremony and insist on his maximum demands. Can you think of any art business that would take you to Palestine ? "

" I can't think of any offhand, but no doubt I could learn of something in the libraries, and I could get one of my clients to write me a letter giving me a commission. I suppose that archaeological research has been suspended for the duration, but I might be talking over plans for something to start up when the war is over."

" Good ! If you wanted a museum to commission you, that could be arranged. Have you used up that money I gave you ? "

" Only a small part of it, Governor."

" Well, use the rest on this."

" One thing more. My wife is a shrewd woman, and in California she served as an extra pair of eyes. She talks to the women—something a man can't do in Arab lands."

" Take her along, by all means. I want you to have a talk with Harry, he has a lot of ideas. Choose your route to get there, and Baker will fix you up. Good-bye, and take care of yourself."

" The same to you, Governor. You are in more danger than I, because so many people are trying to kill you with overwork."

" Don't worry, I've got a rabbit's foot in my pocket ! I am predestined to see this job through."

XI

" Harry the Hop " was in his room, sitting in front of a log fire, slumped down in a chair—he was never content until he had got onto the back of his neck. He was a tall gaunt man, in wretched health, but there was animation and friendship in his eyes. He offered Lanny a drink and a cigarette, and then put him through a grilling as to what he had learned in Germany and Italy.

Lanny found it a pleasure to answer the questions of a man who knew what he wanted and who got the meaning of every sentence before it was finished. " Hurry up ! " his mind seemed to say. " We have to get on with this war ! "

He told the P.A. a lot about Palestine, the factions he would find there and the problems that had to be solved. He pushed a writing pad across the table and dictated the names of books Lanny should read and people he should meet in New York before he started. Lanny made notes, and by the time that briefing was over he understood what his job was, believed that he could do it, and said so. This pleased the President's helper, who was that sort of man himself.

By way of reward he favoured the son of Budd-Erling with many details of the world-shaping conference in Teheran. He confided the rather horrifying fact that the Soviet government had been carrying on secret negotiations with the Nazis practically all the time since the repulse of the Germans in their first rush at Moscow. The agents had been, first, a Russian emissary in Stockholm, then one in Bulgaria, then the Japanese Ambassadors in Moscow and Berlin. The object of the Russians was to get out of the war with the most territory they could ; and when Lanny expressed his dismay, Harry the Hop smiled and said that a man who had lived most of his life in Europe ought not to be so naïve. European diplomacy had always been the same ; each for himself and the devil take the hindmost.

" I thought the Soviets represented a revolutionary tradition," objected the P.A. ; and to this the reply was, " That is true to a certain extent, but less so when you get behind the scenes. It appears to be a principle of revolutions that they degenerate, and I fear that Red Russia is no exception. All leaders think about themselves and their own power, and the longer they hold power, the more true that becomes. It is a fact that must be faced, that the aims of the Soviets are identical with those of Peter the Great : an ice-free port on the Baltic and one on the Pacific ; access to the Persian Gulf and control of the Dardanelles. All those proposals came up at Teheran."

" And did we give in to them ? "

Harry the Hop smiled his quiet, slow smile. " We gave enough to stop the negotiations with Hitler, at least we hope so. We shall keep track of developments and make sure."

" I hope you have better agents than I ! " remarked the son of Budd-Erling apologetically.

" I wouldn't say that," chuckled the other. " We have many in different places, and the whole is always greater than any of its parts. We find amusement in fitting the pieces together ; but that isn't saying that we like the picture when we get it ! " A plain-speaking fellow was this former social worker, and he made many enemies that way.

XII

It was after midnight when Lanny was returned to the hotel. He had forewarned his wife, and found her sitting up in bed, reading. When he told her that she was a duly appointed presidential agent, she didn't want to sleep that night, but to ask questions, not merely about the Palestine job, but about all the last five or six years. The husband didn't mention Germany or Italy, but revealed that he had been working for Roosevelt, and how their meetings had been arranged and the secret kept. Laurel said, " I was fairly sure what it was ; but I never hinted about it to anyone else."

She plied him with questions about that great man whom he was so fortunate as to know. She exclaimed, " He's so much better than we deserved ! " That was her constant theme : the American people were so ill-informed that they would never have elected Franklin Roosevelt if they had known what they were going to get. He had had to use his political arts, and his command of the radio, to keep them in line—and then only by a narrow margin ! " What would have happened to us if he hadn't tricked us into getting ready ! And inventing dodges like lend-lease to help our allies ! " Lanny told her how " That Man " had put Robbie Budd " on relief," ordering him to build fighter planes and paying him out of W.P.A. funds, intended for the unemployed. F. D. R.'s argument was unanswerable ; were not unemployed airplane builders as deserving of jobs as any other sort ?

Lanny and his wife were going to have another honeymoon, this time in the Holy Land. As a writer, Laurel began thinking about local colour, and the sort of stories in which she could make use of it. " When the war is over, you must tell me many stories, Lanny ! " And he promised her an " exclusive." Then he persuaded her to go to sleep, saying that he was tired from the long drive, and had another before him in the course of this new day.

But even after he had put his head on the pillow and closed his eyes she wanted to know, " How shall we fly, Lanny ? " When he told her that they would have a choice of routes, she wanted to know on which one she would see the most. He realized how much this meant to her, this new status, this new vista opening before her. It was like being married all over again. " So far I have had less than half a husband. Your work is the most important part of you."

He chuckled and told her, " You're in the Army now ! "

XIII

In New York they had much to do. Lanny ordered the books which Hopkins had recommended and packed them to be taken on the trip. More important at the moment was to find out what art there was in Jerusalem, and especially in private hands, so that it might be purchased, or at least negotiated for. For that the best authority was Zoltan Kertezsi, whose mind was a world catalogue of painting and sculpture. He must have observed long ago that his friend developed these sudden curiosities only as to parts of the world where the American armies were about to penetrate ; but he never asked any questions. He was at once a wise and a kind man, and he disliked the unwise and unkind Nazis as much as Lanny did.

He informed his associate that there was under way a movement to establish a Jewish Museum of Art in New York ; it would contain not only Jewish ritual instruments, Torah, candelabra, ancient coins, and so on, but mosaics and architectural fragments, and modern Jewish paintings as well. Lanny could be looking for such things, and Zoltan offered to take the burden of arrangements off his friend's shoulders. He went to the libraries and also to the dealers, and after two or three days he came back with a small dossier on the subject, enough to provide a P.A. with perfect camouflage in both Jerusalem and Tel-Aviv.

The next person Lanny wanted to talk to was Johannes Robin, wise man of the world, who knew the Jews in the only way it was possible really to know them—by being one. For the past few years he had managed the New York office of Budd-Erling, and had received a very good salary. That was far different from being the great financier that he had been in Germany; but Johannes said that he would rather work for a day labourer's wage in America than be the richest man in Naziland. He had bought a comfortable old house about half-way between New York and Newcastle, and there he had assembled his family: his devoted old wife, whom they all called Mama; the son of the murdered Freddi, who bore his father's name; the mother of that son, who had remarried and had a husband and three children; and, for the past two years, the two children of Hansi and Bess. They all stayed together, because they had learned so dreadful a lesson of the world's cruelty; they had been taught love by their fear of hatred.

Lanny and Laurel went out to spend a Sunday with this household. He had known them since his boyhood and had been a sort of Prince Charming to them, being so elegant and rich, whereas Johannes had then just begun to accumulate his fortune. Lanny, Hansi, and Freddi had made a musical trio, piano, violin, and clarinet, and they had been enraptured— each with the others. The part which the grandson of Budd Gunmakers had played in trying to get Freddi out of the clutches of the Nazis had made him for ever the adored hero of the family and there was nothing they wouldn't have tried to do for him. When he came to visit, Mama prepared an elaborate Jewish meal and did her best to make him eat more than was good for him. The children had been taught to hang upon his every word, and sat gazing at him with their beautiful dark eyes.

Now Lanny was going to visit Palestine with his wife. He said it was to collect art works, and the children no doubt believed it. The grandfather, a hard man to fool, must have had his guesses, but he wouldn't say anything, even to Lanny when they were alone. However, he would talk about politics, and the dreadful problem of Arabs versus Jews, and what could be done about it. The Jewish race, or people, or whatever name you chose to give them, had been scattered over the earth, and it was their fate to be used as footballs, to be kicked here and there in other people's games or battles. The British had the job of defending Palestine, so the Nazi-Fascists incited the Arabs against the Jews as a means of making trouble for the British and interfering with the functioning of oil pipe-lines from Mesopotamia. Johannes said sadly, " Wherever we go we are in somebody's way." And he added, " There are several pure Anglo-Saxon country-club members who think they could manage the New York office better than I do."

Johannes himself was not seriously interested in Judaism as a religion ; he took the ceremonials as grown-up Christians take Santa Claus, as something that gives pleasure to the children. He had no interest in Zionism for himself, but thought it would be a good thing for those miserable millions of brethren whom he had left behind in the Polish ghetto. When the zealots came to him, he would write a cheque for them, at the same time explaining that he was no longer the rich man he had been and that he had a large family dependent upon him.

All the grown members of this family took part in the discussions with Lanny, and he was especially interested in the attitude of young Freddi, who had just had his sixteenth birthday, and was the living image of his father as Lanny remembered him when he had first visited Bienvenu and played the clarinet. Tall and slender, with beautiful dark eyes and wavy black hair, young Freddi was making a good record in high school, but all his ambitions were centred upon the day when he would be old enough to volunteer for the Army. He wanted so to be in time, and he hoped that the president of Budd-Erling Aircraft might somehow be able to pull wires and have him assigned to the invasion of Germany.

After that, everything would be simple. He would find a sympathetic officer to hear the tale of what the Nazis had done to his father, and would assign him to the unit which would march or perhaps parachute into Bavaria, so that Freddi might be one of those who would deliver the ten or twenty thousand captives of Dachau. It might be that there were men who had managed to survive ten years of that horror and would remember Freddi's father and tell about him. Freddi had cross-questioned Lanny Budd, and had studied the maps in the public library, and knew exactly how he would get to the small market town which lies some nine miles from Munich. He dreamed of rolling in a jeep up the well-paved highway, and he had figured out the strategy of taking a concentration camp which occupied more than a square mile and was surrounded by a high concrete wall with electrified wire on top.

Quite solemnly this shepherd boy out of ancient Judea discussed with Lanny his project of storming the castle on the height, and there setting up artillery with which to shatter the power plant and the entrance gates. No less solemnly the well-instructed Lanny explained, " The first military objective is always the enemy's armed forces. If you defeat and rout them, Dachau will be pretty sure to surrender. A concentration camp is not a fortress ; it is built to keep prisoners in, not to keep an army out."

XIV

Johannes had a friend who was a Zionist and had lived in Palestine ; so Lanny and Laurel paid a visit to another Jewish household. Here were people of considerable wealth and high culture—they were interested in Lanny not so much because he was the son of Budd-Erling, but because he was the half-brother of Bessie Budd Robin, whom they had heard in concerts. There were a father and mother, a grown son and three daughters, all people of modern ideas. The father had fallen under the spell of Jewish racialism and had decided that it was his duty to help rebuild the Zion of his ancestors ; he had sold his home and taken his family, his furniture, and all his belongings to Palestine.

They had lived for a couple of years in the new city of Tel-Aviv; but the father had had to give up because of the discontent of the young people. All four thought of themselves as Americans before they were Jews, and none of them had the least interest in pioneering. They didn't want to learn Hebrew, and they had little sense of kinship with the pitiful oppressed people who were being brought from Central Europe, in great part with British and American money. They missed the crowds, the bright lights, and the cultural opportunities of New York, and they had banded themselves together to break down the resistance of their father and shatter his dream.

And yet—a curious thing—now that they were back, they chose to remember the good side of their Zion; they wouldn't have liked it if Lanny had agreed with them too heartily. It was a pleasant dream to look back on, and they chose to blame themselves rather than the New Jerusalem. They were not tough enough; they were too sophisticated; they had become worshippers of the golden calf. They had been seduced by the lures of New York—the limousines, the fashionable shops, the smart conversation. People who had never known these things could be happy building dams and irrigation ditches and planting orange groves in deserts. Let them do it, and in another generation the university and the libraries would have grown, and there would be more concert halls and theatres, and something to talk about besides the rights and wrongs of Israel.

Lanny was amused by a heart-to-heart remark made to him by the son of this family, a newly trained Air Force officer home on a brief leave. This young man took him aside and said, " I'll tell you the God's truth, Mr. Budd. I got tired of seeing so many Jews. I found that I liked a variety of faces ! "

XV

Lanny might have met some Arabs in New York, but he figured that he would meet enough at his destination. He knew their religion, because he had met so many Moors, and his stepfather had become a sort of lay brother to the Mohammedan scholars and marabouts of Morocco. Lanny would stop in Marrakech to ask questions and get letters of introduction, and pose as being on the verge of becoming a convert to the seventh-century camel driver's creed.

Baker arranged matters, and the favoured couple were flown to Key West, and then to Belém in Brazil and to Dakar in West Africa—a delightful journey in midwinter. In Marrakech they spent a couple of days with Beauty and Parsifal, and Lanny found that his mother was greatly worried over not having heard from Marceline ; he, of course, said not a word. He told all the good news about Frances and the rest in Newcastle ; also he improved his education by meeting an Arab propagandist who was stirring up his co-religionists in French Morocco on Nazi funds.

The next stage was Cairo, where they spent a night in the famed Shepheard's Hotel, favourite resort of British and American officers. Lanny didn't meet any Mohammedans there, for this would have attracted unfavourable attention. Next morning the couple were packed closely in an Army dispatch plane, and in a few minutes were being flown over that rugged Sinai Desert where Moses had caused the water to flow from the rock. It looked exactly like the desert of Tunis where Lanny had come so near to losing his life, and indeed it was a part of the same vast tract, extending from the Atlantic Ocean deep into Asia Minor.

The journey had taken the children of Israel forty years, and it took a fast airplane less than an hour. Below them were vineyards and orchards, and Lanny leaned to his wife and called above the roar of the engine, " The Holy Land ! " Presently they were over a much crowded old walled city on tumbled hills, and as they swung round to come down to the airport, they passed a hill with stunted trees and a temple with a round dome on top. Once more Lanny leaned over. " The Mount of Olives ! " he said.

18

Promised Land

I

As a child, Lanny Budd had been taken all over Europe, and being the near-stepson of a painter he had gazed at innumerable stained-glass windows and paintings and statues of blessed virgins and saints. He had listened to technical discussions of these figures as art works, but it hadn't been until the age of fifteen that he became curious about them as historical characters. He had asked questions of an elderly Swiss diplomat, and so had been told about an ancient work of literature known as the Bible, pretty well forgotten by fashionable society on the French Riviera. Alone and without guidance he had read the story of Jesus, four times over in four varying accounts ; tears had come into his eyes because of the mistreatment of that good and kind man, and the figure had lived in his imagination all through the years, making him more concerned to do good and more ashamed to do evil.

As for Laurel, she had been brought up in a proper Episcopalian family, and had learned all the Bible stories as a child. However her view might change as she grew older, they would continue to shine in her memory and to be a vital part of her culture. She had hundreds of names of persons and places in mind, each one connected with scenes and stories ; she had sung hymns about them, she had seen pictures of them, and few had been the days when some of them were not brought into her thoughts. The Holy Land ! And now here she was, actually treading its soil ! The faces, the costumes, the animals, the landscapes—everything was here, and it was like having your childhood come back to life.

They put up at the King David Hotel in Jerusalem, for of course you had to have the physical comforts, no matter where you went in your mind. Poverty and primitive life were fascinating to imagine and to employ as art subjects, but you wanted your orange juice cold and your toast hot in the morning and must not forget your waterproof coat when it rained. They engaged a dragoman, or guide, to show them the sights—it wouldn't do to go out on their own, for there was such a tangle of civilizations here, so many etiquettes and taboos, that they might have made a host of enemies without having the least idea of offending. They wanted to see the country as a preliminary to meeting anybody ; and there were dangers, even as there had been nineteen centuries ago.

The guide was an Arab, his name Hafiz. He was elderly and lean, and wore a red tarboosh and a not very clean white robe ; also a smile which was meant to be ingratiating, but unfortunately his teeth were bad. Lanny wondered if there was a school for dragomans, where they learned their elaborate discourses ; there wasn't a village, a ruin, a hill, or object of other sort about which he did not know everything and have a prepared spiel, with names, places, and dates—and this regardless of whether it was a Mohammedan, Hebrew, or Christian object. The tourists learned that it was best to let him reel it off, for if he was interrupted he would become disconcerted and unhappy. There was an etiquette for dragomans !

II

" Jerusalem the golden, with milk and honey blest ! " So ran the hymn which little Laurel had been taught to sing. Perhaps it was a heavenly Jerusalem, a transported and transmogrified Jerusalem which the poet had had in mind ; surely it could not have been this walled slum through which the American pair groped their way. They had travelled through China together, so the shock was reduced ; this was the mess out of which human civilization had climbed, and it was the same on all the continents of the Old World : narrow, crooked streets, many of them roofed, swarming with dirty, ragged people with many signs of disease ; camels, goats, and donkeys threading their way through the crowds and leaving their dung behind them ; children playing underfoot, the older ones following the foreign visitors and begging for baksheesh. Such was every " old town," all the way around the Mediterranean littoral.

They found it the same in the Arab quarters and the Jewish; the costumes and the language differed, but the poverty and the smells were alike. All the trades of primitive times were carried on in full view of the throngs. Workmen with their trousers rolled up trod the oil from sesame seed in vats, and in the next dark place a camel harnessed to a pole went round and round, working a press which squeezed olive oil from loads of the fruit; the camel had a hood over his face, so that he wouldn't see what he was doing, and might dream that he was out on the desert trails where he had been born. Next came an underground forge, where iron was heated and pounded out by hand—the method by which swords had been shaped and this land kept drenched with human blood for centuries beyond reckoning.

The bazaars were most of them mere booths, hung with sackcloth, offering bread and meat and fish and produce from the country. Nothing was ever sold without arguing; everything was pawed over, and the heavenly powers invoked against extortionate prices. Presumably the different tribes came to the shops where their words were understood; or perhaps they relied upon gestures, facial expressions, and the counting of fingers. So many human kinds were here, so many languages, faiths, customs, and costumes. The Jews wore round black hats and beards as long as nature made them; the dervishes wore tall felt caps; the Druses wrapped their heads in white cloths; the Turks wore red fezes and the Arabs their embroidered headgear. There were Syrians and Armenians; desert people in nondescript rags; peasants straight out of the Bible; and all the various religious orders—Coptic priests, Greek priests with black beards cut flat across the bottom, white-robed Dominicans, and brown-robed Franciscan friars. In the better streets one saw British troops in varied uniforms and a variety of people in European costumes.

Jerusalem has been destroyed and rebuilt many times. The dust of the centuries has settled over it, and new buildings have been erected on the ruins of the old, often with the old materials. Egyptians and Jebusites, Hebrews and Babylonians, Assyrians, Romans, Persians, Saracens, Crusaders—and now it was the British, holding power under a mandate of the League of Nations. Somebody had to keep order and forbid these fanatical tribes to squabble and tear one another to pieces. Also, in modern times, somebody had to guard oil pipe-lines for a great fleet.

There is a high wall which belongs to the Moslems ; it is supposed to have been a part of the Temple of Solomon, so the Jews have chosen it as a place to come and mourn for the departed glories of their nation. They come, mostly bearded old men, many having travelled from far places to this sacred spot ; they are so moved that the tears run down their cheeks as they kiss the stones. They sit before it and murmur, or they stand with open ritual books in hand and chant or recite or pray. Sometimes there will be hundreds of them, shouting in chorus, always, of course, in the sacred ancient Hebrew. Lanny read a translation of some of their liturgies : " For the palace that lies desolate, We sit in solitude and mourn. For the temple that is destroyed, We sit in solitude and mourn. For the walls that are overthrown," and so on and on. Laurel had heard such litanies recited in the Episcopal churches as a child and had joined in the responses. The only difference was that she had been praying for her own soul and its welfare, whereas these cries were for a nation. " We pray Thee, have mercy on Zion ! Gather the children of Jerusalem. Haste, haste, Redeemer of Zion ! Speak to the heart of Jerusalem."

Here at this Wailing Wall Lanny and Laurel got their first glimpse of the problem they had come to solve. Hafiz told them of the dispute which had arisen here only a few years ago. For some reason the Jews had taken up the idea of fastening pieces of matting to this holy wall. Why they wanted to do it Hafiz didn't know—he was too contemptuous of their nonsense ever to have asked. The wall was claimed by the Arabs, and they didn't want it defaced by hanging rags, so they had forbidden the practice. The Jews had persisted, so a wave of fanaticism had run through the two quarters and had been fanned to fury by agitators. There had been riots, and a number of people killed, and British troops had intervened. The dispute was carried to the League of Nations in Geneva, where bewildered elder statesmen, labouring unsuccessfully to stave off World War II, had to stop and listen to harangues in strange tongues on the subject of pieces of matting being hung on an ancient weed-grown wall.

It was necessary that the visitors should make a tour of the old city and inspect the various shrines which the dragoman had to show them. Each had its sacred associations, and Hafiz had a spiel which he reeled off. He was positive in every statement that he made : here was the portal through which Jesus had passed in entering the Temple, here was where He had sat in front of the Temple, here was where He had healed a leper, here was one of His footprints, miraculously preserved in stone. But Lanny could read in his Baedeker how, a hundred years after the death of Christ, the Romans had completely destroyed Jerusalem, ploughed its site over, and erected a new city with a new name and no Jews admitted. So he was sceptical about these venerated spots ; but there was no use hurting the feelings of their guide, and they let themselves be led down into ancient crypts and through tunnels which had been excavated by modern archæologists. The Bible events might not have happened in this or that particular chamber, but they had surely happened somewhere in the neighbourhood. To a modern political investigator what mattered was not where they had happened, but where living people believed they had happened, and were ready to fly at one another's throats to defend their beliefs.

III

The tourists also wished to see the country. This required a car, and the dragoman said it would be easy to hire one, but difficult indeed to get gasoline in wartime. Lanny had a secret to which he would not refer even by a smile ; he went to the address the O.S.S. had given him and presented the engraved visiting card reading " Mr. Franklin Delano Roosevelt " and commending the bearer to favour. Matters were quickly arranged with the British so that the President's friend could buy what he needed. Incidentally, he was warned that native drivers were apt to be reckless of their own lives as well as of their passengers', so he rented a car to drive himself. To arrange that he had to deposit cash in a bank. It appeared that in this Holy Land men did not trust one another so readily as in more secular places.

They set out, with Hafiz riding in the back and delivering

his speeches as if addressing a large audience. The highways were few but good, having been built by the British for war purposes. Eastward was the Dead Sea, only fifteen miles distant; the route was downhill all the way, that sea being the lowest place on the globe, the deepest depression in the earth's crust. It has no outlet—the rivers flow into it from all sides and the water sinks into the sand. It is a kettle of salt some fifty miles long and ten miles across, and a commercial concern was engaged in extracting potash on a great scale.

Palestine is a tiny country, not much bigger than the state of Vermont, and all its history has been crowded together. At the northern end of the Dead Sea the River Jordan flows in, and they drove northward along its bank. On the way the dragoman told them that tourists, coming in great numbers before the war, had been accustomed to collect water of the river in bottles and take it home to be used in baptizing their posterity. Just now the river was yellow with mud, it being the rainy season, and Lanny did not collect his share. He and his wife had heard the singing of spirituals about crossing over Jordan, but they could look across and see that the same tamarisks and poplars grew on the east side as on the west. There were bridges by which they might have crossed, but beyond were only the Moabite hills of Transjordan, and no cities with streets paved with gold.

A couple of hours' drive up the river brought them to the Sea of Galilee, where they watched fishermen hauling their nets. This really moved them both, because their interest was in human beings, and these were without doubt the authentic types which had been doing that same work nineteen centuries ago. Lanny could not talk to them, except through a bad interpreter; but he wondered, if he had known their Syrian Arabic dialect, and had told them to leave their work and follow him, would they have obeyed? A well-dressed European in a motor-car, he could no doubt have offered money and obtained their services; but could he have won them without pay, and for a doctrine, a cause? He might have said, " I know a way to end poverty and war upon this earth, and it is only a question of persuading people to understand and follow." But could he have got them to believe him?

The difference was that Jesus had spoken in the name of God, and modern men had lost that habit. Lanny had prayed only when he was in deep distress ; but now, standing on this historic shore, and recalling his deep emotions when he had first read the story of Simon and Andrew, and of James and John, the sons of Zebedee, he found himself aware that the men of his time had lost something important from their lives.

The tourist couple did not stop to make any Socialist converts. They drove a few miles to the town of Nazareth, and enjoyed a good lunch at an inn kept by an English woman. Then they drove about this collection of white stone buildings spread out on a hill slope, and looked at places with legends and traditions which you were free to accept if it gave you pleasure. There was the church where the Annunciation had taken place, the cave in which Joseph had worked, the table at which Jesus had eaten, the well to which Mary had gone. The only one of these which seemed plausible was the well, for these do not change through the ages, and if filled up with debris can be cleaned out again. This will be done whether it be Crusaders or Saracens, Beibars or Allenbys who have conquered the district.

What struck the tourists about this tiny land was its resemblance to the much more extensive land which they had visited only recently. Except for the buildings, and the costumes and speech of the people, they would have thought they were in Southern California. The climate was the same —rainy in winter and entirely dry in summer, blazing hot when the sun shone and nearly always cool at night. There is a joke about Los Angeles weather being always " unusual," and it was the same here, for the combination of sea, desert, and mountains frequently caused the winds to box the compass in the course of twenty-four hours. Most of the hills were bare ; the fig, the orange, and the olive grew only where they were planted and irrigated. The mountains were not high, and when you came down from them toward the Mediterranean it was like the San Gabriel plain.

This was the promised land, the land of Canaan, the land flowing with milk and honey. " In the same day the Lord made a covenant with Abram, saying, Unto thy seed have I given this land, from the river of Egypt unto the great river,

V

The travellers went back to Jerusalem, paid off their guide, and settled down to their secret task. The first step was to establish themselves as art experts, and to this end they presented letters they had brought and began inquiries as to what there was in the ancient city which might be purchasable and worth purchasing. Mostly it was the Jews with whom they would deal, for the Prophet of Islam had forbidden his followers to make images—this in order to save them from idol worship. Apparently he had been right—if you had art you would have idols. The innumerable statues and paintings of madonnas and saints which the Catholics had in their shrines were idols in some senses. The Mohammedans, forbidden to have paintings and statues, worshipped shrines and tombs and two hairs from the beard of their Prophet—they were here in the Mosque of Omar, kept in a golden box and exhibited to true believers on special occasions. Here, also, was the stone from which Mohammed had ascended into heaven.

The dealers had things to sell and were prepared, in oriental fashion, to spend a long time bargaining. Lanny, who had purchased carved doorways and fountains for ablutions in Algeria and Morocco, understood this game. He knew that as soon as he made his wants known, the word would spread all the way from Dan to Beersheba, and his door would be besieged by those who possessed treasures, ancient or modern. He would be polite to them all, inspect what they had and hear their stories—mostly untrue. He would ask the price and hint that it was somewhat high; he would promise to think the matter over, and then in the most tactful way would lead the conversation to what they had observed of conditions in this historic land. The time was so tense, the feeling so high, that no man, regardless of his race, religion, and occupation, could help having ideas and explaining them to an important lady and gentleman from the richest and most powerful of nations. Lanny and his wife would listen, and after the visitor had gone they would compare impressions and make notes.

That was the way to work, quietly and unobtrusively, without giving offence to anyone. It appeared that there were not merely dealers, but persons of wealth who had fine homes with *objets d'art* which they were happy to show to an American expert. In this polyglot city were Jews and Gentiles from all parts of the world ; there were innumerable social sets, military, official, commercial, religious, and just plain idle rich who liked the climate and had fled here to get away from the war. Once you had drunk coffee with them, or visited their homes, they would pour out stories of the mess the world was in—and particularly this small corner which had been " promised " to too many different people.

It wasn't as easy to meet the Arabs as the Jews. The Arabs kept to themselves, and few of them aspired to be thought of as cosmopolitan or sophisticated ; they had peculiar notions and customs, which called for special tact. But Lanny's stepfather in Marrakech had obtained for him a letter of introduction to a Moorish rug merchant who had established himself in Jerusalem and become a financial supporter of the Pan-Islam movement. Lanny called upon him in his fine shop —Laurel staying at home, since in the Moslem world the ladies do not take part in business or political discussions. Lanny managed to down a cup of what in that world is called coffee, a very sweet and thick brown paste, and told this gentleman about his researches into Moorish architecture and archæology, his father's former activities in the New England-Arabian Oil Company, and, more especially, his stepfather's researches into Mohammedan literature and practices bearing upon religious healing.

This black-bearded merchant, who wore a red fez and a white linen robe in his shop, was immensely interested to meet a Nazrany—a follower of the Prophet of Nazareth—who had actually read the words of Allah's greatest prophet and understood them. Lanny told how he had met Adolf Hitler, whose propagandists had succeeded in making him something of a hero to the Mohammedan world ; and how the Führer had taken him to his secret retreat on the top of the Kehlstein, near Berchtesgaden, and there had revealed his great admiration for the Arab camel driver who had known how to found a religion and make it stick for a dozen centuries. Lanny, of course, said that he was not a political person of any sort, but a lover of peace and a student of mankind's great teachers and prophets through the ages. He knew that Mohammed had recognized both Moses and Jesus as God-inspired, and had advocated a union of the entire Semitic world, including the Jews. Why could it not even now be brought about, the swords beaten into ploughshares and the tanks converted into tractors ?

The rug merchant opened up and told the grievances of his race against both Jews and Christians. Afterward he told his friends about this just and considerate Frankish person—this name meaning not that Lanny had lived most of his life in France, but that the Moslems still remembered the Crusaders ; through a freak of language, Frankish and frank meant the opposite. But the son of Budd-Erling was both, and the merchant invited him to his home to meet his friends—all men, of course. Later, when the friendship had become established, Laurel was invited to meet the ladies, and so had an interesting story about women under a religious system which allowed four wives to every man who could afford such a luxury. What did these women think about the world that was for ever at war and for ever demanding that their sons be thrown into the slaughter pit ? Like all the other women whom Laurel had met—in America, England, France, Germany, China, and the Soviet Union—she found them convinced that it was the evil nature and intention of other peoples and governments which made it necessary for the sons of women to be armed and drilled.

VI

After a couple of weeks the travellers moved down to Tel-Aviv. This was an even more interesting city, for here were the intellectuals, the specialists, and professional men who were providing plans for the building of a new-old nation. Architects and engineers, scientists, agriculturists, teachers —trained mostly in America—they were alert, full of enthusiasm, and all had political and social ideas to impart to friendly guests. They were too polite to ask how it came about that an art expert could bring his wife on a holiday jaunt through or into a war zone. No doubt they knew enough about America to take it for granted that the son of a great airplane manufacturer would enjoy special privileges. Anyhow, here the couple were, and they wanted to see everything and listen to everybody's ideas, and nothing gives more pleasure to the propagandist type of mind.

To Lanny this was a holiday, to be compared only with his visit to Yenan in Red China. For the past decade, with that single exception, he had been obliged to conceal his real beliefs and feelings, to avoid the people he liked and associate with those whom he despised. But here he was in the company of young Socialists, men and women who were working all day and studying or discussing modern ideas most of the night. They were building the New Jerusalem—not in England's green and pleasant land as William Blake had called for, but in their own racial heritage, the Promised Land of their history and their religion. They were combining the very oldest and the very newest in culture, the messages of their ancient prophets with the tools and techniques of modern science. They had a nation in their hands, and were shaping it and seeing it grow day by day.

Co-operation was their keynote. One young couple got into the car with the Americans and shepherded them on another drive to the Dead Sea. Their goal was one of the *Kibbutzim*, the collective farms, which had been established in that most unpromising region, twelve hundred feet below sea-level and with a climate hotter in summer than Arizona. More than a hundred persons had come here, pledged to carry out their biblical formula of making the desert blossom like the rose. The soil was saturated with alkalis and had to be washed before anything would grow in it ; by prodigious labour they had diverted the waters of the Jordan to this purpose, and now were planting bananas, and also growing carp in ponds which the river filled for them. The members of the co-operative got no wages, but lived like the early Christians, having all things save women in common. Half their members worked in the potash plant nearby and brought their wages to pay the interest on the debt incurred for building materials and tools.

The co-operatives had ancient Hebrew names, and this one was Bet Haarava, which means " House of the Wilderness." Lanny and Laurel sat at one of the long wooden tables in the communal dining-hall and partook of a lunch consisting of buttermilk, whole-wheat bread, and the young onions and radishes which are the first-fruits of any agricultural enterprise. He pleased his hosts by quoting those immortal words of the Prophet Isaiah, which have long had their place in Socialist textbooks. He and Laurel told about what they had seen in Yenan, where the same kind of young people were trying the same communal life ; only it was a cold climate, and the Chinese were living in caves, and did not have plentiful water. The texts they quoted were not from Amos and Isaiah, but from their founder, Sun Yat-sen, and their ancient philosopher, Wang An-shih. There had been some twenty thousand workers in Yenan, and Lanny was told that there were already thirty thousand in the agricultural co-operatives of Palestine.

VII

Wherever you talked with these people, in the meeting places of the workers or the drawing-rooms of the well-to-do, there was never any difficulty in guiding the conversation to international and inter-racial affairs. The world was being rent by the most dreadful of all wars, and the task of keeping this nascent nation alive through the storm was one which engaged the attention of every man and woman in it. The Jews were in a state of agony over what was happening to their brethren in Central Europe ; fugitives were continuing to put in appearance, telling ever more frightful tales—the most merciless slaughter of a race in recent times and perhaps in all history. To save as many as possible was the desire of every Jew, and it was hard indeed for them to face the fact that the British government and military would not permit them to admit and care for the refugees. And this is how they argued.

According to the so-called Balfour Declaration, issued before World War I, the Jews were to be permitted to establish their homeland in Palestine. Why had the British backed down and violated this pledge ? The answer was written plain for all the world to read—written in a substance that was thick and black and greasy, and very difficult to erase. Every Jew, and also every Arab, knew that the oil from the great Mosul field, British-owned, was pumped through a pipe-line across the deserts of Transjordan to the port of Haifa, on the Mediterranean near the top of Palestine. To that port came a constant stream of tankers, and the oil was essential to the operation of the British Navy, the British Merchant Marine, and even British industry at home.

Jewish immigration had stirred up the Arabs and led to the forming of the Arab League and the financing of a swarm of agitators, calling for united action by the seven states which made up the Arab world. First Mussolini and then Hitler had taken up this cause, proclaiming themselves near-Moslems and friends of all followers of the Prophet. That, no doubt, was why Adi Schicklgruber had taken the son of Budd-Erling up to his mountain hideout and there informed him that he considered the one-time camel driver the greatest man who had lived, prior to Adi himself. Anything whatever that would cripple the British Empire and enable Adi to get down to the Mediterranean and the Dardanelles ahead of Stalin !

Now the issue was being decided by war, and all the Jews with whom Lanny talked wanted the Allies to win ; but there were a few who could not see very far and hated the enemy who was nearest to them. The British were here, governing in their rather cold impersonal way. In order to keep from driving the Arabs to frenzy and causing them to destroy the pipe-lines, British officials had to keep Jewish refugees from pouring into Palestine. These refugees came in wretched tubs, likely to fall to pieces in the first storm ; the passengers would try to get ashore, even by swimming ; and what a hideous thing to send them back to sea with no destination—and after having caught a glimpse of the land which the Lord their God had given them !

So a wartime truce was being broken, and there was an underground war between the British troops and a Zionist organization called the Irgun. Some refugees were always getting in, and the Arabs took note of that, and their agitators fanned the flames of hatred. A complicated situation indeed ! Lanny Budd talked to these different kinds of people and heard their arguments ; he did not try to answer, but said that it was all very complicated and troubling to a foreigner. A young Jewish engineer, no fanatic but a man of science, compared it to the situation between the Indians and the white settlers on the American continent. The Arabs were a primitive people, ignorant and helpless, with a culture many centuries out of date; the Jews brought machinery and machine techniques, and modern knowledge of a thousand sorts. Was it not in the interest of progress that they should replace the inferior culture?

Lanny assented, but pointed out that the Americans had come to be troubled in conscience over the way they had treated the Indians, and that you could not do in the twentieth century what your forefathers had done in the sixteenth and seventeenth. To this the Jew answered that his people were prepared to grant the Arabs full political rights and all the benefits of education. The trouble was, the Arabs didn't want to be educated, at least not in modern ideas; they were content to have their children sit on a dirt floor and scratch fleas and learn to recite texts out of the Koran which had no remotest relationship to modern life.

Lanny, trying to draw the man out, said that he had seen Jewish boys at school in Poland under precisely the same conditions, only the book from which they were learning was the Talmud instead of the Koran. Yes, that was true, the other admitted; but modern Jews had a different sort of education and the Palestine they built would be different from the old.

There were at the time about a million Arabs in Palestine, as against a half-million Jews; therefore, in a democratic state, the Arabs should have been able to keep control. But when you talked to the Arabs you found they were afraid of the superior ability and aggressiveness of their rivals; the Jews could talk faster, think faster, act faster. Moreover, they had money coming in from the outside world, and money was power; just as it was buying up the land, so it could buy up elections, and the control of public opinion. The Arabs felt that the immigration that was going on was an artificial thing, and was unfair; a few more years of it, and the Arabs would be a minority, reduced to the status of labourers and serfs.

VIII

So ran the arguments, pro and con. Most of the young Jews Lanny met were Socialists where they were not Communists,

and one and all they pointed out that political affairs did not
work out in modern states as they had formerly. Give Palestine
self-government, and wait a few years for the issues to be
clarified, and you would not find Jews voting against Arabs,
you would find propertyless Jews and Arabs voting against
well-to-do Jews and Arabs. That was true everywhere, as
soon as the people began to realize their true interests. In
New York you didn't find Jews voting against Gentiles ; in
Detroit and Chicago you didn't find Negroes voting against
whites ; all over the North you found New Deal Jews and
Negroes and whites voting against reactionaries of the same
races.

But the trouble was, you couldn't tell that to the Arabs :
few of them had ever heard of either Socialism or the New Deal.
The Arabs held it as their creed that everything was predeter-
mined by Allah, and that there was no use trying to change
anything. They lived under a primitive tribal regime, in which
the sheiks and their relatives and friends absorbed all the
surplus value and left the masses hungry, ragged, and sunk
in superstition. All that immense wealth which the British
and American oil companies paid for drilling and pipe-line
concessions went to kings and shahs and regents, and was spent
for palaces and motor-cars, jewels and banquets ; the toiling
masses got little or no benefit from it.

Such was the East, which Rudyard Kipling had said would
never meet the West, but he was turning out to be a poor
prognosticator. Right here in the land of Canaan East and
West were meeting every hour, and the whole community was
in turmoil caused thereby. They were meeting in China, and
in India, and even in the far Pacific islands, where black men
and brown were getting to know G.I.'s, and riding in tractors
and jeeps, and having their thoughts turned upside-down by
radios and gramophones and motion pictures. The new was
replacing the old because it had more intelligence, because it
could understand the old, whereas the old could not understand
the new—or if it did it became the new. That was a world
process, and the only problem was to keep the old from
destroying the new by sheer physical force and animal cunning
—something which had happened in Italy, Germany, and
Spain.

Lanny and Laurel could observe the fires of fanaticism smouldering in this tiny stretch of land and ready to burst into flame at the slightest breath. Wandering about in the Mosque of Omar, supposedly built on the site of Solomon's Temple, they had observed the Moslems at their prayers and had stopped to watch ; they had observed that the worshippers were becoming restless, casting side glances at the strangers and muttering to one another. The dragoman had nudged the couple and whispered that they should move on. Under the British law they had a right to be there—with big canvas overshoes on their feet, so as not to pollute the sanctuary ; but the Moslems believed that their prayers were rendered ineffective by the presence of unbelieving dogs, and if the dogs had insisted upon staying, they might have started a *jehad*, a holy war, that January afternoon.

It was the same when you went out into the country and met the desert Arabs—black, filthy, and covered with gunny sacking almost falling off them in rags. Lanny and Laurel met a band of them, a wedding procession escorting a thirteen-year-old girl ; they were dancing, singing, shouting in excitement. The tourists thought it would be safe to stop and watch this scene ; but instantly the band forsook their child bride and surrounded the motor-car, screaming for baksheesh. Hafiz had warned them never to give anything, for the crowd would only clamour for more. They must reply sternly, " *Imshi !* " —which means literally, " It is nothing," and is presumably the Arabic equivalent of the American " Nothing doing." Laurel was frightened, and both of them did their best to appear fierce ; but Lanny had to start the car and pretend that he meant to run over these wild people before they would give way. Again it was the East ; to the nomads another form of bargaining, in which generosity is taken for weakness and regarded with contempt.

IX

The two explorers had been sent not merely to observe these phenomena, but to advise what should or could be done about them ; and so, each night before they slept, they spent an hour discussing what they had seen and what they made of it. The longer they stayed, the more clearly they realized the complexities of this problem. It would be hard indeed to persuade the Arabs to dwell in unity with the Jews in a democratically controlled state ; also, there were many Christians, Roman Catholics, Eastern or Byzantine Catholic, Armenian, Coptic, and even some Protestant sects who were scarcely less unwilling. Jerusalem was the Holy City of all these groups ; they had their shrines here, and the trouble was, so many of them wanted the same shrines, and to decorate them with their own kind of tinsel and jewels, and perform their own kind of exclusive rites in front of them.

The founders of all these groups had been men of peace and worshippers of one God, whatever name they gave him. Lanny never failed to remind the Mohammedans that their Prophet had recognized both Moses and Jesus, and he reminded the Christians that Jesus had told His disciples that the Gospel must be published to all nations ; He had taught love and forbearance, and His commands were read in all the churches. But, alas, it is far more difficult to hunger and thirst after righteousness than it is to repeat a formula or to wear a charm or to make a magical sign on your chest or forehead. He had said that when you prayed you should enter into your closet and shut the door and pray to your Father in secret ; but, again, it is so much easier to let some priest do it for you, and to drop a coin in a collection box for his hire. St. Paul had warned that the letter killeth, and the spirit giveth life ; but it is so hard to be kind and just, and so easy to bury yourself in the study of ancient texts, and to become learned in the interpretations of this or that church father, or pope, or learned doctor of the law.

So all these groups, the three great monotheistic religions which had become the bases of Western civilization, had hardened and become dogma-ridden ; they had forgotten mercy and become brotherhood, and had become the means of livelihood for ecclesiastical establishments, and, worse yet, a means whereby the propertied classes kept the poor contented with their lot. Every Church organization fought for its own, and made a virtue out of excluding the others ; so Jerusalem, the Holy City of God, had become a cauldron of seething hatreds, a nest of vipers—even worse, for vipers do not sting one another. Here as elsewhere Lanny observed that it was the young Socialists, many of whom called themselves materialists, who were preaching peace and reconciliation, and it was the Grand Mufti of Jerusalem who was proclaiming a holy war throughout all the Arab world. The rabbis and the priests passed one another on the streets and glared with hatred hardly to be restrained.

Lanny spent an evening with Rabbi Judah Magnes, who had been head of the richest congregation in New York City, and was now President of the Hebrew University in Jerusalem. A rare spirit and an independent thinker, he pointed out that there was a precedent for a multilingual free nation in the case of Switzerland, where people of German, French, and Italian descent had managed to live together in peace for six or seven centuries. He maintained that the partition plan so widely recommended would be ruinous, because every section of the chopped-up land would have its discontented minorities. First of all, there must be education in tolerance. Said he, " The very idea of compromise—the word itself—has been made abhorrent to too many of the inhabitants of this little land. Their political education has not yet taught them that political compromise is the very breath of life of the Western democracies."

Lanny wrote a report once a week, telling what he had observed, and making it short for the busiest man in the world to read. According to orders, he sealed these reports and turned them over to the American Consul, to go in a diplomatic pouch by air mail. He gave his conclusions as he arrived at them : that after the war there would have to be some sort of international government to control the hostile forces throughout Palestine and the district immediately surrounding it. Either that, or there would surely be a civil war. The same thing was true of many strategic points on the globe— Trieste, for example, and the Dardanelles, not to mention China and India and the East Indies. There would have to be some international organization, a revived League of Nations, with real powers to prevent civil wars and to keep the peace in areas where rival claims were not especially hot. " Either that," wrote the P.A., " or we have got nothing out of the war."

X

All this time Laurel was making notes, of a different sort and for a different purpose ; some day she would write stories about Palestine, fact stories and fiction based on the facts. Landscapes and buildings, costumes, faces, and the tragic and touching episodes which people told her, all were being stored away for future use.   The impressions of a mature woman were being mingled with those of a child—for before she was old enough to read there had been read to her a book called " The Story of the Bible," profusely illustrated with drawings of this Holy Land and its people, their flocks and herds and tents and temples.   Such impressions are indelible, and now, day after day, Laurel's own childhood and that of the Jewish people were mingled with the present and the guessed-at future.

Manifestly, her subconscious mind would be deeply involved in all this ; and Lanny had suggested that they try a séance. They tried two or three, but nothing of interest came.   Then, just as they were getting ready to leave—the early springtime was spreading over this storied land—they had a strange experience.   It developed that Madame Zyszynski had travelled with them to Palestine, by whatever means of transportation these psychic entities use, and here she declared that she was sitting on a hillside in bright sunshine, and on the top of the ridge, outlined against the sky, was a small flock of sheep, tended by a half-grown boy.   As it happened, that was exactly the view which Lanny and Laurel had commented upon that morning, standing at the window of a little inn on the outskirts of the Galilean village of Capernaum ; so Lanny was not greatly impressed.   He said politely, " Could you speak to the boy, Madame, and ask who he is ? "

The boy was too far away, the old woman answered ; but perhaps he could come to her.   Presently she said that he was standing by her side ; he was rather tall and thin, had a staff in his hand, and black hair which hung to his shoulders.   That was the way Lanny had pictured the Robin boys in his fancy, and he wondered if he had ever told that to Madame.   He said, " Ask him his name," and she replied, " He speaks, but it is a strange language and I cannot understand a word."

Very baffling; after a few tries Lanny suggested, " Try pointing to him repeatedly and perhaps he will give his name." Madame tried that and reported, " He says ' Peretz.' " Lanny said, " I don't know what language that name belongs to. Speak to him one word at a time, and perhaps he will do the same, and I will write it down."

Laurel was lying on the bed in her trance, and Lanny was sitting by the bedside with a dim light, making notes with a pad and pencil as he always did. The voice which came from Laurel's lips began to speak strange syllables one by one, and Lanny wrote the way they sounded, hurriedly, and without any idea what the language might be. " *Ani Peretz ben Jehuda,*" he wrote; and then, " *M'shephet Jehuda.*" This went on for several minutes and Lanny recorded every sound he heard. He couldn't ask any questions—at least not until Madame stopped speaking. Finally she said, " The boy waved his hand and called his dog and now he has faded away."

" Have you any idea where you are, Madame ? " inquired the observer.

" No," she replied, " but it's a different land and it's warm. I feel that I know it very well, but I don't know how."

" Could it be the Bible land, where Christ lived ? "

" It might be that ; I cannot tell."

" You don't know how you came to be here ? "

" I came because I wanted to be with you. You know that I promised to come whenever I could."

" Can you stay a while now ? "

" No, because your wife is tired ; she is complaining that she has no more power."

Sure enough, Laurel had begun to moan, and that was always the end. She came out of her trance ; and this time Lanny could tell her everything that had happened. He read over the strange syllables to her, and she exclaimed, " Did I really speak all that ? And can it be a language ? "

XI

Lanny had read of numerous cases of persons in a trance who had spoken languages which they had never known or heard ; it was a common phenomenon—but no matter how much you may have read, it gave you a thrill when you came upon it in the flesh, or, to be more accurate, in the atmosphere activated by flesh. They went to the Hebrew University in Jerusalem, and Lanny introduced himself to a scholar connected with the library, an elderly gentleman with a black beard turning grey. Lanny didn't say, " My wife is a psychic medium and spoke these words in a trance." No, for he didn't want to attract attention to himself, and possibly get his name in the newspapers ; he was still a secret agent, and the first word in his code was silence. He said, " I wrote down these syllables at the dictation of a little shepherd boy out in the country. I wonder if you can tell me what they mean."

The grave old gentleman took the paper and glanced at it. A look of great surprise came upon his face. " But this is ancient Hebrew ! " he exclaimed.

" Indeed ! " said Lanny, and did not have to pretend his own emotion.

" This phrasing has not been used by our people for many centuries, Mr. Budd. Where was this boy ? "

" He was on the road to Capernaum. I did not make any special note of the place. What do the words mean ? "

" ' I am Peretz, son of Jehuda. We are of the tribe of Jehuda. We are descendants of Abraham. We have seven sheep and eleven goats. I have a twin brother.' " And so on. " That is really a very strange thing, Mr. Budd."

" Perhaps the boy heard the words in a school, sir."

" They are not words that would be taught in any school. They sound like a boy's conversation. In English it would be Phares, son of Judas, and we have such a person in our Book of Genesis ; there is a story about him—that he was the first-born of a pair of twins, and the midwife tied a red string upon his wrist when he was the first to emerge from the womb. The name means ' the breach.' That was well over three thousand years ago, according to our reckoning."

" Very curious," remarked this unimpressionable American. " We must suppose that the lad was told the story in his Sabbath school, and perhaps had been required to compose a dialogue as an exercise in Hebrew."

" It must be," said the learned gentleman. " But it is not what we do in our schools and it seems hard to believe."

Lanny wrote the translation in his notebook. He wanted to learn all he could about this Peretz, alias Phares, and in the library he obtained an English Bible and a Concordance. It took but a moment to learn that the ancient one was named in the New Testament as well as in the Old. As Pharez, son of Judas, he was in that long line of ancestors who had been listed for Jesus by both Matthew and Luke, and listed differently—thus providing ammunition for the scoffers. It had seemed strange indeed to Tom Paine and Robert Ingersoll that a man who had been miraculously conceived should have had his paternal ancestry traced back through an earthly father to Jacob and Abraham.

But Lanny was on the trail of a different mystery from that. They tried one more séance before leaving Palestine, but this time it was the over-sophisticated international banker who came upon the scene, demanding to know what the devil they were doing in this unlikely place. He didn't know anything about the shepherd boy out of ancient Judea, and when Lanny told him the story he exclaimed, " Really, I don't see how you can believe such foolishness ! It is unworthy of an educated man."

BOOK SEVEN

HUMANITY WITH ALL ITS FEARS

19

Lull Before Storm

I

FROM Palestine Lanny had written a letter to Captain Denis de Bruyne, who had been fighting at the front in Italy. He had received a reply, telling him that Denis was in Algiers, wounded again, this time severely. Lanny and Laurel planned their return trip by way of that city, so that Lanny might visit the *capitaine*, also Robert Murphy, and other friends he had made there. He was in no hurry, for his report had gone in and he had nothing to add to it except anecdotes and sociability.

First Cairo. They took a trip up the Nile to see the Pyramids and the Sphinx ; they were driven along the banks of the river and permitted the driver to show them the precise clump of bulrushes in which the infant Moses had been found by the Egyptian princess ; they explored excavated tombs, and in the great museum in the city inspected the relics of the Pharaohs. They might have seen as interesting specimens in the Metropolitan Museum of Art, but they hadn't found time in busy New York. They rode on camels, and Lanny forbore to say that he had ever done this before ; he kept all his misadventures to himself, for there was no use supplying his wife's imagination with fuel.

When friends meet in strange places, they always remark that it is a small world. They forget that they make it small by promoting more and more travel. This war had shrunk the world to the dimensions of an Air Force officers' club. The P.A. seldom stopped at an airport without meeting some man whom he had chatted with in some far place, Hollywood or Hongkong, Bermuda or Belém. This time it was the banks of the River Thames in Buckinghamshire ; there came striding through the lobby of the picturesque Shepheard's Hotel a British officer in khaki shorts and shirt with wings over the pocket and the desert tan on his arms and legs ; an officer extremely young and what the British call " leggy," meaning that he hadn't had time to fill out his sudden growth. When Lanny had last seen him he had been a schoolboy, punting on the river while a girl read some modern poetry to him ; she had read some to Lanny and he had wondered what the deuce it was about, but had been too polite to say so. Evidently words are wonderful things in themselves, and if you string enough of them together they exercise an intoxicating effect upon the young.

This was one of the grandsons of Sir Alfred Pomeroy-Nielson, Bart., and they called him " Scrubbie," for what reason Lanny hadn't inquired. Here he was, bubbling with delight to meet this old friend of the family. He was only nineteen, but what a story he had to tell ! He had been wild to get into the " show," and already at his age had been all the way through and come out at the far end ; they had grounded him, because he had been on the maximum number of missions permitted to anybody. Beastly stupid, because he was quite fit, but all he could do now was to train others. He had piloted a bomber on that mission to wipe out the Ploesti oil-fields in Rumania ; few had come back unscathed. Oil-fields had proved unexpectedly tough targets ; but they had cut the German production by at least half for the present.

This sprig of the aristocracy wasn't the typical Englishman, who is supposed to cultivate reticence as the greatest of dignities, and to discuss his military exploits only in monosyllables. At lunch Scrubbie told these Americans everything they wanted to hear ; not merely what he himself had experienced, but what this wonderful Combined Air Force was achieving against the foe. They had got together under one command, and without rivalry or jealousy were giving everything they had. Now there were magnificent bases in Sicily and Italy ; Egypt was becoming a training centre, far behind the front. The driving back of Rommel had been an airmen's

job, and they were going to do the same all over Europe ; more
and more were getting ready, all around the perimeter. The
Budd-Erling was the world's wonder, and Lanny promised to
pass that information on to his father.

Also, of course, talk about home. Lanny explained that he
had taken his little daughter to America, and so didn't get to
England as often as previously. The bomber pilot had been
home for a couple of weeks' leave and reported that the Pater
was working hard at his writing jobs. Alfy had got caught in
a " tip and run " raid on an airfield in Hell's Corner, and had
got laid up but was all right again. There was a lot of talk
about the Germans having a new weapon, a flying bomb, and
did Lanny know when it was coming ? Lanny knew more than
he was free to tell.

II

From Cairo to Tripoli, a city where Mussolini had built
monuments to his glory, and which now the British were well
pleased with. From there to Algiers, a city which the French
had taken from the Moors and now called a part of *la France
métropolitaine* ; a city like all the others on the Mediterranean
shore, with an Old Town of wretched slums crowded with the
poor, and suburban streets with modern apartment houses for
the middle class, and up on the slopes overlooking the sea
magnificent estates with villas and palaces for the rich. They
became rich because they owned the productive land and the
natural resources and the means of manufacturing and transportation ; they stayed rich because they had " inherited that
good part." Lanny Budd, who moved freely among them,
didn't point this out, because they wouldn't have liked it and
he would no longer have been able to hear their conversation ;
instead he told them that they were elegant and gracious and
possessed exceptionally good taste, and that he knew where
there was a remarkably fine Ingres or Renoir or whatever
would go well over their dining-room mantel.

Lanny's first duty was to see Denis *fils*, in one of the hotels
which had been taken over as a war hospital. Lanny didn't
take his wife, giving the excuse that Denis wouldn't feel free
to talk about military affairs in her presence ; the real reason
was, he wanted to tell the *capitaine* about having met Denis

père, in Paris, and also the news about his younger brother. Lanny found the Frenchman pale and wan, having got a severe thigh wound from an exploding shell ; his life had been saved by blood transfusions. Now he would have to be a desk man, he remarked sadly ; but he had done his little bit to redeem the honour of *la patrie*. Had Lanny heard about the fine record which General Giraud's men had been making all the way up the eastern coast of Italy ? Yes, Lanny had heard it ; they were all doing well, even the American Japanese, the Nisei, who had the special motive of proving themselves Americans and wiping out the shame of Pearl Harbour.

Lanny told about his meeting with the father, and the messages which the aged man had sent to his sons. There was nothing that either Lanny or the younger Denis could do about the situation. Lanny hadn't been able to see the *capitaine's* wife and children, and could only pass on the word of the *père* that they were alive and well. As to the younger brother, it was odd indeed that he was staying in Lanny's old home in Juan-les-Pins. " Taking care of it ! " Denis said. " We all know how troops take care of things ; but no doubt Charlot will do his best. He is a conscientious fellow, even though his ideas are so cruelly perverted."

Poor Denis ! He couldn't get it out of his head that if only he could get a chance to talk with his beloved younger brother, he could bring that lost sheep back into the fold. The *capitaine* brooded over it all the time. He was so sure that he was right in co-operating with the Americans, and so unable to conceive of any reason why a Frenchman should co-operate with the Nazis ! Lanny took the part of the devil's advocate for the nonce, explaining the younger man's idea that the only victors in this war would be the Russian Reds, and that the French people would find that they had laid themselves open to the march of revolutionary Communism. Charlot had explained this in detail to Lanny, and Denis now explained why it wouldn't necessarily be that way. But convincing Lanny was not the same thing as convincing Charlot.

Lanny said, " I'm not telling any secret, but just guessing that before this year is over we shall be landing somewhere on the Riviera. I could be useful to the Army in that locale which I know by heart, and I am hugging the idea that I may get an assignment to help prepare the way. If so, I may drop in on Charlot at Bienvenu and have another argument."

The elder's reply was, " Do for God's sake keep him out of the hands of the French, for they will certainly shoot him. There could be no other verdict ! "

III

In his capacity as presidential agent Lanny Budd had made many acquaintances in Algiers. He had made them among groups both rich and poor ; he had made them among those who had ardently desired the American landing and among those who had guessed that it was coming and had jumped to be on the winning side. Among the former was the Jewish physician, Dr. Aboulker, and his two sons, who had made their home the headquarters of the youth group, the Chantiers de la Jeunesse, which had seized the city government and held most of it until the Army had got ashore. They had risked their lives, and now they found that they were completely out of everything ; no one paid any attention to them—unless it was the police spies. The elderly crippled doctor had been kept under detention for some time.

Those who were in power were the rich, the big business group which had been exploiting the colony, and were so close to Fascism that it would have required an expert to find the dividing line. Now they had all changed their colour ; they were all for General de Gaulle's formula of " liberation first and then liberty." " Big Charlie " had at last succeeded in his long struggle with General Giraud, and was now the head of both army and government. The French trusted him, but Lanny felt sure that in his heart he had no idea but to restore the old Catholic, military, autocratic France. His creed was very close to that of Marshal Pétain, except that surrender to the Germans was excluded from this picture.

This was the sort of government the American Army wanted in order to win the war quickly, and it was the sort they would want after the war, with no nonsense from reformers and crackpots. The big business men were those who got things done; they were the men the "big brass" dealt with in Washington, and whom they understood and liked. In Washington they had fine homes and gave elaborate parties, and in North Africa it had turned out to be no different. Lanny and his wife were invited to a soirée at the home of the French General Juin, who had married an Algerian heiress and lived up on the heights in an ancient Arab villa, large in size, square in shape, and yellow in colour. The visitors bought proper clothes in order that they might appear at this and other functions ; they met a wealthy provincial hostess, who had been so anti-American that Lanny had been warned against her. Americans in her eyes were democratic, they were enemies of property, Jew-lovers and even Freemasons !

But now all that was water over the dam ; the lady was all smiles and charms, all pearls and diamonds ; her drawing-room was full of French, British, and American uniforms, the tiptop of the armies in this main thoroughfare to the war in Italy. Lanny listened to groups of these men discussing their problems, and he did not hear of any plans to establish democratic government in these colonies, which included such large numbers of dark-skinned peoples—whom some of the officers referred to as " niggers " and others as " wogs."

General George Patton had come ashore at Casablanca, flourishing his two pearl-handled revolvers and roaring for action. He had swept all the way across North Africa, a couple of thousand miles ; he had swept across Sicily and was now on his way up the Italian boot ; he had boldly announced his intention of conducting the same sweeping operations in France and Germany. Georgie was the man for the times, loving his job, sharing Othello's delight in " the neighing steed, and the shrill trump, the spirit-stirring drum, the ear-piercing fife, the royal banner, and all quality, pride, pomp, and circumstance of glorious war." The P.A., desiring victory in this war but also victory in the peace, had heard with dismay how Georgie, in a company like this, had expounded his idea that war was the natural and inevitable condition of mankind. " Man IS war ! " the commander of the Third Army had proclaimed. He was not content with the formula, " In time of peace prepare for war," but wanted it to read, " In time of war prepare for the next one."

So everything would go back and be what it had always been. The swarms of the poor whom Lanny and his wife had seen crowded into the slums of Jerusalem and Cairo, and whom Lanny in past times had seen in Barcelona and Marseilles and Cannes and Nice and Genoa and Naples and Athens—all around the perimeter of this great midland sea—they were going to stay right where they were, sunk beyond hope in poverty and ignorance ; meanwhile the capable intelligent gentlemen who exploited their labour would continue to live in palaces on the heights, deck their wives in pearls and diamonds, and give dinner parties to the fancy-dressed foreigners skilled in the use of instruments of killing. That was the programme ; the near-Fascists would rebuild Fascism with the label changed—probably to something religious.

IV

Ambassador Robert Murphy, genial and kindly Irish-American career man in the Department of State, had a juggler's job of balancing himself between the two factions in that faction-ridden organization. The old-liners, the permanent staff, were tight-lipped conservatives, most of them Republicans ; on the other hand, some New Dealers had crept in, and these had the backing of the Chief, who might step in and upset anybody's apple-cart at any moment. The genial Bob must have guessed by now that the son of Budd-Erling was far from being a proper " striped-pants " man ; but he was a friend of the Big Boss, and carried the most powerful visiting card in the world. Lanny would never know what Murphy really thought of him, but found him friendly and obliging, and that was enough.

What Lanny wanted was to get in touch with two of his old friends : one, Jerry Pendleton, who had been his tutor away back before World War I, and recently had helped to put through a job on the Germans prior to the Casablanca landing. Jerry was an O.S.S. man, so one didn't ask what he was doing or anything of that sort. One said, " I have an important reason for seeing him," and when the answer was that he was probably still in Casablanca, Lanny said, " Can you get a note to him ? " He wrote, saying that he was going to be in Marrakech in a few days. He didn't sign his name, because Jerry knew his handwriting.

The other person was Raoul Palma, Spanish-born Socialist, whom Lanny knew to be working with the underground in the Midi—that is, if he was still alive. Lanny explained to the Ambassador that he had lost contact with this old friend and wanted the O.S.S. to get a message to him if it could be arranged. It wasn't proper to ask the name or address of the O.S.S. head in Algiers ; it was enough that Murphy would forward a note. Lanny wrote, asking Raoul—who was working under the name of Bruges—if he had found any worth-while paintings ; he signed this letter " Neuchâtel," knowing that Bruges also knew his handwriting and would understand that he was to reply to Newcastle.

The Budds were flown to Marrakech, and there was Lanny's mother, enjoying the elegance of the Hôtel Mamounia—she too had " inherited that good part," or at any rate had won it by her combination of endowments and efforts. She and her husband and grandchild and maid were costing a lot of money, but then Robbie was sending his regular thousand dollars a month, and Zoltan was selling Detaze paintings and putting the money in a New York bank. You couldn't live for ever, and might as well have the good things of this world while you were in it. Impossible to find even a small cottage to rent, and you could thank your stars and your social talents that you had made yourself popular in a great hotel, so that you and yours were the last persons they would turn out on the demand of the " brass."

One thing tormented Beauty's soul, and that was the continued silence of her daughter. She besieged Lanny on the subject, and all he could tell her was that he could think of no circumstance under which friends of Marceline in the Allied world could do anything but harm to her in the Axis world. If she was dead, or in a concentration camp, she was equally beyond help for the present. If she had gone into hiding—as many people in Germany had done—the last thing she would want was any effort to find her. If she got out, she would surely let them know ; meantime she was one of many millions lost, missing, displaced, or whatever the word might be, on the tormented Continent. Lanny pointed out to his mother that Marceline had a powerful friend in her Junker lover ; she had made many other friends by her art. It might well be that the friend in Switzerland who had been relaying messages for her had died, or that some law had been passed forbidding the practice. Beauty's daughter was a capable young woman and would surely not be wanting help from enemies of the land where she had chosen to make her home.

The voyaging couple were free to tell what they had seen in Palestine, and Lanny was free to tell his stepfather about the various religions which were supposed to be agencies of love, but which somehow had been taken over by Satan and his minions. How else could a religious man account for what was happening in the world? Your adversary the devil, as a roaring lion, walketh about, seeking whom he may devour! So Peter had warned, and he was the Rock on whom the Church was built. Parsifal was deeply grieved by what Lanny told him of the sectarian wars over the tomb of Christ; Beauty took her son aside and asked him not to talk too much about this subject, for fear that Parsifal might take up the notion that he had a call to go there and preach love and brotherhood to the warring factions. Let a white-haired old gentleman stay in a luxury hotel and love his wife, and surely that would be sufficient in the sight of God.

V

Jerry Pendleton came to Marrakech on the crowded, dusty, and rather dilapidated train. To Lanny he was the same young companion, and it was hard to realize that he had passed fifty and that his hair was turning grey. They had played tennis together, swam and fished and sailed together, and Jerry had risked his life for Lanny in their secret war upon the Nazis. Now the ex-tutor, ex-lieutenant was a full-fledged O.S.S. man, and wasn't permitted to talk about what he was doing, even to Lanny who had got him the job. They had to deal in generalities; Lanny could say that he and Laurel had been to Palestine, and what they had seen there, but not who had sent them.

Good old Jerry was much worried about the war and how it was going. The month was March, and the armies in Italy had been making no gains worth mentioning; they were stuck in front of Monte Cassino and had been pouring out blood there for weeks ; they had made a landing at Anzio, a beach below Rome, and had barely been holding on by finger-nails and toe-nails. The censorship was keeping the facts from the public, but all the world was coming to realize that we weren't winning this war.

Lanny answered, " We knew that campaign was going to be tough, Jerry ; up one mountain and down to another."

" Yes, but if we can't take Italy, how can we expect to take France ? "

The P.A. was far from contented himself, but he knew it was a test of endurance, and every man had to attend to his own spirit. " You know where the real war will be," he said, " and it's not in Italy. We're keeping a dozen or a score of German divisions occupied there, and keeping them away from the Russian front. That's our winter contribution, and you see the result—the Russians are in Poland and also in Bessarabia."

" I wish I could share your contentment," replied the other. " Hasn't it occurred to you that the Germans may be going easy on the Russians, and that when the Russians have got back everything that belongs to them, they may make a deal and quit on us ? "

" I've heard talk about that, Jerry ; but I put myself in Stalin's place and invite myself to trust Hitler and I can't see it. My guess is, the Russians will put the Germans to work for a generation to repair the damage they have done."

" Maybe so ; but they may prefer to make Commies out of them, and we won't like that either." It was a complicated situation, all over the world, and every time you talked with a new person you got a new angle.

Lanny was free to tell his friend what Denis had reported about the fighting in Italy : the men were lying out in foxholes in the cold rain and snow, facing the fearsome new weapons which the enemy had contrived to make misery for them. There was a thing which the army called a Beetle ; a crewless tank, guided by radio, low and flat, and carrying a heavy charge of explosives ; it came hurtling along and crashed into an ammunition dump or other objective. There was a device for destroying railroad track, which ran on the track it destroyed ; it had an immense hook at the back which ripped up the sleepers ; also, on each side a sort of trough, in which bombs slid down every few seconds and exploded after the hook had passed on. And whatever door a man opened, or whatever obstacle he removed, there was sure to be a booby-trap designed to blow him out of this world. There were devilish little devices not much bigger than a fountain-pen that shot up a bullet between a man's legs, just enough to ruin him for life.

Such were the things to which the German scientific brain had been devoting itself ; and the Allied brain had been forced to follow suit. That appeared to be the way of all evil, it compelled the good to cease being good and to meet evil on its own evil ground. " Don't worry," Lanny said, " we have some surprises prepared for the Jerries, and it won't be long before they find it out."

The American Jerry's answer was, " I'm sick of waiting. All the Moors here are beginning to turn up their noses at me ; and some of the French too—the high-toned ones who didn't want us in here and are glad to see us in trouble."

VI

Lanny had wanted to meet this old friend because he had an idea in his mind, important enough to justify him in breaking the rule of secrecy. " I'm going back to Washington," he explained, " and they will ask me what I want to do next. I'm not allowed to go into Axis territory any more, for reasons I can't go into. I have the idea that I might be able to be of use in Spain, and I wondered what you would think about it." Lanny was fairly sure that Jerry's duty was keeping track of Spanish agents working in French Morocco, and perhaps keeping contact with American agents in Spanish Morocco. The border was long and mountainous, impossible to keep closed.

The old friend replied, " No doubt you could be useful, but don't imagine that it would be safe. If the Nazis have got onto you, they could have you kidnapped and carried into France."

" I think that would be what we call a calculated risk, Jerry. Strictly between you and me, I don't know how much the Nazis have found out about me, or what their attitude may be. I have old friends in Spain, some of them important persons—General Aguilar, for example. It might be I could convince him that I had been lied about and misunderstood. Anyhow, it would be worth trying."

"If you're asking about my end of it, Lanny, of course I'd be delighted to co-operate with you and I've no doubt you could get your stuff out. Washington would have to give me the orders."

"The point is, I want to be somewhere near France—I'm sure it's no secret to you that the big push is coming there. The enemy knows that we are getting ready the biggest smash in all history. I don't know where it will be—I have carefully kept from asking—but I'd bet all I own in this world that we haven't been loading up the British Isles with troops for the purpose of holding parades. It happens that I know France better than any other part of the world, and I try to figure out what I can do that will count for most, this spring and summer and afterward. I'll consult the people in Washington, of course, and hear what they have to advise ; but I'm pretty sure that at the end they'll say, ' Well, what do you think ? ' You see, I've been at this game for ten years, and most of the others have only had a year or two of it."

"You ought to be bossing the whole show !" exclaimed the ex-tutor.

"God forbid !" replied his friend. "I've learned to work on my own, but I don't know how to boss other people. If I had all those files on my mind, and the fate of all those thousands of men and women on my conscience, I'd never get to sleep at night !"

VII

That was the end of Lanny's duties in North Africa, and of the interest of both husband and wife in the region. He wanted to get back to F. D. R., and she thought more about the baby than about the blue skies and snow-white mountains and dark-green date orchards of Marrakech. They consulted the Air Force officer who had charge of their flight, and he told them that the quickest way would be on one of the big transports which flew from Marrakech to New York. These

had no bunks and carried wounded men, and it was no trip
for a lady. Laurel asked, " Do they sometimes have women
nurses ? " and when the man said, " Yes," she answered, " I'll
help." The officer could understand that attitude, and she
didn't have to add that she was a writer and that everything
was copy to her. She was even willing to suffer so as to make
sure how it felt. Everything but getting killed, because then
she couldn't write it !

So a delicately reared lady from the Eastern Shore of
Maryland sat on a camp-chair and talked with wounded men
and heard their stories, and when she was tired out she slept
for an hour or two on a cotton pad that was not much better
than a floor. Meantime the four engines roared steadily, and
the winds, blowing westward, helped them on their way. It
was a routine flight, the navigator assured her ; but many
more flew eastward than came back. The pilot set them down,
feather-lightly, on the runway of the great airfield on Long
Island. A couple of hours later the tired mother had her baby
in her arms—and the baby hadn't forgotten her, as she had
feared.

Lanny phoned at once to the President's man. He learned
that the President had gone south, and that there would be
a delay. That was agreeable to Lanny, who had a lot of mail
waiting, and business to attend to. He had found in Tel-Aviv
a young painter of talent, and now he sent photographs to
several of his clients. He told Zoltan about his adventures,
and learned how many Americans had chosen Detazes as an
investment for some of their war profits. An ancient but
ever-strange state of affairs—where some men bled and died
for their country, and others made huge fortunes out of it,
and it was perfectly all right. Lanny drove his wife to Newcastle, and there were Robbie and all his friends and associates
who had invested in Budd-Erling stocks ; they were all making
fortunes, and surely thought it was all right. If you had
asked Robbie he would have replied, " What the heck ! We
couldn't help it if we wanted to."

Frances was well, going to school with the other children,
and entirely happy. Nobody had tried to kidnap her, and the
town had got over its excitement at having an heiress come
to stay. She had kept her promise to write every week to

her mother, and after long delays there came replies ; Frances read the latest to her father, and it contained a sentence : " No bombs have fallen anywhere near us, and there are fewer of them every day." That implied, possibly, a hint of rebuke for the father, the idea that he had taken the child away under false pretences. The flying bombs, the V-1's, were still only a rumour among the insiders, and Lanny said nothing. It could be that the British and American flyers had found the launching sites and destroyed the hellish things. Only time could tell.

Irma Barnes, Lady Wickthorpe, was another Budd-Erling investor, and her fortune was surely increasing in wartime. Somewhere in the Wall Street district was the office of the J. Paramount Barnes Estate, where an ageing brother of that long-deceased traction king still guarded the securities in a vault underground, kept the books, paid the various taxes, and invested the surplus in " blue chip " stocks. Lanny no longer had anything to do with it and never mentioned the subject to his daughter. Let the Barnes half of her deal with those matters !

VIII

There came a telephone call ; Harry Hopkins was at a New York hotel, and when Lanny went there he found Professor Alston in the room. So he could make two reports in one. As always they pumped him dry about the subject he had been studying. In the main they agreed with his conclusions. He said, " If we divide Palestine, somebody will surely have to keep the Arabs off the necks of the Jews." Hopkins smiled one of his dry smiles and responded, " I can see our Congress voting funds for military establishment over there ! "

Alston, diplomatic adviser from the days of the Paris Peace Conference, recalled how the British and the French had there tried to put off on the United States a mandate over Armenia ; but Woodrow Wilson had been wise enough to duck that one. Nations wanted mandates only where there was oil or gold or coal. The three in this room were at one on the proposition of an international authority having an armed force, and a big one. They all looked forward to a long struggle over the issue. Harry the Hop remarked, " This has to be the last war, or there won't be anybody left to fight."

Lanny had dinner with the white-bearded old gentleman who had been his first employer—his only one, in fact, since Lanny was a volunteer so far as F. D. R. was concerned. They spent an evening talking over old times and new problems. Lanny wanted Alston's advice as to his new project, but didn't feel comfortable talking in a hotel room to a person so well known as this presidential " fixer." It happened to be a mild evening, so he suggested that they take a stroll. They went up Park Avenue, and the P.A. made sure no one was following them.

" You know, Professor," he explained, " Jerry Pendleton and I fixed up a scheme to persuade the German agents in Morocco that the American Army was planning to land at Dakar. I really believe we succeeded, and had something to do with the fact that there were so few U-boats off Casablanca —only a couple of them, I've been told. Now I have the idea of going to Madrid and trying the same stunt, or something like it. I haven't been able to formulate a plan that satisfies me ; but at the least I should be able to collect some information as to what the enemy is thinking, and as to conditions in the Axis lands."

" You would go as yourself ? " inquired the old gentleman.

" I couldn't go any other way ; too many prominent people know me there."

" It would be a pretty dangerous assignment, Lanny. Spain is for all practical purposes an Axis country. And if the Nazis have found out about you——"

" I'm not sure how much they have found out, Professor. It's quite possible they just wanted me for questioning. I have a spiel ready for them : I am hurt by their suspicions, and by the fact that Hitler has permitted some jealous person to tell him lies about me. I wouldn't want to try that in Berlin, but it might be good for Madrid. I'll be careful about going out on the street alone at night."

Alston agreed that something might come of such a mission. He would recommend it to the Boss, and Lanny, of course, would go to the O.S.S. and be introduced to their Spanish section and get all the information and advice they had to offer. Said the " fixer," " I will tell you something. The invasion is set for this spring, probably May, and it will be across the Channel. I don't know the exact area—that is the General Staff's secret."

Lanny replied, " I had already guessed as much as you have told me. It seems inevitable."

" I doubt if it will be so to the enemy. I expect him to underestimate both our forces and our nerve. He certainly did so on the North Africa proposition, and that was why you could persuade him to send his submarines to Dakar."

IX

A quarter of a century had passed since these two men had begun working together, and seven years since they had been co-operating in the service of the man they referred to as " the Governor." In that time Lanny had never asked a question about secret matters, or passed on to others anything that had been confided to him. So Alston knew him as a man to be trusted. He had lived most of his life in Europe, and had been there, and all around the world, while Alston was tied down to exhausting conferences with politicians and industrial magnates and brass hats and miscellaneous persons who held power or craved it. So now the ex-geographer plied Lanny with questions, not merely about Palestine and North Africa, but about the whole Mediterranean area. Would the British-trained Arab Desert Force be loyal to Britain or to their compatriots ? Had Franco learned his lesson and would we be safe in reducing our garrison in French Morocco ? What was the present attitude of labour in the various lands ? How strong were the Communists among the Partisans, and would they follow Russia or their own people in the end ?

They had a long stroll ; and before they got back to the hotel Alston asked suddenly, " Have you forgotten everything you learned in Princeton ? "

It was a reference to atomic fission, without speaking those forbidden words. Lanny answered, " I've forgotten a lot, but not the essentials. The Governor saw fit to trust me with a tip a little over a year ago—that the first chain reaction had been achieved. I didn't ask where or how."

" I think you ought to know a little more because your course of action may some day depend upon it. You understand, this is the most closely guarded secret in the country. We are rushing to completion three enormous plants in widely scattered districts. The cost will go to a billion or two, and I think it's the first time in the history of industry that full-scale operational plants have been erected without even a pilot plant to test the procedure. We have plunged into it with top priority, solely on the word of the scientists that their formulas are correct."

" That comes from having a Boss who believes in science," remarked the P.A.

" Partly it's belief in science and partly it's a gambler's temperament ; he's a man who loves to take a chance. It will be the biggest bust in all history—one sort of bust or the other." The one-time geographer didn't smile.

" I hope it happens where it's supposed to happen," said Lanny, " and not over here." He knew enough about the subject to appreciate what he had been told. We were hoping to make an atomic bomb and end the war with one bang !

They walked on, and just before reaching the hotel Lanny ventured, " While you're trusting me with secrets, Professor, there's one thing I've worked on and that I wonder about a lot. I brought my young daughter to this country because of what I had learned about the new weapon the enemy is getting ready. But nothing seems to happen."

" According to my information, you made no mistake. Our English friends are in for a tough time. We'll do what we can to help them, but I fear it won't be much."

" What I'm worrying about, Professor, is that the enemy may be saving up that thing for D-day."

" Nothing is more likely ; but worrying won't help us. We have to do the best we can and take our losses. We have the fixed purpose to get ashore and invade Germany. The whole future of the world depends upon our carrying out that plan, and I don't think we can be stopped."

X

Lanny called up Major Jim Stotzlmann and invited him to lunch. " I have a story for you," he said, and when they met he explained it might be a true story or not, but in wartime no clue was to be overlooked. The Major was one of those charged with the safety of the port of New York, and this came within his domain. In Haifa Lanny had got into conversation with a sailor who claimed to know the German agent who had set fire to the great French liner, the *Normandie*. That beautiful vessel now lay on her side by the pier, as big as a dozen dead whales, and it was too late to do anything for her ; but according to the story the German agent was still in New York, and that was something to be looked into. Jim promised to report it to the right place.

Then he asked about Palestine. He knew some of the rich Jews who were financing that enterprise and could tell about their state of distress. They hadn't expected such a fury of reaction from the Arabs, and now they were accusing the British of perfidy, and F. D. R. of cowardice and vacillation. Only a small percentage of Jews were Zionists, but the horror in Germany had awakened their sense of solidarity. Surely it was right that there should be some corner of the world where a persecuted people could seek shelter, and bring in their relatives and friends ! Surely the British government ought to stand by their pledged word, and the American government ought to make them do it !

What made the matter more urgent was the fact that a presidential election was coming this fall, and no party that wanted to carry the Empire State could forget the Bronx, which had more Jews in it than Palestine. Twice as many Jews in New York City as in the Jewish homeland, and now they were all buzzing like a swarm of angry bees. The Governor was worried about it ; there wasn't any Arab vote to speak of, but there was Arab oil, and our fleet, as well as the British, was using all it could get. So it was a mess.

The scion of the Stotzlmanns had just been down to Washington. He was another man who entered the White House by the " social door " ; he liked to tell his friends that F. D. R. had been present at his christening. They had both of them become what Jim called "mavericks," that is to say, unbranded cattle, individuals who had stepped out from the herd and taken the risk of being run down and devoured by the wolves. Jim adored Franklin, calling him the greatest man in the world. Franklin would have had to be more than human, or less, if he had not been touched by such devotion. They were both of them big fellows, both warm-hearted and full of fun, and both heartily despised the majority of their own class—so blind with greed, so stiff with pride, so dull beyond believing! exclaimed Jim.

"Oh, why should the spirit of mortal be proud?" a poet had inquired, and no one had yet found an answer; but that didn't keep the spirit from continuing the practice. To hear Jim tell about that clan of his, famous throughout America and indeed throughout the world, was as good as a visit to a circus. Jim was fond of the clan's head, who was well over eighty, but he said she had no more comprehension of his New Dealish ideas than if he had come from the other side of the moon. She lived alone in a palace with seventeen servants, and could not give up the idea of being a social queen even in the midst of war; forty people for dinner was a normal event. She would scold the servants unmercifully, but when one of them wanted to quit and go into war work she would burst into tears and say they were abandoning her in her old age and that she would die without them; so they would stay.

Jim said that in 1940 he had laboured hard to persuade the Governor to run for a third term; but this time the "old man" wasn't needing any persuasion. His dander was up, and he was determined to see the war through, and the peace. He thought he could do it without any campaign, but Jim said, "They'll smoke him out before it's over; and God knows how he's going to carry the load. He insists that he's all right, but he looks exhausted, and it's beyond imagining how a man can stand up under such pressure."

XI

After a winter of colds and influenza the doctors feared a break in the President's health and had persuaded him to take a month's vacation. He had gone to the plantation of his friend Bernard Baruch in the tidelands of South Carolina. Lanny was asked to visit him there; and since there was no hurry, and Laurel would enjoy the trip, he chose to motor. It was the familiar Highway One most of the way, and then off on a side road. They did not go to Georgetown, the nearest town to the plantation, for they knew that the hotel there would be full of reporters. Lanny left his wife at a hotel in Andrews, met Baker by appointment, and was driven to Hobcaw Barony, as F. D. R.'s hideaway was called.

It is a fish-and-game preserve some six miles square, in the tideland swamps of this subtropical coast. Lanny was surprised to see a very elegant two-story mansion of red brick, surrounded by immense live oaks draped with Spanish moss. He was taken in at night, directly to the President's room, which was on a ground-floor corner. Baker had said that the Boss had been catching catfish from the dock, and Lanny knew that this must mean that he was far from well; he was a deep-sea fisherman, and proud of his prowess.

Even with this warning Lanny was shocked by his appearance; his face was drawn and without colour. Every time the P.A. came, at intervals of two or three months, he could see a difference for the worse. The plain truth was, the presidency of the United States was a murderous job, and especially so in wartime. This President was waging three wars at once, one against the Nazis, one against the Japanese, and one against his political foes; a civil war, no less a strain because it was fought with political and propaganda weapons instead of arms.

He had been told about Lanny's Spanish proposal, so he was ready with one of his cheery greetings, " Hello, Don Quixote ! " pronouncing it in the old English fashion, " Don Quicks-ut." He wanted to hear all about Palestine, the scenery and local colour as well as the political problems. Many questions Lanny couldn't answer—nor any other man. How far would the Jewish fanatics go in their war on the British authorities ? There had been an answer since Lanny had left —several British soldiers shot from ambush. How far were the Arab threats bluff, and where was the Grand Mufti hiding ? Lanny answered questions for an hour, and had the belief that everything he said would be stored away in that extraordinary mind.

Then the problems of Spain. Lanny's proposal had come at a crucial moment, the Boss explained ; trade relations had been broken off with Franco, to pry him loose from his Axis pals. " We mean to penetrate even his dull brain with the fact that we're going to win this war."

" It's truly inconceivable to him," put in the other.

" I know ; but he saw something in North Africa, and he'll see something in France before long. Meantime he gets no oil, and he won't be able to hold out. But it'll make matters hard for you—he and his gang don't love Americans."

" I don't need their love ; it will be enough if I can make them think they can get some dollars out of me."

" My impression is that the Franco government doesn't permit the exporting of art treasures."

" Nevertheless, Governor, I managed to get some out, and I imagine it will be possible now. All Fascist governments are corrupt, and Franco's will be worse even than the Duce's. The country is poor, the officials are underpaid, and if their families are to eat they have to make something on the side."

" You plan to become a bootlegger of art works ? "

" I'll have to be guided by circumstances. If I'm only going to stay a short while, it will suffice if I whisper about being a bootlegger. So long as I don't do anything, I can't get into trouble ; I'll make friends, or pretended friends, and make alluring promises which I won't have to keep. According to what I hear, war profits in Spain are going to a very small group, Franco's big business friends who put him in power and keep him there. Many of the old families are poor and dissatisfied, and they are the ones who have the art works and might be willing to dispose of them. Also, they are in position to pick up gossip, and they usually talk freely among themselves."

" That sounds all right ; but what will you do about the Nazi agents ? "

" I just have to wait and see about them. It's inconceivable that they won't get reports about me, but what will be in those reports I can't guess. If I meet them, I'll never know whether they are telling me the truth; I'll just have to watch and wait. Tell me what you particularly would like me to get."

"There are so many things that it's hard to know where to begin. Anything that will help us in the invasion of France—which is coming. Anything that will enable us to undermine the Axis, or to starve them. We have been getting tungsten, or what they call wolfram, from Spain and Portugal under what is called ' preclusive buying '—paying hold-up prices, of course. I'm told we get about three-quarters of it, and one of the demands we are making of the little fat Caudillo is that he shall stop all shipment of wolfram concentrates to Germany. We demand some Italian ships that he is holding, and that he kick out certain Nazi agents we have named—the O.S.S. will give you that list, and you will watch out for them. We demand that all German agents shall be put out of Tangier, where they keep tabs on our shipping through the Strait of Gibraltar and keep the U-boats informed. Quite a list, you see, and it's like pulling out Franco's teeth—but we're giving him the gas." The Boss chuckled.

"I've a wild idea in my head," declared Lanny. "I might look up some way to make the Nazis believe we're going to invade through Holland instead of across the Channel. What would you give me if I could do that?"

"Golly! I'd make you major-domo of all the art museums in the U.S. I've recalled pretty nearly every spy story I ever read, trying to figure out how we could do it."

"I've done the same. But I fear I can never get the Nazis to trust me again. It might be that I could have some secret documents and let their agents steal them."

"Go on—you got that out of E. Phillips Oppenheim. Go and talk with Wild Bill; he knows the story and I'll O.K. anything he approves."

XII

Lanny drove his wife back to Washington, and put her up in a hotel while he paid a visit to the old brick building by the gasworks. First he met the genial stoutish Irish-American, who disarmed you by his friendly manner—but don't be fooled, for he had a shrewd lawyer's mind and didn't miss anything. He would call in two or three of his top people, also a stenographer, and they would put the visitor through a grilling—every question exactly to the point and nothing overlooked. Lanny spent a couple of hours with men who were experts on Palestine ; and after that the Spanish section took the rest of the day, part of the night, and some of the next day.

The P.A. knew Spain fairly well ; he could speak the language enough to get along—especially since educated Spaniards know English and French. He had motored through various parts of the country, inspecting paintings and buying several. During the civil war he had stayed for weeks in a town of Western Spain called Caceres, and hoped that nobody knew he had helped in the escape of an English flyer named Alfred Pomeroy-Nielson from a dungeon in that town. More important yet, he had been sent by the elder de Bruyne to interview Marshal Pétain at the time that quavering old gentleman had been the French Ambassador to Madrid—the period called *Sitzkrieg*, before the German invasion of France. All the Rightists had been clamouring for France to make terms with Hitler and get out of the war before it was too late. Lanny had had proper credentials, and had met all the " best " people, including General Aguilar, commander of the military district of the capital.

Wonderful, wonderful ! the O.S.S. people agreed ; the only question was, had he spoiled it by getting exposed or suspected in Germany ? If this had happened, the Spaniards would be sure to know about it ; and what would they do ? Let the Nazis kidnap the false friend and carry him into France ? Or pretend to accept him, watch him, and find out what the Americans wanted to know, who their agents were, and where their " post office " was situated ? Lanny would be in danger ; he would have to use many precautions. They told him these, one after another, and it made a long list—a stenographer typed them out for him so that he could study them. But he wouldn't take them into Spain !

What was he going to find out ? That was another list, of which such things as tungsten, alias wolfram, were only a small part. Franco, who owed his job to Hitler and Mussolini, was doing everything he dared to aid his benefactors : shipping critical materials to them ; spying on the Allies in every land and turning over their secrets ; giving fuel to U-boats, and information about Allied shipping ; permitting Nazi sympathizers to attack Allied consulates—in short, everything except getting into the war. Recently he had gone too far, and the Allies had cut off his oil supplies, which would make it hard for Lanny or anybody else to get about in Spain.

What was this P.A. going to use for camouflage ? He told about his acquaintances in Madrid and Seville and Barcelona who were art lovers ; also about two of his clients at home who apparently suspected what he was doing, and obliged him with letters ordering *objets d'art* in any part of the world he desired to visit. He would renew old friendships in Spain and delicately hint to certain officials that they could earn generous fees by helping him get permission to take paintings out of the country. " I may take some," he said, " and you will have to fix it up so that I don't get jugged for trading with the enemy."

XIII

There remained the most important subject of all : the possibility that this art expert might be used to give the Germans the wrong idea as to the goal of that colossal expeditionary force which the Americans were preparing in most of the harbours of the Atlantic seaboard. The O.S.S. experts on spy stories were called in for consultation : men who had spent their lives thinking up new wrinkles in " Whodunits " and now saw their imaginings turning into grim reality. Believe it or not, there was a man from Hollywood who claimed to have written a hundred and forty-seven such works of fiction, and to have turned more than half of them into screen treatments. There was an elderly lawyer who asserted that he had put himself to sleep every night for forty years by reading such stories. There was the head of a police department " crime bureau " who had spent a couple of decades probing the minds of criminals and finding out what they believed and what they tried to get other people to believe.

A strange place, and a strange assortment of occupations ! At lunch-time, by way of recreation, the bespectacled young college professor who sat next to Lanny entertained him with accounts of some of the things they were doing. They had little pamphlets, top-secret, of course, on the details of committing most of the crimes known to man : how to open any ordinary lock with little strips of celluloid ; how to open safes —they had men who in ten minutes could open a safe that had printed on it the manufacturer's statement that if you lost the combination there would be nothing you could do but have the safe blown. There were treatises on lifting seals and replacing them, on steaming letters open, or reading them without opening, by means of tiny lights inserted in the corner of the flap. There were teams of men working all over the country, trained in the details of entering an office at night, making photostats of thousands of documents, and leaving everything in perfect order, even to the dust on the desks and the floor. The owner of the place would never know it had been entered, not even if he had set traps, or if he made tests for fingerprints and so on.

In this case it was a question of how they were going to persuade the suspicious Nazis to believe the opposite of the truth. The professor of criminal psychology pointed out that when an American told something to a Nazi, the Nazi would naturally assume that it was false. But the Nazi might be capable of one degree of subtlety and figure that the American might be telling the truth, knowing that the Nazi would assume it to be false. Or the Nazi might be capable of two degrees of subtlety, and assume that the statement might be false, because the American would assume that the Nazi might assume it was the truth. This might go on without limit, like the girl pulling the petals off a daisy and reciting, " He loves me, he loves me not." The Nazis would always try to be one step ahead of their enemies in subtlety.

How could a supposedly innocent art expert convey information to the Nazis ? If he had it in his suitcase for them to steal, they would assume that he had put it there to be stolen ; and in that case, would it be better to put true information or false ? It might be that Lanny could receive a letter from his father, a man who would have inside information ; but would the father be indiscreet enough to write it to his son in Spain ? Or could he write that he was sending important documents to some secret place where the son could get them ? Pretty surely the Nazis would be reading the son's letters, and they would contrive to steal those documents—but even then, might they not suspect a " plant ? " Just so, declared the Hollywood writer, did half a dozen men sit up all night in a story conference, thinking up complications to tickle the jaded palates of movie fans !

Lanny's guess was that the Nazis would know him for a secret agent, but would pretend not to ; and what then ? Obviously, they would assume that anything he had was false. But suppose he posed as an agent who had " turned," one who was serving both sides for the money there was in it ? Suppose that a couple of known American agents, say, at Cadiz, were to make an attempt to carry Lanny off and put him on board an American ship, and suppose Lanny were to appeal to the Spanish police and get rescued—surely that would cause the Franco crowd to think well of him, and the Nazis to come running to him with their hands full of gold ! Lanny said, " Yes, but it would be pretty sure to get me into the newspapers, and that is the one thing I've always managed to avoid." The Budd family never got into the newspapers, and especially not as traitors to their native land !

After hours of pro and con this story conference agreed that the wisest course for a presidential agent would be to proceed to Madrid and feel out the situation. When he had made a choice of the best-seeming plan he would drop a note in code to the American " post office " in Madrid. The word would be radioed to Washington, which would provide all the props required for the most elaborate super-feature film. Code words were agreed upon and stowed away in Lanny's memory, and a copy sealed tightly and locked up in the super-secret files of the Office of Strategic Services. Let it be hoped there was no Hitler spy among those who kept the files !

20

Red Laugh of War

I

BAKER provided the P.A.'s passport, made out for Portugal, Spain, and North Africa. Lanny got a Portuguese visa in New York, but thought it best to wait and apply for the Spanish visa in Lisbon. He was flown comfortably on a Clipper by way of the Cape Verde Islands, and when he was set down in the harbour of Lisbon, he betook himself to the best hotel, put in his application for permission to enter Spain, and then telephoned to General Aguilar in Madrid. He had come, he said, because he had heard that Spain had excellent modern painters and he wanted to see their work ; incidentally, he had interesting news about world affairs. The elderly commander was cordial and promised to see that the visa was granted at once. Lanny thought to himself, The Nazis haven't told him about me !

" At once " in the Spanish language meant almost a week, Lanny discovered ; he called at the Consulate every day, but the clerks shook their heads. *Infelizmente, Señor*—but there was a routine which required time. Lanny revealed no impatience ; he had all the company he wanted. Here in the greatest spy centre of Europe there were people of all sorts, male and female, eager to talk to him in English, French, German, or Spanish. He was polite to them all, and happy to express his opinions of paintings, from those of the Aurignacian caves to Picasso and Dali. When it came to the present state of the world, he said it was very bad, and the only thing that a lover of art could do was to refuse to let the subject gain admission to his thoughts.

There were some of these persons who remembered him of old, for he had been coming through here since the days of the Spanish Civil War. He recalled well the Japanese, excessively polite little men, wearing the same black frock-coats and pin-stripe trousers, bowing like automatons and wearing smiles that showed their large teeth to the gums, both upper and lower. Because of previous acquaintance, they presumed to speak to American gentleman in spite of unfortunate war so greatly regretted. American gentleman replied no less politely; he too greatly regretted, having nothing of personal ill will, most happy to learn concerning new Japanese painters in wartime, perhaps making use of new themes? So went this urbane conversation, Lanny knowing that he couldn't fool the Japs and guessing that they knew they were not fooling him. He could believe that there was real sincerity in their regrets about this war, for by now the American task forces had got under way among the Pacific islands, and planes from American carriers were shooting down flocks of the best-trained flyers the Japanese had been able to turn out. Their supply was not unlimited.

Official Portugal was carefully neutral in the whole conflict. The newspapers published the communiqués of both sides, and both were permitted to lease store windows and mount their propaganda for passers-by to read; the Nazis won out in this, because their propaganda included photographs of blonde Aryan females exhibiting everything with which nature had endowed them. Big-business Portugal was likewise impartial, taking in dollars, marks, and pounds sterling in the process of preclusive buying. On the Avenida da Liberdade —which meant in practice Avenue de Laissez-Faire—you saw fine shops with jewels, furs, and every sort of luxury goods; you would also see bare-footed peasant women carrying huge loads of farm produce on their heads.

Wages had gone up slightly—from fifty cents per day; this being another land where birth-control was banned or unknown the population pressed inexorably upon the limits of subsistence. The well-to-do had the poor always with them and found it most convenient, because one could always get servants. Pleasure resorts were being developed, and all you had to do in order to enjoy them was to harden your heart to the starving refugees who sought you out and told you their tragic stories, imploring you for small loans or for help in getting passports to some part of the world where they might find conditions less difficult.

II

At last, a smile upon the face of the clerk in the Spanish Consulate ; it took but a few hours to pay the fees and have all the various documents properly signed, sealed, and delivered. Customs papers, passport controls, money controls, ration card, hotel triptych—these and several other papers you must carry and be prepared to show at any time.

Lanny took the first plane on which he could get a seat, and a couple of hours later came down upon that Cuatro Vientos airfield, which he knew so well. Rick's oldest son, Alfy, had been flying a fighter plane from it in the days when Madrid had been the capital of Republican Spain. Now it was the capital of Falangist Spain, and it still had the marks of war upon its face ; the ruins had been cleared out of the streets but not from the rest of the ground. Franco and his men were very poor builders ; they had no idea how to proceed to restore the land they had seized.

Lanny put up at the Ritz Hotel, home of elegance, with a gleaming white front facing the great square of the Cibeles. Here everything was as if there had never been any trouble in Europe. The waiters all had long-tailed coats and the small bus-boys wore white spats. Lanny got a comfortable room and bath fronting on the court for only a hundred pesetas a day ; the peseta was worth ten cents officially and five cents on the black market. You'd have no trouble in finding the latter ; it would follow you down the street and give you for your American dollars large wads of Franco's paper money, very thin, black, and greasy, making you think of wilted lettuce out of a garbage can.

Prices were high, and many common things were unobtainable except on the black market ; all you had to do was tip the porter, and he would show up with whatever you wanted. Spain had been under economic siege for a couple of months ; the Allies were trying to break her will by depriving her of *la gasolina*. This meant the slowing up of traffic and, still worse, scarcity of goods, and the newspapers were filled with enraged protests, blaming Yankee imperialism for this insult to the dignity of a great nation. Lanny took refuge in a formula which had served him in past times : he had been born in Europe and had lived most of his life there ; he was a Frenchman in his tastes and a Fascist in his sympathies, and he was humiliated to contemplate the role which the land of his forefathers was playing in world affairs.

He called up General Aguilar and invited the old martinet to dine at the hotel. This was the test. What, if anything, had the military commander of the Madrid district been told by his German friends concerning the son of Budd-Erling ? Apparently he hadn't been told anything ; or perhaps he couldn't resist the temptation of an elegant dinner, *vin compris*. Anyhow he showed up, in full regalia, with all his medals and decorations, and white whiskers flowing both sideways and down. He hadn't grown any younger since Lanny had seen him a year ago ; his hands trembled and his memory was less keen. It didn't really matter, for he had competent subordinates, and he lived in glory upon his reputation as head of an army corps of Moors, Italians, and a few Spaniards, which had marched all the way from Cadiz, northward along the Portuguese border and then across to the east, through the Guadarrama Mountains to the rear of Madrid.

At the least sign of interest the old boy would tell you tales of those heroic days—and be sure that a visiting art expert did not fail to indicate such interest. The dinner cost him some six hundred pesetas—about fifty dollars—but was well worth that to him just to be seen in this dining-room in such eminent company. The wealthy and highly placed guests would notice it, the hotel staff would do the same, and all the hangers-on, the spies and agents of the Spanish government, the German, and the other interested lands.

Who was this good-looking and elegant stranger, and what was he after ? He gave the General his carefully prepared story, that he had heard Spain had some important living painters. There was no law against the export of contemporary art works, and it was a part of the Franco propaganda that the new Spain had cultural activities of the very highest quality. Painters ? Those of Spain had always been the greatest in the world, and never more so than now. General Aguilar didn't know their names, but Lanny did, and told them. He wanted to inspect their works and perhaps obtain examples for the National Gallery of Art in Washington and other great institutions. Had the General ever had his portrait painted? Had El Caudillo done so? And would it be possible for Lanny to inspect the work and perhaps arrange for the painter to make a copy for one of Lanny's clients?

The son of Budd-Erling went on to explain that it was his father's influence that had made possible this trip; and that, too, sounded plausible to an old soldier who knew all about the great firm and took it for granted that the president of such a firm would have influence and would use it on behalf of his son. Spain had always been a land of nepotism, and the old commander was busily collecting perquisites for the members of his large family. When he had got them jobs he was proud of it and would boast of the importance of the Aguilar clan. The name, accented on the second syllable, means eagle; the bird is predatory, and in Europe as well as in America has been taken by poets and statesmen as a symbol of worldly pride, pomp, and power. The word also means a gold coin—and that surely did not diminish its prestige in Spain.

III

There really were painters in Madrid, men who had managed to live through a revolution and a cruel civil war. Some of them painted portraits of the rich and great, the generals and the ecclesiastics, and these were able to live comfortably. Others painted landscapes, peasants at work or dancing in fiesta costumes, and these had managed to escape persecution, but not destitution. Picasso, who had painted a symbolical portrayal of bombed Guernica, had fled abroad, and so had others who had painted the people's army. Having met all sorts of artists from boyhood, Lanny knew exactly how to talk to them. Very soon he was a friend of the bohemian world, giving a few pesetas to some poor devil of talent, and purchasing several works which he thought had real merit.

Also there were dealers in art, and owners of paintings, from whom Lanny had purchased works in days before the war. He renewed these acquaintanceships and made himself agreeable wherever he went. In any sort of company, when the subject of world politics came up, he would smile and say humbly that the situation was beyond his capacity to form a judgment; his speciality was painting. Elegant, superior, and opulent, he spread his fame in the art world, and numbers of people came to call at his hotel. He took it for granted that every other one would be an agent of some sort, and he said exactly the right, careful things to them. He left his suitcases unlocked, and they contained letters on fashionable stationery, bearing the signatures of Americans whom any agent could look up in *Who's Who* and discover to be well-known collectors. From first to last there was nothing wrong about this *conocedor d'arte*, and no reason for the most suspicious of governments to interfere in his affairs.

All this took constant watchfulness, the guarding of every word, every facial expression, the very pulses of his blood. This ancient, proud land of Spain stood in Lanny's imagination as a symbol of the evil that ruled the modern world. "Truth for ever on the scaffold, Wrong for ever on the throne!" Spain was supposed to be a land at peace, but it was a land crushed and writhing in suffocation. Francisco Franco's crime of state had filled Lanny with fury, not merely because he had been here and witnessed it stage by stage, but because it was a crime against the future, against the faith by which Lanny lived.

Ever since his youth he had been telling the workers, and the friends of social justice wherever he met them, that the way to peace and freedom lay through the ballot box, that the democratic process would enable them to take power without bloodshed and chaos. The people of Spain had followed this course and had established a duly elected parliament pledged to long-needed reforms. Then had come the man of blood and terror, the assassin of the people's hopes; puppet of Nazi-Fascism, he had opened his country to the German and Italian bandits and had permitted them to use the people of Spain as practice targets for the new techniques of warfare—tanks and Panzer divisions, screaming dive-bombers and area bombing to wipe out the civilian population of whole towns.

The result had been to provide the Communists with an argument difficult indeed for a democratic Socialist to answer. "Look!" they would say. "You tried it in Spain and what did you get?" Lanny must have heard those words a hundred times in arguments with Jesse Blackless, his "Red" uncle; Laurel had heard it more recently in her discussions with Bess. "How many more people's governments do you have to see murdered in order to convince you that the capitalist class will never surrender power without a fight?"

Lanny was putting his hopes in Franklin Roosevelt—and what bitter laughter that brought from the Reds. What had Roosevelt done to help the people of Spain, except to deny them the right to purchase arms in the sweet land of liberty? The first time in history that a legitimate and duly elected government was denied the right to buy arms for its own defence! Franco could get all he needed from Hitler and Mussolini, but democratic Spain couldn't get anything, even when it came with gold in its hands! "*Conspuez Roosevelt!*" Lanny had heard the workers of Paris shouting at a mass meeting to demand airplanes for Spain. "*Des avions pour l'Espagne!*" But not even the Socialist Blum had dared to heed the cry.

On his return home Lanny had heard the President's defence. The country was without arms and in no position to take up the challenge of the three dictators. Britain was in an even worse position, with the menace at her very doorstep. Neither country was prepared militarily, neither was prepared ideologically. In America were the Southern senators, and the Catholic vote in the big cities, and the Church hierarchy cheering for their Spanish Defender of the Faith. Eight years ago this had been, and a presidential election coming on, even as now. "Politics!" Uncle Jesse had sneered; and Roosevelt's answer had been, "What is the democratic process but politics? And if I lose the election, what good will that do the people of Spain? Will they get what they want from the Republicans?"

So Lanny had to bite his tongue off, as the saying goes, and watch that wholesale murder for nearly three years. Now he had to bite every day, observing the crude luxury of Spain's wealthy classes, the great landowners and holders of state monopolies, and the higher clergy, who owned half the arable land of the country and made speeches denying the right of any other form of worship, thus inciting the Falangist rowdies to raid and destroy Protestant churches. Contrasted with their obesity was the sheer naked starvation of the masses in their rickety slum tenements, many of them still unrepaired after bombing.

IV

Germans came to see Lanny, and others who said they were Swiss or Danes but who, he felt sure, were Germans. They were all lovers of art, and some of them really knew about the subject. They took an interest in Lanny's ideas, and he was friendly to them, inviting them to meals and talking " shop "—that is, painters, and the prices now being paid for their works in the various centres of culture. The visitors hinted at secret business to be done, and Lanny was politely interested but refrained from committing himself ; they might be genuine black-marketeers, and again they might be agents of the Gestapo, trying to find out why he was here, and to get some pretext for having him expelled, either westward or—God forbid—eastward.

He was really interested in painting, and he was content to bide his time. Sooner or later he might pick one of these gentlemen as the one upon whom to try some device. Or perhaps it would be the lovely blonde lady named Fridolin, who had twice invited him to her room, and hadn't taken offence at his refusal, but greeted him with unfailing smiles in the lobby. He would be friends with them all and try to make up his mind about each one. He agreed with them that Communism was a nightmare threatening the world, and that the Allies were making a frightful blunder in not helping Germany to overcome it ; but he added that politics and world problems upset his mind and disturbed his aesthetic sensibilities. It was his special task to help the peoples of both Europe and America to have beautiful paintings to contemplate. *Ars longa, vita brevis !*

This cat-and-mouse game went on until one morning a telephone call and a familiar voice. Lanny exclaimed in delight, " *Ist's möglich ? Was machst du in Madrid ?* " Heinrich answered that he would tell him about it. When could he come ? Lanny said, " *Gleich !* " And, to himself, " Hitler has sent him ! "

Yes, that was a pretty safe guess. Heinrich Jung was a desk man, and so far as Lanny could recall had never been outside his Fatherland. He was the logical man for the Führer to choose in order to solve the mystery of Lanny Budd's disappearance from Germany and his reappearance in Spain. Lanny's mind had been intrigued by the thought of both the *Nummer Eins* and the *Nummer Zwei*, and what they would be making of his escape. Heinrich wasn't the cleverest man that Adi could have found, but he was the most honest, and the one whom both he and Lanny would be most apt to trust.

The Jugend leader came, wearing civilian clothes, a grey tweed suit. This was the first time Lanny had seen him out of uniform in something like twenty years, and it was a mistake from the enemy's point of view, because it made him seem unnatural. But Lanny saw the same round, blue-eyed, rather dull countenance, and underneath the tweeds the round belly slowly but steadily expanding. After their cordial exchange of greetings Heinrich explained that he had been sent to consult with the Falangistas as to their educational techniques, which hadn't proved as successful with the youth of Spain as the methods of the Hitlerjugend in Germany. Heinrich had come as a civilian because—and he seemed a little embarrassed as he said it—the Spaniards were having trouble with the Allies just now and were trying to keep German officialdom a trifle less conspicuous. That might be true or it might be invented; no doubt Heinrich had been coached as to every word he was to say.

Of course Lanny wouldn't show the least trace of doubt. They were the same good companions they had been from boyhood; they carried on their conversation exactly as if the fates had not put their countries on opposite sides of a world war. " What on earth made you leave so suddenly ? " demanded Heinrich. " I was planning a party for you at my home."

" Too bad," replied the other, and he became very solemn in voice and aspect. " Has nobody told you anything about me ? "

" Nothing, Lanny. What do you mean ? "

" Himmler came to see me and asked me a great many

questions, which made it plain that somebody had been sowing distrust of me in his mind. Then one of my friends tipped me off that I was in danger. You know what an awkward position I was in—an enemy alien in the Fatherland. I was a foredoomed victim of any slanderer or intriguer."

" *Aber wie Schade!* What did they accuse you of ? "

" How could I know ? I suppose of not being a true friend to the Führer, of having abused his confidence."

" But why didn't you go to the Führer and have it out with him ? "

" I had already seen him and realized what an overburdened man he was. I thought it would be a poor act of friendship to worry him with my problems. And how could I expect him to believe my word against that of his security chief, the man upon whom he depends for his very life ? You know how it is, Heinrich—the Führer is surrounded by men who compete for his favour. I suppose I have made some of them jealous by enjoying too much of his trust and by being able to see him when they weren't able to."

" I am shocked, Lanny, and I'm sure the Führer must be shocked if he knows about it. He is always loyal to his old friends, and it must have hurt him that you deserted him."

" I haven't deserted him, Heinrich. I have been working just the same, doing what he asked me to do."

" How on earth did you get out of Germany ? "

" I'm not free to tell you that. There are people near the Führer who distrust Himmler and consider him an evil influence. They provided me with transportation." The P.A. wasn't making this up on the spur of the moment ; he had thought the matter out and decided that he might cause a little worry to both the Führer and the Gestapo head. Take their minds off the war for a while !

" Lanny, I think this is dreadful ! " exclaimed the Jugend leader. " I'll finish my duties here quickly and go straight to the Führer. He has never refused to see me no matter how busy he has been. I'll tell him what you have said, and I can promise you he'll pledge you safe conduct and let you come back and confront your accusers."

" That's very fine of you, *mein alter Heinrich*, and what I would have expected. Of course I want to clear my good

name ; and I'll come if you can arrange it, provided that I
can manage another trip. It grows more difficult every time.
My father's influence can do a lot, but it can't do everything,
and the American authorities are very suspicious of my
travelling. You see how I am—between two fires ! "

V

Such was the beginning of a duel of wits between two men
who had begun as friends in boyhood and had been made into
enemies by irresistible social forces. Lanny had been deceiving Heinrich for a matter of fifteen years, and all that time
Heinrich had been sincere. What a shock it must have given
him to learn that this adored friend had been an enemy of
Heinrich's adored cause ! Lanny was guessing that Heinrich
had been told this, and that he had come here for the purpose
of deceiving Lanny and paying him back. But there was
always a chance that Lanny might be mistaken, that perhaps
the Gestapo hadn't really had anything definite against him
and had merely wanted to question him. Perhaps they had
sent Heinrich just to try to get Lanny back into Germany,
without telling him anything against his friend. Such compli
cations lent piquancy to the duel of wits.

Heinrich attended to the urgent business which he said had
brought him to Madrid : meeting the leaders of the Falange
youth groups and telling them the wonders which the Führer
had been able to achieve with the bodies and minds of the
children of Germany. As a concession to the Allies, Franco
had recently abolished the Falangist militia ; but that, of
course, merely solidified his control of the country through
the Army. El Caudillo had surely not given up his dream of
" forging an empire," and all Spanish children were being
taught that this heaven-sent leader was going to restore the
country's ancient glory by retaking all the once-Spanish lands
—South and Central America, the West Indies, Mexico, Texas,
California. Then Spain would be really prosperous, and every
Spaniard would be a lord. Heinrich mentioned this programme
to his friend, and Lanny wondered, was he really naïve, or
was all this a subtle pose to make Lanny believe that he was
exactly the same old comrade, having no idea that Lanny was

in any way different from what he had always been ? If Heinrich had been coached it would surely have been a good coaching.

Amid his pressing duties Heinrich managed to find time to dine with Lanny and spend the evening now and then. As usual, he let Lanny take the bill, because he was a poor man. Was he really poor, or was he afraid it would look suspicious if he had an expense account for entertaining American spies ? At every turn Lanny had to occupy his mind with speculations like this ; yet he mustn't seem to be watching, he must be glad to see an old friend to hear the news from home. How was the family ? A large and steadily growing unit—eight children, and they had all been given old Germanic names, Baldur and Horst-Michel, Ingomar and Chlodwig and Wilfried. Lanny had made it a point to remember these names, and every time he had left Germany he had given each of the little ones a present ; that had made him into an American rich uncle, and Lanny wondered if the father had told them the shattering news that their benefactor was a spy and traitor to the Fatherland.

Baldur, the eldest, a tall lad, blue-eyed and yellow-haired, had just entered the Army, proudly and gloriously ; in a few weeks he would be at the front. Naturally that led the talk to the war and its progress ; Lanny, who knew what Heinrich believed, was careful to believe exactly the same. The Americans had taken a couple of months to capture Cassino, and at that rate it was obvious they weren't going to reach the Alps this year. As for the Eastern front, the German retreat was clearly strategic ; they were leading the enemy into a trap, and as soon as the ground was dry this fact would become apparent to the world. Not since Hannibal's crossing of the Alps—successful at first but a failure in the end—had there been a madder military undertaking than the American proposal to invade and conquer the Axis lands. Lanny said it was well known in America that this programme had been forced upon the Army by a Jew-dominated President.

Lanny had undertaken to find out about this Herr Rosenfeld for the benefit of Herr Schicklgruber, and he told how he had travelled across the American continent upon that errand, and what sentiments he had heard expressed by the powerful

R

rich in New York, Washington, Chicago, Detroit, Hollywood, and Los Angeles. What he said didn't have to be true ; he could follow Hitler's own formula about lying. Lanny had given thought to getting just the right sort of stories, stories which Heinrich would accept and which might cause even Heinrich's great Leader to wonder if he had not made a mistake in doubting the good faith of this scion of American big business. It was so utterly impossible for Hitler to conceive how a man like the president of Budd-Erling could be giving aid to the Russians and not realize what a trap he had fallen into. And the fact was, Robbie was almost as puzzled about the matter as Hitler thought he should be.

Heinrich promised to report this news to his Führer at the first opportunity, and Lanny was pretty sure he would do so. Air mail went to Berlin at least twice a day, and no doubt Heinrich could send a letter by diplomatic pouch. Adi might be at his headquarters in the Ukraine, or in the Hürtgen Forest, but he would get such a letter quickly. And sure enough, three days later the Jugend official came, rosy with pride and delight, bearing a note on the private stationery of the greatest man in the world. " I have read with attention what you tell me about Herr Budd, and you may assure him that I shall be, as I have always been, pleased to receive a visit from him. Of course I will grant him safe conduct, both from and to Madrid, and I hereby authorize you to escort him to me and bring him back to Madrid whenever he is ready to come."

To the humble and adoring Heinrich Jung, that was the greatest achievement of his lifetime. He bubbled with German adjectives : " *Prachtvoll ! Herrlich ! Beispiellos !* " He was chagrined when Lanny began explaining that he could not leave that very day. *Unglücklicherweise !* Lanny had incurred obligations, he had promised one of his clients to make a thorough investigation of contemporary Spanish painting, and he could not break his word to any client—no, not even to clear his good name in Naziland, not even to help eliminate Herr Rosenfeld from World War II ! Lanny promised to come soon ; and meantime he prepared a formal report for Heinrich to transmit to the Führer. Also, he started another report, signed " Traveller," which he would turn in at the American

Embassy ; but he thought the idea over and burned the document, deciding that it was too risky and there was not enough
to be gained. Herr Rosenfeld would have to wait for this
item !

VI

April had come, and was going. The Germans in the course
of their strategic retreat had abandoned Odessa and been
surrounded in Sebastopol. The Allies were slogging their way
from one mountain to the next on the Italian peninsula, and
the people at home read stories of rain and mud and blood,
and waited, doubting and despairing, for the Army or somebody to carry out some of the wonderful promises which had
been made to the world. Hope deferred maketh the heart
sick !

Lanny had managed to get himself pretty completely
surrounded by Nazis and Nazi agents in El Caudillo's capital.
This had come about gradually and naturally ; they had
sought him out, and he had to like them ; he spoke their
language more fluently than Spanish, and all his life he had
admired German culture, played German music, sung German
songs. He introduced the others one by one to Heinrich,
smiling inwardly as he did so, for he guessed that the Jugend
leader knew them. In all probability they had come first and,
finding that Herr Budd would talk only about paintings, they
had picked out an old friend to come and break the ice.

Anyhow, it was broken, and Lanny was, as of old, the Nazi
admirer and collaborator. He talked about his many friends
in the Fatherland, and about conditions in America, and the
prospects of the war. Occasionally he dropped items of
information, nearly always things which he could be sure the
Nazis already knew—though perhaps not these particular
agents. F. D. R. had told him more than once that it was
permissible to give the enemy small items which it didn't
possess, provided that one was getting things of greater
importance in return. Money was to be spent without limit ;
so Lanny entertained as became an open-handed playboy.
He was amused to observe that the blonde Fräulein Fridolin
was willing to accept Heinrich as a substitute for Herr Budd ;
this was in accord with Nazi ethics, but, all the same, Heinrich

mentioned to Lanny that it was a subject not to be referred to in Berlin-Grünewald where his family resided.

Everything was just lovely in this Axis *Liederkranz*. Lanny had a piano in his apartment, and they sang every time they met. They ate hearty meals in the dining-room—and perhaps none of them ever noticed that all this hospitality took place in Madrid's swankiest hotel, and that Lanny never came to their places, never went out alone with them, and never got into a motor-car, not even a taxi, with them. He wouldn't even visit the Velasquez Club, where all the diplomatic set played tennis and swam in the pool. The Germans used one end and the Allies the other ; the Spaniards circulated in between. Now and then the Japs came, and then all the others got out and left.

A shy, solitary man, not fond of outdoor life, he seemed content to have paintings brought to his apartment and to spend hours studying them and talking about them. No doubt the Nazis observed all his habits ; if so, they discovered that he read newspapers from half a dozen countries and marked and clipped only passages having to do with art matters. They discovered that he was entirely without sex—they proved it by making several tries, with both women and boys, and of course they would not fail to question the porter and the bell-boys, who always know what is going on in hotels.

A strange man indeed ! Could he possibly be what he pretended to be, an ivory-tower art lover, wrapped up in his speciality and indifferent to the outcome of the greatest war in history ? He seemed determined to know everything about Spanish painting ; next to that came the Dutch—he read papers from Holland, all that he could get in Madrid, and others that he had ordered by mail. He persisted in inquiring about living Dutch painters when everybody knew the Dutch weren't doing anything worth while in any of the arts—how could they, when the efficient Nazis had taken them all and put them at war work ? This Budd fellow spent days in the National Library in Madrid, reading about Dutch painters and trying to find out which were still alive. Of course the efficient Nazis wouldn't fail to track him, and to find out what books he had consulted and what questions he had asked. Imagine thinking he could keep any secrets in this Fascist city, with the Gestapo and the Spanish police working hand-in-glove on security problems !

VII

The secret came out when the American revealed to his dear German friend that he had in mind to get in touch with an odd character of the Dutch art world, Hans van Meegeren by name. This unsuccessful painter had discovered several remarkable works by the old master Vermeer. They were said to be of extraordinary merit ; Reichsminister Göring had paid an enormous sum for one of them called " Christ and the Adulteress." So that was it ! This *Bursche* Budd wanted to get van Meegeren to find him a Vermeer, so that he could smuggle it out to America and sell it to some of his father's rich friends for a million dollars ! From the German point of view that mightn't be so bad, because any money that van Meegeren or any other Dutchman got the Nazis would take away from him, and it would show up as *valuta* to buy wolfram in Spain or steel in Sweden.

Lanny talked frequently about this Dutchman, who seemed to fascinate him ; he wondered where he could find the man's address, and whether the German government permitted the mails to go freely from Spain to Holland. Heinrich undertook to find out and reported that a letter could be sent, subject, of course, to German censorship ; it seemed unlikely that there could be objection to an inquiry about an old master. Lanny talked about the extraordinary " Christ and the Adulteress " and another he had heard about, called " Visit at Emmaus," which showed Christ appearing to two of His disciples after the crucifixion. Heinrich thought that was rather silly, but Lanny replied that it was a favourite art subject and, besides, had cost a million marks. " Don't be a Hottentot," he said.

The Jugend official worshipped power and station, and surely didn't want to be that inferior thing ; so he talked with other Germans and came back to report that some experts believed the alleged Vermeers to be frauds. To this Lanny replied, " The Reichsmarschall asked my opinion. I told him I believed the painting to be a Vermeer, but even if it weren't, it was so good that it was worth the money. Indeed, it might be worth more, for a man who could fool so good a judge as Göring would be an historical figure, and collectors would want his work as a curiosity."

" Is that why you're anxious to get one ? " inquired Heinrich with unexpected shrewdness.

" It's part of the reason," was the reply. " The main thing is that I liked the painting, and so did one of my clients."

" Then," said the German, " I can't understand why you don't go and see the Führer and clear matters up, and then, on the way back, meet this van Meegeren and see what you make of him." Heinrich kept steadily insisting, and Lanny kept steadily refusing.

VIII

Across the foot of a mountain canyon a great dam is erected, by the labour of thousands of men and at a cost of millions of dollars. The waters of a river are pent up and form an artificial lake. A power-house is built, dynamos are installed, and transmission lines are run over mountain-tops and down into valleys. All is made ready, and then one day an engineer in a control room pulls a small lever, and the waters of the lake rush down through the penstocks ; giant turbines begin to turn, electric current leaps in a fraction of a second, and in cities hundreds of miles away an infinitude of factory wheels begin to turn and machines to roar and pound.

So now it was with the son of Budd-Erling : everything had been prepared, and the time for action had come. He had no lever, only a fountain-pen with ink in it, and a scrap of paper on which to write words. He wrote only five, all of them short and none especially impressive : " My roses are in bloom." He sealed the paper in a plain envelope, stamped it, and addressed it to a so-called " post office " in Madrid. He hadn't been told the details of what would happen, but he knew the game well enough to imagine every step. The message would be radioed to Washington, and within an hour after it arrived an O.S.S. agent would take off by plane for New York and from there to Newcastle ; he would interview Robbie Budd, even if he had to wake him in the middle of the night, and would present a letter which Lanny had composed and left in the keeping of General Donovan's office. Robbie would summon his trusted private secretary and dictate the text of that letter, have it typed on his impressive stationery—" Office of the President "—and then sign it himself. The O.S.S. man would take the document, and it would be flown in a diplomatic pouch to Casablanca and delivered to Jerry Pendleton. Jerry would pack his suitcase, provide himself with an American passport and a forged Spanish visa, and be flown by way of Tangier to Madrid.

Lanny waited three days, according to instructions, and early one evening he slipped out of his hotel, taking every precaution to make sure he wasn't being followed. After circling several blocks he walked to the Salon del Prado, a natural place for an art expert to be strolling. Out of the shadows a man stepped forth and whispered, " Jerry." Lanny replied with his own name, and that was enough ; an envelope was placed in his hands and he slipped it into the breast pocket of his overcoat. He did not stop walking, but whispered, " Wish I could have a talk with you, but it's too risky."

" Sure thing," replied the other, and gave him a pat on the shoulder. Ordinarily he would have said, " So long," but since Lanny had been in Palestine his former tutor thought it was fun to say, " *Sholem.*" He turned and disappeared in the darkness.

Lanny got safely back to his hotel, hugging that precious missive which had cost so much in time, thought, and money, and the services of so many persons. When he got into his room he locked the door and then opened the envelope. He knew the contents pretty nearly by heart, but he had to read it to make sure it was correct.

DEAR LANNY :

Information has come to me from one of your clients that you are contemplating going into Holland to inspect paintings. I am deeply concerned, and am going to the expense of sending this letter to you by special messenger. You have many times told me that you are a grown man and have to have control of your own destiny ; but for this once I am hoping you will respect your father's judgment and grant my request to drop this most dangerous project. I do not need to tell you that I have special information, which I dare not put on paper. I simply say to you, with

all the urgency at my command: DO NOT GO INTO THE LOW
COUNTRIES.

Surely there is no art matter important enough to justify
you in disregarding this warning from your father.   The fact
that I am paying more than a thousand dollars to get this
message to you without censorship ought surely to convince
you that I have reasons for what I am saying.   Stay where
you are until summer : or if you must meet your friends,
meet them in France.   The climate in Holland is damp and
unpleasant in spring, and I understand it is a time of bright
sunshine in Spain.   If it is money you need, for heaven's
sake draw on me.

I rely upon you to destroy this letter as soon as you have
read it.

Your loving father,

ROBERT BUDD

P.S.   I am telling your client that I have written this,
so you need not worry about failing to keep your promise
to him.

IX

Lanny didn't destroy that letter.   What he did was to put
it back in the envelope, and then take his nail scissors and
carefully cut some threads in the lining of his suitcase, and
slide the letter down between the lining and the suitcase frame.
He figured that the enemy would not fail to find it there, and
he took the trouble to set a careful trap to make sure.   The
O.S.S. men had told him about the minute precautions they
took to conceal their photostating of documents, and Lanny
had no doubt that the Gestapo men would know all the tricks.
Lanny didn't do anything crude like sprinkling powder, or
leaving a piece of paper with an edge sticking out of the suitcase.   This had to be a really fancy job.   He carefully removed
one thread from the lining, a brown silk thread two or three
inches long ; being the colour of the lining, it was inconspicuous,
and he didn't lay it over the envelope, where it might be
noticed, but carefully laid it between the lining and the
envelope, held by the pressure between the two.

When the envelope was pulled out, the thread would drop
to the bottom of the narrow space.   Lanny tried this several
times, making sure that its smoothness would keep it from

sticking. It would fall into the narrow space, where there was no chance of its being seen ; when the envelope was shoved back into place, the thread would be at the bottom, and not where Lanny had delicately hung it. So he would know that the envelope had been removed.

The suitcase was on a chair, and Lanny locked it. He locked his hotel room, being sure that the enemy would be equal to opening these. He went to the telephone and called the Jugend man ; the evening was still young, and Lanny had some important news. " Come on over ! "

Heinrich came and heard the extraordinary story that an American millionaire had sent a special messenger from Connecticut to Spain in order to carry a letter to his son. What Robbie Budd had said was—so Lanny told Heinrich— Lanny must under no circumstances go into Germany or any Axis land again ; the United States government had become suspicious of him, and he would almost certainly be arrested for treason, and his family would be blackened and shamed. Lanny was terribly depressed over this; it knocked all his plans into kingdom come. So he declared, and Heinrich quite certainly believed him.

" Lanny ! " he exclaimed. " This is your great opportunity ! Why don't you make a clean break ? "

" Just what should I do, Heinrich ? "

" Come over to us ! Come with me to the Führer and explain everything. Give out a statement that you are with the German people in their struggle against Russian barbarism, and that you know they are going to win this war."

Lanny, playing his carefully thought-out role, looked taken aback. " What good would that do, Heinrich ? My statement would be suppressed by the censors in America and it would end my usefulness to the Führer."

" You could talk over our radio and reach the entire world, Lanny."

" I am nothing of a speaker. There would be some curiosity about me, but it wouldn't last more than a few days ; the newspapers would set me down as a crackpot, and that would be the end of my influence. You see, I have never been at liberty to tell you what I have been doing for the Führer ; I have brought him much information, and he has acknow-

ledged its importance. I have done the same for Reichsmarschall Göring ; I have told him not merely about the
Budd-Erling plane, but about other war weapons. The
Führer sent me to Professor Salzmann of the Kaiser Wilhelm
Institut to tell him what I had found out about American
work on jet propulsion, and to Professor Plötzen to tell about
experiments in atomic fission."

" *Aber*, Lanny, you won't be able to do anything like that
now ! "

" I expect to go right on doing my best. I can come here
to Madrid, and perhaps the Führer will let you come and meet
me. You know, I am fortunate in having independent means.
Both the Führer and the Reichsmarschall many times offered
to pay me for what I was doing, but I have never taken a
pfennig from them. So I don't need their consent to go on
with my work."

" What a shame, Lanny, that there is a misunderstanding
between you ! "

" It is something that was bound to happen sooner or later.
They have honoured me with their friendship, and it was
inevitable that I should excite the jealousy of persons around
them. I am an enemy alien, and how could I expect to come
and go without awakening suspicion ? I'm not going to let it
get me down ; I'm going on working for what I believe, and
when the victory has been won I'll take chances on being able
to clear my name."

Would Heinrich believe all this ? Lanny had no means
of guessing, because he didn't know how much Heinrich had
been told ; he didn't know how much Hitler was able to tell.
He knew that Heinrich wasn't very bright ; he was fond of
Lanny and would want to believe the best. So now Lanny
looked mournful, yet courageous, as heroic as any movie
actor in Hollywood.

He had the movies in mind, for a special reason. Suddenly
he said, " Let's take our minds off our troubles for a while,
Heinrich, and perhaps one of us will get a hunch as to the
wisest course. I was passing a cinema today and noticed that
they have a German film, *Friedrich Barbarossa*. Have you
seen it ? "

" I don't have any time for shows, Lanny."

" How would you like to go with me now ? "

The Jugend leader thought for a moment. " I have an engagement, but I could call it off."

" Fine. There's the telephone."

Heinrich hesitated. " Let's go downstairs. I have to look up the number." Lanny smiled to himself, it was exactly as he had guessed. Heinrich had something to say over the phone that he didn't want Lanny to hear. And Lanny thought that he could guess what it was.

X

In the sumptuous lobby of the Hotel Ritz the P.A. waited, well away from the phone booth. He didn't sit down, but strolled about, looking at faces—it was the fashionable hour, and there were many elegantly dressed people. Lanny was hoping to meet somebody he knew ; and here sat a young Army officer whom he had met in General Aguilar's home, El Capitán Gonzaga, all dolled up, his last button polished, his boots shiny and immaculate, his little black moustache waxed and twisted to points. Lanny stopped before him and said, " *Bien venido*," and then, with his best smile, " Waiting for a lady ? " It took no clairvoyance or other occult art.

The officer, arising to return the greeting, spoke with unexpected frankness. " Damn her soul ! She is late, as women always are."

" Too bad, too bad, *capitán*. Why don't you teach her a lesson ? Let her bad fortune be my good."

" What have you in mind, Señor Budd ? "

" I am on my way to a cinema and it would delight me to have your company. A German film, very high class, I believe."

" *Caramba !* I don't like their barbarous language. They have forced me to learn to read it, but when I listen to it I am not so good."

" Fortunately I have a German friend who is going along. He can sit next to you and answer questions. It is an historical picture and will improve your education, to say nothing of that young lady's." So one plays with life in the smart world.

A great discomfort was removed from Lanny's mind. He

had been smitten by the thought that his Jugend friend, instead of telling the Gestapo to come and get a photostat of a letter in Lanny Budd's room, might tell them to come and pick up this double-crossing spy and whisk him into France from one of the airports which they controlled. But now there would be three in the party, one of them a staff officer of the military commandant of this district, with his sword on his left side and his automatic on his right. It might seem strange that a gentleman should appear thus accoutred to take a lady out for an evening, but it was not strange in Spain. The country was supposed to have been at peace for five years, but it was really in a state of suppressed civil war. Up in the Guadarramas, not more than an hour's drive from Madrid, the desperate guerrillas still hid, and raiding parties came down during the night and held up motor-cars on the highway ; not infrequently the rebels stole into the capital, hid in the aged five-story tenements, and conducted bold raids from there. No well-dressed person would dream of going into the slums at night, and few ventured there even by day.

Heinrich came from the telephone, and he betrayed no displeasure when he was introduced to a Spanish officer. The three of them strolled down the brightly lighted boulevard and into the darkened theatre. Lanny kept his promise and put Heinrich next to the *capitán*, and they watched the career of the red-bearded king of the Germans, here presented not as a Christian crusader, but as a champion and prophet of German racialism, making speeches that might have come out of *Mein Kampf*. Lanny soon forgot the dull show, thinking about the far more exciting one which he believed to be going on in the hotel. He felt pretty sure that Heinrich and his Gestapo masters were not overlooking the opportunity which he had so carefully provided.

XI

Back in his room Lanny turned on the light and locked the door behind him. First, like any timid old lady, he looked under the bed and into the closets ; then he went to the suitcase on the chair. He surveyed it, and the carpet around it ; there was no change that he could note. He had no doubt that any fingerprints would have been wiped away, and anyhow he had no fingerprint apparatus. With care he held the suitcase steady, turned the lock, and raised the cover. Again there was no sign that anything had been touched ; he didn't expect it, being sure that this important job would be done by experts.

There was just one point—the tiny silk thread. Where was it ? The least touch or jar might cause it to drop ; so Lanny pressed his left hand firmly against the side of the lining to hold the thread in whatever position it happened to be. The envelope was there, he could feel it through the lining, and he began pulling the lining back, a quarter of an inch at a time, looking for the thread. It wasn't there.

Still holding firmly with his left hand, Lanny worked the lining loose with his right, all around the envelope ; but there was no thread—until he got to the bottom of the cavity after taking out the envelope. He could feel sure that someone had come and opened that suitcase and taken the letter out, no doubt to photograph it, something which a skilled operator could do in a few seconds. The whole operation, what the O.S.S. called " surreptitious entry," would not have taken the American outfit more than a few minutes. Lanny had given the Gestapo more than two hours.

He had lied to Heinrich Jung about Robbie's letter, and Heinrich would find that out. Lanny had planned it that way, for he wasn't trying to win back Heinrich's trust, nor Hitler's ; he had the idea that both of them would find it easier to believe that he would lie to them than that he would tell them the truth. Now, when he got into bed, he could speculate for hours as to whether or not he had guessed their psychology correctly. The Gestapo had in their possession a photostat of a letter which the president of Budd-Erling Aircraft had taken the trouble to send to his son by special messenger, and which that careless son had failed to destroy. The envelope itself was evidence, since it bore no stamp and no postmark. It wouldn't take the Nazis, with the help of the Spanish secret police, very long to find out that an American had been flown from Casablanca to Madrid on that day— and that he had been flown out again that night.

The letter implored the son of Budd-Erling not to go into

Holland, but to stay in Spain or in France. The meaning o
that was obvious, and the only question was whether the lette
was a genuine warning or a "plant." Here was something to
make the chiefs of the Gestapo lie awake at night ! Lanny
could be sure that copies of the letter were already on their
way by airplane to Berlin. They would be widely distributed ;
Himmler would have one, and Göring, and all those who knew
Lanny Budd would be called in to discuss his psychology.
Experts of many sorts would wrinkle their brows over the
problem. *Der Dicke* would take many more benzedrine pills
because of it. Adi Schicklgruber, who slept badly and took a
variety of drugs on that account, would be another who would
torment his brain. " He loves me, he loves me not ! "

The verdict would depend in part upon how much and
exactly what the Führer and his advisers had found out about
this son of Budd-Erling. If they had found very little and
had merely wanted to question him, they might still believe
that he was something of a boob, a *Tunichtsgut* who wanted
to come blundering into a war zone, trying to buy what might
be a Vermeer and might be a van Meegeren. On the other hand,
if they had discovered him to be a viper who had crept into the
Führer's bosom, then they would be apt to judge the letter a
clever device.

But they could never be entirely sure ; the doubt would
stay in everybody's mind and come up at every *Generalstab*
council on strategy. It would affect military minds and alter
the balance in every decision. If it should have the effect of
causing a single division, intended for the Channel Coast, to
be held back in Holland, if it caused a single battery of high-
powered cannon intended for Cherbourg or Dieppe or Le
Havre to be mounted instead at the mouth of the Scheldt or
the Rhine, then thousands of American lives would be saved,
and the labours of Lanny Budd and the Oh-So-Secret gentlemen in Washington would be justified many times over.

21

Into the Cannon's Mouth

I

LANNY BUDD stayed on in Madrid although he hated it. He was afraid that if he left suddenly he might convey to the Nazis the idea that he had come in order to plant a letter with them. Also, he had made the acquaintance of an official who knew about wolfram concentrates and talked freely. Moving in fashionable society, one heard much conversation about the war, and now and then somebody would drink too much good wine and blurt out a secret. Man is by nature a gregarious animal, and the impulse to share knowledge with other members of the horde is difficult to resist. There was talk about the " Blue Division " fighting on the eastern front and getting severe punishment ; about sabotage being practised in Spanish industries ; and even about the plans for a revolution against Franco, whom the old families despised.

The industry of the country, deprived of oil, was grinding slowly to a halt, and the fat little Caudillo was forced to humble his pride ; in the month of May he gave way and accepted the Allies' terms. He would expel the German agents whom the Allies had listed ; he would stop the attacks of Falangist rowdies on Allied consulates ; he would release to the Allies the Italian ships ; and he would limit the sale of wolfram concentrates to Germany to ten per cent of his total production. Would he keep that last promise ? Franco's officers joked about it in the presence of a genial art expert ; there was a black market, and it was notorious that there had always been smugglers in Spain. These jokes were reported in the weekly letter which, with infinite precautions, the art expert managed to deliver to the American " post office."

One result of this settlement was that Lanny lost some of his Nazi friends. Heinrich had already gone ; and now others took their departure, including the lady Fridolin. But the Allied list had apparently not been complete, and Lanny turned in the names of Germans who were still active ; also of Spaniards and alleged Danes and Swiss and what-nots who had taken the places of the departed. The new arrivals cultivated the acquaintance of the charming art expert who had so much more money than they did. Now and then one of them offered to sell him secrets, but he did not take this bait. They showered him with gossip about El Caudillo's succession of favourites, and he listened but refrained from comment. When they brought him bad paintings, he politely feared they wouldn't appeal to his clients. Once they brought him a good painting, and for this he paid a little more than it was worth.

II

May is a lovely month in the land of Castile. The sun shines, and the sky is clear ; showers fall, and tiny jewels gleam on every leaf and blade of grass. There are delightful gardens, where every sort of flower blooms and the bees and the birds are busy from dawn to dark. Lanny had loved such sights in boyhood ; and now a wealthy landowner gave him the use of extensive grounds, with smooth green lawns, a summer house covered with a trumpet vine, a pool with water lilies and gold and silver fish, a sundial, and many mischievous little statues —cupids, fauns, and satyrs. Best of all, there was a library, and Lanny would take into the garden an old volume of Lope de Vega, full of a wild kind of melodrama which had thrilled Spanish audiences for more than three centuries.

Yes, the world was full of delightful things, and always had been for the grandson of Budd Gunmakers and son of Budd-Erling. There were times when he enjoyed them wholeheartedly ; but now he was restless, anxious, and troubled in conscience. What right had any man to be happy in such a critical moment of history ? The month of May was the time when all the military experts agreed that the second front must be opened, if ever. The English Channel and the North Sea were unquiet bodies of water at best, and their south shores were those upon which the winds beat hardest. There was no use putting an army ashore unless you meant to keep it supplied, and the days in which you could do that were passing. The newspapers of the whole world explained this and speculated about the date which the Allies called D-day and why it was delayed.

Lanny watched the papers and listened to a radio when he got a chance, expecting news every hour—but none came. The Allied armies in Italy were now fighting their way toward Rome, and that was something, but very little. Where was the big army, the big push ? Day after day passed and nothing happened, and there wasn't a soul of whom he could ask a question or with whom he could have a frank discussion. He had to listen to the jeers of his Axis friends and admit sorrowfully that they were right ; the Yankees had given new meaning to the word bluff, also the game of poker in which you succeeded by means of it.

Once a week Lanny wrote to his wife, and now and then to his father and his clients. There wasn't supposed to be a censorship of mail between Franco's land and Roosevelt's, but Lanny was sure that letters to him had been opened, and he took no chance with letters going the other way. Those to Laurel were addressed to Agnes Drury and dealt with his art activities, his health, the pleasantness of the climate, the courtesy of the Spaniards, and similar innocuous subjects. Letters that came from Laurel were equally non-committal : the baby was thriving, her work was progressing satisfactorily, and New York was another place where the month of May was delightful.

But at the end of the month came a different kind of letter, brief and businesslike : " This is to tell you that I have sold three paintings dealing with the life of Moses and am sailing for England in a few days. I have information concerning a fine portrait of the Duke of Marlborough, and the owner has arranged for me to come and view it. If it is possible for you to join me and give me your advice, I should be pleased. I am sure you will be able to interest one of your clients in this unique work of art. My address will be the Savoy Hotel. Affectionately, Agnes."

That surely gave Lanny a jolt. He had married a feminist, and once more she was letting him know that she meant it. She had borne him a baby, but she wasn't going to settle down and take care of it ; a baby would keep, but this war wouldn't, and an aspiring writer was going to see some of it for herself.

He had no trouble reading her code. " Three paintings dealing with the life of Moses " meant magazine articles which she had written about Palestine ; and as for the Duke of Marlborough, he had successfully invaded the Continent, and now his lineal descendant was planning to give a repeat performance. The " owner " of this " painting " doubtless meant some magazine which had commissioned her to write about the war. Lanny was left to guess whether it was the magazine's idea or whether Laurel's own lively brain had hatched it. Also, whether she would be going as Mary Morrow, Laurel Creston, or Mrs. Lanning Prescott Budd. Surely it couldn't be as Agnes Drury !

III

The P.A. had been thinking for some days that his work in Spain was about done. He had looked at all the paintings he could find and had tried in vain to think of some other device to persuade the Germans that the Allied armada was going to Holland. Now he found himself thinking about London ; it had been so long since he had been there, and he really had a lot of information which he could turn over to Rick, a capable journalist who would use it in ways that would not point to an art expert as its source. In England he could surely find out what was going on and break the suspense that had become all but unbearable.

He sent the customary cablegram to his father, saying that he had some art business in London, and was on his way to the Avenida Palace Hotel in Lisbon. He packed his suitcase and his paintings and betook himself to Salazar's capital, certain that Robbie would pass on his message to the mysterious telephone number in Washington and that results would come. He waited two impatient days before a message was brought to him that he had a seat in the plane the next day. How those miracles were performed he never knew ; he was in the hands of higher powers, such as mankind had dreamed of all through the ages—the flaming chariot which had come down for the prophet Elijah, the flying carpet which had borne Sinbad the sailor, the *deus ex machina* who had solved all problems for the Greek dramatists.

It was a land plane this time, English, and very comfortable, meant for distinguished passengers : officers in uniform, couriers with dispatch cases which they never let out of their hands, and preoccupied-looking business men. Nobody talked about his affairs, and few wanted to talk at all. Lanny had newspapers and magazines for which he had paid multiple prices, so he was content to be quiet. Most of the way he had to read by artificial light, for one of the aircrew came through the saloon and fastened black covers over the windows. Nobody was going to look down upon that sea ! Lanny occupied his imagination with what might be there. Once he had seen a convoy, hundreds of vessels, spread out in long lines and leaving a trail of black smoke a hundred miles behind them. This time, he knew, there would be thousands—three thousand, four, five—surely the greatest congregation of ships since men had gone down to the sea.

The P.A. hadn't been told where this plane was going to land, and he doubted if anyone else had. They were ordered to buckle their safety belts, and soon they began to feel the crackling in the ears which told them they were coming down. There was a high wind blowing, and everybody was a bit nervous, but nobody would show it. They felt the wheels touch the ground and discovered that they were at Bovingdon, an airport the P.A. had not seen before. He didn't see much of it now, for there was a bus waiting and they were put aboard and driven at top speed to London.

A funny thing to have a wife and not know her name ! Lanny decided that he wouldn't go into a swank hotel and ask for several ladies ; he found a vacant telephone booth—something not so easy in this crowded time—and called the hotel. No, there was no Mary Morrow registered. When he asked for Laurel Creston, yes, a lady from New York, but her room did not answer. He left word that Mr. Budd would call and then checked his bags and went for a walk around this unconquered city, the greatest in the world, built on the "unsinkable aircraft carrier." Lanny recalled the joke to the effect that there were so many American soldiers on the island that it would have sunk if it had not been for the barrage balloons holding it up. The Americans were swarming on the streets in many different uniforms ; the balloons were visible also, huge fat silvery sausages bobbing about in a heavily clouded sky.

There were almost as many people in uniform as in civvies, the P.A. decided ; and more than half the uniforms were from overseas. Some of the G.I.'s hurried, others strolled and gazed, getting their last look at this storied town, noting differences rather than resemblances to home. Two years and a half had passed since these tall lads had begun pouring onto the island, marching and drilling, rehearsing manœuvres on the beaches and the downs, in the forests, wherever there was uncultivated land. The islanders had got used to their unfamiliar words and nasal tones, and made a duty out of taking them into their homes and making them feel comfortable. It had been discovered that some were good and some not so good, just as was the case among the natives.

IV

Lanny went back to the hotel, and this time Laurel Creston was reported in. He went up to her room and oh, what a sight ! Could any husband have imagined it ? A wife in uniform, a natty khaki blouse with pockets all over, a short skirt, a saucy cap, and insignia—a captain, no less. On the sleeve was a white brassard with a large letter " C " ! That wasn't for captain, but for correspondent. She had up and done this all by herself, and now she was amused by her husband's consternation. It was a feminist's holiday, and he pretended that he didn't dare to touch her until she commanded, " Kiss me, sir ! " Only after he had done so did she tell him that hers was only what the Army called a " simulated " rank.

She was only a woman after all and burning with eagerness to tell him this exciting story. It had occurred to her that she was missing a lot of history, and she had gone to the editor who had accepted her Palestine report and inquired, " Why don't you send me over to do the invasion of France ? " He had been interested, and there had been an editorial conference in which they had put her through a grilling. The upshot was that they had made application to Washington and the request had been granted. She was not to get near the front—no woman was to have that high privilege—but she would follow behind the armies and write what she saw, subject, of course, to the censors. She had had to fill out half a dozen documents in quintuplicate, and to take half a dozen medical shots, and then they had shipped her across.

It was going to be not merely the greatest invasion in history, but also the most completely reported. Its Commander-in-Chief was a man who believed in publicity—loved it, swam in it like a fish in water—and he had sent that impulse all the way down the line. This was a people's war, and the people were going to know everything about it that would not give help to the enemy. Army, Navy, and Air Force, all were going to have their historians, working in teams and equipped with filing clerks and secretaries, photographing outfits, messengers and chauffeurs and jeeps. All the important newspapers and magazines would have their correspondents, and these would wear uniforms and enjoy military privileges. The women would be "simulated" W.A.C.'s —Women's Army Corps, and one of them would be "Captain" Laurel Creston!

"When is it coming?" Lanny asked. It was the question in everybody's mind, if not on his or her tongue. Laurel said, "No one is told, but there are many signs. Our men have been pouring through London, and all going south. Today I noticed what I believe is the crucial sign—the correspondents are disappearing. I wanted an item of information this morning and I phoned a colleague and was told that he was out. I tried another and it was the same. My curiosity was aroused and I tried half a dozen and got the same result. They have been told to disappear, without saying a word to anybody."

Lanny answered, "I was struck by the number of uniforms on the streets. I've never seen anything like it before. The day I left Madrid the newspaper *Arriba* reported there were fifty American divisions in Britain and the same number of British troops equipped for combat. That means something over a million and a half. Of course it comes from German sources and represents what the Germans believe."

" Or what they want the world to think they believe,"
remarked the wife sagely. " Both sides are doing their best
to keep the other in the dark."

Lanny smiled and didn't say what part he had been playing
in that effort. He thought he would try out this observant
lady. " There seems to be an impression in Madrid that the
invasion will be by way of Holland," he commented.

The answer was, " It could be." He was amused to see
her doing to him what he had done to her for so many years
—keeping secrets !

V

Laurel's first article was to deal with Britain on the eve
of invasion. She had been here about a week and had been
going about incessantly, interviewing all sorts of people and
taking notes. A wonderful people, at a great moment in their
lives ; they had fought for survival and endured terrific
punishment ; now their rations were low but their spirits
were high. From top to bottom in the social scale everyone
knew what was coming, and Laurel hadn't met one who
doubted the outcome. The common people expressed their
feelings with exuberance, for they were the most sociable of
humans and full of what they called ginger. Even the upper
classes unbent in the presence of a woman soldier, but never
any heroics ! Laurel told with amusement of an elderly
dowager who had inquired, " My dear, have you seen the
tulips in Birdcage Walk ? "

Lanny's reply was, " Let's see them ! " That was after
they had had lunch and had decided to treat themselves to a
holiday. No use hovering over the radio, for D-day couldn't
begin until the small hours of any morning, and there wouldn't
be a whisper about it meantime.

They strolled through streets crowded with traffic and
looked at landmarks which Lanny could tell about, for he had
been visiting here since childhood, off and on. Many of the
landmarks were gone, alas ; there were whole blocks that had
been laid flat, and few streets that did not have gaps in them.
Lanny compared them to the mouths of the Cockneys, who
couldn't afford dentistry, and when a tooth ached, out it came
and that was the end of it.

Bombing was infrequent by now; but people had heard about new weapons on the way—the Nazis had been boasting about them over the radio for a year or more. By now most people had stopped taking them seriously. Lanny said this was a great mistake. His wife repeated what she had been told, that the reason for the delay was the successful bombing of Peenemünde, where the devilish things were being contrived. Lanny could have said, " I know quite a story about that," but he didn't. He expressed fear that the new weapon might be ready now, to be launched against ships and beaches. All conversational roads led to D-day.

They strolled in Hyde Park and admired the lovely flower-beds, a source of delight which war had not taken from the people. There was a long path with lawns on each side, and this was the famed place where the Britons who never would be slaves came even in the midst of war to exercise their right of free speech. On a Sunday afternoon they would bring soap-boxes or light platforms and take their stand and begin to orate, and you could stroll along and take your choice of half a dozen different social doctrines and as many religious ones, not to mention astrology and numerology, the evils of tobacco, vivisection, meat-eating, and divorce. You might laugh and jeer, or ask questions, but never enough to keep the speaker from getting his proper hearing. Here and there a bobby strolled, keeping watch, but he seldom had anything to do; he never interfered with the speakers, not even if they called for somebody to murder the King. It was the British idea that the reason they never had assassinations was that they let everybody come here and blow off steam.

There was Rotten Row, a wide bridle path, with a walk for people, and a wooden railing between. Now there were few riders, for most had gone to war, and so had the horses. " What an odd name for a bridle path ! " Laurel remarked, and her husband explained that it had once been the " Route du Roi." He took the corruption as an expression of the old-time Englishman's contempt for foreign lingo, and indeed for everything that wasn't on his tight little island.

And then Birdcage Walk, a rather dull parkside walk, but made lively by the beds of tulips. They were of every colour and pattern, and nature offered few brighter spectacles.

Lanny recalled the days before World War I when his father
had been doing business with Zaharoff, the munitions king,
and they had called at the Greek gentleman's Paris mansion.
He had a Spanish noble lady whom he adored but couldn't
marry because she had an insane husband ; the lady had loved
tulips, and she had told a little American boy about them.
" I remember bizarres and bybloemens," the grown-up boy
remarked, " but I have forgotten what is which."

The flowers bowed gently in the wind—not a gale, but what
the sailors would call a stiff breeze—and that brought their
thoughts back to D-day. It was from the north, and Lanny
said, " That will be bad on the beaches. They'll hardly try it
tonight." It wasn't until later that he heard the story, that
the sailing had been set for the previous night but had had to
be called off on account of bad weather. Now General Ike
and his staff were in a dreadful state of anxiety. Their
meteorologists expected the wind to die down, but they might
be mistaken, and in any case there would be swells on the
beaches. On the other hand, if the landing were postponed,
it would have to be for another month, on account of the
tides ; and here were the ships in the harbour, many with
troops already on board, and all exposed to enemy bombers ;
here was a vast armada approaching from the Atlantic, four
thousand vessels in all, and no man could guess how many
U-boats lurking in wait for them. To go or not to go, that
was the question.

VI

Husband and wife strolled back to their hotel. He had
been accustomed all his life to have what he wanted when he
wanted it, and now he wanted a radio set. The hotel had none
it could spare, so he went on the hunt and found a dealer who
could not resist a double price for a week's rental. It had to
be brought right away, and it came to the " goods " entrance
of the hotel in a wheelbarrow. After that the couple could
sit and listen to news from all over the world : the British
were swarming northward out of Rome, and it was not believed that the Germans could hold anything below what
they called their Gothic Line, defending the River Po. The
Japanese were being driven back in New Guinea, and oil

plants were being bombed all over Germany. About that too there was a story that Lanny could have told, but his lips were sealed.

Concerning D-day you heard, from the Axis radio, speculation, scepticism, and ridicule, and from the British and American radio complete silence. Every day the B.B.C. warned the French Partisans to make no move until they received instructions in the French voices which they had been taught to recognize. Every day the Axis threatened the conquered peoples with dire penalties and reassured their own people by quoting the victory promises of *Unser Hermann*, the fat man whom they adored, though not so ardently as formerly. " The invasion must be beaten off, even if the Luftwaffe perishes," he had declared ; it was that kind of war, and both sides were girded for a life-or-death struggle.

The couple talked about Göring, whom Laurel had never seen except in photographs without number. Lanny had told much about him, but nothing in recent years. He was amused to discover that he was slightly embarrassed by the thought of this old-time robber baron. *Der Dicke* had been his host, and Lanny hadn't been able to help liking him in some aspects. Now, how much did Göring know, and what was he thinking about this false friend, this snake in the grass, this double-dyed deceiver ? It might be that Hermann's sense of humour would dominate, and he would burst into a loud guffaw over the idea of having been fooled. Lanny had made up his mind that that was how he himself would take it if ever he should meet the *Nummer Zwei*, in this world or the next.

With Hitler, of course, it would be different. Adi was a man with no trace of humour, a man who identified himself with God and took an offence not merely as *lèse-majesté* but as sacrilege. He was a man without mercy and, strange as it might sound, without guile. He thought of himself as a man of infinite guile, but he had gone and put it all into a book and had circulated seven million copies. To be sure, he could figure that nobody but Germans would read the book, and that if others read it, they would be unable to believe it. But in the end all the salient passages had been dug out and quoted, and all the world had caught up with this man of maniacal ego. Lanny could look forward with no pleasure to meeting him, in this or any other world. As for Laurel, she loathed him with a special and peculiar kind of horror. If Adi Schicklgruber were ever taken captive he need look for no mercy from " Captain " Laurel Creston of the Women's Army Corps !

VII

The happy couple slept soundly, and no spirits or psychic entities came to warn them that this would be the great day. During that night a hundred thousand men boarded ships and landing craft in Southampton and other harbours on the English south coast. During that night another enormous convoy came stealing in from the Atlantic Ocean, a couple of thousand vessels, transports, freight ships, tankers, repair ships, hospital ships. Leading the way and bringing up the rear were hundreds of war vessels of every kind and size, battleships, cruisers, destroyers, and small escort vessels darting here and there at speeds up to forty miles an hour. All were equipped with marvellous new devices which enabled them to detect vessels under the sea or on the surface, and planes of any sort in the air. Radio Detection and Ranging was its full name, and the ships had automatic guns of a hundred sizes which could be turned, some of them in the fraction of a second, upon an enemy object thus reported. Their anti-aircraft shells were provided with proximity fuses, incredible little radio devices which drew the shell close to the target and caused it to explode when it was near. Keep out of the way of this new scientific armada !

Sunrise had come early, and the landings had begun a few minutes later. Transocean, the German radio, began telling the news at once ; the Germans had nothing to lose by telling —they could be sure the enemy knew what it was doing. The Allies, on the other hand, couldn't be sure how much the Germans knew, so they kept silent. Lanny and Laurel listened to German accounts, in the English language. They told of forces coming ashore on the beaches, all the way between Le Havre and Cherbourg, a distance of about a hundred miles, and of swarms of parachutists being dropped upon the country-side, as far back as Rouen, forty miles from the sea. They were seeking to seize strategic points, destroy bridges, mine roads ; the Germans said they were being mopped up, and that, of course, was according to formula.

Three hours passed before the B.B.C. made itself heard, and then it was only one sentence. General Ike's press aide, who had a good voice, interrupted a programme with the statement, " In ten seconds I shall make an important announcement." He solemnly counted, " One–two–three–four–five–six–seven–eight–nine–ten." Then, " The invasion has begun on the northern coast of France." Exactly ten words, like a telegram ; the Americans were learning reticence from the British. Nobody was going to accuse them of boasting, of making claims, or in any way resembling Hitler and Göring and Goebbels.

Later in the day the correspondents were turned loose to tell what they saw with their own eyes ; all carefully censored, but no less thrilling for that. Lanny, who had been over all the war zones, talking with all sorts of men, knew the details and could supply them to his wife. He had watched the landing at Algiers and had seen the paratroopers with their faces and hands blackened for night operations—the Moors had thought them a new race of dark-skinned people, amazing to behold. He had had to bail out from a plane, but he didn't tell Laurel that ; he described it as something he had been told about. Besides the parachutists there were airborne troops, whole divisions of them, packed into glider planes, towed by elastic ropes, and turned loose to glide to the ground. During the night preceding the landing the British and Americans had dropped four such airborne divisions and two parachute divisions, somewhere between sixty and ninety thousand men. The planes which had dropped them would return for more, and for loads of supplies. The men had ground-to-air radio equipment and could tell in code where they were and what they needed ; within the hour it would be dropped to them.

Such a coming and going of planes had never been in the world before. During the entire time, a couple of weeks, that Lanny spent in London, the roar of planes was never once out of his ears. It was a sound like nothing else on earth, a multiple drone made up of hundreds of individual ones, no one of which could be distinguished. The sound never died for an instant, because as some planes passed, others came on, and all going north or south, pointing the way to the war.

The correspondents told of scenes near the beaches : the transports and large landing craft trailing barrage balloons, to keep dive-bombers away ; the P.T.-boats darting in every direction, searching for U-boats ; the great battle-wagons parading slowly, several miles offshore, their spotter planes picking out the targets and radioing the data. There were a dozen American battleships here, more than there had been at Pearl Harbour ; some had been sunk there, and had been lifted and made over, better than ever. Some of the old fellows were no longer fast enough for sea fighting, but here, protected by cruisers and a swarm of destroyers, they were moving fortresses, hurling a tremendous weight of metal against the smoke-blanketed shore line.

The Germans had had three years to fortify this coast. They had surveyed and plotted every beach and knew the exact angles and distances. They had mined the entire shore and all the paths, and had blocked every approach with ingeniously constructed obstacles. But on that fateful night midget submarines had crept in and laid beach-markers, and a hundred or two minesweepers had worked all night, protected by airplane bombing. Channels had been cleared to the beaches, and up on the bluffs the paratroopers were raiding the pill-boxes and dropping grenades into the firing slots.

In some places all this succeeded, and the swarms of landing craft came through the surf and let down their ramps ; the combat men poured out and raced over the sand and up the pathways to the top. In other places there was less success, and men were trapped on the beaches and had to dig themselves in under a hail of machine-gun fire. Many died in the surf and in the soft sand ; tanks were wrecked and landing craft sunk ; but more came, and all day long the guns of six hundred war vessels and the bombs from several thousand planes found out the enemy's hiding-places and wore down his fire-power.

VIII

Lanny wanted to do nothing but sit by the radio, and his wife stayed with him. Once he saw tears running down her cheeks; he knew that she was thinking about those pitiful boys, some of them no more than eighteen, trapped in the midst of that concentrated horror, pouring out their life's blood and enduring agonies of pain and fear. He said, " You're going over there, darling. You asked for it, and you'll have to keep your nerve."

" I know, I know," she said, " and I will." But the tears continued to flow, and he shut off the radio and put his arms about her and let her sob on his shoulder. There was something about women which made this necessary; in some mysterious way, physiological or psychological, it did them good. When Laurel dried her eyes she said, " I'm all right now; I'll see it through."

" We have to see this war through," he told her. " Then we have to prevent the next one."

" I keep wondering, Lanny—will any war ever prevent the next one? I hate the whole thing, and in the depths of my heart I'm just as sorry for the German boys as for the American."

" You'll have to keep that out of your articles," he said, smiling, " or your editors will drop you."

IX

Lanny phoned Rick, who came over to the hotel. Nina came into town—impossible to stay quiet on such a day. Now there were two military experts, and two respectful wives to absorb their wisdom. Lanny hadn't seen Nina for several years; she was thinner and her hair was beginning to show grey; she brooded over her boys, but did not let it interfere with her household duties or her support of her husband's cause. Lanny was pleased to tell her good news about her youngest son, her baby; he was in a safe place, for the Germans rarely got a chance to bomb Egypt. Nina exclaimed, " I wish the airplane had never been invented!" Lanny thought, but did not say, " Wait until you see the flying bomb!"

The two men listening to the news agreed that its most surprising aspect was the almost complete absence of the Luftwaffe from the scene. Göring had said that it must stop the invasion even if it perished; but up to noon of that crucial day no more than fifty of its planes had showed up. The conclusion was irresistible—*Der Dicke* simply didn't have the planes to defy the eleven thousand which the Allies had at work. What Göring he was saving for the counter-attack by which the Reichswehr was promising to drive the invaders back into the sea. Another Dunkerque, which Radio Transocean was incessantly predicting.

This much was certain by the end of that day : the landing had been achieved. The invaders had taken beach after beach, including the fashionable *plages* of Trouville and Deauville, which both Lanny and Rick had visited in happier days. The invaders had climbed the bluffs and were spreading out, joining their paratroopers and glider men, over a front of some sixty miles. The people who were praying in all the churches wouldn't have dared ask for more, and might easily have got far less. The radio reported that in Brooklyn the bearded old men of a Jewish home for the aged had put on their prayer shawls and skull-caps and marched through the streets, blowing the *shofar*, the ram's horn.

Another question—what were the Partisans doing, the French ? That was news for which the public would have to wait for some time. General Ike had said over the radio, "The hour of your liberation is approaching." He had told the Partisans to perform those duties which had been assigned to them, and he had told the rest of the population to keep out of the way and do nothing to provoke enemy reprisals. Both Lanny and Rick knew that an elaborate underground organization had been built up ; plans had been flown in at night, supplies had been dropped, and a secret army had been equipped. Now, all over France, that army would go into action, blowing up bridges, wrecking rail lines, chopping down trees to block highways, raiding enemy munitions dumps and oil storage depots. These Free French knew the country they lived in, and nothing could be hidden from them ; what they couldn't destroy they would let the Allies know about, and the Air Force would come and do the job.

The result of this uprising would show gradually and in negative ways—there just wouldn't be any German counter-attack. Plenty of resistance, desperate, hard fighting, step by step backward, but no mass advance, no driving the Allies into the sea. The Germans couldn't get the forces up. They couldn't run trains and they couldn't travel the highways except at night because of the incessant bombing. They would learn the bitter lesson, which they had been teaching the rest of the world, that it is impossible to win a modern war without command of the air ; also, that it is impossible to win when the Commander-in-Chief is six hundred miles away from the battlefield, and when he does not trust his commanders, and will not let them move troops without permission.

Oskar had told Lanny about this preposterous situation, and Göring had told him about the helplessness of the Luftwaffe ; so Lanny could speak as one having authority, even though he did not name the authority. Eric Vivian Pomeroy-Nielson, an authority on air forces, reminded him of the occasion, in the spring of 1914, when Robbie Budd had taken the two boys to visit Salisbury Plain, where the English Army had been making its first feeble efforts at military flying with a few old biplane " crates " held together with piano wire. The pilots were hoping to shoot at the enemy with automatic pistols, and one bold man had the idea that he might carry a machine-gun, lift it with his two hands, and fire it before the plane started into a dive. There had been no augur or diviner to tell the boy Rick that within a couple of years he would crash while flying one of those planes, a crash that would cripple him for the rest of his days.

X

All over the world people sat glued to their radios ; uncounted millions in their homes or in public places, hotel lobbies, cafés, cigar stores, wherever they could find a radio set. It was a new way of life, a new kind of adult education that had been developing for the past quarter century and met this great occasion well prepared. The men in the studios read the news bulletins, they commented and explained, they introduced experts, they shifted back and forth between New York and London and the actual war scenes. With the help of those in power who had learned to love publicity, they would set up their apparatus on a battleship and let the public at home hear the great guns going off ; then it would be a tank rumbling out of an L.S.T., or an airman just returned from a flight over the battlefield.

By the end of the second day it was clear that the invasion had succeeded; the troops were ashore along a sixty-mile front; they were from five to ten miles inland and were holding while reinforcements and supplies continued to pour in behind them. The bombardment went on, for the big guns of the ships had a range of twenty miles or more and were hurling their shells into enemy entrenchments far inland. The weather was making trouble, but not too much, and the airmen maintained cover over the whole scene, keeping the enemy miserable and blocking the roads behind him.

The four friends stayed together, listening and discussing, arguing and exulting; for each it was a personal triumph, something for which they had waited long years. Eleven years and a half, to be exact, for Lanny and Rick had agreed from the day Hitler took power that sooner or later the democratic world would have to put him down. In the early years it would have been easy, but now it necessitated this colossal battle, which was just beginning and might go on for a year, two years—who could guess? Surely not anyone who was talking over the radio.

Laurel's first article was to deal with the English people in these exciting days: what they thought, how they felt and behaved. Nina and Rick were English people, among the most intelligent, and their minds were laid bare in this crisis. The four would go out and get a meal, and then come back to their vigil. They would telephone to friends, and these were more English people. The chamber-maids in the hotel, the bell-boys, the porter, the clerk at the desk—all had something to say, something lively and odd to American ears. The people on the streets were bursting with delight, hardly able to keep their feet from skipping, their lips from breaking into song. " Ow, that ole 'Itler ! 'E's gettin' 'is ! " The old women who sold flowers—the young ones were all in the factories these days —would pat the soldiers on the back, Americans as well as British, and cry, " God bless yer, laddie ! " Laurel would come in and scribble in her notebook. Ere the fleeting hour go by, Quick, thy tablets, memory !

XI

The Cotentin Peninsula thrusts up from France into the Channel, and at its head is the great port of Cherbourg. Now it was becoming plain that this port was the first goal of the American Army. They held the western part of the beachhead and the British had the eastern ; the British goal was the railroad town of Caen, and it was a harder assignment, because Germany lay in that direction, and also the great network of railroads through Holland and Belgium and the industrial part of France. The bulk of the German armies along the Channel were east of the invasion zone, so the British would have their hands full holding on, while the Americans were able to advance. That might be hard on British feelings, but there was no helping it ; they had been holding on for nearly five years, all over the world, and it had become their speciality.

The American plan was to cut across the base of the Cotentin, thus isolating Cherbourg, and then taking it. Normandy is the name of the province, and it was from here that William the Conqueror had launched his invasion of England, not quite nine hundred years before. It is a land of granite rocks, and the houses are built of them, and each house makes an excellent fortress—from the point of view of those who hold it. Even when it has been shelled and bombed to ruins, it will be discovered that some of the enemy have stuck it out in the cellars and then come up with machine-guns.

The rest of the rocks have been patiently dragged off the fields on sledges and built into fences, or more properly, continuous stone heaps ; the underbrush has grown up through them and covered them, and so the enemy had a series of ready-made fortifications, mile after weary mile. The *bocage* country, it is called, the French word meaning copse. Some of the fields were pasture ; others were apple orchards, and in June they were in full foliage, making a cover which could never be entirely destroyed. No matter how much the hedgerows were bombed, there would always be Jerries left in the trenches, with weapons and ammunition in abundance ; it meant that thousands of American and British boys had to die among the poppies, or be wounded and carried back to hospitals in the English coast towns.

Such was the Army's job. Tanks and guns had to be unloaded on the beaches and carried up to the roads. Trucks had to follow, bringing fuel and ammunition. Dive-bombers and artillery had to blast holes in the *bocage* so that tanks could force their way through, while planes were bombing the next *bocage* to keep the enemy there from interfering. How many *bocages* to the mile depended upon the size of the farms ; there might be a dozen or there might be two dozen ; each had to be taken, and there was no such thing as outflanking them, because the whole country was the same.

Lanny knew this land, having motored through it on his sort of honeymoon with Marie de Bruyne, when he had had only half as many years as he had now. That too had been summer-time, and they had thought it marvellously beautiful ; they hadn't happened to think of it from the military point of view. Lanny had just missed World War I, being too young, and while he predicted direfully that another was on the way, he didn't let it keep him from being happy with music and art and poetry and love. Now he described the country to the others, its farm-houses of granite, its chests of ancient oak, its sturdy horses, its sweet cider, and another kind of cider that was sour, with a powerful kick. There were aspects not so pleasant to contemplate—bed-bugs, for example. A pious land, with a shrine at every cross-road, it had been a centre of reaction through all French history. Now, alas, its crowded little towns would be blown to rubble.

Thus the map of the great adventure was unrolled and spread before them. The British were expecting to take Caen, and then the great harbour of Le Havre ; the Americans would block off Cherbourg, and then turn southward and block off the peninsula of Brittany and take the harbours there. Harbours were what the forces had to have, and quickly, if the expected counter-attacks were to be repelled. It was only after Lanny got back to America that he learned from Alston of the devices which had been prepared to meet this situation ; they were the most elaborate devices ever used in war : two artificial harbours, each as big as the port of Dover, built in movable sections and towed across the Channel.

A job for the Royal Engineers; at twenty-seven different sites in muddy coves scattered around the shores of the British Isles they had dredged out great basins, and in them had built a total of a hundred and fifty caissons made of concrete, each as big as a house. They weighed up to thousands of tons, but they would float because they were hollow; when they were completed, the water was let into the basins, and they were floated out and towed by tugs. Anti-aircraft guns were mounted on top, little P.T.-boats darted around them to keep off subs, and they dragged barrage balloons against dive-bombers. Thus guarded, they moved at three miles an hour until they reached the invasion shore. Each caisson had its appointed spot, marked by a buoy, and it had stopcocks so that water could be let in to sink it in an hour. There was a mile-long line of them, behind which great fleets of ships could lie safely. It was a brilliant British invention.

The sides of this artificial harbour were made by bringing in old ships, assembled from far and near, and blowing out their bottoms with dynamite. Outside, beyond the line of caissons, was a breakwater made of large water-tight steel boxes, the shape of cigar boxes; they were securely anchored and served to break the forces of the immense waves which beat upon this coast during storms. Inside the artificial harbours were piers made of floating steel boxes ingeniously contrived to rise and fall with the tides—tremendous tides in this Channel, as high as twenty-two feet. As many as seven Liberty ships could unload against these piers at one time. The artificial harbours were known as Mulberry and Gooseberry, and all their various parts had code names, Phoenixes and Bombardons and Whales; the old ships were Corncobs, and the invasion itself was Overlord. In his youth Lanny had wondered who gave all the names to the Pullman cars, and now he wondered who had the job of thinking up these odd military appellations.

XII

The colossal meat-grinder was now working at full speed, grinding up German bodies, and German tanks and planes and guns and transportation. It would grind British and American and Canadian, also—the difference was that the

Allies had more of everything than their foes and could bring in replacements. It was a war of attrition, and the side that had something left at the end would be the victor. No use shedding tears over it, that was what the world was like, and you had no other world to live in. The Allied chiefs had said unconditional surrender, and that meant no talking, only fighting.

Laurel tore herself away from the radio and wrote bits of her article. She would bring each one to Lanny and wait eagerly while he read it. He was glad they were good—for what would he have done otherwise? She would write, and then become dissatisfied, and put in something else, and then change her mind, back and forth. John Burroughs, the naturalist, had once declared, " This writing is an uncomfortable business ; it makes your head hot and your feet cold and it stops the digestion of your food." Lanny, who had been married to a writer for two years and a half now, decided that it was worse than having babies.

At last he persuaded her that the manuscript was good enough, and then she had to submit it to the censor, another ordeal. While awaiting his verdict, she went to see her commanding officer, a much harassed lady, for this was the first time women had ever been taken into the Army, and it was still a man's world. Laurel wanted to get across that Channel ; she would never feel happy until she was sharing the danger and the pain. But they wouldn't let her across ; it was no place for a woman. After arguing and pleading and cabling her editors, all she could get was a promise to send her down to one of the Channel ports—on the English side—and there let her talk to the men going across and those who had come back to the hospitals. Surely there was story material in that.

Laurel's husband was having trouble with his conscience, too. He was too comfortable in a de luxe hotel. There ought to be something more he could do to help fool Hitler. He wondered, had he accomplished anything in Spain ? Days passed, and the great counter-attack did not come ; and had Lanny had anything to do with that ? Were the Germans worrying about the possibility that this Normandy landing might be a feint, and that the Allies were planning a still heavier stroke in front of Calais, or farther east, in Belgium or Holland ?

A picturesque situation over in Normandy : the German commander, Rommel, was facing his old enemy from North Africa, Montgomery. Rommel was the violent man, and it would be his temperament to hit the invaders with everything he had or could get hold of. But the over-all commander was General von Rundstedt, whom Lanny knew from the old days at Berchtesgaden, and also through Emil Meissner, whose friend he was. Rundstedt was a cautious man, who would weigh the consequences and not stake his everything on one throw. Among the factors he was weighing, would there be a letter from the president of Budd-Erling Aircraft, warning his son under no circumstances to go into Holland ?

XIII

Lanny cabled Robbie in the usual way and waited for his airplane ticket to show up. Laurel was to leave on Saturday morning ; and on the evening of Thursday, the 15th of June, they went to a show, and afterward had a bite to eat. You were always hungry, because meals were so strictly limited ; if you had bread you couldn't have dessert. They came in about midnight, and just as they entered the lobby an air alert sounded. They went down into the shelter, the fashionable guests and hotel staff mixed together, something which would never have happened in Old England.

Here was one more chance to observe the English people, and Laurel learned that their reaction was one of boredom ; they had thought they were through with this sort of nuisance, and that it was the Germans' turn. Everybody was tired and sleepy and nobody talked. They waited, and listened to the rattle of ack-ack, and felt the ground shake with heavy explosions. Usually these ceased quickly, for there were only a few German planes and they passed on or got shot down. But this time the shaking of the earth continued, sometimes heavy, more often light. Disgusted rich people sitting on benches leaned back against hard walls and used bad language under their breath. They had to stay all night, and all day too, unless they got sick of it and decided that they would just as soon be dead.

The P.A. leaned over to his wife and whispered, " This

must be it—the V-1's." He had told her about them at the
time he had brought Frances to Newcastle ; but so much time
had elapsed that she had decided he must be mistaken. Most
English people had decided that it was just another of Dr.
Goebbels' bluffs, an effort to keep his people hoping and
working. The German people had decided the same. In
Spain Lanny had read that their question had become, " *Wo
ist die Wuwa ?* " Where is the Wonder Weapon! Even B4,
the British Intelligence, was divided on the question ; some
reports said yes and some no.

But here the damned things were at last ! In spite of all
the bombing of launching sites, the enemy had got enough
of them ready so that some three hundred could be sent over
in the first twenty-four hours. A period of stormy weather
had been chosen, so that British flyers would have trouble
in finding the objects in the sky and couldn't see the sites on
the ground. But the people on English ground could see
them, and hear them too. They made a loud hissing noise,
and a sort of put-put-put like an old Ford engine, but much
bigger. So long as you heard the sound you were all right,
for the thing was going overhead ; but when the sound ceased,
as it did suddenly, then look out for yourself ! It meant that
the power was shut off and the thing was coasting down ; you
had about two seconds in which to dive into a ditch or a
foxhole before it hit the ground and exploded.

What you saw in the air was a plane fifteen or twenty feet
across and twenty-five feet long. It had no propeller, but shot
out a streak of flame behind. Its speed was about three
hundred miles per hour, and only the fastest pursuit planes
could catch it ; often the thing was over London before they
shot it down, and what good did that do—since it exploded
just the same ? It had the force of a one-ton bomb, and
Londoners knew what that meant : houses blasted, fires
blazing, people having to be dug out of ruins, dead or dying.
It meant women cowering all night in damp and chilly
shelters, and children having to be sent out into the country
again—all the miseries that Londoners had been enduring for
four years and a half.

Laurel said, " You were right about Frances "—and that
was some satisfaction, but not enough. Lanny had called Irma

on the telephone and told her about the child. He hadn't offered to see her, and she hadn't asked him to come. When his daughter was there he had a right to visit the Castle, but when she was not there it would have been bad taste—besides being a bore. Apparently the new weapons were all aimed at London, but many of them went astray, just as Lanny had predicted, and nobody in the southern half of England could feel safe for a moment.

Rocket planes, robot planes, flying bombs, buzz bombs, doodlebugs, junebugs—the British people had many names for their new tormentors. It didn't take the authorities long to gather up fragments and learn just what was hitting them : steel-bodied, pilotless planes, jet-powered and not radio-controlled. Search planes and bombers would have to be sent after the launching sites, and pursuit planes would have to patrol the coast day and night, find the objects by radar, and get on their trails in the few seconds their speed allowed. In that way more than half of them would be stopped ; but London and its environs would never again be free of terror until their armies had fought their way eastward along the coast and captured the nests from which these stinging hornets flew.

Laurel was going to Southampton, and Lanny would have had to get a pass to accompany her ; he couldn't because his own ticket might arrive at any hour. Business as usual, in spite of all the instruments in the devil's armoury ! Lanny saw her to the station, and there they parted, as people do in wartime, knowing that they may never see each other again. " If anything happens to me, take care of Baby," she said, and of course he promised, but added that she would be all right, not so many of the *Wuwas* were hitting that far south. He didn't make a similar request of her, but left her to think that he was going to be safe in the land of his fathers, at least for some time. He didn't suggest the possibility of her giving up this assignment ; she had put her hand to the plough and he knew she would go to the end of the furrow. Standing in Waterloo Station, he let her have a little cry on his shoulder ; he had tears running down his own cheeks, and didn't have to be embarrassed, for it was one of the commonest sights all over this realm, this England.

BOOK EIGHT

ACTION IN THE TENTED FIELD

22

Thou Hast Great Allies

I

LANNY was flown by the familiar northern route, Prestwick to Newfoundland. The earth was at its summer solstice, and afforded an all-daylight trip. When he was set down on Long Island, the first thing he did was to phone Baker and tell him to call back at the New York apartment ; then he made haste to inspect that wonderful baby, now twenty months old, who toddled about and gazed with wonder at this big tall man who came in so suddenly, smiled at you so agreeably, tossed you into the air, and taught you new fascinating sounds. The big man went to the telephone and kept his promise to his wife, sending her a cablegram saying that everything in the world was perfect. Then he called his father to report on his own family and ask about the father's. Having performed these duties, he sat down in front of the radio to hear what Raymond Swing and H. V. Kaltenborn and the rest had to report about progress on the Cotentin.

Lanny's appointment gave him several days, time enough to get a car from his father and to call on some of his clients and report on the state of the arts in Spain ; time to write a lot of letters and have a talk with Zoltan and consent to another raise in the price of Detazes. Shameless profiteering, but then, what is the value of a painting except what people are willing to pay ? The supply was getting lower, and Beauty Budd had to live, and Marceline would need money if ever she got out of Germany alive. Art was art, but it was also business, and objects of beauty were surrounded by hordes of speculators, talking eagerly about prices, and the changes in taste which unaccountably swept over the world and made some things "the rage" and others "old hat." You had to guess; if you had guessed Cézanne and van Gogh you rode on a wave of prosperity, and if you had guessed the Barbizon school you were sunk.

Alston was passing through New York, and somehow he always knew where Lanny was. They spent an evening together, driving up the Hudson on a lovely moonlit night, talking secrets for which the Nazis would have paid many millions of dollars. The old gentleman was beginning to feel his years; he looked tired, as everybody did who was carrying the burdens of this war. Lanny's heart was sad and he wished he could do more. Alston said he helped by being cheerful and keeping a clear view of the ultimate goals. Perhaps also he had been the means of persuading Rundstedt to hold an extra division or two in Holland—who could say?

The slugging match was continuing, and, as always, it wasn't going as fast as you wanted it, as you had dreamed it. They were having the worst June weather in some forty years, high winds and heavy overcast making co-operation between land and air forces almost impossible; the Phoenixes were shifting their positions and the Corncobs were breaking up; the American Army's artificial harbour was about half ruined. Cherbourg, although surrounded, was still holding out, and Monty had been beaten back from Caen. More than a million men had been put on shore, and the efforts to get them what they needed was breaking the back of S.O.S.—Services of Supply. It was by accident that the designation of this Army branch happened to be identical with the emergency call of ships at sea, but the ex-geographer said it fitted exactly in this crisis.

II

Lanny motored to Washington, with the memory of Laurel in the seat beside him; he missed her, but kept himself happy thinking of the service she was rendering. He had brought a carbon copy of her manuscript in his bag, by way of precaution; he called up her editor—not saying that he was husband but just friend—and learned that her copy had arrived and was thought well of. He imagined her under the

buzz bombs, talking to wounded men in improvised hospitals
—schools, theatres, any sort of place that would give shelter.
She would suffer poignant grief, but then she had to suffer in
order to write.   He recalled the remark of Liszt concerning
some woman with a voice lacking in temperament.   He had
said he would like to marry her and break her heart in order
that she might be able to sing.

Highway One was crowded with trucks, never so many.
They went loaded to the ports, to Philadelphia and Baltimore;
they were emptied in record time and came back with raw
materials for the factories.   Great clouds of smoke poured out
from tall stacks all along this route; America was maintaining
this greatest war on a hundred fronts all over the earth.
Americans were proud of it, and few stopped to reflect that
we were exhausting the resources of a continent, sinking the
products in the sea or scattering them over the earth—wrecked
planes, trucks, tanks, guns, not to mention countless billions
of shell fragments that would never be collected.

He put these melancholy thoughts behind him; he bathed,
shaved, dressed, and ate a delicious dinner of soft-shell crabs
fresh out of the Chesapeake, and lettuce, tomatoes, and strawberries from Maryland—" Anne Arundel strawberries ! " he
had heard a hawker call as he passed through Baltimore.
He sat and read the evening papers; Cherbourg had fallen.
The port had been badly smashed by the Germans, but the
American engineers wouldn't take long to clear the entrance
and rig up some makeshift docks.   The American armies
were turning south, to keep the Germans from sealing them
in the Cotentin.   " Keep them moving ! " was General Ike's
formula.

So the P.A. wore his most cheerful smile when he was
escorted to the upstairs bedroom in the White House; he
found his Boss grinning like the Cheshire cat.   " We did it,
Lanny ! We did it, and it can't be undone ! " They exchanged
a strong handclasp on that, and Roosevelt went on, " Winston
is the British bulldog, he never lets go."

" But now it's Rommel he's got by the nose," chuckled
Lanny.   Then he added, " And Rommel is throwing pepper
into his eyes."   He meant the buzz bombs, and of course the
President wanted to know what his agent had seen and heard

in London. He had before him a report on a launching ramp which had been captured near Brix, on the way to Cherbourg ; it was covered by from sixteen to twenty feet of reinforced concrete, and the engineers declared that a twelve-thousand-pound bomb wouldn't penetrate it, even by direct hit. " The infantry will have to take them all," said F. D. R.

It was a long session, because there was the whole story of Spain to be told : the attitude of the Franco regime, and the extent to which they would keep their word, if at all. " Portugal has just signed up to send no more wolfram concentrates to Germany," the Boss revealed. " We are convincing them, step by step." Lanny said that the taking of Cherbourg would help, but a better persuader would be the taking of Paris. He described the state of shell-shock in which the Spanish people lived ; one business man had remarked that he would rather have another hundred years of Franco than another hundred hours of civil war.

The best story was of Robbie's letter, which Lanny hadn't risked mentioning in his reports. He had no copy of it, but he could recite it pretty nearly by heart, and the President slapped the bedcover and gave his favourite exclamation, which was " Golly ! " When Lanny said he would never know whether his trick had worked, the other said it was very significant that Rommel had held off and made no real counter-attack. Lanny was pleased, but at the same time wasn't sure how much of this Roosevelt really meant ; he was such a kind-hearted Boss and so liked to make people feel good !

III

" What do you want me to do next, Governor ? " Lanny took it as part of his duty not to take up the time of this busiest man in the world.

" Something has turned up that is right up your alley," was the busiest man's reply. " We are organizing a team to handle the works of art that we recover from the Germans. I don't need to tell you what a tremendous job that is going to be ; they've been plundering the Continent, and we shall have tens of thousands of priceless objects to dig out of hiding-places, and protect, and restore to their rightful owners. I've appointed a commission, and it occurs to me that you might be the man to take charge of the field work."

"Governor, you're paying me a great compliment, but I'm surely not the man. I've never had any experience in managing other people—I've had all I could do to manage myself. That job calls for an executive, a fellow who knows how to open an office and pick a staff and assign duties and see that people do them. I don't know anything about giving orders. I'd hate it so much I couldn't be a success."

"I hate it too," confessed the head of the United States government. "It hurts me to find fault with people, and when I find that a man I like isn't equal to his job, I lie awake nights agonizing over how I can tell him. Generally I wiggle out of it by writing him a letter."

"Or by kicking him upstairs," suggested the P.A. "Giving him a job with a bigger title and fewer duties." This brought a chuckle, and the P.A. went on, "You know, I'd do anything on this earth for you, but it's no good starting on a job that I know I'm not fit for. You find a big, strong-jawed, hard-fisted business man to run the team, and let me go along and whisper into his ear. I can be a good adviser. I know the languages and the people. I know the salt mines and the castles where the pictures will be hidden, and I know the Germans who have the secrets. I know the threats that will scare them and the bribes that will tempt them. All that might be a lot of fun ; but running an office and keeping records and signing cheques would worry me to death."

"All right, Lanny. I've already asked the advice of some of the people at the Fogg Museum, and no doubt they'll suggest the right director. I'll give you a card to them, and you can get their ideas and give them yours. But don't say anything about the secret work you've been doing."

"Of course not, Governor. But, may I take a minute or two more of your time ? I've an idea of my own that I think might be important."

"By all means. Shoot ! "

"I'm not asking any secrets, but I take it for granted that we'll be landing in southern France sooner or later and going up the Rhône valley. That's the country I know best in all the world ; I lived most of my life on the Riviera, and I am certain I could be of use and help prepare the way for the Army."

"You mean to go in ahead of the landing?"

"It wouldn't be as risky as it sounds. I have so many friends there, and some would shelter me. There is one special situation that has fascinated my mind: I think I have told you about the de Bruyne family, whom I have known intimately. The old man is in Paris and I saw him there the last time I came through. There are two sons, who are practically my godchildren—their mother commended them to my care on her deathbed. The elder, Denis *fils*, is on our side, and is now in hospital in Algiers; the younger, Charlot, went with the Vichy crowd and is now a captain in the French auxiliary force which helps the Germans to keep order. The last I heard he was quartered in my mother's old home at Juan-les-Pins, and sent me word that he was keeping it safe. I want to get to him and persuade him to do a Darlan."

That was a phrase which had come to be current in the war; it meant coming over to the Allied side, in the nick of time, just fast enough to keep out of jail or away from a firing squad. "But suppose he won't do it, Lanny?" asked the Boss.

"I think I know how to fix it so that he will. It is my idea to get a letter from his father, ordering him to come across. You know how it is with these St.-Germain French, the family and the Church rule their lives. The old man made the boy's marriage for him, and he'll make his Darlan for him."

"What is the old man's attitude?"

"Denis *père* is a business man, and the last time I visited him I could see that he was ready to come over; he's a heavy investor in Budd-Erling stock and can't possibly want to be on the losing side. By now he must know that National Socialism is *fini*."

"But how can you get to him, Lanny?"

"The Air Force is putting little planes down in cow pastures all over France now, and I can draw them a map of a field not more than a mile from the Château de Bruyne, which is in Seine-et-Oise close to Paris. I was a member of the family, to all intents, and I know the country so well that I could get to the château on the darkest night. The old

servants know me and would never give me away. If Denis
is in Paris, they can call him home. I'll get the letter to
Charlot, and incidentally a lot of information, and the O.S.S.
can pick me up and fly me out. It sounds like a dangerous
stunt, but it's routine for them and easy compared to some
that they do. The point is, Governor, I might not merely
bring over Charlot, but all the officers in his group. If he
throws his lot in with us, he won't stop there, for he's a bold
man, and something of a fanatic. It's my guess he's been in
the Nazi service long enough to hate their guts ; and even if
he won't take my advice, he surely won't betray me. His
mother's ghost would rise up before him."

" Well, you know, Lanny, I hate to risk losing you——"

" You won't lose me, Governor. I promise. And anyhow,
I'll meet your Fogg Museum people first and unload everything
I have, so nothing will be lost. After that, I'll be expendable."

" All right, old man, if that's what you want, I can't say
no. When would you want to go ? "

" I figure that I ought to be in Juan about a week before
the landing. No use going too early, because any plot is bound
to leak in course of time. I learned in Algiers that it's a mistake
to strike too early."

" I would tell you the date of the landing, but I don't know
it. Everything depends upon landing craft—how soon we
shall be able to spare them from the Channel. We've lost a
number of them, and there's a continuing clamour for them
from the Pacific. All I can tell you is, we shall invade France
from the south on the day we can get the ships and the planes
there."

Said the erudite Lanny, " The Rhône valley has been the
gateway of all conquerors of Western Europe ever since the
beginning of history."

" Exactly so ; and when we get to the top we'll just walk
around Switzerland and into Bavaria, and block the Nazis'
little plan to hole up in the mountains there and make them
into a fortress."

" O.K., Governor, it's a date ! "

" What you do is to talk the whole thing out with O.S.S.,
make your plans, and let them call you when the time for
action comes. I won't be here, because I'm going to take a

long trip." (It was to the Pacific, as Lanny learned later.) " Meantime you can be helping the art people. Also, maybe you can give some tips to another outfit we're getting together —a bunch of young scientists who are going to dig out everything about the German secret weapons, atomic fission and jet propulsion and the rest that you know about. O.S.S. will put you in touch with them too."

The P.A. said, " You make my heart jump up and hit me under the throat ! " He jumped up himself and held out his hand. " I've no right to take any more of your time, Governor. I've got my career laid out for the rest of the war ! "

IV

In the old brick building by the gasworks Lanny went through the usual routine : he told his story to General Donovan and his top people, and was plied with questions about the Nazi-Fascists in Spain and about London under the buzz bombs. Everything he said was taken down—they had a marvellous new instrument which recorded what you said on a tiny aluminium wire, and it lasted for ever, unless you wiped it off with a magnet. Later they turned him over to the Spanish section, and then to the section which had to do with Operation Anvil, the invasion of the French Riviera.

An interesting experience to the grown-up playboy of Bienvenu ! They had detailed air photographs of every foot of the French coast from Mentone on the east to Port Bou on the west ; all were numbered and indexed, and you could get anyone in a fraction of a minute. Lanny could look down on his mother's home, and the beach where he had played with the fisherboys, and the rocks from which he had dived ; he spent hours with a young Air Force lieutenant, marking these maps and answering questions about winds and waves, the temperature of the water, the depths and visibility, the character of the bottom. Maybe the Commander-in-Chief of Army, Navy, and Air Force didn't know when this invasion was coming, but it looked as if this young lieutenant did, for he confined his questions to conditions in midsummer—and summer was already here !

Also, the shore : how high were the rocks and how solid,

and what were the buildings made of ? Especially important, the photographs showed structures which hadn't existed when Lanny had last visited Bienvenu, two years ago. They might be camouflaged block-houses, radar stations, anything military. They were studied through a microscope ; then an extra set of the photographs was brought and two were placed in a stereoscope. Amazing—the houses, the trees, the rocks rose right up before your eyes !

And then questions about the population : what sorts of people could be trusted and what not ? Lanny explained that it was a miscellaneous population, mostly parasitic, and its industries were parasitic. This puzzled the young officer, who had specialized in photography, not sociology. Lanny explained that what they produced on the Riviera was pleasures for the idle rich. He added, " A sort of very old Miami." That was a satisfactory translation.

He couldn't say how many of his old friends were still there. The Americans would have been interned. He named some of the French, including Jerry Pendleton's wife, who was presumably still running the *pension*, perhaps for the Germans —who could guess ? Jerry would, no doubt, welcome an assignment to go in there and help prepare the invasion. Lanny desired especially the collaboration of Raoul Palma, Spanish-born Socialist who had conducted a workers' school in Cannes for some years and recently had given the O.S.S. important help in Toulon. They told Lanny that Raoul, alias Bruges, was now the head of an active group of Partisans in the Midi, and they would arrange to have him on hand when the time came to put the P.A. ashore at Juan.

And then the affairs of the elder Denis de Bruyne. The O.S.S. couldn't or wouldn't say whether or not the Army meant to take Paris, and certainly nobody could say when they would be able to ; progress was discouragingly slow at present. But to set a man down among the estates and farms of Seine-et-Oise, and to pick him up one or two nights later would be easy enough. Cub planes were going out every night from England, and now from the Cotentin, carrying arms and supplies and money and instructions to the Partisans ; since the invasion it had become a big business. No movie writer could imagine anything more exciting, and it was hard for the young people in this organization to keep from telling about their triumphs. But they were all under oath, and they just grinned and said, " We're doing it, all right—and we'll do it for you."

Everything was planned, and code words agreed upon, and the whole project, with a name of its own, Operation Bienvenu, was sealed up and put on file. Lanny was to call a certain man once a week to find out about the prospects. That ended that; and he was turned over, first to the art section, and then to the most secret of all sections, which had to do with German weapons and scientific discoveries. It bore the odd name of Alsos, which nobody could explain. It was so hush-hush that men in the same department had no idea what the others were doing, and a P.A. was warned that when he talked to a jet-propulsion man he mustn't mention atomic fission, and vice versa.

The German section, too, in which he had made many friends, wanted some of a P.A.'s time. All the Germans he had met in Spain had to be indexed, with everything he could tell about their activities and characters. Sometimes the smallest detail might lead to some important conclusion. What was their mood as to the war's events? Was the bombing of civilians breaking their nerve or stiffening it? Was the formula of " unconditional surrender " a help or a handicap to the Allied cause? What had the Nazis tried to find out from a well-informed American? Were they still in love with their Führer, and what would be the effect upon them if the effort to kill him were to succeed?

Lanny never asked questions; but he too could learn things from the questions asked of him. Obviously, those Germans who sought peace by the method of eliminating Hitler would be stirred to fresh activity by the Allied landing in France. O.S.S. men revealed that they were keyed up over this subject and were expecting something to happen. They had a code name for it, Operation Breakers; they asked questions about this prominent Reichswehr general and that, and Lanny was astounded, for it seemed to indicate that this one and that were involved in the plot, and he could hardly believe his ears. But no one had heard anything about either Oskar von Herzenberg or Marceline Detaze.

V

The P.A. drove back to New York and from there to Boston, where, just across the Charles River, the famed Fogg Museum is situated. An old Puritan city, very proud of its culture, calling itself the Hub of the Universe, and not much interested in the spokes. Politically speaking, it had been taken over by the Irish ; but its wealthy old families didn't speak politically, they withdrew themselves in cold reserve, and sent their sons to Harvard and their daughters to Radcliffe. When these young people came out, they felt desperately adventurous when they made contacts outside their narrow circle. There were stories such as the one about the New York banker who wanted an employee and made inquiry of a friend in Boston. The Bostonian recommended a young man and gave full details as to his ancestry : to which the crude New Yorker replied, " I want a man for business, not for breeding purposes." The New York wits also delighted to tell about President Lowell of Harvard in the days when William Howard Taft was President of the United States. A visitor came to Lowell's office, and the prim secretary informed him, " The President has gone to Washington to see Mr. Taft."

Franklin Roosevelt was a Harvard man ; Robbie Budd had got his more hard-boiled education at Yale, which was perhaps one more reason for disliking the New Deal. As it happened, Esther Budd's family were Harvard, and she had a niece who was a graduate of the School of Art, connected with Harvard and the Fogg Museum. This well-brought-up and delightfully rich young lady had been put on full view before Lanny some three years before, when his stepmother had been hoping to find him the right sort of wife. Lanny had dutifully taken her to dinner and a show, but then he had disappeared on his business of trying to save the world from Nazi-Fascism, and Peggy Remsen had become a memory.

He knew that she had completed her course and was a perfectly educated museum director, looking for a museum to direct. In spite of being rich, she must have a job, that being the correct thing for a modern young lady in wartime. That she would get one was certain, for all museums have to raise funds, and none in New England would overlook a chance to gain the favour of two families such as the Remsens and the Budds. Lanny had thought of her the moment that F. D. R. had mentioned the Fogg; it was natural for Roosevelt to turn to Harvard, and it was natural for Lanny to wonder if Peggy Remsen would be one of the experts selected to take temporary control of the museum industry in the Axis lands.

There was nothing especially secret about the Monuments, Fine Arts and Archives Section of the Office of Military Government, United States Army; so when Lanny stopped off to visit his father's family in Newcastle, he mentioned where he was bound and what he had been asked to do. Sure enough, Esther remarked, "Peggy is working with that and expects to go overseas. She is greatly excited and considers it as the opportunity of her life." A curious thing about war, Lanny had observed, it provides opportunities for everybody, even more than there are people to take them. His mind was led to wonder, why couldn't this be arranged in peacetime also? But he didn't say that to his very serious and conservative stepmother, for it might have been taken for a Red remark, or at any rate Pinkish. He said, "I'll look her up and give her any help I can. I've managed to pick up quite a lot of information." He had never given his family a hint of having been in the Axis lands, but it could be that Robbie had guessed, and if so, he might have told his wife.

VI

Lanny found these people in Boston very nice indeed; they were intelligent, conscientious, and completely absorbed in their jobs. They were all in the Army, and wore uniforms, but that was more or less a formality; the Army had recognized them as specialists of a special kind and had put them off in a corner by themselves, so to speak. Family influence might have had something to do with this, but mostly it was the Army's awe of a subject as remote as the other side of the moon. What would a West Pointer know about telling a Titian from a Tintoretto, or how to repair a torn canvas, or how to prevent mildew in an old tapestry, or even how to pack an Aphrodite Anadyomene for shipment in a truck?

Obviously, if a young man or woman had spent years acquiring such knowledge and had a diploma to prove it, you wouldn't send him to basic training camp or set her to pounding the keys of a typewriter.

Not when you had to discover, rescue, and protect property which had a money value of hundreds of millions of dollars, possibly of billions ! There were single old masters which had been sold for half a million dollars, and others which were literally priceless, because the owners wouldn't have thought of parting with them. No one could guess how many tens of thousands of art treasures there might be, or what condition they might be in, or what difficulties might arise in locating and possessing them. People of the utmost integrity were needed for this job, and President Roosevelt had appointed Justice Roberts of the United States Supreme Court as the head of a commission, and he had turned to the leading museums of the country for the people who were equipped and whose character was such that when they found the crown jewels of the Holy Roman Empire they wouldn't steal them.

Lanny discovered that these young people had a great respect for him. They knew that he came from an old New England family, and that he had made purchases for the Winstead collection, the Taft collection, and others. He had lived abroad, whereas they had merely paid visits ; he spoke the languages freely, whereas they were self-conscious and classroomy. Most impressive of all was his acquaintance with the top people in the various countries. He actually knew the Nazis ; he was reticent about it, but evidently he had done business with them prior to the war. It was a bit suspicious, but he showed them a card from the President, and after that they guessed he must have been a secret agent—which put them still more in awe of him.

He was there to answer questions, and they gathered round in long sessions. For the first time they met a man who knew at first hand their opposite number, the German organization which they were to check and outwit. The E.R.R., the Einsatzstab Reichsminister Rosenberg, was named for the Baltic-born racial fanatic who was one of the chief Nazi propagandists. The word *Einsatz* means an enterprise or underaking, and the whole word is equivalent to our naval phrase "task force." Theirs was a task force for looting, very certainly the most colossal of its sort ever known in the world. The young Americans had read about it, and now listened to the details which Lanny had observed in Paris and Berlin and especially Karinhall.

The looters had taken the Musée du Jeu de Paume, the former handball court of the Bourbon kings, as a sort of clearing house for French art. Everything was brought here, and the best was exhibited to the insider, and they took their pick. Hitler, of course, had first choice, but of late he had been too busy to exercise it. Göring had second choice, and he was the world's greatest exerciser; he had his men on hand all the time. In various storage places which Lanny could tell about he had more than ten thousand of the greatest paintings of all schools. The best examples decorated the great rooms of Karinhall, which was intended to become a museum, and really was that now, only the public was not invited.

The son of Budd-Erling, who had been invited many times, told about the old-time robber baron's henchmen. The head of the Einsatzstab in Paris was Baron Kurt von Behr, an elderly aristocrat who had once lost his diplomatic post because of swindling. But that didn't matter in these days; he was now head of the German Red Cross, which gave him a pretext for being in Paris, and for having a permanently reserved table at Maxim's for the entertainment of his friends. He was as vain as his chief, and designed himself as many uniforms. He had the most elegant manners, and Lanny told these young people that if they captured him he would chat with them most charmingly and do his best to pull the wool over their eyes—and he would probably succeed, because it would be impossible for anyone who had been born and raised on Beacon Street to imagine such age-old corruption as this Baron represented.

Also there was Dr. Bunjes, head of the Franco-German Art Historical Society, Göring's own special looting group. He had published a pamphlet defending the procedure on the ground that the French might exchange the art works for planes and tanks. And there was Hofer, Göring's "curator," who was doing a good business on the side and might be a good person for the Army to catch. Even better might be Dr. Friedlinder, who had been the director of the Kaiser Friedrich Museum in Berlin. He had been arrested and brought before Göring, and *Der Dicke* had given him a choice of destinies, either to go into a concentration camp or to become one of Göring's art experts. The director exclaimed, " But I am a Jew! " To that the reply was, " *Wer Jude ist, bestimme ich.*" Who is a Jew is for me to decide !

Another person worthy of their attention was Bruno Lohse, Baron von Behr's assistant, young, blond, tall, and handsome. They must be warned against him, because he would lie to them. This would not be because he liked it, but because it was his duty. He was a true Nazi, and would remain one. That might be difficult for the Americans to understand unless they had read *Mein Kampf*; Lanny made them all promise to read it, for what was the use of going into a foreign land and wasting your time learning by costly mistakes when you could find it all clearly set down in a book that you could buy for two dollars ?

VII

The P.A. saw a good deal of Margaret Remsen, called Peggy. She was twenty-one or two, fair-haired and fair-minded, and very agreeable company. Like Laurel she was a W.A.C. captain, and looked natty in her new uniform. If Lanny hadn't been sent off to find out about the atomic bomb in Germany, and if he hadn't got wrecked in a plane and laid up in a hospital, and if Laurel Creston hadn't come aboard the yacht *Oriole*, sailing to the Far East—if all those things hadn't happened, it might well have been that Lanny would have asked Peggy to marry him. But the other things had happened, and that settled the matter ; for whatever modern ideas this granddaughter of the Puritans might hold, Lanny was sure there wouldn't be any about sex. She was unmarried, and so far as he could find out, unattached ; he hoped she hadn't been cherishing memories of him, and by way of precaution he talked about his wife and what she was doing, and about the little boy who was about to be brought to Newcastle to spend the summer.

Peggy's parents lived in Boston, in a fine home, and that

was a pleasant place to come and meet the other " Monuments " people. (There just had to be some way of abbreviating " Monuments, Fine Arts, and Archives Section of Supreme Headquarters of the Allied Expeditionary Forces ; so they called themselves the Roberts Commission or Monuments officers or outfit or people.) They would come for tea, or for the evening, and listen to the radio a while, and then talk shop. They were full of eagerness, like small children being put to bed on Christmas Eve to wait for Santa Claus. Lanny Budd, one-man " Intelligence," was asked to explain why it took so long to break through at Saint-Lô, and did it mean that the Germans were really invincible, and how far would the Army have to get before they would come upon art objects to be salvaged and stored ?

Nobody could have imagined the immensity of this job, and even Lanny was surprised by the thoroughness with which the Army had gone in for it. When the Commander-in-Chief—Cominch in the technical lingo—said " everything," he meant just that. The libraries and museums of America had been ransacked for catalogues of collections, both public and private, all over Europe. Individuals had sent in data —refugees and plundered owners, not merely at home but throughout the non-Axis world. The O.S.S. had contributed the knowledge its spies and secret agents had brought in. There were photographs of every castle, and sometimes of its rooms ; photographs of monasteries, caves, salt mines, and numerous other places where treasures might be hidden.

The young art experts of America were going into the most romantic adventure in the whole long story of art. What were the treasures of Captain Kidd and Sir Francis Drake and even of Aladdin's Cave compared with the gems of the Rothschild family and the crown jewels of a dozen monarchs ancient and modern, to say nothing of the altar-pieces of the cathedrals of Ghent, Louvain, and Cracow, Michelangelo's statue of the Madonna and Child, and whole rooms full of paintings by Rembrandt, Van Dyck, Rubens, Velasquez, Raphael, Titian, and so on through a list that was like an index to an encyclopaedia of the art of painting ?

The Monuments people wanted to know, would the Nazis destroy all these treasures, or bury them underground, or carry them up into the last-stand fortress which they were reported to be planning in the Bavarian Alps? And which side would get to them first, the Anglo-U.S. or the Russians? Would the captured Nazis try to buy their freedom with information? And what would be the attitude of the ordinary Germans, would they hinder or help? The young experts thought Lanny was joking when he said, " Take along plenty of cigarettes and chocolates. They will be the currency."

VIII

Then there were the Alsos people, a quite different sort of learned folk. Many were young, like the Monuments, but they were less burdened with family and social traditions and dignities. Some had been farm-boys who had got their education the hard way ; without exception they were serious-minded persons, and growing more so every day under the pressures of this war. At first it had seemed a marvellous idea, to have all the world's resources at your disposal, to have A-1 priority on everything ; but by now they had discovered several flies in this ointment. For one thing, you couldn't ramble, you couldn't follow strange ideas which might flash into your mind ; you had to keep yourself pinned down to one special thing which had been assigned to you. And this business of secrecy, not being able to talk freely with any-body but a very small group whom you knew too well, not being able to publish, or to read other people's publications !

So far all scientific progress had depended upon the free and rapid exchange of ideas. A woman in Copenhagen made a discovery, and it was telegraphed all over the world, and within a few days a hundred different men in laboratories from Tokyo to Chicago were at work on the idea, testing it, and speculating as to its corollaries. But now all that was over ; everything was hush-hush, and there was a man standing over you with the threat of a jail sentence if you dropped the least hint of what you were doing. Not even to your wife could you tell it, and some wives got cross about it and were harassing their men.

Worst of all was the realization that all your discoveries were being turned to ends of destruction. If you came upon some idea for the production of health and wealth and happiness, you were told, "Yes, that'll be fine, but only after the war." And then you began to wonder, Would there ever be any "after the war"? Suppose this one went on, and another got started, and another? Talking with these young physicists, Lanny discovered that a new and strange set of ideas was beginning to burgeon in their minds. So far they had been entirely wrapped up in their speciality, which they proudly called exact science, with emphasis on the adjective; they had thought that was enough, and some had even thought it was everything and would solve all the problems of mankind. But now they were beginning to doubt, and to confront the horrid idea that they might have to meddle in some of the sciences which were so far from exact that they were hardly worthy to be called sciences at all. Politics, and economics, and ethics, and even religion—for what was the good of giving men tremendous new powerful tools if the only thing they could find to do with them was to kill one another?

"So far in history," said young Professor Oppenheimer, "wars have been fought by soldiers, and it was they who died; the people at home went on working and living. But now war has been brought to the women and children, and we are providing the military men with the means of wiping out the human race."

It was the new weapons that were frightening the physicists out of their wits. Morse's phrase, "What hath God wrought!" had been changed to "What Satan hath wrought"—and the nuclear scientists were Satan, or at any rate his imps. They had gone and done it, by this summer of 1944 they were sure they had done it, and their minds were torn, one-half pride and eagerness to finish, and one-half horror at the thought of what it might do.

You had impulses to turn back and throw the whole thing into the middle of the ocean. But you couldn't, because the enemy might get it. You were in a trap; the brass hats had got you and would never let you go. You had harnessed the power of the sun for them, the power that had kept it blazing for a billion years and would keep it blazing for a billion more, at a temperature of twenty or thirty thousand degrees Fahrenheit. And now the "brass" was going to use it to shrivel up this pitiful little planet and make it uninhabitable for the rest of time.

IX

In a room of the Physics Laboratory of Columbia University the P.A. had a meeting with four of the Alsos men. They were not the top-flight physicists, but had been chosen because they were young and vigorous and had asked for the adventure. Washington had told them that Budd shared the most crucial of all secrets, so they talked freely in his presence. Like the Monuments people, they looked up to him because he was older and had been all over the territory they were planning to visit. Nobody ever expressed any doubt that they would go there—the only question was how soon. Lanny told them how he had spent two months at Princeton, being tutored by Dr. Braunschweig under the supervision of Professor Einstein, in order that he might know what questions to ask about nuclear fission in Germany. They were immensely impressed and did not lose this feeling even when he added that he had forgotten nearly all the formulas in three years.

The traveller told how he had made contact with Professor Schilling in Berlin. This very important man was just waiting for the Americans to come and get him : he was old and tired, but his head was full of knowledge, and he hated the Nazi gangsters. No doubt he would know others, whose names he had not been free to mention to a secret agent. Lanny told about Plötzen, another top man, whose home he had visited ; Lanny had posed as an American traitor, a Nazi sympathizer, but it was possible, of course, that the physicist had guessed something different. Espionage and counter-espionage made a complicated game, and you could never be entirely sure of the ground you were standing on. Plötzen was wealthy and elegant, and Lanny's guess was that he would know how to get along with his conquerors. Give him a laboratory and he would go to work cheerfully and make jokes about wha had happened under the grotesque Nazis, the *Spitzbuben*.

Salzmann was a different proposition ; a grim old Junker, and no doubt a patriot for any German government however barbarous. But he would be sure to hate the Russians, and if he saw he had to choose he would prefer the Americans.

Nine-tenths of the educated Germans would, Lanny was sure —for the Russians lived near by, while the Americans lived a long way off and the habit of disliking them was not so deeply rooted. There would be a race for Berlin, and a hunt for scientists even more eager than that for the crown jewels of the Holy Roman Empire. The nuclear physicists had something that would melt all the jewels in the world to a glaze !

It was not only the atom bomb these Alsos men were after ; they wanted every scientific secret in the Axis world, and every kind of scientist who might be willing to work for our side. And they were doing the same thorough job as the art people ; they had every sort of catalogue and photograph and scientific record, index and card file and map and programme. They didn't need Lanny to tell them about the Kaiser Wilhelm Institut, or Peenemünde, or Rjukan.

What they did was to ransack his mind as to every personality he had met and every hint he had picked up as to secrets. All about V-1 and V-2 and V-3 ; about Red Erickson and the oil refineries, and about Dr. Stoffel and the new process of making wood into sugar—had they heard of that ? These particular men hadn't, but if the report had been turned in to O.S.S. no doubt somebody would be working on it. And then there was Bernhardt Monck, alias Braun, alias Vetterl, and half a dozen other names ; he was now in Stockholm, and had once helped to smuggle out a new type of airplane supercharger for Robbie Budd ; he had known a whole chain of anti-Nazi people in Germany, and probably most of them were dead by now, but you couldn't be sure. Monck was certainly a man who ought to be taken on by Alsos.

There was also the old watchmaker who had helped Lanny to escape from Germany the last time. He was a Socialist, and Americans had the habit of thinking of a Socialist as some kind of " nut " ; but it would be well for the Alsos people to realize that the German Socialists had a philosophy a century old and were the people upon whom any democratic government would have to rest. No production or even scientific work could be carried on without workers, and these workers learned about what they were doing and often understood it better than the bosses. Lanny suggested that one of the first aims of Alsos should be to get in touch with the Socialists wherever they went in the Axis lands, tell them what was wanted, and see how quickly it would be produced. He had given this same advice to the Monuments outfit, for you couldn't move thousands of paintings without workers, and those workers might have no sympathy with the job or the masters and would enjoy revealing the secret hiding-places of jewels and *objets d'art*.

X

Laurel wrote once a week as she had promised; and here was another person whose mind was torn. She was witnessing terrible scenes in the hospitals; her heart was wrung and it made her hate war worse than ever. But, on the other hand, she wanted this war won, and it couldn't be won except by fighting men, and they couldn't fight unless you kept up their courage and faith, and your own. Laurel wrote, " I hope the censor will let me say this," and the amused censor had written in the margin, " O.K."

The letters came by a delightful new process, called V-mail; they were photographed on microfilm, which was shipped across by airplane and printed on this side. The addressee received a queer little envelope with the address printed on one side and the letter inside; it was folded and sealed by machinery, and the process was quick and saved an enormous lot of transportation. The same thing was done for letters in reverse direction, and it was a great booster of morale; nothing pleased a man in a foxhole or a hospital so much as to get prompt word from the people he loved.

Laurel sent her stories a few pages at a time and left it to Lanny to put together—a great mark of confidence. The most marvellous stories, and all true. She could never know whether somebody had got some particular episode and cabled it, so she asked Lanny to cut out anything he had already seen in print or heard over the air. Episodes both horrible and humorous, the way they are in war. There was one concerning D-day on Omaha Beach, the code name for a landing place where the invasion ran into severe German resistance. The swells were high, the confusion great, and the enemy fire incessant. One G.I. was clinging to something in the water and a landing craft came drifting by. " Throw me a rope ! "

he shouted, and the men on the craft shouted back, " You don't want to come on board, we're sinking ! " The reply was, " I don't care what you're doing, throw me a rope ! I'm sitting on a mine ! "

Lanny wrote back and acknowledged every letter. He couldn't reveal what he was doing, only that it was useful and that he expected to return soon and would look her up if possible. He told about the baby and about various relatives and friends ; that, of course, was the sort of thing the censors wanted you to write about. He could say that the war appeared to be going well and that he hoped she wasn't in any danger. It was better not to mention what the danger might be. Plenty of love and kisses—but don't make " X " marks for the kisses, for they might be a code.

XI

Lanny got together with Jim Stotzlmann, and they talked war and then politics. The Republican convention had been held just after Lanny's return from England ; they had nominated Governor Dewey of New York as their Presidential candidate—a gentleman of whom it had been said that you had to know him well in order to dislike him. Jim said that F. D. R. knew him that well and would take great pleasure in thwarting his cherished ambition.

Now, the third week in July, the Democratic convention was due in Chicago, and Jim had been given leave so that he might attend. He urged his friend to come along, but Lanny said he might have a date with destiny. They discussed the prospects : there was no doubt that Roosevelt would be nominated for a fourth term, so the excitement centred about the vice-presidency. A great many persons, both friends and enemies, doubted that Roosevelt would be able to stand the strain of another four years, so it was possible that in naming a vice-presidential candidate the Democratic party would be choosing a future President of the United States.

The P.A. took in the show by way of the radio, which reported it entire. Nominating conventions are a curious and fascinating aspect of the democratic process ; this one lasted three days and nights, with something over a thousand dele-

gates and alternates attending, and an immense concourse of
spectators who had come from all over the land, and who
spent their time singing and shouting for four years more to
add to their twelve. The various state delegations placed
their "favourite sons" in nomination and then turned out
and paraded through the aisles behind canvas placards bearing
the names of their states. To one who had been brought up
in Europe it seemed a strange method of determining the
future of the richest and most powerful country in the world ;
but that was the way it was done, and if you didn't like it
you could go back where you had come from.

The fight centred about the then vice-president, Henry
Wallace, a man who had made for himself a host of friends
and an equal host of enemies. As Secretary of Agriculture in
the days of the great depression it had been his sad duty to
order the ploughing underground of crops and the slaughter
of millions of little pigs ; and millions of people took that
as a sign that he was insane. They could not understand
that they were living under an insane economic system, which
produced enormous quantities of food but didn't give the
people enough money to buy it ; so farmers and merchants
would go bankrupt, banks would close, and that would be
called "hard times." After a few years people would regain
confidence, they would borrow money and bid up the prices
of goods, and that would be a "boom." Every boom was
automatically followed by a bust, but you would be unpatriotic
if you mentioned that historic fact.

Also, Wallace had said that it ought to be possible for
every person in the world to have a pint of milk every day.
His enemies took that as evidence of his impractical mentality ;
they picked out the Hottentots as the most unlikely folk they
could think of and said he wanted to give a pint of milk—presumably American—to every Hottentot. The statesmen from
the South bethought themselves how awkward it would be if
every coloured person got the idea of having a pint of milk
every day, so they didn't want Henry Wallace to have a
chance of becoming President of the United States. They
were astonished and a little frightened by the clamour of the
workers in Chicago, who did want Wallace and came to the
convention hall and said so. All the same, the delegates cast

their votes for Senator Harry Truman, whom they knew and liked, and of whom they could feel certain that he didn't have any eccentric ideas. In so doing they were making more history than they dreamed—something which happens frequently to humans, who are fated to live in the present, to forget the past quickly, and have no means of penetrating the future.

It was just at this time that excited reports reached America, to the effect that a bomb had been exploded in Hitler's headquarters, injuring him. How seriously no one could be sure. The man accused of the attempt was a Colonel Graf von Stauffenberg, a name not known to Lanny. He read eagerly every word he could get, fearing that the name of Oskar von Herzenberg might come up ; but it didn't. Lanny couldn't even be sure if it was the same group of Army conspirators ; it was entirely possible that separate groups were working to the same end. Many executions were taking place, and of course that would weaken the Wehrmacht and bring the defeat nearer.

XII

The break-through in Normandy came in the latter part of July. The British didn't gain much ground in front of Caen, but by constant pressure they held six out of the nine armoured divisions which the enemy had, and that made things easier for the Americans. Fifteen hundred heavy bombers saturated the lines in front of the latter—ten bombs to the acre—and after a couple of days of heavy fighting narrow gaps were opened up, and the tanks poured through. The Germans close to the sea had to fall back to avoid being surrounded, and the tanks got among them and cut them up. In a few days the German line had been forced back to a place called Avranches, at the entrance to the peninsula of Brittany. The Americans were out of the *bocage* country at last, and in places where freshly landed tanks could operate freely.

It was the American Third Army, headed by that war-loving old Episcopalian with the two pearl-handled revolvers. Georgie Patton was in his element now, doing the job for which he had been preparing all his life ; he was wild with impatience, dancing with excitement, bellowing at his officers and men to keep moving, to get the supplies up, to keep hitting the enemy so that he wouldn't have a chance to recover his balance. The correspondents told about it over the radio, and the whole country listened, the non-Axis world listened, and saw that this was something new, this was the beginning of the end. American industrial power was at last making itself felt, and it was hard not to share the sense of glory—even though you had a traitor pacifist hidden in your heart !

The way of the public throughout this long war had been to alternate between depression and exultation. During the tedious periods of preparation you heard people say it could never be done, we could never conquer the whole of Europe ; as for the business of " island hopping," had anybody ever taken the trouble to count the thousands or tens of thousands of islands in the South Seas and how many troops it would take to occupy them ? They would watch the mounting public debt and talk about inevitable national bankruptcy ; they would look at the casualty lists in the papers and make themselves ill with grief. But then would come a time of action, a landing in North Africa or Tarawa or Normandy, and everybody would cheer up suddenly and begin to figure out a time-table to Berlin and Tokyo.

Lanny had trained himself to resist those mass moods ; he had realized from the outset that it would be a long war. But he had a map, and stuck little pins in it, and soon realized that this was a serious break-through. The armoured columns, supported by planes overhead, were racing south across Brittany, to seal off that peninsula and its important harbours. Other columns were turning eastward, and that was the way to Paris, not more than a couple of hundred miles away. So Lanny called up the O.S.S. man in Washington and said, " It looks as if it might be time for the first half of my job." The answer was, " Your papers will be ready tomorrow. Come prepared to leave at once."

He hadn't much packing to do : one suitcase, and he guessed he wouldn't take that any farther than London. He went out for a walk in the park to think things over. It was the beginning of August, and a warm day, but he walked briskly because he was so excited. Many times before he had taken trips when it was hard to have hope ; but this one seemed like a holiday. He was going to take Bienvenu out of the hands of the Nazi despoilers ! He was going to see the G.I.'s with their heavy packs wading out of that blue water and onto the brown sand of the Juan beach, where he had played and swam and fished since the earliest days he could remember. At any rate, that was what he imagined, and it made his step light.

XIII

The P.A. phoned his father to send for the car and then took the midnight train to Washington and got his papers : a passport in his own name, authorizing him to visit Britain, France—we had some of France now !—Spain, Portugal, and North Africa ; also a French *carte d'identité* in the name of Henri Jean Marie Girouard, a *permis de séjour* and a *permis de circuler*—all forged, of course, but so well done that they would convince any gendarme or S.S. man who might inspect them. There were other papers for Lanny to have in his pocket : a receipt for payment of a grocery bill, a bill for payment on a life-insurance policy, a letter from the imaginary wife of this imaginary Girouard in an envelope with a French stamp and postmark ; an entirely satisfactory job, and all Lanny had to do was to study them and remember who he was and the details of his affairs.

He was flown from the Patuxent airport in an A.T.C. plane, a big one fixed up for the V.I.P.'s, with seats such as you found in Pullman cars and even an antimacassar where you rested your head. At night the berth was made up and you slept comfortably, if you were not nervous. Lanny's orders were to report to a secret address in London, and when he did so he was taken in hand by a couple of O.S.S. agents, who then proceeded to brief him, in a quiet businesslike way which seemed to imply that they had handled a dozen cases that day and had another dozen waiting. They told him that he would be motored to a near-by field, and from there would be flown across the Channel to the American sector. Beyond that they knew nothing and asked not a single question. They would take care of his suitcase, his passport, his American money, his watch, and other belongings ; he must have nothing on him that wasn't French. One of them took him to the " wardrobe room " and saw him fitted with a complete outfit of clothing that had come from France and that had obviously been worn for a long time.

He had just time to write a postcard to Laurel and tell her that he had arrived and would be busy for a few days but would get in touch with her later. She knew enough to feel anxious, but to have no hurt feelings. He wasn't told where the airport was—so many new ones had sprung up it was rather hard on British agriculture. He was driven in a jeep, and put in a two-seated dispatch plane, along with some sacks of mail. He was flown westward and then south—this to reduce chances of encountering a German flyer. These came rarely now, the pilot said, but it was no good making things easy for them.

The course was across the Channel, and Lanny could look down and see the hundreds of ships of all kinds and sizes, which at a height appeared to be standing still. He could only hope that among their watchful gunners there was no one who would fail to recognize the American star and circle painted underneath his plane. Presently he passed over Cherbourg, and he observed the hulks of sunken vessels and the live vessels coming and going. There were the Army encampments, the trucks, the tanks on the roads, and many wrecks that had been dumped off the roads in a hurry. There were the smashed farm-houses, the whole panorama of war, seen in a bird's-eye view. Suddenly they were coming down, into a couple of pastures which had been made into an emergency field. Two or three bumps, and the plane came to a halt.

The sun was just going down, and the sky was golden and pink. Lanny got out of the plane, and a young Air Force lieutenant came up to him and said, " Bienvenu ? " Lanny nodded, and was escorted into a tent sheltered by a tall plane tree. There was a folding table with a map on it and a couple of camp-chairs. Lanny was invited to look at the map ; it was one of those wonderful air maps, and there was a spot marked with a cross in red ink. The polite young officer said, " That is the place where you are to be set down tonight. Study it carefully and make sure it's the right place and that you will know where you want to go in the dark."

23

Outrageous Fortune

I

THE plane was tiny; it had to be, because, as the pilot said, it must be able to come down on a half dollar. It flew as low as possible in order to escape detection by enemy radar. To be sure, that made a danger of church steeples and tall trees in the darkness; but then, as Frederick the Great had said to his troops, "Do you want to live for ever?" The main protection was that so many planes went out at different hours and to different goals that the enemy couldn't keep track of them all. The pilot had an automatic in his belt, but that was for possible use on land; in the air he was helpless and had to take his chances.

How would he find his goal, out there in the black night? He didn't say, and Lanny didn't ask. Obviously, the course could be plotted on a map; such a point of the compass and exactly so many kilometres, and there would be the pasture. But there was wind to be reckoned with, and wind is not reliable. Could it be that the Partisans had been provided with a sending set, and sent out a beam which the young Air Force lieutenant would get on his instrument board? Anyhow, they flew for something more than an hour, and suddenly ahead Lanny saw little pinpoints of flashing light, two rows, three on a side. "Right on the nose!" shouted the pilot above the noise of the plane. He dived, and down they came into the blackness. There were two or three bumps, and then the engine died and all was still.

Men came running from all sides. This was the crucial moment, for if the plot had been betrayed, these would be Gestapo men, and they might start shooting; Lanny would see the flash of guns, but might be dead before he heard the sounds. Or, worse yet, the inquisition and the torture chamber for the false friend, the double-dyed deceiver, the worst enemy the Nazis had.

But no, it was all right this time. The nearest man half whispered, " *Bienvenu ?* " and Lanny answered, " *Bien.*" He had been carrying a package on his lap during the trip ; he handed it out to the man and then climbed out himself. There were other packages stowed in the plane, and the pilot passed them out quickly. Only a few words were spoken, and these low. Half a dozen shadowy forms seized the plane and turned it about and backed it some distance—evidently it hadn't come the full length of the field. At the far end torches began to blink ; no doubt there would be a hedge there, and perhaps tall trees. The pilot started his engine, then gunned it and bounced away out of sight ; the sounds told you that he was rising into the air.

In the few minutes of turning and starting a hand was laid on the P.A.'s shoulder and a voice whispered, " Lanny ! " A woman's voice, vaguely familiar, but he was too surprised to recognize it. " Who are you ? " he asked, and the reply was, " Julie Palma."

Raoul's wife ! How on earth had she got here ? He couldn't refrain from asking, and the voice said, " I was ordered. Everything is O.K." He guessed that possibly she hadn't told the others the identity of this secret arrival, so he said no more. She took his arm and guided him, and the others just melted away into the darkness. Obviously it wouldn't do for a group to be seen on any road or path at night. The coming of the plane must have been heard in the neighbourhood, and enemies might be hurrying to the spot. Silence !

II

The last time Lanny had seen this old friend she had been working in Paris against the Nazis. Later he had heard that she had gone south to join her husband. Had she come back, or had she been sent especially for Operation Bienvenu ? Lanny had told the O.S.S. people that he would like to have the help of Raoul Palma at Juan ; it was likely that Raoul had suggested his wife to help at the Château de Bruyne. Perhaps Julie herself might not know how it had happened, but had just been told to come. All day and night the B.B.C. was beaming programmes to France, and in them would occur strange sentences which seemed to have no meaning. " Violets are blooming," or " Cleopatra has a cold," or " Aldebaran has been calibrated." In secret places all over France men and women would be listening for the phrase or sentence which had a meaning for their particular group.

Lanny was walking on a dark night with a woman, and he knew that this was the safest thing he could be doing ; it had been planned that way, and that was why the men had faded so quickly. A lovely warm night in August, with Aldebaran and several thousand other stars in the sky ; there must be thousands of Frenchmen doing the same thing, and even some Germans, and they might all be disposed to let one another alone.

The couple walked. Lanny noted that they were on small footpaths, not roads ; he soon became confused, for this wasn't the way he had planned to come. He whispered, " Are we going to the château ? " Julie answered, " I have studied the way." He had confidence in her, having known her for more than twenty years. She was competent as well as devoted, and had kept the workers' school going in Cannes during the years when her husband had been helping the Spanish Republican government. She was risking her life every hour that she carried on these intrigues against the Nazis.

They came to a stile with which Lanny was familiar ; he had often crossed it on his walks, and it was only a hundred yards or so from a side entrance to the château grounds. The woman said, " We are safe here," and they sat and talked in whispers. Julie told him, " I don't know what you are here for and I don't ask. The orders were to guide you ; there will be two armed men in the shrubbery, and you can call them if necessary."

He answered, " I don't think it will be. I just want to have a talk with the family ; it may lead to something important." It was then about eleven o'clock, as well as he could guess. " I may have to arouse them," he added. " There is one possibility that troubles me—there may be some new servant who does not know me and who might talk, or even telephone the police."

"There is no new servant, Lanny. Our people here know all about the place and have prepared for your coming."

"I was afraid the old gentleman might be in Paris and they would have to send for him."

"He is here, at least he was this afternoon."

"They used to have a dog."

"They have an old one and keep it indoors at night."

"*La vieille Fidèle!* She will make no trouble for me."

"How long a talk do you want, Lanny?"

"I can't be sure, but an hour or two ought to suffice."

"Make it short, for there is always a certain amount of risk. What do you plan to do then?"

"I was told that your friends would be able to send word, and a plane will come for me."

"That is true. It can come tomorrow night. But where will you spend the day?"

"I had the idea of letting them hide me in the château."

"We advise strongly against that. The reputation of these people is bad, and there are too many of them."

"I have a special relationship with this family, Julie——"

"I know, but I didn't feel at liberty to tell our friends about that. They object that there are children, who can hardly be kept from talking; the whole situation is unsafe, and they want you to leave as quickly as possible and let them hide you. Even if an alarm should be given, the enemy will not be able to find you, and the plane will come to a different spot."

"O.K.," Lanny said. "I'll come out as soon as I have got what I have been sent for. You will wait?"

"I will hide near by. *Bonne chance!*"

III

The P.A. walked quietly to the château, by the drive which led to the delivery entrance. The buildings were old, of red brick; they were not large enough to deserve any name but villa, but the neighbourhood had seen fit to honour the family. Beyond the drive was a high brick wall with a solid wooden gate; it led into the garden, where Lanny knew every tree and shrub; this place had been one of his homes for the half-dozen years that he had been Marie de Bruyne's lover and a family friend, in the accepted French fashion known as *la vie à trois*. On the other side of the wall the apricot trees had been trained to grow like vines, and the fruit would be ripe now, each one carefully tied in a tiny paper bag—that is, if the old gardener was still alive. The peaches would be ripe, and the grapes would be ripening. The lawn would be smooth and green, and no doubt the grandchildren played croquet there, as Lanny had played with Denis junior and Charlot.

The gate was fastened, and it would have been difficult to climb over, on account of broken glass on top. He retraced his steps and came to the front of the house, where there was another lawn, shaded by ancient beeches. All the windows were dark, and he would have to rouse the family ; so he lifted the brass knocker and gave three raps, which resounded like gunshots in the silence of the night. He waited ; presently a window was opened in the second story, which is called the first all over Europe. A woman's voice asked, "*Qui est là ?*" Lanny recognized it as the voice of Annette de Bruyne and answered softly, "A friend with a message from Denis *fils*." The voice said, "*Attendez.*"

He "attended," and presently a light was turned on and the little window in the front door was opened. Lanny whispered his name, and the bolt was shot back, and there stood young Denis's wife, wearing a *peignoir* ; the light made a halo about her blonde hair. Lanny knew her well—she had once telephoned him in distress when the police were about to arrest her husband for his activities with the Cagoulards. She had aged and had lines of care in her face, and, of course, a look of great surprise. " Lanny ! " she exclaimed, and he said quickly, " I have an urgent message for *le beau-père*. Is he at home ? "

The answer was that he was in bed, and Lanny said, " Let me go to his room." One would not have suggested that in a conventional French family unless it was urgent indeed ; even so, the woman hesitated. " I have only a short time," Lanny said, " and it is important. Please don't say anything to anyone else until I have talked with *le beau-père*."

She invited him in, closed the door and fastened it, then led the way. " We have put him on the *rez-de-chaussée* now,"

she explained, and Lanny could guess that the aged man's
health was failing and he could no longer climb stairs. They
had no *ascenseur* in this old mansion, and couldn't get one in
wartime even if they had been willing to introduce anything
so modern, so *à l'Américaine*. She tapped on the door of what
had been the billiard room, and when a feeble voice called,
" *Entrez*," she stepped decorously back and let Lanny enter
alone. She closed the door, and being the well-bred daughter
of an old Catholic family, went promptly away.

IV

Lanny did not know exactly how old this French financier
was, but he knew that he was in his eighties. Lanny had
never before seen him in the state in which he was now, with
his false teeth in a glass of water by the bedside, his sparse
white hair in disarray, and a startled look upon his wrinkled
face. It was taking an unfair advantage of him, but Lanny
had planned it that way, meaning to jolt him into action and
put the job through without a wasted moment. The P.A.
had no desire to risk his life for the sake of a man whose ideas
were repugnant to him and whose evil ways had wrecked the
happiness of one of the sweetest and most loving women Lanny
had ever known. A young American endeavouring to repair
that damage had been scrupulously polite to the head of this
household, but he surely didn't owe him anything, not even
truth.

" *Pardon, mon ami*," he began quickly. " I have come at
great risk and dare not stay long. My father arranged for me
to be brought here—a difficult undertaking, as you can
imagine. It is because of his deep concern for your safety."

" *Mais*, Lanny ! " stammered the other. " Who will wish
to trouble a broken old man like me ? "

" The American Army is approaching Le Mans ; it cannot
be many days before it is through the Orléans gap ; the plan
is to surround the whole Seine district, and all the Germans
in it will be prisoners. The Partisans will rise, and those
whom they consider *collaborateurs* will be in the gravest
danger."

" But, Lanny, I have been out of politics for so long ! "

" Memories are longer, Denis. You gave money to the Cagoule, and that fact is well known in this neighbourhood. You have given support to he Nazis——"

" *Jamais! Jamais!* "

" Perhaps you didn't realize what you were doing ; but the Partisans know, and my father is informed through secret Army sources that they have you on a list."

" *Nom de Dieu!* What does your father wish me to do ? "

" He begs you to come over to the American side before it is too late. You must realize now that the Allies are going to win. I have had to reconcile myself to that fact and take steps to protect my own safety, just as I am urging you to do."

" But, Lanny, I am without any power. I am old and my health is failing. The Germans are still here, and if I tried to do anything they would shoot me."

" Robbie has a definite step in mind and has sent me to tell you about it. I was in Algiers a few months ago and had a talk with Denis *fils* ; he is in a hospital, with a severe wound caused by a shell fragment in the thigh. His life was saved only by transfusions ; he is recovering now and will not be lame. But he is dreadfully unhappy because of Charlot. He begged me with tears in his eyes to find some way to persuade Charlot to get out of his present position and save his life. I promised to do what I could ; you know, *mon ami*, how Marie prayed to me on her deathbed to take care of them and help them. I gave my word, and I am trying to keep it."

" I understand that. What can be done ? "

" Charlot is in the most dangerous position imaginable. All those Frenchmen who have helped the Germans with arms will be treated as war criminals, and either shot out of hand by the Partisans, or else court-martialled by the French Army that is fighting now in Italy. That applies especially to the officers, and Charlot has been one of the most active among them. He is a marked man."

" It is a dreadful situation, Lanny, and I have not failed to realize it." Tears came into the old financier's rheumy eyes, and his little white goatee quivered. His voice was muffled because of his missing teeth, but he was seemingly too agitated to realize it. " What can I do ? "

" Charlot is a man with real power, and he is the one who

must be induced to act. I tell you in strict confidence—the Allied Armies are about to land on the south coast. I do not know the time or the place, but the event is certain and cannot be more than a week off. The German defences there are inadequate, and the entire Riviera will surely be in Allied hands. Charlot and his little force will be surrounded and captured. That is my father's judgment, and you must take his word that he knows."

" I have taken his word before and never been misled."

" Robbie has become one of the most powerful men in America. He is turning out planes by the thousands, and the Air Forces are dependent upon him. The sums that will be due you on your Budd-Erling stock when the war is over will be many millions of dollars, and that is a stake worth playing for."

" *Naturellement*, Lanny, but what can I do here ? "

" You must use your authority and bring it about that Charlot comes over to the American side at once. You know how it was in North Africa—the men who joined us not merely escaped with their lives, but have kept all their property. I was present in Algiers when Darlan made his choice ; and now there is exactly the same situation. It is the hour of decision for your whole family."

" Speak, Lanny, I am in your hands."

" I know how set Charlot is in his opinions, and how proud and stubborn. I am afraid that he would not heed my pleading. So I want you to write him a letter, not advising, but commanding. Use your authority as *père de famille* and tell him what to do. He respects you and will obey as a dutiful son."

The old man's hands were trembling so that he had to clasp them together to stop it. " *Mais*, Lanny ! That might be suicidal for all of us here. If that letter fell into German hands, we should be taken out and shot."

" That is true, *mon ami*, and I wouldn't ask you to take such a risk. What I want you to write is that Charlot shall take my advice in the matter. Tell him to obey *me*, and I'll take the risks."

" You have a way to reach him, Lanny ? "

" My father has arranged everything. I will get to him

and put the facts before him. He won't like them, but unless he is entirely out of his mind he will see that he has no other choice."

"God grant that it may be so. But what are we here to do about our own situation?"

"Your helping Charlot will make all the difference. My father will tell the Army Intelligence people what you have done, and they will inform the Partisans. So, when they come to your door it will be to crown your heads with flowers instead of putting them on pikes."

v

With trembling hands the *père de famille* wrote under the visitor's dictation. Just two lines, on a plain sheet of paper, and with no names: "*Mon fils: Faites ce que notre vieux et cher ami désire. C'est un commandement de votre père.*"

Lanny pledged himself not to reveal the names to anyone, and least of all to the Germans if he should have the ill-fortune to be caught. He did not stop to discuss his own change of front or any other news. He said, "It might help if Eugénie were to add her word," and *le père* assented. He got his skinny shanks out of bed—Lanny considerately looked away until he had put on his silk dressing gown. Seeing that he was a bit wobbly, the visitor took his arm, and they went out to the drawing-room, where the wives of the two sons sat in a dim light, waiting patiently for whatever the head of the household might see fit to tell them.

The doors were closed, and the agitated old plutocrat briefly told them his decision. Lanny wasn't called upon to say anything; he left France to the Frenchmen—it was the Army's programme. To Annette, wife of the elder son, the announcement came as a shock, for she had political convictions of an intensely reactionary sort. If her signature had been asked, she might have refused. But Eugénie, the younger woman, was the old-fashioned sort; all she wanted was to get her husband back, with no bullet holes through his body. She gladly wrote under her father-in-law's words, "*C'est aussi ma prière.*"

So the P.A. had what he wanted, and he stayed only a few

minutes to tell the agitated ladies what he knew about their husbands. They offered him food, but he said no, he was exposing them to danger every minute he stayed in their home. He folded up the paper and put it with the other documents of Henri Jean Marie Girouard, and pledged the three de Bruynes not to mention his visit to servants or children or anyone else. He went out by a side door, and they closed it silently behind him ; he stood for a while, waiting for his eyes to get used to the darkness. Neither friend nor foe appeared, and he walked quickly by a path which he knew well to the stile where Julie Palma was waiting.

VI

When the former school directress came out of the shadows he told her, " Everything is done. What next ? " She told him that a comrade would be coming soon. He had got through more quickly than they had expected.

They talked in whispers, a man and a woman in the darkness of a warm summer's night, but it was not the sort of talk that was to be expected under such circumstances. Julie told him that she had a job with an importing firm which had offices in Paris and Marseilles so she had a pretext for travelling and had been a sort of liaison officer for the Free French. She had made a score of trips, carrying messages, always in her head. She reported that Raoul was well and exultant over the events of the past two months. Apparently she did not know that Lanny was expecting to go south and to meet him, and Lanny didn't tell her that. He said, " I have been able to help a little, and I'm still trying."

What Julie wanted to know, most of all things in the world, was when the Americans were coming to Paris. He warned her, " Do not be disappointed if they pass you by. Remember, the goal of this battle is not Paris but Berlin. I have heard talk that we may go through the Orléans gap and straight across France to the Rhine."

This horrified the Frenchwoman, who exclaimed, " Oh, Lanny, Lanny ! You mustn't fail Paris ! " just as if he had been the head of the Allied Combined General Staffs ! She went on to point out what the Nazis might do to that most beautiful of all the world's capitals ; and how simple it would be to take it, just a few tanks and armoured cars flying the American flag ! When Lanny ventured to doubt if it would be quite that easy, she went into detail about the situation : three million people, burning up with hatred and ready to explode, just needing someone to give the signal, to speak the word. And they weren't helpless ; some had managed to save weapons from the days of their great disaster, and many of the young fellows had managed to steal weapons from the Germans or to get them from the Allies. All that was needed was to see the Stars and Stripes coming down the Champs-Élysées, and Paris would rise to the last man and woman. But they must know that the enemy couldn't come back !

This nervous, high-strung little woman—she was at the age where women are like that—came near to forgetting the danger of her position and Lanny's at that moment. She couldn't accept his statement that he had no influence with the military authorities ; she was sure he must at least know people who had. Hadn't he given Raoul and his friends proof of the fact that he knew President Roosevelt and was able to get to him ? All right then, let him give the great President—hero to the French as well as to the Americans—this report from one who was living and working with the Free French in Paris and knew all the groups and the parties—the Gaullists, the Socialists, the Communists, and the plain humble people who had no one to speak for them.

They had suffered such indignities, such horrors, and above all shame, that they would be willing to die by the thousands in order to wipe out the disgrace of having had to surrender, and to live under the hated Boches and see them strutting in the streets, pulling wads of paper money out of their pockets and buying up the best of everything in the city. The Nazis had kept the Parisians down by the most abominable system of hostages, a thing that had not been known in Europe since the Middle Ages. Men and women would be seized, perfectly innocent persons, just because they were respected and beloved, and would be held in prison, and ten would be shot if some Frenchman lost his head and stabbed or shot a Nazi in the streets.

" Oh, Lanny, you must liberate Paris ! Think of the

prestige, the moral effect! All the world will know it, all France will rise up and go into action. For all the rest of our history they will tell how the American Army did it, and our gratitude will become a national tradition!" Raoul's wife became so excited over this chance to send a message to President Roosevelt that her voice began to rise, and Lanny had to whisper, "*Prenez garde.*" He told her he agreed with her and promised that he would find a way to pass on the information. She said, "We have comrades who can tell you exactly what strength the Germans have, and what we of the Resistance can assemble." Lanny answered, "By all means let them do so."

VII

There came a low whistle from near by, and Julie said, "We must go." She led the way, and presently there was a man walking in front of them, just near enough to be followed. They walked on cross-country paths and came to a patch of woodland, and in it was a hut. The man had disappeared, and the woman said, "This won't be very comfortable, Lanny, but it will be safe. You will find sacks to make a bed, and you can fasten the door on the inside. Food and drink will be brought to you, and the password will be Bienvenu."

"Fine," he replied. "How long do I stay here?"

"Until tomorrow night. Of course if a plane does not arrive you will have to wait longer. *Bonne nuit, camarade.*"

By the light of the stars, to which his eyes had grown accustomed, Lanny could make out that this was somebody's wood hut and that it was nearly empty. He hoped the farmer had no dogs. He found a pile of sacks, and he wondered how many saboteurs and agents had slept on them in the course of four years. He locked the door and lay down and thought over his problems; he was just making up his mind to sleep when he heard footsteps. There was a tap on the door and the password was whispered low. He got up and opened the door. The form of a man was outlined against the faint light. The man held out a bottle and a package wrapped in newspaper. Lanny said, "*Merci,*" and took them.

"Monsieur," said the man very politely, "I should like to talk with you if it would not be any trouble."

"Certainly not," said the P.A. He backed into the hut and sat down on his sacks, and the man sat beside him.

"Monsieur," continued the visitor, "I am a man of the Fighting French, a follower of General de Gaulle. I have two comrades, one a Socialist and the other a Catholic democrat. There are some things we think you ought to hear, and if it is not too late and you are not tired—" He stopped, and Lanny answered: "I am not at all tired, and I shall have all day to sleep."

The man whistled, and two others came in, closed the door, and fastened it. Evidently they knew the place and took seats on the piles of wood. Lanny never saw their faces; they did not strike any light, perhaps because they had no tobacco. They spoke politely, yielding to one another, and Lanny identified them by their voices as Tenor, Baritone, and Bass. Baritone was the one who had come first, and he was evidently an educated man, a doctor or lawyer. Tenor was apparently a slight and nervous person, and young; Lanny identified him with Montmartre and imagined a bow tie and a beret, except that he knew the Nazis had banned the wearing of berets, which was classified among "demonstrations harmful to the state." Bass had a country accent, and Lanny thought that he might be the owner of the property on which this odd *réunion* took place.

The P.A. guessed that Julie Palma had told these men that he was a person of influence, a friend of the great; their first concern was to defend the honour of *la patrie*, letting the outside world know that Frenchmen were daily risking their lives and many giving their lives in resistance to the hated foe. They had no means of knowing whether this fact had reached the outside world, and they hoped this important Monsieur Bienvenu might find some way to make their voices heard.

The world must not suppose that this Resistance had begun only since the Allies had landed; *non, pas du tout*, it had been going on from the first hour of defeat. Thousands of young Frenchmen had wrapped their weapons and buried them, and later had dug them up and taken to the mountains or the *maquis*. The French word for underbrush, *maquis*, had come to be the name for the men who hid in it and came out to carry on sabotage against the enemy. "Monsieur," said

Baritone, " we have the enemy's own figures that more than forty thousand Frenchmen have been executed during the occupation, and a hundred thousand are in concentration camps in Germany. This in addition to the quarter million who have been deported."

Lanny assured them that the news of this heroism had not failed to reach America. He listened to dreadful stories of Nazi repression, and to figures as to the number of bridges which had been blown and trains which had been derailed in the neighbourhood. Just now the whole population was holding its breath, expecting the arrival of the Anglo-Americans. Evidently Julie had told them that Paris might be by-passed, for this was the subject they talked about most. They knew Paris, they knew the mood of the people, and that nothing but machine-guns and grenades and tanks and artillery kept them in subjection. All that was needed was a small armoured force at the city's gates, and the population would rise and barricade the streets behind the Germans and hurl building stones upon their heads. " Monsieur," said Tenor, " I was in Paris only three days ago, and I know on authority that there are now only two German divisions there ; but one is armoured, and that is our trouble."

No use for Lanny to plead that he had no authority, that the military would decide this question on military grounds. The three voices trembled as they pleaded : there were three million people in Paris, including the refugees, and they all wanted to work for the liberators. They would produce goods for the Army ; they would restore bridges, rebuild railroad track, repair damaged vehicles, be a colossal force behind the armies. " Three million friends are not to be by-passed, Monsieur ! " And Lanny assured them that Paris would not be forgotten, Paris would be delivered just as quickly as military security would permit. No use to drive the enemy out and then have him come back and blast the city in a siege.

VIII

The P.A. slept, and only the hedgehogs disturbed him. He slept through most of the day, and then thought about his plans, which had gone well thus far. He waited patiently, and after twilight had fallen in the woods he ventured to open the door and peer out; there was no one in sight, and he locked himself in again. It was about ten before he heard a step, and then a voice whispered the password. He opened the door. It was Baritone. Lanny followed him without a question, and they walked on country paths for perhaps half a mile. Then they came to a pasture, and on the edge of it they hid in some bushes—the *maquis*. " *Ne parlez pas*," the man whispered, and they made not a sound.

Suddenly Lanny's escort sat up and cupped his hands behind his ears. The sound of a plane. Instantly the *maquis* sprang into life, the flashlights began to wink up toward the sky and down again. The roar of the plane came near; it dipped fast and came to rest on the meadow. The flashlights went off; the men ran out, and there was the same business of taking off packages and turning the plane about and backing it to the limit of the field. It was one of those tiny cub planes, perhaps the same which had brought Lanny, but the pilot was different.

Baritone had escorted the passenger and given the password; now he said, " *Montez*," and then, " *On les aura*." The engine started up, and Lanny held his breath; it was truly a frightening thing in darkness—suppose the field wasn't long enough or the trees too tall? But no doubt the field had been measured and photographed, and possibly the trees had been topped; anyhow, the plane rose. The mysterious silent man at the throttle knew what was below him and what was in front; the passenger had nothing to do but sit there and hope that no wandering Heinkel or Junker night fighter would swoop down upon them, a hawk upon a carrier pigeon.

IX

Not that kind of bad luck, but another! They were flying west, toward the American sector. Black clouds loomed ahead, hiding the stars—one of those sudden thunderstorms which come from nowhere on summer nights. Lanny didn't hear the thunder for the noise of the plane, but he saw lightning flashes and realized that they were heading straight into the heart of the storm. The pilot swerved and shouted into the passenger's ear, "We have to keep out of that!" He began talking into his radio telephone, and Lanny couldn't hear what he was saying; he knew enough to be sure that the pilot of an unarmed plane would never call the ground except in an emergency.

The P.A. had been in a plane wreck once before and surely didn't want another. He had no parachute, and apparently the pilot had none; they flew too close to the ground to make such recourse possible. Lanny could only sit and wonder. Did the pilot plan to fly around that heavy black storm, or was he looking for a place to land? They were headed toward the south, and he guessed they were looking for that strip of *la belle France* which the American forces had taken in their eastward drive.

The helpless passenger thought that there must be some routine for situations like this; surely these little cubs couldn't stand heavy weather. The plane came lower, and suddenly bright lights flashed forth, directly ahead, and there was a field, with planes lined up on each side of it. The pilot dived, and down he came, and in half a minute they came to rest on the ground. The instant the wheels touched, the lights went off again. The glimpse Lanny got suggested another cow pasture but a bigger one; and so it was. The moment the Army made sure of a new district, their first procedure was to clear an "airstrip," so that "flying boxcars" might bring in supplies and fighter planes might be that much nearer to the enemy.

The pilot stepped out and his passenger followed, and in a jiffy the little plane had been run off the field into one of the waiting rows. The pilot said, "That storm will blow over in a few minutes, and we'll go on." Lanny replied, "O.K." But then, as a field officer came out to get the pilot's report, another idea occurred to him. He asked the officer, "Where are we?" And the answer was, "Air headquarters of the 117th Division, Third Army." Then Lanny asked, "Are the general headquarters near?" And the answer was, "We don't give that information. What is it you want?" Lanny said, "I am an O.S.S. agent, and I have some news that might be of immediate interest to your commanding officer. Could I have a telephone?"

The officer escorted him into a tent. There were several phones on a folding table. The officer took one and gave a number, just as if he had been calling in town ; he reported what Lanny had said, listened, and then hung up. " This way, please," he said, and took Lanny outside and put him into a jeep with a soldier. " Take this man to General Young." Lanny stepped in, and they went bumping down a road without any lights ; how it was done he couldn't figure, but presumably no one minded if the jeep turned over, because it was so light that you could set it back on its wheels, anywhere except on the side of a house or in the ocean.

X

They came to gates and turned in to what evidently was a fine estate, with a gravel drive and a double line of trees ; unfortunately a number of the trees had been either shot down or cut, and pushed off to the side. They halted at a large mansion ; many staff cars were parked before it. The mansion loomed high in the starlight, but large sections of it were missing and you could see the stars where the walls should have been. They went up some steps partly blocked with rubble ; two sentries stopped them, but passed them when the soldier said, " The General's orders." They went into an entrance hall and then into what had been an elegant drawing-room. There were two or three candles burning inside, giving just enough light to see rugs and tapestries, upholstered armchairs and well-polished tables, and also that one corner of the room had been shot away and the wreckage dumped back against the wall.

Seated at a table, with maps spread before them, were two officers, one a two-star general and the other a colonel, both tired-looking, overworked men who hadn't time for a bath or a shave. Lanny was aware that he himself didn't look like the glass of fashion ; he was purposely ill-dressed and had had no chance to wash his face or hands. The officers introduced themselves, and Lanny gave his real name and explained that he had been to the outskirts of Paris on a confidential mission and had talked with four members of the Resistance there, one of whom had just come out of the city. He repeated what they had told him about the strength of the German forces and the attitude of the population.

After they had asked some questions the superior officer said, " The Chief ought to see this man." The other assented and remarked to Lanny, " General Patton is here on an inspection trip. He'll see you if he isn't asleep."

Lanny replied, " If necessary, I'll wait, because it's important. My plane can go on without me, and you can send me to England when you have a spare bucket seat."

The colonel rang for an orderly and gave him a message. The man went away and came back with a report that the General would see Mr. Budd. Lanny followed the orderly to a part of the mansion which the shells had missed and was escorted into a very elegant lady's boudoir, all fixed up in French fashion with ormolu and pink silk, double curtains at the windows, ruffles and lace on the bed, and perfume and rouge bottles on the dressing-table. In the middle of these incongruous surroundings sat the khaki-clad warrior, on a gilt Louis Quinze chair with spindly legs, in front of a table of the same super-elegant period. He was reading, and the binding and shape of the volume told Lanny that it was a Bible ; his quick eyes took in the fact that it was open at the last third, and he wondered if Georgie Patton was preparing himself for the conquest of Germany by reading the Sermon on the Mount.

XI

Fully accoutred, and wearing the two pearl-handled revolvers, the commander of four hundred and fifty thousand men looked up but did not rise. He was nearly sixty, and his hair was white and sparse ; his face was long, and in repose somewhat melancholy. Without any preliminaries he demanded, " Well, what have you to say to me ? "

He was one more tired man, and Lanny made allowances for him and came at once to the point. " General, I was sent on an O.S.S. errand into Seine-et-Oise, close to the suburbs of Paris, and I have learned that the Germans have only two divisions in Paris, that the whole population is ready to rise the moment the first American troops appear."

" Who told you this ? " snapped the commander.

" I talked with four active leaders of the Free French——"

" I don't pay any attention to those bastards. They are a bunch of Reds."

" The one who gave me the first-hand information, General, is a Catholic."

" It don't make any difference ; they're all yellow. They quit cold, and we're not counting on them. We're winning this war with Americans."

" I understand, sir, that the French have been doing very well in Italy——"

" Goddamit, man, who sent you here to argue with me ? " The warrior's lined and tired face took on the colour he so intensely disliked.

" I'm not trying to argue with you, General ; I'm telling you facts. I have lived most of my life in France and I know the people. The moral effect of taking Paris would bring you millions of allies——"

" Goddamit, man, I tell you we're not taking Paris, we're taking Germany ! " Georgie was an old-fashioned cavalryman, and his every sentence contained a mention of either the First Person of the Trinity or the Second ; Lanny observed that he never mentioned the Third—perhaps he had overlooked it, or perhaps he was afraid of it. He had a great variety of invocations and expletives, and two modes of speech, or dialects, one of which he employed in the presence of men and the other in what was called mixed company. Lanny had been about the world enough to know that this was supposed to be the way of a " he man," and he thought it rather silly. Also, he knew that he was poorly dressed, and unshaven, and that this declassed him.

" General," he continued patiently, " it would take an armoured force not more than three hours to drive from Orléans to Paris, and Paris is nearer to the Rhine than Orléans."

" Jesus Christ, man ! Have you come here to tell me how to run my Army ? " The warrior hit the spindly table a thump with his heavy fist.

" No, General, I'm just telling you that if you don't send a task force to take Paris you will be making the worst blunder of your career."

Patton leaped to his feet. His face was purple now, and he called Lanny a very bad name indeed, and didn't smile while he said it. But Lanny smiled, for he thought he knew his man, and that it was essential to stand up to him. "Keep your temper, General," he said. "I am here as a friend, trying to save you from a humiliating experience. If you don't take Paris of your own impulse, you will be made to."

"You are an insolent dog and I ought to have you shut up in the guard-house."

"No, sir, you won't do that, for you're not a Nazi, even though you try to appear one. I have risked my life going into enemy territory with false papers in order to get information, and I bring it to you free of charge. I make allowances for the fact that you are carrying a heavy burden, and perhaps are overstrained and short of temper. That is why I do not resent your bad manners and report you."

"Report me? Who the hell would you report me to?"

"You command the Third Army, General. Don't forget that there is General Bradley, and General Eisenhower, and General Marshall, and finally a Commander-in-Chief."

Such were the steps in the military ladder; and there was something in Lanny's tone which caused this half-soldier and half-actor and whole-boy to stop and reflect. "Who the hell are you?" he demanded.

"My name is Budd, General."

"Budd, what Budd?"

"You have heard of Budd-Erling, no doubt. I think some of our planes are overhead now."

"So you're telling me that you're Budd-Erling?"

"It happens that my father, Robert Budd, is president of that company and its founder."

"You expect me to believe that?"

"I don't know what to expect, General. I was surprised to discover that you had so little self-control. In the book you've been reading it is set down that he that ruleth his spirit is better than he that taketh a city."

"Now look here, Budd." The warrior's tone had changed with surprising suddenness. "How am I to know when a man comes in on me without any credentials and starts telling me my business——"

" I point out to you, General Patton, that a secret agent going into enemy territory does not carry credentials. I have none on paper, but I have some in my head. Suppose I tell you that on one of my recent visits to President Roosevelt I told him about a letter he had sent you to be delivered to the Sultan of French Morocco, and how you insisted upon revising that letter without the President's knowledge or consent."

" The hell you say ! May I ask how you knew that ? "

" It happens that I am a friend of one of our vice-consuls in Morocco, who brought the letter to you. I am sure you must remember the incident."

The blood had gone out of the warrior's face, and it looked even more drawn and tired. Lanny waited, with malice afore-thought, to compel him to reveal the curiosity he felt. " And what did the President say ? "

" He wasn't amused, General. But I think he will be amused when I tell him about this interview. Also, I haven' the slightest doubt that he will agree with me that it would be a grave error of strategy to leave the people of Paris at the mercy of the Nazis an hour longer than necessary. The city is like a boiler with the safety valve tied down ; there is bound to be an explosion, and perhaps a frightful massacre, and not merely all France but the whole world will ask why we didn't prevent it when we so obviously had the chance. Be sensible, General, and listen for a few moments : you naturally think about military power, but the President has to think about moral power too—prestige, morale, whatever you choose to call it. He is playing a game of world politics and knows what it is to electrify our friends and to depress our enemies. Paris is not merely a centre of romance, of beauty, *la ville lumière* ; it is a great manufacturing centre ; the enemy is getting the products now, and we can have them for the taking. You will have to fan your armies out—they can't all move on one road—and if you fan a hundred miles to the north and go through Paris, that involves very little delay. Believe me, you won't have to hold the city or to govern it ; the French are all ready to take over, as I saw them do in North Africa. And the road from Orléans to Paris is a fine highway ; I have driven it scores of times from my home on the Riviera."

There was no more cursing. " All right, Budd," said the

two-gun warrior. " I'll think it over. And no hard feelings,
I hope."

" None whatever. Perhaps I was tactless in my approach."

" I like you, Budd. I respect a man who stands up to me."
He held out his hand and they exchanged a clasp.

" Thank you, General," said the P.A. and started to leave.
He was stopped by a word from the fighting man. " And by
the way, Budd, do you have to tell the Cominch about the
bad reception I gave you ? "

Lanny was tickled, and a grin spread over his features.
" Patton, I'll make a deal with you. I love Paris. I have a
host of friends there, the real people, not those who live by
preying on tourists. I hate to think of what those Nazi beasts
might do to the city. You send a few tanks there and save it,
and I promise to sing your praises for the rest of my life, and
never say one word that isn't glory."

The whole-boy Georgie Patton had a sense of humour too.
" Go to hell ! " he said. " I'll do my duty, and you goddam
highbrows can make what you please of it."

XII

The pilot of the cub plane had waited. The time was nearly
up, for his orders forbade him to be caught over the Channel
by daylight. But he had been told that Lanny was with the
commander of the Third Army, and he was impressed. The
storm had long since passed. The plane took off without
incident and flew low toward the west, and then north, re-
tracing the path which the famed Third Army had taken in its
victorious rush. No enemy planes appeared, and Lanny was
set down on a secret American field near London—we had
built them all over the " unsinkable aircraft carrier," and when
the war was over they would be a problem, because the English
people would need potatoes more than planes.

The P.A. wrote out his report and entrusted it to the O.S.S.
men to forward ; it would be in Washington in twenty-four
hours, they assured him. Then there was another briefing ;
he was to be flown at once to the Mediterranean—he had barely
time to telephone to Laurel and let her know that he was alive
and well and sorry that he couldn't come to see her.

Since he was going back into France, the clothes he had on would serve; he wouldn't need his passport, because O.S.S. would give him a special card that would save him questioning and would be taken up at Ajaccio, on the island of Corsica, the last Allied point at which he would call. He wasn't allowed to write his instructions down but had to learn them; and while doing this he had a chance to take a bath and shave. He was flown to the Bovingdon airport, and with an armful of newspapers and magazines he settled in a comfortable chair on a D.C. 4 transport, strapped his belt around him, and absorbed himself in the latest news of what the Third Army had been doing. Oddly enough, the news was two days behind what he had seen with his own eyes, for the Army never gave out the names of places until after the enemy had broadcast them. What the enemy didn't know wouldn't help him.

A wide swing to the west to avoid the perils of Francoland, and the plane came to the Rock of Gibraltar. It had once been a symbol for security, but now, with its crowded harbour and still more crowded airport, it would have been a " sitting duck." Göring had known that and had been ready to put it into his bag; the Führer had broken his Number Two's heart by changing his plans suddenly and attacking Russia instead. Most of the powerful guns which *Der Dicke* had installed on the land side, in Spanish territory, had been taken away and set up on the Channel coast, where they hadn't been good enough. The wild monkeys which hopped about in the trees on top of the Rock were still alive, so, according to the tradition, the British title to the place remained valid.

Lanny changed planes and was flown to Algiers, a hot and sultry spot in August, and a place for him of many memories. A wide ample harbour, ringed with tall white houses, and a background of green hills and high, barren, brown mountains, it was now a great Allied air and naval base, a distribution centre for several fronts. Lanny had just time for a visit to Denis *fils*, who was now moving about on crutches, waiting for strength to come back into his damaged leg.

The P.A. was not free to tell Denis where he had been or where he was bound for; but for the *capitaine's* peace of mind he made up a story to the effect that *le père* had managed to get a letter smuggled out to Robbie Budd, saying that he and all the family were well. This, of course, did Robbie no harm and did Denis a world of good. He said, " You wouldn't tell me if you knew, Lanny, but I have learned from many signs that an invasion of France from the south is impending. I am praying God that poor Charlot may find some way to escape."

XIII

The plane that took the traveller to the island of Corsica was another bucket-seat job ; it carried freight, laced tight with a spider-web of ropes, and passengers were a superfluity. Fortunately the trip took only a couple of hours. With Lanny there rode two other civilians, both young ; one gave it out that he was a specialist in citrons, a sort of large thick-skinned lemon which was grown on the island, and the other said he was a specialist in the various disease-bearing parasites which interfered with work at the harbour. From the first moment Lanny had a different idea about them both, and he was not surprised when they turned up to continue the journey to the mainland.

The P.A. had never been to Corse, as the French call it, and knew only two facts concerning the island—that it was the birthplace of the Bonaparte family which he did not admire, and that its high mountains were inhabited by bandits. When the plane came over the harbour of the capital he discovered a well-enclosed bay, and a city crowded into a small corner of it. Amazing how human creatures like to pack themselves together ! Here were buildings as tall as those in Algiers, and streets so narrow that Lanny saw two laden donkeys unable to get past each other. Ajaccio was a place of laziness and poverty, but like all other places in the war zones it was enjoying plenty now ; there was a market for everything it could produce, and ships crowded its docks. There was a swarm of the new American landing craft, and the P.A. didn't need to ask anybody what that meant.

The new arrival was in the hands of the Navy. A wide-awake Intelligence officer took him into a small cubicle in an office building and informed him that he was to be taken in one of the fast motor-boats and put ashore west of Cannes at approximately midnight. The distance was about two hundred miles, and they would leave an hour before sunset, the first part of the journey being in waters well guarded by American land-based planes. His further instructions were contained in a sealed envelope, marked " Bienvenu," which the officer gave him. When he opened it he found some well-worn French money, and orders to report to an address in the Old Town of Cannes with which he was thoroughly familiar—it was less than a block from where the labour school had been conducted in an old warehouse.

The traveller was free to take a walk and stretch his legs, and find himself a razor, a toothbrush, and a comb of French manufacture. He observed that the town was full of Allied soldiers. He got a bath, a shave, and a meal, and promptly at the hour specified, no standing around and attracting attention, he reported at the dock. The speedboat waiting there was about twenty feet long and had a one-inch gun in the bow, one that could be aimed either horizontally or vertically. Lanny was amused to see the two young " scientists " make their appearance ; the three smiled knowingly, but talked only about the weather.

The little vessel pulled away from the dock, put on power, and shot out of the harbour. The weather had been delightful now for weeks, grand fighting weather for Georgie Patton's tanks and the planes which covered them, and the same for all operations in the Midland Sea. There was a breeze, just enough to kick up green and white waves, which the speeding little boat lifted up by its bow and scattered in showers over the deck. The passengers went below, for it wouldn't do for them to be wet when they came ashore. A member of the crew handed each of them a small can ; he hoped they wouldn't need it, but his smile belied his words.

And sure enough, the wind rose, and the craft began to leap and buck. The three civilians became violently sick, turned a pale green, and lost their interest in helping to win the war. Sucking fresh lemons from Corsica did them no good, and the best the crew could do was to give them hard sea biscuits and candy to keep in their pockets, so as to restore their strength when they got ashore. Sea biscuits of French baking and candy of French manufacture—Naval Intelligence overlooked no smallest detail.

XIV

It was a miserable five or six hours, shut up in a tiny box with barely room to move their elbows ; Lanny thought that the human race had never appeared more disagreeable ; he would lean back and doze, but then somebody would waken him with violent retching. No wonder that seamen looked down upon landlubbers ! These were very new seamen, but the weaklings had been weeded out. They knew that the passengers were going in on dangerous errands, so they tried not to patronize them.

Time passed. The violent heaving of the little craft died down, and a young ensign touched Lanny on the shoulder. Lanny followed him up the companionway, and when his eyes got used to the dim light of the stars he perceived that there was a still smaller craft on board the motor-boat, one of those tiny kayaks which had set Lanny ashore south of Rome. It was made of wood and canvas, shaped like a bath-tub and no bigger. The engines of the motor-boat had been running slowly and softly, and now they stopped, and the craft drifted and came gradually to rest. The city of Cannes was blacked out, and so was the harbour, and Lanny could see nothing ; but he had been shown a map with the spot marked where he was to be put ashore, outside the harbour, west of the mole. Now he trusted to a well-trained navigation officer who had secret ways of knowing exactly where he was.

Everything was still but the lapping of the waves. Not a word was spoken, and the men on deck wore soft overshoes ; the enemy had his own secret ways of protecting his coast, and at any moment searchlights might flash out and a torrent of fire be poured upon the tiny craft. The officer in command gave a signal, and the kayak was laid down upon the water ; a seaman stepped carefully in, and a paddle was handed to him. The passenger was helped down and took his seat, with his legs bent up and his feet packed out of the way of the seaman's. The kayak was pushed away by hand, and the paddler went to work. Lanny could tell by the sound of the surf that they were near to the shore.

When they reached it they did not touch the rocks. The

seaman whispered to his passenger to lean to one side, to balance the craft while he got out on the other side. After he procured a footing on the slippery rocks, in water above his knees, he had Lanny stand up and take a piggyback ride, for Lanny must not be wet. After setting him ashore the seaman went back to the kayak, dragged it ashore, and dumped out the water which had splashed into it. He managed the feat in silence, then launched the kayak again and paddled away. Presently Lanny heard the engines of the motor-boat start up, not too loud, and heard the sound fade into the distance.

Lanny was in France again, this time among the scenes of his childhood. He couldn't see them, but fond recollection presented them to view, and he enjoyed the wonderful sensation of being on something that didn't leap and buck and upset the tiny balancing apparatus in his ears and thus throw his whole nervous system out of order.

24

Tongue in the Thunder's Mouth

I

THE Traveller restored his strength by eating French biscuits and candy. He was in no hurry, for he was sure that no alarm had been given ; the searchlights would have been used if such had been the case. He relied upon the Navy enough to think that he knew where he was, and there was plenty of time to reach his destination before dawn. When he felt stronger he got up and tiptoed over the rocks, away from the sea.

There were buildings, looming large and dark. Presently there was a path, then a highway, and then a railroad track ; Lanny realized that the Navy had slipped up and put him too far to the west ; he was close to that Villa de l'Horizon which had belonged to Maxine Elliott, retired American stage star. The railroad passed so close to her house that when a train roared by everything shook ; you could hardly keep from closing your eyes, as if you expected to be hit. On the side toward the sea there was a swimming pool, and by it Lanny had sat and listened to Winston Churchill, clad in a red dressing-gown and a big floppy straw hat. He had been writing his memoirs of World War I, and had declared that his political career was over, his party had put him permanently on the shelf. How little the cleverest of men understands his world !

Lanny didn't mind walking on the Route Nationale by starlight. He kept a careful watch ahead for flashlights, a sure sign of the enemy, for civilians could no longer get batteries. When he saw one he made a wide detour, and so came into the Old Town, with warehouses and small factories and whole blocks of tall tenements, ancient and ill-cared for and packed with human beings. In times of peace, on warm summer nights like this, you would have seen people sleeping on doorsteps or with their backs against walls ; but now they stayed indoors in spite of suffocating heat, and Lanny couldn't be sure whether it was because of a curfew, or because the Gestapo and their hired French agents were roaming the streets, picking up men of all ages, shipping them off to labour in Germany or on fortifications along this coast. The P.A. realized that his pocketful of papers wouldn't help him much, for the more he convinced them that he was Henri Jean Marie Girouard, the more certain they would be to give him a job. When he heard voices he crossed the street, and when he saw several people together he backed up and went along another street.

He knew the streets well. As a boy his Uncle Jesse had taken him into one of these dingy tenements and introduced him to a woman Syndicalist, his first contact with the labour movement. She had struck a spark in his soul, and he had grown up to become a young idealist, out of touch with the life of this Coast of Pleasure, the playground of all the wasters of Europe. He had met Raoul Palma, a clerk in a shoe-store, and had helped him to start and keep going a workers' school, where Socialists and Communists and Syndicalists and all shades and varieties of these could meet and argue their ideas. Lanny had been the friend of all, and he wondered what had become of them, and which, if any, he was going to meet now.

II

The address given him was a tobacco shop, and it was shut up tight at this unlikely hour. There was a narrow alley alongside it, and, knowing the ways of the underground, he guessed that this might be the reason for its being a place of rendezvous. He groped his way into the alley and found there was a side door; he tapped on it softly, and it was opened so promptly that it startled him—there must have been somebody sitting right by the door, waiting. He whispered, " Bienvenu," and a woman's voice said, " *Entrez*." The door was shut and bolted behind him, and he followed down a dark passage; the woman struck a match and lighted a candle, revealing a small store-room with a cot in it, and a man lying on the cot. The slight sound awakened him; he sat up, and Lanny saw his old friend Raoul Palma.

This Spaniard had been in his youth one of the loveliest human beings that Lanny had ever seen; a painter had chosen him for the young St. John the Evangelist. He had delicately chiselled features, rich dark colouring, and an expression mild yet ardent. His dream was of a happy world order, to be attained by the co-operative working classes, and he had clung to that dream through a quarter of a century of disappointments. He lacked a sense of humour, but had loyalty and a quiet determination which shrank from no danger. Now when Lanny saw him it was a shock, for the bones stood out in his face and his colouring was gone; he was younger than Lanny, but he looked like an old man and one who hadn't had enough to eat for a long time.

That did not keep him from starting up with an exclamation of delight and two kisses delivered in French fashion. Lanny noticed that he didn't call him by name, and Lanny took the hint. The last time they met Raoul had been Bruges, but he might be someone else now.

The woman had left the room without a word, closing the door, and these two friends sat on the cot and spoke in whispers. Raoul said, " I have been so worried about you. You must not go out on the streets. They are picking up every stranger, and they are out day and night."

" How are you managing it ? " Lanny asked.

" I am used to it and know the tricks."

Lanny didn't say how many tricks he himself had been forced to learn. He replied, " When I asked for your help I expected to take your advice. Have you been told what I'm to do ? "

" I was told nothing except that ' Bienvenu ' wanted me. I came from Toulon, and it was a difficult trip. Yesterday we got the code message over the radio that you would arrive tonight, so I was expecting you."

" Good service, I must say ! You have a group here ? "

" A strong one, and on tiptoe for action."

" You know that the Allies are about to invade ? "

" We have known that for weeks ; everybody knows. They say a hundred thousand people have left the Riviera in the past month ; everybody who has the money, or any place to stay in the interior."

" How did they know it, Raoul ? "

" Oh, there are reports of shipping activities in near-by Mediterranean ports ; the assembling of landing craft there ; the bombing of Toulon and Toulouse and military objectives all along the coast. Your planes have bombed out the radio-finding stations, and when you did that in Normandy the invasion came only a few days off."

" I see you are well informed, old man."

" There's the logic of the situation ; everybody knows the defences here are weak and that it's a long way from Germany. You will land here and march up the Rhône valley, join with the northern armies, and cut France in two."

" Just how weak are the defences ? "

" There's a lot of stuff on the coast, but it's a shell ; there's nothing much behind it. The moment we rebels get the signal, we'll cut all the communications. What the Germans have here now is all they will ever have. If only you bring enough to get ashore and stay."

" I'm sure we have no other idea. That too is the logic of the situation."

III

Lanny knew that he could trust this friend, and, more important, he was authorized to do so. He told about the false papers he carried, his visit to Seine-et-Oise, and his meeting with Julie. Since her husband had not heard from her for several weeks, this was glad tidings. Lanny described the visit to the Château de Bruyne, the letter he had got there, and the use he planned to make of it.

The Spanish Socialist's voice was grave as he answered. " I thought of this as something you might have in mind, but I turned it down as preposterous. I must warn you that the man you have in mind is one of the very worst of our enemies. He is Darnand's right-hand man, and Darnand is perhaps the most hated man in France, not even second to Laval. We know him from of old, because he operated here in Nice, where he was one of the leading Fascists. Now he's the Gestapo's French agent ; his hands are stained with the blood of thousands of French patriots."

" I know all that ; but we are trying to win a war and to save the lives of Frenchmen as well as of British and Americans. Don't forget that there are going to be French divisions among those which attempt a landing on this coast. If we can seduce Vichy Frenchmen away from opening fire on them, is not that what you call the logic of the situation ? "

" I grant all that—if it can be done. But the idea sounds like madness to me."

" You must leave that to me, old man. I have been thinking about it for a couple of years, ever since we were planning the landing in North Africa, and I met Denis *fils* there. You must understand, both these brothers are honest men who sincerely believe in what they are doing. I have known Charlot since he was a boy, and I have a special hold upon him."

" You must realize that you'll be taking your life into your hands when you go among that gang."

" A lot of our men are taking their lives in their hands, and they'll be doing it on the Côte d'Azur very soon. If I can manage to have some of the guns badly aimed against them, it's surely worth the risk."

U

"Then what do you expect to do, Lanny? Convince our crowd that young de Bruyne has come over to them?"

"I expect to tell them the truth, and I expect you to back me up. They don't have to love Charlot—they can call him a time-server and a double-crossing scoundrel—but they'll have to let him alone, as they did Darlan and Lemaigre-Dubreuil and the rest in Algiers."

"And let your Army put them in power over us as they did there!"

"That's something for the future; that's for the French people to decide, and you will be free to have your say and cast your vote. But you can't do it unless we win the war."

Raoul gave up. "*Bien*, you want to meet de Bruyne. How do you expect to do it?"

"That is something on which I seek your advice. I was told that he was living at Bienvenu. Is he still there?"

"So our people report."

"I might just go there and ask for him. But that might embarrass him, whichever way he decides. He would have to account for me, and it might awaken suspicions. On the other hand, if I sent a note to him, the messenger might be questioned, or the note might be read by someone else. I'm inclined to think the best way would be to telephone; he would know my voice and would come wherever I told him to."

"But if he came over to our side, the enemy would get busy on every clue. A telephone call can be traced."

"It should be from a public booth. And where shall I tell him to come?"

They both knew the city and discussed various places. In the end Lanny decided upon a programme of boldness; he would go to the fashionable Hôtel Métropole and register as Henri J. M. Girouard, order a room, go upstairs, and telephone Charlot to come there. Under police regulations Lanny would not have to report himself for a full day, and meantime he would be through and gone. Raoul objected that it might be suspicious for a man to arrive in Cannes when everybody else was leaving; but Lanny said that suspicions took time to crystallize, and he wouldn't stay long enough. Raoul said the *maquis* had friends among the hotel staff, and a guard could be set up to protect Lanny in case of trouble; but the P.A.

vetoed that. He was relying upon persuasion and surely wouldn't take the chance of telling a number of persons what he was doing. If there were spies in a palace hotel, there would also be spies among the Partisans.

IV

Dawn was approaching, and Raoul would not let his friend walk into the fashionable part of the city. He asked for an hour's time and went away; when he came back, Lanny followed him out to the street, and there, dimly visible, was a small one-horse cart such as French market-gardeners use. A woman was driving, and Raoul whispered, "Cover yourself up, and if anyone lifts the cover she will say that you are ill." Lanny could guess that he looked it, for the few bites of food he had had were a poor substitute for what he had lost.

"I will telephone the hotel tonight," Raoul said; and the P.A. climbed in and drew the canvas cover over him. The cart rumbled away at a walk, as French farm horses go unless violently disturbed. After half an hour of bumping the cart stopped, and the woman's voice said, "*Ici, M'sieu'.*" He got out and saw that he was at the side entrance of the hotel. He said, "*Merci de tout mon cœur.*" She deserved it, for she had risked the death penalty for him. He did not offer to pay, for it was not that kind of service.

He brushed himself off and walked into the hotel. There was no one in the lobby at that hour, and he was to discover later that there were few at any hour. The patrons of palace hotels had read accounts of what had happened to Cherbourg, Caen, and other places on or near the Channel, and they wanted none of it in their lives. Better to pack up a couple of valises and go and sleep in a wood hut in a forest, with only the hedgehogs for company.

Lanny registered and explained that his *bagages* had gone astray. Being a rather seedy-looking customer, he put the price down on the desk, and that made him respectable. He was escorted to the room, gave the bell-boy the proper tip, and then locked himself in. His first step was to search the room for wiring and for peepholes; he even moved the bureau and crawled under the bed to make sure there was no listening hole into the next room. Then he took a bath, as well as a man could do with cold water and no soap ; he shaved, under the same handicap, and then lay on the bed to rest and think and wait for daylight to make a telephone call less of an intrusion and an anomaly.

The number was that which he knew best of all numbers : the villa where he had spent his childhood, on the road which runs through the village of Juan-les-Pins and southward along the rocky shore of the Cap d'Antibes. As Lanny waited, he imagined the phones ringing—one in the drawing-room and the other in the long hall near the pantry. He assumed that several officers would be quartered in the house, and they would have orderlies to wait on them.

When Lanny called, a man's voice said, " Villa Bienvenu," and Lanny replied promptly, " Capitaine Charles de Bruyne." He waited, and when he heard the familiar voice he said quickly, " This is an old friend. No names, please. I have just seen your father and your wife, and they are well. They have sent you an urgent message. I am at the Métropole and can't stay long. The room number is seven-fourteen. I have no means of transportation. Can you come to me at once ? "

The answer was prompt, " I will come."

" Room seven-fourteen, the Métropole. I am staying with a friend named Girouard." The French pronounce it " Zheer-wahr," and Lanny took the precaution to spell it.

V

Two years had passed since Lanny had seen Charlot, and he was not surprised to discover lines of care in his face. The world had not been going the way an ardent and aristocratic-minded young Frenchman wanted it to go, and now, according to his point of view, it appeared about to slide over a precipice. But the *capitaine* was well set up, his figure trim and well corseted, his dark hair closely cut and his uniform faultless. His face was pale, and this brought out the scar which he carried as a badge of honour, having got it in battling with the " Red " mob which had rioted in Paris shortly before the war. He hated that mob and still burned to put it down.

They exchanged a handclasp, and Lanny took the precaution to look out into the hall before he closed the door. Then he said, " Charlot, I was at the château a few days ago. I saw *le père*, and Eugénie and Annette. They are well and told me the children were well. Having a garden, they are not doing badly. They begged me to get a message to you and I promised to try."

" Lanny, how on earth do you manage these things ? "

" It was my father who made it possible. He was concerned about *le père*, as both a friend and a business associate." The P.A. signed his friend to a chair and drew up another. "*Cher ami*," he said, " I come as a herald of what I fear is bad news. I have taken a risk to come to you, and I have to pledge you to hold what I tell you in strict confidence."

" Of course, Lanny, you don't need to say that. What on earth has happened to you ? "

" As you know, I continued to visit Germany and do what little I could on behalf of our cause. But on the last trip I was warned by friends that I was in an unsafe position. Both Hitler and Göring are surrounded by jealous persons who could not endure to see an American enjoying their trust, and these evil ones have been whispering rumours and slanders. I saw that my position was becoming impossible and made up my mind to withdraw entirely from this hateful civil war. That is what it is to me, for I have made my friends among Germans and French and British and Americans alike, and I cannot get any pleasure out of seeing them destroy one another. I decided to become once again an art lover, as your dear mother so often begged me to do."

" I can understand your decision, Lanny, and perhaps it is the wisest thing for a man of your gifts."

" I found that my father had entirely changed his position under the pressure of events. He likes the so-called New Deal as little as ever, but he has become convinced that the Americans are going to win this war."

" How can he bring himself to believe that Germany can be conquered, Lanny ? "

" He is in touch with the men who mean to do it. He himself is turning out a fabulous number of planes—I have never seen anything to equal the mushroom growth of the Budd-Erling plants. There is no resisting air-power, Charlot.

It gives the ability to land on any coast and to roll in any direction. From what I have been told I believe the last German soldier will be out of France within the next month, or two months at the outside."

"You may be right, Lanny," admitted Charlot humbly. "I have been unpleasantly surprised by recent events."

The P.A. got up and went to the door and opened it suddenly. He had left it unlocked, so that he could do this. Then he came back and resumed in a still lower voice. "Believe me, Charlot, my father has made it his business to know what is coming. He became greatly worried about your family. He says that between the time when the Germans withdraw and the Allies arrive, there will be a period of disorder in which great numbers of people who have aided the Germans will be shot out of hand ; later, when a pro-Allied French government is set up, many of the Vichy leaders will be tried for treason and sentenced to death. You must know without my telling you that you are one of the most vulnerable."

"Certainly I know it, Lanny. It will not trouble me too greatly, for I have no desire to live under a regime of the rabble."

"Robbie sent me to explain matters to *le père* and urge him to change his position and make some contribution to the de Gaulle movement. I spent the better part of an evening with him and found that he had already taken this step. His one fear was for you, and he begged me with tears in his eyes to find a way to see you and transmit to you not merely his wishes but his command as *père de famille*. He wanted to write you an explicit letter, but I pointed out that if such a letter fell into the hands of the Germans he would be shot, and his property confiscated, and his grandchildren left in destitution. I persuaded him that it would suffice if he told you to follow my instructions, for I was sure you would not question my good faith in this matter."

"No, surely not, Lanny."

The P.A. took the letter from his pocket and put it into his friend's hand. Knowing the letter by heart, Lanny followed in his mind what Charlot was reading : "Do what our old and dear friend desires. It is a command of your father." And beneath it the words of the wife : "It is also my prayer."

VI

Charlot looked up from his reading and gazed hard at his friend. " Well, Lanny, what is it you want me to do ? "

" It is not what I want, Charlot, but what your father commands and your wife prays. I am only their messenger. First, let me inform you, in the strictest confidence, that the Allies are going to invade this coast. It may be at any moment now."

" We know that well, Lanny. We have made all preparations to receive them."

" Do you think you can withstand them ? "

" That is in the lap of the gods. My only concern is to defend my honour."

" You are aware, Charlot, that a considerable part of the force will be Frenchmen, under the command of General de Tassigny ? "

" He is under the political control of the wretched de Gaulle, whom we consider a traitor to *la patrie.*"

" I am surely not among his admirers, *cher garçon*, but it appears that he is the man the so-called Free French want."

" The Free French are a bunch of Reds and assassins, and we do not consider them our countrymen."

" Let me assure you, I have talked with some of de Gaulle's supporters, men whom you were glad to call your comrades in past times. Whatever his faults may be, he surely has no trace of sympathy with Communism. If he has accepted the help of Reds, it is as any military man accepts the help of any ally in war. *Le grand Charlie* is a devout Catholic like yourself ; a graduate of St. Cyr, and they do not train social rebels. If he should gain power he would quickly divorce himself from every trace of radicalism and proceed to make France the kind of country you desire. Yet you are fighting him ! "

" It is he who began it, Lanny, by setting himself up against the legitimately constituted government of France."

" I cannot debate those questions with you, Charlot, because they seem to me metaphysical, and I am no abstract thinker. No words can alter the fact that you are going to fight an army of Frenchmen, and an army that is bound to win. You remember, we Americans had a revolution in our country ; if George Washington had been defeated, he would have been a traitor under British law, and he might lawfully have been hanged. But he won, so he is called the Father of his Country."

" That is a cynical way to look at it, Lanny. I have heard you quote some American philosopher about the worship of ' the bitch-goddess Success.' "

" Yes, but you are a military man, and that means that you accept the arbitrament of arms ; you consent to have the issues of history decided that way. Surely there could be no other reason for a Frenchman to fight on the side of Germans against a French army."

" What do you want me to do, Lanny, run away ? "

" Again I remind you, I am not telling you what I want ; I am repeating a message from your father."

" *Bien.* What does *le père* wish me to do ? "

" He wishes you to live. He points out that you are the heir-apparent to half of a great property. Also, you are the father of a family, and you owe it to them not to throw your life away and leave them in destitution. *Le père* wishes you to take part in the shaping of the new France which will emerge from this war. He wishes you to work by your brother's side for those ends. I must tell you that I have seen your brother several times, and he is in an agony of distress about you ; his pleading was one of the reasons which induced me to risk this journey. Denis was severely wounded and in hospital, and is only now beginning to get about on crutches. He begged me with tears in his eyes to persuade you to come over to the Allied side before it is too late. I do not need to tell you what will happen to you if you fight the French Army."

" I have faced that issue, Lanny."

" You must know," continued the P.A., " that the moral struggle going on in you is no new thing to me. I saw it with one Frenchman after another prior to the Allied landing in North Africa. Hundreds of your old comrades came over to the Allied side, they risked their lives, and they do not have to feel that they besmirched their honour. General Giraud,

General Juin, General Béthouart, Admiral Fenard, Admiral Battet—I could call a long roll of the men I saw making up their minds, and without any help from me, because I hadn't made up my own then. Now these men are commanding French divisions or French ships. The hour has come when you Frenchmen on the Côte d'Azur have to make the same decision. It seems to me it should be much easier for you, because in North Africa there were no Frenchmen landing and no Germans giving orders to Frenchmen."

VII

This was the beginning of an argument that lasted all through that day. As a man who did not wish to be convinced, Charlot took the argument back over the same ground again and again. *L'honneur*, which means so much to a Frenchman, and *la gloire* and *la patrie*, and *la légitimité*. Who was this Big Charlie? A mere brigadier-general who had dared to rebel against *le vieux maréchal* and to vilify him to the world? And the boy who had shot the French admiral, Darlan, for his treason, was he or was he not a patriot and hero? And what were the prospects for France if it was set free and entrusted to the politicians, to democracy *à l'Américaine*—would it not become a Red satrapy? And what would have happened if Vichy had had its way—would Hitler have ever kept his promises to withdraw?

Lanny had the advantage of having come fresh from the Allied lands; he could tell of the colossal preparations being made for Operation Anvil. What were the defences of the Midi compared to those along the Channel? What was the roughness of the Mediterranean compared with those northern waters? Raoul had told Lanny there were few reserves back of the Riviera, and Lanny now pretended to know this, and Charlot admitted that it was true. The big battleships would pound the shore installations to pieces, the planes would do pinpoint bombing on what was left, the parachutists would seize the bridges, power plants, and airfields, and the tanks would be coming ashore in a few hours and racing everywhere. The Germans who stayed to defend the towns would be surrounded and made prisoners, and the younger son of the de Bruynes would be tried and shot. And what good would it do to his *honneur*, his *gloire*, or his *patrie* ?

Charlot had four persons against him, his father, his elder brother, his wife, and his near-godfather ; and that was about all a Frenchman could have in the way of family authority. Lanny had an especial hold, because up to recently he had believed as Charlot had. It did not occur to Charlot to doubt that such was the case, and when Lanny described the steps his conversion had taken, he was preparing a path for the younger man's feet. When Lanny had come to Vichy, his job had required him to buttress the *capitaine* in all his convictions ; and now that he had changed, his example was equally convincing. He had recently been in London and could knock out the Nazi propaganda that the city was in ruins and the population in a panic. Of course the buzz bombs were nasty, but could anyone imagine that the killing of a few thousand more civilians would cause Britain to give up ? It was just a question of digging out the launching sites, and already the British armies had broken out of Caen and were forcing their way eastward along the coast.

And then—the Germans ! Had Charlot been able to get along with them ? Were they kind masters ? Did they respect the honour, the dignity, of their French partners ? Just as Lanny had guessed, the high-spirited young *capitaine* had been ill-pleased with his comrades-in-arms. They had become more and more exacting and less and less patient. As things went against them, they demanded more of France, and when it was impossible to meet the demands they became insolent. Would it be too unbearable to see a French army come in and knock them off their perches ?

And then, Charlot's colleagues, the former Jeunesses Patriotes, now evolved into the Francs-Gardes—were they all patriots and heroes ? Their *capitaine* was forced to admit that some of them were blackguards and others of low intelligence. In short, Lanny dragged out of him the fact that for a long time he had been unhappy in his occupation and in despair for the future of his country. Once started, he poured out his confession, and Lanny gathered enough information to make his journey worth while, even if he did not win the soul of his friend.

But he meant to win, and he kept on until evening. The argument which clinched the matter was Lanny's statement that by coming over in time Charlot might be saving not merely himself but his whole family. Lanny would bear witness to the part which *le père* and *la femme* had played in Charlot's conversion, and the Partisans would know of it. Charlot bowed his head to hide the tears that welled into his eyes. "All right, Lanny," he said, "I will do what you advise." And suddenly it seemed to his near-godfather that Charlot turned back into the shy and sensitive lad whom his mother had introduced to Lanny at the château more than two decades ago, in that quiet garden, with the apricots and the grape-vines in blossom, the jonquils and the narcissus filling the air with fragrance. Lanny thought, oh, God, if children knew what was going to happen to them, would they consent to stay in this world ?

VIII

The younger de Bruyne was not the sort of man to wish to run away. If he was coming over to the Allied side, he would take an active part, and Lanny talked to him on that basis. Who was there among his associates who might be open to persuasion ? What strategic places were there which might be occupied at the critical moment ? The German garrison in Cannes greatly outnumbered the French group, so there could be no outright revolt ; but saboteurs might blow up munitions dumps, set fuel stores on fire, put guns out of commission, render vehicles inoperable. Above all, a mass of information might be turned over to Allied agents, so that they would know when to strike and where to meet their Partisan friends and give them support.

Lanny reported what he had seen in North Africa. At Casablanca the conspiracy had failed, and as a result there had been two or three days of fighting between the French on the shore and the British and American invaders ; General Béthouart, who had tried to help the Allies, had come near to being shot as a traitor. But in Algiers the conspiracy had been more widespread and there had been little fighting. Unfortunately the conspirators had gone into action too early, and their opponents had had time to rally; if the opponents had been Germans, great numbers of the conspirators would surely have been shot.

The next step was for Charlot to meet the Partisan leaders, and this was a matter of some delicacy. Lanny warned him that he would meet some he did not like and hear ideas which were anathema to him. He had to make up his mind to work with any and all who were willing to fight Germans. Lanny was expecting a telephone call from Raoul and told about this old friend who was in contact with the Partisans here. Charlot had been hunting these people and might have a hard time convincing them that he had come over. In all probability some of them had known Lanny in the old days and believed that he had become a Fascist enemy; they would feel sure that Raoul was being led into a trap.

They got some food delivered to their room—Charlot had a card which enabled him to order what he wanted. Soon after dark came the telephone call, and Lanny told Raoul to come to the room. In spite of the fact that Charlot and Raoul were old friends of Lanny's, they had never met, for Marie de Bruyne had been out of sympathy with Lanny's political opinions and he never introduced her boys to his socially undesirable acquaintances. In those days the grandson of Budd Gunmakers had lived in two idea-tight compartments, the world of Raoul and Rick, and the world of his mother and his *amie*.

Now these two worlds met and mingled, and if the occasion had been one of less deadly seriousness Lanny would have been amused. The scion of the de Bruynes was very stiff and correct; he was " St. Germain," which is the same as if you said " Beacon Street " in Boston or " Berkeley Square " in London. When Charlot met his social inferiors, they were servants or common soldiers with whom he did not shake hands. Now he was meeting a peasant's son who had fled from the police of the Spanish monarchy and who might on some occasion have fitted a pair of shoes on Charlot's feet in this city on the Coast of Pleasure. Whether or not that had happened, it was certain that if the *capitaine* had caught him twenty-four hours ago he would have had him shot forthwith. The distinction between Red and Pink was vague in Charlot's mind, and he took it as wholly fraudulent, a camouflage.

But Raoul had his own form of dignity and thought just as well of himself as Charlot did of Charlot. They were like two Indian chieftains smoking a peace-pipe—only Raoul did not smoke. What they did was to talk business, and soon they forgot everything else. Lanny said that Charlot was a man of honour and that when he gave his word he could be trusted to the death. That was enough for Raoul, and after a while he offered to go back to the hideout where he had met Lanny and try to persuade the leader of the Resistance in Cannes to come to the hotel for a conference. Raoul himself had been working in Toulon and had in Cannes no contacts which would enable him to transmit information to the Allies.

IX

The one-time school director went away, and the *capitaine* and the presidential agent talked about their families and about the war. After an hour or so Raoul returned in the company of another man, swarthy and dark-haired, who spoke with a strong Provençal accent. He was stocky and had once been powerful, but now, like nearly everybody on the Riviera, he hadn't had enough to eat for some time. Raoul introduced him as Ribault, which might, of course, be a name for the occasion. His manner was guarded and suspicious, and he did not offer to take the hand of this hated policeman of the Vichy gangsters. He spoke directly and to the point, and the substance of what he said was that the lamp still held out to burn and the vilest sinner might return. (Not that a leader of the *maquis* had ever heard the hymns of Isaac Watts !)

The *capitaine* replied with dignity that hitherto he had seen no possibility of getting rid of the Germans, but that now, when the possibility appeared, he was ready to do his part. Actions would speak louder than words, and if Monsieur Ribault would make notes, the *capitaine* would tell him everything he could. Raoul volunteered to do the writing—perhaps the other man's heavy fist was not adapted to the task. Charlot proceeded to pour out information about the number of troops in the garrison and near by, who commanded them, and what weapons they had. He gave the facts about fortifications, the number of the guns, their calibre and range; the location of oil and other stores, and of radio-ranging stations not yet bombed. He said that the Germans had seven divisions in Southern France, two of them armoured; only three were at the coast, but others were on the way. He said that all the best troops had been taken to the north; many of those left behind were badly trained divisions, older age groups, and convalescents; the way to deal with them was to attack boldly and push on, not worrying about your flanks. He answered every question promptly—and Ribault was in a position to judge the answers, for it had been his business to gather such facts and no doubt he had many.

When the session was over he got up and shook Charlot's hand. "*Monsieur le Capitaine, vous êtes un camarade,*" he said, and that was meant to settle it. The leader took the paper and hid it in his jacket, saying that he would get the information to the Allies before the night was over.

What were the others going to do? Raoul wanted to return to the neighbourhood of Toulon, his post of duty, and he had a way of getting there. Lanny's problem was more complicated; not knowing how long his job in Cannes might take, he had made no arrangement with the O.S.S. to be taken out of France. He had told them that he knew where he could hide out in the hills and wait in safety until the invasion was over. He asked Charlot to drive him to the neighbourhood of this place, and Charlot agreed.

First the Provençal left the hotel room, followed by the Spaniard. Then Charlot went down to his car, telling Lanny where it was. After a short interval Lanny put his razor, his comb, and his toothbrush into his pocket—all he had in the way of luggage—and slipped out of the Hôtel Métropole unobserved. He had already paid for his room and for the food. It was then after midnight, and Lanny could have used some sleep, but he dared not stay longer in the hotel without registering with the police. He stepped into the car, and after that he was safe, for not even the Germans would have held up the car of a captain of the Francs-Gardes.

On the way Lanny explained that his destination was the home of a peasant family, several of whose members had been

servants at Bienvenu in past years. He didn't want to be
driven there, because the sight of Charlot's uniform might
trouble them ; all peasants fear all authorities. Charlot
agreed ; he didn't want to be seen with Lanny any more than
Lanny with him.

They drove on a road which led up into the mountains ;
it was lined with the gates to fine estates, and after they had
gone a considerable distance Lanny said, " I think this is far
enough to be safe." Charlot assented, saying that he must
get back to his duties so as not to excite suspicion. They
exchanged a warm handclasp and words of friendship and
trust. " You were right," said the Frenchman, " and I am
sure I shall never regret it." They were the last words that
Lanny was to hear from his friend.

x

The P.A. climbed for a while, and then his breath began to
come hard, and he realized that he was short on food as well
as sleep. Bordering the road was one of the forests of pine
trees which cover the slopes of the mountains, and he found
a smooth place and sat down to rest. It is chilly on the Riviera
as soon as the sun goes down, and when you climb it grows
even more so ; but he didn't wish to approach his destination
in darkness, so he curled up into a ball for warmth and with
one arm for a pillow fell fast asleep.

When he wakened dawn was spreading, and he was stiff
with cold. He listened to the tinkle of sheep bells, then got
up and started climbing again. But presently came another
sound, one that stopped him. Thunder ? No, bombing ! He
had been hearing it off and on for some eight years—the first
time having been in Barcelona. He was an expert and could
tell the difference between big ones far off and little ones near
by. These were distant, but not very.

He looked about, and as the light grew brighter he found
a spot on the mountainside that was clear of everything but
brush. He pushed his way into it and stood looking down
upon a scene veiled in early morning mist. Through the mist
were flashes of orange-coloured fire, quick and sharp, like the
gleam of fireflies. Here, there, all along where Lanny knew

the coast would be, he saw these fire-bursts, one after another, so many that the sounds were incessant. He stood fascinated while the light spread and the sun came up. He knew the view from boyhood : beautiful white villas below him, their grounds planted with ornamental trees from all over the world ; orange groves of dark green and olive groves of silvery grey ; and beyond them a rough and rocky coast with white stretches of sand here and there, and the Midland Sea, green in the shallows and deep blue all the way to the horizon's edge.

The mist lifted, but its place was taken by a cloud of smoke, so Lanny could not see the coast. What he saw was a swarm of planes, flying high, and diving down, dropping their deadly loads and then turning out to sea. He had expected to observe ships, but this was an air bombardment ; so he knew that D-day wasn't yet. The fire flashes extended from Cannes as far to the westward as his vision could reach, and this told him, as it told everybody in the world, the general location of the coming invasion. His heart ached for the beautiful city of Cannes, which he loved in spite of its corruptions. He wondered, was it getting an area-bombing, like Berlin and the other German cities ? Hardly likely, for this was France, and the Air Force was doing what it could to spare the civilians ; the planes would be spotting military targets, and Lanny wondered, had they received the information from Ribault in time ? It was possible, for a radio-sending set didn't take long to work, and everything in this war was faster than ever before.

XI

Lanny watched for the smoke to rise ; but there were fires, and more smoke from them. The sun came and warmed him, and he waited for hours before he was sure there were no fires on the Cap d'Antibes, and that the familiar buildings which stood out in Cannes were apparently undamaged. Then he climbed into one of the small side valleys, where lay the little farm of Leese and her family.

This capable Provençal woman had been the cook at Bienvenu when Lanny was a child, and she had risen to the post of *majeuse-dome*, a word which the playful Lanny had coined for the occasion of her twenty-fifth anniversary. Now she was old, and might be dead for all he knew ; but her numerous relatives would be at the place, and the Budd family held royal rank in their eyes. In the early days of the war, before Beauty had fled from Bienvenu, they had been her bootleggers by exclusive appointment, keeping her supplied with every sort of farm produce. No doubt the money she had paid them was still hidden in mattresses or buried in some pot at the foot of a tree on the farm.

An unpaved road led into the little valley where the farm stood on a steep slope. Tiny gardens had been terraced, every cupful of soil was saved, and vegetables grew in plots no bigger than your handkerchief. The house was built of rocks—so plentiful, alas ; the house was mainly kitchen, having a great fireplace of rocks, made tight, like the house, with plaster. There was the inevitable French manure pile, but reduced in size because the Boches had left them only one old cow and one tiny donkey. But the ancient olive trees stood, and the apricot and peach trees and the vines ; everything perfectly tended despite the fact that there was only one old man left in this family, and one middle-aged man with his right arm and part of his shoulder lost ; there were three women, two of them with husbands at war, and half a dozen children, all of whom worked.

They had heard the bombing ; but would they stop work for that ? No indeed ! They had been hearing such sounds from the Mediterranean off and on for almost five years. Such sounds, in their view, concerned the people in the cities, the great and powerful who lived by collecting taxes and drafting young men into armies. What peasants did was to keep alive and get the highest prices they could for what products they could spare. Every hour there was work that had to be done, and no time to think about matters that were far away and beyond understanding.

The arrival of a stranger was no novelty just now, and they hardly looked up from their labours. But when this city man smiled and said, " Don't you know me ? " they looked, and then cried, " Monsieur Lanny ! " Everybody came running, and shook both his hands, and patted him on the back, and introduced him to the children, most of whom were too young to remember him. They wanted to hear about Madame Detaze—so they called Beauty—and Monsieur Dingle and the little boy, where and how were they and would they come back ? They took him in, and there was Leese, shrunken but still alive, bedridden but propped up, doing the family mending and knitting, and giving all the orders for the place He kissed her toil-worn hand, just as if she had been a *grande dame*, and she patted him, as if it had been the good old time when he was a little boy, racing about the estate or learning to pound the piano.

So much there was to talk about, and so many people ! He had a little daughter, a big girl now ; he had a new wife and a baby boy, and when would he bring them to Bienvenu ? When *les Boches* were gone, he told them ; the Americans were coming to drive the evil ones out. So that was what the shooting was about ! Well then, they would be glad ; they knew how the Americans had come last time, and had paid for produce with good money, whereas *les Boches* paid with money that lost its value fast. But they came and made you take it and you didn't dare to say a word, but hid all the produce you could, and ate as much as you wanted. You got fat to spite *les Boches* !

Lanny said, " Don't say a word about my being here. It would be very bad for me. I came up to hide until the Americans have got ashore." They all promised, even the children promised, *pas un mot !* They had hidden some of the Maquis now and then, their own sort of people, fighting the harsh-voiced foreigners who came to search the peasant's huts and store-rooms and carry off his grain and olives and fruit and poultry, all the means of life he had laid up for the coming winter.

That was what war meant to peasants all over Europe, to those fortunate ones who happened not to be in the line of march of armies or on the ground chosen for battles. It meant lugging your produce out into the forest and hiding it in caves, or in hollow trees, or in pits dug and bricked in. It meant the children keeping watch, and when the alarm was given, the women fleeing into the mountains and being hunted like wild animals by lustful men. It meant paper currency that presently became worthless, so that peasants learned to take only hard money, and change it into gold, and put it in a sock and bury it under a loose board or hearthstone.

XII

Also, it meant refugees, pitiful people fleeing from towns and villages, from battles and bombardments. That was what it would mean this very day; they knew it and discussed it with sombre resolution. *Les pauvres gens*, of course one was sorry for them, but there had been too many of them, and farm people had to survive if farms were to continue to be worked. "Thousands have come, Monsieur Lanny, and we have given more than we can spare. What good will it do if we starve in the winter and are unable to work the fields in the spring?" It was a cruel world, and perhaps only the hard-hearted were fit to survive in it.

The flood began to arrive late in the morning. People had leaped out of bed, for city people do not get up with the dawn. Some wore pyjamas; they had not even stopped to put their clothes on. Others rolled bundles in baby carriages or children's carts. One woman had nothing but a gilded cage with her pet canary. They had toiled up the foothills and spread into the valleys, and one and all seemed to think that farm people had nothing to do but take care of them. They were exhausted, terrified, helpless; they begged and pleaded, with tears in their eyes. Surely they could sleep in the barn, in the half-empty store-room, or with the cow or the pig! Any place but out in the wild forest among the rocks, and only *le bon Dieu* knew what sorts of wild beasts! They held out money, the paper money printed for *les Boches*; the peasants had no idea how that money had come into existence, but they knew it would buy less and less, and they wanted less and less of it, "*Non, non, madame, monsieur, rien, rien! Il faut partir!*" The wretched ones didn't want to go, for where was there to go to?

These scenes went on, day and night, all the time that Lanny stayed on the place. There was an incessant stream of refugees, and they had to be scolded before they would move on. They wanted water, and you couldn't refuse water, but you tried to make them understand that wells in these hills often went dry and that water was as precious to a farmer as food. They begged to sleep under shelter, and would swear that they had no matches or tobacco. But you couldn't believe them ; the old man declared that many a farmer who had done so had lost his barn for his kindness. Lanny observed the deeply rooted mistrust of the peasant for the city person. The city was a parasite upon the farm ; the bourgeois slept late and wore fine clothes and did no real work, but charged the peasant high prices for tools and clothing and all the things he had to have.

Against this would be the claims of common humanity. A mother wept and pleaded for a little milk to save her baby's life. They gave her a little milk, even though their cow was going dry and there was not enough for their own children. And then, of course, the mother wanted to stay ; she had found kind people, she had made a dent in the hard crust of this cruel world ! An old man, apparently a gentleman, fainted from exhaustion, and what would they do about him ? Who was to tell if he had really fainted, or if he was only pretending, as so many of these clever folk had learned to do ?

Lanny's food choked him, but he ate a little, because he too had to survive ; each person thinks there is some special reason why he should do so. To these Provençal peasants Lanny was a privileged being, an old friend, besides being heir-apparent to the Bienvenu estate. He had climbed here as a boy and a youth, loving these mountains and the country sights. He had come to the festivals and learned the songs and danced with the girls to the music of fife and drum and tambourine : a quick little waltz, and a jerky polka, and the farandole. He had sung " *Oh, Magali, ma tant amado,*"— Provençal being a cross between Italian and French. He had learned a lot of their words and had not forgotten them now ; he would amuse them by exclaiming, " Name of a good little man ! "

They locked him and themselves inside the house so that others might not see them eating. They cut him a slice of whole-wheat bread, and put on it a slice from a large onion. With a handful of dried olives that was a meal for any farm worker, and it was a meal for Lanny. A cup of wine went with it, and they drank the wine exactly as the sun crossed the meridian. He didn't know why they did that, and they couldn't tell him ; it was a custom. They kept him out of sight, for there might be spies among these refugees, or there might be Boches running away from the Americans. Later the Boches would be licked and would surely come then—and the peasant women would join the refugees and sleep in the forest. *C'est la guerre !*

25

Le Jour de Gloire

I

EVERY morning Lanny would hear the sounds of bombing, and walk out to the mountainside and look for ships. But he saw only planes and the line of shell bursts and clouds of black smoke ascending. Three days he watched that sight and noted that the most numerous bursts and the heaviest smoke were to the west. He decided that that was where he wanted to be, and he made a bargain with the one-armed peasant to escort him to the farm of one of Leese's nephews, who had worked at Bienvenu as gardener and would surely be glad to welcome his former employer. The one-armed man, a son-in-law, didn't want any of the paper money, but was glad to take Lanny Budd's cheque on a New York bank; that would be good for dollars, and he knew the day would come when he could cash it.

The mistral had started blowing, that cold wind which comes from the north and spoils the joy of tourists on the Riviera. The pair set out early and took the whole day. The streams have cut their way down to the sea in gorges, and it is not always easy to cross them ; but a man who has lived here all his life knows the trails and the fords and how to keep out of sight. The mountains had suddenly become full of people, and how they were going to subsist was a mystery. Lanny and his guide walked all day toward the west, and spent the night safely in a cabin in the forests of the red Estérel mounains, behind which Lanny had seen the sun set all through his boyhood and youth. The owner of the cabin was a cork worker, small, black-haired, and swarthy, his features recalling the fact that the Saracens had many times invaded this land.

Before sunrise Lanny again sought a view of the sea, and there, looking down from a clear spot amid a forest of rugged cork oak trees, he saw at last the sight he had been expecting. The ships ! The whole sea was spotted with them as if they had been sprinkled out of a pepper-pot ; they extended in all directions as far as the eye could reach. He did not try to count them, but later he learned that there had been more than eight hundred. And all headed toward the Côte d'Azur !

Ahead came the tiny P.T.-boats and destroyers, darting here and there, on the lookout for the subs. Then came the majestic battleships and heavy cruisers ; they turned in lines parallel to the shore and at once opened up with their big guns, the mightiest cannonade that Lanny had ever heard or imagined. He saw the tongues of yellow flame shoot out, and saw the shells burst on the shore before he heard the report from either explosion. But it was only a few seconds before all the reports had become a blur, a roaring as of all the thunder in the world. All the warships of all sizes were bursting with flames, and swarms of planes over the shore were adding to the racket. Even through the smoke Lanny could see that the shell bursts were bunched at certain spots ; he was glad he was not on any of those spots, and wondered how many of them had been listed in the information which Raoul and Charlot had furnished.

This bombardment went on for so long that the observer couldn't guess the time. Here and there through the smoke he could see other kinds of ships coming in from the sea and knew that what the Armed Forces called H-hour was at hand. The transports and other vessels came in and halted, and the swarms of landing craft set to work. Some that were big came to the shore with the loads they had brought ; smaller craft were let down from the transports and the men came swarming down on rope nets on which scores could move at the same time. Lanny knew that everything had been rehearsed over and over, so that every man who took part in the enterprise knew exactly what he had to do.

The mistral which was still blowing made no trouble for

them because it was a lee shore. Very soon the swarms of boats were moving in toward the beaches, and when batteries on land which had survived the bombardment opened up on them, the guns of the warships opened on the batteries, and planes overhead dived down on them with bombs. Surely an unusual sight, and worth crossing an ocean and climbing a mountain to see ; Lanny hoped that none of the spotter planes would call the attention of a battle-wagon to two civilians sitting on a mountainside !

II

The P.A. kept count and observed seven waves of men coming ashore in the space of a couple of hours. They were entering a little bay, full of fishing boats. He said, " That is St. Raphael, is it not ? " The guide confirmed his guess. Lanny knew the town ; a lovely place, especially favoured by the art lovers who wanted to live cheaply and away from the fashionable atmosphere of Cannes. " The G.I.'s will like it," he remarked.

He was joking, for he knew they wouldn't stay long. The other man replied, " They may be driving the Boches this way, Monsieur." Lanny took the hint, broke off his sojourn, and went back to the cork worker's hut and spent a night among the fleas and the refugees. The latter were nearly as thick as the former ; the cork worker didn't mind their sleeping in his backyard, for he had no farm and nothing that would be of use to them. They wanted to keep out of the cold wind.

Early next morning Lanny got up and listened. There was still a lot of shooting, but not so much as on the previous day. He decided that it was time for him to move and said good-bye to his friendly host. He went out to the place of observation and saw that there was resistance in the direction of Cannes, and some toward the west, but in other places the ships were shooting into the hills, doubtless at enemy tanks and transport. In front of him there was no sign of trouble ; the ships were not bothered by the offshore wind, and the landing craft were gliding to and fro like ferryboats. The wonderful Navy put a hundred thousand men ashore in two days, on a seventy-mile ront between Cannes and Toulon.

The cork man had pointed out an obscure path which led down along the mountainside and would take the traveller into St. Raphael. Lanny started down; there were refugees toiling up, and he was no longer afraid of them. He asked some of them for news, but found that their only idea was to get away from news. There came German soldiers, laden with their packs, and Lanny stood aside respectfully and let them file by. No Gestapo any more; nobody requiring French civilians to show their papers. He observed a baby carriage standing by the path, empty; somebody had found the going too steep, and he or others had emptied it of contents. Farther along was what had been a gun emplacement; its concrete had been knocked to pieces, and one gun was standing on its nose, the other sticking up at a crazy angle. The traveller got by that spot as fast as he could, lest one of the hovering planes should not be entirely satisfied with the job.

III

The nearer he got, the better he could see that show, and it was one to remember and tell his grandchildren about. The big L.S.T.'s came up to the beach and opened their huge jaws; tanks came rumbling out, or tractors towing heavy guns. Pack-laden soldiers looked like waterfalls pouring down the sides of ships. Every sort of little boat was bringing them in, and the tiny harbour of St. Raphael appeared to be solid with craft. Lanny would stand and look for a few minutes, and then descend to a lower level and a closer view.

Presently there was some sort of structure on the slope that he took to be connected with the waterworks of the town; there were several men guarding it, and, glory hallelujah, they were G.I.'s! Lanny stopped and spotted their leader, a private first-class. " Hello, soldier," he said.

It was a little dark fellow, sprightly of mind, and Lanny guessed that he was from Brooklyn. " Hello," he replied. " You American ? "

" Happily, yes."

" Seen any Jerries up where you come from ? "

" A dozen or so, getting away as fast as they could. Tell me, where shall I find your command post ? "

" What's your business, Mister ? "

" I'm an O.S.S. man."

" What the hell's that ? They dish up so many of these initials."

" Intelligence Service."

The " P.F.C." appeared suspicious. " What's your name, Bud ? "

" That's my name," said Lanny with a smile, " Budd."

" Yeah ? " The tone indicated that this was taken for fooling. " Any relation to Budd-Erling ? "

" My father is president of the company," said Lanny, amused.

" Zat so ? My name is George Washington, and this guy here is Abe Lincoln."

" Pleased to meet you, George and Abe. But tell me where to find your commanding officer, because I have information that I was sent to get."

" Abe, take this Mister Budd-Erling to the Captain ; and make sure he ain't Benedict Arnold."

IV

So Lanny went on down the path to the highway, and, glory hallelujah again, here was the Army ! All over the place, and none waiting around to see what was going to happen ; all moving out into the countryside to make it happen. Dispatch cars, trucks, and jeeps all along the Route Nationale ; wicked-looking tanks and motorized guns—everything loading up and starting after the Jerries. By the roadside, under a pepper tree, on the ground covered with its berries, were several folding tables and camp-chairs with officers sitting in them, studying maps, reading dispatches, listening to telephones. The command post, no doubt, and Lanny prepared to tell his story in the fewest possible words.

But he didn't get to it, for on the way he ran into another kind of Jerry ; ex-tutor, ex-lieutenant, ex-*pension*-manager, ex-travel-bureau-manager, ex-O.S.S. agent Jerry Pendleton ! Jerry in uniform, a second lieutenant again ! They were so glad to see each other that they hugged and almost wanted to kiss French fashion. " What on earth are you doing here ? "

asked Lanny, and the answer was, "Franco appears to be on the shelf, so they took me for an interpreter. What are you doing?"

"They sent me to Cannes on an errand, and after it was done I decided to get up into the hills. A lot of other folks, including Germans, had the same idea. Tell me, has Cannes been taken?"

"No, the garrison is holding out."

"That's bad news for my friends. I tried to arrange for an uprising. When are we going in?"

"They don't tell things like that to interpreters, Lanny. Let me introduce you to our Intelligence man."

The P.A. was led to one of the tables and introduced to a Captain Harris, who heard his story and inspected his forged papers. Since Lieutenant Pendleton vouched for him so emphatically there was no question as to his good faith. The Captain said he didn't know the plans concerning Cannes; since Lanny was urgent, he called his superior on the phone and told the story. As a result, Lanny was put into a jeep and whirled down into the fishing village and tourist resort of St. Raphael.

He had a chance on the way to observe an Army in the process of getting itself in order. Already an air-strip had been cleared, and scout planes and small fighters were coming back from pursuit of the enemy; no doubt the site had been picked in advance and everything needed had been rushed to the spot. Gasoline, packed in square tins to save space, came ashore by the ton as soon as combat troops had cleared the beaches. Thus planes could be flown from carriers, and refuelled and worked at short range; and thus a jeep could hustle an O.S.S. man into the headquarters of the Thirty-Sixth Infantry Division of the Sixth Corps of the Seventh Army, Major-General John E. Dahlquist commanding.

Lanny talked with the General, who looked very handsome in a uniform belted with a gold buckle and a trick scarf around his neck on which was printed a map of Southern France. Lanny talked fast, urging the importance of Cannes as a harbour and prestige point; but he couldn't insist, as he had done with Patton, because Cannes was not Paris, and the life of one French captain was surely not as important as the lives of many American soldiers the Army's strategy meant to save. The General didn't say why he hadn't taken Cannes or when he would take Cannes; he just said politely that Mr. Budd's information was of interest and that full use would be made of it. Lanny was free to go off and worry about Charlot all he pleased; he couldn't do a thing in the world to help his friend.

V

The P.A. had promised to return and have lunch with Jerry on the outskirts of the village. A cloudy day, and the mistral was still blowing, but they sat outdoors; they were leaving in a few hours, and it wasn't worth while to put up shelter. An orderly brought hot soup out of a can, and then pork and beans, and while they ate Jerry asked, " What are you going to do next ? "

The answer was, " I have finished my assignment, and I suppose I'll go back to Washington and report."

The ex-tutor had a better idea. " Why don't you come with us ? The Army's always looking for interpreters, especially one who knows French and German and a bit of Provençal. You'd have a grandstand ticket to the show."

" What would they do with me, Jerry ? "

" Give you a temporary rank and put you in uniform, as they did me. I've already spoken to the Captain about it. You know how it is, they all think it's rather wonderful to be the son of Budd-Erling. They'd make you a captain, and you could boss me."

" Don't be foolish, Jerry. I'd need you to tell me what to do."

" My own briefing was short and sweet. They wanted me because I know French and a little German—you learn everything in the travel business. Think about it seriously, Lanny. We have the idea this is going to be a parade ; we have the stuff, and the Germans down here are third-raters. We're going up the Rhône valley—we'll be on our way this afternoon. Unless I miss my guess, you could be in Paris in a month, and there'll be nothing to prevent your getting word to O.S.S. meantime, and if they have another job for you they'll let you know."

" Would the Army let us stick together ? "

" Sure they would. I've told them how we worked together on the job before the Casablanca landing. This is a tiptop outfit, and you are the very guy to interview German prisoners, the *maquisards*, the peasants, and all the other sources of information."

That was the way the next stage of Lanny Budd's life was determined. The procedure was unusual, but the need for interpreters was extreme ; the bag of prisoners was so heavy, it suggested the complete collapse of the enemy. So a man who had come into the camp with only a safety razor, a toothbrush, and a comb, was fitted with a brand-new field uniform with various objects in its many pockets and a holster which contained, appropriately enough, a Budd automatic ; Budd Gunmakers was still working for the Army, even though Robbie and his family no longer owned it. They gave him a physical examination which took only a few minutes because he was sound. They gave him some shots against disease, which soon made him feel as if he had all the diseases and more. They put a " dogtag " around his neck with a number on it—a number up in the ten millions. They gave him identification papers, and let him keep his forged French papers on the chance that they might come in handy. So far he hadn't had to show them to a single enemy person.

They also gave him time to write several letters : one to the President's man, saying where he was ; one to O.S.S. in Washington, one to Robbie, and one to Captain Laurel Creston in London—she would exceed him in seniority, which would give pleasure to a feminist ! The letters would go by V-mail —that is, assuming that the censor approved them. By that time Lanny would be—he didn't know where, but the Army would know, and the answers would find him.

VI

The new captain had been told that he would move out immediately, but the orders were changed. There were so many prisoners, and so much to be learned from them ! He and Jerry were escorted to separate rooms in a commandeered inn, and Germans and a few Frenchmen were brought to them one at a time ; a stern G.I. stood guard and a male stenographer took notes in English as Lanny told him what to put down. The Army had been taken by surprise by the suddenness of the enemy's collapse ; ten thousand prisoners had already been taken with losses of only five hundred. The " shell " had been broken, and it appeared to be empty. Everybody had to improvise, and an interpreter was put to work with not more than half a dozen sentences of briefing.

The son of Budd-Erling, who had said that he didn't like to give orders, had to put on all at once a stern and terrifying look. He remembered the *Feldwebel* he had seen, the Prussian drill sergeants barking orders, ready to kick the lout who failed to respond fast enough. He had a threat as alarming as any *Feldwebel* had ever employed : " Do you want to be turned over to the Russians ? " Of course that wouldn't be done, but the prisoner wouldn't know it until later. On the other hand to " Do you want to be sent to America ? " they would answer eagerly, "*Ja, ja, mein Herr !*" He would say, " If you tell me the truth I will have you sent to America, and if you lie to me I'll send you to the slave camps in Siberia."

He would start asking, " Where do you come from ? " and " What is your unit ? " and " Who is your commanding officer ? " and " Where has the rest of your outfit gone ? " and " How many tanks have they ? " and so on. Generally the prisoner would tell what he knew, but now and then one would say that it was *verboten* to speak. Lanny would look his grimmest and reply, " *Im Gegenteil, jetzt ist es Befehl* "—now it is commanded. Incredible as it might seem, that would work in case after case ; orders were orders, regardless of who gave them. This was true especially of the peasant *Burschen*, most of them from Bavaria ; Lanny knew their dialect—it had helped to save his life and now it helped the Army. The soldier's face would light up, and he would talk eagerly.

The Prussians were tougher, and Lanny didn't waste much time on them ; there were so many more, and time was racing. Now and then came an intelligent man who really knew things and would tell them. " I hate the Nazis," he would declare, and Lanny would ask, " *Sind Sie Sozial demokrat ?* " If the man answered that he was, Lanny would say, " *Ich auch* "—

me too ! But he wouldn't tell that to the stenographer. He
would add, " There is going to be a democratic Germany.
Help us with everything you know."

An amusing circumstance : Lanny was permitted to
question enlisted men, non-commissioned officers, lieutenants,
and captains, but under the Geneva Convention he was not
permitted to question anyone of rank higher than his own.
The German officers were always informed as to their rights
and would refuse to answer. After a few days Lanny's own
officers realized that his knowledge of languages was excep-
tional, and so they put him in a colonel's uniform ; thus he
was able to deal with majors and colonels. But no generals—
it was against regulations for him to wear any stars !

He was not invited to be present when the high " brass "
digested the data he had collected ; but he could see for himself
what the conclusions would be. The enemy had known for
weeks that the invasion was coming but had not been able to
prepare. Whole divisions had been drawn off to try to stop
the attacks in the north, and there was no way to replace
them. Fortifications had been begun but not finished, and
few of the guns had enough ammunition. A good part of the
troops were Poles, Czechs, and even Russians, and these had
no stomach for the fight. One and all, they desired not to fall
into the hands of the Partisans, who were infuriated and might
shoot them ; what they wanted was to be politely taken by
the fabulously wealthy Americans and given hot coffee that
wasn't ersatz and three meals a day of American canned food.
Lanny mentioned these things frequently, and he could see the
light in dark Bavarian eyes and sometimes even in blue
Prussian eyes.

VII

The Army wasn't sitting and waiting for the result of such
inquisitions. As fast as tanks and jeeps and armoured cars
got ashore, the men would pile into them and they would go
off, by one road or another, to find out for themselves where
the enemy was and how eager he was for a fight. When they
found groups assembled by the roadside with their hands in
the air, waiting to be captured, they would radio word, and
ground forces would come in trucks to disarm the prisoners and

keep the Free French away from them. Two divisions of American paratroopers and airborne troops had been dropped at strategic points, and these had seen some fighting, but now most of them were guarding prisoners and waiting to be relieved of the burden.

After darkness fell Lanny and Jerry were treated to a meal and then told to be ready to move. Hours were irregular in the Army, and surprises frequent. Jerry had been sure they would travel up the Rhône, and that would mean first going westward, across the delta lands of that great river. But they were put into a car and driven to the north, into the mountains from which Lanny had come. These roads were mere shelves along the sides of precipices and the cars were using only dim parking lights. There was nothing Lanny could do to help, so he leaned back and closed his eyes, and when he fell asleep he dreamed that he was shut up in a concrete mixer, one of the modern sort that turns round and round as the vehicle moves along the road. Perhaps it was the guns which he heard up ahead, echoing among the mountains like thunder ; but thunder sometimes stops, whereas the guns went on and on. There would be few hours of the day or night when Lanny wouldn't hear them during the next month.

He had become a camp-follower of the Army. He would follow just close enough to get all the backwash ; to hear the shooting but not to be in danger from it ; to see the ruins and the wreckage ; and to hear the groans of wounded men, but not himself to suffer anything worse than discomfort. He was a part of the Army brain, which had to be kept safe ; they told him that, and it should have satisfied him, but sometimes he tried to help where he shouldn't, and gave his food away to women and children for whom he was sorry. When the discomfort became too great he would recall the ribald song he had heard the recruits singing on route marches at home, in which they told one another that they were in the Army now, they were not behind the plough, they would never get rich—and they called themselves a bad name which happened to make a rhyme.

VIII

This " flying column" came to a town where there had been fighting, but it was over. Lanny was put up in a second-class inn—the Quartermaster Corps had a squad car which followed behind the troops and picked out the best for the higher " brass" and the second and third-class for riffraff such as translators. Anyhow, there were bed-bugs, and Lanny wasn't surprised or shocked, for he had taken walking trips through Provence and knew what goes with the romance and picturesqueness of the Old World. After two or three hours he was glad to go to work again and get his sleep while riding in a concrete mixer.

Here were not only more " krauts" to be interrogated, but also the Free French, the *maquisards*. They came down from the mountains, on bicycles, in horse carts, in wood-burning buses which sometimes gave out and had to be pushed up the small hills so that they could coast down the long ones. They were for the most part young fellows, of draft age, high-spirited and unwilling to be enslaved ; they were tough and inured to hardships, the sort with whom Lanny had hidden out in the mountains of north-eastern Italy. They were enraptured to meet a comrade, and they told hair-raising stories. They were armed for the most part with hunting rifles and some had old-fashioned pistols fit only for museums ; with these they had fought Germans armed with machine-guns, and had not done so badly. They had wrecked the railroads and most of the bridges in this mountainous land, and perhaps they had made a mistake, they said, laughing, for it would slow up the pursuit.

What they all wanted was to get a Garand rifle and a bandolier of cartridges, and be allowed to go after the enemy. The Army took them on as scouts, paying them the French equivalent of two dollars a day, which was magnificent. They had to swear that they would not kill the German stragglers or the French *collaborateurs* ; both were to be made prisoners, the former to be shipped off to the prisoner camps which had been built for the fighting in North Africa, and the latter to be imprisoned and tried under French law. After that the Partisans would go happily off, and the Army would be kept well supplied with facts about the Nineteenth Germany Army it was pursuing. Wherever the enemy stopped to resist, the Army would radio the location to the nearest air-strip, and the planes would come and make his life hardly worth living.

Such was the P.A.'s life for the next month. He learned, as men do, to accommodate himself to rough circumstances. He learned that the Army had a marvellous new insecticide called D.D.T. ; it was made into bombs, and you turned a little screw and it shot out a fine spray ; a few seconds of that over and in your bed and you could sleep ; it also came in the form of a powder, and you dusted your clothing with it to ward off lice. You learned to help work your car out of the mud when it rained, and when the earth dried you learned to eat grey dust and like it. You learned to carry some food with you, and to heat it with a little gasoline poured into sand or soft ground. You had a warm overcoat and put it on at night—for the high Alps, covered with snow, lay only a few miles to the east. You learned to sleep whenever you were not working or eating.

IX

The route led straight to the north, through the towns of Valensole and Castellane. It was famous as the road which Napoleon had taken on his return from Elba ; the French had flocked to him then as now they were flocking to the Americans. The modern French have divided the province into departments : Alpes Maritimes, Alpes Basses, Alpes Hautes—that is, Sea Alps, Low Alps, High Alps. In the first group the rivers flow to the Mediterranean, and you travel along the sides of gorges. When you get farther north, the land drains into the Rhône, to the westward ; there you climb through one mountain pass and go down into a valley, cross a swift stream and then climb into another pass, each higher than the one before. When you came to a bridge that had been blown up, you had to wait while the combat engineers, who boast of having hairy ears, put a new bridge together out of ready-cut sections of steel. Watching that sight, you could be proud of your country.

Indeed, Lanny Budd was proud all the time. Surely if you were going to have war, this was the right kind to have : war

x

in which other people had done the job of tiring out the
enemy, and all you had to do was to chase him three or four
hundred miles, for which purpose you were provided with an
increasing swarm of vehicles. Lanny didn't see much of the
infantry—they didn't have time to catch up. The motorized
men considered themselves the crack troops and would do the
job and let the " dog-faces " clean up and collect prisoners.

The " old man " who directed this chase was a Brigadier-
General Butler, and Lanny never saw him. Later he got a
glimpse of General Patch, commander of the whole of Operation Anvil; a tall, nervous-appearing man, who bore the
nickname of Sandy. A couple of days after the landing he
issued an order which was read to groups of the men wherever
they could be reached, telling them that the enemy was
stunned and that they should " press on, regardless of fatigue
and possible shortages of food and equipment." Thus the
team of Lanny and Jerry occasionally had to forage for their
grub. It was no trouble, for the peasants came out with
chickens and eggs and all the kindly fruits of the earth, ready
to swap them for American luxuries or even give them for love.

Lanny recalled Browning's poem : " It was roses, roses,
all the way, and myrtle mixed in my path like mad." The
people in the villages put out bed-sheets in token of surrender,
or the tricolor, or crude imitations of the Stars and Stripes as
tokens of joy. They had waited so long for this day, and they
hadn't expected it so soon. They stood by the roadside and
cheered ; they tried to drop peaches and pears into the men's
laps, and the girls climbed onto the running-boards and hugged
and kissed their deliverers. " This is the damnedest ever,"
the men said, and it made them feel proud of themselves ;
they tried not to think about the buddies who had missed the
show by getting drowned in the surf or shot while storming
the fortifications. This was still going on—there were always
gunshots ahead, and men coming back on litters, often with
a blanket over their faces.

As a rule, men at the front know only the tiny sector where
they march and fight ; but Lanny, being in close contact with
other officers, could ask questions. He had told them why
he was so concerned about Cannes, and they reported that
the city was being pounded by sea, land, and air. It held ou

for ten days, and of course that meant that whatever Charlot had tried to do, he had failed. Lanny had no way of finding out what had happened to him. Jerry Pendleton was also on tenterhooks, because his wife and children were in Cannes. After the surrender he could hope to find out what had happened to them and to the *pension*.

Marseilles, the great port which the Army had figured to take on D-day-plus-fifty, was taken in eight days, and Toulon in twelve. In the former city there had been a revolution, and the Germans and their collaborators were hunted like wild beasts. Both those ports would be put to immediate use ; their capture would mean supplies not merely for Operation Anvil, but for the armies in the north via railroads and highways.

X

And what about Paris ? Lanny, who had risked being put in the guard-house in the effort to get help to that city, learned that it had been liberated on August 25, the same day as Cannes ; but he had no way to learn what had happened to the de Bruyne family or to Raoul's wife and her friends. By that time his flying column had come into the department of Isère, a high land of forests and vineyards, pastures for cattle and horses, fields of wheat and rye, and mulberry trees for silk culture. It was harvest time, and the peasants were hard at work in the fields ; they stopped to wave to Americans and let them know that they had come at the right moment—to keep the Germans from sending all the food away. In the middle of Isère, on the river of that name, is the ancient city of Grenoble, with a famed university, and factories that made twenty million pairs of gloves every year. The workers told Lanny that they would have to change their models now, American hands being longer and thinner than German.

From there were roads leading westward, downhill into the valley of the Rhône. The strategy of this bold dash became apparent ; it wasn't to take a lot of mountain scenery and glove factories ; it was to outflank the enemy who had been putting up stubborn resistance all the way up the Rhône. Fast columns rushed down the valleys of two rivers, the Isère and the Drôme, that empty into the Rhône. They posted themselves on the heights which overlook the narrow valley, and their artillery fire wrecked the enemy vehicles and blocked the roads. The enemy forces, raked by machine-gun fire and bombed incessantly from the air, had to fight their way through a twelve-mile stretch of death and destruction. It was a badly shattered Nineteenth German Army which got through and fought its way on up the river.

The team of Lanny and Jerry stayed with the column which rolled north-westward and came to the Rhône at Lyons, a great manufacturing city, which welcomed them with a fervour they would never forget. More roses and more myrtle ! After that the route was northward, a main highway over which the son of Budd-Erling had motored times beyond counting. There was enemy resistance all the way, but only what the military men call delaying action. Back where the translators worked there was the sound of guns, but no steel or lead. The Allies had command of the air, and only twice during this long anabasis did Lanny and his pal have to dive into a ditch.

Most of the time it was routine business, asking the same questions of unshaven and exhausted, dust-caked and stinking Germans. Some were frightened and some surly ; by long practice Lanny had learned to recognize different types and what technique would work best with each. By comparing one statement with others he could be sure which were lying. There was nothing he could do to the liars, and he didn't want to ; poor devils, they were trying to help their country. The easiest way was to tell everything, and perhaps get a cigarette as a reward.

Some of these unfortunates were grey-haired old men, and some were boys of sixteen. They had endured incredible sufferings on the Russian front, the Italian front ; they had lost fingers and toes, noses and ears, by freezing. One old man had had his legs run over by a tank, and had survived, as he said, because the mud was so soft. One boy, tending an anti-aircraft gun in Berlin, had been deafened by a bomb-burst and recently had been wounded because, being deaf, he did not dive into a ditch as fast as the others. All had been promised an easy time ordering Frenchmen about ; now they told with horror of Allied planes which had chased them on the roads and made life a nightmare. To the last man and boy they had swallowed Dr. Goebbels' propaganda, and they talked about the " Wuwas " that were going to save Germany. One boasted that all South England was already in ruins and that twelve million people had been killed. Another talked proudly about the " V-4," of which Lanny had never heard mention, which was designed to blow up the entire main island of Britain !

In the course of a month of such service the P.A. interviewed several thousand men, and only once did it happen that he was recognized. A sturdy S.S. sergeant had been in Hitler's Leibstandarte at the Berghof, on duty at the gate, and had seen the Führer's American friend arriving and departing several times. The days of Lanny's posing as a Nazi were over for ever, so he didn't have to worry. He knew that he wouldn't get much out of that fellow, and he didn't. Let him go back into the horde, and be shipped to North Africa, and from there to America ; he would be well fed in stockade, and in due course would come back to Germany to make another try at world domination. Lanny had no hope for the men who had grown up under the Nazi discipline, but he thought that something might be done with the German children, if anybody was willing to take the trouble.

XI

The route followed the River Saône, which flows into the Rhône at Lyons. Straight north, and it was more of a picnic than ever. The enemy was in flight, and didn't have far to go, for at points to the eastward troops of Georgie Patton's Third Army were waiting. At Dijon some twenty thousand of the enemy were caught between the two forces and brought to surrender. That meant a respite for the translator team, for when a whole army has surrendered what it knows becomes of interest only to historians ; the military men move on to new fields. Lanny had time to beg a couple of Paris newspapers from Third Army officers, and to read them and learn what a lot of history he had been missing in one fateful month.

The General with the two pearl-handled revolvers had been having a joyride wilder than had ever been dreamed by any

Napoleon or Alexander. His armies had romped all the way
across France and into Luxembourg, and he was now defending
bridgeheads which he had established across the Moselle River,
between Luxembourg and Germany. Whole divisions had
been surrendering to him. At the same time the British had
broken out of Normandy and had been making an equally
spectacular dash, getting across the Seine and rolling along
the coast of the Channel, thirty or forty miles a day, surrounding and investing one small port after another. This
included Dunkirk—and what pleasant news that must have
made for Rick, who had been there with Lanny ! More
important yet, it meant taking one after another of the launching sites of the buzz bombs which had been making London
so miserable. The newspapers reported a partial lifting of the
blackout in that long-suffering city.

Other items had been left out of the papers, but Lanny
gathered them from officers whose friendship and confidence
he had won. The sudden and unforeseen gains had put a
tremendous strain upon the American Army's transport.
Their artificial harbour had been pretty much wrecked by
storms, and the enemy garrisons were still holding on to the
principal ports. Le Havre had only just been taken, and
Boulogne and Calais were still under siege. To carry supplies
the long distances to the front the Army had set up a system
called the Red Ball Express, an endless chain of trucks rolling
eastward on one highway and coming back on another. New
York City had got used to one-way streets, and now Europe
was being taught about one-way streets three or four hundred
miles long ! So great was the demand for gasoline that pipe-
lines were being laid on the bed of the Channel, and also across
France. Patton's Army was being supplied by air, and had
come to a halt because it couldn't get enough.

XII

Lanny had given his family the designation of his unit ;
you didn't give an address, for you never knew where you
would be, and even if you had known you wouldn't have been
allowed to tell. It was the business of the A.P.O., Army Post
Office, to find you wherever you had been sent ; and soon

after Lanny's Seventh Army made contact with Patton's Third, he received a letter from Paris. Captain Laurel Creston was there ! She had managed at last to get permission to cross the Channel, and now was completing an article about how the French had welcomed their liberation. She wanted so much to have Lanny read it and was sending a carbon copy, taking the precaution to put it in a separate envelope. Lanny received the letter, but not the manuscript, and he never knew why—it was the way of things in war.

Straightway the P.A. made application for a week's leave to visit Paris. He wanted to make sure that Washington knew where he was, and that there was no call for him ; he promised to come back and work for another month unless there was a call. His Seventh Army had been taken into what was to be the Sixth Army Group, and it was heading eastward, presumably for the Belfort Gap, a wide valley leading into Germany just north of Switzerland. Jerry was going along ; he was a very happy lieutenant-translator—having received a letter from his wife. Cerise had boarded a lot of German officers during the war, but they had not molested her—they had been trying to win the friendship of the French. She added that they hadn't looted the *pension* before their surrender, the reason being that they had been surrounded.

Lanny managed to wangle permission to be flown on a transport plane which was taking permanently incapacitated men home via Paris. " Sad Sacks " they were, but the very thought of home gave them new life. The P.A. chatted with as many as he could, but he only had an hour or so before he was set down at Le Bourget.

Laurel was quartered in a W.A.C. hotel, and he couldn't visit her there. He had no trouble in getting a suite of rooms, for half the hotels of *la ville lumière* were empty since the Germans had gone. The telephones were working again, and he arranged to see her after he had got a bath and a shave— with cold water because there was no fuel in Paris. When she came, they ran to each other's arms, and then held each other off and took a good look to make sure there was nothing missing. Such a lot of adventures they had been having, and such fun it was to tell them ! Ladies first, of course ; Laurel narrated how one of her editors had pulled wires and had got her the chance to come to Paris only three days after the Germans had left. She had witnessed the parade of the American forces through the Arc de Triomphe and the frenzy of the massed inhabitants, the most thrilling sight of her lifetime. It had been dangerous to be an American that day because everybody, men and women, wanted to kiss you!

She had made a story out of it, and Lanny pleased her by asking to read it right away. An enthusiastic story, a little bit hysterical, like Paris itself. Four years of shame and suffering, of hatred and loathing pressed down by terror; and then had come the landing in the south, and the news of uprisings among the Partisan forces everywhere. The Germans in Paris and its environs began rounding up the Resistance leaders, and that had brought matters to a head. The Paris police declared a strike, and an insurrection of the whole city followed. The Free French seized the central portions and the government buildings; barricades were thrown up in the streets, and for four days there was fighting. This forced the hand of the Allies, just as Lanny had told Georgie Patton it would. Georgie wasn't the one to act, being far out to the east. It was General Ike who made the decision, and he politely picked out a French armoured division to have the honour of making the first entry.

Supported by American forces, General Leclerc had fought his way up from Orléans. And what a story that made for a writer of fiction! His real name was the Marquis de Haute-cloque, and he had been twice captured by the Germans and had twice escaped. He had made his way to Lake Chad in Central Africa, and there had organized an army of Senegalese troops, and had led them across the Sahara Desert to take part in the fighting in Libya. Now, a general of division, he had been landed across the Channel, and French history for all time would celebrate him as the man who had delivered Paris from the Hun.

XIII

Lanny's leave in Paris was spent mostly in beauing his wife around and watching her work. She wasn't satisfied with what she had got, but wanted to collect more details and spend a lot of time weighing them and deciding which were the most effective. She wanted to walk in delightful autumn weather and savour the taste of the most elegant of cities in the midst of one of those great convulsions for which it is famous. She had learned her French from books, and wanted to hear it spoken. She wanted to see the sights of war before they were cleared away: the burned-out tanks, the broken walls, the proclamations posted everywhere, first by Nazis and then by patriots.

Lanny introduced her to Julie Palma, who wasn't hard to find; all the Partisans had come out of hiding now, and in most places had become the government, replacing the Vichy masters who had fled with the Germans. The various Resistance groups had come together—the Francs-Tireurs et Partisans Français, the Front National, the Mouvement de Libération Nationale, and Ceux de la Libération. Now they called themselves Comac, for Comité d'Action Militaire, and had set up staffs to direct the struggle all over the land.

Julie, who had been in the thick of things from the beginning, told inside stories about the conduct of the struggle and about the supposed-to-be truce of which Lanny had heard reports. There had been a crucial debate in the headquarters of Comac, at which Julie had been present. The Consul-General of Sweden had been in negotiation with the Germans for several days, and he had pleaded with the liberation chiefs to be patient. General von Choltitz, the German commander, had wanted a truce and threatened that if it were not agreed to and kept he would wipe out the city. Many of the Partisans had wanted to agree because they had so few weapons.

But the fighting men had argued that the way to get weapons was to take them; to form small squads and raid the German stores, to capture German cars and tanks and turn them against the enemy. That was the way the Partisans had been getting weapons all over the country, and surely the capital city must not lag behind. If Paris let this German garrison get away, they would merely be condemning the smaller cities and towns to destruction by the same foes. So the vote was for fighting, and the barricades went up, and the German squad cars discovered that they could no longer race here and there to put down trouble the moment it started.

For four years Laurel's husband had been declaring that

the realities of this war were exceeding anything that fiction writers had thought up, and here was the proof once more. Julie took her two comrades to the place where the historic debate, so vital to the future of *la ville lumière*, had taken place. The underground fighters had made their headquarters in a fortress built literally underground, and in which surely no fiction writer would have asked his readers to believe. Eighty-five feet beneath the city's surface, protected by a layer of limestone sixty feet thick, with steel doors, gas-proof, and a ventilating system pumping fresh air through it ; with its own lighting and heating plant, telephone connections, and tunnels running to every part of Paris and even to distant suburbs—such was the military hideout which had been constructed by the French Minister of War in the critical year of 1939. And that secret had been kept from the German occupation for four years.

The tunnels were for the most part ancient, for through the centuries Paris had been mined with a vast network of quarries, catacombs, sewers, and finally the *métro*, the city's underground railroad. The whole thing made a labyrinth in which you might have lost yourself and never come out. Julie's friends were taken in by way of the *métro* station at the Place Denfert-Rochereau ; because the elevators were not working, they had to go down a hundred and twenty-eight steps to the fortress doors. She gave the password, and they were admitted. Later they were introduced to Colonel Rol, the one-time sheet-metal worker who had been the active head of the Resistance all through the war.

Blond and blue-eyed, precise and elegant in manner, this man would have been taken for a poet or a scholar, and his age would have been guessed at no more than thirty. Laurel tried to get him to talk about himself, but did not succeed ; he wanted her to write about the army of school children, so he called them, trained under the very noses of an enemy who thought he had the last word about youth training and also about secrecy. Colonel Rol showed them one of the textbooks which had been used in this liberation school, an innocent-looking little pamphlet with a cover showing a peasant ploughing and a happy boy waving his hat. When you opened the book you read : " Chapter I : German Weapons. (A) The

German Pistol. (B) The Automatic Rifle. (C) The Machine-gun."

XIV

The next day Julie took them to the scene of one of the battles, the Préfecture de Police. It is situated on the Ile de la Cité, an island of the Seine in the heart of Paris. The grandson of Budd Gunmakers had a most vivid recollection of the place, inside as well as out, for just after the Peace Conference in the year 1920 he had fallen under suspicion of the Deuxième Bureau for having in his possession some Communist literature belonging to his " Red " uncle, Jesse Blackless. They had made Bertillon measurements of him, and a commissaire with a black spade beard had put him through a severe interrogation. Then it had seemed amusing, but during the days when Lanny had been playing a Fascist role it had caused him many a qualm to know that his identification was in the possession of both the Paris police and those of Rome.

Now Paris was in the possession of the Reds and the Pinks, plus General Charles André Joseph Marie de Gaulle. How they were going to get along together was a problem about which there were as many opinions as there were Frenchmen, not to mention women. Julie discussed it on the way to the Préfecture. When they came to the Boulevard du Palais she stopped to tell them how, at this very spot, she had had to throw herself on the ground to escape German machine-gun fire. Then she had run to the Préfecture, and the door of the courtyard had been opened to let her in. The place had been full of trucks and weapon carriers captured from the enemy ; and up in the windows had been men with English, French, American, and German weapons, all clamouring for more ammunition of their special sorts.

That had been a day which a former schoolmistress was never going to forget. She had gone to the place to make a report on the activities of her group and had been caught by an attack of the S.S. upon the ancient building. She didn't know about shooting a gun, but had worked a switchboard at the school now and then, so she took that duty while the fight was going on, knowing all the while that if the place were taken she would be stood against a wall in the courtyard and shot. The German tanks had come in the afternoon, and their guns had blasted the door leading out to the cathedral square. The opening was blocked by trucks and sandbags, and the fighting men were filling bottles with gasoline to use upon the tanks if they tried to force their way in. The enemy infantry didn't dare come up because of the fire from the building.

As a result of such activities Raoul's little wife had become quite military in her conversation. She explained that city buildings, made of stone, and with windows, stairways, and roofs, are surprisingly good places for ambushes; you can shoot quickly and get away unseen. Street barricades slow up traffic, and a car going one way can shoot up a car going the other way and make its escape while the shot-up car is trying to turn, assuming that the driver is alive to try. As a result of such factors, and of careful rehearsing and " dry runs," the losses of the Partisans during the ten days of fighting were surprisingly small compared with those sustained by the enemy. The German trucks and cars just couldn't be protected against the numbers who were setting traps for them, and when the Allied armies arrived ten thousand of the enemy were surrounded and forced to surrender. Hitler had given orders that Paris was to be destroyed, but the orders had not been carried out, and Lanny had a guess as to the reason; General von Stülpnagel, Military Governor of France, had been active in the plot against Hitler's life, and had managed to see that the Paris garrison was commanded by officers who shared his hatred of the Nazis.

The result of these days with Julie Palma was that Lanny's wife fell in love with the ex-schoolmistress and wanted to put her into the magazine and perhaps into a book. It was inspiring to meet people who had lived their faith and held on to it in spite of all disappointments. So many turned into tired radicals and took to living off the movement, or quit and lived by denouncing the movement. So many human organisms were unequal to the strain of being heroes, or martyrs, or saints—whatever name you chose to give to people who accepted new truth, spoke it boldly, and stood by it regardless of consequences.

Laurel voiced that sad idea, and Julie said, " We are having a flare-up of hope and excitement now ; but there is a long stretch of privation and struggle ahead of us, and maybe we shall split up into factions as we did before. People who hope for a peaceful and co-operative world have a long job of education to do, and perhaps we shan't live to see the end."

The literary lady from *outre-mer* put her arm about this nervous, high-strung little Frenchwoman. " Come and let us feed you at least one square meal," she said with a warm smile.

BOOK NINE

FEATS OF BROIL AND BATTLE

26

A House Divided

I

LANNY had the de Bruyne family very much on his conscience, but he put off communicating with them, hoping that he would get some definite news of Charlot. He had written to Raoul at the Toulon address, asking him to write to Ribault in Cannes to inquire what had happened. Presumably mail service along the coast was restored ; the trouble was, Lanny had left his military unit, and how prompt would they be in forwarding a letter ? He had written also to Jerry Pendleton's wife, asking her to find out if she could ; but the same trouble applied there also.

The news reached him by a different route. Julie Palma came with a letter from her husband in Toulon, telling how his group had blown up the bridges and railroad lines in a semi-circle about that city, and had received the surrender of many groups of Germans. He added, " If you see Lanny Budd, tell him that Charlot gained the support of several officers in Cannes, but their movement was betrayed, and several days after the Americans landed Charlot was taken out behind the ice house at Bienvenu and shot. Poor fellow, he changed his mind too late. But I suppose it will help his family up north."

So Lanny had to go as the bearer of this sad news. He took Laurel along, because she was a writer and wanted to know the French people, and this *gratin* sort were not so easy to meet ; also, she had a normal curiosity concerning a family that had played an important part in her husband's life. The hotel porter managed to find them a small Citroën car, with no questions asked as to the *essence*. They drove out into the country to the north-west, by the route which the American

troops had followed in reverse, coming in under the Arc de
Triomphe through the madly cheering throngs. Now those
jours de gloire were over, and the highway was empty of
everything except military cars and a few peasant carts bringing in produce. The autumn rains had come and the landscape
was dreary.

When they got near to the place Lanny pointed out the
landmarks. Here was where he had stopped his car and
Marie had joined him when they had gone away together for
a summer-time trip through Normandy and Brittany and the
" château country." Just over there was the stile near which
he had sat talking in whispers to Julie Palma a couple of
months ago. And here was the red-brick villa called a château ;
here was the rear entrance with the gate into the garden, and
here the front drive with a box hedge now permitted to
grow wild.

And here was the family manservant, almost as old as his
master ; and the drawing-room which Lanny had so often
described to his wife. While they waited to be announced
she did not stand on ceremony but went straight to the
fireplace in which a wood fire was burning. Over the mantel
hung a portrait of a woman with delicate, rather pale features ;
a woman in a light summer dress, standing by a rosebush.
Laurel stood gazing into her dark brown eyes ; woman spoke
to woman, and Lanny stood in the background, watching, but
not interfering.

II

" So you are Marie de Bruyne," said Laurel. " And you
loved him."

" I loved him as long as I had life," said Marie.

" I can see that you are kind," said Laurel. " You are
lovely, and he was not deceived about you."

" Surely I never tried to deceive him," said Marie. " You
do not have to be ashamed for him."

" I have tried not to be jealous," said the wife, with just
a trace of a smile.

" He is a better husband for what I taught him," said the
amie. " It was a long time ago, but he has not forgotten."

" No, he will never forget," said the wife. " I have given

up wanting him to forget. It is a little hard, for sometimes I think that he loved you more than he loves me."

"There is no grading in love," said the *amie*. "No two human beings are exactly alike, and no two women can give a man the same thing. Let us be kind in our memories of each other."

"Oh, you are very sweet!" said the wife. "I cannot love him unless I love you too."

"I would have loved you if I had known you," said the *amie*—and did the portrait smile? "But you would have had to look for another man."

"Perhaps you are right," said the novelist. "I am thinking of putting it into a story. Would you mind?"

"Not at all," said the Frenchwoman. "But you would have to understand our customs."

"I have tried to," said the lady from the Eastern Shore of Maryland. "I am still trying. You will help me."

"Take good care of him," said the mother. "He is not a difficult man to manage, but you mustn't let him know that you are doing it."

"Oh, surely not!" said the wife. "It has been a great relief to meet you."

"Perhaps we shall meet again, somewhere in the next world," said the memory. "It will be a pleasure to compare notes."

"Yes indeed," said the living one. "I have the better of you now, but then, perhaps, matters will be reversed."

III

Laurel Creston, novelist, had been advised by her husband to read one of the great American novels, *The Ambassadors*, by Henry James, whom Lanny described as the leisure-class historian. The central figure of this story is a young American of independent means who has chosen to reside in Paris. The members of his strait-laced Boston family wonder why, and after some years have passed they send over two of their number—the ambassadors—to find out. They meet a charming and cultured married lady, somewhat older than their young relative, and after they have come to admire her they make the shocking discovery that she is the young man's *amie* in the French significance of the word ; she has made the young man over into an urbane and cultivated person, and the dilemma of the family as they come to realize this fact is presented with the quietest possible humour by a shrewd observer of the well-to-do and well-pleased-with-themselves. Henry James has been described as a novelist who wrote like a psychologist, while his brother William, the psychologist, wrote like a novelist.

It was a picture of two civilizations, the puritan and the hedonist, confronting each other. The teller of the story took no side, he told you what happened, and left it for you to understand if you could, and to draw what conclusions seemed proper. To Laurel, reading it, the story seemed like a paraphrase of the one which Lanny had told her from long ago—only a little more than two decades, but what a cycle of history had intervened !

As a wife, she had perhaps not been wise in asking for all the details, but as novelist she had not been able to resist. The story had not been in accord with Maryland *mores*, but she was trying hard not to be or seem a provincial person ; she wanted to know all there was to know about the world she lived in, and not merely America, but Britain, France, Germany, even Russia and China. Her husband adored the memory of the woman who had been his friend, his guide, and his guardian for a matter of seven years ; he had assured Laurel Creston that she was a happier wife because of that aid he had received.

The situation had been dominated by two facts : first, Marie's husband had cherished a secret vice ; and second, the family was Catholic and therefore divorce was unthinkable. Laurel had heard much about that old man who " had to have virgins," and had wondered about him, and now here he came into the room, and she had to steel herself to meet him, telling herself that she was going to be a woman of the world. She had asked Lanny if she would be supposed to shake hands with him, and Lanny had told her that that was, for ladies, a crude American custom, and she would simply bow.

Whatever he had been, he was now a poor pathetic figure

with a sparse white goatee, a skull-cap on his head, and trembling hands. His face revealed intense anxiety, for he had had no news of his younger son and could guess that Lanny was bringing some. The two women followed him, and poor Eugénie could hardly wait to acknowledge the introduction to Lanny's wife, so great was her suspense.

There is no sadder duty than to be the bearer of news of a bereavement. Lanny had copied the words from Julie's letter and he read them without delay. For once the customs of France and America were the same, and the young wife burst into uncontrolled sobbing; her sister-in-law came and put her arms about her, and the old man hid his face in his hands. The two visitors sat in silence, for there was nothing they could do or say. Lanny knew they would wish to hear the story of his meeting with Charlot, and what the *capitaine* had said and promised to do; he waited decorously until the first shock of the disclosure had passed.

There was no longer any reason for secrecy, so he told all that had happened. They told him in return that they had received a letter from Denis *fils*, who did not know anything about his brother's fate, but reported that he had obtained a leave and hoped to be home soon. Lanny pointed out what the elder brother's attitude would be toward the tragedy—he would consider that Charlot had saved his honour and the honour of the family by what he had done. Lanny refrained from adding that Charlot had also saved his father's life and the family fortune. The old man would know that many of his friends and associates had been jailed as *collaborateurs*, and that nothing had saved him from the same fate but the fact that the Partisans knew that Denis *fils* had been fighting with the Free French in North Africa and Italy; also, their leaders here in Seine-et-Oise had somehow been informed of what had happened to Charlot.

The present attitude of the three persons was something that didn't concern Lanny. He knew that Annette had been a Fascist without reservations; but no doubt she would find a way to adjust herself to her husband's career. Eugénie would put on full mourning and teach her children to revere the memory of their father as a hero and martyr. The old man's opinions would be determined by his property interests, as always, and no doubt he would be a loyal adherent of Budd-Erling. The internationalism of big business is a phenomenon with which Lanny Budd had been familiar since boyhood, and he was used to hearing it called law and order, honour and justice, free enterprise, individualism, and a lot of other good-sounding names.

IV

Back in Paris, Lanny wrote letters to his family and friends, telling them where he was and what he had been doing ; he was going back to the Army, where new letters might come. He wrote to his father and his little daughter, and to his mother in Marrakech ; to Nina and Rick in England, to Raoul in Toulon, and to Capitaine Denis in Algiers, taking the precaution to send a copy to the château. Laurel was staying on in Paris, for she wanted to see Belgium and Holland liberated and to get at least a glimpse of conquered Germany. How would that arrogant people behave in defeat, and what course would they choose when the Nazi yoke was lifted from their necks ? Had they really loved and wanted that yoke, and what would they find to love now ? Laurel Creston was another novelist who wrote like a psychologist—or, at any rate, desired to.

The night before they parted she asked very solemnly, " Lanny, are you going into Germany any more ? "

" Behind the armies—I hope so," he told her.

" But not in front of them ? "

" I couldn't, darling, if I wanted to. They know me too well."

" You must know I have guessed that you have been going into Germany. You didn't fool me."

" I was under orders, Laurel. This much I have a right to say : my orders are not to go into Germany any more."

" But you went into France while it was the same as Germany."

" Not quite the same, darling. I had a lot of friends in France, and they took care of me. But the Germans have found out about me, and not many would take care of me there. Put your mind at rest on that score."

" I'll put my mind at rest when this war is over, and when there is an international government with a police force to keep the peace."

" Just a little thing like that ! " He smiled. He did not tell her any of his adventures, for he was sure they would disturb her sleep. Let her collect data from persons who were not quite so near and dear !

V

Lanny's time was up, and he was about to report and be returned to his division, which was at the Belfort front ; but he was called to the telephone and asked to call at O.S.S. headquarters in Paris, a top-secret address. He said to his wife, " That probably means I'm wanted in Washington." He went, fully expecting such a notice ; instead, he was told that an Intelligence representative of S.H.A.E.F. in Paris— Supreme Headquarters, Allied Expeditionary Force—wanted him " for special interrogation purposes." That sounded intriguing indeed, and Lanny went to call upon a Major Hartman of General Eisenhower's staff. He received an order to report at once at G-2 of Third Army, whose head-quarters were now at Nancy. The Major didn't tell him what he was wanted for, and it wasn't up to Lanny to ask. He was handed a pass, thanked the Major, saluted, and departed. He wondered how the all-powerful S.H.A.E.F. had come to hear about him. Later he learned that G-2 of Third had asked S.H.A.E.F. for him, and S.H.A.E.F. had asked Paris O.S.S. about him ; Paris O.S.S. had never heard of him, but had checked with Washington, and so had learned that he was with Sixth Army Group, and Sixth had given his Paris address. Quite a roundabout.

Lanny was driven to his hotel to collect his few belongings and say good-bye to his wife. On the way he tried his best to imagine what this call could mean. Could it be that he had made such an impression upon Lieutenant-General Patton that that busy man had kept him in mind for nearly two months ? Nothing could have seemed more unlikely. Or could it be that somebody at " topside " had spoken about him and awakened interest ? Lanny, completely in the dark, was taken to a near-by field and put on board a "flying boxcar." Another bucket-seat trip, but it was only an hour or so; the front of the Third Army was from Luxembourg to Saarbourg, along the Moselle and the Saar Rivers, roughly within a hundred miles of the Rhine.

On the trip Lanny recalled what he had heard about Patton's forces and their present situation. In their astonishing sweep across France they had had casualties of less than thirty-five thousand and had inflicted four times that many upon the enemy, besides taking a hundred thousand prisoners. The Third had been brought to a halt early in September, but not by the enemy. Supplies had run out, and a motorized army couldn't move without hundreds of thousands of gallons of gasoline.

Who was to blame? There was a bitter controversy going on, and the G-2 officers of Lanny's Sixth Group had talked about it in semi-whispers. The shortage wasn't because the supplies couldn't be brought by air to rapidly moving troops, but because S.H.A.E.F. had diverted them. Patton, wild with excitement, wanted to rush on to the Rhine and across it into Germany; he insisted that he had the enemy hopelessly demoralized and that the same thing could be done in Germany that had been done in France. Keep moving, and let the enemy do the worrying! At the outset Georgie had addressed his staff, " I don't want to get any messages saying ' I am holding my position.' We're not holding anything. Let the Hun do that. We are advancing constantly and are not interested in holding anything, except onto the enemy. We're going to hold onto him and kick the hell out of him all the time."

But S.H.A.E.F., which carried the responsibility, wasn't willing to stake everything on such a gamble. S.H.A.E.F. believed that fighting in France, where the population was with us, was different from fighting in Germany, with the population against us. S.H.A.E.F. knew that the Germans had immensely strong forces in the north, and that Patton's stretched-out line in the south might be broken and several hundred thousand troops cut off from their base. S.H.A.E.F. considered that the Allied forces on the Continent were in a bottleneck because of the lack of ports capable of handling the immense quantity of supplies required for a war that grew bigger every day, and also more distant.

The British, in their rush up the coast, had taken Antwerp with its port facilities intact; but unfortunately Antwerp lies some distance up the River Scheldt, and the Germans still held strong fortifications in that flat land which is the delta of several great rivers—the Scheldt, the Meuse or Maas, and the outlets of the Rhine, known as the Waal, the Lek, and the Yssel. In the effort to take that district the British landed an immense airborne force, some of it as far to the north as the Dutch town of Arnhem, across the Lek; but the weather was against them and they had to retire from Arnhem in the face of strong enemy attacks. That was a serious check, but the work of opening the port of Antwerp was going on, and when it was completed the advance could be resumed all along the line.

VI

Lanny's plane was landed in a rainstorm, with visibility close to zero. He knew about autumn weather in the Saar, wet and cold without limit, and had bought from Army stores a raincoat, boots, and gloves. He was taken at once to C.P., as it was called—Command Post; there was a whole Army lingo made of initials, code, and slang, and you had to learn it or you were lost. This post was in an old barracks which had been built by the French, occupied by the Germans, and bombed now and then by the Allies. He was introduced to a tall, thin gentleman, a G-2 captain; he was head of Interrogation and lost no time in interrogating the visitor. "Thanks for coming, Captain Budd, we had quite a hunt for you. Would you mind telling me if you have any friends among German generals?"

Said the P.A., "I have had opportunity to meet quite a number of them. It has been my job."

"Is there anyone whom you know particularly well?"

"Emil Meissner is the first who comes to my mind. I have known him since we were boys and I visited in his home."

"Would you mind telling me what you know about him?"

"I met his youngest brother at a dancing school in Hellerau, near Dresden, when I was thirteen years old. Kurt Meissner grew up to be a famous *Komponist*. I was invited to visit the family at Christmas, and there I met Emil. From then on I would run into him occasionally. In later years I had dinner at his home in Berlin. We didn't have much in common, but I liked him and had the impression that he liked me."

" He mentioned you as a friend, and that is why we sent for you. What sort of man is he ? "

" Well, he's a professional soldier, highly trained ; a Wehrmacht officer and a Prussian gentleman, which means that he is conservative and strict. His father was business manager of the Stubendorf estate, and that meant that he was an old-fashioned Prussian ; not a Junker, which means an aristocrat, but completely Junker-minded."

" Is Emil a Nazi ? "

" I couldn't say flatly because I never asked him. His brother Kurt is an ardent Nazi and a personal friend of Hitler. If Emil had been the same, I believe he would have expressed himself in my presence. The fact that he kept silent I took to mean that he was not altogether in sympathy with Kurt. You understand that from 1937 on I was acting as a secret agent, and it was my role to agree completely with Kurt. So Emil would have avoided discussing the subject with me, and he did. The Nazi troops and the Wehrmacht officers did not see eye to eye, as you no doubt know."

" Tell me this : would you be surprised to hear that Emil was implicated in last summer's attempt to take Hitler's life ? "

" I should be surprised, but not too much so. As a man trained in strategy, he would bitterly resent the Führer's taking over the direction of the war."

" I should inform you that Emil is our prisoner, and he tells us that he was one of the few conspirators who escaped suspicion."

" If he tells you that, I would feel certain that it is true. He is a very proud man and would not stoop to seek favours from the enemy or to increase his own importance."

" He has been treated with every consideration due his rank. We are being careful in conforming to the requirements of the Geneva Convention, hoping that the Nazis will do the

same with our people. We have been working on Meissner
in a polite and careful way ; he has shown signs of coming
over to our side, and of course that would be important to us,
for we expect soon to go after Metz, and it seems that he has
special knowledge concerning that fortress."

" It is very likely that he would, for he has learned all
there is to know about fortification. He had little models in
his home, and he also had a lot of toy soldiers and moved them
around on a big table. He has that sort of mind ; he likes to
play chess, which, I gather, is a sort of miniature war."

VII

So Lanny understood what he had been brought here for.
They wanted him to call on his boyhood friend and " work
on him," try to persuade him to tell what he knew about the
fortification of one of the great strongholds of the old Maginot
Line. The Nazis had had four years and more in which to
turn it around and make it face the other way, and maybe
Emil had had charge of the work, or at any rate had been
consulted about it. He had already become convinced that
the German cause was hopeless, and Lanny might be able to
convince him that the best thing would be to get it over
before the last German city had been turned to rubble.

The P.A. said that he would be glad to try. Captain Morgan
—formerly a professor of psychology at a Middle-Western
university—took him to the officers' mess and gave him a
good dinner, prepared by a cook from New York's Chinatown
—" best damn cook in the Army," they called him. Then
the officer took him to a room and gave him a couple of hours'
briefing on General Emil, who had surrendered at Châlons in
the course of the Third Army's mad rush across France. There
was a dossier on him, including reports of conversations by
various officers. Lanny was left in no doubt that they attached
importance to the information this Wehrmacht specialist
could give.

The P.A. had a choice of courses. He could tell Emil that
he had been anti-Nazi from the beginning, or that he had been
convinced by recent events that German defeat was inevitable.
It was the latter course he had decided upon with Charlot,

and it had worked so well that he was inclined to try it again. Lanny would tell Emil about Charlot—but not about his sad fate. He would tell what he had seen of American and British and French military power, and about industrial power as he had seen it in Newcastle, Connecticut, and Budd, New Mexico, and Los Angeles, California.

VIII

Emil had been separated from the other prisoners and was on parole ; he had a room in a large villa occupied by American officers in the suburbs of Nancy, and his meals were brought to him. The place was guarded outside, but that would have been the case even if he had not been there. Lanny tapped on his door next morning ; he found the officer sitting at his desk, writing ; the visitor got a momentary glimpse of a long and pain-drawn face before it lighted up with recognition.

After that they had a pleasant time, for nothing can take the place of age in friendship, and the people we knew when we were young have a reserved section in our subconscious minds. This high Prussian officer, still in his uniform, sitting as erect and looking as alert as if he were still commanding an army corps, was to Lanny Budd the magnificent tall cadet who had walked into his father's home for a *Weihnachts* celebration. Rosy-cheeked he had been then, whereas now his cheeks were colourless and a bit flabby ; but the scar on the left cheek which was the mark of his caste would be the same as long as he lived. He was fifty, and his close-cropped hair was grey.

How different now were their circumstances ! Lanny apologized for his own. " I couldn't hold out, Emil. My father gave way, and then everybody I knew. The last time I met Hitler I was forced to realize that he was not the man I had believed him. Perhaps he had been once, but he had lost his character, his judgment, even his senses, I fear."

That made matters easy. " You are exactly right, Lanny," said the officer. " I saw a great deal of him and I decided that his self-esteem had run away with him. The handling of great armies is a science and requires a lifetime of study and the closest application. Excitement and fervour and raving cannot take their place. I cannot find in all history any calamity like that which has befallen Germany, to have so much power entrusted to hands which are incompetent to wield it."

Lanny might have said, " I am told that you had something to do with the effort to remove him," but he thought it better to talk about old times and re-establish their friendship before he approached the crucial subjects. First, he satisfied Emil's curiosity, telling him that he, Lanny, had been acting as a sort of liaison officer for Budd-Erling, interviewing flight officers in the field to find out about the performance of the new models and collect suggestions for possible improvements. That gave him a chance to describe the mushroom growth of America's aircraft industry, and to add, " What a calamity that it had to be against Germany ! "

He asked about Emil's family, and especially about Kurt : did he still cling to his faith in the Führer ? The elder brother replied that he never discussed the matter ; there had come to be such a tense situation in Germany that a man couldn't speak frankly even to his own brother. Lanny took that to mean that Kurt was still a Hitlerite ; but he didn't say any more because he saw that Emil was heart-sick on the subject.

They talked about old friends in the Fatherland, and it was a melancholy roll call. Emil's second brother, Fritz, was missing on the eastern front, and that almost certainly meant dead. The Berlin palace of Graf Stubendorf had been destroyed by bombs and fire. Lanny told how he had been in the palace of the Fürstin Donnerstein when the same fate had befallen it. He didn't say that he had since met Hilde in the Obersalzberg, or how he had got out of Germany. Instead he remarked, " I wonder if you ever met Oskar von Herzenberg."

" I have met him casually," replied Emil. " Poor fellow, he undertook to fight the regime, and he was unfortunate in his choice of confidants. Himmler had him shot."

Lanny didn't have to pretend to be shocked. " *Fürchterlich !* " he exclaimed, and added, " That concerns me greatly, because my half-sister, Marceline Detaze, was his close friend, and we have had no news about her."

" *Leider*, I can tell you nothing. I have heard people speak of her as a dancer, but, as you know, I am a family man, and I rarely went to night clubs. But the fact of my not having heard anything about her may be a good sign, because I heard the names of many who fell into disfavour for one reason or another. I knew practically everyone who was involved in the attempt on Hitler of last July, and it was a terrible thing. The S.S. went into action at the first moment, and it was enough to cause your arrest if you had ever been seen in the company of one of the conspirators, or if they had your name or number in an address book."

Lanny now thought it safe to say, " They tell me that you had knowledge of it in advance."

" I had been discussing the subject with a few friends for more than three years, ever since Hitler began taking control of the Wehrmacht and setting aside the decisions of the General Staff. One law that we had considered fixed was that Germany should never again become involved in a two-front war. The attack upon Russia seemed to us sheer lunacy, but we were helpless. Men who ventured to speak of tradition and experience were rudely shoved aside, and the plunge was taken."

IX

After that the P.A. had nothing to do but listen. A Prussian officer's dignity, his self-respect, were involved, and that of his caste, his profession, his people ; the control of his country had been seized by a band of low fellows, gutter rats, frenzied malcontents born of the defeat and despair of World War I. They were criminals and degenerates, unworthy of the name of Germans ; every nation had such creatures, but no nation with a civilization worthy of the name had ever before fallen into such hands.

The thing that made it hardest for Emil was the fact that his own youngest brother had been a supporter and even a friend of the head gutter rat. The elder apologized for him, saying, " Kurt is a man of genius, and they have never been distinguished for judgment about practical affairs. They mistake the intensity of their own desires for reality."

Lanny replied humbly, " *Unglücklicherweise*, I haven't the excuse of being a genius. I took my father's word that

National Socialism was Europe's only recourse against Bolshevism."

"To me they are the same," said the Wehrmacht man. "And when you have won this war you will have another to fight."

The P.A. didn't comment on that, but asked about the conspiracy, and for hours listened to the details of a struggle which antedated the war, and concerning which he had picked up only a few hints during his visits to Germany. The anti-Nazi movement which Lanny had known had been that of the Socialists, the workers; but here was a movement of the aristocracy, the old masters of the Fatherland, and it had included some of the most highly placed personages, some whom Lanny had met without having the slightest idea of what was inside their heads.

There was, for example, Admiral Wilhelm Canaris, head of the Abwehr, the Counter-espionage Division. Lanny had met him several times at the Berlin home of Graf Stubendorf. He was a nervous little man of Levantine appearance, and was known as "the little Greek." Lanny had taken him for a thick-and-thin Hitlerite; but now he learned that Canaris and his assistant, Major-General Oster, had been working ceaselessly upon the Wehrmacht officers, right under the noses of the Gestapo. One of their allies had been Colonel-General Ludwig Beck, Chief of the Wehrmacht Generalstab. Another was Colonel-General Werner von Fritsch, whose treason was detected; the Nazis shot him on the Russian front—or perhaps he shot himself. The story given out was that he had been killed in action. Emil called a roll of such personalities, and as Lanny recalled them it seemed to him that Adi Schicklgruber had been completely surrounded by traitors in his own home.

"It wouldn't have done any good to kill just the Führer," the General explained. "We had to get enough of his gang and to have a sufficient organization to act at once and seize control of the government; otherwise we'd merely have exchanged Hitler for Himmler. In the early years Canaris and Oster made the mistake of thinking it couldn't be done until the war had started. But then Hitler won so many victories that they knew it would be impossible to turn the German people against him. The opposition had to wait for defeat;

which meant they had to sit helpless and see the country embarked on a two-front war."

The man who had approached and converted Emil Meissner was General-Major Henning von Tresckow, First Staff Officer of the Central Army Group. He had seen the tragic significance of the failure to take Moscow in the autumn of 1941 ; and when America was drawn into the war he knew that it would be the story of 1918 all over again. Emil told about the controversy inside the movement between the civilians who were afraid of making Hitler a martyr and wanted to take him prisoner, and the military men who insisted that he must be eliminated. They worked out elaborate plans for the seizure of control in Berlin and the other principal cities. They had won over General Kluge, who commanded the Central Army Group on the eastern front ; but Kluge deserved his name, which means shrewd, and backed out at the last moment, after the conspirators had lured the Führer into a visit to Kluge's army.

" That was early in 1943," said Emil. " We tried to get Hitler with a time-bomb as he was flying back from that visit. We had a special kind of English bomb, and Oberleutnant von Schlabrendorf, a young lawyer in uniform, made a bold effort and got it on his plane returning to Berlin. But the thing failed to explode ; and Schlabrendorf, who had wrapped it as a package containing two bottles of brandy, had to rush to Berlin by the next plane and try to get it before somebody opened it up."

X

The P.A. got many surprises in the course of this talk, the strangest being when Emil mentioned the name of Heinrich Himmler. Lanny exclaimed, " Surely you don't mean that *he* is involved ! "

In reply Emil told him a strange story, having to do with a Berlin lawyer by the name of Langbehn, a man whom Emil knew well. Some years before the war this lawyer's little daughter had been invited to the home of a schoolmate, and upon the father's inquiry had said that the schoolmate's name was Himmler and that her father " had something to do with the S.S." Out of this had grown an acquaintance, ripening into friendship ; and after the German defeat at Stalingrad the lawyer had ventured to talk confidentially with the head of the S.S. about the tragic position of Germany, whose military affairs were in the hands of a man without military training. Herr Langbehn had made the discovery that Himmler, the ex-poultry grower, had become intoxicated by the power he was wielding and was convinced that he was better fitted to deal with the emergency than was his Führer. Out of that had grown a separate and smaller conspiracy with the aim of removing Hitler and putting Himmler in his place. One of the group was Dr. Popitz, a lawyer and Reichsminister.

"Emil, you take my breath away!" exclaimed the American. "Himmler came to the New Chancellery and put me through a questioning, scaring the daylights out of me. And now I wonder—maybe he was sounding me out, with the idea of taking me into his confidence!"

"Nothing is more likely, Lanny; but you would have been in just as great danger. The Langbehn conspiracy came to the ears of Bormann, who is Himmler's furiously jealous rival, and he reported it to Hitler. Himmler was able to persuade the Führer that he had been engaged in leading the conspirators on. Both Langbehn and Popitz were arrested and have been in prison for a year. Just recently I got word that they were being secretly tried; and the fear that they might mention my name was one of the reasons I decided to surrender my division. I much preferred an American jail to one of the S.S."

The Junker-minded General went on to tell the story of his own efforts. After the failure of the airplane attempt he and his friends had spent another year winning over important officers and preparing plans for a new government. Another amazing thing to Lanny: among the men they had won to their support was Lieutenant Dietrich von Bose, an official in the Führer's field headquarters whom Lanny had met several times there and had despised as a time-serving Nazified aristocrat. Emil had twice been flown to that place, supposedly to interview Hitler, but really to get from Bose the details about the Führer's personal habits.

Said the General, "I volunteered to try to shoot him at the military conference which took place about noon every day. It would have been difficult because he kept himself so surrounded by S.S. men, and everybody had to be searched.

My friends insisted that it must be done by a bomb, and I had moral scruples against killing all the persons who might be in that room. They picked another man, Colonel Klaus Schenck von Stauffenberg, who was Chief of Staff in the General Army Office ; he came of an old Catholic family in Bavaria, and had been badly mutilated in the fighting in Italy. He carried the bomb into the conference room in a brief-case and set it by a table near the Führer's seat. Unfortunately it was in another man's way, and he moved it behind a pillar. That is why the evil genius of Germany is still alive."

Lanny remarked, " I know only the story the Nazis gave out, and one never knows whether to believe that."

" Half a dozen men were killed, and Hitler was deafened and had his right arm badly hurt. At first we thought he was dead, but then we heard him speaking over the radio, denouncing his enemies. First and last, about ten thousand men and women were arrested and questioned, many of them under torture. I thought that my time would come at any moment. Tresckow told me that he was afraid he couldn't stand torture, and he went out and blew his head off with a grenade. Stauffenberg and Olbricht were shot immediately, and Beck was allowed to take his own life. They are still trying people and executing them ; a long list : Goerdeler, Oster, Hassell, Witzleben, Hagen, Oertzen, Dohnanyi, and Werner von der Schulenburg. If your armies are having an easy time in the invasion, Lanny, you must attribute it in part at least to the fact that a madman has shot out the best brains of the Wehrmacht."

" Yes, indeed," said the P.A. " And we also understand why a number of high officers have surrendered rather easily." This was putting it tactfully and was balm to the wounded spirit of an extremely *korrekt* Prussian general.

XI

They talked about the war and how it was going and why. Lanny knew a great deal that Emil didn't, and he was free in pouring it out. He had been in London and could convince a military man that the new victory weapon had little military significance. The big ones, the rocket bombs called V-2's, had just gone into action ; two had landed in English fields, and no doubt more would come. Many might hit London, level a few more blocks of houses and kill a few more hundreds of civilians ; but they surely wouldn't stop the war and they couldn't be aimed at targets smaller than a city.

Emil said yes, but there was a V-3, bigger yet, and it might be better aimed. To which his friend replied, " You know, old man, my father has special information, and now and then he whispers something to me. Do not think that I am playing tricks upon you—I pledge you my good faith as a man and a friend. This is something that is probably not known to a dozen men in our armies here : American scientists with the help of those from several other countries, including Germany, are preparing a bomb upon an entirely new principle, never before known in the world. It will be capable of wiping out not a city block, but a city, killing hundreds of thousands of people in a fraction of a second."

Lanny waited to let that sink in ; and after some thought the German remarked, " I suppose that what you are suggesting is the much-talked-about atomic fission."

" Don't guess, Emil, because I can't say yes and I can't say no, and it seems rude to say nothing."

" Can you tell me how soon this is likely to happen ? "

" It may be six months, or it may be eight. If the war is still going on, some large city in Germany, or perhaps in Japan, will see the thing tried out. When I got my first hint of it I made up my mind that I wanted the war to end before that, because the power is something too awful to be trusted in the hands of the sort of men who rule our world today."

Again the other sat in thought. Finally he said, " You have come to urge me to give information to your side ? "

" I came because I was ordered, Emil, and when I got here I was told that you had mentioned my name. I won't deceive you—I know that I couldn't anyhow. I came over to the Allied side because I found little by little how Hitler was deceiving the German people. He has broken every promise he ever made to them, as well as to the outside world. Now I have only one thought, to get this horror of blood and destruction over with as quickly as possible. I am telling you facts and answering your questions as far as I am allowed to. I am not going to do any persuading—I leave it for you to make your own decision. You say you couldn't bear to plant a bomb that would kill some innocent men ; well, both sides are dropping bombs on thousands of innocent men, women, and children every day, and that will go on until one side or the other gives up. I can assure you there isn't the remotest possibility of the Western Allies giving up. We are going to clear out the Lowlands and turn the port of Antwerp into the greatest base in Europe ; we'll restore the railroads, and bring new locomotives and cars, and unload billions of dollars' worth of ammunition and fuel and food. The men we have put ashore so far are not one-fourth of what we have in readiness ; and, believe me, I have been all over America and know there is not the remotest chance of our weakening in the will to win this war."

" Our madman has done that for us," said Emil sadly.

" Exactly. We didn't want to get in, but Hitler declared war on us. Now every day a few more hundreds or thousands of German factories and homes and public buildings are being turned into rubble. It is for you to wrestle it out with your conscience and decide what you can do to save that part of Germany which hasn't yet been laid waste. Surely you know us well enough to know that we are not going to destroy anything after the surrender. All we want is to knock Hitler out and then give the people of Germany a chance to set up a decent government."

XII

The harassed officer wanted time to think, and Lanny gave it to him. He went out and entertained himself making the acquaintance of some of the staff of " Lucky "—such was the code designation of the Third. He had discovered that armies were a curious kind of one-sexed family ; rent with factions, pulled and hauled this way and that by rival ambitions, greed for fame and promotion, jealousy and spite. There was a great war going on against the enemy, and there was a string of little civil wars within the organization.

In " Lucky " everybody was in a frenzy over the ill-luck which had befallen, the " sit-down " which had been imposed upon a triumphantly advancing host. They blamed it upon S.H.A.E.F., which couldn't bear to see one army more successful than all the other armies put together. So " Lucky " had to sit down, chafing and champing, while the Germans in front of them got time to reorganize and to bring up reinforcements. They had forty thousand slaves working on the Siegfried Line, strengthening its defences, and now it would cost thousands of lives to take what might have been had free of charge if Georgie had been allowed to have his way.

They all called him Georgie, and all swore by him, even while they chuckled over his foibles. He had infected them all with his cockiness ; they all put on fancy dress, wore ties in the field, walked with a swagger, saluted smartly, and boasted of being the best damned army in the whole world. The rest of " topside " was afraid of their commander, because he hogged all the limelight, and now S.H.A.E.F. had taken to censoring his utterances, claiming that his frank language might shock the folks back home. The real reason was that the correspondents took such delight in Georgie that they gave the impression he was winning the war all by himself.

Georgie was here, there, and everywhere ; flying in a cub plane from one air-strip to the next, exhorting his men and blessing out his officers if they came down off their toes for a moment. Then he would fly to Group headquarters and beg and plead and scold. They were taking whole corps away from him and giving them to his rivals ; they were wasting the precious hours, and the enemy was getting its courage back, even daring to conduct reconnaissance in Patton's territory, dropping spies by parachute all over it. Hot damn !— and add all the curses you know.

Lanny ran into the two-gun warrior once, in the corridor of the headquarters building. Georgie stopped, stared, and exclaimed, " Hello ! Aren't you Budd ? "

" Yes, General," said Lanny.

" What the devil are you doing here ? "

" I'm one of you now, sir."

" The hell you say ! What are you doing ? "

" I'm interrogating prisoners."

" Well, go after them ! If they don't answer—" Georgie's advice was that Lanny should apply his pedal extremity to the posterior of the illegitimate German, but of course he didn't say it in that Latinized language.

XIII

Lanny spent the better part of two days and nights with his special German target. He listened to the incredible story of how the German Army was being managed. Hitler, in Berlin, was growing every day more suspicious of all his old-line generals—and with abundant reason. He would send them elaborate detailed orders, from which they were not permitted to vary by a hair's breadth, on penalty not merely of their jobs but of their lives. He was insanely unwilling to withdraw from any foot of land he had taken, and would insist that the men must stand and die. In that way he had lost half a million at Stalingrad, and in the last three months twice that many in France.

Worse than that, he would keep his orders secret from everybody but the officers who had to carry them out. " The man next to me would be told to attack," said Emil, " and I wouldn't be told of his move, so we would lose contact and leave a gap for the enemy to plunge through. I had anti-aircraft units which came from the Luftwaffe and wore its uniform ; Göring insisted upon keeping command of them, so I couldn't tell them where to go and they were never of any use to me. I was told that I was to get a new division, and when I sent it orders I learned that all that had been sent was a division commander, a medical officer, and six bakers. I got whole regiments that had had only a week's training and had never fired a gun. I got what were called *Magen* battalions, men who had been set apart because they had stomach ulcers and had to have white bread and milk—but I had no way to get either."

And always there was that insane raving, that cursing and brow-beating over the telephone ; there was the threat of being ordered back to Berlin, not knowing whether you were to be shot, and your family for good measure. Field-Marshal von Kluge had wanted to withdraw from Falaise and Hitler had forbidden it ; when the army was pocketed, Hitler had screamed that Kluge had done it on purpose, to prove that he was right. Ordered home, the Field-Marshal had taken poison on the plane. General Rommel, hero of North Africa, had been reported dead in an automobile accident, but Emil said that he too had taken poison. Hitler had ordered it, partly because he had failed to stop the Normandy invasion, and partly because he was believed to have known of the plot against his Führer. " I am very well content with my fate," said Lanny's old friend dryly.

The P.A. did not push him, but waited until Emil himself brought up his problem of conscience. Emil did this many times, but still couldn't make up his mind. At last Lanny gazed into the eyes of his old friend and said, " Emil, you aren't being entirely frank with me. You have something on your mind that you haven't told me. What is it ? "

The other looked away with a face of misery. Finally he broke down. " Yes, Lanny, there is something I haven't the right to tell you."

The P.A. shrugged his shoulders. " All right, old man. If that is so, I'm wasting my time and yours."

" If you would only let me tell you something in confidence —I mean, as one friend to another."

" You know I'm not here for social reasons, Emil. I am here as an officer in the American Army. If you tell me anything that has to do with the Army and its interest, I can't promise to keep it to myself."

" That is what has been worrying me. I want to put a price on my help, and I want your advice about it. I want to talk it over with you, as between friends and not between officers of enemy armies."

" I'd have to ask my superiors about that," was the American's decision. " If they give me permission, then of course I'll pledge my word."

" And keep it under all circumstances ? "

" Of course I'd keep it, Emil. You wouldn't be talking to me unless you knew that." Lanny sat with knitted brows for a space, then said, " Let me ask you one or two questions, Emil. You may answer or not as you please. I've an idea that your concern has to do with someone other than yourself."

" That is true."

" Some member of your family ? "

" Yes."

"I am guessing that it can only be Kurt."

"I'd rather not say, Lanny."

"Some member of your family has done something, and you want to buy immunity for him with your information. Is that the idea?"

"That is it."

"You want to ask my advice about it, and I am not to be free to mention it to anyone else without your consent. Is that it?"

"That is it."

"All right, I'll see about it."

XIV

Lanny took the problem to Colonel Koch, the G-2 of "Lucky," that is to say, the staff officer in charge of its Intelligence Section. A quiet, scholarly man, as unlike his chief as possible, he listened to the life-story of a German *Komponist* whose reputation was known to him. Lanny said, "Kurt is a metaphysician who has drugged himself with long words and mistakes them for reality. He was teaching me Hegel's formulas when I was thirteen and he was fifteen. He convinced himself that Adolf Hitler was the embodiment of all that lofty idealism, and now I suppose he thinks he has to die with his hero. Emil wants to try to save his life, at least that is my guess."

Said Colonel Koch, "The fact that Kurt Meissner has been a Nazi propagandist for the past couple of decades is known to all the world. There can hardly be anything confidential about that."

"No, and so I'm guessing it must be something that Kurt is doing now. I have not forgotten that after World War I he came to Paris as a secret agent of the German Army to stir up the French Leftists against the peace terms. I was young then, and swallowed the propaganda myself, and helped him to escape into Spain. I surely wouldn't like to have Emil put anything like that up to me now."

"You don't have to worry," responded the Colonel. "The hint you have given already is enough for G-2; we can very quickly get photographs and descriptions of Kurt Meissner, and if he is operating as a spy anywhere on this front we can find him."

"That's all right," said the P.A., "so long as you are acting on my guesses and not on what Emil may tell me. The question I should like to have answered is this : suppose that Emil reveals something of that sort and asks my advice, what am I to tell him ? Would you bargain his life in exchange for the vitally important information that Emil could give you on the subject of German defences and fortifications and troops ? "

"That is a difficult point, Captain Budd. The Army has an over-all policy to avoid all types of immunities."

"So I have been told, Colonel. But everything has its price in war. Emil may be the means of saving many thousands of American lives ; and surely they are worth more than the life of one spy."

"It is a problem I would have to refer to a higher authority."

"Let me point out to you that Kurt Meissner was a captain in the German Army at the end of World War I. Could he not be treated on that basis when we catch him ? "

"He would be—provided that he was in uniform."

"Use your imagination, Colonel. Let us assume that O.S.S. has a lot of uniforms of the enemy, taken from dead bodies. They must be using them in their business."

"That is a fair assumption." Colonel Koch smiled.

"And suppose that I went along when Kurt was to be taken, and I persuaded him to put on the uniform ? I would take the responsibility, and it wouldn't weigh very much upon my conscience. A well-known musician would be sent to a prisoner-of-war camp instead of being shot, and we would get everything that General Meissner knows about the Metz fortifications. Don't you think that if that were put up to Georgie, he might consent to break one of the regulations ? "

"I couldn't say, Captain Budd ; but I'd be willing to ask him. Of course it would be conditioned upon General Meissner's coming through with the real stuff. He'd have to answer questions and his answers would have to be right."

"That goes without saying, Colonel. Let me urge you to get the decision as quickly as possible ; the only difficulty I see is that Kurt might be captured by some other unit of the Army, and I don't suppose they delay very long about trying and executing a spy."

" Indeed not ! " said the G-2 man.

XV

The deal was made, and Lanny went back to Emil Meissner and made the proposal. He saw at once that he had lifted a ton load off the General's shoulders. " You have guessed correctly," Emil said without hesitation. " Kurt was operating as a secret agent in my territory, and that is within General Patton's territory now. He didn't come to me for permission —he went directly to the O.H.K." (*Oberstes Herres Kommando*, the Army High Command.) " I was never sure whether they assigned him to watch me or to watch the enemy ; the split in our Fatherland is that terrible. Two weeks have passed since I was captured, and I don't know where he is now, but I can tell you the name he was using and the place where he was staying."

" Was he operating alone or was he part of a group ? "

" We Germans are always part of a group, Lanny. But he did not tell me the names of the others, and he will not tell them to you. He is posing as an art expert, representing a dealer in Berlin who has a way of smuggling German-captured art treasures out of the American zone. That, of course, is what he tells the Germans ; what he tells Americans I do not know."

" He has taken a leaf out of my notebook," said Lanny, somewhat amused.

" Of course," replied the other. " He has heard you talk art on a hundred occasions, and it has become a second speciality with him. He has grown a beard as further camouflage ; but he cannot conceal the fact that he has a crippled left arm."

" I understand that Hitler has the same, and so did the last of the Kaisers."

" I have not failed to note the coincidence, Lanny. We old-timers look back upon the *Kaiserzeit* as the happiest in all German history. I suppose that is a habit of the aged and a sign of premature ageing. The world is going into something new and strange to us. Perhaps you can foresee it; I can't."

"I can foresee this much, Emil; either the Anglo-U.S. are going to get to Berlin first, or the Russians are. You have to make your choice between those two—and which will you say?"

"You hardly need an answer to that."

"All right then, get busy and tell our people what they need to know in order to break through the Siegfried Line and get across Germany before our bombers have knocked every last stone off the top of the next one."

27

A Friend in Deed

I

THE deal was closed, and Emil provided the G-2 Section with a detailed description of his brother; he was five feet ten and weighed seventy kilos, about a hundred and sixty pounds. His face was long and thin, with deep lines at the mouth; his eyes and hair were grey. He could move his left arm, but slowly and without much power in it. He had heavy scars on the left chest. In the library at Nancy they found a good portrait of him and made a photograph of it, and Emil drew in the beard and moustache as he had last seen them; these were painted in by an artist and then another photograph made, and all the G-2 agents went out with this. Emil knew that his brother's hiding-place was in Toul, but knew only the general locality. "It won't take us long to find him," said Colonel Koch.

Meantime Emil was provided with an American uniform, for reasons of security, and installed in a villa with a G-2 staff. They brought him their wonderful photo-reconnaissance maps, and he sat at a big table poring over them with a reading-glass;

he put little numbers on certain spots, and then wrote out a list of emplacements, giving a detailed description of each, its depth, amount and kind of armament, and the forces it contained. He told its strong points and its weak, and how it could best be taken. He did this for all the fortifications of Metz, from Forts Kellerman and Gambetta on the north to l'Aisne on the south, from Bordes on the east to the row of defences on the west : Guise, Jeanne d'Arc, de Vaux, Driant, de Verdun—a territory of some thirty or forty square miles. The American officers could check many details by their spies, and they said that Meissner's memory was beyond belief.

Emil, for his part, said that American coffee, candy, and cigarettes were *himmlisch*. He was particularly pleased with apple pie, and when the officers of the friendly enemy came to a party in the evening he served it to them proudly. When the time came for the jump-off, they had his German uniform newly cleaned and pressed ; and took him into a large drawing-room with an immense map on the wall. The commanders of all corps and divisions of Third came in, and Emil stood, pointer in hand, and gave them a briefing, showing them where to attack and how. He spoke in excellent English for two or three hours without a break. Lanny wasn't there at the time, but he was told about it later, and how freely the American generals had expressed their admiration. They said that only one thing would have improved the occasion, and that was to have Adolf Hitler among the auditors.

II

During the P.A.'s sojourn with the Third Army it still had the Moselle River before it and was permitted to fight only for " limited objectives." But with Patton that meant a lot of activity, especially as the enemy seemed to be in the same mood. The front was " fluid " ; each side kept stabbing at the other, and units found themselves now and then behind the enemy lines. The sound of gun-fire was incessant ; and as Lanny wasn't supposed to get into danger, they would pick him up and with other G-2's move them away. The rain was incessant, the mud was horrible, and men were in misery from head to foot—head colds and trench feet. The air-strips were so soggy that planes couldn't get off, which gave the enemy a great advantage.

But G-2 went on working, and after a couple of weeks they reported that they had located Kurt Meissner. They wouldn't take him right away. That, they told Lanny, was the weakness of the Gestapo : they were so full of hate that they couldn't restrain themselves and would grab one man ; but the Americans were calm and calculating and would watch their man for a long time and get all his associates. Lanny wasn't allowed near the place for fear of being recognized ; he spent his time interviewing prisoners who were brought in every night from the raids. The officers had promised that they would let him be present when Kurt was taken ; they wanted his help in handling this prize catch, soothing him down, and possibly getting information out of him.

The day came, and they put the P.A. in a staff car with two other Intelligence men. Lanny had his comforting Budd automatic in a holster, and by his side on the seat a large bundle, carefully wrapped and tied ; it contained a complete outfit for a Wehrmacht *Kapitän*, five feet ten and weighing about seventy kilos. It had been taken from a dead man and was newly cleaned and pressed, and included everything except the arms and the insignia. The wardrobe department of O.S.S. thought nothing of equipping a score of men every day with different outfits, each exactly what it ought to be. Some of the outfitters had come from Hollywood and had been doing that sort of thing for thirty years.

The party was preceded by two other cars and followed by two more, under supervision, with men specially trained to take particular prisoners and not let them get away or commit suicide. The amount of brain power and hard work which had gone into this war would have solved most of the secrets of the universe. Or so, at any rate, thought the pacifist son of Budd-Erling, as he sat looking out upon a rain-soaked landscape, shivering slightly, and wiping his nose now and then—for he had an undignified cold, like so many others of those who would never get rich in this man's army. The car skidded now and then on a slippery highway, and twice they had to get out and wait while the G.I.'s lifted it out of the mud and set it onto the paved road.

But they were coming to the town of Toul, and Kurt was there, and Lanny had been waiting for this D-day a long time; so he perked up, and by the time that darkness fell and they were coming into the town, he found his heart thumping with excitement. However, the way things happened wasn't at all picturesque or dramatic; the caravan stopped by a sidewalk, and Lanny was told to sit there and wait, and he did so. He knew that the men were surrounding a certain house, but he didn't see that house, except later as a dark form looming. He had been told that the telephone wires would be cut, and that what was called a " surreptitious entry " would be gained; that is, they wouldn't ring the bell or batter in the door, but would pick a lock or cut a pane of glass out of a window, while having on one hand a sticky glove that would keep the pane from falling when it was pushed in. So many tricks there were —and so many unsolved secrets of the universe !

III

Lanny was prepared to hear shooting, but there wasn't any. A sergeant came and reported, " Everything is ready, sir." Lanny asked, " You have them all ? " And the answer was, " All that were in this place." Lanny got out, took the bundle of clothing under his arm, and followed the man to the house, which was one of a block, only dimly to be made out. They went in by a doorway where two soldiers stood guard; they went up a flight of stairs by the light of an electric torch. There was an open door at the top and light pouring from a room. Lanny stopped in the doorway, and there, in the middle of the room, sitting stiff in a straight chair, was Kurt Meissner, and perhaps ten feet away a G.I. with a tommy gun at the ready.

Lanny took in the scene at a glance. The room was somebody's study, and had bookcases against the wall, and a flat-top desk at which Kurt had probably been sitting, for there were papers scattered over it. He was wearing a dark-grey business suit, and his beard and moustache were as the artist had drawn them. Lanny thought, he is thinner and paler. Poor fellow !

" Hello, Kurt," he said aloud.

The other turned his head. " Oh, so it's you." His voice was cold and said very plainly, no nonsense here !

Lanny set his bundle down, then spoke in German, very gently, " Kurt, an old friend wants to have a talk with you."

" You may talk as long as you please," was the reply, with no change of tone. " I am your prisoner."

" One thing I ask, Kurt. Your word of honour that you will not attempt to escape or to commit suicide."

" I am not interested in what you have to say, and I don't see why I should bother."

" Believe me, what I have to say is important to you, not to me. I am not going to ask you to betray anybody or to tell any secrets. I know you too well to expect it. I am trying to help you ; take my word for that."

" All right," said the *Komponist* grimly. " You give me your word and I give you mine."

" *Richtig*." And then, speaking English, " Sergeant, you and this man may go downstairs and wait."

The sergeant looked troubled. " Are you sure, sir ? " he asked.

" Quite sure," was the reply. " I have known this prisoner a long time."

The sergeant and the private with the tommy gun went out, and Lanny closed the door behind them. Then he went to his bundle, slipped the cord off, unwrapped it, and took out the uniform. He held it out, saying, " Put this on quickly."

The other could not conceal his surprise. " What is this for, Lanny ? " It was the first time he had spoken the other's name.

" In the clothing you are wearing, you are a spy and would be shot in a few hours. In this clothing you will be a prisoner of war and will be sent back with the other officer prisoners."

" Who is doing this ? "

" I asked for your life, and my request was granted. This was one time when it was good to be the son of Budd-Erling."

" And what is the price of it ? "

" No price whatever, Kurt. I am paying an old debt of friendship. Be quick ; I have reasons for haste."

Without another word the ex-*Kapitän* took off his civvies and dressed himself according to the rank he had held a quarter of a century ago. He had trouble with his bad arm, but Lanny didn't offer help, knowing the sort of perverse pride the German had. There was a cap and a sword-belt, but, alas, no sword. Lanny rolled up the civilian suit and wrapped and tied it—O.S.S. would have use for it whether it was German or French or English. He tucked the bundle under his arm and said, " You understand, Kurt, you are still under parole ? " When the other assented, Lanny led the way downstairs and out to the street.

To the sergeant he said, " Lend me your flashlight." He took it and turned it down the street, away from the prisoner. Some of the men might notice the change of clothing, but they knew it was G-2, or perhaps O.S.S., whose doings were frequently beyond comprehension. Suppose that this captured man had been an American agent posing as a German ; suppose that now he was to be dressed in a German uniform and put with the other officer prisoners—whose business was it to inquire, or even to guess ?

Lanny escorted his man to the car and put him into the back seat, with Lanny on one side and one of the officers on the other. Several more prisoners had been taken, and they were put, handcuffed, into the other cars. The cortège drove through the streets of this ancient town which had once been the capital of a Roman province. A great bulk towered up to the stars and Lanny guessed it was the cathedral. Presently they were out on the slippery roads again ; as they couldn't afford accidents, they drove more slowly and got back to headquarters very late.

IV

Lanny had asked the privilege of interrogating his special prisoner, so he took the prisoner up to his own room. He was sure that Kurt would not reveal any secrets and that he would take such a request as an insult ; Lanny had promised not to request it and he didn't. But he was curious as to his own affairs, and Kurt would know about some of them. How much had the Gestapo found out about the Führer's one and only American friend ? How had they found out, and how had the Führer taken it ? Above all, would Kurt by any chance mention Marceline ?

" Well, Kurt," began the P.A., " this is a strange way for you and me to meet."

" I see you have gone into the Army," was the unpromising response.

" Yes, Kurt. There is a limit to the amount of pressure a man can withstand."

" You were always a weakling," remarked the other ; and Lanny didn't mind—he had known for thirty years that this German man of genius held that opinion of him. It had been useful of late years ; and maybe it was true, who could be sure?

" I should like you to know," said he gently, " that I have never done any fighting, against Germans or anyone else. I am here as an art expert to see that cultural treasures are properly cared for."

" And to ship them to America, I suppose ? "

" You suppose wrongly. They will all be returned to their original owners."

" Even if they are German ? "

" If they belong to German museums, they will be returned without question. If they belonged to private parties, it will depend upon who those parties are."

There was a pause. " Well," said Kurt, " what do you want to question me about ? "

" The Army wanted to question you, Kurt, but I convinced them that you would never tell them anything that would do harm to your cause."

" Thank you," replied the *Kapitän*, but his tone was one of sarcasm, and there were no thanks in his soul. " Would you mind telling me how you came to be mixed up in my affairs ? "

" A pure bit of luck, Kurt. A friend mentioned that you were in danger of arrest. I went to one of the higher officers and persuaded him that you belonged to a special category, and he gave permission for you to be changed into a prisoner of war. You will be treated according to your rank and, I presume, will be shipped to America. The officer prisoners who give parole are spending their time in comfortable summer hotels and have a money allowance. You will have no trouble in getting music paper and will be in a position to write that piece of music which the Führer commissioned."

This was a bait, but Kurt didn't take it. He sat in silence. Lanny could be sure he was recalling the scene in the air-raid shelter in the garden of the New Chancellery. Adi had promised to provide the funds for a new *Götterdämmerung* ; and what a piece of irony if the funds were to be provided, not by the Führer of the Germans, but by his despised foes, the materialistic, the Judeo-pluto-democratic Americans ! Bitter bread indeed for a German *Komponist* to eat while he did his work ! He could taste it in his imagination, and he set his lips together tightly, refusing it.

V

The humble American made an effort to change the conversation. He said, " I want you to know the reason I left Germany, not to return. I learned that jealous persons in the Führer's entourage had lied to him about me, telling him things that cast doubt upon my good faith."

" And so you came and put on the uniform of his enemies ! " This was a sneer, and the tone was bitter as gall.

" I did the best I could, Kurt. I could no longer help the German government, but I am helping German art and culture."

There was silence ; the two men looked at each other, a duel of eyes. When the *Kapitän* spoke, it was with quiet contempt. " If there are questions which your duty requires you to ask me, do so. Otherwise I prefer to end the conversation."

" All right, Kurt. There is nothing else. Some day, perhaps, we can meet under happier circumstances." He rose, and Kurt rose. Lanny held out his hand, saying, " *Viel Glück !* "—which means, " Good luck to you."

Kurt's two hands stayed by his side. Facing his old-time friend, and standing close to him, he spat full into his face.

And so Lanny had the information he wanted. He stepped back a pace or two, took out his handkerchief, and carefully wiped his face. Then he took the Budd automatic from its holster and held it in his hand. He said, in the same cold tone the other man had employed, " Precede me downstairs."

Kurt said nothing but obeyed ; and when they were down, Lanny said to the waiting sergeant, " Take charge of this man. Guard him carefully, because his parole is at an end. Have you other men with you ? "

" Yes, sir, there are wo outside."

" All right. If you handcuff him, be careful, because one of his arms is lame."

" O.K., sir," said the sergeant.

Lanny went upstairs to his room and shut the door ; he sat on the bed, and tears ran down his cheeks, and he did not wipe them away. Strange as it might seem, he had loved Kurt even while he was deceiving him. The deception had been for Kurt's own good, but Kurt had not appreciated it.

Lanny had his information now ; he knew that Kurt knew that Lanny had been a false friend and a spy all through the years that he had been visiting Hitler. Lanny knew more than that—many things : what the Nazis were going to be after the war was over ; how they were going to feel about Americans and how they would behave when they were let out of prison camps ! He knew that the Nazis were Germans, the old, old Germans, the *Drang-nach-Osten* Germans of Wilhelm II, the *Blut und Eisen* Germans of Bismarck, the Pomeranian-grenadier Germans of Frederick, called the Great ; yes, even those Germans who had poured out of the dark forests wearing bearskins, and helmets with cattle horns on them, and had burned and sacked the cities of ancient Rome !

Lanny had seen such Germans as a boy but had refused to believe in them. He had seen them in elegant expensive uniforms, strutting on railroad platforms, clanking their swords and twirling their upturned moustaches. He had seen them drilling on immense parade grounds, galloping on horseback or rolling in huge machines, raising dust that floated across the country for miles. Worse yet, he had collided with the spirit behind this drilling ; in Kurt's home he had come upon it in a little song book prepared for children. " Now, brave sword, show honoured your worth ! Break, bare steel, our woe with flaming lightning ! Crush to earth those who dishonour our horde ! May the blood of the brute besprinkle our threshold ! " So it went—iron and steel, sabre, sword, and spear, flags and banners, trumpets and drums, defiance and hate, blood and death !

VI

Lanny made up his mind that he would not tell anyone about that painful episode. He would never let himself hate Kurt, no matter how much Kurt hated him. He told the officers that the prisoner had refused to say anything of significance ; he did not suggest that they should put the civilian's suit back on him, but turned that suit over to the O.S.S. to be worn by some American spy. He told Emil that Kurt had been bitter, but he did not say how much so. It had been agreed that Lanny would give the younger brother no hint that he had met the older.

The P.A. forbade himself to brood over the episode. It was a small part of a war which was an infinite tragedy. Curious that Kurt himself had been a spy, yet he despised Lanny for being one ! No doubt Kurt would say that Lanny had been spying on friends ; but maybe Kurt had made some French friends in Toul ; very certainly he had made some in Paris years ago. The real difference was that Kurt had been spying for Nazi-Fascism, while Lanny had been spying against it ; also, perhaps, that Kurt had failed in his spying, whereas Lanny had succeeded. Let this be an omen for the fate of the two systems !

The son of Budd-Erling reported to his superiors, and they wanted him to stay with "Lucky". It was the beginning of November, and the Army was about to jump off for the Moselle crossing. Then it would be "view halloo" to the Rhine ; a good show for everybody, but best of all for the Patton mob. Lanny said that was all right with him, but he had promised to rejoin his old friend Jerry Pendleton with Sixth Group. The reply was that if Jerry was as good as Lanny said, he really belonged with Third, and they would try to find a way to wangle him, or maybe to kidnap him.

But before this plot had been worked out there came a message from O.S.S. in Paris : Lanning Prescott Budd was to report at once for a return to Washington. Lanny knew that meant F. D. R., but he didn't say so. He was glad, because he was tired of rain and mud and of having a running nose. He packed up his few belongings, and said good-bye to his new friends, and promised to see them again if it could be arranged. He got a seat in a fast plane and was set down in a Paris airport an hour later.

Laurel was still at the W.A.C. hotel. He had been exchanging letters with her and had persuaded her not to return to London. The new rocket bombs were sudden death out of the sky, and there was no defence against them; why should a woman expose herself when she could write just as well in Paris? Now he said, "Why don't you go down to Cannes and get warm? There's a story there: the taking of the Riviera, and how it was under the Germans, and how it is now under the Americans; Monte Carlo in wartime, and the international refugees there, and the British and Americans who were interned and now presumably are liberated. People at home will want to know about those matters."

The writing lady said, "Fine!" And Lanny told her to go and stay at the *pension* with Cerise Pendleton, and gave her a letter to the authorities, both Army and civilian at Juan-les Pins, authorizing her to take charge of the Bienvenu estate. Since the Vichy Armed Forces had had it, presumably the American Army would have it now; they would expect to pay rent, and could pay it to Laurel, who would forward it to Beauty. Laurel would send Beauty a report on the condition of the place. Incidentally she would find out about Charlot; and she might also get in touch with Raoul and have him come over from Toulon and tell his adventures. Wonderful to realize that France was free once more and that people could travel where they pleased—provided they had the price and could squeeze themselves into a train.

VII

O.S.S. asked Lanny how he preferred to travel, and he chose the southern route; he would get warm for at least a few hours. Also, he would like time to have a chat with his mother; they routed him via Marseilles and Marrakech, and from there direct to New York. He kissed his wife good-bye, promising to write her often, and to see the baby as soon as possible. She didn't go to see him off at the airport, because it was a miserable rainy day, and anyhow it frightened her to see a plane rushing down a runway and perhaps not rising into the air.

But it rose ; and Lanny was set down in the greatest of Mediterranean ports, where he would have liked to stroll and see the damage that had been done in the small civil war, and ask about how the new government of the Free French was making out. But he saw only the airport, and the harbour crowded with shipping ; within an hour he was off again, across that blue sea which had been the centre of his life—for swimming, for sailing, for fishing, for travelling in everything from pleasure yachts to armed motor-boats. The rain had been left behind, and the wrinkled sea looked like a sheet of the fabric called seersucker, spread out below him as far as his eye could reach in every direction. Here and there a vessel cut a temporary path across it ; the biggest looked small, and the small looked like tiny specks, motionless, with two little stripes sticking out, resembling the antennae of insects.

They skirted the coast of Spain, just far enough away to give Franco's guns no chance to practise on them. Then it was Africa : first a shore, and then plains, mostly barren, here and there flocks of sheep, and white spots which Lanny knew were *marabouts*, little round shrines. There were tumbled ranges of mountains on the left, and behind them the tall Atlas range, at this season mostly white with snow. Now and then a town came into sight, or an oasis with palm trees and herds of cattle mixed with camels. At last there was Marrakech, a great city, at least geographically speaking, spread out with gardens and orchards, and here and there tall pink mosques with gleaming domes, and the white villas of wealthy foreigners, and a great hotel famous for luxury. Two years had passed since the American forces had come here, and now the airport was one of the biggest and busiest in this war-busy world.

VIII

Cablegrams were slow and planes were fast, so Lanny dropped down unexpectedly out of the blue and surprised his mother and stepfather. How glad they were to see him, and what cries of delight and what bearhugs they gave! He had a night to stay, and spent most of it answering their questions.

Kurt Meissner had been Beauty Budd's lover for a matter of eight years, and there was no secret about it ; the story of what had happened to him was one that Lanny could tell, all but the climax, which would have caused Beauty too much pain. " Oh ! " cried the mother. " Are you *sure* they won't shoot him ? " Lanny could say that he was quite sure.

He told about Laurel, what she had been doing and what she was planning to do. Beauty hadn't been able to get any word about her home and of course was anxious. " Lanny, I suppose you've got just the sort of wife you wanted," she said, not for the first time, and Lanny assured her there could be no doubt about it. There would always be a little humiliation in this for a mother who had tried so many times to find her son the sort of wife that he really and truly ought to want. Irma Barnes had been the best of all possible guesses, and the fact that the marriage had fizzled was a wound in Beauty's soul that would never entirely heal.

But Laurel Creston was a fact too, and had to be accepted ; so was her little son, whom Beauty knew only by snapshots. She had to be told all about him, and about Robbie and the fortunes he was making—colossal, only he had to pay an income tax of eighty-two per cent, and to pay it before he made it. This almost broke his heart every fifteenth of March —" Caesar, beware the Ides of March ! " It almost broke Beauty's heart to hear about it at the beginning of November, and Lanny had to remind her that the money had been spent to take Bienvenu from the Germans and restore it to its lawful owner. That was something, of course.

Beauty had had no word from Marceline, and neither had Beauty's son. The Army was going in there soon, and they would find her. Lanny had to tell about his visit to Patton's Army ; Georgie was the sort of man that Beauty Budd adored, and she had met him at a party in Marrakech ; she had done her best to charm him and thought she had succeeded. Poor soul, she fought so bitterly against old age, and couldn't bring herself to face the idea that she was launched into her sixties. She was taking part in the social life of this community of millionaires in pleasant exile, and was full of chatter about who was who and who was whose.

Also, there was that lovely little boy, Marceline's son and

Lanny's nephew, who was allowed to sit up late in order to renew his memories of his suddenly-coming and suddenly-going uncle. Half Italian, one-quarter French, and one-quarter American, he had lovely dark eyes and eager intelligence. War did not frighten him, for he had never seen it ; to him it meant gay-coloured uniforms, and airplanes flying overhead, and stories of dramatic and delightful events. He listened to Lanny's stories until he fell asleep and was put to bed.

28

The Paths of Glory

I

UP in a plane over the Atlantic Lanny Budd busied himself catching up with the news. In Marrakech he had bought New York newspapers and magazines that had come by air and cost a dozen prices. He read about the unending British battle for the delta of the Rhine, and about the American landing in the Philippines. There had been a three-days naval battle in Leyte Gulf, in which a good part of what was left of the Japanese fleet had been wiped out.

Very pleasant indeed to be warm after being so wet and cold ; very pleasant to refresh your mind after the boredom and ignorance of war. A hot political campaign was near its climax at home. Lanny had heard about it in the Army, but it had been something remote and hard to make real. He had applied for an absentee ballot, and had cast it, giving the address of his apartment in New York. Here and there he heard men talking about the campaign, but for the most part they left it to the folks at home, who had time for luxuries. In the Army you thought about getting in out of the wet, and getting a chance to put on dry socks and rub salve between your itching toes ; then maybe about getting a bit of freshly baked bread or an egg that was real. What you wanted from home was a letter telling you that your wife hadn't forgotten you, and that the baby had got over the croup, and that the interest on the mortgage had not been overlooked. Politics, hell ! The politicians were getting themselves re-elected, and when the war was over they'd be helping the guys who had got rich out of the war and forgetting those who had been sitting in foxholes full of rain.

When Lanny arrived at the La Guardia airport he called Baker, guessing that the summons had come from him. He was told that Baker was out campaigning with the President ; when Lanny gave the code name, Traveller, he was given a telephone number in Boston and called there. It was Saturday, three days before election day, and that night the candidates one and all would be closing their campaigns at the biggest meetings their managers could assemble.

The President's confidential man said, " The Chief didn't think you'd get here so quickly. He wants to see you right after election. He told me if you called to tell you to come to Hyde Park for supper on election night."

" Fine ! " said the P.A.

" Come early, because the returns begin to come in at about seven. Tonight we're putting on a grand show in Fenway Park. All Boston will be here, except Beacon Street. Why don't you fly up and take it in ? "

Lanny thought for a moment. " I'm just getting over a cold," he said, " and it will be a raw night. I'll take it over the radio."

II

He got a morning paper, so as to see how the campaign was shaping up. Then he took a taxi and was driven to the little ferry which crosses Long Island Sound. From this it was only a short ride to Newcastle ; and there was the family, always glad to welcome him, and to hear his stories of the world of blood and terror. There was Baby Lanny, now running about on sturdy legs, and no longer in doubt about this tall smiling man who called himself Daddy. The little fellow had been here ever since summer, with Agnes to take care of him and a nurse to help her ; it was much better for him than being shut up in a New York apartment. There was a governess for the grandchildren and also a music teacher, three ladies who had their meals together in the breakfast room. Robbie and Esther always had everything exactly right—in spite of having to pay eighty-two per cent of their income to the federal government !

When Lanny telephoned, Robbie left his office and came home in the middle of the afternoon to hear about the Budd-Erling planes in Europe and what the Army was saying about them. Incidentally, of course, he was interested in learning about Kurt and Emil, both of whom he knew ; about Laurel and her writings ; and about Jerry, and Raoul, and Beauty and her small family in Morocco. Lanny could talk more frankly now and told what he had seen and done in France ; he still didn't say anything about Marceline or about having been in Germany.

Robbie talked about his family, and how things had been going. Robbie Junior had the flu, and Percy's wife was expecting another baby. At the plant, production had reached its peak, and it was something to come and see ; but already the head of the concern was starting to worry, for fear they were beating Hitler too fast and there might be a cancellation of orders. That led to politics, on which Robbie had been spending a lot of the firm's money, listing it as advertising— imagine the Budd-Erling plane needing advertising with the news dispatches full of its exploits ! Robbie said the election looked very close ; the polls gave Roosevelt a tiny edge, fifty-one per cent, but that might not be enough. There was a still better chance of the Republicans carrying Congress, which would at least be a brake upon the insane extravagances of the New Deal. Under that head Robbie listed various kinds of " social security " ; you could be sure that he wouldn't list any purchases of military planes.

Lanny remarked cautiously that he had been out of touch with politics for a long time. To that Robbie replied that Governor Dewey was making his closing speech that Saturday night at a mass meeting in Soldiers' Field, Chicago, and the family would assemble in the drawing-room to listen over the radio. That would give Lanny a chance to hear the issues of the campaign carefully explained ; and Lanny said he would see what he could do about attending. It was pathetic—for just thirty years Robbie Budd had been hoping and scheming to bring his first-born to a proper set of political and economic beliefs. He had never succeeded and never would succeed, but he would go on trying.

What Lanny did was what the schoolboys at St. Thomas's Academy had been wont to call a " dirty Irish trick." He saw Agnes Drury going out with the baby, and he went along. He explained to her that the family wanted him to listen to Thomas E. Dewey in Chicago, whereas he wanted to listen to Franklin D. Roosevelt in Boston. Did Agnes have her small radio set in her room ? Agnes was slightly tinged with Pink sentiments—she could hardly have failed to be, having lived for years with Laurel Creston. She was tickled still pinker by the idea of committing this crime of *lèse-majesté* against the Budd tribe.

She whispered the secret to the other governess and the music teacher, and the governess was willing to join her ; the music teacher was afraid and went obediently to the drawing-room and listened respectfully while the Governor of the Empire State told a hundred thousand people in the great Chicago Stadium and perhaps a hundred times as many more over the radio that this election represented an effort to turn America over to the Communists. Meantime Lanny and the other two sat in Agnes's room with the radio turned low, chuckling while they listened to the warm caressing voice of Lanny's Boss telling an equally great audience that Governor Dewey in one city had threatened that the victory of the New Deal would mean the establishment of Communism in America, and in another city that it would bring about a monarchy in America. The Governor should have made up his mind which he wanted, for surely he couldn't have both !

It had become a fighting campaign, and this was a fighting speech. Roosevelt had been roused to indignation by the falsehoods told about him, and about his family, and even about his little dog Fala. The President's four sons were all at the front, doing their duty, but that had not saved them from charges. The President himself had been accused of bringing on the war, and he answered that the war had been brought on by the Japanese attack upon Pearl Harbour, and by the declaration of war against the United States by the

German and Italian governments. He said that he had been reluctant to run for a fourth term, and had not cared much whether he was re-elected; but " since this campaign developed I tell you frankly that I have become most anxious to win." The thunder of applause which this remark brought made it necessary for Lanny to turn the radio still lower.

To the son of Budd-Erling this speech was thrilling, because he knew the ex-Governor of New York State so well and could visualize him and every detail of the scene. He had discussed the issues with him—long ago, before the campaign had shaped up, before the war had begun. This was Lanny's fight, and had been since his boyhood, and he gloried in having a champion who could defend his cause before the whole world.

Yet at the same time his heart ached for the tired, over-driven man, the cripple who was carrying the burden of the future upon his shoulders, and who had been goaded by his enemies into coming out and " taking the stump " in his own defence. Lanny had been reading accounts of him, travelling about the east and the north-east, and as far west as Chicago, addressing outdoor mass meetings at night, and speaking from his motor-car and from railroad platforms—this man who could not stand even for a few seconds on his heavy steel braces without pain. Campaigning was the American custom, and his supporters expected it; he himself enjoyed it, or insisted that he did; but what a ghastly strain upon a man who was Commander-in-Chief of armies, navies, and air forces all over the world, and had to carry on diplomatic negotiations that might decide the future of the world for centuries.

III

Lanny rested, played with the baby, and wrote letters to Laurel and to all his friends abroad. On Monday Robbie loaned him a stenographer, and he dictated letters having to do with his long-neglected art business. The fond father wanted to send out a hurry call to all Rotarians in Newcastle and have them come to a luncheon and meet this traveller from overseas. They would give him a circular piece of cardboard with his first name printed on it, and he would hang it on his buttonhole so that everybody would know what to call him ; they would feed him and then call upon him for a speech, and when he told them that Hitler was on his way out they would cheer him lustily and pat him on the back. But Lanny didn't want any publicity and wouldn't have had his picture in the *Newcastle Chronicle* for anything he could think of.

He had to face a reception of the Budd tribe ; there could be no getting away from that. There were old ones—they lived to vast ages. Some were recluses, but they would come to meet Lanny in order to disapprove of him ; some were quiet and scholarly, some were worldly and chirrupy ; all were rich. There were young ones, male and female, and in-laws ; some of these were modern and full of curiosity about a strange, left-handed relative who could travel all over the world in wartime and was full of evasions and suspected of unorthodoxy. Election eve, and he had already voted in the Army, but he wouldn't say how he had voted—he just smiled and said he had forgotten.

Election day morning he went and looked at the plant. It never stopped running, day or night, Sundays, holidays, even Christmas. There were three shifts of men and women, and enough in each shift so that one-seventh could be spared each day in the week ; many of them slept in beds that never grew cold—one man got in as another got out. Some kind of aircraft rolled out of that plant every few minutes, and each one already had a load of high-octane gas in the tank ; it went under its own power to the flight field, and after its engines had got warm it rose into the air and circled a few times and then disappeared, never to return.

Lanny came back for lunch, and then put his belongings into the little car which he was accustomed to drive, and set out up the Newcastle River. He didn't say where he was going—just a business engagement. It was a wintry day, there had been snow, and he was headed north into the Berkshire Hills, and then westward to the Hudson River. He took his time. The scenery was beautiful, not so different from that of the Moselle country, except that it was peaceful and still ; no rumbling of guns and no heavy transport rushing over the roads ; only farmers going to town with loads of straw or cordwood. Thank God for the peace of America, and pray that it might endure! The sun was shining and the squirrels were out, and tracks of rabbits and foxes gave life to the blanket of snow on the hills.

So, towards sundown, Lanny came to the city of Poughkeepsie, the "Reed-Covered Lodge by the Little Water Place," and turned north up the Albany Post Road, now a broad, paved highway. He came to the village of Hyde Park, made famous by its citizen known as the Squire of Krum Elbow. The Squire had come in that morning and had cast his ballot. Scores of reporters had been there to see what happened, and cameramen and newsreel machines. They had wanted him to pose; everybody had to pose—this was America! The voting had been by a machine, and it hadn't worked the first time; an official had had to show the voter what was wrong. He didn't tell how he had voted, but nobody would have much difficulty in guessing.

The polls were still open, and Lanny stopped across the street and watched for a few minutes. There was an American flag on a staff before the old white frame town hall, the polling place, and a few people waiting in line—but no loitering, and no electioneering within a specified distance of the sacred spot. He had seen people fighting one another on so many parts of the earth's surface, and how he longed to teach them this dignified and orderly way of settling their problems.

IV

Lanny drove on and came to the sentry box which had been set up at the entrance to the Krum Elbow estate. He gave his name to the officer on guard and was given a nod. A long drive lined with trees led to the grey house, part stone and part brick, with a semicircular portico in front. Several cars were parked in the ample drive, and Lanny added one more. A Negro man opened the door for him, and a secretary led him down a passage to the President's study.

Eight or ten people were there ahead of him, and the Chief said casually, "Hello, Budd. Make yourself at home." It was "Budd," not "Lanny," and the P.A. understood that he was to be inconspicuous and semi-incognito. If newspaper-men asked about him, he would be "a friend of Mrs. Roosevelt."

The First Lady had a host of friends, and many of them were odd fish; they were not supposed to have political significance, and the less said about them the better. Lanny's uniform did not make him conspicuous, for there were ten million in the Army now. He slid into a chair and sat watching and listening.

His first thought was of the Chief's appearance. His face was thin, and exhaustion was written in every line. He was playing the host graciously, as always, but what he did was an effort; he had put all he had into the battle with his foes. Presently he remarked, " We shall get all the answers tonight." And the P.A. wondered if, deep in his heart, he might be longing for the answers to be no, so that he could sink back in his comfortable chair and rest. He told his friends of his love for this place, and how happy he would be to stay in it and write history.

Seven years and four months had passed since Lanny had first sat in this spacious room and listened to the creator of the New Deal expounding his political philosophy : " Mr. Budd, I cannot go any faster than the people will let me." Lanny had never forgotten his simile of a man driving a three-horse team, what the Russians call a *troika*. The first job of anybody who wanted to effect social changes was to stay in power, and for F. D. R. that meant guiding his three wild horses, keeping them from baulking and getting in one another's way ; feeding them on patronage, keeping them in harness, and choosing a course they would consent to follow.

Every four years he had to submit to the whole people the decision as to his competence as a driver. He had done it three times, and received a verdict of approval ; today was the fourth, and pretty soon he would be getting the answers from some forty-eight million voters, who would say thumbs up or thumbs down on his conduct of the war and his competence to make the peace. There could be no half-way verdict ; either it was Roosevelt and his party or it was his opponents, who had falsified so recklessly about him, and his friends and family, and even about the little black Fala, who now lay peacefully snoozing at his master's feet, having no idea that this was one of the crucial days of history.

The dining-room with its big table had been given over

for the night to men from the press associations, who received by telephone the telegrams which came from the President's friends all over the country. The guests were served a buffet supper of scrambled eggs, and Lanny sat next to his hostess, telling her a little of what he had seen in France. She was a woman of tireless curiosity, also of tireless kindness. She was busy all of every day doing services for other people, and the excitements of the campaign hadn't seemed to trouble her at all. She had set a new standard for " First Ladies," one they would have a hard time living up to. She watched over her husband, guided the conversation, got the important people next to him and the bores away from him. It was a lesson in social tact to watch how she got people out of the room while the handicapped man was being shifted from his seat in the dining-room to his wheel-chair, and then how she showed them paintings and other objects of interest to keep them from entering the study until he had been shifted from the wheel-chair to his seat in that room.

The radio was turned on, and the scattered returns began to come in, a precinct at a time. The President had a book in his lap, giving the votes of each city and state in previous elections, so that he could form an idea what the new returns indicated. Everybody was burning up with anxiety, but it wasn't good form to show it ; the way the excitement revealed itself was in mid-evening, when the returns were pouring in fast, and it was evident that the Chief was doing a shade better than the sample polls had promised.

Presidential elections in America are conducted upon a system which would be puzzling to a foreigner. The people do not vote for candidates, they vote for a slate of " electors," who go through the form of choosing a President. Each state has a number of electors in proportion to its population, and the slate is elected as a whole. Thus Roosevelt or his rival might carry New York State by a very small margin, yet win all forty-seven of that state's electors. That was the way it was happening now. By midnight it was plain that Roosevelt was getting a little more than half of the popular vote in the whole country, and more than three-quarters of the electoral vote. That made it look like a landslide, and everybody in this Krum Elbow study chose to take it that way. Only the partisans of Governor Dewey were surly enough to point out that it was really a very close decision.

You could laugh at them, because a victory was a victory ; the ins were in and the outs stayed out. Everybody laughed and cheered, and drank cider and ate doughnuts. At eleven o'clock there came the sound of thumping drums and tootling fifes—a red and white torchlight parade coming up from the village. It was a Republican village and a Republican neighbourhood—the Squire of Krum Elbow had never once been able to carry his own Dutchess County. But there were enough Democrats to make a rousing hurrah. The Squire was bundled up and wheeled out to the semicircular portico and made a little speech, with the reporters taking notes and the newsreel cameras grinding. He told the crowd his boyhood memory of the election parade which had come here to celebrate Grover Cleveland's victory, more than fifty years ago. The paraders cheered and shouted their slogan of triumph : " Four—four— four years more ! "

V

Captain Budd had kept himself inconspicuous, and he was prepared to steal away and get in touch with Baker again ; but the secretary came to him and said that he was to spend the night. His bag was fetched from his car and he was taken upstairs to an old-fashioned mahogany bed in which—so he was told later—the Queen of England had slept ; also, he could guess, that ancestor of the Roosevelt fortune who had been a ship captain in the China trade, not entirely unacquainted with smugglers. The guest slept soundly, undisturbed by ghosts ; and when he came down in the morning he had his orange juice and toast alone with the secretary, nobody else having appeared. He glanced over the delightful election news, magically provided in the New York morning papers ; also he read that the Third Army had launched a heavy attack south of Metz and had taken a dozen towns. Lanny could eel that he had had something to do with that. Elated, he went for a stroll among the Squire's Christmas trees, soon to be cut for the market.

The host was busy in his study and did not appear for lunch. Lanny found himself a book and kept out of the way.

When at last he was summoned to the presence, he made bold to say, " Governor, it's a lovely day. Why don't you let me take you for a drive ? "

He didn't know whether that was protocol or not ; but the response put him at his ease. " Fine ! " exclaimed the Chief. " The only way we can escape the telephone ! " He pressed a button, and Prettyman, his Negro valet, brought the black naval cape and the old fedora hat ; the master was wheeled out to the portico, and Lanny tactfully talked to the Secret Service men while the Boss was lifted into the comfortable sports car and had a robe well tucked about his legs. It must have been someone's business to tip the operatives off, for there they were, and four of them in a car fell in behind Lanny's car and followed it as if the two had been connected by a cable. Those capable men, whose duty it was to guard the Chief's life, had the most elaborate training you could imagine. They boasted that they could shoot out a man's eyes at fifty yards. The President used to recite some lines from a children's poem by Stevenson :

I have a little shadow that goes in and out with me,
And what can be the use of him is more than I can see.

F. D. R. knew these roads as well as Lanny knew those about Juan-les-Pins. He indicated his choice with a movement of the hand, and they went up into the hills where the views of the river were glorious. A land of much history—for the New World—but they did not talk about it. The busy executive was plying his friend with questions about Europe : first, Lanny's own adventure, which hadn't accomplished very much, he was afraid. F. D. R. replied that Operation Anvil had been a whopping success, and there was credit enough to go round. Certainly General Meissner had given help—the President had already heard that story. As for Kurt, who could guess how much harm he might have done the American Army ? Roosevelt had never met the composer or heard any of his music that he could recall, but he had been hearing about him from Lanny, and it was like the continuation of a serial story.

VI

" What are we going to do with Germany ? " demanded Roosevelt suddenly ; and Lanny smiled a little and replied, " A lot of people would like to know, Governor—including all the Germans."

" We are going to have to settle upon a policy before long, and I am taking all the advice I can get. You know the Germans well, and that's why I called you home."

" I'll tell you anything I can, Governor ; but don't expect me to pull a formula out of my sleeve. It's a tremendously complex problem."

" Henry Morgenthau wants to turn the industries over to the nations which have been plundered and make Germany into an agricultural nation. That way they would never be able to attack their neighbours."

" That's quite true ; but the trouble is, you'd have twenty or thirty millions of the population as permanent objects of charity. They couldn't be fed from German soil and they'd have nothing to export. We couldn't very well let that number of people starve to death, and I don't know any place they could emigrate to."

" But if we let them rebuild their industry again, they'll start rearming. We have learned how easy it is to convert heavy industry to military purposes."

" We'll have to police the country for a long time whatever your long-range programme may be ; also, we'll have to supervise the educational system and try to raise a different sort of German. In the long run, I don't think there is any chance of avoiding war in Europe so long as its big industry is in private hands. There are many causes of war, but in modern times the number-one cause is the race for raw materials and foreign markets."

" You are just as much a Socialist as ever, Lanny ? "

" More so every day, Governor. You are going to have to move in that direction because of the state of mind of the new people who are taking over the governments behind our armies. The Partisans in Italy and France are Socialist or Communist almost to a man ; even the Catholics have been brought to realize that the old masters of industry are nearly all *collaborateurs*, and that the days of wholesale exploitation are over. It is just unthinkable that we should turn industry back into private hands when the peoples are so set against it."

"Hasn't it occurred to you, Lanny, that a state which had all big industry in its hands would be more powerful for war than one in which the power is divided?"

"I have thought about it a lot, Governor. I think your picture is deceptive because you fail to realize that in pre-war Europe both industry and government were in private hands. The steel and coal and armament industries in Germany were one strong combine, and they fixed prices and ran the country, under the Kaisers as well as under the Nazis. Hitler was their creature; they paid for the weapons which put him in power and he would never have got anywhere without them. To be sure, he ran away with them for a while; but notice he is shooting great numbers of his generals, but no members of the cartels."

"That is one aspect of the situation that has not been put before our public."

"It is true, I assure you. My father has dealt with these men and I have sat and listened ever since my boyhood. They hold the power, and they have no idea of giving it up. They are the same sort in France, and right now they are working on our top "brass", wining and dining them, and persuading them that they are the people who know how to run the country, and that it mustn't be allowed to fall into the hands of a bunch of Reds. Imagine Georgie Patton, for example; can't you hear him snorting at the idea of letting the Partisans take power?"

"Yes, Lanny; and I can also hear our newly elected congressmen snorting at the same idea. It is from them that I'll have to get the appropriations to carry out any programme."

"What you have to show those congressmen is that they have to choose between a parliamentary and democratic Socialism and a violent and fanatical Communism. There is no other choice. If we try to keep the people of Germany from socializing their industries after this war, we shall simply be putting our armies in the place of the Kaiser's armies and Hitler's, doing the same job of repression. Automatically we shall find ourselves in alliance with every reactionary force on the Continent—and, believe me, you won't like some of them. They will like you only so long as they can get money and arms out of you."

"Oh, Lanny, Lanny," exclaimed the tired man. "I am trying to end one war, and you are trying to start another!"

Said the P.A., "The war I am telling you about has been going on in Germany ever since the Peasant Revolt, about four centuries ago."

VII

When they finished with Germany they discussed Italy, and then France, and at last Russia. Roosevelt said, "I am going to have a settlement with Stalin before many months. I have waited, to be sure I was going to be re-elected. Since he won't come here, I suppose I'll have to go to him. I'll take you along, as an expert on the subject."

Lanny smiled. "On the basis of a two-hour talk with Stalin! But, as it happens, I have known many Communists, and I understand their party line."

"I wish I did, Lanny. It seems to me they change it every week."

"That is because you don't distinguish between temporary situations and fundamentals. Lenin was an opportunist; he ordered the N.E.P., the New Economic Policy, but that was just until he had got production started after the civil war. What every Communist has as his fixed goal is a Communist world, and he counts on the discontent in every capitalist state to bring it into being."

"And what are we supposed to do about it?"

"We have a choice of two courses. We can cling to our competitive commercialism, through one depression after another, and repress our social discontent; in that case we'll get a revolution, sure as shooting. Or we can proceed to put our big industry on a production-for-use basis, and thus do away with the possibility of depressions."

Said F. D. R., "It seems to me, Lanny, that the Communists hate the Socialists even more than they hate the capitalists. So what good would it do us to turn Socialist?"

"It's puzzling, Governor, I admit. But the reason th

Communists hate us Socialists is because they don't believe the changes can be brought about peaceably; therefore they call us betrayers of the workers' hopes. But if you once put industry on a co-operative basis, that attitude would dissolve. The attraction between the two systems would be irresistible and they would be drawn into a truce. With capitalism, of course, there is no possibility of a truce, because capitalism is forced by its very nature to expand. Within five years after this war is over we shall be producing twice as much goods as our people can purchase. We shall either have to take all the foreign markets in the world, or else face the worst depression in all history."

The President thought for a while and then remarked, "What I have to worry about is the immediate problem, whether Stalin will make a deal with us, or whether he is going ahead with a programme of expansion after this war."

"I would wager that he will make a deal; but the question is whether he or any man can prevent the conflict between Communism and capitalism from increasing. There are countries all along the border of the Soviet Union which will be in collapse, and their Communists will be in a state of revolt, clamouring to join the Soviet system. The reactionaries will be putting them down. And what will we be doing?"

"You don't promise me much rest in my fourth term, Lanny." The tired man said this with a smile, but Lanny knew he meant it.

VIII

The P.A. kept quiet, waiting for the next question. None came, and looking out of the corner of his eyes he saw that Roosevelt had leaned his head back against the seat of the car and closed his eyes. Whether he was thinking or dozing Lanny didn't know, but in either case the Chief was the one to speak first; Lanny sat as still as was possible for the driver of a car. He thought about the problems his Boss had raised and what more he ought to say. Every man of power is surrounded by courtiers who make a business of telling him that everything is fine and that his judgment is perfect; but Lanny had never been one of these, and he knew that was why Roosevelt called upon him. The son of Budd-Erling thought that the world was in a God-awful mess, and he feared it would get worse because of the blind passions and the sheer ignorance of men. He couldn't say otherwise—and especially not to a man who might have the power to dispel some of the ignorance and allay some of the passions.

He decided that the President was asleep; but as time passed he became uneasy. Out of the corner of his eyes he could see his face, so pale and drawn, and he thought how people sometimes died in their sleep; propped as this man was, he might stay in position. But at last Roosevelt opened his eyes, smiled, and resumed the conversation without apology. " What are you planning to do next, Lanny ? "

" I came for orders," was the reply; and the President stated his idea: that Lanny should follow the Army into Germany, meet as many people of all sorts as he could, and find out their attitudes, and what classes and groups could be depended upon for the building of a democratic government.

" I don't think you ought to spend your time interviewing prisoners, Lanny; that is a job for the military. What I need to understand is civilian opinion and how to organize it in support of a civilized regime. I don't care whether it is Socialist or what, provided it is willing to stand by democratic principles and the process of free discussion."

" All right, Governor," said the P.A. " I'll do the best I can. What shall I use for camouflage ? "

" I leave that to your judgment. I think you had better continue in uniform, so that the Army will give you help without your always having to show credentials."

" There are two groups that I might work with nominally ; one is the Monuments people, who are looking out for the art treasures, and the other Alsos, who are after scientific secrets."

" Which do you think would be better ? "

" I might shift from one to the other, meet both kinds of people, and follow whatever leads they give me."

" O.K.," said the Boss. " Baker will arrange it that way. You should run down to Washington and report to O.S.S. and tell them what you have told me. Doubtless they will have suggestions."

Lanny said, " I'll start as soon as you turn me loose."

IX

Having returned his charge to Krum Elbow, Lanny crossed the Hudson by the Poughkeepsie Bridge and sped down the west bank of the river, where the towns were fewer. He joined the Skyway and followed Highway One, and got into Washington well after midnight. Baker had telephoned a hotel reservation for him—he had to share a room with a genial salesman of metal pipe from Cleveland. In the morning he reported to General Donovan and spent the whole day and most of the night with various sections of the O.S.S.

Next morning, Friday, the President was due to arrive at Union Station at eight-thirty, having taken a night train from Hyde Park. Half a million people were expected to greet him ; the opening of schools had been postponed, and all government workers were permitted to be late for their jobs. Unfortunately it was a rainy morning, which discouraged many ; but Lanny had his waterproof coat and came early. He had watched French crowds celebrating victory, and he was interested in comparing an American crowd with them. Besides, he felt victorious himself and had some pent-up enthusiasm.

He did not join the throng at the station, but listened to the resonant voice from a loud-speaker in front of a radio store. The President was thanking his friends, and especially the faithful government workers. Lanny walked on Pennsylvania Avenue ; a heavy shower had come up, but the people stuck it out. There was a forest of umbrellas, and the rain from one man's umbrella ran down the neck of the next man ; but they stood patiently, just to get a glimpse of the face of their new-old Chief. The residents of the District of Columbia have no votes, and perhaps that is why they wanted so much to use their voices. A vast wave of cheering rolled up the wide avenue as the little procession moved slowly by. In spite of the rain, the President rode in an open car, a long one known as a phaeton ; he was wrapped in a waterproof, and let the rain run in rivulets off his head as he raised his hat to the cheering throngs.

His face shone, for he loved these demonstrations and the

people who made them. He believed in the people, in their right to choose their own destiny, their ability to look after their own interests. He believed in the whole democratic process, by which he appealed to them and got their response. Three days ago he had won their endorsement in the greatest number of votes ever cast in an election in the United States, and very probably in the whole world. He was on his way to the Executive Mansion, from which he expected to carry out another four-year mandate, and the government employees who made up most of the crowd were the humble subordinates who were going to help him in the task. Eight moist bands shook the water out of their trumpets and tubas and played the Sousa marches which have become standard for American manifestations.

The procession passed, the crowd scattered, and Lanny strolled on into the business part of the city, which is very close to the White House grounds. The rain had slackened up, and he was meditating upon his experiences of the last three days and the conclusions to be drawn from them. The papers reported that Patton's Army was continuing its fierce drive south of Metz ; it was the route which Emil Meissner had recommended, and Lanny could feel that he had had something to do with that. Everything was coming his way, and there was only one thought to disturb his peace of mind—the glimpses he had got of a harassed and exhausted man dozing in a motor-car. That face would light up with excitement for a victory parade, but afterward its owner would be so tired, oh, so tired !

X

Lanny came out of his unspoken prayer and saw that he was on a run-down business street ; Washington is a mixed-up city, and in the very centre of a block of handsome houses you will find the most abominable tenements, considered fit only for the Negro population. Lanny did not know the street he was on, but later he discovered that it was Tenth, and across the way he saw a dingy red-brick building resembling a warehouse. He recollected having had it pointed out to him ; it was the old Ford's Theatre, where Abraham Lincoln had been shot nearly eighty years ago. It was now the Lincoln Museum.

Lanny recalled the story of the frenzied Southerner, an actor himself and brother of a famous actor, who had sneaked past a drowsing sentry into the President's box and put a bullet into the back of the Great Emancipator's head. Then he had leaped down to the stage, catching his foot in a flag used as drapery and breaking his ankle. He had shouted his melodramatic cry, "*Sic semper tyrannis!*" and had made his escape on horseback. A dreadful story, and a dreadful calamity for a nation; for Lincoln, the Emancipator, had also been the Conciliator, the merciful man who had pledged himself to bind up the nation's wounds. He was the one man who could have allayed the furious hatreds of the period, and his death meant that the country had to go through the blunders of Reconstruction, and be set back by a generation of partisan strife and corruption.

Lanny had been riding with another President, and thinking about assassinations and death, sudden or slow. He considered Franklin Roosevelt another Emancipator, and an even more practised driver of political mad horses. Once more the country was coming to the end of a cruel war, and once more the wise man, the man of mercy, would be needed to bind up the wounds, this time of the world. He was such a tired man—a sick man, as Lanny believed, in spite of all the optimistic pronouncements of his physician. Lanny stood at this scene of old-time tragedy and tried to imagine what would happen to mankind if Roosevelt went under—the confusion, the unleashed hatreds, the helpless drift to calamity in both hemispheres. Despair seized him; he felt himself growing dizzy and had to turn and walk quickly away from that haunted spot. Abraham Lincoln had been too good for the American people, a piece of blind luck; and that was exactly the way a presidential agent felt about his Chief in this world crisis. Where would they find another like him?

CONCERNING THE CIRCULATION OF THE WORLD'S END SERIES

In the following record the volumes of the series are indicated by their numbers in order of publication:

Vol.	I.	WORLD'S END	1941
Vol.	II.	BETWEEN TWO WORLDS	1942
Vol.	III.	DRAGON'S TEETH	1943
Vol.	IV.	WIDE IS THE GATE	1944
Vol.	V.	PRESIDENTIAL AGENT	1945
Vol.	VI.	DRAGON HARVEST	1946
Vol.	VII.	A WORLD TO WIN	1947
Vol.	VIII.	PRESIDENTIAL MISSION	1948
Vol.	IX.	ONE CLEAR CALL	1949

In the United States, the total number of copies printed, including book club editions, is 1,314,139.

In England, Mr. Sinclair's publishers, T. Werner Laurie Ltd., report their total as 351,304. All paper obtainable was used in printing these books, and editions were sold out in a month or so. Foyle's Book Club offered to take 140,000 copies of Vol. II., but paper was not obtainable at that time.

Other countries in which translations have been published are listed in alphabetical order:

ARGENTINA	HOLLAND	POLAND
BELGIUM (French language)	HUNGARY	RUMANIA
BRAZIL	INDIA (Tamil)	SWEDEN
BULGARIA	ITALY	SWITZERLAND (German language)
CZECHOSLOVAKIA	NORWAY	U.S.S.R.
DENMARK	PALESTINE	